THE FEAST OF SAINT ANNE

ROBERT J. STAVA

Deathwatch Books

ROBERT J. STAVA

www.wyvernfalls.com

ISBN: 0615820301
ISBN-13: 978-0615820309

The Hudson Horror Series novels:

At Van Eyckmann's Request

The Feast of Saint Anne

By Summer's Last Twilight

Nightmare From World's End

Short stories set in Wyvern Falls:

Famous Artist's Course

The Haunting of Tanya Gonzales

Top Five Ways to Return from The Grave
(Plus how I killed myself using this weird little trick)

Municipal Lot #9

Blynd Haus

Dipper Don's Last Dance

The Dying Dream of Major Andre

The Anteater

Last Halloween

Other Novels:

The Lost World of Kharamu

Neptune's Reckoning (Coming 2018)

to Ray Bradbury
who got so many of us spooked out by carnivals,
and to my good friend Tom
- part of us never really did grow up, did it

CONTENTS

ACKNOWLEDGMENTS

My heartfelt thanks to all of those who helped make this book happen; my wife and first critic Tomiko for her unwavering support and feedback, RJ Cavender, Tam Hernandez, Anna Cabrera and Jennifer Laemlein for editing, Anne Rice and Michael Marshall Smith for encouraging words and taking time to respond to my frustration-laden emails, and all my family, friends and neighbors - you're really a terrific bunch.

...and of course to whatever mysterious forces are at work here along the Hudson River Valley that continue to fire my imagination....

INTRODUCTION

HEY THERE, you're just in time - summer has just officially arrived here in the lower Hudson River Valley.

Now for a lot of people that could be defined in a variety of ways.

Some will point out it's in the subtle way the bright spring foliage has darkened into the richer greens now seen along the Palisades cliffs and others, the proliferation of sailboats that are now clustered around the yacht basins as if seeking safety in numbers. Or, if you're an art enthusiast, you might have concluded its how the river has shifted out of that muddy brown spectrum from the spring run-off into that deeper greenish blue so often seen in those Hudson River School paintings.

But for most of the people in Wyvern Falls there is really only one, and that's the annual carnival known as 'The Feast of Saint Anne'.

It's a scenic place this village, if you recall (it hasn't been that long now, has it?) just like so many of those sleepy towns one finds tucked up along the Hudson, all sloped streets with old brick buildings and Victorian houses. Except the harbor as you can see, is sheltered by the large peninsula we're on that juts out into the river like a flattened - some say *Wyverns* - wing. This is Raadsel Point. It's always over there, in that open field off to the right, just before you get to the campgrounds, that the carnival is held.

Now as far as I know, the 'Feast of Saint Anne' is a Wyvern Falls exclusive in this part of Westchester County. There were those who complained there used to be a few too many Catholics running around there (and still do, between all the Latin Americans and Portuguese in our little demographic pie) and somewhere after the Great Depression they co-opted the older yearly carnival and stamped their saint on it. Since then the carnival's been arriving at the end of June; 'Regular as the Pope's bowel movement' as one local old-timer used to say, when his Catholic friends were out of earshot.

Let's get back to the carnival, though. You can see for yourself – we'll be there in a minute.

It was a big deal back in the old days for every generation's grade school years, a dazzling portal defining what used to be that limitless event horizon known as 'summer vacation'. Actually, I'd say it still is, based on the hefty turnout of kids we've been passing. Even with a recession full on.

Now if you grew up around here you'd know that the carnival here has always been one of those reliable milestones that will kick off (and break up) many relationships, result in a few under-aged teens being indoctrinated into the sacred World Of Drinking and for many subsequently to the not-so-sacred World Of Puking In A Field. Not much has changed over the years. There's still the predictable transfer of funds from local wallets and purses for rickety and tired-looking rides to the pockets of the rickety and tired-looking people running them. The kind of people with the hard miles and uncertainties of their lives written in the deep lines of their faces. And all those rides that look like refugees from the nineteen fifties or earlier probably are, though now they're mixed in with a few modern neck-wrenchers like *The Octopus* and *Evil Weevil*, with their predictable hypnotic blitz of lights and heavy metal music *thwumping* out of bass woofers.

So, here we are.

The midway looks like it's pretty much the same drill as last year . . . they've got *Johnny Pirates' Rope Ladder Climb*, *Dunderberg Ring Toss* and *Whac-A-Mole*. The *Sleepy Hollow Haunted Horse Ride* and *Half Moon Boat Ride* on either side are locally-themed variations. Can't say I've ever seen those other ones before though. A 'Magic Show and Ventriloquist Act'? You have got to be kidding. You can go later if you like. I've always hated those God-damn things, especially since the time I saw that movie 'Magic' with Anthony Hop— oh now look there, '*Fate and Fortunes told by the Countess von Richtofen, the Red Baron's Daughter*! No doubt a predictable amount of cryptic pseudo-mystical bullshit from that one, five will get you ten. But every carnival is required to have one like it, it's probably right there in the fine print in the permits. Come to think of it, I'd heard they even talked about having an old-style Freak Show at one point. But the Rotary Club – that's one of the carnival co-sponsors – balked. I don't blame them. I thought it was sick when they used to have them forty years ago and just as sick today.

Now beyond that I see there's the usual gambling distractions like *Rat Roulette* and *Wheel of Luck*. Towards the back; that's the Vegas Tent where the old farts play poker and Black Jack and drink premium brews like Budweiser-in-a-plastic-cup. Or if you're a real hardliner, Kentucky Bourbon or Jack Daniels.

If you were to continue out past the picnic tables, you'll see there's a large blue and yellow open tent which features live music. In more recent years, they've had mainly local cover bands, some pretty decent, some, like Todd Wunderman's 70's progressive rock tribute band, *Thunkit*, clearly delusional regarding their musical talents.

Last are the food concessions with the usual spectrum of fried foods though in recent years a few diet-conscious alternatives have appeared, like the frozen yogurt stand, the fruit smoothie stand, and the forlorn-looking vegan burger stand with its forlorn-looking Vegan Dude in tie-dye and knit cap. By and large though, we all know that half the fun of the Feast of Saint Anne's Carnival is kicking off the summer by eating everything one is *not supposed* to eat.

Now, like many such small town rituals, the Feast of Saint Anne's has developed into a sort of touchstone for the Wyvern Falls community. As in any recurring event over many generations it's become woven into the deeper fabric of the village social structure: one of those opportunities to 'hang one's towel out' so to speak, to step up to the local stage of life and play one's role and to have that role acknowledged, whether good, bad, or indifferent. It's another of those simple reassurances we look toward where we pause and say "hey . . . still here . . . still *alive!*" while having an acceptable excuse to get drunk, eat too much artery-clogging food, and gamble away funds one most likely cannot afford to lose.

That's it. Yep, it's pretty much like any other carnival.

And yet . . . it's not.

Sure the clams are good, the wind is fabulous and so is the view of the Hudson out here at Raadsel Point when you're at the top of that Ferris Wheel, creaking and swaying, like that couple up at the top there. See, he's got his arm around his date and I'd be willing to bet she's edging in a little closer precisely *because* of how much it's creaking and swaying.

But there's something else you should know. Wyvern Falls isn't exactly like all those other towns up and down along the river. *No sir.* And not everything that happens here gets printed in the local Gazette, if you catch my drift. Don't get me wrong, it's a beautiful village, yet, I'm not sure how to put this . . . it can be kind of a *strange* place. There's a witching influence in the air here and the dead don't rest easy in their graves. A lot of violent things occurred in the past, some of them brutal - like the particularly gruesome way the Dutch soldiers massacred all those Indians back in 1643 under Governor Kieft's orders, butchering the woman and children in their village that used to be on the Point. And there always seems to be a fair amount of unexplainable, supernatural sort of stuff going on around here. Did you hear about terrible business that happened up at the Van Eyckmann estate last year? Cripes, what that maniac did to those businessmen was gruesome! How he mutilated their bodies and tore out their—

You know what? Forget what I just said. It's Friday evening and the *Feast of Saint Anne's Carnival* has begun. Look how that sun is sinking down into a fiery blaze towards the cliffs on the opposite shore and the shadows are reaching longer - not at all like sharp-nailed fingers I might add - even as the first lights flicker into life . . .

-R.J.S

I. THE RED BARON'S DAUGHTER

We loop in the purple twilight
We spin in the silvery dawn
With a trail of smoke behind us
To show where our comrades have gone

So stand to your glasses steady
This world is a world full of lies
Here's a toast to the dead already
…and hurrah for the next man to die!

-WWI aviator's song adapted from "The Revel"

-1-

THE TWO BOYS standing in line had exactly eighteen dollars and fifty-three cents between them. Hardly a king's ransom but enough to do a little damage at the carnival on a Friday night.

The older was a sharp-featured thirteen-year-old named Luis Dimas, from a local third generation Portuguese family. Dark-skinned and on the slight side, he'd inherited his mother's striking looks and father's agile mind. Even at a glance it was obvious he was the leader of the two: like his older brother Ricardo he possessed a natural, easy going charisma and confidence that went far beyond his years.

The younger was Armando Ortega, whose family had landed in Wyvern Falls the previous August after a four-year overland trek from Ecuador, a journey that was an epic story in itself. A heavy-set kid a half year younger than his friend, Armando had the unmistakably broad, inscrutable face of his Indian ancestors that masked an absurd sense of humor. His father Eduardo had quickly established himself in a landscaping business and equally as quickly gotten past his ears in debt. His mother was an expert seamstress who was currently helping make ends meet waitressing at *Los Choza*, an Ecuadorian restaurant up on Route 9B.

By whatever means in which the universe mysteriously works, Luis and Armando had immediately become best friends from the moment they'd first met. That had been during lunch period on their second day in 7th Grade at Wyvern Falls Middle School. Gerry Miller, arguably one of the biggest and most physically developed of their class, had been harassing Armando over his lunch for no particular reason other than something to do. He'd gotten as far pouring the Ecuadorian's milk over his spaghetti when Luis, who had been quietly observing this from across the table, stood up, walked over, and with no warning belted Miller in the mouth.

There had been a moment of stunned silence as talk died out in the cafeteria. Blood trickled out of Miller's nose.

Gerry was no stranger to fights, but as anyone who's ever taken a punch square in the upper teeth can tell you, it has a way of momentarily scrambling your senses. Even so, he would have belted Luis right back but for the murderous look in the kid's face that convinced him otherwise.

Discretion being the better part of valor, Miller had simply shaken his head and grinned like it was all part of the plan. With a shrug he'd turned walked out, probably to sneak a cigarette behind the school gym and nurse his injured pride. Before he did however, one kid, Andy Krueger, had snickered but was silenced by a homicidal glance from Miller that squashed any other further outbreaks.

Armando had said nothing. He'd simply raised his eyebrows in surprise as Luis sat back down and resumed eating as if this was all part of a normal 7th Grade eating ritual. Armando simply put his fork and spoon to his lunch as if spaghetti with meat sauce and whole D milk was just another typical American school lunch.

Then as they had gotten up to leave he'd said quietly *"Gracias."*
Luis had grinned and clapped him on the back. *"Sem problemas."*
Something unspoken connected between them, and that was that.

Being the first Friday of not only the carnival but of the kick-off weekend for the entire wide open vista known as *Summer Vacation,* for these two boys the night was the threshold of the event horizon of limitless possibilities tailored to this Hudson Valley town: mountain biking expeditions to be launched, ruins of old mansions to be explored, historic (if highly imaginary) battles to be fought, and pilfered selections of old porno magazines to be examined in Luis' tree house. Progress notes on particular females of interest (also in the highly imaginary category to date) to be compared. They had also bought tickets for the 'Pirates on the Hudson' event being held in Philipse Manor over the Fourth of July weekend and invested in a decent cache of bottle rockets through another friend, Peter Vogel, who'd just returned from a family trip to Pennsylvania loaded with contraband fireworks.

Thus the depleted state of finances between Luis and Armando, neither of whom came from particularly well-off families but who were both reasonably industrious at earning their keep. Luis ran a New York Times paper route. Armando worked weekends and off hours with his dad's landscaping business and, lacking that, mowed lawns in the summer, raked leaves in the fall, and shoveled driveways in the winter. One thing that the Ecuadorian had learned over the last four years: you worked wherever and whenever you could, period.

It was moments after they'd made it to the midway and surveyed the offerings that Luis, with a discriminating eye, zeroed in immediately on the one they'd never seen before. Putting his hand on Armando's shoulder he'd pointed and said excitedly "Whoa, check it out *Amigo*! How cool is that?"

Armando had squinted and given one of his trademark shrugs.

Three booths down from the Rope Climb they'd just wasted two precious dollars from their budget on was a strange looking tent with an even stranger looking sign above it:

> *Countess Lorelei von Richtofen – The Red Baron's Daughter!*
> *Fortunes Told, Mysteries of the Past, Present,*
> *and Future Explained,*
> *Spirit Readings, Lost Items Found, Past Lives Revealed*

The antique-looking billboard depicted a stern yet mysteriously attractive middle-aged woman in pre-1920s costume surrounded by a combination of WWI biplanes (including the infamous red Fokker Triplane, of course), soldiers in trenches, skull heads, magic symbols and an Egyptian-looking all-seeing eye gazing down from the heavens. The Baron was pulling up and looking down from above, his expression grim and determined, having just dispatched an enemy Nieuport biplane to its fiery death. In the background two more enemy planes – Spad VIIs – also flamed out into oblivion. If one looked carefully, one could just make out a flailing smudge suggesting that one pilot had leaped to his death rather than be roasted alive. It was a surreal combination of classic carnival illustration, WWI dogfighting, and a strangely provocative-looking woman.

Luis, who had gotten into a WWI dogfighting sim on Xbox called "Richtofen's War" via Pete Vogel only a few months earlier, was instantly curious. The Richtofen game, which was a reissue of an old classic once put out by a company called Avalon Hill, recreated the "glorious" days of aerial fighting over the Western Front during World War I as a first-person combat flight sim using the latest in 3D gaming technology. The title referred to Germany's most legendary WWI ace, Baron Manfred von Richtofen, nicknamed the 'Red Baron' for his tendency to paint his aircraft in an all-red scheme. Richtofen's War had been the runaway neighborhood gaming hit that spring.

Recently however, Luis had found his interests becoming a confusing tangle between games and girls and here he was, confronted by something tying in both.

Correction: not girls, a *woman*. With a seductive look. Dozens of feverish fantasies formed in his mind. Not missing the gleam in his friend's eyes (it was subtle, but there) it was clear he wasn't alone.

Neither had to say it – both of them bee-lined toward the tent.

The line was short even though it was peak time at the carnival, just after 8:00 p.m.

Luis and Armando found themselves behind a couple of college kids who looked like they'd put in some bonus rounds at the beer tent. Just in front of them, Luis noticed the stunning Sabina Torres – how could any non-catatonic heterosexual male not – and quickly noted her latest Neanderthal, 'Vince The Mince' (a name coined by their friend Adam Carr whose older brother used to have something on with Sabina), who was looking around with the indifferent malice of a German Panzer tank on patrol in a subjugated country.

A knuckle punch in Luis' left shoulder as he was waiting snapped him out of his Sabina reverie. Cliff Ducat was standing there with a couple of his buddies. Cliff, a tall, good-looking black kid from the Barrows currently occupied a unique position on Luis' 'Friends and Enemies' roster:

He was on *both* lists.

In fairness, it was Cliff who was the wildcard in the deck and there wasn't a lot of logic to how or when his status might change at any point. One day they might bum around together or even doing a sleepover in Luis' tree house; the next they might be outside the school yard trying to beat the hell out of each other, typically because Cliff would get fired up on some unrelated matter – usually something going sour on the home front – and just pick a fight out of the blue. And Luis, though he liked Cliff, would be obligated to take it up with him in what had become an almost ritualistic dance. Cliff was tall and powerful, Luis was fast and agile. Neither boy ever got a significant upper hand and pretty much every fight ended in a draw, usually when their respective friends pulled them apart or some random adult came along and actually intervened.

Which was part of the ritual.

On this occasion however they were on *Neutral Classmates* status. The knuckle punch was (like most things Ducat) one of Cliff's blunt and effective ways of getting one's attention.

"*'Sup.*"

"*Aló!*"

Cliff screwed up his face and squinted as he looked up at the placard and back at Luis. "*Psssshhh!* What you doing standing in a line like that? That's sissy stuff."

Luis smiled. "Then how come you're not in line with us?"

Cliff looked up again at the sign, but didn't look quite as sure the second time. In fact, he saw something he didn't like at all – a series of symbols along the bottom that suggested something disturbingly familiar. The Ducats were an old local family that could trace their origins to Congolese slaves originally brought over by Frederick Philipse in the 1600's. Once, playing in the attic at his grandmothers with his brother and sister, he had discovered a forgotten box in the rafters with strange stuff inside. *Black Magic* stuff. Along with an old book containing formulae and similar symbols that had haunted his dreams for weeks.

He looked at Luis, his air of goofing now a little forced. "You should stay away from that shit, man. We're gonna score some brews at the tent. My brother's working tonight. You up?"

"Maybe in a bit." The line shuffled forward. Cliff's older brother Mark had worked out a clever system for sneaking them beers under the noses of the guys who ran the tent, who were usually too plowed to pay much attention regardless.

Something was bugging Luis about the whole current situation though. He sensed something was off, but he couldn't pinpoint what. Perhaps, he wondered, in the age of the internet people just weren't as interested in having their fortune told by anything that wasn't an app for an iPad or Droid. Or perhaps it was simply the oddness of this attraction: it suggested "traditional" but didn't quite add up.

He glanced around; Armando appeared to be lost in his own world, his default look. Cliff was shaking his head and walking away with his three buddies. Any further thoughts were interrupted as their friends Pete Vogel, Adam Carr, and Henry Van Dorn cut into line behind them. Not that the Red Baron's heir-apparent was a top draw this evening, only a handful of people were strung out in back of them. Even Luis was able to sort out the math enough to grasp that this whole thing was some sort of charade: if the Red Baron in fact had a daughter she would have to be, at the very least, ninety-two years old, since the Great Ace himself had bought the farm in April of 1918. He had already concluded it was highly unlikely that she would be running around on the Carney circuit at that spry age, and definitely not the hot ticket displayed on the sign.

Luis was startled as Pete clapped him on the back. "What gives, my good man?" Pete asked.

"Hey guys," Luis answered, "Thought we'd get our fortunes told. Looks kind of cool, with Richtofen and all."

Pete tilted his head back and gave the sign a critical look. "Hmpf. They've got the Red Baron wearing British goggles," was his only comment.

Luis rolled his eyes. At the same time however, it was good to have the only three other kids he could really call his friends alongside him.

He'd known Pete Vogel since kindergarten. Squat, Pete was built like a bulldozer with square features, tinted glasses, and short, cropped red hair.

A spray of freckles highlighted his bulbous nose and cheeks. He had a love for all things military, particularly anything involving exploding things, and, not unlike a bulldozer, pretty much plowed through everything in life with unwavering certainty. At thirteen one of those certainties was that his future path lay directly to West Point. He'd told Luis recently that his mother was already looking into various military academies to facilitate 'polishing off his rough edges' (of which there were quite a few) before then. The problem was that Pete's Dad had run off years ago and the family's finances were still on shaky ground, so for the foreseeable future he was stuck in the Wyvern Falls public school system.

Pete Vogel may have been forged in a world of unwavering certainties, but he hadn't quite figured out that the rest of the world was not.

Luis knew Adam Carr from around the neighborhood but hadn't really gotten to know him until they'd played Little League together. Adam was small, dark-featured and had a much older brother, Nick, who was back from college under a cloud of failure. Adam may have inherited his Dad's intense looks but personality-wise he pretty much stuck to the classic younger brother profile: upbeat, easygoing, quick to please and quick to make friends. He had an older sister who was a tolerable nuisance – fun, cute, not to be taken too seriously – but he talked about his older brother with a mixture of awe and adoration like he was a combined pioneer, talented rebel, and trailblazer. In this sense Luis found him as unwavering as Pete Vogel: any derogatory comments (and sometimes they hung in the air as thick as an artillery salvo) about his brother Nick from parents, teachers, or friends bounced off him like Teflon. Nick Carr was gold-plated and that was that.

Henry Van Dorn was really Pete's friend, so technically just a 'Buddy-in-law' to Luis. The most introspective of the bunch, he was a broad-shouldered kid with horn-rimmed glasses, an unruly mop of straw colored hair and the oldest of three brothers. He also had an older sister, Katherine, who was a junior in high school. Henry shared Pete Vogel's interest in most things military, as his father was an ex-marine. Mr. Vogel ran a masonry quarry just outside of town and a part-time gun shop out of his basement. He was also a mean drunk who kept the Van Dorn household in a perpetual state of fear and awe, from what Luis had heard. Beds were made with sheets tight enough to bounce quarters off and the word 'mess' was something to be assaulted, subdued, and summarily eliminated without mercy. Any violations of the Van Dorn Code of Household Conduct were met with the harshest words and, if the occasion warranted (or if the liquor flowed that night), an additional lesson involving Heinrich Van Dorn's belt or even fists would be in order.

Mrs. Van Dorn put on the brave face of the assertive housewife – in fact she worked as a head nurse over at Philipseburg Memorial (in the trauma unit, ironically enough). But it was all a brittle façade. Few of her friends suspected the truth: that she lived in terror of her husband and they slept in separate beds. Luis sensed this on the few times he was over visiting – like the time she'd made them lunch with trembling hands and he'd seen the ugly bruise peeking out of her collar – but any attempts to bring it up with Henry went nowhere. After the third try Pete had yanked him aside and asked him never to mention it again.

The line moved forward as Pete and Henry got into a heated discussion about the accuracy of the biplane pictures on the placard. Pete could be a lot of fun to hang out with, but to Luis still seemed utterly oblivious to the existence of the opposite sex. For those topical discussions, he had to rely on Armando who, for all his nonchalance, was *extremely* interested in the mysteries and activities of the female species.

Luis tried to contain his irritation as Pete launched into a vocal simulation of a WWI dogfight just as Sabina and her date emerged from the tent. Like a lot of boys his age, Pete had an automatic act-like-an-annoying-knucklehead response that was set off by the proximity of any attractive females. Luis discreetly took a few steps away in a vain attempt to suggest he wasn't really associated with this geeky demonstration but Sabina didn't even glance his way. Whatever fortunes from the future the Red Baron's Daughter had imparted to them apparently hadn't been of the *you-will-be-unbelievably-rich* or the *you-are-eternal-soul-mate's* variety. Sabrina was wearing the flat-eyed look of someone who had just been informed by their bookie they'd picked the wrong horse at the track and Vince, who looked like a homicidal version of the clueless muscle-head in the old Planet Fitness "I pick things up and put zem down" television commercial, had a grim expression that suggested that whatever he put down would be minus its head and probably both arms and legs.

It seemed the two college students had been in but a matter of seconds before Luis and Armando were ushered into the gloomily lit tent. Luis hadn't even seen them exit. There was little time to weigh on this as, to his surprise, Pete, Adam, and Henry were brought in as well by the usher, an odd little man who looked like a less sawed-off version of Toulouse-Lautrec, right down to the top hat and narrow spectacles.

"Come, come, all of you boyzz . . . yes yes . . . *all* five at once," He muttered in an odd accent.

The tent was circular and had a small round table set up in its center where a pole would typically be, surrounded by a set of folding wooden chairs. Even that was odd. At a glance, the tent seemed like no other Luis had ever seen before. For starters the material looked like a patchwork of old doped canvas with the suggestions of curved struts, not unlike an old aircraft. The table was a gothic-looking thing. The top was painted with weird occult-looking symbols in concentric rings outside of a pentacle with symbols at each corner. In the center appeared to be a crystal ball on a stand covered by a black velvet cloth. From the amount of wear and tear on it, the table looked like it had traveled around the world more than a few times and maybe even dragged behind the wagon on a couple of them.

The room was lit by a series of old kerosene lanterns suspended from the ceiling by metal hooks, the kind one might have found on an old aerodrome in France during the First World War. Propped up in one corner was a pair of honest-to-God Spandau machine guns. With them was a Vickers MG that was banged and dented. There was also an antique wooden coat stand with a blood stained pilot's uniform on one hook, a pair of fleece-lined boots beneath it, and a display case containing a bunch of old and faded photos – pilots and old biplanes, with what appeared to be a nude female photo or two. Some of the pilots were standing by their planes, some in groups, some were in a group hoisting beer steins in a tavern. Looking closely, one could see that most the pilots looked gaunt and had haunted, faraway looks in their eyes: the look of men gazing into oblivion.

Last, opposite the coat rack was an old Victrola phonograph atop a wooden cabinet, its huge fluted speaker the type known as a 'Morning Glory'. As the boys filed in, music was coming out of it: The German National Song or *Deutschland Uber Alles*, though none of the boys would have recognized it. The man singing it, Carl Schlegel, had a rich baritone and an almost mournful delivery. It was definitely not the bombastic "Let's Stomp the World into Submission" version often associated with Nazi rallies.

Most of this was lost on Luis, however, who only heard a scratchy antique-sounding song floating around the vaguely moldy atmosphere of the tent like an insubstantial ghost. Hardly the pounding, transistorized assault of 21st Century rock he was accustomed to. Yet for a moment he felt a faint stirring of sadness somewhere in his heart, a momentary intuition that the reckless and sunny days of youth were fleeting and the darker waters of adulthood might hold un-named dangers . . . perhaps even *horrors*.

If nothing else, the Red Baron's Daughter knew how to set a stage.

She also knew how to make an entrance.

After the usher had glided out of the tent with a cryptic "Do not touch zenny-thing or Frau Velt vill not be pleased . . . be good little boys now . . . she vill be here very soooon!" They were left to their own devices for a few minutes. And boys being boys, the quickest way to get them to do something was to warn them not to.

Pete and Henry went straight to the bloodied pilot's tunic. From the Royal Flying Corps emblem on the breast, the original owner had been British. And, from the four bullet holes around the chest area (and a more gruesome looking one around the short collar), it was a reasonable guess he hadn't survived the war. The fleece-lined flying boots looked lumpy, the leather was cracked and dried with age, and in many places the finish was flaking off. The two boys were examining the flyers' clothes like they were holy relics from Jerusalem. Luis meanwhile was fascinated by the table and its mysterious markings and was running his hands over its surface. Armando fell to studying the Victrola as if it was some sort of alien artifact while Adam was galvanized by the trio of machine guns propped in the corner.

All these investigations came to a freezing halt as the curtain at the back was flung open and the Fraulein herself stepped into the room. Except for the weighted swish of the fabric and the faint crunch of the earth under a laced-up old-fashioned boot, there was an expectant silence in the room as the five boys focused on this other-worldly apparition.

The Fraulein, or *Red Baron's Daughter* as had been advertised, did indeed look as though she had stepped straight out of that very era where puffed shoulders, piled up hair and tight-waisted dresses were still the rage – when the formless flapper fashion of the Roaring '20s was still lurking in the future and corsets were riding out their last hurrah.

The *Red Baron's Daughter* was beautiful in a regal, high-cheek-boned way. She had an imperious mouth that would have made Marlene Dietrich envious and strongly arched eyebrows over riveting violet-blue eyes. Her face was alabaster white with a heavy pile of chestnut-colored hair. The dress was in a league of its own: below the waistline, it was heavy black damask which hung in sculptured folds. Above, it was cream and wine-red silk with black lace and a series of Egyptian-motif patterns that followed the bust line, then ran up and over the shoulders. Contrary to the conventions of the time, however, the bust was provocatively low cut and there was no mistaking that the dress was fashioned to pull attention to the Fraulein's ample cleavage.

She entered and every boy's eyes went immediately to her breasts.

Then the spell was shattered as Adam's shoelace snagged some protrusion on one of the Spandau's and, with a deafening clang of metal, the three heavy guns went toppling over.

The Baron's daughter pulled up short, shock, then outrage flaring in her eyes. The rest of the boys were busy staring at Adam as if he'd shown up naked in the school cafeteria. Adam looked stricken and about to burst into tears. Luis was the first to run over. A second later Pete and Henry jumped in and made a valiant effort to put the guns back to rights. Heavy and cumbersome, it took three tries.

In the meantime, the Fraulein had regained her composure and like a queen to her courtiers gestured they should take up seats at the reading table.

She produced a small metal box and carefully extracted five 7.92mm machine-gun bullets which she fanned out on the table. Her fingers were long and suggested a much older woman, the pointed fingernails painted a deep glossy red as if dipped in blood. Then, inclining her head, she produced a smile and looked at each boy. The illusive lantern light served only to accent her cheekbones and the mystery of her eyes. It was an enigmatic smile that might indicate anything: indulgence, tolerance, friendliness, (sexual?) interest. Or it just as easily was something more sinister.

Luis felt an uneasy tingling somewhere deep in his gut. Partly it was the uncomfortable proximity of a mature and commandingly attractive adult woman with no supervising adults around, partly it was the intuitive sense of loss one has as the final days of childhood slip away into the more uncertain currents of adulthood. Partly it was the first pricks of fear that they might have somehow stumbled into some kind of trap that none of them were experienced or knowledgeable enough to comprehend.

Whatever picture it was suggesting was quickly scattered as the song on the Victrola wound down to its end and the needle skipped. Luis was expecting her to stand up and change the record but she simply sat there, eyes half closed, looking into space. Abruptly the needle was engaged by some sort of mechanism which lifted it up, swung it back to the outside of the disk and lowered it back to the first groove.

Only this time, impossibly, a completely different song played. This time the song was an instrumental that sounded like some sort of opera. It was: Puccini's Allegro Don Libre. The Fraulein waved her hand palm down over the bullets and, like a conjuror's trick, each was suddenly standing upright in front of each boy.

Suddenly she let out a little laugh and spoke: "Ah boys . . . so much trouble. Always misbehaving . . . *ja*? Well, you wish your fortunes told. No? Then take a magic bullet . . . each are the Baron's Bullets, and hold it tightly in your hand, like so." She demonstrated by holding her hand in the fashion one would hold a key or lucky rabbit's foot charm. Luis didn't like the feel of it – cold and heavy and dead.

Then: "Let us see what the future holds for each of you! We should ask the Baron himself I think!" With a flourish she pulled the velvet cloth from the object in the center.

There was a collective gasp from around the table.

It was a human skull.

-2-

THE SKULL looked old – the bone was yellowed and had a mellow patina from being handled by countless human hands over so many years. And there was a groove along the upper side of it where perhaps a .303 bullet had creased the skull (if it really was von Richtofen's) on that nearly fatal day back in July of 1917. That day when a lucky shot from an English rear gunner had almost ended the Baron's career.

It certainly drew everyone's attention like a magnet.

This was no Halloween-store fabrication or cheap prop that had arrived via FedEx from some mysterious virtual store on eBay, but a bona fide *human* skull. For a bunch of kids raised in a world of console games, e-books on demand, and Wi-Fi, there was something morbidly creepy, fascinating, and terrifyingly final in its realness.

This had once belonged to a living, breathing, human being.

Who was dead.

However, they weren't given much leeway to dwell on it. The Baron's daughter made hypnotic whirling motions around it with her slender old fingers. Her eyes seemed to deepen in color to the tint of the darkest reaches in the oldest stretches of the universe. Though no-one could swear to it, the temperature in the little tent actually cooled. Goosebumps appeared on bare arms.

Their host's lips were quivering. Faintly whispered words/sounds that suggested ancient incantations, moldering black remains in forgotten tombs, the sliding gasp of gossamer wings unfolding. Goosebumps became even more pronounced. The words and sounds rose in intensity. ". . . tell me show me tell me show . . . *ngasssi samma ara rouche . . . ara . . .* death and bullets, oil and fire!" Then the daughter's face took on a diabolical, leering look. Her eyes and nostrils flared and her fingers, tightening into claws, dug into to the vacant eye sockets of the skull. The atmosphere felt electrically charged.

Then she gasped: "Show them! Show these boys from behind the veil of the grave . . . see and *learn*!"

Luis was squeezing the German bullet in his hand so tight he briefly wondered if he might set it off through sheer pressure. Then he felt himself

flip/switch

He was *flying*!

It took his confused senses a few minutes to sort through the overload of unfamiliar stimuli to understand this:

First, the goggles over his eyes constricted his vision and the buffeting wind (which was making a concerted effort to suck every molecule of air out of his lungs) and the blast and roar from the propeller only slightly diverted by the small glass windscreen in front of his face made it hard to breathe. Then there was the unfamiliar sensation of jolting around not in one or two but *three* dimensions. Toss in the rough and unfamiliar clothing with a stiff collar, tight-laced boots, a heavy shearling-lined leather overcoat and a tight-fitting cap. A silk scarf was wrapped around his neck, covering his mouth and nostrils against the fine mist of cod liver oil coming from the engine. Looking down he saw his hands encased in clumsy, thick leather gloves with gauntlets that ran nearly to the elbows.

"*Mon dios!*" he thought, "what in the—?"

Then his overtaxed thirteen-year-old brain made some sense out of the maelstrom of unfamiliar inputs and processed new observations: the thrum of the cables and struts, the heavy wings, the dull sheen of the ass-ends of twin Vickers machine guns mounted just fore of the cockpit. The wooden instrument panel and stitched padded leather trim framing him in.

An open cockpit.

He was in a biplane!

Holy Shit!

For a moment he was seized by a tight fist of panic. This was compounded by a sudden lurch as the plane hit an air pocket. His hands and feet seemed to be operating on their own instructions, even so the Xbox controller seemed like ridiculously simple child's play compared to this. Within minutes, he was soaked in sweat despite the numbing chill of the wind. It was June. How was that possible?"

Then he understood he was looking at a primitive altimeter on the control panel. The thick and thin hands in the clock-like window were indicating he was flying just over twelve thousand feet!

Of course!

If that wasn't surreal enough, glancing out to his left and right he saw he was flying in a formation of heavy looking biplanes. He even knew what they were – Spad XIII's. And from the screaming Indian Chief face painted boldly on the canvas fuselages, aircraft of the 103rd Aero Squadron. *Americans.*

The planes were flying in two loose 'finger four' formations, just as they always did in the computer game. Forward and lower to Luis' right was an older-looking man with a bushy mustache he'd never seen before. But the two flyers fanned out farther to his right – correction, at three-o'clock – he most definitely knew.

They were Armando and Adam.

They looked as bewildered and terrified as he did.

He risked taking one hand off the control stick (it bucked and fought in his hand like it was alive) and made a tentative wave to his friends. Almost immediately the plane slewed sideways in a sickening motion and he had to fight it back into position again. Armando's eyebrows shot up in alarm and Adam fished up a ghastly looking grin. Then, getting his aircraft under control, Luis managed an 'OK' sign with his thumb and forefinger. A moment of terror shot through him at the thought that this flimsy contraption of canvas, wood and wires with an engine that sounded more like an over-taxed lawnmower was the only thing keeping him ten thousand feet above the earth – with a lot of empty air between.

The whole idea seemed utter lunacy when one really considered it.

Followed by the thought: *guys were expected to actually maneuver and kill each other in these freaking things?? That's just lunacy squared.*

Then another truth chased that away:

Holy Shit! he thought again.

I'm flying! I'm really flying!

The thrill was incredible.

The aircraft bobbed and weaved through the sky, inexperienced hands struggling with the unfamiliar controls, and the world beyond the little plane seeped into Luis' observations. For starters, this was nothing like any computer game he had ever experienced. And nothing at all like riding passively on a big commercial jet. The Spad felt like it was jumping all over the damn place like a toy. Random air pockets would cause the plane to suddenly jump up, or to drop tens of feet, resulting in the uncanny sensation of one's heart jumping up into one's throat. The high-pitched whine came from an engine that sounded barely capable of keeping the whole thing up in the air. But after a few minutes Luis settled in. The skies were gloomy caverns of stacked cumulus clouds – a study in washed blue-grays – and it appeared to be something of a rainy afternoon. Down below were occasional flashes on the deeper gloom of the earth's surface, artillery presumably. In the distance floating specs of other aircraft formations flew over the front, too far to determine if they were enemies or not.

This was incredible! He thought. *How cool!*

It was as though they had all been dropped into the most amazing simulation ever conceived. Nothing at all like the clumsy hydraulic things at Disney World or the NASA Space Center!

Craning his head up and backwards at the higher formation, he wasn't surprised to see Pete and Henry in the fore, looking otherworldly with their goggles and leather flying caps. Pete grinned and made a thumbs-up gesture with his left hand. The other two pilots he didn't recognize. He also realized, with a start, something coming down at them from higher up, what looked like the front silhouettes of other planes…coming to join them or…?

Then he noticed the winking pinpricks of light from the front of the planes bearing in on them.

"What?"

Then dread seeped through his whole body. His heart pumped ice through his veins. He felt paralyzed with fear.

A whizzing sound. Like angry hornets.

As if by magic a series of holes stitched along his lower wing. "Oh God! *Germans!*"

All hell broke loose.

Without thinking, Luis jerked the joystick up and kicked the rudder pedal over so hard he wondered if he might put his foot through the floor of the plane. The air seemed filled with tracer bullets, each one swerving right at him. The two formations of Spads scattered like deer as the enemy aircraft cut through them.

Blunt nosed aircraft – Fokker D.VII's with purple, green, and brown fuselages. A glimpse of crudely painted screaming skull and crossbones streaking by. Large black crosses on white squares. Shredding canvas and snapping wood struts.

Screams.

Chaos.

The Spad was an unwieldy aircraft, but durable. Even so, Luis did a reasonable wing-over and, leveling out, found his plane dipping past a plane piloted by a man with mustache – the name Major Ned Pearson popped into his mind from somewhere – then he realized that one of the Fokkers had locked onto the Major's tail and was pouring bullets into it. This plane wasn't like the others – it was completely black except for the white squares highlighting older-style Maltese crosses and the skull painted on the side. It was also immediately clear that this pilot was diabolically good. He matched the Major's maneuvers as if he was predicting them. Even as Luis watched, the Spad began to disintegrate and the Major's body jerked as several

Maxim bullets punctured it. A white plume of smoke appeared – fuel – which quickly erupted into flame as the tracers set it off. In a ghastly gesture, the Major saluted Luis in a 'carry-on' gesture as his plane became enveloped in fire within moments, then it plummeted earthward, shedding flaming debris. A moment later, the body tumbled out and pin wheeled down into the murk.

Luis looked back at the enemy pilot and screamed.

Something out of a Teutonic nightmare was piloting the German craft.

At a glance it appeared to be a sort of grinning corpse – a skull covered with dried, blackened flesh – but with a battery of elongated teeth the color of tarnished metal (Maxim) bullets. The features were a caricature of a human's with its sharp cheekbones and jutting chin. The leather flying cap was a dark, moldy green brown with a Maltese Cross on the forehead. The goggles had strange wing-like attachments and a knot of rotted scarves flapped from the neck in the slipstream. And the eyes – glowing white orbs with slitted vertical pupils like a reptile's – immediately locked onto Luis'.

The Fokker began a quick roll to lock onto his six.

Scared out of his mind, Luis wrenched the control stick back into his stomach and the Spad shot upwards. He had just watched a human being burn then fall to certain death after being shot up by this creature, but there was no time to dwell on that thought further:

Get away! Get away! His nerves were screaming. More bullets whickered through his wings. A Fokker zoomed beneath him, doing a lazy barrel roll. Improvising, Luis kicked the rudder pedal again and pulled the stick further into his stomach, trying to execute an *Immelman* maneuver.

Altitude! Get altitude!

The Spad responded with all the sluggish grace of a refrigerator – but he managed to just do a wing-over at the top of his climb without stalling the plane. At least some of those countless hours in front of the TV with the Xbox were paying off! He looked around wildly to see what had happened to his friends. Planes appeared to be shooting through the cavernous skies every which way in a chaotic dance. The German D.VII's seemed everywhere. He saw Adam's riddled plane cut underneath him at an angle, huge holes in the fabric of the upper wing, cables whipping freely in the slipstream. His face was locked in rictus of fear. Henry was close on the tail of one of the Fokkers, twin Vickers blazing, but two more swung around onto his own six. The German planes seemed to be able to hang and maneuver on their propellers.

Luis was screaming "Henry!!! Behind you!" But of course Henry couldn't hear him.

More bullets came through his own plane, one smashing the fuel gauge and sending glass shards every which way.

Luis glanced back and saw a truly terrifying sight:

The Black Fokker was right back on his six!

Then he had another surprise: behind the German was Armando, who began firing in earnest at the German. He almost screamed in relief. For a moment, he thought the steadfast Ecuadorian would destroy the thing on his tail. His elation was short lived. With a snarl, the German bobbed and weaved as if he could almost sense where the bullets were aimed, then a moment later another D.VII flew into Armando's Spad, clipping the outer wing and sending him spinning away into the clouds. Luis screamed "Armandooooohhhh!!!" but there was no time – the black Fokker dropped down and locked onto his six again.

While he'd never flown an actual aircraft before, Luis hadn't been unbeatable in the neighborhood playing *Richtofen's War* for nothing. He had amazing hand/eye coordination that older generations could only gaze on with envy. He did a snap roll and dove straight down, nearly vertical. His heart threatened to stop beating and his stomach lurched. It was almost like one of those elevator rides at Six Flags where you drop straight down ten stories. Except on this particular ride, death was right on top of you and doing his damndest to riddle you with machine gun bullets.

Luis dove past Pete's Spad, which was banking around after one of the Germans, its tail getting chewed to pieces as another German blazed away at him. Then Luis was falling away into the gloom, pulling the stick around to put the plane's dive into an erratic spiral, trying to make himself a more difficult target.

The German, if that's what it was, followed him with uncanny precision. Terrified, Luis began to comprehend that his remaining life expectancy was being reduced to minutes and seconds.

He was running out of tricks.

He dropped out of the undercast with his altimeter spinning below a thousand feet, the control surfaces shuddering from compression and the wind whining through the cables and stays. A less sturdy plane would have ripped its wings off in such a dive. Below him the trenches came into view with a sickening spin. He could clearly see the twisted, hellish moonscape of No Man's Land, a charnel house of torn-up earth, twisted wreckage and bodies, stitched on either side by the zig-zag of trenches. The smell that came up was unbelievable: years of death, decay, and the putrification of men and animals.

He was quickly losing altitude.

Bullets zinged around him as he manhandled the Spad out of the dive and leveled out a few hundred feet above the ground. Whatever this thing was, it was apparently inescapable.

More bullets buzzed around him. A hot sting on the left side of his neck. Metal ricocheting off the engine. A dull punching sensation in his right leg. Blood spattered around the cockpit.

The 220 Hispano-Suiza engine began to make ratcheting sounds, like a fatally-wounded animal whose breath was beginning to hitch. Luis felt a dumb resignation begin to seep over him like a heavy cloak. It seemed inconceivable he was about to die.

But there it was.

Thirteen years old and death had found him already, though it didn't seem to make much sense.

Perhaps it never would?

He briefly considered whether he should just roll over and auger the plane into the ground, just to get it over with.

The bullets abruptly stopped.

Not quite correct: there was the staccato drumbeat of machine gun fire further back.

Luis looked back, puzzled.

The black Fokker was breaking left. Behind it was another plane he had never seen before – a sky-blue Sopwith Snipe. The blunt-nosed British aircraft was blasting away at the German and this time the enemy had no choice but to break off.

The Snipe pilot attacked as though he were possessed.

The German veered to the right, then did a snap roll to the left, an almost impossible maneuver at such a low altitude and given the torque of the engine. The British pilot was quite skilled however, and clung tightly to the German's tail like a terrier with its blood up, letting off few more quick bursts from his guns. The Fokker bobbed and weaved away towards the north. As the British fighter turned to follow, Luis caught a brief glimpse of the pilot – a rugged but kind face with steely grey-blue eyes – who acknowledged him with a quick nod even as he banked away after the German plane.

Luis however felt his aircraft lurch and had just enough time to see the ground zooming up at him and . . .

Screamed.

Jumped up from his chair.

What his eyes were registering was horrible and he continued screaming.

The other boys were regaining consciousness. Heads shaking, eyes fluttering as though coming out of a deep, trance-like sleep.

Something was wrong about the woman . . . even as he watched she was *changing back* but . . .

What looked like a floating web of thin tendrils or tentacles was reeling back into her hideously distorted mouth. Whipping through the air. He had an afterimage that moments before they had been gently touching-caressing-probing the young boys' faces . . . necks . . . groins?

Luis kept screaming.

-3-

JOHN EASTON snapped awake in his chair.

Without comprehending what he was seeing, he found himself gripping the thick armrests with whitened knuckles, eyes staring-at-but-not-seeing the large Sony widescreen LCD television across from him, his ears still trying to process the sound that had escaped his throat.

Had he been yelling in his sleep?

He had just about pitched forward onto the coffee table and upset the remains of a glass of Scotch where he'd left it. The chair was one of his few real indulgences around the house – one of the high end leather ones known as a "Cigar" chair, its leather smooth and creamy to the touch. The kind of chair manufactured specifically for cool rainy days and reading favorite old books.

On the forty-two-inch screen, a sooty-faced George Peppard was clambering out of the cockpit of his Fokker Triplane, only to get chewed out by his commanding officer. The only area of his face not smeared in engine oil was where his flying goggles had been. Flying was apparently dirty business back in the good old days. The movie was *The Blue Max*, a 1966 classic Easton had ordered through his Video-on-demand.

He blinked slowly several times.

The dream had been incredibly lucid. He felt he was still half in it. He looked at his watch: 9:48 pm. Vivienne said she wouldn't be back before eleven. A major e-commerce client had decided to rethink their branding strategy mid-day and the company CEO had made it clear to her boss that if he didn't see the revisions by tomorrow morning (before his usual Saturday morning tennis game) not only his company but, from the sound of it, the very future of Democracy and the entire world would be in jeopardy, perhaps even irrevocably destroyed if his website wasn't updated.

So for Easton his Friday night had redirected from heading over to the carnival with his girlfriend to a couple of drinks, Thai take-out from The King of Siam and an On-Demand movie. Which, after a considerable amount of fuckery, he was able to figure out how to order and download to his TV set.

He never thought he'd be nostalgic for a video store until they all vanished one by one. Gotham Video on Main Street had closed back in February. The "Re-Opening Soon Under New Management!" placard in the soaped-up display window was now torn and yellowed.

He found the remote and after a few moments of fumbling buttons managed to figure out how to put the movie on hold. He hated technology and the older he got he was getting increasingly convinced that it hated him back twice as much. Vivienne had talked him into swapping his old cell phone for a Droid. Every time it randomly announced itself by saying "Droid" in its flat mechanical monotone, he felt an inexplicable urge to rip the damn thing out of its holder and chuck it as far as humanly possible. Preferably in front of the nearest moving vehicle.

That was one issue about the generation gap between them that he hadn't been able to address or even admit: certain new technologies like iPhones, apps, Droids, Facebook, and ordering movies through TV sets filled him with fear in a way all the horror and death he had faced in his life could not, perhaps because it made him think that he might be skating along the edge of old and obsolete. One of those fuddled and confused old fogies one finds in nursing homes, shuffling along the final stretch in life with the dazed look of someone at a complete loss as to what happened and at what point the entire world zipped on by into the future.

Then he caught himself: *Chill out old man, it's just technology. And it can get useless really quick when the electricity stops.*

He picked up his Scotch – a mellow Aberlour Single Malt - and walking over to the front windows, looked idly out at his street. This particular neighborhood favored houses from the early 1900s interspersed with the odd Victorian. Easton was drawn to it as the house, at 56 Irving Avenue, was on the high side of Route 9B and from his front bedroom windows had a scenic year-round view of the Hudson River.

Getting the house had been something of a coup since the bottom fell out of the market a few years back. The owner, Rick Edwards, had lived there his entire life but had been looking to dump it and move to a gated condominium community. Built in 1915, his father had purchased it in 1923 after finally returning home from the First World War in Europe. Edwards, a retired plumber and local volunteer fireman, wasn't born until just before the Second World War, the unexpected child of a late marriage. His mother had passed away in the early '50s, leaving her son to be raised in a neat, strict, and, from the sound of it, unhappy household. The place had been a steal. Upon showing up with his realtor, he was even more surprised when he found that the purchase included pretty much everything in the house "as is." Apparently Edwards wasn't overly sentimental about his family history. The house had all the signature details of a classic Craftsman design: six-over windows, a tapered post front porch with heavy stone piers, tan stucco siding, and dark wood trim. The steep-pitched roof was a side-gable design with heavy knee braces and exposed beams with a fieldstone fireplace chimney on the south side. Inside, it was all square oak paneling, stained glass, and wide plank floors. The furnishings were all original Mission-style pieces.

The Edwards may not have been warm and loving family but they knew how to take care of a house. The wood positively glowed from years of hand oiling and waxing and everything was meticulously maintained. Easton was incredulous at the offer. After walking around the place once, his realtor, an immaculately dressed Italian named Peter Nicocci, had stopped in the living room, turned around and shook his head. Then, letting out a low whistle, he said. "I just don't get it. The furniture *itself* is worth a fortune. Basement's dry, roof is new, maybe a new coat of paint on the outside and you're good to go."

Easton had nodded. "Great stuff. Strange the son would be so quick to get rid of *everything*. Mustn't have been a very happy home for him."

Nicocci had looked up at the heavy beamed ceiling. "To hell with happiness, if you ain't going to buy the place, I may just have to."

Easton had the offer in and accepted that afternoon.

During the closing, his realtor had insisted the place be "swept clean and move-in ready" but Easton had told him to drop it and hired a local cleaning service to tackle it instead. As the lawyers were filing out, he had a chance to shake hands with Rick Edwards. He still felt a little odd moving into a place fully furnished with someone else's belongings, so he said, "Thanks. I really like the house. But if there's anything you want back, just knock on the door."

Edwards, a stern-looking man who looked vaguely like Spencer Tracy, shook his head sadly. "It's all yours. I took out the few keepsakes I needed. It was always my dad's house. I was just a guest there. Not even really a welcome one."

Vivienne, the twenty-nine-year-old web designer Easton had been dating, could hardly contain herself when he'd shown her the place. She'd run around the first floor like a little kid, practically screaming with delight. A moment later he could hear her upstairs jumping up and down on the master bed.

"This place is . . . is awesome!"

Easton had to agree.

Irving Avenue was dead quiet. Most the families would be over at the Feast of Saint Anne Carnival out on the Point. Easton had only lived there since February but he had developed a pretty good sense of the neighborhood's rhythm and flow. Although hardly a wild street (aside from the random weekend party), this amount of hushed stillness for a Friday felt strange.

He gave the dregs of Scotch a swirl and finished it off.

The tattered afterimages of his dream flitted around the edges of his consciousness.

A plane. He had been flying a plane. A *biplane* for god sakes. Goggles. Oil. The buffeting wind of an open cockpit. An emergency. Something about a kid. *A kid?* Why would a kid be flying in the other plane? Death.

A new form of death he had never seen before. Didn't understand. Glimpse of the kid's intense face, blood . . . nothing. Even as he grasped at them, the images seemed to flutter out of reach, dissolving back into the deeper pools of his subconscious.

No doubt the movie had something to do with it. Quite obvious, actually, when you thought about it. He'd dozed off watching *The Blue Max*, the sounds of the movie infiltrating his dream state.

That added to what he'd found in the attic the previous week.

Easton loved the house but still found it strange, sad actually, that someone would just leave behind so much personal stuff. It spoke volumes about Rick Edwards' childhood. Still, as the saying goes, one man's trash is another's treasure and this house was a fully stocked trove. It wasn't until the previous week that he'd finally gotten around to going through the attic and the contents of the closet under the eave.

The attic had been partially finished early on and looked like someone had given up halfway through, probably Edwards' old man. The front half had open rafters and some naked bulbs in black metal sockets that might be from the 1930s. The floor was planked with unfinished tongue-and-groove pine that was scuffed and dinged from years of use. There wasn't a whole lot of stuff left up there: a few pieces of furniture, a box with an old 16mm movie projector from the 1940s, a case of old 78 LP records and a few miscellaneous crates. But on either side of the large dormer on the west side of the house where the roof line dropped to the eaves, large closets had been boxed in. One of these had a door that looked like it hadn't been opened in decades. The black enamel lock mechanism was rusted and Easton had to make a trip down to the drawer in the kitchen that held a box of miscellaneous keys to get it opened.

The closet was empty except for a footlocker and, propped up along the corner, an old wooden aircraft propeller that looked nearly eight feet tall.

The footlocker was a big one, almost the size of steamer trunk, with heavy steel bands, leather straps, and a bad-ass looking padlock. Neglected spider webs hung in loopy, dusty curtains; apparently even they'd given up on this particular real estate. It took a fair amount of effort to haul the locker out into the main area. One of the leather straps, brittle with age, broke in the process. Kneeling over it, he brushed aside the cobwebs and blew away the dust on the lid. Against an olive drab background was a red-blue-white roundel with a pair of crudely-painted eagle wings on either side. Below that in black letters with red outlines was written:

Air Service. U.S. Army.
Property of Lt. Luke A. Edwards
103rd Aero Squadron

Below that was a diamond shaped black and gold metal tag that read:

Henry Pollack Trunk Co., Dallas, Texas

Easton considered for a moment whether he should try to contact Edward's son about all this but then dismissed the idea. Whatever was going on behind why the house was left pretty much as is (it was almost as if Nick Edwards had simply packed a suitcase and left), it was probably best to let the whole thing lie. He poked around in the metal key box from downstairs but couldn't find anything that remotely matched the old padlock. He stood for a moment, tapping his chin with his finger, and thought about his grandfather's house back in Cornwall and a locked cabinet he'd had in the basement where he'd kept "A bunch of rubbish from the war your Grandmum would rather see tossed into the ocean." He walked over to the closet doorway and groped around along the top of the door frame and, after a minute, found, sure enough, what he was seeking hanging from a nail out of sight.

The footlocker held a fascinating and. as it turned out, quite bizarre treasure trove of history. The top half was a removable tray lined with striped cloth, stained with age. The overwhelming aroma of mothballs and cedar wafted up, and with it the memory of every old person Easton could ever recall meeting when he was a kid. The tray contained a whole host of personal artifacts including Lieutenant Luke Edwards' dress uniform – a remarkably preserved tunic of olive drab wool with a stiff collar and embroidered pilot's wings over the left breast pocket, a leather Sam Brown belt and shoulder cross-strap – along with a cracked leather flying cap, goggles, and brown leather flying boots. Pants, leggings, and personal effects were all neatly folded and stored. There was a set of silk scarves, log books, and training manuals, a Bowie knife, and a standard issue 1911 Browning .45 that looked like it had seen some action. Next to it was a German 9mm Mauser pistol. Setting this all to the side, Easton pulled out even more stuff: heavy bearskin boots for flying, a set of gloves and gauntlets a second tunic with bloodstains on it, a box filled with old photographs in a second box with medals and a leather folio of what looked like letters, promotions, etc.

In other words, what one might expect to find in a WWI aviator's footlocker.

At a glance it was a collection worthy of a museum.

It was in a tray at the bottom that things began to get a little odd. A bunch of torn swatches of airplane fabric, some with German and some with American markings, bullet holes, stains, and such; a small brown leather notebook that appeared to be a sort of diary; and a heavy scrapbook. Easton put aside these last items and went back to retrieve the propeller. It looked original and had seen a lot of action if its nicks and scratches were any indication. The blades had dented aluminum trim on the outer edge and a circular emblem in the center of each that read "SPA". Cleaned up, it would probably fetch a couple of thousand dollars. He left it propped next to the closet door and took the diary and scrapbook downstairs to the den he had converted into a home office.

This room, at the back of the house, was a mix of old and modern.

The original ceiling beams, quarter-sawn wainscoting, and plank floor, along with the bookcases, desk, and small fireplace all said classic "Craftsman". The high-backed leather executive chair, large widescreen monitor, sleek black computer and keyboard, and brushed steel halogen desk lamps added "Yes, but hi-tech" to that description. The room managed to look cozy and slick at the same time. Which was just the way Easton intended it.

He'd laid everything out on his desk and looking at nothing, took a minute of slow breaths to clear his mind. In his old life, his pre-Wyvern Falls life as it were, he had been a Detective (Assistant) Superintendent with the Royal Turk and Caicos Police Department and it was an old technique he still found quite useful, a sort of mental reset that cleared the decks of distracting debris/thoughts that tended to collect there.

He found himself reaching for the scrapbook.

The scrapbook held a story, though what it was wasn't exactly clear to an outsider. Instead of the usual chronology of a veteran's career from boot camp to shipping overseas to combat, this book, through a series of photographs, scraps of notes, and yellowed newspaper clippings, appeared to obsessively follow the career of a particular German pilot named Klaus Richtenstein. It wasn't much – apparently Richtenstein was a minor ace who chalked up nine kills before disappearing in combat along the Ypres sector in the summer of 1918 – and the one photo showed a thin, diminutive man with sallow cheeks and small dark eyes. The chin was small and the mouth almost feminine. In the photo, Richtenstein wore an expression that all but screamed aristocratic disdain. In short, he looked like the type the bullies in the schoolyard are pretty much obligated to torment. There was some reference indicating that he had been a doctor in civilian life and came from a wealthy industrial family.

There was a clipping about a hunting lodge in western Germany and several maps, including one of the Western Front from the latter part of 1918, with Allied and German airfields marked in pencil and repeatedly changed. There were also several other maps of Germany with all sorts of scribbled notes on them, some theater programs including, oddly, a Russian performance of a play called *Kashchey,* as well as a bunch of articles involving what appeared to be unconnected murders. Those articles were from German newspapers dated through 1921. Apparently Luke Edwards' peculiar hobby had gone on well after the war had ended. Then, to round it off, were a series of clippings including strange illustrations torn from books that depicted a skeletal, nightmarish-looking creature. One image was a postcard of a painting depicting the creature as a cadaverous old man leering over a terrified maiden.

Easton wasn't sure what to make of it. Ultimately, he decided to put it on hold as something to look into on a rainy day. It all may have been nothing more than an eccentric ex-pilot's hobby horse, though Easton had a hunch there might be a more interesting story going on once he started digging. On the surface though, it just seemed like a collection of unrelated random stuff that had no correlating logic except to the person who had put it together and, according to what Easton had been told, Luke Edwards had died back in 1978.

Still the topic kept nipping and pecking around the edges of his thoughts over the months. He'd just wrapped up a messy theft and impersonation case over in Chappaqua a few days before that had left him vaguely depressed. A husband-and-wife con team impersonating a maid and chauffer had ensconced themselves in a wealthy and half senile art collector's household and had then proceeded to help themselves to substantial amounts of his collection and bank account over the ensuing two years. Easton had been hired by the collector's nephew (who lived in Vancouver) after word had gotten back to him that the "maid" had been recently soliciting the widowed collector for marriage. Easton had notified the FBI once he sorted out what was really happening.

He'd been paid well for his services but the nephew had been a narcissistic and neurotic asshole and the art collector himself had acquired several of his rare pieces through highly dubious means – paintings that had previously belonged to several distinguished (and, courtesy of the Nazi "relocation" program, annihilated) Jewish families living around Prague and Vienna until WWII.

Which was how he found himself with little to do on a Friday night in June with his girlfriend working late. His friend, Jim Franks, had called before and asked if he'd like to tag along to the carnival, but Easton wasn't much in the mood for playing third wheel. Plus, truth be told, he was a little chagrined that his girlfriend Vivienne was working late while Franks, who as Art Director for the same small interactive media company was technically her boss, was running around enjoying a little R&R.

So Easton's Friday night plans had been reduced to deciding which restaurant to order take out from. The options had come down to either Pancho's Villa, a local Tex-Mex restaurant of as dubious a quality as its namesake was of character, or Thai. Thai won – with Scotch. Hell of a combination.

And of course there was the movie.

Easton had dozed off somewhere around the midpoint and had lost track of the plot. George Peppard was playing an "up from the trenches" German pilot mercilessly intent on earning the German Air Force's highest medal, the coveted *Pour le Merite* – also called the Blue Max – at any cost. Peppard, playing Lieutenant Bruno Stachel, was coming off as gutsy and likable in a sociopathic anyone-between-me-and-my-medal-is-expendable sort of way.

The dogfight scenes were fairly impressive if sometimes puzzling. Mixed in with some vintage Fokker D.VII's, D.I Triplanes and reasonably done British SE5A mockups (actually modified post-war Tiger Moths) was the Red Baron, inexplicably flying a 1931 French Morane Saulner MS.230.

Easton refilled his Scotch and sat down to watch the conclusion. The German Air Force general finds out that Stachel, who's become a heroic German ace, has been faking kill claims and fucking the General's wife to boot (played with breathless sexiness by a young Ursula Andress). After being informed that a new German monoplane fighter being tested is really a structurally-unsound death trap, the German general, played by James Mason, realizes it's the perfect answer to his dilemma. He orders Stachel to take it up and challenges him with – ". . . let's see some *real* flying!" – knowing full well what the result will be. Sure enough, minutes later there came the whine of an aircraft falling and a moment later the plane crashes in the airfield outside the general's office window. *Voila!* Stachel's career is *finito*.

Muting the sound as the credits rolled, Easton let his mind wander back again to the dream he had just had. Only gossamer fragments remained. He had been flying an aircraft of sorts – a biplane – and there was something about the enemy pilot he was pursuing that was connected to a deep loathing and fear. And something about *purpose*.

And there had been that other plane. The Spad. Flown by a *kid* for god sakes. He thought about the bloodied face looking up at him from the splintered cockpit. The kid couldn't have been more than twelve or thirteen years old.

What the hell had that been about?

Easton shook his head as he walked back into the kitchen to refill his Scotch.

"I need to get out of here, take a vacation and get the hell away from all this old history crap," he said to the empty room.

Another thought followed on the heels of that: he was thinking *I*. Not *we*.

He had a hunch it wasn't just old history he needed to get way from.

-4-

LAZY BARS of sunlight were slanting through the thicket of bamboo and reeds. The morning tide was out and the aroma of swampy mud hung thick and sweet in the air like something one could touch, something greasy and unpleasant. Unfortunately, this particular morning the mosquitoes and black flies around the rough plank platform that defined the northern part of MacGregor Town seemed particularly motivated.

It wasn't really a "town," *per se*, unless one was adventurous enough to call the Frankenstein assemblage of a pint-sized shacks built out of found lumber, scrap doors, carpeting, and windows on the stretch of land south of Shadow Pond a "Town." That was just what the kids who put it together christened it after the two brothers who had originally put it together some years back. It was more like a "Base of Operations." For local kids.

Luis swatted another black fly on his neck, cursing. The only thing the Deep Woods Off was good for this day was as a pungent *Eau du Chemical Pine* cologne. Armando, however, seemed as impervious as ever to the squadrons of black flies and mosquitoes. Luis had no idea how he managed it. Must be some secret ingredient his mother snuck into his enchiladas or something, he decided. Or maybe Ecuadorians were just genetically protected.

A couple of crows squawked off in the distance.

Over the years, MacGregor Town and the surrounding bamboo thicket had served as a malleable backdrop for whatever games Luis and his friends cooked up on the spot: Marines in the jungles of Guadalcanal, Rambo seeking his abandoned squad-mates from the clutches of the diabolical North Vietnamese, or a special forces operation sent into the deep jungles of New Guinea to rescue a downed air crew from the headhunting cannibals. Most of the military themes were courtesy of Pete and Henry. Once it was even the setting for a half-baked "Survivor: Wyvern Falls" (only once – it had resulted in multiple fist fights) and on many occasions the "Half Moonies" version of *Lost*.

"Half Moonies" was the name Armando had unwittingly christened their little group after mishearing Pete Vogel heckling the Croton Tigers at a varsity football game the year before. (*Somos half munìs?* he had muttered in his odd pursed-lips manner of talking). Armando's ears had an uncanny tendency to mangle English phrases into equally mangled Spanish phrases. It had taken Luis awhile to figure out this was in fact his way of expressing his peculiar sense of humor. *I guess walking across a continent for four years will do that to you,* he had figured. What Pete had actually yelled was "Whatta a bunch of Half-Moroonies!" a Vogelism for those not meriting the title of a full moron.

But *Half Moonies* had stuck.

Plus, it kind of connected them to Henry Hudson's ship.

Today, however, there were no *Marines Kicking Jap Ass* or *Smoke Monsters Swallowing up Hapless Airplane Wreck Survivors*.

Just two boys, a hot June morning, and the sickly smell of drying mud. Along with the insects, of course.

And something else that hung like a frightening pall over the morning, a suggestion of dread that nibbled around the edges of what should have been a quintessential summer vacation day.

"Henry's gone missing," Luis said quietly.

There was a moment of silence. Then Armando shot back, *"Qué!?"*

The two boys were sitting on a section of a fallen pin oak that had been salvaged out of the woods nearby and manhandled (or boy-handled) onto the low rise that served as a meeting place and forum for the Half Moonies. Their respective bikes were propped up against Shack #2 nearby. Luis had phoned his friend and told him to meet at MacGregor Town "stat!" Pete and Adam were on their way.

Luis went back to fiddling with the piece of reed in his hands.

"Pete called me this morning. Mrs. Van Dorn called *his* mom in hysterics at 7 a.m. Henry went home when we all did last night, but this morning, when he didn't come down for roll call – I mean breakfast – his Dad went ballistic. They found his room empty. His bed was slept in, but empty. And *unmade*, which is like, unheard of. Dude, that's like fucking KP duty for a year over there, *after* his Dad kicks the living shit out of him. The police are over there now. Word is they think he ran off. Or ran away. I don't know, man. Something's not right. Henry wouldn't cut out without a word. At least to Pete."

The reed in his fingers continued to roll back and forth. He was still skating around what was really bothering him, but he wasn't sure how to bring it up with Armando without sounding like a complete whack-job. He was already embarrassed at what had happened at the tent last night.

What really did happen last night?

Hypnosis? A group trance? Hallucinogenic gas?

Did he just doze off and have an awesomely lucid nightmare?

He had been screaming like *uma rapariguinha assustada* – a scared little girl – and had made quite a scene. A bunch of adults (including the stumpy-looking usher) had quickly stormed into the tent fully expecting to find nothing less than someone being horribly murdered only to find an indignant (and angry) fortune teller with a bunch of confused-looking boys with slow blinking eyes.

Madam Red Baron had been glaring daggers, hunched over her table with her hands over her ears. Once it was established that the extent of Luis' outburst was nothing more than a bad case of hysterics, the usher quickly hustled everyone outside muttering "Itzall right . . . itzall right . . . nothing to vorry about!" Like a mantra that, if repeated enough, would become truth.

Luis' friends had tried to console him but he had been red-faced with embarrassment and his thoughts a maelstrom of fear

[Gleaming Maxim-bullet teeth. Blood. Death.]

and confusion. He just wanted to get away and be alone. One concerned parent had offered to call his parents (God no!) or at least give him a ride home, but Luis had shrugged them off, still sobbing, not wanting to see the equally embarrassed and concerned looks of his friends.

Armando had been there, looking at him worriedly (and something else?) but not saying a word. Luis had wiped his now-snotty nose with the back of his hand and, humiliated, walked off by himself.

Later, at home, as he sat on the edge of his bed turning the evening over and over again in his head, he remembered the bullets. They had all disappeared when the adults came in. (God, had Sabina been one of them!!? That would be the ultimate humiliation!)

What had happened to the bullets?

Nothing added up.

And Armando? He had a hunch his friend knew.

Luis shivered as he recalled the filaments-like tentacles he had seen (Did you, *amigo?* Really?) issuing from the gaping maw of that woman – who, *what* was she?

It would have to wait. But the Half Moonies would have to meet ASAP in the morning. Even through the stink of humiliation, Luis knew something, weird, very weird, had been going on in that tent and the cold knot in his stomach was telling him it wasn't over yet.

He had looked up at the framed picture of the Virgin Mary his mother insisted keeping over his bed and crossed himself.

The next morning, he found out Henry had disappeared.

Finally, he stopped spinning the reed.

Pulling together his resolve, he looked his friend in the eye. "Armando . . . last night. At that tent. Did you see anything; you know…like *weird?*"

The way the Ecuadorian's eyes darted to the ground and stayed fixed there answered his question.

Luis sensed this was uncomfortable territory for both of them, but he pressed on.

"C'mon, *amigo*, I need you tell me what you saw. What did you see that woman doing?"

But Armando was shaking his head. Once, twice - four times. Luis knew he could put red hot coals to Armando's heels and still not get an answer if his friend wasn't ready to give it. Like when he'd pushed Armando for details about the time when the Ecuadorian had accidentally seen his older sister Sonia naked in the bathroom.

Nothing. Wall of silence.

Christ, sometimes I'd like to wring his neck! Luis thought.

That train of thought was interrupted by the arrival of Pete, who came crashing along the back trail on his mountain bike with all the subtlety of a charging rhino. He was followed a moment later by Adam with his ever-present skate board tucked under his arm. The board was a beat-up looking thing covered in worn stickers but it had been a hand-me-down from his older brother and, like all things from Nick, was handled with a combination of awe and solemnity.

Pete was wearing cargo shorts and a striped Gator shirt with big crescents of sweat under the armpits (his nickname in their little group was "Sweatmonster-P", a title which he actually seemed to relish) along with his ever-present backpack. On any given day, it might contain any combination of war games, a water bottle, matches, and an assortment of fireworks or some sort of flammable substance and, if their activity occurred over lunch, a couple of bologna sandwiches on white bread with *French's* mustard. Luis was convinced Pete Vogel was the only remaining human on earth who still ate bologna sandwiches.

Pete stumped up and took up a seat on one of the large rocks that ringed the meeting area, Adam joining him. He wiped the sweat off his brow with the back of his hand (and a hearty "Phew!") and went through the ritual of cleaning and adjusting his glasses before pulling out his water bottle and taking a few swigs. It took Luis a moment to realize Pete was just as uncomfortable about bringing up this morning's news as he was. The silence began to drag out uncomfortably.

The smell of mud and river and rotting vegetation continued to hang in the air. A few more black flies and mosquitoes showed up with their friends.

After a few more slaps and curses, Luis finally spoke up, "Any word on Henry?"

Pete shook his head, lips compressing. "*Nada.* The police said it was too early to file a missing person's report and I heard a lot of their questions were directed at his dad. Most of them actually. Not their first courtesy call to the Van Dorn domicile, if you catch my 'incontinental' drift."

Luis did. In fact, he'd already heard pretty much the same thing via the local Portuguese hotline, which carried news as fast as any internet connection.

Pete picked up a stick and started making aimless lines in the dirt. "I texted him a few times but nothing. This ain't good." He said suddenly, voicing everyone's thoughts, "This isn't a Type Five Henry move." (This was another *Vogelism* he'd coined to describe Henry's more hare-brained schemes.) "It's more like a . . . like a—"

"—Fuckchopped ballbender?" Adam ventured, recalling a phrase he'd heard his dad use, usually when the elder Carr was waxing philosophic out in the garage (or workshop) on his cell phone to his buddy, Carl Atkins. The first time he'd heard it, his dad had been describing the ninth inning of the previous season's opening game between the Yankees and the Braves. Adam had no clue what a "Fuckchopped Ballbender" really was, but it sounded kind of cool.

Around him there was a moment of stunned silence while Adam's friends processed this unexpected *bon mot.* Luis was the first to burst out laughing. Peter quickly followed suit. Armando pulled out one of his rare big smiles and then, unable to contain himself either, doubled over and, after a moment of suppressed sounds that came out something like

"Brffffttt!" joined in the chorus.

"Fuckchopped ballbender? *Fuckchopped ballbender!!?*" Luis howled. Pete was actually slapping his thighs. Adam smiled and looked down at the ground, secretly pleased he'd finally made everyone laugh.

After a minute, things faded into a few dying snickers.

The pall of Henry's disappearance reasserted itself.

Luis' face grew serious and he looked at each of them in turn. "We need to talk, *amigos.* About last night. About what happened in the tent." Even at thirteen Luis had a natural directness and sincerity that would win him more than a few cases as a trial attorney many years down the road. Today, however, he began by looking Pete in the eye. "Pete, what did you see after that . . . that woman put that old bullet in your hand?"

Pete went through his glass-cleaning ritual again. "It was kind of cool . . . I mean *uber* cool! It was like I . . . we . . . were all in the coolest WWI flight sim in the world. *Richtofen's War* on steroids. Remember the Meuse Campaign? Where the 103rd Aero takes on Jasta 13? It was exactly like that. Actually, it *was* that. Aw, man, when those Germans came in . . ." Pete, carried away with memory, made his fists into machine guns and started making airplane noises. "Arrrrr . . .takka-takka-takka . . . nrrraaarrrhh!"

"Pete! *Amigo*!!" Luis was practically yelling.

Peter shook his head and blinked. "Huh?"

"This is *serious*, man. Focus!" He looked over at Adam. "You too? Like a super real flight sim?"

Adam nodded.

Luis had dropped the reed and started ticking off items on his fingers. "Okay. Number One. Fraulein Fortune Teller gives us each a bullet, a . . ."

"-Live bullet." Pete cut in.

"What?"

"They were *live* bullets. *Real ammo*, bud. I checked. The primer was intact. German 7.92mm. The same used in the Spandau machine gun - original WWI ordnance, I'd bet."

"Okay. She gives each of us a live bullet. Suddenly all of us are plugged in to this . . . let's call it a *simulation*." That wasn't quite right, not by a long shot, but Luis was trying his best to work out a cohesive narrative of what happened without a lot of digressing. "Suddenly, all of us are flying the unfriendly skies of France. Then a bunch of Germans show up and there's the mother of all dogfights. Then—"

"—Jasta 13." Pete interrupted again. "They were from Jasta 13. I know those markings like the back of my hand," he added, talking like he was a veteran of the Great War himself. Luis sometimes seriously questioned which version of reality his friend lived in.

One that clearly involved a lot of guns, stats and ammo. And unit markings. Don't forget all the unit markings.

"Okay. Jasta 13. Fine." Luis echoed, his tone sounding like: "whatever the hell that has to do with the price of tea in China. "Adam, you hip to all of this? You found yourself flying a biplane too, *sí*?"

A quick nod.

"Right. So all of us wind up in this simulation, somehow, and then we get attacked by a bunch of Germans-"

"Boche." Peter corrected

"*Boche*, then. Fine. Great. And then this monster comes flying through the pack in a solid black plane with a big skull on it and—"

"—What!?"

"*Oi chata*, Pete, will you knock off with the interruptions?" Pete didn't appear to be listening. His mouth scrunched to one side of his face as he contemplated something.

Luis looked at Adam. "Didn't you see him? The Black Plane that shot down that guy —Major Ned Pearson (how the heck could he have known that?) – who was shot down by the Black German Fokker who—"

"—Nope." Peter said firmly, shaking his head.

"*Nope?*" Luis realized, not for the first time, he could hit Pete Vogel over the head with a two-by-four and Pete would still go on being Pete, doing Pete things.

"Nope," Pete repeated. "Jasta 13 was flying Fokker D.VII's at the Meuse campaign, September 1918." He was looking up at a distant point in the sky above as if recalling all of this by rote, "Black, brown, purple green Markings. Sky blue undersides. No black planes though. Jasta 7 did, and of course, Voss's D.I in Jasta 2, but with a green nose cowl. But Jasta 7 was nowhere close to the Meuse campaign. Are you sure it was black, all black? A Fokker D.VII?"

Luis was trying to process all this. "It was black alright. Solid black. Propeller to rudder. With a big bad-ass white skull on the side and those big crosses…" He picked up a stick and quickly drew in the dirt:

Peter looked at it, brow furrowing, and shook his head. "That's the old-style Maltese Cross. Phased out by then." He took the stick from Luis' hand drew this next to it:

"That's what it should have looked like." He put his chin down and looked over the tops of his glasses at Luis like the world's youngest disapproving professor.

"Are you sure?"

"Sure as *merda* on a hog, bro. You didn't see the pilot? The one that looked as though he had crawled out of *Tales from The Crypt*? Skeleton face? Glowing white eyes? Rotting leather cap?" Pete looked at him like he'd grown an extra head or two. Adam was shaking his head as well. Armando didn't say a word, although he stared at the ground and crossed himself again.

"Well, I did. It was the freaking scariest thing you could imagine, and that includes Mrs. Cararez' *pita*." he added, referring to the anatomy of the Wyvern Falls High School history teacher, who was so overweight she'd given birth to a son the year before without any of her students being aware she was ever even pregnant. He looked at his friends, trying to process this. "Seriously, you didn't see this dude?" Thinking: *maybe for the best – whatever the damned thing was, you wanted to stay the hell off its radar.* Then he turned to Armando.

"But you saw it, *amigo*. You tried to shoot it off my six. Right before that other Kraut creamed you."

A long pause. Then Armando nodded reluctantly.

For a moment no-one said anything. Finally, Pete spoke up.

"So . . . what does this, this German in the black plane have to do with Henry disappearing?"

Luis had been trying to work that out himself. It still didn't add up.

And yet he knew it was so.

"Dunno. But there's more. After we, well after *I* came out of the simulation . . .

[the ground rushing up . . . you were already dead]

. . . I saw something else. Something really, *really* weird." He told them as best he could what he'd seen: the gaping, nightmare mouth that had become hideously distended...the gossamer tentacles glistening in the dim light . . . the smell . . . that vaguely recalled nearly-dead fish floating on the surface of the water. He'd forgotten that detail until now. Even as he described what he'd seen in the tent last night, goosebumps ran up and down his forearms.

Any rational adult would have scoffed at Luis' recollection, dismissed it as the product of an overactive imagination and one too many video games or *Twilight Saga* movies. But Luis could tell by the rapt expressions that his three friends, sitting there in the glistening heat of an early summer day, in the same spot where their overactive imaginations had fabricated all sorts of fantastic scenarios, believed every word. Even Pete, the most ardent pragmatist of the Half Moonies, slowly nodding his head in acknowledgement.

Luis stood up, walked over to the water's edge. The tide was now coming in and, on the rippling surface of Shadow Pond, opposing currents could be seen, suggesting the more dangerous deeper currents underneath. He flung the stick in his hand out into the water, then, again in an unconsciously lawyer-like gesture, turned to face his friends with a dramatic flourish.

"That fortune teller is some sort of monster, *amigos*," he said forcefully, "A real, bona fide monster. And don't ask how I know this, but I think she has something to do with Henry disappearing. We have to go back tonight and find out who and what she is . . . *si?*"

"Shouldn't we just tell our parents? Or the police?" Adam suggested. Pete let out a snort and glanced sideways at him. "Sure, Chief, good plan. And they'll throw us into straightjackets and send us on a Thorazine vacation right afterwards."

"Pete's right. We need to do this ourselves. Like Assassin's Creed."

"Nah," Peter said, "'Call of Duty Four'. And ladies, I think I have an idea . . ."

-5-

WITH A burbling roar, the red Fokker Triplane zoomed by, did a tentative dip and, banking left, began to trail a thick plume of grey-white smoke. A moment later, there came again the staccato rap of machine gun fire from the cream-colored Spad tailing it and the Triplane did a sluggish skid to the right, dropping down towards the airfield as it looked for a place to land.

"Looks like the Baron is done for this time!" boomed the announcer's voice through the loudspeakers hung from the nearby wood poles. A sporadic round of applause broke out from the spectators lining the side of the aerodrome as if the crowd was unsure whether or not this was a good thing.

". . . Really toned it down – a *lot* – not like the old days when they'd really put on a show. Especially back when Cole Palen – he's the guy responsible for all this – was still around. Now that was some *real* dogfighting." The old man in grease-stained overalls was wiping his hands out of reflex on an old rag he'd produced from his back pocket. "After the crash in '08 that all changed. Now the sheriff has to send a deputy down to every show to make sure our pilots play it soft and easy-like. Court order."

Next to him, John Easton shielded his eyes against the early afternoon sun. The whine and roar of old aircraft engines in the June air was giving him a boyish thrill he hadn't even known he'd forgotten. Standing by the entrance of the hanger at the far end of the airfield with the older man, he realized with a start he was grinning with excitement.

He felt like an eight-year-old kid again.

"What happened?"

"Dunno. Nothing unusual that morning. Same old dogfight. It was a Nieuport 24. New one up from New Zealand. Just spun out and augered in just over the trees yonder."

Carl Steneck was a pilot, veteran mechanic, and chief curator at the old Rhinebeck Aerodrome. He was also a bottomless well of information when it came to antique aircraft and pretty much anything involving the First World War. As a young man, he had met and talked at length with many surviving pilots of the Great War, men who in the twilight of their lives found themselves all but forgotten, eclipsed by the interest and immediacy of the Second World War.

Easton had first stumbled across Steneck the previous autumn when he'd shown up one dreary day to poke around the old and dusty exhibit hangers across the road from the aerodrome. The brochures had made it seem a little quaint and kitschy. The reality had been even stranger. Stepping onto the grounds of the aerodrome had been like stepping through a window in time with its antique-looking hangers festooned with antique signage, the old vehicles, and assorted aircraft paraphernalia – wooden props, wing and fuselage parts, a swatch of canvas with a roundel on it here, a propped up flag there, the smell of oil and grease and gasoline. With the morning mist seeping around the undercarriage of the German Albatross that had been wheeled out to be prepped for winter storage, it was easy to imagine one had simply strolled into the year 1918.

It was in the display hangers across the road from the aerodrome that Easton had met Steneck poking around the exhibits which were an oddball mix of vintage planes, parts, old vehicles, signage dust and cobwebs. Without prompting Easton had received a wealth of information about the pitfalls of flying, including the real reason behind the legendary silk scarves– it wasn't so much to prevent the chafing of the pilot's neck from the perpetual 'rubbernecking' to spot the enemy as it was to keep from inhaling the castor oil used on the engines back then, which blew straight back into the cockpit. As Steneck dryly pointed out, there was nothing worse than getting a bad case of the shits at ten thousand feet when some enemy pilot was busy trying to drill your ass with lead. He also elucidated the various differences between flying a biplane versus, say, a jet, and how being a licensed pilot didn't automatically qualify one to fly both. A point underscored a few years previously when a hotshot colonel from West Point, who was a veteran F14 pilot, was allowed to take up one of their Fokker DR.I Triplanes. The big PR event had gone awry when the colonel, unfamiliar with the stall speed and torque of the Fokker, pulled up too fast on take-off and smashed into the trees by the runway. The colonel survived with little more than a bruised ego but the plane had to be scrapped.

So while Luis and his friends had been over by Shadow Pond contemplating the mystery of Henry's disappearance, Easton had gassed up the Maserati, packed up the strange scrapbook from the attic, and driven up to the Old Rhinebeck Aerodrome. He could have done a fair amount of research online but Easton figured a good place to start was talking to a living, breathing human being who was arguably the best local resource on the subject.

Plus, it was a convenient excuse to get out of town and go see a little bit of flying history. Not to mention postponing what he knew would be an unpleasant confrontation with Vivienne, who'd rolled in around two in the morning, drunk as a sailor.

It was a beautiful Saturday morning: a bright June sky with a few clustered puffs of cumulus clouds drifting along, apparently not in any rush to get wherever they were going.

The rag found its way back into Steneck's back pocket and he fixed Easton with eyes as faded a grey as his overalls. On the short side, he had a lean, compact frame and a squarish face that suggested the long-forgotten Oswald Boecke – Manfred von Richtofen's ill-fated mentor and friend.

"So what can I do you for today, Mister . . .?"

"Easton. John Easton."

"Ah yes. You're the detective fella that was up here last fall." Steneck had an oddly steady way of talking, Easton noticed, as if every word was measured out and evaluated before being spoken. "I remember you. Margie told me you'd called this morning about something you wanted to have a look at. That it?" he added, nodding toward the leather satchel tucked under Easton's arm.

Easton grinned and ran a hand through his unruly thatch of straw-colored hair. Since his whirlwind romance with Vivienne that started seven months ago, he'd let it grow out from its usual regulation cut. He was good-looking in a rugged sort of way but, having just brushed past forty a month before, he was at a loss as to what the young web designer saw in him.

Or if what she saw was still there.

He padded the leather satchel. "Anywhere we can sit down and go over this?"

Steneck motioned towards a 1920s-looking white house across from the entrance. "My office" he said.

The house was part office, part living quarters, part WWI airplane-parts storage. The kitchen they entered through had an old coffee maker, the remains of a pizza in a box, and the exhaust assembly off an Albatross sitting on the counter. Steneck's office was a small whitewashed room on the second floor packed to the gills with old posters, parts, shelves overflowing with magazines, and various large-scale models stacked on top or hung from the ceiling. It looked as though a cyclone had ripped through just before they'd entered.

After clearing a pile of debris from the center of his desk and rescuing a footstool for Easton to sit on, the old mechanic sat himself in an old wooden swivel chair and leaning forward with his arms on the rests got right down to business.

"So what have you got?"

Easton pulled out the scrapbook and handed it over. "That's what I'm hoping you can tell me. I found this in the attic of my house. Souvenir from the previous owners."

Steneck took the book delicately with both hands and set it front of him like it was a holy relic. Producing a set of reading glasses from his front pocket, he opened the cracked leather-bound cover, careful to touch only the corners of the folio pages with his fingers. His brow furrowed as he gave the scrapbook a quick once-over, then a twice-over. The third time, he pulled out a magnifying glass from one of the desk drawers and went back and forth over the pages repeatedly. Easton was curious to learn what Steneck was thinking but contented himself by looking over the wall posters with half-feigned interest. A warm breeze wafted through the half-open window carrying the mixed aromas of fresh grass, honeysuckle, and engine oil. Over on the airfield, Easton noticed a Rolls Royce Silver Ghost (painted yellow) being chased by a pilot on a vintage motorcycle and sidecar. He wasn't sure exactly what was going on but it was apparently all part of the show. A man dressed up as a German pilot was at the wheel of the Rolls. In the back seat was a "kidnapped" young woman in period dress, "'bound" with heavy ropes. Easton wasn't sure if she was waving to the pursuing pilot in distress or telling him to kiss off.

The chair creaked as Steneck sat back and removed his spectacles. "Hmmmm . . . if I didn't know better I'd suspect this is all a very strange practical joke. A goddamned *antique* practical joke. These pictures all look authentic and the clippings certainly are." He half-turned in the chair.

"Where *exactly* did you find this?"

"A closet in the attic. Inside a footlocker. Full of all sorts of interesting stuff. Luke Edwards — the previous owner's father, was apparently in a squadron known as the 103rd Aero. Ring a bell?"

"Ayuh. Rings a bell or two all right. Hundred and three was a famous American outfit. Originally they were a bunch of American volunteers known as the Lafayette Escadrille, commanded by William Thaw — one of the few surviving aces of that ex-pat squadron who stuck it out when they had to go legitimate. Never heard of no Luke Edwards though, but I can look it up quick enough. There's a One-Oh-Three Squadron history around here somewheres . . ." He gestured vaguely toward the bookcases on the opposite wall, which appeared to be buried under a landslide of books.

"What about Klaus Richtenstein? You ever hear of him?"

"No. But I can dig around. There were thousands of pilots on both sides in that war and for much of it, their life expectancy was an average of two weeks. Not much of a long-term choice for the career-minded."

"Neither was the infantry, I heard"

"Nope. Not that either."

Easton noticed Steneck's finger tapping absent-mindedly on the scrapbook cover.

"Anything else come to mind? As weird as it all looks, it's a pretty compelling story in those pages."

Steneck thought a moment. "Well . . ." He tilted his head and gave Easton a one-squint-eye' look, his finger paused in mid-air. "Well, Mister Easton…"

"John is fine."

"John, then. Well, there's no doubt this Edwards fellow was obsessed with this German pilot. But, well, I get the idea you might have had a gun firin' in your direction once or twice, and might have been doing the firing yourself once or twice, but pardon me for saying – and don't take offense at this – you ain't a combat veteran, are you?"

Easton smiled. "Can't say I am."

Steneck tapped the book again.

"Airmen were – are – just as much a superstitious lot as any sailor. I flew F104s and F101s in Vietnam, so I can speak to some of this first hand. Where I'm going is that, whenever you have men dying and killing each other day in and day out, you'll have bogeymen."

"Bogeymen?" Easton wasn't sure he'd heard correctly.

"Bogeymen. Just like it sounds. World War Two has plenty of accounts of this. German fighter planes painted in schemes that never existed. Accounts of Japanese fighters painted all black or black with cherry blossoms. I have one autobiography by a veteran pilot that goes on and on about a Japanese plane he called the "Black Predator" that became the terror of his squadron. But you see, such a thing in that case doesn't even make any sense."

"It doesn't?" Easton wasn't sure he was seeing at all.

"It doesn't. Not if you understand Japanese culture. It would be unthinkable to any Japanese pilot to individualize his aircraft in such a way. It would be considered tasteless and egotistical. Not to mention that there has never been a single Japanese account on record even mentioning such a thing. And then there are tales like that of Tokyo Rose. You know about Tokyo Rose now, don't you?"

Easton shrugged. He had some vague recollection, mainly from old movies, about the infamous Japanese female propaganda announcer who taunted the allied servicemen over the radio waves throughout the war. Still, he was at a loss where the curator was headed with all this. Steneck leaned back in his chair and crossed his fingers.

"Tokyo Rose was the bane of the U.S. servicemen in the Pacific during the War. Every night she would come on the airwaves in her "Hey, Joe!"

sing-song voice and taunt them with everything from jokes about what their wives were doing back home with the milkman to uncanny intel on what had happened that very day, such as the names of an aircrew that had just been killed or who had just been transferred to what airfield or such. Anything to psych out the Americans and make like the Japanese were some omniscient, all-powerful enemy, all-seeing and all-knowing and all-undefeatable. The books in my library are filled with references to her, much quoted accounts of her broadcasts, how much the soldiers both despised and were amused, even entertained by her on those lonely nights far in the middle of the Pacific. There was only one minor problem with Miss Tokyo Rose."

"Which was . . .?"

"She *never* existed."

"Come again?" Easton considered having his ears checked out by a doctor.

"I'll say it again: *She never existed.* She was a myth. There was no Tokyo Rose. Oh, there was a network of female Japanese propaganda announcers that put on broadcasts throughout the war. But absolutely no record, and more importantly no evidence, *ever*, of any woman announcer ever calling herself 'Tokyo Rose'. But that's only half the lunacy of it."

"What's the other half?"

"The other half is that by the end of the war the *idea* of Tokyo Rose had become so firmly embedded in the American psyche that, during the war crimes trials, they took it to the extreme of producing a scapegoat, accused her of being *the* Tokyo Rose and, in predictable kangaroo court fashion, they sentenced her to life imprisonment. It wasn't until the late 1960s that the farce was put to rest when President Nixon pardoned the poor woman but even today most people don't know squat about that. But that ain't the point now, is it?"

"What *is* the point?"

"The point is this: even grown men, men dealing with the horror and reality of death day in and day out can invent– and completely believe in – something that is utter and complete BS. To the point of putting that BS on trial and convicting it, just to convince themselves it was real. I'd be happy to poke around about your Luke Edwards fella here as a matter of history – local history, mind you – but for the record, I would say he was probably just another pilot who went off his rocker, quite a ways off his rocker in this case, in pursuing his own private bogeyman. Christ, it's sad really, most of these guys, even the great Red Baron, all went pretty much insane by the end because of all the killing. And they were so young." Easton considered this for a moment. And considered a few things he'd Googled on the internet that morning. He was sure his next question would undermine his credibility with the old curator, but he was here and they were talking and what the hell.

"Have you ever heard of a *Liche*?"

"Nope, can't say I have." Steneck eyed him carefully, as if suspecting he was about to get his leg pulled. "Sounds like some sort of moss. Or maybe a fungus."

Easton chuckled. "Well, not exactly. It's an old Slovakian legend. There's a playbill in the scrapbook of a Russian play called *Kashchey*. I looked it up. It's about an old king who, through sorcery, extracts his soul into a container, in the process turning himself into an undead creature who can't be killed by conventional means. Of course he captures a beautiful maiden and forces her to become his wife and a young prince attempts to rescue her. But it's his obsessive fear of death that drives him to such extraordinary measures."

"Sounds like a good children's story."

"It certainly does, doesn't it?" Easton was leaning against the wall, hands in pockets and watching the ongoing melodrama outside. The pilots had jumped back into their aircraft and were chasing each other across the airfield. He looked back at Steneck. "Well, if you wish to keep the scrapbook for a few days, I would be curious to know if you could find out any more, shall we say, *less whimsical* information regarding Mister Richtenstein and Mister Edwards."

Easton pulled out his wallet and gave Steneck one of his business cards. "My pleasure. Not too often I get a request to dig around for anything new on the Great War." He glanced at the card. "So this Edwards fella was from Wyvern Falls?"

"Far as I know. He certainly wound up there. Does that suggest anything?"

Steneck was looking thoughtfully at the business card he held between his thumb and forefinger. "Lived there long yourself?" he asked, as if not hearing Easton's question.

"About eight months, give or take."

"Well . . . kind of a strange place that village is."

"In what way?"

Steneck smiled a little. "Just that it has kind of a reputation of sorts hereabouts. Let's just say it somehow don't surprise me this Edwards fella is from there. Not a bit."

-6-

THE BASEMENT room smelled of mold, rot, dead leaves, and animal shit.

And hot urine.

The latter was fresh and pungent as it had just recently run down the leg of the boy shackled to the old stone wall.

The shackles were old and rusted, something right out of a medieval dungeon. They were also a size too small and bit painfully into the wrists and ankles of the boy, emaciated as his limbs were.

He couldn't remember how, or even when, he had gotten here. His thoughts felt fuzzy and disjointed. He remembered something about

[*a bullet*]

a woman, a very sensual and attractive *older* woman.

Had she unzipped his pants? The cold caress of alabaster fingers. A glimpse of swollen breasts as her robe opened and the darker mystery was revealed between her legs.

Naughty thoughts.

Only a slight twinge from the penis in his shorts. He was vaguely, fuzzily aware that he had peed himself, because most of his attention was now focused on what he was seeing in the archway opposite, suggested by the dim bars of sunlight filtering through the rotted floorboards above. The face that had materialized there seconds (minutes? hours?) ago.

It was a nightmare visage.

Watching him.

A blackened skull, gleaming gun-metal teeth and sunken eye sockets with orbs the color of rotted egg-whites. Gaping slits where the nose had once been.

Blood seeped from where the shackles were cutting into his skin. The fingers of one hand fluttered weakly. The boy heard a sound and realized it was coming from his own lips. It was the whimpering gibber of a terrified animal. His father would have been disgusted at such weakness. He would have . . .

All thoughts of what his father would or might have done flew away. He didn't remember seeing the thing move, yet the face was right before him in a blink. Too close, invading his personal space, one might say. Someone needed to alert Child Welfare.

The smell was overwhelming. Rot and decay. And dirt.

You need to clean up your act, mister. The absurd thought vanished as the boy became aware of a strange sensation, like a million needles probing his skin and pores.

The mouth of the skull opened.

Like something you might see in a bad carnie doll, the rotten egg-white orbs rolled and two slitted pupils – a reptile's eyes – fixed him, barely an inch from his own.

The needle pricking sensation increased. Almost exquisitely painful. The boy heard a thudding, pounding sound in his ears and realized that it was his own heart, fear turning it into a frantic sledgehammer. A milky, wispy substance was drawing off his skin and mouth and he realized that the needling sensation wasn't of something *entering* him, rather it was something being drawn *out* of him.

And into the gaping mouth.

A choking sob. Desiccated, skeletal fingers cupped his chin in an almost sensual embrace, forcing his jaw open.

He felt cold. Terribly cold. The heat was draining out of his body. The boy realized, remotely, that he was about to die. There would be no graduation, no more weekends gaming on the wii, no more Hot Pockets and Coca Cola and no falling in love and maybe losing his virginity with a girl named Sally Meyers he'd set his sights on . . . nothing but the rushing black abyss of death.

From somewhere in that hideous maw, a tongue darted forward, a blackened slug. Wet and ice cold, probing along the boy's lips and nose. Testing. Tasting.

Like a ship slipping its moorings, his mind went.

The jaws clamped down on his lower face, and chewed.

It always liked the boys. Boys were the easiest.

After a few minutes, the screaming stopped.

-7-

THE LATE SEPTEMBER *morning is unusually cold. The mist that lingers around the aerodrome at Lisle-en-Barrois drifts in ghostly fingers around the outbuildings and parked vehicles. In the distance there is an occasional boom of artillery from the trenches at Verdun, muffled and sporadic. From one hanger comes the telltale clinks and clangs of a plane being serviced, a Spad XIII that was badly mauled in the squadron's mash-up over Dun-sur-Meuse the previous evening. Of the twelve aircraft in the 103rd Aero Squadron's inventory, four are burnt and mangled wrecks behind the German lines, two are being patched together in the hangers, one is being dismantled for whatever usable parts it might still have, and five are out on the morning sortie looking for payback.*

By the corner of one of the hangers sits a pilot on a folding chair, a bandage wrapped around his head where a German bullet nicked his skull the previous day. His arm is in a sling, the left hand heavily bandaged where another bullet passed clean through his palm, miraculously not breaking any bones. Under the tight olive-drab tunic and uniform shirt, a third bandage wraps his abdomen where yet another German bullet passed through his right side, a shallow but painful wound that creased the lower ribs. His right chin and cheek have a spray of small scabs where splinters from the dashboard of his cockpit were removed.

He's an intense looking man with a thatch of sandy-colored hair sticking up in crazy tufts around the head bandage, but his bloodshot eyes have a hollow, haunted look, his cheeks are sunken, and the scattered pile of French cigarette butts around his chair are a clear indicator of his current state of mind. If they weren't, the two trembling fingers of his right hand holding the still-lit cigarette certainly are.

Lieutenant Luke Edwards takes a drag off his smoke and stubs it out under the heel of his knee-high leather boot. Although smoking is a relatively new habit to the American flyers, he's had enough to know the French cigarettes taste like burnt manure and are only eclipsed in sheer awfulness by their German counterparts which Edwards sampled only once on a dare.

By all rights, he should be convalescing in the nearby field hospital but he simply walked out, despite the doctor's and nurses' protests. He also refused any painkillers, even a handful of the relatively new Bayer aspirin tablets, saying, "I've had enough godammed Hun medicine in the last twenty-four hours, thanks." In a perverse way, he somewhat relishes the pain and the way it sets his thoughts and teeth on a tight edge. Relish or not, his orderly or 'bat' has provided his silver flask with some decent French brandy that had been scrounged up and at least took a little of that edge off.

The Lieutenant Edwards that sits, elbows on knees, cigarette in trembling fingers, on this cool autumn morning in France is angry, upset, and in a fair amount of pain. But, behind the hard, bloodshot stare, he is also wrestling with fear and terror. Fear of sharing the same horrible, burning death so many aviators experience, terror of the particular instrument of that death during yesterday's evening mission. At his hip is a regulation 1911 forty-five caliber pistol in its stiff leather holster. The running half-bluff he has told his fellow pilots is that, if his aircraft catches fire, he will use it on himself rather than endure a slow screaming death falling through the sky. Now the thought has crossed his mind as to whether he would use it on himself before his plane caught fire, before facing again the nightmare that dropped out of the clouds and sent four American pilots to their deaths the day before.

The mission started out normally enough: a routine patrol over the trenches of Verdun after a week of bad weather. Edwards and his fellow pilots were eager to mix it up. Just after five pm, they'd jumped a pair of Junkers J.I observation planes lumbering along at about 2,000 meters on the German side of the front, Edwards putting his fair share of bullets into the second one, which, despite its all-metal fuselage and armored pilot tub, suddenly did a snap roll with flames erupting out of the engine. Edwards was watching in morbid fascination as the German aircraft went into its death spin, the rear observer/gunner jumping to his death as the plane became a fiery coffin arching down through the heavens. Then it seemed the sky around him was filled with the angry buzz and whine of bullets, directed not at him but at Jim Roundtree's Spad flying alongside. Edwards realized he had made a classic rookie mistake — target fixation — but there was no time for second thoughts. Certainly none for Roundtree, whose head erupted in an explosion of blood, gore, and grey matter as Edwards looked on in horror.

Edward's hands and feet already responded automatically, kicking the rudder and wrenching the Spad's control column up at an angle that would minimize his target area, even as his head snapped up to see what proved to be the most terrifying thing he had ever witnessed.

Edwards was expecting to see that they'd been jumped by a German squadron waiting to ambush them from higher altitude. That would make sense — sending in the observation planes as bait, then pouncing on the unsuspecting enemy — but in the drawn-out split seconds that followed, he grasped that this is definitely not the case. It was a lone German aircraft, a Fokker D.VII, painted solid black with Maltese crosses and a large skull-and-crossbones on the main fuselage but no other specific unit markings.

But it was the thing piloting the Fokker that riveted Edwards' attention: a skull wrapped in blackened parchment-like flesh with a rotting leather cap and reptilian eyes with whites the color of rotting egg-whites. It was unlike anything he had ever seen before but there was no time to analyze the atavistic revulsion that seized him: whatever this thing was he knew with certainty that it was the very incarnation of death.

The how and the why were irrelevant as the tight formation of Spads broke up and the engagement began.

There had been rumors traveling up and down the front as these things do: rumors of a frightening, skeletal-looking German pilot, usually preying on small groups of planes; that he is invincible and diabolical in his ability to kill; that he is able to fly his plane in a manner that is impossible; that his guns have unlimited ammunition and that his bullets never miss their mark.

There had been a spike in casualties these past few weeks along this section of the front, and the last few days had seen a rise in mission aborts, particularly among the observer craft. Edwards had heard the stories along with the rest of his squadron, but he'd dismissed them as the whisperings of overwrought imaginations and as hysterical episodes that occasionally come upon men, even whole units, after extended periods of unrelenting stress.

Until now.

In a blink, his whole perception of reality was turned on end, along with his concept of death. Still, he was first and foremost a pilot and a trained killer and he acted without overanalyzing.

Despite this, the situation quickly went south. Within five minutes, two more 103rd Spads were describing their funeral arcs through space and Edward's own plane was riddled by two passes of the demonic German. At least one aspect of the rumors had been proven false, he noted with grim satisfaction, or he wouldn't still be alive. There was no time for strategy, hand signals, fancy maneuvers, or anything but survival. The pilot, or whatever it was, was unnervingly good and handled his Fokker with inhuman skill. Bobbing and weaving, impossible to hit but still squeezing off deadly bursts at its foes. More than once, Edwards had the black Fokker in his sights only to have it jump right back of them out as if the enemy had eyes in the back of his head and was anticipating Edwards' every move. The Spad was hardly the most maneuverable of aircraft but it is at least rugged and fast. A minute later the senior officer on this flight, Captain McDonnell, had the struts of his upper wing severed and along with it his head as his biplane became instantly converted into a monoplane. The top wing broke off and pin wheeled away. Edwards had to fight down his rising gorge as he saw his leader's Spad, once a marvel of aviation engineering, flop gracelessly end over end, quickly tearing itself into pieces and catapulting McDonnell's headless corpse out into the ether.

More than once Edwards swore as he saw machine gun bullets passing through the German pilot's body with no apparent effect. "Impossible," he thinks. Part of his brain considered that this might simply be some sort of insane joke, that the death's head was some sort of mask put on for effect, to psych out his opponents, but it quickly became apparent that this wasn't the case. At one point the Fokker was momentarily alongside Edwards' Spad and the death's head flicked in his direction and, impossibly, the grin *appears to widen. Edwards felt the blood in his veins turn to ice.*

He also realized another first had occurred in all his missions to date: the squadron had been routed. Blind panic seized the veteran pilots of the 103rd Aero against this unstoppable, invincible enemy. Edwards was hit twice at this point and blood was filling the left side of his goggles. His heart was going like a trip hammer and from his throat came an animal snarl as he saw the Fokker's bullets riddling yet another plane – it looked like Howard Crushank's Spad – and he saw another Spad falling away, trailing white smoke, diving towards the safety of the Allied lines.

Edwards saw the black Fokker falling in behind Greg William's aircraft and, shoving the rudder hard right, slewed his own plane behind the German. "Got you, you bastard" is all he thought as he yanked the lever on his twin Vickers to clear the action and fired. He was barely fifty yards away and his bullets chewed pieces off the rudder and fuselage of his target, marching their way toward the engine nacelle. Edwards had just figured out one important thing: the creature may be impervious to bullets but the plane its flying was clearly not.

The Fokker staggered under the fire and then suddenly the hammers on Edward's guns fall silent except for empty clicks: he'd just run out of ammo. Cursing a blue streak, he slammed the throttle forward intending to ram his enemy but the Fokker, despite its damage, suddenly bobbed up, flipped and performed a split-ess – gracefully – then dove away into the lower cloud cover.

Edwards followed him. His vision – he could only see out of his right eye at this point – grayed out and he realized that his injuries were more serious than he realized. He leveled his plane again and instead pulled up alongside Williams' aircraft to assess his situation. Williams appeared to be uninjured but signaled that his control surfaces were damaged; his aerilons were barely usable but he at least had rudder control. Both pilots looked down over their cockpits but the lone German had vanished. It was nearly dusk when they made it back to the airfield. Williams had to make clever use of his throttle and rudder to see-saw his plane in for a semi-controlled crash landing. Edwards, weak with blood loss, managed a textbook landing but nearly collided his Spad into a hanger while taxiing and, barely conscious, had to be lifted out of the cockpit by the ambulance and ground crewmen.

He woke up in a field hospital and, after managing to hitch a ride back to the aerodrome, arrived only to find that he was too late: the squadron had taken off with the remaining flyable aircraft to hunt down the Black Fokker.

Two hours passed but still there was no sign of the squadron. Edwards pulled out his pack of cigarettes again and was just about to shake one out when he heard the muted ring of a telephone from the small brick building that served as their headquarters. After what seemed like an eternity of seconds, the front door opened and Major William Thaw, the 103rd's commanding officer, materialized in the doorway.

His square, blunt looking face was emotionless, his mouth a compressed line under the thick mustache.

Even at a distance, Edwards could see from his demeanor that, whatever news had just come through the telephone, none of it was good. Edwards jammed the cigarettes back into his pocket and, standing up carefully, a slight wince in his right eye betraying his pain, marched into the hanger where the mechanics were patching together two of the Spads with whatever parts they could cannibalize from the wrecks of other planes. Gerry Rosenthal, the crew chief, looked up with a grease-stained face as Edwards walked in, the stub of an unlit cigar clenched on one side of his mouth under a heavy bandit's moustache. The smudged and creased pillbox cap jammed on his head appeared to be an afterthought and the leather apron and overalls looked like they were last washed inside an engine block. Even the whites of his deep-set brown eyes appeared stained with oil. He'd been working through the entire night along with his crew to get the aircraft in some sort of flyable shape for the day's missions and the lines and wrinkles of his face only further illustrated the depth of his exhaustion.

Edwards glanced at the nearest Spad. Rosenthal read his look quickly enough.

"One hour, mebbe hour and a half. Still need to check the . . ."

"Now. I'm taking off *now*." There was no margin for interpretation in Edwards' response. But the Major had been explicit when he visited Rosenthal in the hanger the previous evening: "There'll be a patrol in the morning. I need at least four aircraft on it. Five if you can. The remaining two ready by this afternoon. And nobody, absolutely nobody, goes up without my clearance, understood?"

Rosenthal looked down at his feet, his brow creased. He was intensely loyal to the pilots whose planes he services but he was equally loyal to the Major as well. Major Thaw wasn't some desk jockey, more interested in getting results to impress his superiors and garner a promotion. Thaw was a veteran pilot himself who had volunteered for the Lafayette Escadrille and was a confirmed ace with five victories. There was no question he has the squadron's best interests at heart. Rosenthal responds with "I'm sorry, Lieutenant, but Major Thaw's orders are—"

He was interrupted by a heavy click and looked up to see the business end of a 1911 government-issue Colt .45 automatic in front of his face. The glassy look in Edwards' eyes wasn't quite sane.

"Now." Edwards repeated evenly.

Moments later, the Spad, ready or not, sputtered out of the hanger, blue smoke puffing out of its exhaust pipes. Major Thaw was still in the doorway of his headquarters, his moon face a study in anger and alarm, but Edwards didn't even glance in his direction as he taxied out onto the grass field. There'd be consequences to be tallied later – a narrowly avoided court-martial and being grounded for the rest of the war – but for the moment the Lieutenant was purpose personified. And that purpose was to avenge his fellow pilots and destroy this new inhuman enemy they are up against. Exactly how he could succeed where the rest of his squadron had so far failed never even enters his mind.

The Spad took off into the late morning gloom and disappeared over the horizon.

The cockpit clock was reading just past noon as Lieutenant Edwards patrolled along the front. He'd already spotted the wrecks of four of his squadron mates scattered across the blasted moonscape of no-man's land. Still, there was no sign of the Black Fokker and its dreaded pilot. The late September sun had burned away the undercast but the cumulous clouds piling up through twenty thousand feet are developing into thunderheads, with dozens of ominous caverns where the enemy may very well lurk in ambush.

Edwards cruised along around fourteen thousand feet and was just about to pull into a slow bank out of his latest crisscross course when the hairs on the back of his neck start tingling. Already light-headed from the thinning oxygen and sub-zero temperatures at such an altitude – in an open cockpit no less – it was the pain of his injuries and an undiminished fury that kept his senses alert. He was aware that his reflexes will not be at their sharpest after over an hour in such an environment.

It was a sudden double strobe flash of lightning off to his right that saved him.

The enemy had chosen its approach well – the black Fokker was all but invisible against the cavern of bruise-colored thunderheads behind it and it was only the brief flare of light that revealed him. There was a momentary lag caused by a morbid fascination as Edwards saw the German plane racing along in a sweeping arc to get into the kill position on his six, but before he even knew of it his frozen hands and feet already worked by themselves; slamming the throttle forward, clearing the action on the twin Vickers machine guns, pulling the stick in and pushing the rudder pedals into a hard right.

Death was coming for him and he would face it head on.

Blue-black smoke poured out of the Spad's twin exhaust pipes while the engine roared like a spirited horse cut loose after chomping at the bit too long. Bullets whined and whickered through the air as the Spad did a slow roll towards the Fokker, a dangerous but clever trick Edwards developed to throw off his enemy's aim. The D.VII's Spandau machine guns were winking and to Edwards it appeared that the tracer bullets are converging directly at his head – an optical illusion he knows from experience, but still one that is extremely unnerving. As the Fokker rolled into his sights, the Spad's twin Vickers began their own deadly chatter. The

German was slow rolling in the opposite direction and it was almost a graceful duet as the two planes, converging at over two hundred miles per hour, missed each other by mere inches. Edward's face was locked in a bestial snarl; his opponent's was a grinning death mask.

Over the next five minutes the deadly dance played out against the rolling thunderheads and flashes of lightening with neither side gaining a clear advantage or inflicting critical damage. The Fokker was superior in its maneuverability but the Spad was faster. However, there was a third factor that continued to frustrate both pilots – Mother Nature. The biplanes were tossed and battered about by crosswinds and air pockets as the storm gained in intensity. More than one decisive shot went wild as one or both of the planes took a lurching drop or were swatted aside as if by the mischievous fingers of an invisible hand.

Edwards soon realized that time and energy were against him in this battle. He was physically weak from his injuries and loss of blood. He was soaked in sweat from his exertions while his enemy – whatever diabolical spawn from hell it was – continued to function with the unrelenting precision of a machine. Despite his best intent and flying strategy he is time and time again unable to score a critical hit on the black Fokker and, for the first time since taking off from his airfield, the first seeds of doubt began to corrode the edges of his will. Though his grim determination was unrelenting, he understood that, unless he brings the fight to a speedy conclusion, it is only a matter of time before he makes a fatal mistake. Blood is seeping into his left eye through the bandages under the helmet. Both aircraft have already dropped several thousand feet in the constant maneuvering. Edwards mentally banged his head, riffling through everything he knows about the Fokker D.VII: "Think! Think! Think!" It was a plane with few weaknesses and a reputation for making even mediocre pilots look good. But powerful as the German BMW engine is, the 220 horse-power Hispano-Suiza in his Spad has the edge.

And something else he is sure he remembered hearing . . .

There's no time to start second-guessing. The Fokker had just snapped off another few rounds and was looping around to get on his six again. Edwards made a few drunken lurches with his aircraft and slumped forward to suggest he'd has been seriously wounded, then rammed the control stick forward into a steepening dive. The wind howled and shrieked around the struts and cockpit and the soldier's way down in the trenches below looked up with the deepening whine of the plummeting aircraft. Edwards hunkered down behind the small windscreen in front of him, one eye fixed on the airspeed indicator. Playing 'possum was a well-worn trick that wouldn't fool any but the greenest of pilots, but Edwards wasn't concerned with trying to fool his enemy, the trick was to bait him into following him.

The two aircraft arced down into the stormy undercast. The altimeter in the Spad's cockpit was spinning at an unnerving rate. The heavy airframe shook and the control column was shuddering as compression set in on the control surfaces. Edwards' stomach was a cold, writhing knot of fear. He was playing a deadly gamble, caught between a mangled, smashed death waiting in the cold earth below and the hideous grim specter hot on his tail. Glancing back, his eyes widened as he saw that the Fokker was gaining on him, which shouldn't be possible. He steepened his dive even further. The Spad shook and shuddered with increasing intensity. Edwards knew that his mechanic would have done his job well, but what of the assembly line workers who put together this particular aircraft? Was the laborer who assembled the wing struts in a distracted mood that day, thinking about his next cigarette break or perhaps grabbing a quick bottle of wine and cheese with his new girlfriend later, or was he particularly focused on doing the job right?

The Spad felt as if it was about to shake itself to pieces. The airspeed indicator slid into the red zone. Through the murky undercast, the zig-zag of trenches took form and, based on his heading and the way they were situated he knew he was well into the German side of the lines. Bullets whickered through his wings. The black Fokker closed to fifty yards. Behind the winking Maxim machine guns, he could see the blackened skull grinning at him. And, glancing up, something that gave him a glimmer of hope – shreds of fabric peeling off the Fokker's top wing. If what his mechanic Rosenthal told him months ago while sharing a smoke one afternoon was accurate, then this suggested something critical: the structural failure of the upper wing ribs, the Achilles heel of the Fokker model D.VII in a high-speed dive.

The ground was looming up at an alarming rate. Edwards pulled the control column all the way into his stomach and to the right. The compression turned the control surfaces to mush. For a few fleeting, nerve wracking seconds, Edwards wondered if he had miscalculated and would momentarily become so much broken wreckage strewn across enemy soil. But finally the Spad responded. His wheel nearly brushed the churned soil and, as the plane climbed up in a right bank he heard a tearing, snapping sound, one that that pierces any pilot's guts; the sound of wood and canvas and cables pulling apart. At first he feared it was his own plane – but then he glanced back, just in time to see the Fokker's top wing disintegrate, fold up, and fly off in pieces. Within split seconds, what was once a marvel of German aeronautical engineering became an ungainly mass of cartwheeling junk, leaving a twisted trail of debris across an abandoned farmer's field. The coffin-shaped fuselage of the Fokker, sans most of its wings, did a spinning tumble as if mimicking a gymnast, describing four complete revolutions and shedding its undercarriage before landing upside down across a drainage ditch.

Edwards did a slow loop around the crash site which was nearly a mile behind enemy lines. The field looked reasonably flat but even an errant muskrat hole could potentially wreck his landing gear. But he had to be sure.

He brought the Spad down in a rough but successful landing. Bolting out of the cockpit, he ran over to the wrecked German plane, drawing his .45 automatic. The fuselage was broken, bent in the center like a thoroughbred horse that has snapped its back, and the smell of petrol, gunpowder, and oil was strong. But there was another smell too – of something long dead.

Edwards bent over, gun ready, but the cockpit was empty. Puzzled, he looked left and right, then yelled in surprise as his left foot was jerked out from under him. He landed square on his ass to see a nightmare scrabble out of the debris in the ditch and land on his chest, the mangled skeleton of the enemy pilot fastening its gauntleted hands around his neck. The grinning death face was suddenly mere inches from his own, its gleaming gunmetal teeth snapping. The fetid smell coming out of its jaws, the smell of something dried, dead, and putrid, brought tears to Edwards' eyes.

He fired his pistol once, twice . . . nine times into the thing's body with no effect. The edges of his vision grew fuzzy and grey. Only his left elbow saved his face from being chewed off by the thing's gnashing mouth. Finally, he tossed the pistol aside and grabbed the creature's throat with both hands and, with superhuman effort, stood upright. For all its inhuman strength, the enemy pilot was as light as a bag of bones. Its legs were twisted and useless (one was bent around backwards) but the hands and teeth seemed quite capable of finishing this fight, attacking with spastic frenzy.

Edwards glanced over its shoulder and, even as the idea entered his head, he drove the thing up against the fuselage, grabbed one of the steel wing cables still attached by one end to the aircraft and wrapped it several times around the creature's neck, then yank it tight. Then with both hands, he grabbed the thing's wrists and snapping his elbows in, ended the stranglehold by breaking the bones.

A hissing, keening howl issued from the remains of the thing's throat, broken hands flailing as Edwards stepped backwards. A bullet whined overhead and he looked over to see a German patrol approaching from the other side of the field. He was running out of time. The monster was flailing like a trapped spider, unable to get a purchase on the cable wrapped around its neck. Fumbling in his pocket, Edwards found his metal pocket lighter, one he had purchased in Paris on a leave that now seemed years ago. Striking the metal wheel, he looked at the thing and said simply, "Die, fucker." Stepping back, he tossed the lighter at the fuselage. With a muffled *whoomp* the wreckage – and the thing tied to it – were engulfed in flames.

More bullets whined overhead and Edwards had no time to observe his handiwork — he turned, stumbled back to his plane, and leapt into the cockpit amid rifle fire and German-accented shouts.

"Halt!"

"*Surrender!*"

Edwards glanced once at the writhing thing tied to the flaming fuselage, shuddered, then gunned the Spad's engine and, trundling down the field, got airborne in one piece. He was half tempted to loop around and strafe the patrol but knew this might well push his luck too far. Instead he pulled his battered plane up towards the gloomy sky, towards the west and his home airfield.

-8-

OUT ON Raadsel Point, the carnival was winding down its second night. In the old days, the days before skyrocketing insurance rates and policy riders a Harvard Ph.D. would struggle with, the festivities would have lasted long past midnight. Tonight the rides had shut down promptly at eleven, a couple of policemen making a friendly (but very visible) walkthrough of the beer tents, and by half past the hour, the parking lot was all but empty – the lights out and the heavy blue and yellow music tent rippling in the light breeze coming off the river. Here and there came a high-pitched twitter as bats flicked through the sky, doing their small part to keep the local mosquito population in check. From somewhere out in the deeper woods of the point came a yelp that was suddenly cut off. There had been an increase in coyote sightings these past few years, to where the missing-small-pet count in Wyvern Falls had risen enough for upset locals to petition the mayor for some sort of action. But since spring this year, the population had been mysteriously *decreasing* – and, based on a couple gruesome 'discoveries' by the park rangers in the woods, the assumption was that a black bear had moved into the area.

That was apparently of little concern to the few drunken stragglers who had left their cars and were making their way back along the main road that looped around the bay and back into town – word had gotten around that a couple of Roy Hendricks' deputies were in their cruiser near the park entrance and doing random sobriety checks.

Just beyond the parking lot in the copse of spruce trees near where the carnival employee trailers were located came a brief gleam from reflected glass. High up in one tree, Pete Vogel was perched with a pair of Steiner 8x30 military-surplus binoculars, a birthday gift courtesy of his older brother Greg, who was currently enjoying his second tour of duty in

Afghanistan. Adam Carr was a few branches below him. Both were dressed like action movie commandos: black turtlenecks, black jeans, black caps and gloves, faces smudged with camo grease paint. Pete also had a surplus 'Kbar' knife strapped to his belt and a pair of insulated Timberland hiking boots that were making his feet sweat. Adam had to make do with an old pair of Adidas, which he had spray-painted flat black with a can of Rustoleum filched from his dad's workshop. A fair amount of it wound up on his hands, since he didn't understand it was enamel paint and he didn't wait long enough for it to dry before lacing up.

Hidden in the shrubs near the base of the trees were four bicycles and various rucksacks where they'd stashed them earlier.

Pete was on the look-out for Countess Lorelei, aka *The Red Baron's Daughter*, who he estimated would return to her trailer at any minute – the very same trailer where Luis and Armando were currently rooting around, trying to find out something, anything, that would shed more light on who this so-called Countess was and what she might be up to.

The plan was simple enough and Pete was smart enough to know that simple was always best. They'd showed up close to 9:00 p.m., presuming – incorrectly – that the area around the trailers would be mostly deserted. Pete had also reasoned that there probably wouldn't be much in the way of security. After all, why would anyone in their right mind want to break in a bunch of "carnie folk" trailers? The Countess's trailer had been easy enough to spot: it was the RV with the big red Triplane painted on the side and, if that left questions, the words

"The Red Baron's Daughter" in huge old-fashioned scrolled type would put them to rest.

The original plan was "in-and-out" in fifteen minutes. If for any reason Luis and Armando got caught, their cover story would plausible: the two boys were smitten with the Countess and had dared each other to take a camera phone photo sitting on her bed and maybe filching some keepsake out of her make-up kit or something. Pete and Adam were the lookouts and Adam's 'Star Wars Clone' walkie-talkie set was the warning system, set to minimum volume. Earlier, when discussing the 'in' part of the plan it had been Armando who had spoken up, producing a torque screwdriver (along with a small, devious little smile) using one of Luis' catch Portuguese phrases: *Sem problemas* – no problem.

The plan had gone from "in-and-out" to simply "out" when they'd discovered too many people going to and from the trailers. Not a lot – the trailers were near the RV camping area and a long walk from the carnival – but too many to get by unnoticed. It wasn't until close to eleven that the trailer area was empty, presumably because that was around the time everyone was occupied with closing up shop for the night, but by then the window of opportunity had narrowed and the potential for getting caught was high. It was Luis who had insisted on still doing it, showing his reckless streak of daring. And leadership. When Luis got his wind up and that wild gleam in his eyes, things happened.

"We can do this, guys!" he'd said when they'd regrouped out by one of the picnic tables on the point. "In, out, ten minutes. Pete, you just keep your eyes peeled. Armando, you're sure you can get us in quickly?"

A quick nod.

"Done. Let's go!"

And that was that.

The breaking in part had turned out to be almost ridiculously simple. The Countess' trailer was wedged in among the spruce trees, probably to maximize on their shade during the day. Throughout the summer, the area was used for campers, trailers, and RVs (with VWF parking permits) so there were water hook-ups and crude light poles with low-wattage bulbs strung up. After a quick once over, Armando had indicated the shadowed back area of the RV with a cutting motion of his hand and the two boys had run up to it in a sort of crouching scuttle. Armando had felt along the lower part of the trailer siding until he got to one area where there was a panel below a high horizontal window – the kitchenette, Luis had guessed.

Armando produced his special screw driver and, after a quick glance left and right to make sure the coast was still clear, had the six screws holding it place removed in less than thirty seconds. Luis stared at his friend in amazement.

"Where in the hell . . .?" he hissed.

Armando responded with his stock pursed smile and raised eyebrows look. Luis didn't need to finish his question. Sometimes Armando would just do something that was so completely out of whack with his quiet, almost Zen-like personality that it blew his friend's mind. Luis also figured that living on the road for so many years, tight family or not, probably entailed acquiring a few skills not endorsed by the local law enforcement community.

Armando pocketed the screws and the screwdriver vanished. He silently pointed to himself, then to the opening, then to Luis, followed by a stop/pause then a circular gesture that indicated his friend should wait, then loop around to the front.

The horizontal access panel was too small for a grown man to fit through but not for a twelve-year-old boy on the diminutive side. Grasping the top edge of the panel with his gloved hands – Armando had broken out his prized Nike bicycling gloves bought at one of ubiquitous neighborhood tag sales for this mission – he angled himself in on his back and up into the trailer. For a moment when only Armando's kicking feet are visible, Luis had the unnerving impression that the trailer had swallowed his friend up whole, the access panel like an obscenely tiny mouth on the face of a mute, dumb giant.

Then after two long minutes, the curtain parted in the window overhead and he saw the oval of his friend's face along with his right hand making an OK sign with his thumb and forefinger.

Luis acknowledged this with a curt thumbs-up and circled around to the side of the trailer, crouching in the shadows there until he heard the lock on the main door being opened.

There was a nerve-wracking moment when two men suddenly appeared walking right by the trailer, both smoking cigarettes. Luis was alarmed to see that one of them was none other than the Countess' assistant – the odd looking man with the derby and spectacles that evoked the ghost of Toulouse-Lautrec without the tiny bow legs. The other man was someone Luis had never seen before but immediately didn't like. The weak overhead light cast most of his face in shadow, but what was visible was a hawk-like visage with a heavy brow and long silver hair pulled back into a ponytail. He was tall and broad-shouldered with a long 'duster' jacket and scuffed cowboy boots. Something in the tense way he pulled on his cigarette and jerked it out of his mouth with a hand that looked like it could crack walnuts suggested a coiled, homicidal energy.

As Ricardo, Luis' older brother would say, "A man you most seriously do not want to fuck with."

"Toulouse" was doing most of the talking and the tall man was doing most of the listening. Although Luis could only make out snatches of words here and there, it seemed apparent that the assistant was trying to convince the other man that he could provide some sort of service and his demeanor, while subservient, seemed crafty. Luis heard bits like "Yesss-yesss . . . difficult to procure . . . but achievable . . . special delivery . . . shall we say . . . in an hour?"

Luis prayed that Armando had the sense not to open the trailer door (the Ecuadorian hadn't, having heard the conversation outside) and then, for one heart-stopping second, the tall man turned his head and it seemed he was staring right at Luis in the shadows. Time seemed to hang and Luis thought *a man like that, even if he can't see me, he can probably smell me a mile away, like a wolf. He's going to leap over here fast as you can say 'Jack-Rabbit Slim' and snap me in two like a twig.*

But that didn't happen.

"Toulouse" continued talking in his lispy whisper and the tall man was nodding or shaking his head – the movement was too subtle to be sure – when he flicked his cigarette butt off into the darkness with an aggressive snap of his fingers and blew smoke out of his nostrils like some sort of dragon. Then he nodded, once, twice, then abruptly walked away towards the main parking lot.

The assistant stood there a minute longer, holding his own cigarette in his thumb and forefinger but reversed, the lit side palmward in an almost effeminate position. He muttered something that sounded like "*Sbiessehapf*" then walked up to the trailer door. He reached out for the doorknob and, for one heart-stopping second, Luis thought: "he'll fling open the door and see Armando sitting there, caught like a deer in the headlights." But miraculously none of this happened. The assistant hesitated, withdrew his hand and rubbing his chin, did an abrupt about-face and strolled away, back towards the carnival.

Luis realized he'd been holding his breath for the past sixty seconds and let it out in a controlled sigh before poking his head around the corner. For a moment, nothing, then with a soft click, the trailer door opened just a crack. He did a slow glance through his field of vision right to left and left to right – something he saw once in a Mark Wahlberg movie – before dashing around and carefully pushing himself in through the door.

Inside the RV was gloomy and unfamiliar. Weak light filtered in through the windows from outside, revealing that, while the Red Baron's Daughter might have been many things, a dedicated housekeeper she was not. A pack rat, more like. The place looked like the inside of an old East Village antique store. Not only were Luis and Armando not exactly sure what they should look for, they didn't have even the lightest clue where to even *begin*. Glancing around the RV, Luis decided it could take an entire archeological team a solid month to catalogue and tag the contents of the interior and they had all of –what? – fifteen minutes? Ten? Luis produced a small pen flashlight he'd nicked out of his father's workshop. Armando had a $3.99 disposable one, compliments of True Value Hardware. The RV appeared to be of an early 1980s vintage when wood paneling and plaid fabrics – those pinnacles of interior design style from the '70s – hadn't quite been phased out yet.

Juxtaposed within this RV time capsule circa 1980 was a bizarre array of posters, knick-knacks, glasses, toys, and assorted paraphernalia stretching from the early 1900s (WWI era to be more accurate) to the present day, stuff that one might have simply passed off as the hobby horse of a slightly eccentric collector. However, while neither boy was particularly knowledgeable about such things, both were aware that there was something off here, something disturbing about what they were seeing.

There was a collection of antique posters and playbills taped on the walls, including a couple advertising a Parisian fortune teller from the 1950s, a handful for a magician in Vienna from the '30s, and one in German titled *Koschei Alle Glückszustände* showing a skeletal-looking wizard clutching a forlorn-looking princess that, judging from the illustration style, might be from the 1920s. It was this last one that Luis' flashlight beam paused on. The princess, in a heavy-looking indigo blue dress with intricate gold trim and an ornate gold headdress, looked hauntingly similar to the Countess whose trailer they were sitting in. Luis and Armando traded glances. Then without thinking Luis stepped up and carefully removed the poster, rolled it up and placed it in his backpack.

The flashlight beams moved around the counters and shelves. Besides a lot of antique looking items (an old scarf, a child's bonnet, some marbles and a slingshot), there was a clutter of newer-looking items such as a yo-yo, a Red Sox cap, and a blue Smurf with one of its eyes missing. Luis was thrown off by the whole mess. It didn't appear to make any sense. It was almost as if . . .

Luis paused near the front of the RV where there were two swivel bucket seats for the driver and passenger. Something glittering from the rearview mirror caught his eye. Nearby Armando was standing by the kitchenette table, studying a broken pair of horn-rimmed glasses.

Luis reached up and *froze*.

There was a crunch of a footstep in the gravel by the door.

Followed by the jingle of a key.

Luis felt an icepick of panic prick at the back of his neck, then snatched the item off the rearview mirror. It was a gray and white lucky rabbit's foot on a silver keychain.

Just like the one Henry always carried in his pocket.

Grabbing Armando by the arm, he dragged him towards the back of the trailer where they dashed into the larger of the two bedroom closets, pulling the louvered door shut just as the main door of the RV opened.

A moment later there was a whish of fabric as the Countess entered the trailer in her heavy dress, turning on lights as she went. There was a pause while she rummaged around in the kitchenette area, then the light staccato of heels as she walked back into the sleeping area. Luis felt his heart pounding in his chest like a trip hammer and was convinced the Countess could hear it loud and clear. His thoughts were scrambling but he forced himself to think through what limited options there were. The closet they were in was too small – they would be discovered as soon as the door was opened. The question was, "is this the closet she uses most" and "if she opens it, what then?" Scream? Run for it? Or perhaps they could lie low until she went to sleep and then sneak out through the access panel? Does she even sleep?

Or perhaps a simple shrug and 'Sorry Ma'am, we were heading out of the carnival and my friend and I had to take a leak and somehow we wound up in your closet– *lo siento!*"

The questions chased each other around Luis' head while one part of him listened carefully for some sort of clue or tip that would tell him how this scenario would play out.

He quickly figured out that, by standing on his toes, he could maximize his field of vision and look down through the horizontal slats of the door. After what seemed like an eternity of rustling, unzipping, tiny clips, and whatever other mysterious sounds accompanied a woman getting out of a hundred-year-old dress, Luis could just make out that she had pulled out a chair and was sitting at a combined vanity/dressing table in the small bedroom. Through the louver, he saw what amounted to an enticingly-shaped thigh in a stocking and garter and the crisscross lacings of a red corset, not one of the cheap thrills variety seen in a Victoria's Secrets catalogue (which he knew front-to-back) but something handmade, older, and clearly of very expensive quality. He looked at Armando next to him who was also straining to stand on his toes and the bars of light coming through the door revealed that his friend was equally bug-eyed at what they were seeing.

If the Red Baron's Daughter was some sort of monster, she was truly one hot and sexy nightmare.

She was humming a song to herself that sounded like *La Complainte de la Butte*, (which Luis had heard in the movie *Le Moulin Rouge*) when she abruptly stood up and walked to the front area of the RV.

Almost on cue, Luis heard a tiny little cough from his hip and nearly jumped through the doors. He was so tense he almost yelled out "Fuck!" but caught himself. Instead he unclipped the walkie-talkie and turned around, cupping his hand around the piece and jamming it close to his face.

"Luis!?" Pete's voice hissed through the unit. "I swear she came out of nowhere! I didn't see her 'til she got to the door! "

Luis didn't know if this would screw everything up and or if it was a godsend. Without acknowledging he simply hissed back, "Pete, we need a diversion. Fast!" Then he spun the volume dial with his thumb to turn the unit off. He decided now was an excellent time to pray to whatever saints came to mind.

Under his breath he muttered "*Ave, Maria, cheia de graça o Senhor é convosco* . . ."

There was the sound of some rummaging and then the Countess was coming back to the bedroom. There was a pause, then a click of a lighter and a sharp intake of breath. A moment later, the smell of tobacco filled the small room. The silence drew out. The boys heard what sounded like fingernails drumming on a wood-paneled wall.

Then finally the Countess spoke, very clearly and commandingly. "You boys might as well come out of the closet now."

Luis and Armando exchanged panicked glances.

Fifteen seconds passed. Armando looked at Luis again and shrugged.

Then in unison they both pushed the closet doors open.

Shocked silence.

Then a gasp from Armando: "*¡Dios Mío!*"

Lorelei, the Countess, the Red Baron's Daughter, stood before them like an ultimate thirteen (and twelve) year-old boy's wet dream: one arm up along the bulkhead wall, the other holding a smoldering cigarette in an ivory holder. Her lustrous hair had been let out in a disheveled sweep and, aside from the corset, garter, and high-heeled shoes, she was wearing nothing. The corset was tailored to feature her well-endowed cleavage to its best. Below the garter belt, her pubic area was plainly visible, the first either boy had ever actually seen on a grown woman.

There was a hint of a cruel smile and one of her eyebrows described an unmistakably seductive arch.

Luis wondered momentarily if he had completely misjudged the situation. The nearly instantaneous erection in his pants suggested as much, then again he was just getting into that hormone raging age where nearly anything could trigger a hard-on. For one moment the situation seemed to be suspended in time; two boys, twelve and thirteen, suddenly finding themselves in an unbelievable fantasy scenario – face to face with a gorgeous, all-but-naked woman looking ready to seduce them. The proximity of her nudity, the mystery between her legs and the unmistakable musky scent of her sex lurking under the pall of tobacco was nearly enough to short-out their young, eager brains. Luis was no longer aware of Armando – his friend might as well have been standing back in Ecuador for all he knew – his eyes were glued to the woman before them. Her breasts. Her pubic area. Back and forth, back and forth until he thought he might very well just explode on the spot, like the perpetually doomed drummers in that old classic movie *Spinal Tap*.

Bang!

Nothing left but human confetti.

Yet he just as quickly he realized something else as his eyes (which by this point were physically incapable of opening any wider) settled onto hers: he was completely and utterly terrified. Not terrified as in "confronted with the overwhelming mystery of women and sex" terrified, but a much deeper, atavistic terror.

The Countess' eyes were hypnotic, a 'cougar's eyes in modern parlance. Luis realized he was completely powerless against them.

He wasn't alone however: Lorelei had the apparently impossible ability to look at both boys directly at the same time though they were a foot apart. Then abruptly she said, "Well boys, it's time to upgrade your education, yesss?" Without breaking eye contact she took a drag on her cigarette and blew smoke sideways out of her mouth.

Luis couldn't speak. Armando looked like he was about to faint. The air felt charged. Lorelei stepped forward and up to Luis. Her free hand did a teasing caress of his crotch, gave it a tantalizing nudge, then went to his face where she traced his jawline as if with a lover's touch. His nerves tingled, although her fingertips were as cold as mausoleum marble.

He felt completely paralyzed.

The frigid hand reached behind and cupped the back of his head and she bent her face down close to his, lips parting. Her pointed nipples brushed the top of his chest. Again he smelled perfume, tobacco, her sex, but underneath it…something else, something dreadfully unpleasant. The smell of decay? Death? But he was powerless. A tear gathered at the corner of his eye.

Her *teeth* . . .

Suddenly there was a loud bang at the door.

Not a knock, not a tap, but a heavy *whump* as if a battering ram had just swung into it.

The Countess snapped her head around. One of her breasts actually slapped Luis on the chin.

Her eyes flared in rage.

Another *whump*

The rattle of glass, small objects toppling over.

And again.

Whump

The sound of metal buckling.

Lorelei turned around and marched towards the front of the RV, head cocked, absently taking a silk robe off its hook on the wall and throwing it around her shoulders, as if going to deal with some persistent door salesman instead of what sounded like an elemental force of nature trying to burst its way in.

Luis noticed something else: The Countess was changing as she sauntered toward the door. Her fingers appeared to be elongating into claws and she appeared to be growing taller, her hair wilder. He'd never seen such a thing outside of something cooked up by a Hollywood special effects team and he was only seeing it from the back, which he sensed might be for the best.

The Countess was reaching for the door handle when the whole thing pretty much exploded inward.

Something barreled into the front room of the trailer and it took the boys a moment to process what it was, and even then they weren't fully able to comprehend what their eyes were registering.

It appeared to be some sort of massive wild dog. That was if one took a bear, crossed it with a werewolf, and clipped its ears off. It was the size of a mastiff, covered in coarse shaggy fur that was mostly brown and white, with intense brown eyes and a snarling mouth that looked packed with sharp teeth.

It was the scariest looking animal either boy had ever laid eyes on.

The shaggy beast let out a deep growl.

Lorelei responded with a snarling roar that sounded horribly inhuman. From there things became a blur.

Luis grabbed Armando by the shoulder and yanked him towards the back of the trailer. Above the small bed was a sliding window on the back wall and that immediately became Luis' Priority Number One Goal. The boys leaped onto the bed, Luis ripped the curtains aside and scrabbled at the latch mechanism.

He looked back long enough to see the dog-beast launch itself at the countess, jaws gaping Then there was a long *snick* as he jerked the window along its track and then he was forcing his friend out of it. The trailer rocked as the countess and her attacker bounced off the wall in a tumble of fur, flashing teeth and claws and then Luis vaulted out the window, landing and rolling in a bed of dirt and pine needles.

In a panic, both boys tore off through the trailers and trees with no cohesive thought other than to put as much distance between themselves and whatever was taking place in the Countess' trailer. Their escape might have turned into an aimless rout through the woods if not for Pete Vogel.

Pete had been up in his perch biting his fist and trying to come up with some sort of plan to create a distraction when Adam tapped his shoulder and pointed downward. At first, they didn't understand what they were looking at – a four-legged juggernaut of fur that came charging out of the shadows and launched itself at the RV door headfirst.

No warning or context.

Pete's first thought was that it was some sort of deranged bear, though why a bear would assault the Countess' RV didn't make a whole lot of sense. Then he saw the large shaggy tail and realized it was some sort of enormous dog. Though calling the animal he was looking at a *dog* was something like calling a Bengal Tiger a kitty-cat. Then he saw it back up, take a leaping charge, and ram the door again with its massive head.

And again.

"Holy Moly!" he'd thought, even as he climbed down through the branches of the spruce. Staying high up in the tree might have made better sense on one hand, but he had a hunch Luis and Armando might seriously need help and hiding up out of danger's reach might not be the best place to give it.

He was just dropping to the ground, a moment after the thing bashed through the trailer door, when he spotted his two friends drop out of the back of the RV and run off. Without thinking, Pete put his two pinky fingers into either side of his mouth and executed what he called his "Sonic Whistle Number Forty-Seven" which could turn heads from several blocks away (and certainly from the other end of a high school football field).

It definitely got Luis' and Armando's attention. Luis snapped his head around automatically and saw Pete motioning with his hand urgently, then jabbing towards where the bikes were stashed.

"Come on!" the hands were saying, "get your asses over here pronto!" Armando and Luis looped around and then there was a mad scramble as bikes were sorted out, feet stomped onto pedals and dirt flew as the four boys took to their mounts and high-tailed it out of there.

It wasn't until they got to the police checkpoint that they stopped and it became apparent somewhere along the way that one of them had disappeared.

Armando was no longer with them.

-9-

"WE NEED to talk."

Even as the words came out of his mouth, Easton whacked his forehead with his palm. Walking out tired clichés was never a particularly good way to start off a discussion about why the hell their relationship had been heading south on an express ticket. He forced his hands into his pockets, lifted an eyebrow and began again.

"Vivienne, what's happened between us?"

Good Christ! What's next? 'You never call anymore?' 'I've been thinking lately?' Great going, Slick. You can package it up and sell it like a Berlitz audio learning course: The John Easton Easy Break-Up Method. "Repeat after me: 'I've been thinking lately . . .'(I . . . I've been thinking lately . . .)"

Easton put his head against the frame of the bathroom door and chuckled. He'd been talking to his reflection for fifteen minutes and getting nowhere. Hardly a surprise there.

Then again, none of this was really a surprise.

After the whole business the previous fall up at Taron Hall, Van Eyckmann's creepy rock pile just north of town, he'd been a little out of sorts. A little off his game as it were.

A little?

That's like saying the Pope is *a little* Catholic there, mate. That whole Aun-mai-lost-love baloney that had happened there and then suddenly this highly attractive, young and tall Asian woman drops on your head and knocks you sprawling. But she's twelve years younger than you are, how long before those chickens came home to roost? It was a dream, a fantasy.

But...

It felt *genuine*. And there was that . . . tacky-cheeseball as it sounds . . . resolution of a lost love. The sense that they had been guided together by some unseen hand.

Or some other bullshit.

But if such a thing were true, then that was the hell of it, wasn't it? Provided you bought into the whole lost-soul-mates-brought-back-together-after-three-hundred-and-ninety-years shtick, it didn't necessarily follow that such an event would result in a successful relationship, did it?

Someone left that fine print out of the fairy-tale script.

Well, no denying it had been a blast. And there had been that uncanny connection between the two of them for those first heady months. For a while, they were so much in tune and the connection was so intimate that they would unconsciously complete each other's sentences, correctly. Something their small circle of friends at first considered quaint, then somewhat annoying. And Easton was surprised to find, sliding into his middle age, that he had a deep romantic streak he wasn't even aware of. Buying flowers, little gifts here and there, a surprise dinner at that Mexican restaurant out on Route 9, 'Quetzalcoatl's' when he'd arranged for the Mariachi band to play a bawdy version of her favorite song. The same night that had ended with Vivienne dancing on the bar after three Tequila shots and Easton hustling her out the door right after the bra came off and was spinning around her fingertip. It was also the same night she'd all but chewed off his clothes when they got home and had sex standing up in the front hallway. Hell of night all right.

That brought a ghost of a smile to his lips.

It *had* been a wild ride. That reckless holy-shit-here-we-go thrill like the first time he'd gone sky-diving. Of just letting go of everything and letting her rip.

Wild times, fun times and enough gratuitous sex to fill a year's worth of those old *Penthouse* Forums he read as a kid, but those times had been growing steadily less frequent over the past two months and, in the past few weeks a certain sullen resentment had seeped in. Somewhere along the way, the fairy-tale romance had started to crisp and smolder around the edges. Now the air between them was on the verge of going toxic.

The front door closing downstairs snapped Easton out of his depressing reverie. He was getting maudlin and it didn't wear well. That it was almost midnight on Saturday and he hadn't seen Vivienne since she'd left for work Friday morning wasn't helping matters. Downstairs he heard the refrigerator door open and, a minute later, the TV going on.

She was sitting, legs crossed Indian-fashion, on the living room couch. With her black jeans, grey turtleneck, rectangular black-rimmed glasses and hair pulled up in a careless ponytail, she looked like a very hip and sassy librarian. Easton stopped and leaned against the broad archway that connected the front room with the front hallway. It was another thing he had really liked about the house from the start; the layout had a wide and open flavor to it. It was the kind of house that, when you walked in through the front door, you immediately wanted to find a chair, kick your feet up and relax.

"So?"

Vivienne ignored him at first, sipping at a bottle of Honest Ice Tea and pretending to be focused on a HGTV home makeover show that he knew she hated. The silence dragged along until it started to look weary. She *looked weary*, like she hadn't had a good night's sleep in days. Make that weeks.

Finally she glanced at him, like a petulant child.

"*What*?"

Easton felt a cool cloak of calm settle on his shoulders.

"What?" He shot back. There was a whole list of 'whats?' bullet-pointed in his head. "Well, for starters how about 'what the hell is going on?'"

"What do you mean 'what's going on?' I'm home. I'm watching TV. What else do you need to know?"

Easton's eyes made a circuit of the ceiling then settled back on his girlfriend. Who was more and more look like someone he didn't recognize. It was uncanny how someone you had been so intimate with, someone with whom you'd shared the more vulnerable corners of your heart, could slide without your even being aware of it into a completely different person like some sort of B movie. *Invasion of the Body Snatchers*: long lost girlfriend abducted and replaced with Pod Person in the last week, leaving our hero confused and suspicious.

"For starters, what have you been up to?"

Another sullen look. "I've been out. It's not like you own me or anything."

"Never implied that I did."

"Well, you're sounding like you're my father or something."

Ouch.

A muscle twitched in his jaw, but Easton didn't reply, he just kept looking at her with his steady grey-blue eyes like he had all the time in the world, leaning against the arch with his arms crossed.

"What? Nothing more to say?"

Easton had a lot to say, for starters a few questions about where she had been the previous twenty-four hours. The story about working late had been an outright lie; he'd mentioned it obliquely to Jim Franks when Franks had called him earlier to catch up on some other business – something about a librarian who had gone missing the night before – and Franks had sounded genuinely surprised: "Vivienne was working late? Can't imagine why. The Harrington-Cross website was wrapped and out the door with a bow on it by end of day. Client was ecstatic." Easton changed the subject before Franks' wheels could get turning too much. Whatever the situation was, he didn't want to get his friend – and Vivienne's boss – involved in his personal problems, especially when he was wandering in the dark about what those problems really were.

There had been other absences too in the past two weeks. A pattern was emerging and the picture that was forming didn't suggest a happy, smiling couple spending their life together.

He could have said all sorts of things: bitter, accusatory, pleading, confused. After all, weren't two people in a relationship supposed to discuss issues when they came up? Apparently not. And he wasn't surprised to find no words were coming out.

Instead the Droid buzzed at his hip.

Saved by the bell.

The caller ID showed it was from the police station.

Easton tapped the answer key and wandered back towards the kitchen. "Hello?"

"John?" It was Roy Hendricks, the Wyvern Falls Police Chief. Calling from the precinct. At nearly midnight. Three things that together probably didn't add up to a feel-good equation.

"Hi, Roy. What can I do you for?"

"Sorry to bother you this late, John, but I kind of have a strange situation here and my hands are a little full right at the moment. And Bell is out on sick leave. His dad passed away on Wednesday." Hendricks sounded tired and slightly exasperated. "I was hoping you might be willing to come down to the station. *Unofficially*, of course."

Easton had developed a respectable professional relationship with Hendricks since the disaster up at Taron Hall and had "unofficially" helped out the police on a few matters since (including breaking the case on a series of children's murders that had Hendricks and his department on the hot seat for a few weeks back in March). "Unofficial" because, although Easton was now on unpaid leave from the Royal Turk and Caicos Police Criminal Investigation Department and thus by extension a member of the British Metropolitan Police, if push came to shove he could still work in an official capacity. It just made things a whole lot simpler if he didn't. Despite being from another country's police department, he was still a member of that unspoken fraternity.

These days, the two most valuable things (aside from his RTC CID Badge) in Easton's wallet were his private detective license and his pistol permit. But, contrary to the endless fantasies of countless television shows and mystery writers, no self-respecting American police department would involve itself in cases with a private detective.

Unless that detective was an ex-cop.

Darren Bell was the full-time detective they kept on staff with the village police department. Vaguely competent in a dull, 'just-doing-my-job' sort of way, he had all the hallmarks of a late-middle-aged guy riding it out until retirement. Fortunately, the local Hudson River towns in this second decade of the 21st century were hardly hotbeds of crime. Hendricks had hinted at offering Easton the position down the road, though both men knew that the Englishman was a little over-qualified to be tracking down people's lost cats and the perpetrators of such heinous crimes as leaving sneaker prints in a sidewalk the Public Works Department just poured.

In addition to the Wyvern Falls *Village* Police, which only covered the 3.8 square miles of the village itself, there was also the Wyvern Falls *Town* Police, whose jurisdiction covered the area outside the village. They operated out of a completely different station house located over on Breckenridge Lane and were an extension of the Westchester County police force. The only reason Hendricks would call was if it wasn't a serious enough matter to invite the County detectives to come over and start pissing around in his sandbox.

"No worries. I'll be there in a few minutes." Easton answered.

"Thanks."

Easton looked at the now blank Droid screen. What the hell is this about?

When he walked back into the living room, Vivienne was watching an old *Law & Order: Criminal Intent* re-run. Vincent D'Onofrio was demonstrating (again) that the best way to interrogate a suspect was with your head tilted at a crazy angle with ominous music playing in the background.

The level at which Vivienne was ignoring him was becoming tedious. Easton chose a grey blazer off the coat-rack, pulled out his car keys and paused by the front door. She didn't even ask where he was going. He shook his head and stepped out into the night.

-10-

THE VILLAGE of Wyvern Falls Police Station was one of those massive Depression-era buildings built when washed-out brownstone and art deco motifs were all the rage. Situated just off Main Street at the corner of Van Wyck Avenue and Hanson Place, it somehow looked blocky, sleek, modern, and hopelessly antiquated all at the same time. It harkened back to a different era of hard-eyed Federal agents with Fedoras and .45 Caliber Thompson machine guns, policemen with stiff blue uniforms with double rows of buttons, speakeasies, flappers, and John Dillinger. By contrast, across the street was the Municipal Building, an imposing edifice built in the later 1800s. With its heavy brick and elaborately scrolled detailing that defined the words "imposing edifice," it looked like a grumpy old grandfather. Behind the police station was the Volunteer Ambulance Corps with its glass-steel-and-brick design that all but screamed 1970s urban renewal, where one half-expected to see Starsky and Hutch fishtailing out of the parking lot in their equally '70s Ford Torino with its racing stripes.

The local architect who had designed the police station, Fred Baum, had adopted an *O Fortuna/Carmina Burana* theme reflected somewhat bizarrely in the various cast bronze disks and bas reliefs that adorned the façade. Additionally, there were stylized Art Deco wyverns on every corner. Twelve different gods and fates were represented across the building: *Bellum, Pax, Fides, Potestas, Folia, Sapientia, Tempus, Mors, Abstinencia, Justitia, Castitas,* and *Abundantia.* And the central theme of Justice with her two faces: The Dragon of Life and the Angel and Devil cranking the Wheel of Fortune. Mister Baum himself had disappeared somewhat mysteriously after this particular public works project and nothing was known about his fate. In fact, except for this somewhat mystical (and to many, puzzling) building design, not much else was attributed to or even known about Mister Baum aside from a few dusty newspaper articles suggesting he was

77

a strange man obsessed with mythical themes.

Easton walked into the high-ceilinged foyer where the Sergeant on desk duty – a stocky, blunt-looking policeman he remembered as Connelly – was dealing with a semi-hysterical Hispanic woman. At a glance, it was pretty busy even for a Saturday night with all sorts of people hanging out in the waiting area: a couple of policemen dragging in a clearly drunk young man sporting serious tattoos on his biceps, what looked like three generations of an Ecuadorian family waiting patiently in one row of seats, assorted people shouting and yelling and so on. The place was a madhouse.

Easton walked up to the front desk, noting the woman. She was a striking woman in her twenties or thirties and laying into Connelly at about a thousand words per minute in a confusing jumble of Spanish and English that made Easton's head spin. Based on the flashy skirt and blouse and high-heels, he guessed she'd been out on a date. An evening that didn't sound like it was ending on a good note, if her tone was any indication. Connelly was trying to take down her information in his plodding, methodical one-letter-at-a-time manner that suggested he would take all night and tomorrow to get it right if necessary. He looked up at Easton and, still writing with the pencil in his right hand, jabbed with his left thumb towards the stairwell that led up to the police chief's office. A moment later, he pressed a hidden button that released the entry gate so Easton could pass through. He felt the woman glaring at him and heard her pause briefly before launching in again, "Who's he? *I* need to see the police chief now*!* *Sus tres horas! Estamos hablando sobre mi hijo joder!*"

". . . Ma'am, was that address 39 A, or 39 B De Graal . . .?"

Easton knocked on the pebbled glass of the police chief's office.

"It's open."

Normally he would have had to circumvent Hendricks' second line of defense, an old battle-axe known as Beatrice Voight, one of those vaguely middle-aged, stalwart women that one finds in village and town offices throughout America as if part of some obscure government by-law.

However, Beatrice – 'Bea' to the police chief and her few personal friends, "Mrs. Voight" to the rest of the planet – was off duty.

Hendricks was behind his desk, legs crossed, a fistful of reports in his hand that he wasn't really looking at. The office itself reflected its current occupant: neat, clean and functional. It suggested an air of austere authority with its muted walls, well-framed artwork, and tall windows. A new Dell computer was set up on the oak desk, next to a modern cordless phone unit. A huge antique map of Wyvern Falls adorned one wall; on another was a magnificent canvas of the Hudson River done by a local artist, showing the view from Croton Point looking south. He'd just captured the midmorning sun of a cloudy day with dappled shadows bringing out the Palisades cliffs of the west bank. The execution suggested a fantasy landscape like that the Brothers Hildebrandt used to paint, but as anyone with a pair of working eyes can tell you, the Hudson Valley really looks like that. One shelf was a small shrine to one of Hendricks' passion: football. The real incongruity, however, was the wood bookcase behind the chief filled with all sorts of stuffed animals, dolls, and such, along with a few photos and honorary plaques: an accumulation of gifts from kids in the community over the years. Hendricks was big on being a visible and highly engaging (when he dialed up the charm) presence in the community.

As Easton walked in, Hendricks indicated one of the leather chairs in front of his desk. He continued to look off into space for a moment then, with a disbelieving shake of his head said, half to himself, "Jesus H. Fucking Christ." Then, "Helluva night so far, John. Helluva night."

Easton sat back, arms crossed. "Looks like it, Roy. What's going on?"

The police chief looked over at him. He had hooded, grey eyes that had a disconcerting way of boring right through you. *A Destroyer Captain's eyes, quick and sharp*, Easton thought. *Bet he got a lot of confessions right on the spot when he was a patrol officer.*

Hendricks tossed the reports on the desk. "So far tonight I have a missing librarian's assistant, a total of three – no make that four - missing boys, one definite homicide, nine cases of disorderly conduct, four break-ins, one attempted stabbing, two car accidents, five DWIs and a so-called "investigative reporter" from the city whose sole purpose in life is to give me a serious migraine. Did I mention the team from *Ghost Seekers International* up here sticking their infra-red cameras into everything and gasping "Did you hear that!?" every time a god-damn leaf rustles? Christ. Somehow this year's carnival has turned into a three-ring circus."

"Sorry to hear it. About the *Ghost Seekers*, that is. How can I help?"

Hendricks chuckled but tapped his finger on the desk for a minute before answering.

"Not the sort of thing I would normally ever bother you with. We don't have a whole lot of visiting resident CID detectives to call on and I wouldn't want to abuse you as a resource. Anyhow, I've got a couple of kids with Detective Eckhart right now telling stories about monster dogs and shape-shifting fortune tellers that get off stripping for thirteen-year-olds and I really need her to focus on a couple other matters including Miss Olivia Hernandez, whom I'm guessing you observed giving Officer Connolly the third degree when you came in."

Easton nodded.

"Protocol says that with Bell out, I should ring up the County boys at this point but I find myself in an odd position. Nothing exactly at this point suggests this matter is serious enough to warrant that call and the last thing I need is the County cops laughing at me over wasting their time on fairy tales. I'll wind up with boxes of nightlights, teddy bears and little pink "bankies" on my desk. You know how it is."

Easton rolled this over, mentally ticking off the points Hendricks *wasn't* saying. Detective Eckhart was the youth services detective required by the County these days to handle any cases involving minors. If her caseload was full, then technically Hendricks should call in the town/county police for assistance, but Easton knew he would only do that if absolutely necessary. There was a long-standing friction between the village and county police that went deeper than the typical cross-department rivalry, something over a case Hendricks had been left holding the bag on years back. Easton didn't know the details other than it had been something that had seriously pissed off the police chief and that was apparently a rare occurrence. Ergo, bring in good buddy and ex-cop Easton to help fill out the story that the village police department was taking every complaint seriously. The real question was why? Why not just give the kids a reassuring pat on the back and send them on their way with a token "Appreciate your coming in here boys and letting us know – we'll look into it right away."?

"It's no problem, Roy, glad to help out. But I'd kind of like to know what's really on your mind here?"

Hendricks' finger kept tapping the top of his desk thoughtfully. After a minute, he leaned back in his chair, interlacing his fingers across his midsection.

"John, I don't really know how to put this, so I'll just lay it face up on the table. And please don't take this in any way negative – it's not. I know your record as a policeman and it's solid. Hell, I'd hire you in a second. But I also know that, since you went on leave and took up on that private dick's license, you've handled a few cases in the area that were, oh, shall we say 'odd' in their way." When he saw Easton was about to interject, he held up a hand, "Let me finish. What I'm getting to is that you seem to have an aptitude for solving things that have – for lack of a better word – a 'supernatural' aspect. Without getting all gooey and loony and 'aliens abducted my grandmother' about it. You look at these kinds of things as a *cop*. I'm aware there was a whole shitload of weirdness to that business with Van Eyckmann that Knightbridge and you didn't tell me and that's fine. I didn't want to know then and I still don't want to know now." He smiled. "I'm already probably building this up to something bigger than it really is. We're probably talking about a bunch of kids with too many hormones and too much time playing video games. I'm going to have Officer Vance on it for now. But I was hoping I could get you to tag along as an extra set of eyes and ears. Just in case. Because, John . . .?"

"Yes?"

"Between you, me, and the wall something's going on around here that's not right. A *lot* of somethings. I need someone with a different take on things. Gary Vance is competent enough, but I wouldn't ever accuse him of being overly imaginative. He's with Eckhart and the kids right now over in the youth services room. You've probably got five or ten minutes before their parents show up."

Just then, the phone on the police chief's desk rang. Simultaneously someone knocked on the door. Hendricks shook his head. Before picking up the phone, he added, "Let me know what you think. I really appreciate this."

Easton stood up as two policemen he didn't know entered at Hendricks' prompting. He had a hunch the police chief was in for one very long night.

The youth services detective's office was down the hall from the police chief's on the second floor. The second floor of the police station was mainly devoted to administrative offices and, of all things, a reading room. The top floor had a gym and a lecture hall that also doubled as public use space for community functions. The holding cells and garage were in the basement.

Easton passed several policemen (and two policewomen as well) heading back and forth in the hallway. He rapped on the glass with his first two knuckles and a moment later the door was opened by a short, very Dutch-looking woman with brown eyes and blond hair in a policeman's uniform. She was somewhat attractive in a no-nonsense sort of way. Easton pegged her at around forty, give or take. *The kind of forty that suits some women just fine*, he thought. He guessed the uniform was to reassure the kids that they were dealing with a bona-fide member of the police department.

"Can I help you?" She sounded wary and protective.

"John Easton. Chief Hendricks asked me to sit in as a favor." He pulled out his I.D. and held it up.

An eyebrow went up slightly. "Oh, so you're *that* Easton."

"I didn't realize there were that many of us running around town."

That got a slight smile. "Dozens. We can't keep track of all of them anymore. But since you're the only one that showed up you might as well come in."

The room was on the small side, filled with a desk, a bunch of chairs, toys, games, stuffed animals and other entertainments for the younger set. The walls were painted 'Smurf' blue and bright curtains with flowers hung from the old tall windows. A concerted effort had been made to turn a police department office into a reassuring environment for children. It almost worked.

Leaning against the window sill, arms crossed, was a broad shouldered policeman with the kind of natural physique that makes high-school girls swoon, though the face that went with it was square and on the bland side. Seated around a pint-sized plastic table were three tired-looking boys. The one in the middle, Luis Dimas, looked up as Easton entered and his eyes flew wide. "*Puta merda!*" he blurted out, "It's you!!"

Suddenly all eyes were looking at Easton. The ones belonging to the two police officers the least friendly of the bunch.

Easton looked straight back at the Portuguese teen, brow furrowing. "Me . . . who?" He responded.

"The guy in the plane! You were the guy in the plane! That saved us . . . me, from . . . from that German! Tell them, you have to tell them, Mister!" Luis sounded nearly hysterical and overtired. Which was good. Easton looked over at Detective Eckhart with his hands up like a contestant on an old TV game show (*What's My Line* maybe?) who's just been blindsided by a trick question.

He hoped it was convincing.

-11-

TEN MINUTES later, he was in a squad car speeding out towards the carnival grounds. Officer Vance was driving. He'd left the sirens off but was running the blue and red flashers just to remind people they might better stay out of their way. He may not have been a brilliant conversationalist but at least he knew how to drive well. It had crossed Easton's mind more than once since taking up residence in America that some policemen may have taken the job simply to have a legal reason to speed everywhere. Riding in the back was Luis Dimas with his father, Victor. Pete and Adam were sent home with their parents after it had been decided only one of them was really necessary, since it was already pushing one in the morning and they could be brought back that afternoon if needed.

Easton had played out the episode as a simple misunderstanding, which wasn't difficult as neither officer was inclined to believe that he had *really* been responsible for chasing off a demonic German pilot after a big WWI dogfight in which several young boys and a CID detective had been flying over France in biplanes. The boys had obviously been through a stressful experience. Two of their friends were now unaccounted for. Something had occurred out at the carnival that evening; Officer Vance and Detective Easton would go have a look and see if they could ascertain what had really happened. It would be helpful if one of the boys could accompany them to clarify exactly where they had been when the alleged incident had occurred. Luis had calmed down considerably when, on the verge of interrupting Easton for a second time, he caught the detective giving him a discreet wink while asking a series of seemingly matter-of-fact questions. Luis may have been only thirteen, but he was a quick study and caught the message loud and clear: "I gotcha, now roll with me on this.

Your credibility is sliding into negative numbers already, so zip it."

When Easton suggested they have a look around the trailer park while Detective Eckhart dealt with the parents, she'd looked relieved. He had a hunch she'd had enough of spook stories for the evening.

Officer Vance's look didn't reveal much.

The Crown Victoria police interceptor car was trim and efficient, like the policemen it was designed to convey. Easton was studying the shotgun with the orange stock and grip clipped under the squad car's dash.

"Twelve gauge?"

"Yessir." Uplit by the center-mounted laptop between the two men, Officer Vance's face seemed to be capable of only two modes: *expressionless* and *more expressionless*. "Remington eight-seventy. Carries a 'bean-bag' load, non-lethal unless you get hit in the wrong spot. Gets your attention though."

"I'll bet."

He glanced back at the two passengers behind the wire mesh grill. Luis' father had the solid-but-intense air of a man not to be trifled with. Easton didn't know much about him, other than that he ran a masonry and stone supply company over in Croton. He didn't look too thrilled to be racing around in a police car after midnight. Probably an early riser, Easton guessed. Luis looked wired and excited to be doing something other than sitting around a police station with a detective who clearly didn't believe a word he'd said, although a car had been dispatched to the Ortega's house (a multi-family Victorian over on Clinton) to see if Armando had turned up yet.

From the amount of chatter coming through the mobile unit on the dashboard, the Wyvern Falls police department was still having a lively evening out there. Easton heard two 10-01 (vehicle accidents) calls, three 10-08s (fight/disturbance) and one he wasn't familiar with, a 10-10, which he asked about.

"Investigation condition," Officer Vance promptly replied, without elaborating.

He slowed to a stop and lowered his window as they pulled up to the two squad cars that were now parked, lights flashing, on either side of the entrance road that led out to the parking area on Raadsel Point. Two cops sauntered over, hands hooked in their belts.

"Anything?"

The closer of the two policemen, a stocky black man named Russell, shook his head. "Nothing much. A few kids. One group of very drunk *Mexicanos*. Only four cars have passed through in the last hour. All locals.

No one matching your perp's description. Sorry."

"Thanks."

A minute later they pulled into the trailer area. From the back seat. Luis directed them towards the area by the copse of spruce trees. Vance slowed the car down to a crawl and flicked on the exterior searchlight.

Luis had his face pressed up to the mesh. "There . . . it was right over there!" The searchlight probed past the trunks of the oversized evergreens, one of which Pete and Adam had been perched in only hours earlier. Next to it was an open space of dirt, pine needles, and crisscrossing tire tracks. About twenty yards further was a silver Air Stream trailer. The searchlight glinted off its polished surface, then paused.

"That the one?" Officer Vance asked.

"No, it was right there!" Luis pointed at the empty spot. "I swear!"

Vance stopped the car. The radio continued to broadcast calls.

Luis was incredulous. He tried to say three things at once until Vance cut him off with a raised hand. "Wait here," Vance said to the back seat. He and Easton got out of the police car together, Vance pulling a heavy Mag-Lite from his belt and flicking it on. The light beam played over the ground. There was a sparkle of broken glass, and some deep splashes of maroon.

But the Red Baron's RV was gone.

Vance was crouching by what were undoubtedly blood stains. He reached down and, dipping his hand in the dirt, rubbed it between his thumb and forefinger, then sniffed it. Easton was standing next to him.

"So what do you think?"

The policeman grunted, "*Hmpf.* Well it's looking like *something* happened here." He stood up and focused the flashlight on what was clearly a set of heavy vehicle tracks. They veered off to the northeast.

"What's up that way?"

"Another picnicking and parking area. Dead end circle."

"No way out?"

"Not unless our missing RV has wings."

Easton nodded. "Why don't you have a look? I'd like to talk with the some of the residents here. Starting with that trailer right there."

He pulled a pen light out of his jacket pocket flicked it on.

"Roger that."

"And Vance?"

"Yeah?"

"I don't know about you, but I'm not liking this. Not at all."

"With you on that." Vance walked back to the squad car and popped the trunk. A minute later, he returned with a black handheld unit with a clip-on holder.

He switched it on and handed it to Easton. "Familiar with one of these?"

Easton looked it over. It was a Vertex VX920 portable radio. "I've used them once or twice."

"Good. It's already set to the correct channel. Just press and talk."

"I should be able to manage that."

He pointed the penlight at something he'd spotted on the ground. It was a line of paw prints. *Large* paw prints. They led off towards the woods that covered the north half of the point. A few drops of blood went with them.

"What do you make of those?"

Vance stepped over and added his own flashlight. "Christ. I'd say dog. A *very big* dog."

"I'd agree on that. See you in a few minutes?"

Vance walked back to the squad car and half sitting in the driver's seat with the door still open picked up the handset of the car radio and called in his report.

It was the last time Easton saw him alive.

-12-

OCTOBER OF 1919. Luke Edwards has been in the village of Vossenack for three days. The village is in the North Rhine/Westphalia area of Germany and is part of the Hürtgen Forest, or Hürtgenwald, which in twenty-five years will be the setting of one of the most brutal battles of the Second World War. Although still a scenic and rustic town, its economy, like many in the aftermath of Great War, has been decimated and the majority of its male population annihilated in the slaughterhouse of the Western Front. The Reich mark is already spiraling out of control with inflation and food is scarce.

Lieutenant Edwards has grown lean, hungry, and haunted. He has also been officially AWOL from his unit since November of the previous year, although there is no real effort to locate him or bring him up on a court martial. The war is over, most of the American Expeditionary Force has shipped back over the Atlantic and he is one less soldier the Army needs to concern itself with mustering out.

Major Thaw, Edwards' commanding officer, hadn't seen him since the day after the 103rd occupied the German aerodrome at Mars-la-Tour and Edwards took off in a 1916 Peugeot Bébé abandoned in one of the hangers. Aware of his Lieutenant's increasingly obsessive behavior but also aware of his outstanding combat record, Thaw decided to discreetly drop the case into Army paperwork limbo, vaguely citing Edwards' disappearance in the chaos of airfield transfers.

He was unaware that, shortly after arriving at the German aerodrome, Edwards discovered a sheaf of half-burned reports in an oil drum behind the officers' quarters containing a partial log that suggested that the bizarre German pilot might not be dead after all, that the day after being interred in the ice locker, the body had disappeared. Mention was made of a dead German guard and footprints in the mud heading east, towards the woods and the German border. In the same report, he also discovered something even more important: a name.

Hauptmann Klaus von Richtenstein.

The German prisoner who translated this for him – a lowly corporal part of a detail left behind with orders to sabotage the remaining aircraft but didn't – could add little except that Hauptmann Richtenstein had been missing since July; that he had a reputation as a strange, but competent pilot; that he had been a doctor before the war; and that he was from a wealthy family from Aachen.

And there was one more thing that the corporal had been reluctant to discuss. The Hauptmann had developed some sort of bizarre acquaintanceship with Manfred von Richtofen, the Red Baron himself. Apparently, he had taken photographs of the crash sites of the Baron's victims, with a focus on the mangled remains of the dead pilots. Word was that Richtofen had not only taken a keen interest in collecting these 'trophies' but that both men had developed an unhealthy fascination with them, part of the corrosive psychological death wish that could invade even the most stalwart pilot's soul over time. The Baron had become increasingly obsessed with the Hauptmann's morbid hobby until his own death in April of 1918, after which von Richtenstein's proclivities had turned even more bizarre. There was talk of magical rituals and books – he took to painting tiny mystical symbols around his cockpit – and strange lights and voices could be heard in his tent until the wee hours. Already something of an outcast from the usually tight fraternity of pilots, the others began to completely distance themselves from Richtenstein despite his overtures of fresh food and brandy that only a man of very wealthy resources could afford by that point in the war.

But Edwards could get no more out of the corporal, even at gunpoint. At the crack of dawn, the following morning, Edwards packed up and left, soon joining the stream of refugees and demobilized soldiers heading back toward their defeated Fatherland.

He abandoned the Peugeot near Liege, Belgium after running out of gas, a commodity all but impossible to come by. Undaunted, Edwards continued on foot, making his way to Aachen where his inquiries painted an even more disturbing portrait of his quarry. The youngest son of a prominent industrial family, there were rumors of animal mutilations, a rape, possibly even a murder. There were also rumors that he dabbled heavily in the occult and presented himself as a magician of sorts. Passing himself off as a veteran pilot assembling biographies on his German foes for a book he was writing, Edwards obtained a photograph of Richtenstein. It showed a sallow, dark eyed man with a weak chin, straight black hair slicked straight back and large ears. A face that no doubt attracted the interest of the bullies at the Military Academy he attended as a boy. Even the photograph itself seemed unpleasant to the touch and Edwards kept it folded away in his satchel, taking it out only when absolutely necessary.

The trail grew cold for some months as Richtenstein was officially listed as Killed in Action (much to the relief of his family, apparently). Edwards took up residence with a tavern waitress and actress who insisted on dragging him to theater performances (and whenever their meager funds would allow). One night they attended an amateur performance of 'Kashchey the Deathless', a one-act opera by the Russian composer Nikolai Rimsky-Korsakov. Edwards wasn't much of a theater type but this show got his attention, particularly its central theme of an evil, ugly wizard who cheats death by transferring his soul to his daughter's tears and into a container. As long as his soul is in the container, his physical body cannot be killed, though the process turns that body into something hideous and ugly. The container, in typical fairy-tale fashion, is kept inside a needle, which is inside a hare which is inside a duck inside an iron chest under an oak tree. Once the container is destroyed, the wizard is once again mortal and vulnerable.

Edwards' woman friend, a beautiful Austrian whom he's concerned he was possibly falling in love with, was passionately caught up in the predictable "kidnapped princess rescued from the evil wizard" part of the story and its subplot involving the wizard's daughter. Edwards was focused on two key things about the wizard: his skeletal appearance and his trick of immortality.

The following day, he was in the city library where he discovered that the opera, which originally premiered in 1905, was actually based on an older Slovakian legend: Koschei. What he read of this is fantastic and utterly unbelievable, but then so was what he witnessed with his own eyes (and machine guns) over the Western Front. The woman whose bed he now shared – and now his heart it seemed – knew nothing of his true purpose nor can he bring himself to tell her. And one day a week later, a small news item got his attention that he correlated with another bit of information he had discovered. He slipped out of the warm refuge of their bed in the freezing apartment on Donnerstrausse in the wee hours and left without so much as a goodbye.

A farmer in his cart took him southwest to Vossenack, a quiet village in the nearby forest where the private hunting lodge of the Richtenstein family was. It was also a village where ten children had disappeared recently. And, it was a village with a remarkable church where a certain unconventional father, a Slovakian Catholic priest, maintained his congregation. An unusual choice, but these were unusual times. All that remained of the priests' predecessor were a bunch of decaying parts still half buried in the trenches of Verdun. This beautiful building with its elegant steeple will be shot to pieces and mutilated beyond recognition by artillery and tank fire during the next World War at the tail end of what will be known as "The Battle of the Bulge". It will eventually be rebuilt into a blunt, clunky-looking ghost of itself, but that was still many decades into the future.

And so on this ninth day of October, Edwards found himself in the church. It was a Thursday afternoon and the church was quiet. A scattering of gaunt, ragged looking people, no more than a dozen, were sitting or kneeling on the benches. Some were praying. Some simply sat staring vacantly at the large crucifix and its occupant in the vaulted apse as if wondering in shock how He could have allowed the last four years to really happen. It was all supposed to be over by Christmas. Now the great Weimer Republic was in tatters, its great Teutonic leaders and soldiers beaten and bowed.

No one here escaped the ravages of war, the shortages of food, clothing, death.

Edwards cared about none of this. He was there to settle a score, and one score only. It was during his conversation with the priest in his private office in the back that he began to understand how Richtenstein had achieved what he had, that there were things beyond the understanding or even knowledge of the modern "Age of Reason" with its scientists and engineers and mathematicians. Although, given the diabolical efficiency by which this age has contrived to slaughter young men by the millions these past four years,

"Reason" might well be replaced by "Insanity."

But there are darker things and activities being practiced that appalled even Edwards' cynical and war-hardened mind. The priest came from what they call the 'old country' and of a line that was quietly vanishing in this modern age; a priest who knew well the secrets and darker history of mankind from places where myths, legends, and folklore are still a part of the fabric of daily life.

Edwards asked the priest if he knew of Koschei the Deathless.

Paling, the priest crossed himself and Edwards found himself ushered quickly into the back chambers of the church.

"Yes, after a fashion," he finally responded, once a small service of tea had been mustered up. "But what would possess a military man, an American military man, to bring up such a blasphemous topic?" The priest spoke in a thick accent that was almost impossible to understand. "Yezzz, afta eh fachun," it sounded like.

Edwards, never one to be tactful or circumspect, plowed straight ahead: "Because I have good reason to believe that such a creature, such a thing, may be not far from this village. 'After a fashion' that is. And it is my aim to destroy it. Can you help?"

And wonder of wonders, the Priest could, and was willing to help. He too had heard rumors, and he too was aware of the girls who had disappeared. Most were members of his congregation.

The priest talked.

Edwards listened.

Saturday morning found Edwards standing before the heavy beamed hunting lodge on the southern fringe of the Hürtgen Forest. The worn leather satchel hung over his shoulder had in it a Mauser C96 pistol and a ten-round clip of cartridges blessed by the priest. He looked gaunt, hard, and merciless. The crisp collared army tunic he once wore has been replaced by a threadbare surplus German military jacket, his boots are sprung and the grey wool trousers he wears have holes. His thick tousle of dirty blond hair (shaved close on the sides) is unkempt, his jaw covered with stubble, but the eyes are clear and piercing.

This is the face of a man who accepts, and delivers death.

The lodge was large but not ostentatious. With its steep roof and plaster-and-beam construction, at a glance it looked like it belonged on a colored postcard with stout Germans posing in front of it sporting lederhosen, feathered green caps, hunting horns, and rifles. Around it the towering evergreens were like motionless sentinels. Mist crept through the undergrowth, not unlike another autumn day a year (a lifetime?) earlier.

Edwards sensed the house — or something in the house — watching him. The thick glazed windows revealed little but years of dirt and disuse. Some of the panes were broken. Branches from storms long past littered the eaves and balcony. The lodge had a forlorn air — it was clearly falling into disrepair — but it also had a sly, sneaky look.

Like an old bear that was only pretending to be asleep.

Or dead.

The silence had a weighted quality to it, suddenly broken by the harsh caw of a raven which lifting away into the sky, annoyed. Edwards looked up, then to his right, as a movement in the woods caught his eye.

Out of the murky gloom of the forest appeared the largest dog he had ever seen. It looked like a bear crossed with a wolf. Its fur was thick and shaggy, brown and black with white forepaws and a dark face with black lined eyes. Its ears were ragged stumps. At a conservative guess, it was probably in excess of one hundred and fifty pounds. The sound of its giant paws was muted by the pine needles as it sauntered up in its odd 'head swinging low' bear-like gait and it quietly stopped then sat down about two yards to Edwards' right, facing the lodge.

Edwards gave a start but he wasn't surprised. The priest told him of this possibility. It was likely one of what he called non-human 'Bogatyrs' – protectors – led by Polkan, a dog-headed god, although they are known by many names: Gelert, Chuvac, so on. There are stories that their bloodlines can be traced back to Argo, the faithful dog of Odysseus, but no one is sure. Only that they sometimes appear as guardians of men against dangerous things – even undead, unclean things. When Edwards asked where they came from, the priest merely shrugged as only Eastern Europeans do: who knows?

What Edwards did know was that, whatever this unexpected ally was, he was glad it was for him rather than against him. He glanced over and the dog rolled its eyes back at him as if to say, "Well?"

Edwards pulled the Mauser out of his satchel. An ugly, heavy looking thing with a "broom handle" grip, he carefully loaded the ten-round slot clip into it. This was a wartime 9mm model he'd found in the trunk of the car he'd stolen and each bullet had a symbol scratched into its casing by the priest. He snapped the action to chamber the first round and then in unison man and dog walked toward the heavily timbered front door.

It was unlocked.

With a groan, it opened inward, revealing a large, gloomy hall. It smelled of dust, old plaster and decay. And something else. Perhaps a hint of putrescence? Something rotting in its grave? The dog sensed something down there. Edwards heard a deep growl and glimpsed large fangs emerging from the animal's snout.

The hall had a high ceiling with gas globe lights suspended from it. The walls were crowded floor to ceiling with racks of antlers, mounted heads – mostly deer but some boar, reindeer, bear. All were dusty and garlanded with cobwebs. There were doors on either side and an archway at the back. Past the doors on either side was a narrow staircase leading to an upstairs gallery and presumably to the bedrooms. Beyond the archway to the back was the great room, a vast chamber with an open ceiling. Edwards decided to try this room first.

The Richtenstein family had not been to the lodge since before the war but it was immediately clear that someone had been making use of the building. For starters, there was a damaged but intact Lewis machine gun mounted over the fireplace along with a dozen large swatches of aircraft canvas on one wall – at least four were clearly from

American aircraft. Two had bloodstains. Edwards stared at these, eyes widening in surprise, then rage. This was something he didn't expect. Are these trophies from his friends? Probably. He looked over at the massive stone fireplace, seeing the stack of dust-covered logs in the metal hopper along with a box of kindling. He had to resist the urge to simply run over and set the entire place ablaze and burn it to the ground.

Control!

Yes, he must start a fire, but the razing must come later. There is work to do, and not much time. The priest will be here within the hour with a mob of villagers. Edwards was adamant: Richtenstein is mine! Give me one hour, then do what you will. One of us will be dead by then.

Edwards' first order of business was to pull out the second item in his satchel, a battered kerosene railroad lantern, and light it.

The chamber was lofty and ostentatious – the sheer volume of trophies (not including the more recent additions) suggested excess and over-indulgence, neither which sat well with Edwards' Spartan approach to life. Staghorn chandeliers were suspended from the beams of the cathedral ceiling above, rich leather chairs and divans were scattered around the room. Near the center was a large, low circular table. There were a few ashtray stands and an end table with a pipe rack on it. All the furniture had a rustic yet unquestionably Teutonic look to it. The wide timbered floors were hewn of Black Forest oak. To the back of the house, a series of windows and double doors revealed a covered porch and the dense forest beyond. On one wall hung a massive tapestry depicting a hunting scene with what might be a Richtenstein ancestor on a horse. To the left of the archway, a second staircase led up to an open gallery. It was at the door under its landing that the dog, after one complete circuit of the room, stopped.

Edwards guessed that the door led to the basement, but before he could consider that, he needed locate something very important. The legends said that the Koschei kept his soul in an object – traditionally in a needle or an egg or both –possibly in a small chest, buried near a tree. But it could be in anything. The priest believed it would be kept close by, however, as the turmoil and upheaval of the last four years suggested that nowhere was completely safe, buried or not. It would be something inconspicuous, small, and in a convenient location, easy to get if a hasty exit was required. Edwards agreed.

But where, then?

He paced around the room once, twice. Nothing suggesting an egg. There were four small chests, but all proved to be empty (one has matches for the fire, but these are dusty). The dog continued to sit by the cellar door like a statue. Edwards was on his third circuit and about to go up the stairs to search the bedrooms when he spied something on the fireplace mantel. It was sitting far back, nestled amongst various items: a bronze hunting horn with a green leather strap, a statuette of a Teutonic hunter with a bow, an elaborately carved beer stein and a silver shooter's cup.

A single bullet.

It was the only item with no dust on it.

He stepped over, picked it up and examined it. The bullet was a German 7.92mm, the same type used in the mounted Spandau guns on German aircraft. Except that this bullet was odd — the back of the shell casing had no primer, just a smooth steel surface.

Which it was unfirable.

Still it felt loathsome — somehow greasy to the touch — and he shuddered. He slipped the bullet into his front pocket and looked around the room. This was all too easy. It felt like a set-up to him. Still, he loaded some logs into the grate, packed them with kindling and got a fire going. The wood was dry and old and, within minutes, the flames were roaring. He stepped back and paused — there was a thump from the cellar below, and what sounded like the rattle of a chain.

The dog growled again.

Edwards grabbed the lantern and pistol and stepped quietly over. Setting the lantern down again, he worked the latch on the door and, with a protest of rusty hinges, it swung inward.

The stench that wafted up was horrible: dampness, corruption, decay, blood, human excrement. He heard the rattle of a chain again, and a moan. And something else, something he can't quite identify. But it raised the short hairs on the back of his neck. Death, there was certainly death down there. But also . . . un-death. Looking down into the Stygian gloom, he thought that it was the last place on earth he wanted to go, but also understood that there was nothing else to do — turning back was not an option.

He steeled himself, breathing through his mouth, and started down the rough-hewn steps.

More than one creaked as he descended.

At the bottom of the cellar stairs, the ground floor was hard-packed earth. To the left was a door, possibly to a wine cellar. To the right, a small storage room with some crates and what looked like old machinery. Before him, however, was a short hall lined with cells. They looked like they might once have been stalls of a sort, but what they definitely were now are cells. For holding young children.

But before he took more than a couple steps, the door to his left flew open and things shamble out, hissing. One moment, all he could see in the dim light of his lantern were moldy, skeletal faces with needle- like teeth lunging at him; the next, he was knocked flat on his face as, with a roar, the massive dog leapt, jaws open, like some sort of shaggy hell-hound from someone's worst nightmare. As luck would have it, the lantern landed upright and didn't go out or set the basement on fire. Edwards regained his feet, staggering backwards.

The dog was a thrashing machine of destruction, tearing the creature's limb from limb, snarling, snapping. It had gone into its killing zone. One of the creatures got past it and came at Edwards, its gaping black maw of a mouth clicking and hissing, taloned claws scrabbling at the air. It reeked of decay and rotten fish. This was one of the 'Draugyr' — the low dead — that the priest had warned him of, but knowledge didn't lessen his horror or revulsion at all. With only a moment's hesitation, he raised the Mauser and fired point blank into the thing's face. The scabbed head jerked as a hole appeared in its forehead, the back exploding in a spray of gore, and the clicking teeth paused in an almost comical 'o' of surprise. Then the creature collapsed like a puppet whose strings have been clipped.

Edwards' ears were ringing – the retort of the 9mm in the confined space was deafening. One more of the creatures came crawling out with its weirdly glowing pupils, clawing its way along the dirt floor towards him. One of its legs had been torn off at the hip. If the soiled remains of the white dress it was buried in was any indication, this one was a female. Edwards raised the pistol again but, before he could fire, the dog leapt out of the gloom and landed on the thing's back, massive forepaws pinning it. The creature had time to half turn its head before the massive jaws clamped down on it. Then the shaggy head shook and, with a sickening pop, the thing's head was torn off and sent bouncing off the corridor wall like a soccer ball.

The dog, which Edwards was already thinking of as 'Polkan' made a gagging cough as if it has tasted something foul, which it had. Then it looked at him with an oddly fixed expression as if to say "Well?" Edwards noticed the dog's eyes were brown mixed with flecks of gold that glowed in the lantern light. He shrugged and set to examining the cells along the corridor.

There was a dozen of these, six to a side, and here was the answer to the mystery of the missing children. Some of them at least. Only four were still alive and of those, only two looked like they had a shred of sanity in their eyes. The two others stared off into space vacantly, like blown-out candles. The other cells held three corpses, one which looked recent – a little girl coated in filth curled into a fetal position, a small teddy bear still clutched in her small hands. The other two corpses looked like desiccated mummies, their dry husks still chained to the stone walls. Presumably this was how the Liche feeds.

Another cell held what appeared to be a pile of old bones and some moldering clothes.

Of the rest of the missing children, there was no sign.

Suddenly the dog looked up at the ceiling.

Edwards sensed it too.

Something was upstairs – was it a soft thump? A rustle of old clothing? Or just the instinctive feeling that something had emerged out of hiding like a spider appearing in front of its trap.

Edwards had never been more terrified in his entire life.

His heart was hammering in his chest and goose bumps raced up and down his arms. There was a moment where he hesitated, when the rational imp in his subconscious was shouting 'This is insane! You can't stop this thing! You'll be horsemeat!!'' But then that dissenting voice was quietly squashed as cold rage raced through his veins and the killing mind settled on him like a soft cloak. He inched up the cellar stair carefully, back to one side, pistol raised in one hand. The dog followed him, placing each paw on the wood treads with careful deliberation. It was surprisingly quiet for such an ungainly beast. All is quiet except for the occasional creak of the stair tread. Edwards gets to the doorway and glances into the great room, first one way then the next.

Nothing.

The fire is roaring in the fireplace. Shadows play around the walls in the half gloom of the interior. Edwards steps carefully into the room. Could something be lurking in the darkness gathered up in the rafters of the cathedral ceiling? Possibly.

A glance up at the second floor gallery balustrade.

Empty.

The dog crept into the room as well, one paw stepping cautiously in front of the other; he is in stalk mode. Instinctually they move apart in separate directions, Edwards along the wall to his left, the dog towards the archway to the right.

Past the low round table in the center of the room where there is a scattering of chairs the air appears to darken and shimmer and gather into itself; then it resolved into an upright figure of the Liche. Richtenstein. He is dressed in some sort of old Prussian tunic and robe. There was also something large in its hands. Before Edwards could even register what it was, there was a mechanical sliding sound – kacherk – and the dog let out a cry and toppled over, an oversized crossbow bolt protruding from its flank.

Edwards darted to his left towards the fireplace, reaching for the bullet in his front trouser pocket. He had time to register that his enemy was once again intact and to wonder at how that could be – what sort of regenerative powers does the thing have – but the thought is cut short as Richtenstein stands up, casting the crossbow in its hands aside and made a flinging gesture towards the fireplace.

The flames disappeared as if extinguished by a powerful wind.

Then in an instant it's right in front of him, the grinning skull with its blackened flesh and hellish orbs for eyes. Edwards did the only thing he could think of – he struck the face with the Mauser in his hand. Once from the right, then again from the left. There was a dry crack in the air as he did this. Then the third time his hand is seized – the creature has an iron-like grip. The next thing he is aware of is that he's flying across the room.

"Not good," he has time to process and then he hit the far wall, an explosion of pain radiating from his upper back. He bounces off in a cloud of broken plaster and tumbles to the floor, knocking aside a table and lamp but landing on his hands and knees. Shaking his head, he looked up to see the Liche flying towards him and, without thinking, he snatched up the lamp and hurled it. The end table followed it a moment later. He scrambled sideways and for a few minutes the fight took on an almost comical twist as he systematically threw anything he could lay his hands on at his attacker: another lamp, a statue, a glass ashtray.

Then Richtenstein was upon him, his terrible hands scrabbling for purchase around Edward's throat. Arms and legs flailing, the two figures rolled across the floor, finally coming to a stop near the fireplace. Richtenstein was on top, his skeletal, steel-like hands gripping Edward's neck. The awful visage leans towards Edwards' face, its jaws gently opening . . .

Edwards was coming to the realization that he might fail after all and that this will end badly for him. But then another scrap of data surfaced in his scrambled thoughts: heat.

He felt heat on the top of his head.

The fire in the massive fireplace was out – correction: appeared to be out – and yet he can still feel its tremendous heat. And on the coat-tails of that thought: what if it was simply a trick? A sleight of hand?

With that he acted. He stopped his futile attempt to break the thing's grip and with his left hand, reached again into his pocket and felt the greasy cold metal of the bullet and pulled it free.

And tossed it backwards into the grate.

Richtenstein's reaction was instantaneous – he tried to scramble after it. Edwards grabbed onto the Liche's body with all his might and, scissoring around, reversed his position so that one of his heels was digging into the stone hearth and the other was up against one of the oversized andirons. Richtenstein hissed and scrabbled like an enraged cat but Edwards held on with everything he had. His clothes were torn and his skin was ripped in the vicious struggle.

A moment later there was a resounding 'bang!' as the round exploded, sending the bullet ricocheting off the stone somewhere into the room. Sparks flew as one of the log crashed and Edwards rolled away, running for the pistol which he had dropped near the wall.

Richtenstein regained his feet by the hearth, which is burning again, and stood there – a nightmarish and yet puzzled figure, looking at its hands as if seeing them for the first time.

Then there was another loud bang as the Mauser was fired and, as if by magic, a hole appeared in the Liche's hand. It actually screamed, a sound more like a steel nail being dragged across an iron grate, and Edwards fired again and again.

The second shot clipped the Liche in the shoulder and sent it whirling backwards – smoke sizzling out of the hole in the tunic. The third went wild. The priest had spoken the truth. With the bullet destroyed - the vessel holding Richtenstein's essence – he was once again vulnerable. And the blessed bullets in the Mauser can do their work.

Edwards walked, almost non-chalantly towards his enemy, who had landed half propped on one elbow.

Another round was fired into the narrow torso.

The thing hissed, its jaws working in pain. A whorl of smoke curled out of the wound.

Edward's face was expressionless as he raised the gun one more time to deliver the coup de grace, when suddenly he heard his name spoken aloud.

By a woman.

"Luke!"

The gun stopped as the sights settled on a spot on Richtenstein's forehead.

Again: "Luke! You mustn't!"

Impossible! He knew the voice; he knew it well.

His girlfriend.

Still keeping the gun trained on Richtenstein, he half turned.

"Lorelei?"

Out of the corner of his eye he saw her approaching – gliding – down the stairs and threading her way through the toppled furniture and tables. He took a couple of steps backward, confused. Lorelei is dressed in a beautiful, tight-waisted gown, her hair done up in a style already beginning to fade out in more fashionable circles and she looked – impossibly – more seductive than he had ever seen her. This was not the rakish bohemian he had known these past few months, in clothes little better than rags, waking up next to her with her hair wild like a cyclone. No, this woman looked like a temptress, a siren Queen out of a fairy tale (perhaps illustrated by Gustav Klimt) with her high cheekbones and violet eyes.

And she was smiling, a deep smile that spoke of yearning and love and . . . hunger.

The word had barely registered in his thoughts before she was upon him, ignoring the gun and clasping him in a tight embrace. Edwards was completely confused. None of this made any sense. Her dress, her look, her very presence here.

". . . it's me," she said breathlessly. "You don't have to worry about von Richtenstein anymore, my darling."

"No?" He glanced back at the Liche who was still on the floor, though it looked like he had crawled a couple of feet away. Then Lorelei's hand was caressing his cheek. He felt her tongue dart around his ear. Despite the bizarreness of the situation, he felt himself hardening with desire. But he was not there to indulge such things.

He was there to . . .

Lorelei literally leapt onto him and Edward stumbled. The gun went off, sending a wild shot across the room.

"No!" This time her voice was a vicious snarl. He swung the Mauser around toward her, only to have it struck aside, her blow powerful enough to send it flying out of his hand. He blinked in surprise, then for the second time that day, found himself tossed across the room. This time he toppled over the sofa and landed on his back. A moment later she vaulted over the furniture and landed on top of him, straddling with her knees. Both her fists struck in unison, boxing his ears in a double hammer blow. Edwards was stunned, his brain going haywire. This time his eyes made a couple of slow blinks, the slack expression of a stupid man who can't remember if he put his pants on before going out the door that morning. He tried to focus. It was difficult. His ears were ringing. He blacked out for a moment, then came to with a vicious slap across his face.

"Lor . . . Lor . . ." he stuttered.

She had his arms pinned under her knees, looking down at him and looking sensuous and terrifying at the same time. One thing was certain, this was no magician's trick. His throbbing ears could testify to that.

"My poor darling," she said, "He's known for a while you were looking for him . . . he came to me in Aachen . . . with promises of riches . . . and eternal life . . ."

"But I . . . you?" Edwards couldn't even fully articulate the thought.

"You what? Left me without a second thought but for your vengeful quest? Ach du lieber . . . tut mit leid . . ." And she bent towards him, her face distorting horribly, her mouth opening wider and wider. To his mounting horror, he saw what looked like a cluster of silver filaments emerging from the back of her throat . . .

"Halt!" commanded a voice from over her shoulder.

Standing in the archway was the priest, his crucifix held high in one bony hand. Behind him was a ragged throng of villagers with assorted weapons ranging from antique shotguns to axes to farm implements. He was not a great man, this priest from the deeper reaches of what was once the Austrio-Hungarian Empire, not a physically large nor powerful man. But he was a man who would not back down, who would stand up again no matter how many times he was knocked down, and who would not suffer fools gladly.

Nor supernatural creatures, apparently. All this was evident in his unwavering glare and the way he held the cross, which, after all, is nothing more than a symbol to channel something that ran deep in his heart and soul.

Lorelei, or whatever thing she had become, immediately grasped this. Hissing like some sort of feral animal she sprang into a crouch, her distorted features continuing to transform into some sort of hideous goblin face, the mouth ringed with pointed teeth. Her fingers had elongating into sharp talons, the nails quivering in the air as if eager to tear at something. The tendrils of her hair appeared to be animated, like Medusa's wig but in which, instead of snakes, there are living filaments.

She made a short lunge as if to attack the throng but the priest didn't flinch. He simply raised the cross higher.

"You are unclean!" he said in his heavy accent, "Begone!" Edwards swore he saw some sort of flash of light, like an electrical pulse, flair out from the priest and Lorelei leapt backward like a cat landing on a hot plate. She hissed again, then jumped through the window at the back of the house in an explosion of shattering glass and wooden panes.

The priest and the throng rushed in. Edwards was helped to his feet.

"Richtenstein" he slurred, but, even as he said it, he saw that the Liche was gone, the back door ajar. He tried to follow and stumbled, unaware he had suffered a concussion, only vaguely understanding he was not quite right. The priest was at his side, hand on his elbow.

"The dog," Edwards got out.

The dog was still alive, though for how long was a question. The crossbow bolt was lodged in its chest, though whether any vital organs were hit was anyone's guess. It was clearly in a lot of pain and its tongue rolled listlessly out of its mouth, its breath in ragged gasps. At Edwards' insistence, a litter was hastily put together and the animal was lifted out. A dozen of the villagers headed into the cellar and carried out the children, both living and dead.

A half dozen of the villagers set out in pursuit of Richtenstein and Lorelei but they lost the trail after half a mile in the impenetrable Hürtgen Forest. They were old men and young boys – the more able-bodied who would have been more successful at this sort of thing are buried in France. Edwards would spend the next few days in a fever in a bed at the rectory and this time it would be a week before he recovers. He spent the next two years searching for von Richtenstein and Lorelei, and her betrayal was a bitter fruit he tasted for many years beyond that. The dog Polkan survived and, along with the priest, whose name was Leslaw Tőkés – a few more tales may one day come to light. But the trail of the Liche would grow colder until Edwards lost it altogether. Eventually he made it to Paris where he fell in with some American ex-pats including a W.W. Windstaff, another American pilot who became his drinking companion in the popular bars like

Harry's and Jimmy's Falstaff. This spree went on for months until one morning he woke up in a gutter, half smeared with excrement, and he realized how far out of control his life had become. A week later, he was on a boat back to America and from there back to Wyvern Falls, a village he will never leave until the day he died.

-13-

THE BATTLE in the trailer was a near thing and might have ended differently if it hadn't been for another entertainer named Bob Johnson running a little late-night errand.

The thing known as Lorelei was certainly no longer human, but she was also not invincible. The inside of the trailer was quickly in shambles as the Red Baron's Daughter and the shaggy dog-beast went at each other, clawing, biting, smashing into walls. Lorelei was getting the worst of it, since the dog had a thick undercoat that was all but impossible to tear through. Time and again, for all her effort she found herself with nothing more than clumps of wool-like fur in her mouth and nails while the thing's vicious teeth were taking its toll.

It had a mouth like a bear trap.

They had just landed on the floor with the dog on top, Lorelei's hands (claws) locked around the dog's throat, keeping its gnashing jaws just inches from her face when a cheerful voice spoke up from the doorway.

"Holy mackerel there, ma'am! Need some help?"

That the term "ma'am" could only loosely be applied to the Countess at this point – she looked more like a blood-streaked, half-naked demon – seemed to escape the speaker's notice. Looking over the dog's shoulder, she saw the man from the next trailer, Bob Johnson, poking his head through the shambles of the door. His eyebrows were slightly raised, a corn-cob pipe sticking out from his mouth at a jaunty angle, and in one hand was a metal cash till and in the other an odd grey plastic box. From his expression, one would have thought the scene he was looking at was no more unusual than if someone had, say, accidentally dropped their dessert (like a bread pudding, perhaps) on the kitchen floor. He didn't even seem to be aware that one of Lorelei's large breasts had fallen out of the robe and was in plain sight.

She couldn't even think of how to respond, although the dog was still trying to lunge at her face. She saw Johnson make a sort of "oh well" expression and hold the gray plastic box up as if he was aiming it. Then his thumb pressed down on something and the dog froze in mid-bite. Suddenly it gave its head a massive shake as if a bee had landed in one ear, then to Lorelei's shock, vaulted over her head and landed in the middle of the trailer, blinking and cringing. A moment later, Johnson was knocked aside, raising his arms in an exaggerated reaction as the dog shot past him in a blur of fur and teeth. When he looked back at the Countess, she had more or less resumed her human form and was pulling the tattered remains of her robe together. She stared at him warily, unsure how to handle this latest twist.

Johnson looked like he was just here as a friendly neighbor following up on some sort of ho-hum mild accident. The half-smile and merry eyes looked a little put on however.

"Say there miss, you look like you took a scratch or two. Would you like me to fetch a doctor?"

Lorelei got to her feet, making a good stab at regaining her dignity. Should she kill him? Tear his throat out? Tear off the jaw and that dreadful pipe and watch his eyes pop as she sucked the life out of him? He didn't look particularly strong. In fact, with his button-down cotton sweater, Brylcremed hair, and pencil moustache he looked like a home-spun 1940s movie actor. Then she remembered: he was the ventriloquist act with the dummy named Timmy or Jimmy or something. She didn't really care. What she needed to do was get him out of here as expediently as possible. So *she* could get out of here as expediently as possible. The boys had seen too much. The authorities would be nosing around soon, if not already on their way.

She drew up a half smile from somewhere. "I'm sorry, Mister . . .?"

"*Johnson*! Bob Johnson!" He let out a high-pitched chuckle as he said this.

"Mister Johnson, then. You're not going to discuss with anyone what just happened here, will you?" She put on a demure look, which would have worked if one just ignored the terrible bite marks, bleeding cuts and the weird transformation that had just occurred.

Apparently, Bob could.

"Abso-lute-ally, Miss," he responded with the almost-but-not-quite confident staccato of a classic vaudeville performer, "Peas and rice! Wouldn't do to have cops and lawyers poking their noses all over the place!" Then a sly wink. "Us *performing folks* have to look out for each other. Besides, I got an errand to run. Do I do!"

She nodded at the plastic box in his hand. "Just what is that thing?" Johnson looked at the plastic box as if he'd forgotten he even had it. "Oh, this? Gosh! It's a Dazer III. Ultrasonic gizmo. Dogs hate the gosh-darn things! Got it when one persistent fella kept trying to chew the legs off my uh, my uh . . . puppet. Just press this doohicky and . . . Bob's your uncle! Works like charm, eh?" Again came that high-pitched chuckle. Lorelei decided. "Could you leave me now, Mister Johnson? I need to pull myself together if you don't mind."

Again he gave her the sly wink. Again she wondered if she should just kill him after all and be done with it.

"Gotcha loud and clear, Miss! Well, gotta run!"

Another question popped out of the Countess' mouth before she could consider it: "One more thing, Mister Johnson . . . are you for real?"

"Real as a pink plastic peel!" he said enthusiastically and was gone, only a trace puff of pipe smoke in the air marking he'd been there at all. If she had been planning on staying, that nonsensical response might have concerned her.

After closing the door best as she could, she staggered over to the bathroom to clean herself up. The wounds were pretty severe. A normal human being would have been in the trauma unit of the nearest hospital.

The worst was her left shoulder where the dog's fangs had torn out deep divots of flesh. She could see the white glint of her shoulder bone through shreds of ragged muscle. There were punctures all up and down both arms where she had been bitten and a tear in her scalp above one ear.

But nothing fatal or life threatening.

She put one hand over the shoulder and gently closed her eyes. In the bleary fluorescent light of the tiny bathroom, her face was gaunt and drained. She looked like she'd aged ten years in the last half hour. The wound knitted itself together – slightly – then stopped.

She needed to feed again. Soon.

Could she have dined on the overly helpful Mister Johnson? She didn't think so but she would have been hard-pressed to explain why. There was something her instincts told her wasn't right, and those instincts had stood her well over so many years.

First things first.

She did what she could with the portable first aid kit and went back to the bedroom, the worst of the wounds covered with gauze and medical tape.

As she changed into a '70s-looking jumpsuit that had come with the previous owners of the RV (her fashion sense ran from the stunningly tasteful to the stunningly tacky), she had a rare moment of introspection: *what was she really?* She didn't really know.

Richtenstein had combined unconventional medical experiments with his darker knowledge of the arcane – he probably didn't know himself. She had been horrified at their first encounter – he had gained entry to her apartment one night when Luke had been out drinking – but then he had showed her... *things*. Eternal or at least an extended life. Not like himself but by other means he had knowledge of, means by which she could maintain her beauty and youth. Part siren, part succubus, part vampire, part human. And of course there would be wealth and riches.

And in return? What could the desiccated, skeletal creature he had turned into want? Sex? (Hideous, and not practical in his condition.).

Companionship? A maid?

No. All Richtenstein wanted, needed actually, was a *personal assistant.*

Someone who could move about in the real world without attracting negative attention.

To secure his meals.

And be an irresistible lure for what had become his favorite meal of all, young boys.

Lorelei did her job well.

A few minutes later, there was a rumble as the RV's diesel engine turned over. The vehicle rolled out slowly, without its lights, as if unsure of itself. It swerved towards the main exit, stopped, then turned towards a badly-paved road leading up a low rise to the northeast. The top of this rise, which was once the site of a large Setasqua Indian fort (and which had been eventually respected by the time-honored American tradition of being turned into a parking lot) was ringed by a little-used picnic area. Many local residents these days weren't even aware it was there, or had forgotten, which was hardly surprising as the access road looked neglected and the sign marking it had fallen over sometime in the 1970s. These days, its occasional night-time function was as a Lovers' Lane, mainly for high-schoolers looking to make out or get stoned or a little of both. Only a few hard-core members of the Wyvern Falls Historical Society (and maybe one or two village old-timers) could tell you what they *think* happened to that Indian village or at least what the legends say happened to it, but to the average Joe, the only indication at all was a bronze statue of a Setasqua chief or sachem atop a pedestal by the edge of the lot with a small plaque. It had been dedicated by the Boy Scouts in 1904 and subsequently annotated by several graffiti *artistes* with such witty observations as "Sabina is UGLY", "Debby sukz" and "J.D. & Alicia 4evR"

Tonight, however, the statue escaped getting plowed into the once-sacred earth by mere inches as the Red Baron's RV slewed past it and came to stop a few yards past the picnic tables next to a towering spruce.

It was dawning on Lorelei that her injuries were more serious than she originally thought. She needed to feed again, and soon. Lorelei had no idea if the dog (she also thought of them as *Bogatyrs*) would return or not.

And she was tired. Weak and terribly tired.

She mumbled a few words and make a brief gesture and the RV appeared to grow *dim*, not vanish entirely but blend in more with the shadows. Then she slumped over the steering wheel and slipped into semi consciousness.

The iBeam digital sports watch on Officer Vance's wrist was reading 1:03 am as he slowed the police cruiser to a stop near the edge of the parking lot, right near the bronze statue. He had made a complete circuit before the searchlight mounted by the driver's window highlighted the bulky form of the RV by the trees. He couldn't understand how this was possible and yet there it was.

The vehicle looked *dim*.

At first, he wondered if the bulb in the searchlight was malfunctioning and then immediately dismissed the idea. The spruce and river birch trees were clearly visible. The RV was not. It was as if by some sleight of hand, it had been coated by some anti-glare (or anti visible) material, because it was only on the second pass that he could see it was there.

Vance however wasn't possessed of an overly active imagination and he didn't dwell on this little discrepancy in what he knew was reality. Instead, he called in his location, suggested they send a back-up unit, and slid open the partition window to the back seat.

"Be right back." He said to his two passengers.

He approached the vehicle carefully, unclipping the safety strap on his holster and holding the heavy duty flashlight high in his left fist. He noted the battered condition of the door. From the angle of the vehicle and the condition of the bush it had run over, he surmised that the driver had lost control, or lost interest in control of the vehicle and had simply rolled to a stop.

Further inspection revealed the woman occupying the driver's seat, slumped over the RV's oversize steering wheel like a sloppy drunk. He also noted the bandages and blood.

With the light shining through the passenger side window (the driver's side was up against a bunch of birch saplings), he pulled out the mobile unit from his belt.

"Dispatch, this is Officer Vance, over. Looks like we have ten-oh-three here at the Renslaer parking area, better send an ambulance. Copy."

A blare of static came out of the unit.

Vic Carrerra, who was working the dispatcher shift, responded. "Ten four, Gary. Hold tight. Ambulance will be there in five, repeat five minutes. Copy?"

Vance acknowledged and, replacing the mobile, opened the RV door, placing his right hand on his Glock as a precaution.

"Ma'am, are you okay? Do you require medical assistance?"

A pointless inquiry, but he was simply trying to evoke a response. Lorelei stirred, one bleary eye looking at him through a tangle of hair.

". . . Help me," she said in a weak voice.

Vance nodded and planted one booted foot on the running board of the RV.

"Ma'am, an ambulance is on the way. In the meantime, can I see your driver's license please?" He was thinking he had a DUI on his hands, although the wounds looked pretty serious. But seriously injured people tended not to run their RVs off into the woods.

When she didn't respond immediately he repeated, "Ma'am?" She looked at him again blearily, then mumbled, "It's . . . it's in the . . . the glove compartment." She made a half-hearted attempt to reach over and open it, mumbling something else.

Vance reached in to open it for her. "May I?"

She said something again and Vance gave her a perplexed look, not sure he'd heard correctly.

"Sorry, ma'am, could you repeat that?" He had a moment to process that something was going seriously wrong here, the woman's face was elongating, distorting. Her mouth, which was suddenly far too large and with far too many teeth, opened wide. She snagged his wrist in a powerful grip yanking him in close and in a deep guttural voice repeated,

"I said *'I'm hungry'*."

Officer Vance's scream was cut off as Lorelei lunged and clamped her jaws around his mouth. This time there was no finesse, the feeding filaments all but leapt into his throat and began eating. Greedily.

In the squad car, Luis had been watching the cop with keen interest. He'd had a queasy feeling since they'd pulled up and spotted the dim (how could it be so dim?) Red Baron's Daughter RV which Officer Vance had gotten out to investigate.

He was also overtired but keyed up.

In the last two days, his previously hum-drum small town life had cranked into an abrupt turn of real-life drama. Except for a few school fights and the time he'd torn his shin open on a jagged rock while climbing down a gully near the river bank (he'd walked into the kitchen and told his mother "Mom, I need a Band-Aid" - she had gone white as a sheet at his blood-filled sneaker, all but thrown him into the front seat of the car and sped off to the Philipsburg Memorial ER room while driving like a madwoman), most of his excitement came from video games and his adventures with his pals in the village.

But this was off the charts. Tonight he had already seen a stunningly beautiful naked woman (and touched by her breast!) attacked by some sort of monster dog and he was now sitting in an actual police car, with his dad no less, trying to help out on an investigation. He was terribly worried about Armando, and Henry as well, but that didn't lessen how excited he was at the same time.

He was about to ask his dad about getting out of church this coming morning (it was already Sunday) when he saw Officer Vance getting yanked in through the passenger door of the RV.

His father had been leaning back, chin on his fist in a half-doze when he was snapped awake by his son's scream.

"Papa! Oh, no!"

From the RV, Officer Vance's legs were kicking furiously, then suddenly went slack. It wasn't rocket science to figure out that that meant nothing good.

Victor Dimas swore and immediately went for the car door, without success. Like any standard police cruiser, there were no door handles in the back seat. For the moment, they were trapped.

Through the windows, they watched in horror as Officer Vance's back legs seemed to collapse, as if muscle and bone were being drained out of the clothes, which was in a manner of speaking, true. Then there was a shuffle as the blood-soaked apparition of Lorelei clambered out over the policeman's corpse. It took a moment for father and son to register what she was holding in her one hand.

It was Officer Vance's decapitated skull.

Lorelei was feeling much better. So much better.

The wounds slowly begun to heal themselves, but such regeneration ate up a lot of energy. As a rule, one had to be cautious and discreet, but there were occasional situations (like this one) where all bets were off, it was strike-and-run and hope for the best when the shit hit the fan, which it undoubtedly would tonight.

It wasn't like the old days.

Now everything was instant communication, cross-referencing, spy cams, and GPS tracking. It was getting harder and harder.

Still, her blood was up and she felt good. Reinvigorated. There was a certain sense of release at taking the gloves off and letting the claws out so to speak, no more cat-and-mouse games.

She saw the young boy and the man sitting in the cruiser. One more meal and she would need to get moving, quickly.

Luis acted without hesitation. Fear is always a great motivator. Although the access window between the front and back seats was small, it wasn't designed to prevent slim thirteen-year-old boys from getting through and he was able to wriggle his way into the front seat quickly. The first objective was to lock the two front doors, the second was to grab the mike on the mobile unit and get talking.

Easton was in the midst of what he was thinking was the most bizarre conversation of his career with the resident of the Airstream trailer when the portable radio clipped to his belt let out a squawk.

His knock on the trailer door minutes earlier had been answered with the door opening abruptly, as if its owner had been awaiting the moment.

Although it was past 1:00 am and the trailer was dark, Bob Johnson greeted the detective puffing on his pipe and wiping his hands with a rag as if he'd just wrapped up a project in his workshop and was about to kick up his feet with a cool beer and enjoy his favorite television or radio show.

"Hey there, fella! How can I help?" he'd offered while Easton's hand was still hovering in the air in mid-knock.

Easton had pulled out his official badge, hoping the man wouldn't look too closely and ask why the hell a British CID detective was questioning people in the Hudson Valley. But he figured it was a quicker way to get better answers. "Detective Easton, on liaison with the Wyvern Falls Police here. I have a few questions I'd like to ask you, if you don't mind."

Johnson's "mister friendly" expression immediately took on a crafty sideways look, the kind of look an old ventriloquist might make. He'd continued to smile, but it'd stopped well short of the eyes.

"What kind of questions would you be talking about, buster?" *Buster?*

Easton had wondered, *Was this guy for real?* Something was completely off about this man but Easton couldn't place his finger on it.

Also, he'd caught the whiff of something unpleasant, like formaldehyde from an old science specimen jar.

What kind of questions should I be talking about? Was the thought that had crossed his mind, but instead he'd pointed with his thumb and asked, "About your neighbor back there. The Red Baron's Daughter? Did you see anything unusual going on tonight?"

Johnson's eyebrows shot up comically and his head had done an exaggerated double-take. "Over where? I don't see nothin'!" This had been followed by a high-pitched laugh that Easton found unsettling. What had followed had been an elliptical non-conversation with Johnson giving what one used to call "wise-acre" answers until the portable handset had interrupted everything.

"Hello?" He pressed the talk button and waited.

To his surprise, a boy's voice answered. It sounded small and very scared. It took him a moment to realize who it was.

"Hello? Anyone? We need help! Please hurry! Officer Vance has been...he's dead. Really dead . . . and she's coming for my papa and I . . .

oh *meu Deus*!"

By the end of the sentence, Easton was already running, leaving Bob Johnson with his rag in mid-wipe and a surprised (and perhaps disappointed) expression on his face.

He'd been having so much fun with the English detective!

-14-

ARMANDO WOKE up in the front seat of the car just as it pulled out of the police checkpoint at the entrance of Raadsel Park. He'd just missed the driver – the strange spectacled man who was the assistant to the Red Baron's Daughter – saying with a resigned chuckle to the policeman with the flashlight, "My nephew, too much cotton candy and one too many rides tonight, I think." There was no trace of any accent and the three stuffed animals in the back seat made the picture even more convincing. Which was exactly why they were there.

The cop had glanced briefly at the man's license, studied the condition of his eyes and the cadence of his speech, then waved him on. Had he run the license on his computer he'd have been quite surprised. The name and address belonged to a man who had been dead quite some time. The driver's real name was Eddie Gacey, from Neptune City, New Jersey. A place where he would probably be either killed or arrested if he returned to it, depending on which party found him first. Among his many talents, Eddie was an established procurer of goods for a very specialized market, one that involved children and clients of "discriminating" tastes. He'd originally stumbled into his current situation while serving as a 'Backyard Boy' (i.e., gofer) for the carnival before he'd worked up to the role of 'inside talker' for the Red Baron's Daughter tent. Gacey liked to think of himself as a 'Smoke-and-Mirrors Man', a sort of master of illusion who could be everything and anything. What he really was, was a carnie guy who ran a lucrative side-business in the child sex trade. The wacked out Toulouse Lautrec get-up he used for the Red Baron gig was something he put together after accidentally picking up an old art book he'd found in someone's trash.

Gacey was a thin, blond (although his hair was now dyed black) guy who was pushing thirty but usually dressed like a fifteen-year-old. To give him some credit, he could assume a wide variety of disguises – though none that would hold up to any reasonable scrutiny – which, in addition to an uncanny amount of luck and a certain animal cunning, was why he had gotten away with things as long as he had.

The car was a beat-up old Saturn that looked as though it hadn't been cleaned out in a decade. It smelled of cigarettes, fast food, sweat, and fear. It also had a few custom modifications, such as the removed inside locks and special seatbelts.

Armando didn't remember much about how he'd arrived in his current predicament. He had been stomping down on the pedals of his bike and hot on Luis' tail when, just as he passed one of the last trailers, a figure had stepped out of the shadows and strong-armed him across the face. He'd landed on his ass in the pine needles and had enough time to register that he was no longer riding a bike before he was dragged into the shadows and a cloth reeking of something sweet and chemical-smelling clamped over his mouth and nose.

Then it was lights out, *Señor*.

When he came to, he was buckled firmly in the passenger seat. Still groggy, his immediate reaction was to free the seatbelt, which earned him a quick backslap on the cheek.

"Don't even bother, buckaroo. You ain't going anywhere without this." Eddie patted a small key ring clipped to his belt. Then, still steering with his left hand, Eddie pulled something out of his right pants pocket. There was a soft 'snick!' and Armando found himself staring at the business end of a six-inch switchblade. "And one more thing. You make so much as a peep and you'll be wearing a new smile under your chin. *Comprende?* Armando nodded. He tried to focus his eyes on the blade, but it was difficult. He felt so light-headed.

The blade disappeared and Eddie popped a cassette into the car stereo. A moment later, Bon Jovi was blasting through the speakers, explaining to the young Ecuadorian that he was a cowboy and that it was a steel horse he rode. Armando wondered if maybe the cowboy could shut up and call the *policía* instead.

He tried to stay awake and make note of landmarks because he remembered from some show someplace that it was important to remember details when you were kidnapped, but he had a splitting headache and the music blasting through the car speakers was disorienting. They went up Main Street past the Greek restaurant and the old Alhambra Theater (and irony of ironies, right past Van Wyck Avenue where the police station was). It was frightening and painful to be riding past so many familiar places, places that he had ridden or walked by how many times? A hundred? A thousand? Now here he was helpless, kidnapped in some scary dude's car, and they might as well have been a million miles away. Then Eddie cut off the main drag and took a series of zig-zagging turns up into the residential neighborhoods north of Route 9B. He turned the stereo down once they were off the beaten path to avoided unnecessary attention. Armando lost track but thought they were on Clinton when the car quietly pulled into the driveway of a badly remodeled old Victorian, the kind that might have once had nice details but now had multiple additions and aluminum siding. The drive snaked around to the back of the house where Eddie cut the engine.

"Don't go nowheres," he said to Armando. "We have some friends to pick up."

The back area of the house looked like it was half junkyard with a warped looking garage that looked ready to fall over and die. There were a couple of rusted motorcycles and some furniture, including a cheap stove that was once white. All this Armando took in, looking blearily out the window as the porch light came on and some figures appeared at the back door. He couldn't see clearly as the light was blinding, but Eddie talked with the occupant of the house for a minute, then pulled out some sort of envelope from his back pocket and handed it over. Then the door opened and two other children were led out – two young girls, definitely South American, around his age. He had never seen them before, but they looked resigned and sad.

As this was happening, Armando saw another person appear behind the one in the doorway and for a split second a man's face was revealed in the yellow light.

Armando gasped.

It was a face he recognized.

The girls were led, docile as lambs, into the back seat of the Saturn, where Eddie locked them into their seatbelts with the efficiency of someone who had done this task many times before. Armando craned his neck around. One girl looked slightly older – maybe fourteen. She was pretty with deep, soulful eyes and long black hair but she looked like she hadn't had a decent meal in a long time. The other girl looked like she was ten or eleven and had the broad features usually found in the mountain regions. Both girls wore tattered dresses and looked like they hadn't eaten in days.

They had a beaten demeanor that set off something deep inside Armando, an emotion he so rarely felt it was nearly unrecognizable: anger. And, on the heels of that, another first: when the older girl looked him in the eye, he felt his heart skip. In that moment he knew, in that instant and absolutely positive way only kids his age can possibly experience, that he was in love.

The only outward indication was a slight widening of his eyes and nostrils but she stared straight back at him in reciprocal amazement.

"*Pleno.*" He whispered as his eyes flicked towards their captor, "*Ser del otro equipo.*" ("It's okay, he's a homosexual.")

That got a small gagging sound as she suppressed a giggle, and a tiny smile. Armando's heart flew right out the window.

So did his head, it seemed, as, a moment later, Eddie slapped him with a vicious backhand.

"Shut the fuck up, piglet!"

A third emotion flickered across Armando's face: murder. He was batting three for three tonight, it seemed. He risked a second look back, ignoring his stinging cheek, and saw the older girl staring intently back at him. And with that, a certainty resolved itself deep down in his guts. He had no idea who she was or where she came from and he was terrified at what might lay ahead in the near future for the three of them.

But he was also going to get them out of it. Or die trying.

-15-

AS EASTON ran into the parking area, he was processing several things simultaneously. The first appeared to be a nightmare version of one of Charlie's Angels crouching on top of the roof of the police cruiser. The second was the head of Officer Vance on the ground nearby, where it had come to rest after bouncing off the windshield. The third were the terrified faces of Luis and his father trapped in the vehicle. The father had at least found the twelve-gauge and it looked like a stand-off.

Easton slowed to a walk and pulled out his Beretta, steadying the grip with his left hand. He stopped when he was about ten yards away. "Miss, step off from the vehicle and put your hands in the air. Now!"

Lorelei looked over at him and snarled. Her face had distorted into a horrifying amalgam of partly human, partly monstrous features with blazing eyes and an enormous maw of wicked looking teeth. Easton felt the short hairs on the back of his neck rising. She was crouching on her haunches like she was getting ready to leap and for a moment Easton considered repeating his demand, then, realizing that the situation had already gone absurdly beyond any normal police protocol, just said "Oh, fuck it."

The first shot clipped her in the arm just as she leapt off the roof. She landed on a spot about five yards from Easton like some sort of hideous four-legged wolf spider. Easton dropped to one knee in a regulation stance and fired two more rounds into her chest, clearly seeing her shudder with the impact, then she leaped clear over his head. He instinctively rolled to the side and came up firing, but the shots went wild as Lorelei bounded off into the woods in a zig-zag gait.

Easton tried to track her but held off firing again.

He waited, listening as the sounds of her crashing off through the woods diminished, then flicked the safety on and holstered the Beretta. First he walked over and, taking off his jacket, draped it over Officer Vance's head. It was a bizarre sight, looking as if all the moisture had been sucked right out of it, like a flash-dried instant mummy. It was impossible to believe it had been attached to a living, breathing human being barely a quarter of an hour ago. The implications of a creature existing that could do such a thing were extremely disturbing, but one thing Easton was learning well was the ability to simply accept the impossible and just keep rolling forward.

It was either that or crawl under the covers and just keep screaming.

He tapped on the window of the police cruiser.

"It's all clear. Whatever that thing was, it's gone."

Luis had to crawl back into the front seat to unlock the front door and a moment later emerged with his father, both wearing similar spacy-eyed expressions of shock. Easton carefully took the shotgun out of Victor Dimas' limp hands and, after checking the safety, placed it in the front seat and got on the radio.

"He's really dead, that's really his . . .?" Luis couldn't bring himself to finish, but his eyes kept sliding back to the lump under Easton's jacket a few feet away. The father seemed like a decent sort, but at the moment he was half slumped against the police cruiser, one arm on Luis' shoulder, his eyes looking off into space.

Easton knelt down.

"Son, Officer Vance is dead," he said, looking Luis directly in the eye, "And that's a terrible thing to witness. But there was nothing you could do to stop it and there's nothing you can do now to change it. It's just one of those things. But you are alive and so is your dad. And it was Officer Vance's job to ensure that and that's what he died doing." He could see tears running down the kid's face. It had been one hell of a night for him, hell of a night for *all* of them. But he could sense from the determined set of the kid's shoulders that he would be all right. Probably have a few years' worth of nightmares, but he'd make it.

A moment later, the first police cruiser arrived, this time with lights and sirens going. A county-wide, Level Two alert had gone out. Easton had a hunch he wasn't going to be getting much sleep.

An hour later, he stepped out of the RV where he'd been looking over the inside with the police captain, a tall guy named Fowler, and one of his lieutenants. A tow vehicle was on its way to take the RV down to the impound lot but at the moment there was a fast scrabble to find any clues leading to the missing children. Roadblocks had already been set up north and south and east of the village and a search team was already combing the woods for any sign of Lorelei, who had quickly shot to the top of the Wyvern Falls police priority list.

Easton had been circumspect with the facts, suggesting they might be dealing with a deranged, drug-influenced suspect. When Hendricks arrived and, pulling him aside, asked point blank "What in God's Hell happened here!?" Easton had answered, quite truthfully, "I really don't know. But I'll do my best to help you find out."

The search of the trailer had turned up little, although Easton found a blank antique postcard showing a castle-like mansion that looked vaguely familiar, which he showed to the captain.

"Recognize this place?"

"Yeah, that's Castle Krell. About seven miles north of town."

"Can you tell me anything about it?"

"Still owned by the Krell family, though no-one's lived there in decades. It was modeled after a castle on the Rhine owned by a family named Reichenstein or something."

That got Easton's attention. "Could it have been *Richtenstein*?"

"Could have. I can look it up later if you like." Wes Fowler, in addition to being the only captain on the Wyvern Falls police force, was also an amateur historian with an encyclopedic knowledge of local information.

They'd become acquainted over the Muncy case back in April and occasionally met up for a beer.

"Mind if I hang on to this?"

"Sure, just make sure you log it."

Easton looked at the postcard a moment, then snapped it with his forefinger before dropping it in his jacket pocket and walking out.

-16-

LORELEI FINALLY stopped at a bluff overlooking the Hudson. She'd stumbled onto the ruins of a gazebo overgrown with creeping vines and saplings, pausing to get her bearings. So far, this night was turning into one disaster after another and she had now fallen into a sort of desperate panic. She needed to get back to Klaus and warn him.

The men with their guns and dogs would be coming.

A slight breeze sighed through the trees. Over the river, a quarter moon hovered and the sky shot with stars. In other circumstances it might have been a romantic backdrop; perhaps for a clandestine lover's tryst. A couple of large bats darted overhead, making their peculiar sonic cries.

Lorelei was panting heavily. First the dog, then the policeman. The gunshot wounds were bad. Not life threatening, but painful. But she'd left a trail and she had to start thinking better. The trailer was lost – they would have to find another means of transport and get as far as possible by morning.

The current base had been good for some time and it would be a shame to lose it, but such was the way of things. They could start new someplace else – perhaps it was time to try another country. And perhaps a new plan, a new front. That brought a ghost of a smile to her lips.

The Red Baron's Daughter business had been her idea. "Von Richtenstein's Daughter" didn't have quite the same allure. And Richtenstein had known Richtofen after all, had shared their twisted little hobby in fact. It had been important to find a means that kept them on the move without attracting undue attention. Luke Edwards had been the first of many to hunt after them. Just prior to the Second World War, it had become apparent that Europe would no longer be a suitable venue. The

Nazis were far too efficient at tracking down the unwanted in their ranks and, when it was clear the Nazi agenda would involve the conquest of all of Europe, they had looked for better pickings (and banquet tables) abroad.

The one irony was that after so many years and so many miles she had finally arrived in none other than Luke Edward's hometown, though Lorelei was completely unaware of it. Edwards had shared very little of his past in their short time together.

And now . . . what? She had to get moving again. Another shipment would arrive, if it hadn't already. The carnie man known as Eddie would have to be disposed of. It was best to cut any loose ends.

But she would have to be careful.

There was still the dog out there. Was it one of the *Bogatyrs*? It seemed likely. They always seemed to find them. Always at the worst time. She'd wounded it, but it could be tracking her again even now, waiting for the next opportunity.

Lorelei struggled painfully to her feet.

Morning was coming.

-17-

ARMANDO WAS getting a crash course on bad 80s and 90s music, courtesy of Eddie Gacey's CD collection. Bon Jovi had been torment enough, but the compilation CD now blaring out of the Saturn's overtaxed speakers was sheer hell. In the past ten minutes, he had been subjected to Journey, REO Speedwagon and Poison. At the moment the lead singer of Warrant was blathering through lyrics so sub-moronic that if the car engine had had ears it would have seized up.

For a Latin American boy raised on Pasillo and Andean music, he was in a state of shock.

They went north out of town on Route 9B for six miles before turning off onto the old Albany Post Road, then onto an unmarked road that cut eastward up a steep hill. Eddie reached over and lowered the volume (Ozzy Osborne was whining about a Mister Crowley by this point) to a slightly less than earsplitting decibel level so that he could focus on the heavily wooded road, which wound upwards with a steep drop on the left side. Finally, they pulled up before a massive stone arch with an iron gate that might have been borrowed from a medieval castle. The heavy chain and padlock looked like something from a horror movie prop room. It took Eddie a few minutes to go through the sequence of opening the gate, pulling up the car and relocking the entrance behind them, but shortly they were pulling into an overgrown parking area, the Saturn's old headlights revealing a towering derelict mansion that somehow made Armando think of the *Wizard of Oz*.

Krell Castle.

He was familiar with it – nearly anybody who had ever driven up Route 9B during the day was – as the castle (a mansion really) was sited about seven hundred feet up on a ridge overlooking the river, a fairy-tale castle with its elegant spire and steep pitched roofs and gables. It was still owned by the Krell family but hadn't been lived in since the 1960s, something about a family dispute between the heirs that was still yet to be settled. It was one of those glorious old ruins along the Hudson that locals just accept as part of the landscape and which, on occasion, get the attention of some tourist and show up in a back-page article or in someone's blog.

And yet for all the fairy-tale trappings at a distance, the closer reality painted a different picture. The house was teetering on the point of no return – with holes in the roof, a partially collapsed eastern wing, and a general infusion of rot and decay. The decades-old dispute was about to be settled by Mother Nature herself, that all time knock-out champion.

There was some other force at work here, a slumbering, sinister quality about the house and grounds that kept vagrants, nosy college kids, and the occasional nosy reporter convinced that there were more interesting places elsewhere. And that extended to the world of animals and birds as well. Except the crows.

Little of this was on Armando's mind as he was released from the car and a pair of handcuffs was clapped over his wrists. His thoughts were racing along other lines – distances, avenues of escape while Eddie was making the mistake of indulging in a warped daydream while getting the girls out from the backseat. (He was ad-libbing through his own version of those classic self-serving smug Saturn commercials, only this one had Eddie in soft-focus saying *"My name is Eddie Gacey. I'm a carnie guy, drug dealer, and sex-trafficking professional and I like what Saturn's all about . . . and that's what I like to instill in the children I kidnap and play around with . . . like this. . ."*)

Perhaps he over-estimated his ability to keep his latest catch intimidated, or perhaps it was that he hadn't stopped to consider a twelve-year-old of Armando's seemingly placid demeanor would actually try anything.

Either way, the result was the same.

Just as he turned and let the girls clamber out of the car, one hand holding Armando firmly by the upper arm, he caught a blur of an upswinging foot and then his balls caught the first surprise of the evening. The second surprise came a moment later when, as he doubled over, Armando did a switch kick with his other foot and caught Eddie square in the face, breaking his nose. As he crumbled down, stunned, Armando kicked at his head a third time.

Eddie Gacey may have been down, but he was not out. Swift as a snake, his left hand shot out and grabbed Armando's ankle, yanking him off balance, his other hand scrabbling for the switchblade in his front pocket. Armando had survived more than one street fight in his native Cuerto, however, and his next move was pure instinct. Even as he landed on the ground (with a painful grunt), he twisted and lashed out with kick #4 which connected with Eddie's jaw. This time it was "lights out, see you later, alligator, don't forget to write."

"Keys! Keys!" he hissed to the older girl, nodding towards Eddie's pockets. Both girls looked at him wide-eyed, not moving an inch. On the one hand, Armando couldn't blame them. On the other, they had to get out of there quick.

But the girls were petrified.

He looked at the older girl again "What's your name?"

"Carmina."

"Carmina, *aqui* Armando. I can help you, but you must hurry! Do it!"

Carmina made a hurried nod and, gathering up her courage, bent down and rolled Eddie over so she could get at the keychain clipped to his belt. She shrank back as Eddie moaned. The younger girl simply stood there, eyes as big as saucers.

"Don't worry, he's still out. Just get the keys!" Armando urged her on. He knew no such thing, but he did know they didn't have much time. Carmina finally unclipped the key chain and ran over to Armando. It took five tries (and dropping the keys once) before there came a metallic click. Armando was about to toss them aside, then changed his mind. He rolled Eddie over and pulled his arms back, locking the handcuffs first on one wrist, then the other just like he'd seen on countless *Law & Order* episodes. Then he took the keys from Carmina and threw them as far as he could into the woods.

"Come on, let's get out of here!" He paused, realizing both girls were looking at him with something close to awe. It was the first time anyone, let alone a girl (and one as pretty as Carmina), had ever looked at him that way. Suddenly his back became a little straighter, his shoulders a little more squared. One eyebrow went up a little, then he grabbed both girls by the arms and they ran back down the driveway.

As they came around the curve of the driveway, they saw headlights and the blinking red and blues of a police car. Armando never thought he'd ever be glad to see an actual police car, though with his adrenaline up it didn't occur to him to ask why it was sitting *inside* the gates.

Instead he just yelled "Help! Help us, *por favor!*" and ran up to the cruiser. Just as they did, the door opened and a bland middle-aged man in a brown worsted blazer got out, though Armando didn't recognize him. He had a broad face and a thick mustache and looked like a guy that might be the head manager of the local Stop & Shop or Payless. Almost simultaneously, the passenger door opened and another man got out. This man Armando knew. It was the tall man in the trench coat he had seen back in the trailer park, talking with Eddie. He stopped dead in his tracks. The first man would have been recognized immediately by more than a few people in the village of Wyvern Falls, and definitely every member of the police department.

It was Detective Darren Bell.

There was little time to ponder any of this however, as just then both girls screamed at the top of their lungs, a high-pitched hysterical scream that made Armando snap his head around, the hairs on his neck standing up.

Floating down the driveway at them was a nightmare apparition, a skeletal thing with blazing eyes and clawed hands dressed in some sort of antique clothing. Although Armando didn't know its name, he recognized it from the dogfight they had experienced when they were hypnotized in the Red Baron's Daughter's tent.

Von Richtenstein had come to meet his guests.

Then the lights went out as Armando was struck from behind.

-18-

IT WAS JUST after 5:00 am when Easton pulled into his driveway. He parked in front of the two-car garage in the back, noting that Vivienne's Rav4 Mini was gone. He sat for a moment in the Maserati with his head back against the headrest. It had been quite a night. It felt like someone had taken his eyeballs out, rolled them in sand and then stuck them back in his skull. And there was a complex swirl of emotions drifting through his heart – a bittersweet melancholy? Blended with weariness? Depression? Certainly they were in the mix. But there was something else in there too, a form of…elation? He was tired and things were a mess at the moment. The search had been inconclusive, neither the boy nor the fortune teller (who was currently at the top of the Westchester Most Wanted list) had been found and the police chief was quietly furious.

But he couldn't deny it felt good to be involved in, well, an *exciting* case again. Doing what he was good at. Something off the charts. Whatever that thing was that he had shot at, it wasn't human, or wasn't human *anymore*. It was terrifying and thrilling at the same time. He hadn't mentioned that to Hendricks - let the police come to their own conclusions when they finally captured her. He'd only made it clear they were dealing with a homicidal maniac, a deranged woman to be considered armed and dangerous – not that anyone in the department had any doubts on that, after seeing the remains of Officer Vance. Also, an AMBER alert had been issued for Armando Ortega, Henry Van Dorn and now three other missing kids, including a Kevin Hernandez.

Finally, around 4:30, Hendricks had clapped Easton on the back and told him to go get some rest, the County police would help with the second-shift search and he would call him if anything turned up. Easton had already spent an hour giving his report (he'd had to turn over his Beretta as well, as part of the crime scene) and had decided there was little else he could do at the moment.

Now he was home.

An *empty* home from the looks of it.

And somehow that came as no surprise, perhaps something of a relief in fact.

He got out of the car and closed the door – he always enjoyed the expensive-sounding click it made – and stood looking up at the sky, his hands in his front pockets. The sparrows and finches were having an animated discussion in the boxwood tree in the back yard, and from somewhere nearby came the sonic call (it always made Easton think of a submarine) of a blue jay. High up in the cloudless sky, a young bald eagle was soaring on the thermals, the proverbial early bird looking for something meatier than a worm, he suspected.

The air smelled good. A light breeze carried that hint of Hudson River water mixed with the ocean, one of the many things Easton secretly enjoyed about his adopted home.

One hand absently jingled the keys in his pocket.

Then he went in to catch a few hours' sleep.

-19-

EVADING THE search parties had been a near thing, particularly the dogs. But after all the years, it was something Lorelei knew a thing or two about. And a trick or two. About four miles north of the point, she'd cut to the river, then doubled back and gone vertical. Here the trees were close and tall, connected by countless vines and creepers but she was able, with a clumsy grace despite her injuries, to move up to Route 9B. It would throw them off temporarily. Then, near an old drainage tunnel under the road she'd found the skunk. Like many of its kind resident in the river towns, it appeared to have been bred from a mutant strain hooked on growth hormones; it was as large as a beaver. She'd dropped down before it had a chance to react and, snatching it up in her two claw-like hands, held it at arm's length and directed its spray away from her. It hissed and writhed like an angry badger but she daren't kill it – instead she tossed it away to let it spray the area again while she took off through the tunnel.

That would definitely throw the dog off his game.

It was around 2:00 in the morning when she arrived at the gates of Krell Castle.

She found Eddie lying on his back next to his Saturn. His days of illegal trafficking were over, someone had done the world a favor by cutting his throat while he lay unconscious and he'd bled out all over the ground. This was unusual.

She would have gotten rid of him herself – another loose end to tie up before they rolled up the tent – but someone had beaten her to the punch.

The question was: who? And why?

She sidled around the back of the house where there was an abandoned swimming pool from a century ago – it appeared empty but for a few old leaves and branches and maybe a dead bird or two – to a sitting room at the back. Except for a few random pieces, all the furniture had been removed years ago. In many of the rooms, the walls were stripped down to the studs during an abandoned attempt to renovate the house around the millennium, although this particular room still had its original oak paneling. It had gone nearly black with age. This room had a single oak table that dated from the mid-Victorian era – one of those heavy squat-legged objects that looked like it could support an elephant. Behind it was a tall-backed chair that might have been borrowed from an Inquisition chamber and on the table was a tarnished silver candelabra with three candles burning in it.

Sitting at the table was von Richtenstein.

He might have been a grisly statue custom-made for some haunted house, the kind that used only the best and most realistically-made props. He was still dressed in his quasi-military garb that spoke of old money and Kaisers and imperial agendas with its stiff collar, woolen cape, and rotting gold-braided trim. The blackened skin that stretched across the skull retained an echo of his original visage, though it had taken on a burnished sheen after so many years and was cracking in several places. And, as ever, the teeth gleamed like gun metal. Only the eyes indicated what there was still burning in this hideous thing, greenish white orbs like moldy eggs with their peculiar vertical-slit pupils. The magic that imbued the Liche with its unnatural life tapped into forces and entities beyond most human understanding. Its engine ran by means that would make most scientists go insane had they been presented with it.

Lorelei drew open the doors at the back of the room and entered. Wounds and 70's jumpsuit aside, she still knew how to make an entrance. Certainly they made an odd juxtaposition: the un-dead Liche dressed like a decaying Germanic imperial soldier and the beautiful half-demonic and half-mutilated woman, dressed like a blood-spattered Charlie's Angel.

She stood with one hand on her hip, the other raised against the door frame. Then she strolled in, all business.

"*Mein Herr*, I am afraid it is time to find a new location – we must leave here immediately. There's been a complication. The authorities . . ." She shook her head. "It is time for a change. We have been here too long as it is. A new game. I have grown tired of this 'Red Baron's Daughter' and we have grown complacent."

She drew up to the table next to Richtenstein and leaned against it, tracing the surface with her fingers. She was terribly exhausted and in a lot of pain, but she covered it well. She wondered which of the children held prisoner in the basement she would feed on. Richtenstein preferred the young boys. She enjoyed them all.

Richtenstein's hand reached over and covered hers in a gesture that was almost affectionate as he rose. The sound of creaking tendons and old bones moving was that of dead branches rubbing in the middle of the night. Richtenstein very rarely spoke and, when he did, it was a near-guttural whisper of leathery old lungs pushing air through desiccated vocal chords; a raspy sound that was piercing and painful to listen to.

"Ahhhh *Mein* Lorelei . . ." The whisper of his voice was like cobwebs of nightmare and madness spreading from the grave. "It has been so many years...and you have served me so well." His skeletal hands reached up and cupped her face as he drew her close.

That was when she saw the figure standing quietly in the shadows of the archway leading into the rest of the house. She could just make out the harsh-looking features, leather overcoat, and the gray hair pulled back into a tight ponytail. A man she recognized. Eddie had always referred to him as "The Weatherman" or "Mister G" but of course that wasn't his real name, just a label he had lifted from a New York news station in some sort of perverse joke.

The man who preferred little girls.

There wasn't time to ponder this, however, as the hands that now painfully gripped her face forced her to look back at Richtenstein.

"*Nein . . . nein . . .*" He said in his grating whisper, "It is *you* who have grown complacent . . . now where is the vessel . . . my *container?*"

Lorelei's eyes widened. "The trailer, *Mein Herr*, it ist hidden, hidden well. But I can get it . . . I will go back . . . but I must feed . . ."

Her lips trembled.

Richtenstein shook his head slowly side to side, the teeth making a light clicking sound. "Yessss . . . you will go back were the authorities will find you...as it is you they want . . . no? *Auf wiederzehen, mein Fraulein.*"

Before she could even react, Richtenstein's hands did their work with savage quickness. His thumbs pierced her eye sockets - which exploded like grapes - and crushed her skull with a dry pop as he whispered some sort of incantation. Then he stepped back and let her body drop to the floor. In the flickering candlelight, she lay still for a moment, then abruptly her spine arched as her nervous system sent a final mis-fired signal. A blackish liquid with tiny filaments leaked out of her mouth and onto the floor.

The Weatherman stepped into the room.

Richtenstein turned to face him. "Put this body where it will be discovered . . . away from here. My vessel must be found . . . and brought to somewhere safe..."

The Weatherman pulled a cheap cell phone from his pocket, one of the untraceable ones. A non-thinking man would have called then and there. But he knew about minimizing risks and about GPS tracking and staying off the grid. "I'll call the detective. Once I get back to town."

"Of course."

Richtenstein appeared to be laughing.

-20-

EASTON WAS in the grips of a terrible dream.

He was back again on the rear terrace of Taron Hall, Van Eyckmann's estate, fighting the *iffriti* – the thing that called itself Kimmi. Except this time, there were no tricks up his sleeve. This time, in the stormy twilight with lightning flashes lancing across the sky and thunder echoing from the cliffs across the river, he was about to be torn to pieces. Kimmi was larger and uglier than ever, and he had grown extra arms.

The sword – that old family heirloom – was in his hands, furiously parrying every slash of the thing's talons. But his strength was going, and there was this constant ringing. He realized that it was the Droid phone at his hip and it wouldn't stop. What fuckwit was calling him now? *He was fighting for his life goddamnit!*

He was . . .

Easton sat bolt upright in his bed. He was in the master bedroom at the back of his house, in the oak mission-style queen-size bed he'd had custom-built by an Amish furniture builder in Ohio. With the new-style mattresses, he felt like he was sleeping ten feet off the floor. One of these days, he was going to roll out of bed and break his neck.

Sunlight was streaming through the windows.

On the nightstand next to the bed was a mica-shaded lamp, a clock radio, and a telephone, one of those wireless jobs. For some idiotic reason, he'd neglected to put it back in its charging cradle in the other room and left it by his bed.

It was ringing.

The clock said it was nearly noon.

"Hello?"

"Easton? Sorry to bother you." It took him a moment to process it was the chief of police on the other end. "We found the woman. And her accomplice."

"What?"

"Lorelei – no last name. That so-called fortune teller who called herself the "Red Baron's Daughter. Found her body near a car off Route 9B near the old Van Eyckmann estate – remember that old place?" (*"Oh yes, I do,"* Easton thought) "From what we can tell, she got picked up by her accomplice, another piece of work by the name of Eddie Gacey, and they got into an altercation, mortally injuring each other. He was still at the wheel, throat cut. We recovered the knife near her body. Oh, the bodies of two children were in the trunk. Neither was one of the boys we are looking for. We still have search parties out, but it doesn't look good."

Easton rubbed his forehead, trying to process what he was hearing.

"How's that?"

"Well, some evidence we recovered suggested that they may been moved out of the area. As in 'out of the state' out of the area. Sex trafficking is what it's looking like. Not good. None of its good, my friend." Hendricks sounded tired. Easton had an intuition. Despite coming from a deep sleep, he was now wide awake. A light tingling sensation crawled up his spine. Without thinking, the words slipped quietly out of his mouth.

"Because it was staged."

Now it was Hendricks' turn to be surprised.

"Come again?"

Easton put his forefinger and thumb to his chin. "You think the murder scene was staged. Probably by whoever is *really* behind the trafficking."

There was silence on the other end of the phone for a few moments. Then there was a dry chuckle. "John, you know sometimes I like you. And then sometimes I don't. Particularly when you lay on the spooky shit."

Now it was Easton's turn to laugh. "Oh, I think you just enjoy having a mystery man in your life, Roy. When are we going to drop the pretense and tell the world we're getting married?"

That got another chuckle. "I'll call in and make the announcement in the *Gazette* this week. In the meantime, just letting you know Bell is back on duty and going over the woman's trailer with the forensics guys to see what else they can turn up. So you're off the hook. But thanks again for your help. I'll let you know how it all works out. And you should get your Beretta back by the end of the week."

"Got it. And Roy?"

"Yes?"

"I'm sorry about Officer Vance. Nasty bit of business."

"Yeah, he was a good cop. Knew him since he was a kid."

Something in his tone suggested to Easton that it was best to close the topic. Because with it came a slew of other serious questions, like what had happened to Vance's body and what exactly was this Lorelei person? That was going to be an interesting autopsy.

"Thanks for the call, Roy."

"You bet."

After a quick shower, Easton threw on some jeans, a black shirt, and a pair of well-broken-in Kenneth Cole shoes. He was down in the kitchen five minutes later, brewing coffee and poking around the fridge for something to eat, when someone knocked frantically at the front door.

He almost called out to Vivienne to answer the door before catching himself. He realized that their relationship was becoming a widening gulf that was growing colder and bleaker, yet still he was putting off dealing with it. Part of it was that he was angry with her, with her increasingly childish and petulant behavior. And with himself. The thoughts in his head were sounding alarmingly like a stodgy old finger-wagging adult: "crusty old Mister Rules and Responsibility." *Good Christ, when did that happen?*

On the heels of that came another alarming thought, punctuated by the banging on the door.

What if there's been an accident? Vivienne's been hurt. Or killed?

He immediately brushed these thoughts aside.

A moment later, he was standing in the open front door, mug of steaming coffee in his hand. His visitor turned out to be Luis, the kid from the previous night. He looked exhausted, with black circles under his eyes.

He also looked very serious.

No wonder, Easton thought, *He's been through a lifetime of bad shit these past couple of days.*

He was wearing Puma high-tops, cargo shorts, and a t-shirt with a blood-dripping, fanged mouth on it that read "Teenage Vampires Suck!"

"Mister Easton?"

"Yes?"

"You have to help. You have to. I just know it!"

Easton shook his head. "You've been through a rough time, son. But the police are handling it. Let them do their job." Even as he said the words, he heard the hollowness in them.

Neither are one of the boys we are looking for.

Two of whom were this kid's friends. *Sex trafficking. Maybe out of the area.* Nothing good about that.

"Look, Luis, they caught the woman from last night. She's . . . well, she's dead. And they're trying to locate your friends. And they will. Give it time."

Luis shook his head.

"No! My dad got the call too. They told us about the woman. But it's not her! Don't you see, it's not her!" He pushed past Easton and marched into the living room.

"Hey kid, wait, you can't come in here!"

He thought, *Christ! These days having a young kid come into your house alone was a potentially serious problem, whether or not you were a cop. Especially a kid you didn't even know! This is how absurdly out of control our society has gotten these days. An adult can't even conceive of being alone in a room with anyone under eighteen without immediately thinking all sorts of paranoid potential labels like pervert child molester, evil adult! Hell, the neighbors could be on the phone to the police chief right now.* That was ridiculous but he had to get the boy out of his house and quickly.

Luis sat himself down on the couch and pulled something out of his pocket. Easton strode over, prepared to pick the kid up and place him back outside, by force if necessary but stopped short all the same.

Luis looked up at him with a very serious and adult expression.

"You have to help, Mister Easton." He repeated. "You *know*. You were there. You saw that monster, the thing flying the German plane. It was real. I know that's who's behind this! That monster!"

"Boy, there is no monster. That dogfight wasn't real. That was just a . . . a . . . dream. A trick."

Even as he said it, he realized his mistake. The kid didn't miss it either.

Christ, he hated smart kids. They always nailed you.

"See! You *were* there! I know you are . . . you are *supposed* to help. And I found this. In the trailer. It was Henry's."

He dropped the object into Easton's hand. It was a rabbit's foot keychain. It felt oddly heavy. But that wasn't all. No sooner did Easton's hand close around it, than a series of images flashed into his head like exploding bulbs.

Richtenstein. Henry. The Castle. The feedings. Over all these years.

Oh God.

The police chief would never buy this one. He had to think. But there was something else, something rattling around in the rabbit's foot. It took him a moment to figure it out, but, when he unscrewed it, something heavy and dull dropped into his other hand.

It was a bullet.

Easton stood there a moment, looking off into space, wheels turning.

Then he looked back again at Luis. He held up the bullet.

"Was this Henry's?"

Luis shook his head. "No. I mean I don't think so. I never saw it before. Henry always kept things in there, but never a bullet. Isn't that kind of dangerous?"

Easton turned it around in his hand. It felt dead and heavy. Oddly, there didn't seem to be a primer. He also realized something else: it wasn't metal; it was painted ceramic.

"Depends." He said aloud. *Depends on what's inside it.* And with that, another thought, in another voice he didn't recognize (possibly the lost voice of Luke Edwards himself): *this is the key.*

"Luis, go home, stay home. I'll get to the bottom of this. That's my promise to you, all right?"

The boy stood up.

"We have to do a special handshake. It's what the Half-moonies do when we swear to something."

"The who?"

"The . . . never mind. Here I'll show you."

It turned out to be a variation of countless buddy shakes repeated the world over; clasp, over/under fist tap, palm slide followed by a double knuckle to knuckle bump.

"Now you *have* to do it. *You have to save Armando and Henry.*"

-21-

"ARMANDO? *Tengo miedo.*" (I'm scared.)

Armando blinked several times, first aware of a throbbing mass of pain from the back of his head, second aware of fingers lightly tracing his cheek. He was lying on his side in an eight-foot by six-foot cell, one of six that had recently been constructed along the north wall of the basement. Carmina, and the younger girl whose name was Paloma, were in the adjacent cell. Carmina was just barely been able to reach through to touch Armando, who had passed out where he had been dropped hours earlier. He looked about without moving, trying to get his bearings. The basement was vast and gloomy, some parts on the far side lit by shafts of sunlight coming through what was apparently a collapsed section of the house above. There appeared to be other children here, some in mesh dog cages, some in cells. Some were moving; others appeared to be perfectly still. Through a series of arches, he could see the opposite wall some twenty feet away, where a lone figure was hanging from chains against the wall. Armando sat up abruptly, nearly passing out from the wave of dizziness that followed. He managed to grab the cell bars and steady himself.

"Henry?"

The figure hanging from the chains stirred slightly.

"Henry . . . you okay?"

The head managed to rise up enough for the sunlight to reveal what was left of his friend's face.

The girls began screaming.

This time, Armando joined them.

-22-

THE BLACK MASERATI Gran Turismo shot up Route 9B like a bullet, eating up the asphalt like a Formula One race car. Easton made it to the Albany Post Road turn-off in less than half the time Eddie Gacey's Saturn had taken the previous night.

He skidded to a stop at the front gate to Castle Krell, sending a fantail of dirt and leaves into the air. Then he quickly checked the Colt .45 in the shoulder holster under his left armpit, checked that his Droid was clipped securely to his hip, then opened the glove compartment and pulled out the antique leather holster with the Mauser. He had to rig it through his belt at his right hip – it made an awkward bulge in the plaid Ralph Lauren sport coat he was wearing – but there was little to be done about it. The thing felt ridiculously heavy. But he knew he'd need it. Edwards' journal had been clear about that.

He'd phoned Hendricks from his built-in car phone (much easier with its dashboard speed-dial and speaker phone than fumbling around with the Droid) and wound up talking with the dispatcher instead. Apparently, the police chief was over at the carnival grounds dealing another crisis involving that celebrity reporter Lorenzo King (Easton had no idea who that was) and those *Ghost Seekers International* guys and would be back within twenty minutes. If it was urgent, she could put him through to the senior officer currently on duty. Easton said it was and a moment later he was talking with Darren Bell.

'Detective Bell, its John Easton. I have a lead on the missing kids. Have Hendricks meet me at Krell Castle with as few cops as possible, and only those who can really be trusted – you're going to want to keep the lid down tight on this one. No time to explain. See you there."

Bell said that he understood, Easton should stay put when he got there, and he would be there immediately with the cavalry.

He walked up to the gate and looked about. The leaves on the ground had been disturbed recently. Someone had made a cursory effort to cover it up.

He looked at his watch.

Procedure dictated that he should wait until Hendricks arrived, or, more accurately, follow exactly the advice he's given Luis: step back and let the police do their work. But he also knew that in situations like this, time was of the essence.

It was the screams that decided it for him.

Even in broad daylight, the mansion gave off a distinct sense of foreboding. Surrounded by towering Norwegian maples, river birch, English oak, sugar maples and the occasional fir, the trees crowded in close, restricting the sunlight to illusive patterns and shadows that left all perception of depth shot to hell.

Easton clambered over the gate and bolted up the drive. The screams were definitely coming from the house and they definitely sounded like kids. Easton pulled out the Colt and held it with both hands, pointed down at the ground, as he ran up to the house.

The house was built of rough-faced stone and topped by red slate shingles. Up close, most of the wood trim work was either grey with age or peeling. Like the trees around it, Castle Krell was tall and vertical – not unlike its design counterparts along the Rhine back in Germany – and it had a restless combination of gables, balconies and steeply pitched roofs, as if the architect had been unable to make up his mind and instead decided to throw in a little of everything. The one dominant feature, though, was the thin cylindrical tower with its tapering spire and ornate detailing that suggested the Brothers Grimm.

Easton stole a few quick glances in the windows by the entrance but most of the first floor looked empty except for some rolled-up rugs in one room and a random chair or two.

The screaming had stopped, though he thought he could still hear a girl sobbing. Stepping carefully along the spongy carpet of old leaves and debris, he worked his way around to the back of the house. He noted the ancient swimming pool and what was once a formal garden with paving stone walkways, now long grown over with weeds, thorny bushes, and poison ivy. There was a fitted stone wall that ran along one side with a grotesquely carved satyr face that appeared to be leering at him. *Come closer my friend*, it seemed to say, *I've got a secret or two to tell...come close and let me whisper in your ear...*

Easton shuddered.

The whole place was hinky. He could feel it everywhere, the flicker of hidden histories and memories simmering under the surface of reality, tugging at his thoughts with cloying insistence.

The oak tree that used to be behind the outhouse, where the first owner used to apply his belt to his children when they misbehaved...the whipping tree they called it...

The pool where not one but three children had drowned, and where the second wife had killed herself one August evening...

The spruce trees that now stood where a Mohican warrior named Ketchiwa had taken his hatchet to his entire family in their wigwam in the early hours of one October morning, the remains of their bones still among the roots where he had buried them...

The stone bench where a gardener named Harry had once sat for two hours one Monday morning in 1927, staring at that satyr's mask and listening....and finally taking his pruning shears and plunging them up through his chin and into his brain...

All these scraps of images and more flickered around the periphery of Easton's mind. He had to force them down like the lids on a dozen traps with tiny but feral animals trying to scrabble out of them. It was a side to him only his Aunt Bethany knew and understood...that overtly attractive woman with her smoky voice and all the ridiculous charms and crystals and New Age booklets about astral travel and such...He hadn't actually seen her since that terrible business when he was sixteen, but had spoken to her again recently. Right after that mess at the Van Eyckmann estate... Easton knew it was wrong to think of his aunt in any sort of sexual terms, six ways from Sunday wrong to be honest...and yet it was impossible not to. She exuded sexual energy the way some deer exude musk. And, on one level at least, she probably couldn't even control it any more than a person could control their own sweat glands.

At the moment however, the voice of his aunt whispering in his head was not teasing him with sweet nothings – the voice was clear and stern, telling him to be very watchful and to keep his fences up and all the sentries vigilant.

No wonder Richtenstein had holed up here, Easton thought. The place was a magnetic lodestone of negative psychic energy. Hell, he could probably just sit there in the tower and run off it like a battery.

Around the back were the remains of an addition that had never been completed and had partially collapse. The sobs were coming from the basement there.

The million-dollar question of course, was: *where was Richtenstein?* It was one of those crossroads where the decision could have serious consequences either way. There might be a trap – he had to assume there would be – but the priority was to get the children out of there and away to as safe a distance as possible.

But first things first.

He slipped around to the small back porch where Lorelei had entered hours before. He saw the French doors and the short overhang with its peeling trim. To one side, an enormous spider web filled the gap between the short rail and the roof. In its center was a meaty – and, to Easton, just a little intimidating – black and bright yellow spider that was nearly as big as his palm. The dense web swayed slightly from a hidden breeze. The spider seemed to be studying him with the patient malice only arachnids seem to possess.

Come close and maybe a burst of air will land me on your shoulder.

Or neck.

He shuddered and decided to give it as wide a berth as possible.

Once inside the doors he looked over the room, noting the table, the inquisitor's chair, and the odd stains on the barren floor.

He pulled out the rabbit's foot charm and unscrewed it.

It took just over five minutes to locate the cellar door.

There was no electricity, so he had to feel his way down the stairwell using a small penlight he'd brought, once brushing against a thick strand of cobwebs (and hoping its occupant wasn't the cousin of the one hanging on the porch). The treads were sagging with age and claustrophobically narrow. At the bottom was a large low-ceilinged chamber with a dirt floor. Arches of rough stone opened in the wall on either side and in front. Cobwebs hung from the rafters and from the rusted piping. Old cloth-insulated wiring and ceramic insulators suggested the wiring hadn't been updated in eighty or ninety years. Easton had no idea when the power was last on but it was a wonder the place hadn't burned to the ground. He moved toward what he knew was the back of the house, keeping the Colt drawn with the safety off.

The smell was a revolting combination of rot, mold, putrid meat, and excrement and, as Easton walked through the arch and down a hallway lined with small rooms, he began to understand why.

And with that understanding came his realization of the enormity of the horror.

Richtenstein, and his late accomplice The Red Baron's Daughter, had not only been collecting victims here recently, they had been feeding on them here for *years*.

His shock was probably not altogether different from that of the first Allied soldiers liberating the camps in Germany: "How in the hell could this happen?"

Not on the same scale, of course, but a scale unspeakable in a small town along the Hudson River? Most definitely.

Not all were children – even a connoisseur like Richtenstein couldn't dine on caviar every night – and clearly not all were from the local region. Easton could see that from the range of clothes and what he could make out of the faces (though all that were not living were like dry husks, which explained why the smell wasn't permeating the whole area outside).

Richtenstein must have had a wide network to pull this off undetected for so long and Easton had a hunch they would find most of these were illegal immigrants – Mexican, South American, Chinese.

Henry was dead by the time Easton got over to him. He checked for a pulse and didn't find any, knowing from the extent of the mutilation (the entire lower face was missing along with much from the groin down) that, terrible as it was, it was probably for the better.

Perhaps if he'd gotten here ten minutes sooner, an evac to a trauma unit might have saved him. But then sometimes the miracles of modern medicine weren't really miracles at all.

"Boy, do you know where the keys are?"

Easton was squatting by the door of the cell Armando was in. The two girls were clustered in close as well, clutching at the bars, tears streaking their cheeks. The looks on their faces were pleading and naked with fear. Armando shook his head. The look he was giving Easton was clearly wary. Easton didn't understand what the issue was. "Look, I need to get you and your friends out and away from here quickly, understood?" This got an affirmative nod. Easton looked at the lock. It was a standard chain and padlock. "Hold on a second."

He stood up and did a quick search of the basement area and found an iron pry bar propped in the corner. Shooting off locks might look good in the movies but in truth anything that sends flying shrapnel in unpredictable directions is a risky thing. Fortunately, the cells weren't set up to hold hardened criminals. He shot the bar through the chain and twisted it until it snapped. Five minutes later, he had Armando, the two girls, and another boy who couldn't have been more than five or six up the stairs and onto the back terrace.

Easton knelt down again and drew them in close.

"What's your name?" He asked Armando.

"Armando."

"Listen carefully then, Armando. Do you know if there are more children down there? More rooms?"

Armando shrugged. No idea.

Easton thought a moment. "I need to make sure there's no one else down there, understand? I need you to wait here and stay in charge. There's going to be a lot of policemen coming to help within the next few minutes. Can you do that?"

Another nod.

"Good." Easton stood up and put his hand out, palm down. "Stay put. I'll be right back." He pulled his gun out again and stepped through the back porch door.

The basement felt gloomier – and creepier – than before, if that was at all possible. Perhaps it was Easton's senses picking up that there was nothing alive remaining down there.

Anything human at least.

The human sensory apparatus is an interesting thing. Certainly capable of detecting far subtler input than the bullet-point list of five hammered into every grade school kid's skull, as if the very bedrock of what defined a human being depended on it.

John Easton, detective superintendent with the Royal Turk and Caicos police department (currently on unpaid leave) and now private investigator licensed to work in New York, New Jersey, Connecticut, and Pennsylvania, happened to be gifted with what might be described as an 'extra sensory edge'.

A gift and a curse, as he'd discovered in his early teen years, one that had been only recently re-awakened under decidedly strange circumstances that had occurred the previous year with the Van Eyckmann affair. And what that extra sensory edge was telling him, broadcasting loud and clear thank-you-very-much, was that the only things lurking in the moldering recesses of this old mansion basement were things most distinctly unpleasant and *un-dead*.

In addition to Richtenstein, who he sensed was lurking somewhere in the chambers above like some sort of malignant and patient spider. In his mind's eye, he could easily envision him in the ceiling rafters of the tower, waiting.

Something rustled in the darkness. The area under the main floor of the house hadn't been checked and, as he stood on the basement stairs thinking about going back down there, he felt his conviction wavering.

There's no one left down there.

Are you sure?

Quite sure. Okay, ninety-eight-point-five percent sure.

Well, that doesn't exactly add up to one hundred percent, does it, Detective Easton?

No. But maybe close enough for government work.

Except it wasn't and that was the hell of it for men like Easton. He pulled the Mauser out of its holster, unclicked the safety and chambered the first round. It still felt old and ugly and heavy in his hand. But he had a hunch his Colt wasn't going to be quite as effective down here.

This time he went down with the Mauser pointed forward, the penlight pointed with it.

Rustle. Thump.

The central room under the main house housed a boiler that looked like some behemoth out of a Jules Verne novel, with its various gauges, iron grate, and octopus's arms of ductwork spreading in every direction. An old workbench was off to one side and, oddly, a smashed-up -Victorian baby buggy, its fabric hood all but rotted away. The workbench was accompanied by a bunch of old shelves with rusting tools on them. Against one wall was resting a six-foot diameter saw blade, festooned with rust like some relic of the industrial age.

This room looked like it had been half finished at some point, before the owners had given up and gone off to more worthwhile endeavors. The inner walls were partially wall-papered and there were old sagging doors leading into even more rooms. Some were partially open. Towards the far wall, at what would be the front of the house, were piles of old junk and furniture.

The pen light played off an old steamer trunk and pile of old mason jars, some of which had been broken. Clots of fungus spouted out of several of them. A toppled ice-box stood with its wooden door open, racks fallen askew.

The place looked as though it should be crawling with vermin or at least show signs of scavengers.

Unless of course, something was eating them.

Something in the pile of junk stirred. It looked like an old dress. And now he could smell a putrid, almost fishy smell.

Rot and decay.

The *Draugyr*. The low dead.

Then he saw the first one.

It was one thing to read about them. It was a whole other ballgame to actually see (and smell) them, like the ones currently scrabbling upside down along the basement ceiling toward him. Scaly and pale, with mouths rimmed with needle-like teeth pistoning open and closed, they were much smaller than he had imagined, almost child-sized. Hissing like snakes.

Unblinking eyes the color of spoiled eggs.

Jesus Christ!

Easton felt fear ripple through his veins in an icy infusion. His eyes widened and, anywhere there were short hairs on his body, they were standing up full at attention.

Terror pricked around his thoughts and he mentally forced it off. Fear was fine. Terror was not. He could function with fear. Terror would leave him paralyzed until they dropped down and tore him to pieces.

The Mauser sounded like a cannon.

The nearest creature paused as a hole exactly nine millimeters in width appeared dead center in its forehead, barely registering that the back of its skull had been blown out in a spray of blackish gore before it dropped. Easton's heart was hammering and the blood was roaring in his ears but his hand was steady as he swiveled and fired twice more. The second creature caught it in the left eye, the third he shot right through the mouth. There were more coming, some along the ceiling, others along the walls and floor.

Any further thoughts on the subject of search and rescue got cancelled. Instead, Easton backed up into the stairwell where they could only come at him one or two at a time. By the time he was back at the top of the stairs, four of the things were piled up at the bottom. He had no idea if they could come outside or even survive in the daylight, but he had a hunch they couldn't.

Either way, there was only one way to find out.

"Change in plans." He said aloud to no-one.

Easton bolted out the door backwards. He saw a scaly hand reach around the doorframe to the basement as he did so and then he was out on the back porch.

The kids were gone.

In their place was Detective Bell.

"John! There you are! Where are the kids?" Bell's broad face split into a grin.

Easton was disoriented. It was a good question – *where were the kids?* An even better question was: *what was Bell dong here alone?*

"Darren? Where's the rest of the force?"

"Oh, they're all out front! Door was locked. I came around back to see if there was another way in . . . Cripes, you look like you've seen a ghost."

Something wasn't adding up about all this. Bell must have read this on his face because he smiled even wider and said "Oh, yeah. and while I was back here I found this!" Out of his pocket he pulled a small black box. The Mauser in Easton's hand came up even as he registered what it was: A Taser.

Then he was dropping to the ground convulsing helplessly as the sky spun around and around.

-23-

WHEN HE CAME to, he was sitting in a chair in what was presumably the master bedroom of the house. And standing by the broad window with the heavy draperies was, Easton ventured to guess, the Master of the house. This room, unlike the rest of the house, *was* furnished.

In death, or un-death to be more accurate, Richtenstein had elected to furnish his quarters with a little bit of the Fatherland. The room was already enormous with sixteen foot ceilings, a massive Gothic-looking fireplace and heavy oak-paneled walls stained with time and age. The décor was a curious mix that ran from the Medieval to the Edwardian. Much of it had a worn, salvaged look and Easton guessed most of it had been scrounged, though God knew from where.

There was a large canopied bed, a towering armoire with elaborate carvings that looked as if it could hide an entire family, and an overlapping array of Persian rugs strewn across the floor. The andirons in front of the fireplace were the winged double eagles of the Hapsburgs; a collection of beer steins were arrayed on the mantel. There were several chairs and couches that looked late Victorian, a long table with lions-paw legs, a dressing table with assorted bottles and antique looking vials, and a large mirror (with an oddly flawless yet murky-looking glass) that would have been right at home in a Brothers Grimm tale. There were several paintings, some stacked against the wall, and overall the place had an almost Bohemian air, the room of an Old-World scion of an industrial family who had run out of funds yet was maintaining an air of moldering respectability while living in a world that no longer was.

On the long table were scattered several ancient looking books, various photographs, and the Mauser. At the far end of the table sat Detective Bell, his crossed feet up on the table and a toothpick sticking out of the corner of his mouth.

As for his own predicament, Easton was tied with his hands secured around the back of a chair and his ankles tied to the legs.

Through the window Easton could see the sun was setting, which meant he had been out for over seven hours.

"Welcome back to the world of the living, Johnny. For a little bit at least. Gave us some time to do a little house cleaning downstairs. But I'm afraid I think it's our fine host's intention that this will be the last sunset you'll be seeing, on 'this side of the truth' as one Welsh poet put it." Bell worked the toothpick to the other side of his mouth.

"I guess this means the Calvary isn't coming?"

"Bingo."

"And I suppose this is where I ask why you're doing this?"

"I suppose. And I tell you that it was all about money, that I had one too many gambling debts that I couldn't cover on my poor detective's pay, or some old tired shit like that."

Easton thought a moment. "Or maybe you're just a worthless fuckwit who can only get it up with little kids because they have tiny parts like your own. Set the bar low as possible so to speak."

Bell chuckled, "Ooh, sticks and stones . . ." But the glare in his eye told Easton that his barb had landed close to home. The laugh came out forced and at the same time he pulled out a gun. Easton wasn't surprised to see that it was his own Colt automatic. Bell drew the action and pointed it at Easton's head.

Easton decided he didn't like looking down the barrel of his own gun very much. But at the same time he was furious, especially when it came to adults doing things to kids.

Richtenstein, who had been gazing out the window at something below, turned around.

"You will stop with the games." The creaking whisper sent a shiver down Easton's spine. At the same time, he began working at the ropes around his wrists and was rewarded with a little looseness. Bell may have been good at fooling the police force, but a Boy Scout he was not. And shifting his weight subtly revealed that the antique wooden chair he was bound to wasn't too secure either.

His thoughts were running in contradictory directions. On the one hand, he had more than a few questions for this monster. On the other, he just wanted to kill it as quickly as possible. Given the option, he was hoping for the latter.

As for his own mortality, that wasn't even a question at this point. He would simply go until he stopped.

Richtenstein drifted over to the table – the way he moved could only be described as *drifting* – and picked up the Mauser.

"A most interesting choice of weapon. A German officer's weapon. Like one that was used against me many years ago . . . *ja*?" Richtenstein turned the gun first one way, then another, as if it was an object of utter fascination.

"Could be," Easton shot back. "Let's try it out and see if it works any better the second time."

The Liche ignored him. "And I believe you may have something else of mine?"

Easton had wondered about this. How accurate were the thing's senses and how close was its connection to the vessel that held the key? They were about to find out. He shot back another quip. (He seemed to have no shortage of them in his arsenal this evening.)

"If you're referring to your Teutonic Cross boxer shorts, I'm afraid they're still back at the precinct in the Lost and Found."

Although Easton didn't actually see the thing move, the next moment he was acutely aware that Richtenstein was right on top of him, choking him with one skeletal hand. The fingers felt like metal pincers. Easton's eyes bulged in their sockets.

Up close Richtenstein was even more horrifying to look at. The blackened skin stretched over the skull was like having a re-animated mummy right up in his face only twice as awful-smelling. He also noticed for the first time the mystical symbols traced all over the surface of the skin. Even worse, they seemed to be moving of their own accord, like delicate maggots.

Richtenstein's' dried-out lips appeared to snarl. "I could pluck your eyeballs out und eat them like grapes, *mein Scheißkerl*, then enjoy your tongue like a fresh blood sausage . . ."

Well, of course he could. Easton had no question on that account. He also knew that anger was sometimes a good thing and could be used to keep your opponent distracted. He just hoped it didn't wind up costing him some crucial part of his body.

His face was turning purple. Blood began to seep down his neck where Richtenstein's nails had pierced the skin.

Then just as the world was turning grey and fuzzy around the edges, his throat was released.

Easton took a whooping gasp of air, then made a gagging cough.

Richtenstein leaned in close again.

"Where . . . is *it*?" The rabbit's foot key chain materialized and was dangled in front of his watery eyes. "It looked just like this one!"

Easton knew that there was little sense getting coy, so he said the first thing that popped into his head.

"The woman had it. Lorelei." He said hoarsely. That didn't make much sense, but he was improvising. He was also getting a welcome update from his hands – the ropes were nearly undone.

Richtenstein looked over at Bell, who shrugged.

"How do you know this?"

"Because I saw it hanging around her neck when I shot her. Back in the park. I assume she's still wearing it. At whatever morgue they took the body to."

Richtenstein swiveled his head back towards Bell again. It sounded like dry wood twisting.

"*Dummkopf!* You did not check Lorelei's person?"

The stricken look on Bell's face told Easton that the ruse had worked.

Bell dropped his legs and leaned forward.

"Well uh . . . I, ahh . . . hey, you didn't . . ." He ducked as a book was hurled at his head, just missing it.

"*Verdammt noch mal!*" Richtenstein hissed, cutting him off. "Get it. Now! *Schnell!*"

Bell stood up and, looking shaken, holstered Easton's pistol. "Got it." Then he turned and hightailed it out of the room.

Richtenstein walked over to the table with his back to Easton. One hand reached out and traced the cover of one of the books with a finger. Easton watched him carefully, gauging angles and distances carefully. The Mauser was right there. What he didn't want was to give Richtenstein too much time to think. The story about Lorelei was flimsy at best.

"Quite a life you've made for yourself up here. Surprised *Architectural Digest* hasn't done a feature on your digs here yet. Though you may need…"

"I think you are a clever man, *Herr* Easton," said Richtenstein, cutting him off. "But why come here . . . unprepared, shall we say?"

Apparently good manners didn't apply when you got to be . . . what . . . a hundred twenty, thirty years old?

The finger continued to trace the book cover while Easton formulated his response. The most convincing way to fool someone was what his father used to describe as "to skate right up along the edge of a lie."

"Nothing much clever there, I'm afraid. Once I got the word I called the police chief – and got Detective Bell instead. Getting here and getting the kids out was my first priority." (Was that a crash and tinkle of glass downstairs? Richtenstein cocked his head as well, as if listening). "Not much time to plan things, though I left a message for the police chief – with your good friend Bell ironically." Easton kept his tone conversational, calculating how he could get to the ropes around his ankles next.

As if sensing this, Richtenstein picked up the pistol and turned around.

"I am curious where you found this weapon, *Herr* Easton? An interesting coincidence."

Placing the pistol down again, he stepped over and Easton found his head grasped in a crushing grip. Again he found himself face-to-face with the hideous mask, Richtenstein looking at him first one way and then another as if he was studying a particularly interesting species of insect.

"I think you are lying," the Liche said in his grating whisper.

For a moment – an eternity of moments – Easton had a flash of images and thoughts and memories: from von Richtenstein's tormented childhood through his military academy years, an overwhelming sense of loathing (and yet pity too) as he saw the frail young German get bullied and tormented into an insidious creature of fear . . . the strict, brutal yet aristocratic parents raising him more like an object to be polished and refined and put out for show . . . and then the terrible forge of the war, the twisted psychology of a man of means doing any trick to prove his superiority over the other pilots, men he considered brutal and low-bred . . . then the reality of terror at every mission, coalescing into a rabid desire to cheat death at all costs . . . money paid to so-called sorceresses and witches (even a gypsy or two), at first to shysters and charlatans with quack spells and rituals, but then, finally – almost by accident – to occultists and shadowy practitioners who truly dabbled with the darker aspects of the Kabala and other forbidden arts, then to the blasphemous rituals that had been undertaken to transform himself . . . all that followed and more.

To Easton, the stream of experiences felt like a repulsive wave of squirming larvae, nibbling at his own thoughts and mental defenses and he shuddered and clenched his teeth, forcing the thoughts away by sheer force of will. Then he did the last thing his foe probably expected – he reached up with his own freed hands and grabbed the thing's skull and drew it in even closer. At the same time, he used his tongue to roll the object he had been keeping tucked in there so that it stuck out between his clenched teeth. Then, despite every nerve in his system screaming in revulsion, he yanked Richtenstein even closer, as if in some sort of obscene kiss, and jammed the ceramic bullet into his foe's mouth.

"I think you're right," he hissed.

Then his fist pistoned up into the underside of the thing's jaw, smashing teeth and ceramic bullet alike.

Richtenstein let out a screech that felt like razors in Easton's ears and mind but he didn't let go. Instead, he fell onto Easton and they toppled over. Easton saw stars as his head slammed into the floor. Richtenstein's grip was still like steel and he leaned in, broken mouth gaping wide, strange worm like filaments coming up from the back of the throat. Awful images began to probe again around the edges of Easton's thoughts – screaming boys, bullets flying, the endless years of victims disappearing, tears, terror – the whole horrifying spectrum that defined Richtenstein's existence as a perversion of nature.

He wondered what kind of universe could allow such things to exist.

Then vaguely Easton was aware of something entering the room off to his right. He was focused on what horror was about to happen to him next, his hands locked around Richtenstein's neck and trying to force him and the insanity nibbling at his thoughts away.

It wasn't working.

He had time to observe – in an almost detached fashion – that the motions of the glyphs playing across the Liche's skin had reversed direction, then something slammed into the German with the force of a runaway train, sending him flying.

All Easton saw was a flying blur of shaggy fur and legs as it passed over him. Richtenstein bounced and rolled towards the fireplace and the newcomer – Easton could now see it was the most massive beast of a dog he had ever seen – landed and sank its jaws into Richtenstein's arm. Easton heard bones snapping and the German let out an inhuman scream.

Then he grabbed one of the Eagle andirons with his free hand and struck clumsily at his attacker.

The dog let out a cry of pain and backed off as Richtenstein managed to get to his feet, right arm dangling at a sickening angle. The he threw the andiron at his attacker and ran, grabbing what looked like a small scepter or cane propped up by the door. The dog, which Easton thought was one of the strangest he had ever seen, cowered briefly, the torn stumps where its ears had once been twitching (perhaps trying to flatten), then it hurtled after the German.

It took Easton a moment to roll over in the broken remains of the chair, ignoring the bolts of pain shooting up his back where he'd landed, and to free himself. Then he grabbed the Mauser and followed.

There wasn't far to go.

Outside the master bedroom was a stair and rail opening to the downstairs on the right. To the left was a short flight of steps leading up into the turret, which, based on the amount of stomping, cursing, and deep-throated woofs and snarling sounds, was where the party had gone.

Pistol in hand, Easton bounded up the stairs two at time.

The turret wasn't large – perhaps twelve feet across. A spiraling wooden stair led up to an observation platform where a series of tall vertical windows offered a panoramic view of the Hudson Valley. Some of the windows were broken and the many of the wooden slats that formed the ceiling had fallen down. Like many areas of the house it looked like a half-assed repair job that had been abandoned midway.

Richtenstein was on the platform, keeping the dog at bay with the staff (which Easton could now see was a curiously carved scepter with – no surprise – a screaming death's head at its top wearing the old style spiked German helmet). The dog was snapping and snarling, its jaws like a massive bear trap. It looked like a 150 pounds of pure destruction. Easton had time to observe that the animal had both spots and stripes: striated black and brown fur along its back and haunches, white forelegs and belly with a couple of random dark blotches. The massive head had most of the black fur had gathered around the snout and eyes, making it look like the dog had dipped its snout in soot.

Yet even as he brought up the Mauser with both hands, the beast launched itself under the sweep of the striking staff and, with a shatter of wood and glass, the two figures tumbled out the window and were gone.

Easton couldn't believe it. A few shreds of Richtenstein's tunic fluttered in the window frame. What was even more astounding was what he found when he bounded up the stairs and leaned out the window. The window was on the east side of the house where the slate-tiled roof sloped away steeply to the gable overlooking a porch entrance on the south.

Where the roof dropped off was a wide chimney. Beyond that was probably a 35-foot drop to the ground.

The dog had rolled down into the angle formed by the chimney and the roof. Richtenstein had managed to clamber to the top of the chimney itself and was preparing to skewer the helpless animal, which was still scrabbling for purchase.

The wind plucked at Easton's hair and, across the Hudson River, a molten sun was setting over the Palisades, painting the clouds in rich ambers, purples, and evening blues. Easton, his voice already hoarse from the abuse he'd taken earlier, yelled at the top of his lungs.

"Richtenstein! Look here, goddamn you!"

Richtenstein snarled back at him through his broken teeth, one arm dangling useless at his side, the other with the staff poised, aimed at the dog.

Then he struck downwards.

The first shot caught him on the shoulder.

The staff clattered harmlessly on the slate shingles, then tumbled off over the edge.

The next five shots – fired semi-automatically – went into a tight grouping around his heart.

The last shot went right between the eyes.

Whatever last words came out of Richtenstein's mouth at the end were carried away in the wind.

And with that he toppled over and fell away into the darkness.

-24-

THE NEXT FEW minutes where harrowing.

Easton had no immediate answers in his playbook on what to do when you find a massive animal wedged on a steep-pitched roof high above the ground. The dog didn't appear to be seriously injured, but if it panicked, the fall would most certainly be fatal.

A robotic-sounding mechanical voice announced itself from his hip, startling him.

"Droid."

He'd completely forgotten about the phone. For the first time since he'd received the damn thing, he was grateful to have it.

He got another surprise when, after dialing 9-1-1, they patched him through immediately to Hendricks.

"We're already on our way, John. The Ecuadorian kid – Armando – showed up ten minutes ago with the rest who escaped. Fill you in later."

"You'll need a hook and ladder, Hendricks. I've got an emergency situation here with, well…you're not going to believe this one." After he relayed the basic details, he added, "Oh, and Hendricks, you need to collar Detective Bell immediately. He's dirty."

"Copy that, John, the kid gave us a brief statement. An APB is already out for Bell. Hold tight, we'll be there in five."

Easton debated what to do next. It was clear what the animal's views were on Richtenstein and Lorelei, but not on himself, but he wasn't sure how long the dog would be smart enough to stay put. Feeling a bit foolish, he called down to it.

"Stay put! Don't move!"

The massive head swiveled up at the sound of his voice, the deep-set brown eyes almost sad looking. The dog whimpered but stayed in its half-rolled-up position.

Easton ran back down to the bedroom and ripped the curtains off the windows. They were old but he thought they would hold his weight. He bolted back up and was relieved to see the animal was still there. He looped the curtains through two of the windows, then lowered himself down along the roof the ten feet or so down to the chimney, the wind plucking at his hair and sport jacket. Hanging on to his makeshift rope with one hand and steadying himself against the chimney with his foot, he was able to sidle in next to the dog. He put his fist out knuckles first to let it sniff him.

"Pleased to meet you. I'm Johnathan Easton," he said.

The dog looked at him, then simply leaned its head against his leg. He saw it had an old leather collar around its neck, with part of a broken metal tag attached to it. In the fading light he could make out some Cyrillic characters and part of a name written in English characters: "*Rovsky.*"

Easton put his hand on the massive head, gingerly at first, and, when the dog didn't appear to mind, stroked its thick fur.

"Rovsky," he said quietly. "Just what in the hell kind of dog are you?" He didn't expect an answer and didn't get one. "Well, thanks, pal. You saved my neck back there. Now we sit tight until the cavalry arrives."

The view was quite spectacular up here, he decided. *As long as you don't look down.*

He settled in to wait.

-25-

Detective Bell was sitting in his Prius hybrid in the parking area near the Raadsel Bay condominiums where the view offered an excellent panorama of the river. He may have committed some monstrous acts against innocent people, mostly children, under his masquerade as a man of the law, but at least he was doing his part to help save the environment.

All part of the image, he thought, and it had worked. For a while at least. But the gig was now most certainly up. Before he got even close to the impound at the Wyvern Falls Buildings Department, he'd caught the updates on his scanner and heard he was now a "person of extreme interest" to the same authorities he had represented and was to be considered armed and dangerous and apprehended with force if necessary.

The picnic area was a spot he often frequented on his lunch breaks back in that other time when he was operating in the realm of legitimacy. Somehow, parking here with his lunch, usually a brown bag take-out from a local joint like Luciano's Pizza or the Greek place, Xeno's, made him feel calm and at rights with the world.

Good times.

Now, like so many victims whose fates he had assisted, his luck had run out.

Bell pulled out his service revolver – this was the original .38 police issue he'd bought when he'd graduated from the academy and had insisted on keeping – and placed the barrel under his chin.

He thought about his older sister Margaret: Margaret, who in many ways had been the cause of how fucked up so many things had turned out.

A couple of seagulls drifted by, one landing on the wooden post at the edge of the parking area. A wind was picking up across the river as evening settled in, sending cat's paws chasing each other across the darkening water.

Bell looked off into space, his eyes blank and emotionless. Then he pulled the trigger.

-26-

"I THINK it may be an Ovcharka – a Russian mountain dog – but I can't say I've ever really seen one before. He will definitely need stitches. This dog's been in one hell of a fight for sure." He wrinkled his nose. "And a decent bath, I daresay. Make that two."

The man talking to Easton was Cyrano Jones, a local vet who often worked with the police and also ran a kennel just out of town. He'd earned his first name due to his certain facial similarity to the title character in Edmond Rostand's famous play and, also like that character, was gregarious, well-spoken, and extremely intelligent.

He'd worked with the firemen to jury rig a sling (and to give the dog a tranquilizer, just to be safe) and they were able to lower the animal to the ground and get him loaded into Cyrano's van.

"What'll happen to him?"

"Well, once he's healed up and current on his shots, I'll get him evaluated and placed for adoption. Any interest in owning a dog?"

"Not at the moment. I've got enough problems going on at my house." He looked around as there was a commotion by the gate. It looked like the press had arrived.

There were a few minutes of chaos when one sharp-looking Latino guy with a mike in hand broke through and ran around the crime scene asking all sorts of questions. He was followed by a bunch of college-age-looking kids with cameras who had surprised the few officers by the entrance and quickly overwhelmed them. The cordoned area around the castle was momentarily over-run by people with cameras, shouts, flashes.

Some yelled, "What the dilly, Boss? EMF readings are off the fucking charts!"

And: "Holy . . . look at that action!"

Then Easton found the Latino guy (who reminded him vaguely of that celebrity Marc Antony) thrusting the mike in his face and firing a staccato of questions at him:

"Antonio King here, from LiveEYE New York. Sir, can you comment on reports of a sex-trafficking ring operating here at…what do they call this place? Castle Skull? LiveEYE New York viewers are demanding answers! Hasegawa, you getting this all on tape? Sir? Sir . . .?"

Easton, who had been in similar situations before, was smart enough to keep his hands down, his mouth buttoned and his face impassive. To make matters even more surreal, the so-called reporter, clearly intoxicated and smelling vaguely of vomit, was being filmed by a Japanese kid with a tiny hand-held camera. Then out of the corner of his eye he saw the situation escalating as a bunch of the college kids gained the front steps of the castle and, unbelievably, set up a shoot as though this was just another TV set.

Despite the policemen running up to intercept them, the situation might have gotten completely out of control if gunshots hadn't rung out three times, stunning everyone into silence.

Chief Hendricks had gotten ahead of the group on the stairs, drawn his weapon, and fired it into the sky.

He immediately had everyone's undivided attention.

He gave a quick steely-eyed look around him, then said loudly and clearly:

"That's it. You're all under arrest."

Someone protested but was silenced by a fourth shot into the air.

There were no arguments after that.

Easton walked back up to where Hendricks was discussing the mangled body of Richtenstein with the forensics team. The German pilot had landed head first on the flagstones near the entrance. The area was taped off and one of the forensics team, an assistant named Osterman, was taking photographs with a Canon 5d Mark II. If anybody had been paying close attention, they might have noticed the look in his eye was a little *too* interested. And excited.

"Anything you care to tell me about this guy?" Hendricks asked. Easton put his hands in his front pockets. "Not really. He tried to kill me. Now he's dead. So from the looks of things, I'd say his flamenco days are over."

A call came in on Hendricks' mobile unit. He talked for a moment, one hand cupping his opposite ear so he could hear better. "Ah. Uhuh. Got it. Thanks." Then he turned to Easton. "They found your car. Someone trashed it and tried to drive it into a ravine, I'm afraid. I'm guessing it was

Bell."

Then he touched Easton by the elbow and led him out of earshot.

"John, what in the blue blazes is going on here? The press will have a field day with this. Christ, I've already got one media monster running around town sniffing for trouble as it is."

"Roy, you probably don't need me to tell you this, but your best strategy is to put the squash on this whole thing and make it go away. If this gets out past the village limits, you'll have a media shit-storm on your hands that'll make Mister Antonio look like a high-school newspaper reporter. You'd be better off taking that thing's body and burning it, then dropping the ashes in a trash bag and burying it. Nothing good will come of looking too hard and long into any of this, and it won't bring any of those dead kids back." He didn't mention that only a few of the bodies had been found in the basement – Bell had done an efficient job of cleaning up during the afternoon. And of the Dragyr there had been no sign. Which raised a trailing list of other questions. Like who might have helped him? And where had the remains gone?

Hendricks stood there with his hands behind his back, rocking on his heels and looking off into the sunset.

"I was thinking along those same lines. One of these days maybe we'll have a couple of beers and talk about what you *really* know. Or, then again, maybe not. Maybe we should just stick to talking baseball."

"That's probably a better idea."

"Right. But let's get you over to the hospital and get those neck injuries tended to. You look like you've been fighting a vampire or something." Easton felt a chill go up his spine and shuddered. He could still feel the echo of Richtenstein's corrupted thoughts when they had been in their hands-on struggle.

"Or something," he muttered.

-27-

THE FUNERAL for Henry Van Dorn was on Tuesday at 10:00 in the morning. It was held at the Blynd Funeral Home over on Brandreth Avenue, a blocky, oddly-built place with diamond-mullioned windows that suggested its nickname, 'Blynd Haus'. It was a large, squat-looking house to which all sorts of gables and extensions had been added in the years since it had been built, which, according to the village records, was in 1911 by a Dutchman named Otto Hoch).

Besides the Van Dorns and their relatives, there was a broad turnout from the community at large, as well as Henry's friends and their families. The Vogels, Dimas, Ortegas, Ducats, Carrs – a spectrum of family ethnologies that was like a core sample of the region: Dutch, English, South American, Afro-American. A few teachers showed up, as did the police chief and his captain. Easton found himself standing next to the woman he'd last seen at the precinct – Olivia Hernandez – with her five-year-old son who was one of the children that had escaped from the basement of Castle Krell. She was on the tall side, with a dancer's physique (she'd been a soloist with the New York City Ballet at one point, he would discover later) and alluring eyes. She'd pulled him aside at the entrance to the cemetery.

"I wanted to thank you, Mister Easton, for saving my son's life," she'd said, touching him on the arm. That was followed by a fierce hug that left him feeling more than a little awkward. He'd never been good at handling compliments.

"Well . . ." he'd said, pointing over to the Ortega family who were taking their places at the folding chairs near the gravesite. "Maybe the one you should thank is that boy over there, Armando. He's one brave kid. And he was the one that led your son and the others to safety."

Olivia looked down at her shoes and smoothed the front of her already perfectly-ironed dress as if momentarily embarrassed by her own actions. Then she ruffled her son's hair. "Even so, *gracias.*"

Easton gave her a short smile. "*De nada.*"

The minister, Grant Ketchum, was well-liked in the community for his dry wit and no-nonsense approach to Protestantism. He had one of those hang-dog faces that might have been lifted straight out of a Norman Rockwell painting.

The service he gave was short but sincere. Mr. Van Dorn stood rigidly throughout it, only breaking down at the very end (his wife had been sobbing the entire time) when Ketchum cast the first handful of dirt over the casket. Henry's sister and brother simply stood there in shock.

Next to Luis and his family, Armando stood with his own family in his best Sunday suit with his head bowed and hands clasped. Conflicting emotions were swirling though him like the eddies and whirlpools he'd so often seen when playing with his friends along Murderer's Creek. On the one hand, he felt a terrible sadness at the loss of Henry. He'd been the only one of their group to be there when he'd died and it was an image that would haunt him to his own dying day. And yet, mirrored with that was another experience that would haunt him in an entirely different way; his first bona fide kiss.

Carmina.

Just *thinking* her name made his head swim and his heart soar in that intoxicating way only young teenagers experiencing such emotions for the first time can feel. It was one thing to read of such things, watch them on television, or fantasize about them in your daydreams, but the first time that foreign citizen of the opposite (or same, depending on your inclination) sex camp, *really, physically kisses you on the lips*, it's enough to make one's head explode.

The events of that day were still clear in Armando's mind: no sooner had Easton disappeared back into the house than he had sprung into action, convincing the three others that they had to run and run now. It wasn't that he didn't trust Easton and it wasn't that he didn't believe the policemen he said were coming.

But, Detective Bell was a policeman.

And who else was working with him?

No, the one person he could trust, unquestionably, was his friend Luis. His mom and dad he loved dearly, but they were still newcomers in a community which kept to itself and which was careful about sharing its business. They would not wish to make waves or draw undue attention to themselves.

But Luis would know what to do. His family had their feet in both camps.

The next question had been how to get to Luis' house. The answer had presented itself when, fifteen minutes later, they'd emerged from the woods near Route 9B: the bus. Buses (and walking and bike riding) were something Armando knew plenty about. This part of Route 9B was on the #11 bus route, the same one his mother took to work, so it was simply a matter of finding the nearest stop, checking the schedule, and waiting. Out of sight. If Bell (or the Weatherman, although he didn't know him by this or any other name) spotted them, they'd be in trouble. He had enough fare for himself and Carmina; the other two were short enough to ride free.

So waiting until the road was clear, he'd hustled them over to the other side and led them south along the road, far enough into the woods to provide cover. They went half a mile until he spotted the bus shelter, then, after sneaking over by himself to check the schedule (reminding himself it was a Sunday), found they had less than a 15- minute wait. They'd settled in behind a fallen log where he explained his plan. The young boy, whose name turned out to be Kevin, wouldn't stop crying.

"I want to go home . . . I want my mommy."

Armando had grasped him firmly by the shoulders and looked him in the eye. "Don't you worry, *senor*, you will get home and see your mommy, I swear it. But you have to stand straight and be brave, or when the bus comes, the driver will be suspicious and ask questions, okay?"

Some of the conviction in his voice got through because Kevin did stop sobbing, though he still had a fair amount of snot running down his nose. A few minutes later, Carmina pulled Armando aside and behind a nearby oak, claiming she wanted a word with him. Though scuffed and dirty, with her hair a tangled mess, he thought she looked like the most beautiful thing in the world.

"Armando, I wanted to thank you for everything you've done so far. I don't know what will happen when we get to town, but just in case there is no time…" and with that she shocked him by grabbing his face with both her slender hands and kissing him full on the lips. Then he surprised himself by kissing her back just as passionately. It may have lasted only a couple minutes . . . or maybe five (to him it was an eternity) and then it was over, Carmina looked affectionately at him, her face flushed, Armando realized he had even been cupping one of her small breasts (he could still feel the ghost of it in his palm) and was hard as a brick between his legs. "Holy shit," he thought, "she's tongue-kissed me!" But then she took control and dragged him back around the tree to where Kevin and Paloma were waiting, Armando wearing a dumbstruck grin like someone had just walloped him with a Goofy Bat. From up the road came the low rumble of a diesel engine.

The bus was coming.

Five minutes later they'd gotten off in town a couple of blocks from the Dimas house. It felt surreal to be back in the village after all that had happened, as if he'd been gone for weeks instead of three-quarters of a day. The Dimas house was one of those Second Empire Victorians on Washington Place (just around the corner from Easton's house, in fact) that had been "remuddled" so many times over the years that most of the original details were lost, particularly the exterior where some intrepid aluminum-siding salesman had convinced a previous owner that sheathing every inch of one's house in a white painted metal alloy was the ultimate statement in building modernization.

Luis' bedroom was on the second floor at the back of the house. Armando wasn't sure if his friend would be home but it turned out after the third pebble had bounced off the window that he was. The sash went up and an annoyed face popped out, a face that quickly turned to comical surprise, complete with wide bulging eyes and mouth forming a big 'O' when he saw who his visitor was.

"Armando!? *Tchau*, no shit! What the . . .!?"

"Yeah, it's me you, *loco* pork chop!" Armando had said in a hushed voice, "Get down here! We need your help!"

A minute later, they huddled in the side yard under an old chestnut tree while Armando explained what had happened to a clearly shocked and awed Luis.

"See, I told you that the English guy was involved in this . . . and not just as a cop." Luis was staring at his friend as if not believing his eyes, occasionally glancing at the other kids. He'd slept badly the night before but was all eyes and ears now. Luis was particularly thrown by the part about Detective Bell and the mysterious man they'd seen by the trailer the night before and, of course, the truth about what had happened to Henry. He'd even felt a guilty pang of jealousy that Armando had survived such an exciting adventure and was now sitting here with this very pretty (and older) girl who was holding his hand. This was the kind of stuff that would become legendary in their circle of peers. But those thoughts were quickly squashed as he focused on the problem of how to approach the situation. Finally, he'd stood up and said, "We have tell my father. He knows the police chief – they're like old friends. And I think this Easton guy was sent to help us somehow, and we have to help him back."

Armando hadn't been too keen on going back to the police, but in the end Luis was able to persuade him.

After that, things happened quick.

Armando's reverie at the funeral had also a bittersweet aspect to it. Aside from the terrible sense of loss from Henry's death, there was still the unresolved issue of what would happen to Carmina. And Paloma.

The meeting with Detective Eckhart had been a messy scene, with Armando nearly flying into a rage when she had explained in calm (and somewhat patronizing) tones that the two girls weren't here legally and that their birth parents would have to be found and notified. Did Armando understand that the girl's parents would be just as worried as his own had been? (No, he didn't understand why someone – say, the church or his own family or somebody, anybody – couldn't just adopt them so they could all stay together.)

There was much more to it than that, of course, but nothing the Wyvern Falls police would share with a twelve-year-old kid. The girls were to be kept at a foster home handled through Child Services at an undisclosed location while the legalities were sorted out, particularly the immediate investigation into what had been a sex-slave-trafficking operation whose pipeline had run right through this sleepy river-side village. The investigation was proving problematic, the operation having folded up and shut down as mysteriously as it had appeared. There had been no direct connection to the carnival itself, no further leads on the mysterious 'Weatherman', and, so far, no indication that anyone from the police department, other than late Detective Bell, had been involved, though Hendricks was being rigorously thorough and had welcomed an Internal Affairs team from White Plains to assist.

The only item that ran in the Falls *Gazette* was a brief item on the sex trafficking, noting that the detective who had committed suicide in his own car may have been involved, along with a New Jersey man named Eddie Gacey who had been found deceased near his car. There was no mention of Castle Krell or Richtenstein and only a small byline that the Red Baron's Daughter tent at the Saint Anne's Carnival was closed as its owner had been called out of town on an emergency.

The only thing Armando was acutely aware of was that, just as quickly as Carmina had come into his life, she was taken out of it and in its place was a hollow ache that he'd never experienced before, let alone understood. Yet that, too, would be savored as Carmina would become like a sacred relic, to be polished and buffed as the subject of countless daydreams and reveries for many years to come.

Real or imagined he learned, there is never anything as poignant as one's first love.

The following day found Easton at the Philipseburg Memorial Hospital getting the injuries on his neck checked. He'd been put on antibiotics as a precaution (which for the first time in his life he took religiously – God knows what was in Richtenstein's fingernails) and had been dropped off earlier by his friend, Jim Franks, whom he'd agreed to meet with on Friday for a couple of drinks. Vivienne hadn't just left Easton, she'd left town altogether. Franks' girlfriend, Karen Evershaw, had some inside information but she wasn't talking. In the meantime, Easton was carless. The Maserati would be over at Tenny's Collision for a few weeks – Bell had, in a fit of juvenile rage, urinated all over the front dash and left a nice little dump in the driver's seat after leaving Castle Krell – and Easton wouldn't be picking up a rental car until the evening.

He'd run into Olivia Hernandez in the lobby as he was heading out to flag a cab. She'd been with her son visiting an aunt who was suffering from advanced Alzheimer's and had been talking with some family.

"Detective Easton?" She spoke with a trace of a Latino accent but not much. Easton guessed there might have been some serious vocal coaching in there somewhere.

He smiled and offered his hand. "John, please. Nice to see you, Miss Hernandez." She shook it confidently and flashed him a smile in return.

"Olivia. You need a lift back into town?"

"In fact I do. My car's getting cleaned up over at the shop."

Olivia snorted. "That's not what I heard. Word is that shit of a detective mistook your nice Italian sports car for a latrine." She cupped her hands over her son's ears too late. "Sorry, honey, pretend you didn't hear that. Mommy shouldn't use bad words like that."

Easton had a hunch she might have a whole truckload of words like that if she got her wind up and someone got on her wrong side, especially after what he'd witnessed at the police precinct what now seemed a lifetime ago. Yet he also couldn't deny that he found her quite sexy. The fitted summer dress with a large floral print she was wearing and her exotic-looking sandals were an eyeful, although Easton suspected she was the kind of woman who could wear a burlap sack and make it look great. She had a perfect posture and her dancer's physique didn't hurt either. The lack of any serious make-up, the way she wore her hair with glasses up on her head, and the no-nonsense fingernails all suggested a classy woman who was more concerned with being functional than vain. But he was also aware that his own personal life was in shambles and besides, he had no idea what her personal situation was, though he felt tempted to find out.

He couldn't help commenting on her perfume, which seemed tantalizingly familiar. The fragrance was subtle, but it drew his attention.

"Nina Ricci?" He ventured.

That got a smile. "Good call," she said, "*L'Air du Temps*."

The ride back to Wyvern Falls was uneventful. Easton kept the conversation focused on her. In addition to once being a soloist with New York City Ballet, she'd also done a season with the Dance Theater of Harlem but was out of the game now and running a small dance academy in the village where she taught ballet, flamenco and tango. He also found out she had grown up in Wyvern Falls but had been born in Spanish Harlem. She was quite curious about the Turk and Caicos Islands where'd he'd worked as a Detective Superintendent for so many years and she sounded convinced that it was some wild and exotic place populated only by movie stars and famous musicians, despite assurances that that was far from the truth.

Her son Kevin was a cute kid with a mischievous smile and clearly his mother's Latino features but lighter skinned. Easton guessed his father might be Caucasian. Shy at first, he grew excited after getting up the courage to ask about Easton's police experience and how many times he'd shot bad guys and what it was like to kill someone.

Olivia had been horrified. "Kevin, you shouldn't ask questions like that. It's not polite!"

"That's all right, a lot of kids ask that." Easton had turned to look at him in the back seat. "Kevin, it's not like the movies, or television. It's something you never, ever want to do unless your life absolutely depends on it. Because you can't ever take it back. And good or bad, it will always sit on your shoulders. Okay?" For a moment he saw a snippet of one of Richtenstein's memories – Spandau machine-guns blazing at a hapless enemy Spad, the other pilot screaming – and shuddered.

Olivia's son must have picked up on the seriousness of his tone because he quickly changed the subject.

Then as they pulled up in front of his house, she said, somewhat standoffishly "Well, it was very nice seeing you again, John," then surprised him by adding, "Oh, I didn't know you had a dog."

"I don't," he said as he half turned, opening the passenger door, but the words trailed away as he saw the huge shaggy beast sitting there on his front steps, looking like he owned the place.

"What do you call that, then?" she asked.

I don't know that I'd call that thing over there 'a dog', exactly he thought. But aloud he said, more speaking to himself, "Let me, uh . . . let me get back to you on that one." Then he turned back towards Olivia. If there had been a moment there, it felt like it was gone. "Well, thanks for the lift, Olivia. I'm sure I'll see you around. Bye."

"*Ciao.*"

Easton walked up to his house and stood, hands in his front pockets, staring at the massive beast sitting on his front step. The dog just sat there and stared right back at him. The thick forelegs looked like logs, the back ones splayed out on either side. All he needed was a wife-beater t-shirt and some bling and he'd look right at home on a Brooklyn stoop.

Not entirely sure how to proceed, Easton pulled out his Droid, preparing to dial Dr. Jones. Then he changed his mind. When he had returned home on Sunday, Vivienne had been gone. Clothes, suitcase, personal belongings, completely gone. No note or anything. So maybe he was meant to have another roommate. At least the dog had been cleaned and groomed, though he still had the old leather collar on. Easton took a seat next to him on the steps of the porch, forearms on knees.

He looked over at the dog. "Rovsky, huh?"

The big dog let out a single deep "Woof!" that seemed loud enough to flatten the grass in the front yard. Then it leaned against him.

Easton shook his head.

Oh boy.

-28-

Just to the north of the aerodrome, the Fokker D.VII biplane swept in low, guns blazing. The Spad XIII it had been tangling with gunned its throttle, sending out plumes of smoke from its twin exhausts, and banked off to the left. The pilot disappeared over a nearby ridge, skidding the plane as if he was losing control. The Fokker followed. There was a space of a few minutes and then both planes popped back up over the ridge, this time with the Spad chasing the Fokker. More gunfire and the German plane slewed in for a quick landing, trailing smoke. A minute later, the Spad landed behind it, the pilot leaping out of his cockpit with a pistol drawn, chasing his enemy halfway across the field before halting him with a single gunshot in the air. The German put his hands up in mock surrender. On cue, the announcer came over the loudspeakers: "Alrighty folks, looks like the game is up for the evil Baron. Smitty Jones has won the day again! How about a big round of applause for Captain Jones!"

An intermittent applause followed. The audience had seen this routine once or twice before but still enjoyed it.

Half an hour later another, much larger biplane was taking off from the grass runway, this one a 1927 D-25 New Standard with an open passenger cockpit in front and the pilot situated just behind it. In the front compartment, where the plane would have carried bulk mail, were four passengers: John Easton, Luis Dimas, Armando Ortega, and Pete Vogel. All four were wearing leather flying caps and goggles and were buckled in by what appeared to be old car seatbelts.

The three boys looked equal parts scared and thrilled.

"You wanted to see what it felt like to fly in a real biplane, right?" Easton had to shout over the sound of the rotary motor and wind blowing back into the cockpit. He grinned and jerked his thumb back at Carl Steneck, who was piloting the plane. "Let's hope he can figure out how to land this thing again. I heard it's his first time, too!"

That got alarmed looks in response. Only Pete was shaking his head.

"He's joking, guys."

"Really?" Luis asked.

"Absolutely. I heard it's actually his *second* time."

Before Easton could pick up his rental on Wednesday, he'd gotten a call from Captain Fowler offering to loan him his 1972 Ford Mustang Mach 1 with a Cleveland 351 2 barrel V8 —essentially a hot-rod engine mounted on four wheels. When Easton asked Fowler if he was sure about lending the Mustang out, the Captain had replied, "Well, I'm thinking of selling it – my wife is on my case about freeing up the garage. But, to answer your question, no, but I'm sure you'll take good care of her. Otherwise, I'll be the proud owner of a Maserati, right?"

"Yeah. But your wife will still be on your case about the garage space," Easton had replied.

"That's all right, she's Italian. She'll make an exception for a fellow countrywoman."

The next day, he rumbled around town in a classic 70s muscle car, feeling just a little ridiculous. When he'd pulled up at the light on Main Street and South Hudson (Route 9B), a group of high school girls ogled his car. One actually asked him for a ride.

Then he felt *a lot* ridiculous.

But underneath it he had been feeling depressed. He'd slept only fitfully that week, as if his body was going through some physical withdrawal since Vivienne had left. It was one thing when she wasn't there the nights she hadn't come home. It was another when she was completely gone.

And he was angry. Angry with himself for getting involved with a younger woman; angry with her for walking out with no explanation. And angry with fooling himself into thinking it could have worked. It put a strain on his friendship with Jim Franks, who had been her boss at the web design company he ran in Irvington. Franks felt responsible since he'd set them up in the first place.

Easton didn't hold it against him; he just needed time to sort it out. And, more importantly, it was time to get out and just do something new. Exciting.

The carnival was still going on but to Easton it felt like the whole atmosphere had soured somewhat after what had happened. He had a hunch it had soured for a few young boys in the village. *The Red Baron's Daughter. Who had she been really?* From Edwards' notes, she had been an aspiring actress, who had been caught up, along with Richtenstein, in a nearly Faustian tale of eternal life. *And at what cost? What the hell kind of life was that?* Easton decided he much prefer a short and sweet existence to the grim, drawn-out purgatory Richtenstein had created for himself.

He also needed to shake out of his rut. So on Thursday, when he'd received a phone call from Steneck up at the Old Rhinebeck Aerodrome, he'd gotten to thinking.

"Hi John, just wanted to follow up with you. I managed to dig up some info on Edwards and this von Richtenstein guy, but not a whole lot. Edwards went AWOL at the end of the war, but had a good record up until then. As for Richtenstein, I'd almost say there's a curious *lack* of information, as if someone made a concerted effort to wipe him from the record."

"I bet." Easton replied. "Well, I appreciate it. But I may have had enough of Richtenstein for the moment. Long story. But while I have you on the phone . . . I just got an idea . . ."

So Easton had made some calls to some parents. "A day trip up to Old Rhinebeck, his treat. Get the boys out of town, a little adventure, a little history." Only Adam Carr's dad had turned him down, saying, "Well, thanks, Detective, but I think we've had enough excitement around here for the time being. Maybe next time."

Victor Dimas had opted to come along as an extra chaperone, though he absolutely refused to set foot in the biplane. "You go have yourself a good flight. I'll be here with my feet planted on the ground when you take off – and they'll be planted here when you come back."

Luis mentioned that his dad absolutely refused to get on any plane, period. Something about an incident in the past that he wouldn't elaborate on.

Steneck made a low bank and took them out over the Hudson River. At two thousand feet, the air was cool and fresh and, despite the constant barrage of wind and noise, Easton couldn't remember having a better time in years. There was an indescribable thrill in sitting in an open, lurching cockpit so high up in the air, the wind buffeting your face and trying to pluck the breath out of your mouth.

I'm flying. Really flying.

Sitting in a pressurized cockpit on a commercial jet was one thing.

Being socked into an open cockpit contraption made of wood and canvas involved a good deal of faith and a fair chunk of wishful thinking. Easton couldn't help but wonder that guys like Edwards must have possessed a good dose of youthful insanity to not only fly in these damn things, but actually push them to their limits while trying to shoot down some other guy was equally as crazy.

Below, the Hudson Valley was a magnificent rich green vista drowsing in the early summer afternoon, suggesting age, mystery, and hidden tales yet to be told.

Up here, the sky was blue and wide open and full of all kinds of possibilities.

Easton looked at the kids and grinned.

II. THE LONELY DANCERS

The same strange music everywhere
The woven paces just the same
Dancing from out of the viewless air
Into the void from whence they came
Ah! But they make a gallant flare!
Against the dark, each little flame!

—Richard Le Gallienne, The Lonely Dancer

-1-

NICK CARR was upset.

One could pile a bunch of other adjectives on top of that (angry, resentful, hurt, jealous, slightly intoxicated) but sitting on top of all of them, king of the hill this night, was just plain old ho-hum every day *upset*.

Looking at a snapshot of Nick Carr's life might offer us some possible clues as to the cause of this upset. He was 20 years old, gainfully employed full-time at the local True Value hardware store run by Frank Garrety over on Main Street, and making just over minimum wage. He'd dropped out of SUNY New Paltz after just one year of half-hearted creative writing classes and was living under a vague whiff of failure with his parents in their 1892 Queen Anne over on Voelkner Avenue. He drove a 1978 Ford Mustang with a spoiler, a lot of rust, and a bad muffler. It was a blue wonder the damn car was still running, let alone maintaining a legal New York State inspection status (even that was somewhat questionable – Nick 'tipped' a buddy of his forty bucks a year to overlook a few key issues, like the muffler, for instance). He was decent-looking enough with dark, serious features and scraggly, straight dark brown hair in a classic Tom Petty cut even though he was born thirteen years after that illustrious rocker's debut on the charts. He sported pointed mutton-chop sideburns and had the schleppy/rebellious rock-and-roller character down pat.

But he lacked the confidence and extroverted personality to score regular dates and seemed to lack any clear direction for his future other than his regular guitar playing and desultory stabs at writing. Which was hardly a big hit with his father, Valery Carr, a self-made man who ran a roofing and general contracting business and was a twenty-two-year member of the Wyvern Falls Volunteer Fire Department.

So there was plenty of friction and resentment on the home front, mediated only by Nick's mother Liz who had the more forgiving set of genes in the family. He also had a younger sister Anne who was in the tenth grade and more or less a complete pain in the ass. She had her sights set on acquiring his larger bedroom – the one with the bay window at the front of the house – a plan thwarted by his unscheduled return to the Carr domicile. She was the complete opposite of Nick: outgoing, popular, and quite the social butterfly. Then there was his younger brother Adam, twelve years old and in complete awe of his eldest sibling but at ease with his youngest brother role and well socialized. By contrast, Nick was introverted and a loner, increasingly convinced he had been kidnapped as an infant from a pair of normal, artistic, and caring parents and placed in his current unimaginative and uncreative household as part of some diabolical social experiment aimed at testing the effectiveness of prolonged mental torture.

Any of these things might be considered a cause of Nick Carr's disquiet. But the direct source of this of this *upset* was not a *cause* but a *name*: Sabina Torres.

Even the name suggested the striking eighteen-year-old Portuguese beauty with her wavy pile of long black hair, dark eyes under arched brows and devilish smile that could make sane men crazy. If that didn't do it, the buxom figure she'd capitalized on since passing thirteen would have. She liked older men and she liked them on a short leash. Although she did have a sweet side to her mercurial persona, she also had an almost psychotic tendency to torment her suitors the way certain cats will casually break legs off a spider one by one before growing bored and swatting it dead. She had also been, oddly enough, Nick's girlfriend for the last six months of his senior year at Wyvern Falls High.

If Nick Carr had been a slightly more objective type of guy, he would have grasped the obvious: the primary reason Miss Sabina Torres had hooked her claws into his not-so-well-protected heart could be chalked up to high-school politics and the classic teenage fuck-over. Nick had been dumped by his previous girlfriend, Kelly DuBois, over Christmas that year. For Steve Everston, no less, one of his fellow seniors. As in Steve Everston who drove a Corvette, had preternaturally good looks and sandy blond hair, whose father, Chad Everston, owned the Raadsel Bay Yacht Club (along with a fifty-foot Ketch). Who was essentially three things Nick was not: athletic, charming, and rich. To make things more awkward, both Kelly and Nick had been cast together in the senior musical *South Pacific*, which began rehearsals the following February. The same musical for which the then sixteen-year-old Miss Torres was one of the production staff.

For reasons known only in the jealous, competitive, and sometimes vicious hearts of teenage girls, Sabina had it in for Kelly, perhaps for no more rhyme or reason than a cobra and mongoose go at it. It's just simply in their genetic make-up. They probably couldn't have clearly articulated it themselves; there was only the certainty that when Sabina Torres and Kelly DuBois were in the same relative proximity, claws came out, ears flattened and hackles went up.

Only figuratively, mind you.

Both girls acted civilized, even friendly to each other, in front their peers. It was only through the text messaging, out-of-ear-shot school hallway gatherings, the whispered lavatory conversations, and late-night cell phone conversations with their respective girlfriends that the truth came out.

Sabina is a tramp, totally.

Kelly's a stuck-up bitch.

Sabina buys her clothes at Whores-R-Us.

Princess Kelly is most definitely fucking her teachers.

So when Kelly DuBois went for a boyfriend upgrade, Sabina didn't hesitate to put the moves on Nick. Nothing drives a popular teenage girl crazier than to see her ex picked up by an even better-looking girl.

And Nick, on one level a clueless hayseed despite his aloof 'alternative rocker' self-image, was loving every moment of it. Part of it was ego, part of it was youthful naiveté, part of it was just the basic human need to be wanted and accepted on some level. And there was Nick Carr, spurned boyfriend, who in the movie version of his life should be plotting to win back the heart of his ex via some outrageous but ultimately wildly successful ploy (which in one of his fantasy daydreams was writing a killer song that gets picked up by a major label and becomes the breakthrough Top 10 hit of the year, climaxed by a scene where Kelly comes flying up to him backstage with arms open and tears in her eyes, begging "I had no idea how much you meant and oh god –sob– how much I love you! Kiss me!"). But instead, in reality, he finds himself being hit on by one of the hottest tickets in WF High and, much to the utter disbelief and then utter envy and awe of his few friends, winds up being asked out by said hottest ticket. Who could blame him for being side-swiped by such a bizarre – or bizarre – twist of fortune?

It was a wild ride regardless, even stripping away ulterior motives and scheming, and, for Nick Carr the most exciting three months of his life to date. Kelly *was* jealous, though not jealous enough to give up yacht rides on the Hudson or racing around in expensive cars to win back her ex, despite rumors to the contrary. And as for Sabina, she found in Nick an intriguing and interesting and very talented guy, but nothing that could ultimately override her base nature. Nick was convinced she was as head-over-heels for him as he was for her and in fairness that was actually true. Kissing lips may lie but the eyes seldom do. But no sooner did her heart begin to lower its defenses, then that little imp in her psyche ran by and threw the switches labeled "Relationship Self Destruct Sequence" and it all went to hell in a hand basket. In short order, Nick found himself getting needled, criticized, compared to any able-bodied man in Wyvern Falls, and the target of all sorts of wild accusations. "I saw the way you looked at that woman! Why don't you go screw her instead!" "You were talking with Sara M in the hallway? Meeting up with her tonight?" And classics like "You're such a loser, what kind of job will you ever have? Get real! My brother Antonio makes more than you and he's a waiter." This was followed by the increasingly cold looks, increasingly long spaces of time between phone calls and texting until they stopped altogether, with Nick feeling angry, frustrated, and hurt. Then the final bomb dropped; the *coup de grace*: "It's over, Nick. I'm seeing someone else." And the final cruel twist of the knife: "Can't we be friends?"

Then came the days of shock, depression, anger, and blinking disbelief that only someone who has gone from the highest highs his heart can aspire to can imagine; to having his world strafed, bulldozed, set fire to, and blown up until there was only smoldering, twisted wreckage where that heart used to be, his clothes burnt and smoking and hair standing up in screwy tufts with his future prospects looking like a bleak, featureless horizon painted in shades of oblivion.

Or so it seemed to his angst-addled teenage heart.

That summer was one of the darkest on record in the Nick Carr playbook. He bounced back – to some extent at least – the young don't stay down and beaten for long. A bunch of cliché-riddled songs got written or half-written with predictable titles like "Oh, woman" and "Dark Days," though the following summer the Carr song list would be refined by slight more original titles like "Too Late For Sorrow" and the Stones-ish "Thursday's Lady". Nothing that would have made more than a brief spark on an A&R reps radar, but still some indication of potential talent that may or may not be lurking in the wings. He had more than a few drunken nights and more than a few times praying to the porcelain God afterward. Sabina had hooked up with Carlo Vasquez, neighborhood bad boy, driver of hepped-up muscle cars, terrorizer of several under-muscled WF High students, and wearer of several tribal-looking tattoos. Even Senor Vasquez would be dropped temporarily (and two months later permanently when he married his Camaro to a telephone pole one August night at that wicked curve where 9B meets Route 251, eliminating himself and three friends from the gene pool for keeps). By then, Nick's Sabina-Torch-Bearing-Days would be over, eclipsed by a whole new strata and level of maturity of "College Girls Going Wild," courtesy of SUNY New Paltz, leading to more heartbreaks and more songs. Kelly DuBois had become a footnote that following year as well, dumping Steve Everston unceremoniously by the end of the summer before heading off to William Smith College and completely off Nick's radar.

Nick hadn't given a lot of thought to his old flame from Wyvern High. In fairness, he'd returned from college licking his wounds after a one-month fling with a dark-eyed beauty named Francine who was currently top of the charts on the Carr *object d'heartache* list—Francine of the petite figure and feathered haircut and, if he were to call it straight, of feathered brains as well.

Until tonight.

Tonight was Friday, June 24th, the first night of Wyvern Falls' Feast of Saint Anne's Carnival. For Nick Carr, it had been a good end to the work week, as he was off on Saturday, he'd gotten paid, he was looking to meet up with an old friend, Mike Gallagher, who was a bass player with whom he'd been trying to get a new band off the ground, and he was feeling relaxed, energized, and ready to cut loose for a little fun.

In short, he was in a good mood.

All that came crashing down at 9:00 p.m., when, standing in the middle of the blue and yellow music tent where the bands set up, he saw Sabina.

She was in a tight skirt to show off her dancer's legs, a tight tank top to show off her decidedly non-dancer's cleavage, Roman style sandals with leather ties that ran up to her knees, a short cut-leather jacket, and amber earrings winking out of her wild mane of jet black hair. It was possible she could freeze traffic on I-287 at rush hour and she looked like she knew it.

With uncanny accuracy, she looked casually over her shoulder as if she expected that Nick would be standing in his exact position a dozen feet away, gave him the ghost of a smile and, measuring him with a lingering glance, turned back and said something to the man next her. From the sharp profile and chiseled cheeks, he appeared to be Vince Voelker, Nick's old nemesis from high school. And if there was any half-flutter of hope when Nick set eyes on his ex, it was crushed underfoot when Vince casually put his arm around Sabina's shoulder and kept it there.

Nick felt his heart drop through the basement like an elevator with its cables cut. Trying to appear nonchalant, he took a sip of his beer, locked his jaw, and stared straight forward, looking very intensely at nothing. But, as anyone who has been in these situations can tell, maintaining non-interest for any length of time is virtually impossible and Nick Carr's eyes were not exempt. As surely as if pulled by a magnet, they wandered back to his ex and, just as if he'd walked up and tapped her on the shoulder, Sabina turned and looked back at him.

And smiled.

"You bitch!" was the first thing to enter his head, a thought chased away on rabbit's feet a second later, when Vince Voegel glanced over as well with his usual expression that ran somewhere between razor-edged fury and dumb indifference. Nick glanced down quickly at the dirt and flattened grass around his shoes and flushed with shame and anger.

And fear.

For a few moments he felt exposed, vulnerable, and uncomfortable with himself and he hated Vince for it. He was also keenly aware what a *schleppy* figure he cut with his old jean jacket, his *Who* T-shirt, and brown corduroy pants. When he'd changed after work, he thought this made him look kind of cool in a "screw-the-establishment" kind of way. Now he felt like a complete loser. He could thank Mister Voegel for that, too

Further contemplation of his failings were redirected as the emcee ambled out onto the stage, where a drum kit, some amplifiers, and a banged-up Peavey PA system had been set up earlier. It was Frank Percy of all people, looking surprisingly sober for such a late hour (by the Percy clock) with his old man's vest, threadbare swallow-tailed jacket one-size too small, and the kind of pointy shoes they used to call Puerto-Rican roach stompers. He had a hang-dog look and an unruly head of curly iron-gray hair that looked like it hadn't been combed in years.

Clutching the old Sure SM-75 mike with one fingerless gloved hand and lit cigarette - tonight's emcee was a class act – Frank looked up at the tent top with a screwed-up expression as he taxed his brain cells for his upcoming announcement. After a long pause, followed by a few heavy finger taps on the mike (which sounded like hammer blows and triggered a brief wail of feedback and winces) he slurred in his deep gravelly voice: "Gentleladies and men, scholars and rogues . . . and Rhodes scholars . . . it is with pleasure that I introduce to you our next performers on tonight's bill: the unbelievable and over-talented . . . uh . . . um . . . (mumbled words to the side, followed by a "huh?" as if talking with an invisible prompter, followed by a vague wave backwards that trailed cigarette smoke) . . . *ah*! . . . Paul Brammell and the Lonely Dancers! Give it up, folks, they've come a long way to play for you tonight!" Frank shuffled backwards like a hobo-version of Ed Sullivan, as the band – a trio – walked out on stage. As they went through the time-worn band ritual of hooking jacks through guitar straps, second-checking mikes, the drummer settling in behind his kit and making a quick last-minute cymbal adjustment, Nick realized he was standing with his jaw open.

For starters, they didn't *look* like any band he had ever seen before.

They looked kind of British in an old-school sort of way, but, not being much of a big Brit-rock fan (outside of the Who and the Jam), he wasn't really sure. Nick Carr's music tastes tended more towards Queens of the Stone Age, Nine Inch Nails, and Green Day. Compared to those bands, these guys looked like they'd just dropped in from another planet.

The lead singer was tall, thin, and wide-shouldered, with a tousled blond haircut, impossibly tight cuffed jeans, and a sleeveless white-and-red striped t-shirt. He also had white leather high-tops that laced up past the ankles, and Gibson Firebird – the original style with the reverse headstock

– gloss black with gold hardware and a broad white arrow angled up across the body reminiscent of the Who. Over the t-shirt was a motor-cross jacket with red-and-black leather and padded elbows. When he half turned to switch on his amp – a Park on a four-twelve cabinet – Nick could see a British Union Jack, sewed vertically, covering the back. He also had a chiseled face with sad eyes, sunken cheeks, and a nose that looked like it had been broken sometime in the past.

The bass player had a spiky mid-70s Keith Richards haircut thing going with a white V-neck sweater trimmed with navy and maroon, black leather pants, and white sneakers with green stripes. They looked like bowling shoes of a sort. His bass was a black Rickenbacker 4001, left-handed, and he had a real serious, almost hurt look to him.

The drummer was a mess of hair, a cut-off t-shirt with 'The Jam' and the red-and- blue Royal Air Force roundel stenciled on it, red pants that might have been sprayed on, white leather boots that laced up half-way to his knees, and a black biker jack with a Triumph patch sewn on either arm. He also wore black leather gloves with the fingers cut off and had on a set of mirrored aviator glasses even though it was night.

The lead singer gave the audience a once-over, cocked an eyebrow, and said in an English accent, "'ello everyone. We'd like to start with a number off our upcoming album – also called *Lonely Dancers* – that just came out. This one is called "*You're Dreaming*." He turned to his band, gave a curt nod, and started in with a killer riff in B, the Firebird's Humbucker pickups snarling through the hundred-watt Park amp. A measure later, the bass joined in, followed by an aggressive drum roll, before launching into a tight high-hat and snare back beat and they were off like a rocket.

Nick was galvanized.

He felt like he'd been plugged into a 240- volt socket. The hair stood up on his neck, goose bumps broke out on his forearms, and he felt like he was undergoing something akin to a religious experience. In a sense he was – Nick Carr had just been hardwired into the Holy Conduit of Rock, not the homogenized watered-down pap churned out by popular music factories or mechanically regurgitated for reality TV shows. This was the high-voltage, grab you by-the-balls, jump-in-the-car-and-floor-it-as-you-fishtail-out-of-the-driveway rock. Sabina was forgotten; Vince Voelger and his threatening looks were forgotten; his down-at-the-heels future and job and Wyvern Falls were forgotten. The tent and carnival were forgotten.

For a moment in time, he was in an entirely different place. Nick Carr forgot *himself.*

It was clear from the first opening notes of the set that the Lonely Dancers were a tight and professional band. The complex three-part harmonies were spot on. There was no hesitation in the riffs or notes and the bass and drums were as tight as two coats of paint.

The first song verse of *You're Dreaming* plowed through the singer's lament about laying his heart out on the line and getting played for a sucker by this woman – hardly Grade-A original material but the phrasing was clever, as was the twist in the chorus where he almost kisses her on the lips but walks out the door and keeps walking:

You got me down once with my face in the floor
Spinning down the hall and spinning out the door
And now you got me back in bed, you're seeing blue but I'm seeing red
You might think I'm coming b-b-but baby I'm leaving,
Yeah if that's what you're thinking then b-b-b-bay you're dreaming –

Paul Brammell had been burned once or twice and he was still pissed and he was letting the world know it. A sentiment Nick Carr could relate to, praise the God of Rock, amen.

The band blitzed through a forty-five-minute set like they were on fire. Nick couldn't quite place the sound – Brit Power Pop sounded too trite and didn't do justice to the punch and delivery of the lyrics and riffs. Or, more importantly, the humming power going on behind them: a balanced equation of anger, youthful cynicism, wit, wistfulness, and raw energy. The bitter irony of life wove through the songs.

Nick was mesmerized. His definition of cool had just been deconstructed and reassembled again.

The Lonely Dancers ripped through one song after another. Nick was having difficulty following which was which but he caught the title of another song that had his head bobbing and fingers tapping called *One-Way Ticket*. It sounded like a hit single if there ever was one.

And then it was over.

The band disappeared in the shuffle as the next band came on and set up their equipment. Nick found himself at the beer tent with Mike ordering him a refill and all he could say was "Killer Fucking Band," over and over again.

Mike, a tall-dark haired guy who favored outrageous jackets, white-and-black checked sneakers, and monosyllabic responses nodded quizzically and said, "Nnyarrr."

Nick glanced around but there was no sign of Sabrina or the illustrious Mister Voegel. No matter, he felt like he had a contact high from the previous 45 minutes, fired with that sense of euphoric invincibility that comes with any kind of music that connects straight to one's core being. He took a slug out of the plastic pint cup as he and Mike ambled back into the main Carnival area. The next band, also a power trio but led by a hot-looking female bass player with raven black hair and leather pants to match, was introduced as 75RPM. In any other circumstances, Nick would have stuck around, if only to ogle, but tonight, after watching the Lonely Dancers, he had a hunch the best policy was to step away.

He turned to Mike. "What did you think, was that band cool or what?"

"Cool?"

"Agreed." Nick looked at the booths on the midway with a half frown. Suddenly, the flashing lights and blaring racket of bells and whistles seemed even more irritating and obnoxious than usual. Mike's girlfriend, Mary Anne (aka M.A., aka M80), was working one of the food concession stands, so he'd have reason to hang around. "Shit. I think I just want to get the hell out of here and go for a spin." He took a couple healthy gulps of the beer but couldn't have felt soberer. After thinking a moment, he said, "Mike, sorry, man. I think I'm gonna cut and run. Ring you tomorrow?"

Mike shrugged. "No prob."

They tapped their plastic cups of beer together – the salute of champions – and Nick walked away, veering towards the row of Port-a-Johns near the parking area to give his bladder some relief. The route took him past a couple of log cabin outbuildings used as utility storage for the park and, as he passed by, he noticed absently that someone was leaning up against the wall in the shadows under the eave, smoking a cigarette. Out of habit, he gave a half nod as he walked past and mumbled "hey" as the figure flicked the butt away.

The next thing he knew, he was being spun around, then seeing stars as the back of his head slammed against the cabin wall, his arms pinned to his sides in a vise-like grip.

He found himself looking down at the flat-eyed features of his good buddy, Vince Voegel. He also realized, in a detached way, that his feet were dangling off the ground. He had a sneaking suspicion this wasn't a friendly courtesy call.

Vince was peering at his face as if studying an interesting scientific specimen. He reeked of tobacco smoke.

"Sabina is a little *upset*, buddy, and I don't like to see my lady upset. Got it?"

Nick struggled to clear his thoughts. *What in the blue fuck was this all about?* He also felt ice picks of fear in his gut. Victor Voegel was not a man to be trifled with. He had an aura of hair-trigger violence wafting off him. You could smell it under the tobacco. Nick had no illusions that if he didn't play his cards very, very carefully, this conversation would end badly for him.

"Upset . . .?" His voice had a quaver in it that he instantly hated himself for. He could see the cords of muscles standing out on Voegel's neck. The man had biceps made of iron.

"It's not a question. I read her like a book. I read you like a book. You stay the fuck away from my woman or you and I got a problem. I don't like *problems,"* he hissed. "We understand each other?" Without waiting for a response, he pulled Nick forward and slammed him again against the wall.

From what sounded like a mile away, a man's voice was saying "Hey!"

Then, "Hey, what's going on there?"

Vince let go and Nick felt his knees give way as he slid down on his haunches. Vince pointed one stubby finger at him, waved it side-to-side twice, then walked away, brushing past a dark-haired man walking up to them.

Nick felt humiliated – the warm hot feeling in his groin told him the worst – he'd pissed in his pants. The man, a youngish-looking guy with dark hair and intense green eyes, came up and leaned over, putting a hand on Nick's shoulder. "Hey, pal, you all right? That guy hurt you?"

Nick shook his head. Hot tears of shame were welling at the edges of his eyes. The only thing that felt seriously hurt was his pride. He felt like a complete and utter coward. He waved the hand away.

"I'm fine . . . fine. Just leave me alone."

The man stood there a minute longer, not saying a word. Surely he must have smelled the urine but he didn't say a word about that either. Finally, he shrugged and sauntered off in the direction Voegel had gone.

Nick made it to one of the stalls and cleaned up as well as he could, wadding toilet paper in his pants to help soak up the worst of it. Fortunately, his old Mustang had vinyl seats, so that wouldn't be a huge problem. The huge problem was his emotions – he was, in a maximum way, humiliated and upset.

In fairness, the peeing the pants was more physical than fear – getting slammed around with a bladder full of Budweiser was an accident in waiting – but he *had* been afraid. Terrified to be correct. Vince Voegel was not a man for melodramatic announcements, no "I'm going to kick the living shit out of you and then . . ." Or "I'm going to bust your ass into next week." But "You stay the fuck away from my woman or you and I got a problem." Direct and to the point. The rest of the implication was clear as a bell. And Nick Carr had no delusions about his outcome with Mister

Voegel: it would short, brutal, and very painful.

But it begged another question: what did Sabina do or say to set Vince off like a flash burn fuse? And why? And, on the heels of that: *probably anything, you dumb ass, and maybe just for the sheer hell of it. Sadistic bitch!* And then a tiny voice from the Peanut Gallery: *maybe because she still loves you.*

He smacked himself on the forehead with his fist. *Christ, if that was her definition of love, she was certifiably psychotic. Grade A Girlfriend material, Nick!*

That got a little chuckle, and made him feel a little better.

Still, he was angry. Voegel had caught him off guard, and scared him for a moment, two things that definitely did not sit well in the Nick Carr playbook. He found his car in the parking lot, pulled out an old Indian blanket from the back hatchback area, and spread it out on the driver's seat for some extra buffer.

The whole way home he played out a series of increasingly ridiculous scenarios in his head in which he outwitted and defeated Mister Voegel, including one where he delivered a swift kick to his balls followed by two vicious uppercuts that knocked him clean out. One variation had Sabina watching on – first in horror, then in admiration – as she saw Nick for the real man and hero he was and came running over to hug and kiss him. "Oh, Nick, he was such an asshole. I've always loved you, don't you know that? I was going out with Vince just to get your attention, to get back at you, to…oh, please, Nick, Nick –sob – come back!" And he pushed her away and stoically marched off into the darkness, his heart cold as stone…

During the whole drive home, he had completely forgotten about the band. Until 10:45 the next morning.

After that, he convinced God had a seriously deranged sense of humor.

-2-

SATURDAY MORNING was one of those idyllic late June ones that makes you forget just about everything. The sun got up bright and early, the birds chit-chatting a storm outside the bay window of Nick's bedroom, a slight breeze tickling the trees overhead, the sky cast in cerulean blue. And, despite the mixed events of the night before, Nick woke up in a decent mood.

For starters, he had the day off.

He pulled out a pair of Levi's (last night's 501s had gone directly into the washing machine, followed by the Indian blanket) and a fresh-air smelling T-shirt. His mom still insisted on drying clothes on the clothesline in the backyard when it was warm out. He practically bounced down the stairs to the kitchen.

His father was stewing over the sports section along with his coffee and a forgotten English muffin. He could hear his mother down in the basement doing more wash. No sign of his brother or sister. The kitchen was clean in a no-nonsense, ship-shape handy-man sort of way: restored wood cabinets, wide plank wood floor, semi-classy but not-too-expensive hardware. Valery Carr was a thorough if not overly imaginative home improvement type of guy – definitely *This Old House* over *Architectural Digest* material. Doors were plumb, cabinet's level, pots, pans, and cooking utensils in their proper place in the orderly universe of the Carr kitchen. The table was from an old farmhouse that his dad had restored, its nicked and battered surface waxed and oiled to a mellow sheen.

"Morning, Pops," Nick said as he pulled poured what was left from the coffee maker into a Yankees mug. It was an ongoing source of contention between the two of them. Usually the mugs only lasted a week or so. He suspected his dad would take them out to the rifle range and use them for target practice.

"How are the Mets doing?" This earned a slight drop of the paper and a hard-eyed look over the top. Val Carr weighed up whether his son was joking or needling him. Probably both. Rather than dignify that with an answer – they both knew damn well the Mets were having an exceptionally lousy season – he shot back, "Given any thought to what the hell you're going to do with your life yet? Still planning to live at home until you're forty?"

Nick felt his spirits dampen. His Dad always had slightly pissed-off look when he talked to him that said: *I know what I'm looking at. I'm looking at Failure. With a capital F.*

Nick brooded for a minute. Then he saluted with his mug and said icily, "Thanks. You're a real inspiration." Then carefully placing the mug on the table, he turned and walked out the back door.

"Hey – don't turn your ba—" He father began as the screen door slammed shut.

But Nick was gone.

Walking down Main Street to the lower district he paused along the way to side kick a metal public trash can and hiss "Fuck!" under his breath.

Why did his dad have to be such an unrelenting asshole all the time? And what the hell was up with Sabina and her Triple-A asshole boyfriend, Vince Voegel? Was the whole fucking god-damned world in a conspiracy to – what?

Which was when Nick Carr stopped cold in his tracks.

It took a good minute for his conscious mind to catch up to what his subconscious had flagged. On the north side of Main Street as it curved down towards toward the Metro North railroad station, just before it trailed off into a bunch of old buildings near the overpass ramp, was a cluster of turn-of-the-century old brick row buildings, mostly empty these days. One, however, had a pitted sign that read "Tony Accardo's Loan Office: Buy – Sell – Cash Loans – Highest Prices Paid!" i.e. one of those threadbare pawnbroker's young locals like Nick Carr never really paid much attention to. Two dusty display windows with old posters, half-battered goods from someone's garage sale, it was just an unremarkable backwater storefront in the village that he'd never really had cause to look at.

Until now.

Displayed in the window along with a bunch of old saxophones, cymbals, VCR, s and TV sets, computers, a telescope, a faded velvet Elvis painting, and a knock-off Hoffner bass was a black Gibson Firebird guitar, with worn gold hardware and a wide white arrow angled across the body. It had a fine coat of dust and a trace of cobwebs around the headstock.

Not possible.

Nick unlocked his legs and step up to the window. No question, it was a dead ringer for the exact same guitar he had seen Paul Brammell playing on stage last night. And no question that, unless someone was playing some elaborate practical joke, this particular guitar had been sitting here in the window for quite some time.

Only one way to find out.

A tiny overhead bell tinkled as he opened the battered door with re-enforcing bars on the glass and stepped into the gloomy interior. Having never actually set foot in a pawn shop before, Nick felt like he had crossed a threshold into a strange, interesting, and pretty much depressing universe. Inside the shop was a mix of old glass and oak display cases, 1970s wood paneling, and a dazzling array of junk and half junk, illuminated by a few rows of overhead fluorescent lights with a few tubes burnt out, the musty air of defeated dreams and weary desperation shuffled around by an ancient ceiling fan caked with dust. On one side were jewelry cases with old watches and old rings and older necklaces. The one opposite had stamps and coins and miscellaneous collectables. The case that faced you as you walked in had the marginally better-quality items: some antique looking sidearms and swords, the more expensive jewelry (and what might actually be a Rolex Watch or two), and some decent cameras including a few old Leica's. There were wall clocks, an old O-gauge train set, cymbals and beer signs, and what looked like some shrunken heads atop one of the old wall cases. A giant moose head hung over the door with a cigar stub some wit had stuffed in its mouth years back, a stack of various guitar amplifiers was piled against the wall, and a wooden tobacco store Indian stood near the door. There was a coconut head with sea-shell eyes from the 1920s, a pair of tap shoes and top hat from the 1930s, a full army uniform and helmet and spats from the 1940s, as well as dresses, muskets, statues, and a few

Civil War caps next to some Indian scalps.

A collection of the rare, bizarre, and tasteless.

Nick kind of liked it.

Behind the counter was a man in his 50s with an Elvis haircut (Presley, not Costello) and Elvis sideburns, some grey mixed in, and mustache. His face was squarer than the King's, with grey-blue eyes and a slightly rounded nose. He wore a black shirt and black jeans with a small beer gut covering the buckle. In front of him, a Ruger Blackhawk revolver – the classic Dirty Harry .44 Magnum – was disassembled over a soiled-looking cloth. He appeared to be fiddling around with the cylinder. Nick could smell Hoppe's Gun Lubricant and hear the weighted click as the cylinder was carefully spun.

"Morning," the man said without looking up. His voice was clear, deep, and musical; the voice of a favorite uncle who might surprise everyone when the karaoke got rolling at the wedding reception.

Nick made a brief circuit of the shop, taking it all in. A piece of black timber had a certificate verifying that it was from the U.S.S. Constitution.

Next to it was a clay pipe that apparently belonged to George Washington. Next to that was a jar of formaldehyde with an index finger floating suspended in it. The yellowed label said "Pancho Villa's Trigger Finger." Next to that was a bone-handled knife in a scarred and oiled leather sheath with some odd symbols on it. Of all the things inside the shop, it was the knife that really drew his attention, though he'd be hard pressed to articulate why.

Finally, Nick found himself standing before the elderly Elvis. "Are you Mister Accardo?"

Still without looking up, the man aimed his thumb at a framed 8x10 on the wall behind him. It held a black-and-white photograph of an Italian-looking man wearing an unfriendly expression. For no particular reason, Nick said:

"Ah. Will he be in today?"

"Nope."

"Will he be in Monday?"

"Nope."

"Will he be in this year?"

"Nope."

The thumb went up again, this time aimed at another picture on the wall. It was a framed reprint of a photo from the *Hudson Gazette*. It showed a white Cadillac, or what was left of it after it had been blown up. The wreckage was in a parking lot with a bunch of policemen standing around.

"Got it. Are *you* the owner then?"

Finally, the man looked up and flashed his lady killer smile. "Now you're talking, son. Tommy Falcon at your service." Nick found a calloused hand offered to him. He shook it: dry and firm. He noticed Mr. Falcon's eyes twinkled when he smiled. He thought, *I'll bet he could charm the pants right off a woman.*

"Now what can I do you for?"

Nick looked over at the knife. "Just out of curiosity, what's the story with that old knife hanging on the wall?"

It took Falcon a moment of looking around to figure out what he was talking about. "Ah . . . that old thing? Hmmm. Some old Haitian guy pawned it here awhile back. Left town and never picked it up. Ticket's expired so I guess it's mine now." He sauntered back, pulled it off the wall and brought it over to the counter. Nick noticed that he walked with a slight limp and had black cowboy boots.

Regular Johnny Cash, this guy.

The sheath had a leather clasp that held it in place. Falcon flicked it open and delicately laid the blade on the counter with both hands as if he'd been handling a valuable surgical instrument. The knife had a six-inch blade and the metal was pitted and discolored, although the edge looked razor sharp. Definitely a weapon that had seen action. Exactly what kind Nick didn't want to speculate about.

Nick bent over. "What are those symbols carved in the handle? Is that bone?"

Falcon peered closer. "Sure looks like it, chief. No idea what those chicken scratches mean. Hell, never seen anything like it " Then, after a pause, "George. Guy's name was George. Came and went like an autumn leaf. 'Bout as thin as one too. Huh."

The knife had him spellbound. But he hadn't come in here looking for pig stickers. He pulled himself upright.

"Yeah. Cool. Anyhow, I what I was really interested in was that guitar you had in the window."

Falcon carefully sheathed the knife and clipped it shut. "Which one would you be talking about?" He stepped out from around the counter, unclipping a ring of keys from his belt.

"The Firebird? The black guitar with the white arrow on it?"

"Firebird . . . Firebird . . ." Falcon mumbled as he went over to the right window display where the instruments were hung and unlocked a flush-mounted panel. A minute later the guitar was laid out on a towel atop the left display case and Falcon was dusting it off with a rag. "Shit on a stick . . . this old thing?"

Nick stepped up. The strings were rusted but the gold hardware looked in relatively good shape. He wasn't sure but it looked like a mid-70s MKVII model. This one had twin Humbuckers, a Bigsby bridge and whammy bar system and, other than some scratches, had been cared for in its time.

"How much?"

Falcon cut him off with a raised forefinger. "*Ahht.* There are certain rules and procedures to be followed, chief. First, before any numbers are discussed, one must examine the merchandise." He held his hands out, palms up. Nick picked up the guitar, surprised at how heavy it was. It felt like a battle axe in his arms. The neck was the longest he'd ever seen on a guitar. He looked it up and down carefully. Sure enough, it had the Gibson logo on the headstock and the slightly chipped gold Firebird emblem on the white pick guard.

"Can I . . .?" But Falcon was already rolling out a beat-up looking Fender Twin amp from behind the counter along with an old 70s-style coiled jack. After a bit of fiddling, it was plugged into an outlet, the jack plugged into the guitar, then the switches on the back of the amp flipped. The tubes were old and a moderately annoying hum filled the store. Nick sat down on the amp, pulled a pick out of his front pocket, and strummed a tentative G chord. It was horribly out of tune.

Even after a few minutes of adjustments, it was clear the only way this guitar would sound right was to give it a new set of strings and to reset the action, but at least the volume and tone controls were working and would roll smoothly once the pots were cleaned. The pick-up toggle switch was loose as well, but an easy fix.

Once that sucker was cranked up, old strings or not, the sound coming out of the Fender as Nick played a one-note lead was rich and powerful. Unlike most guitars, this Firebird was carved out of a single piece of wood and thrummed like a thoroughbred. For a novice player like Nick, it was immediately clear this wasn't just a guitar you played, this was a guitar you hung onto and hoped for the best. Which begged the million-dollar question: how was it that a valuable guitar like this one came to be hanging, neglected, in a pawnshop window? The going rate for a vintage Firebird was a cool couple grand easy. Unless Mister Falcon was asking an outrageous price for it.

Cripes, there's no way I'd be able to afford this.

A bittersweet thought: the guitar felt fabulous in his arms. The odd-shaped body was counterbalanced by the heavy neck and headstock. He closed his eyes and played out a few leads to one of his own songs, switched into the riff from *Back in the U.S.S.R.* then into a standard blues progression. Falcon had gone back to fixing the revolver on his counter top but looked up as Nick unplugged the guitar and brought it up.

"So, how much?" he asked.

"For that thing? Christ. Two hundred bucks."

Nick was in shock. He didn't say anything right away – he was calculating how much was in his savings account. Falcon must have taken his lack of response as an affront. He carefully took the guitar from Nick and flipped it over.

Now he saw what he'd missed – the guitar body had been cracked and shoddily repaired. Someone had done a botch job of stapling it and trying to fill it with wood putty. His heart sank.

"That's why," Falcon said. "But not a bad deal for the hardware alone." But the guitar had sounded *good*. Great actually. To his ears at least. Defective. It's practically junk. What did you expect?

Then: it looks identical.

And: *it really feels right.*

He decided to make a plunge: "Would you take a hundred fifty?"

Falcon mused over this. The Budweiser clock on the wall behind him ticked through a full minute. He shrugged.

"Yeah, what the hell. It's been sitting there too long as it is."

"You take plastic?"

"Son, this is a pawn shop, not a supermarket."

Nick went pulled out his wallet. Two twenties. Shit. He looked around. "Is there an ATM near here?"

Falcon pointed next to the tobacco store Indian. Squeezed in between it and a dusty Wurlitzer was, wonder of wonders, a cash machine. Falcon must have picked up his expression. "This is a pawn shop. But it's a *21st Century* pawn shop. Appearances to the contrary."

Nick winced at the surcharge he was probably going to pay but decided this was an emergency. He didn't have the patience to go home, get the car, drive to his own bank a couple miles away, and come all the way back again. But this would be an unexpected hit on his meager funds. If his father were here, he'd be blowing a piston. "A hundred fifty bucks on that piece of junk!? Jesus Christ, were you born stupid or did you get that way all by your lonesome?" to quote a classic Valery Carr-ism.

And that clinched it.

Falcon dug up a battered hard-shell case to put it in. Money changed hands. Then, as Falcon went to put the knife back, Nick asked on an impulse, "How much would you want for that?"

Falcon turned his head, eyebrow cocked. His twinkly blue eyes didn't seem as friendly as before.

"This isn't a toy, chief. It's the kind of knife that's built for business. *Got it?*"

Nick tried to think fast. "It'd be for my dad, he's into hunting and stuff." Then he added, "I never got him anything for Father's Day. He'd really like it."

Falcon didn't look like he was buying whatever Nick was selling.

"And who *is* your Dad, chief?"

"Valery Carr."

That got a response. The atmosphere relaxed instantly. "Hmmm, I know Val. We go back a ways."

Nick was surprised. He couldn't ever recall his dad mentioning Tommy Falcon's name or this pawn shop before. Without thinking he added,

"Really? How do you know my dad?"

Falcon chuckled. Merry eyes were back. "That'd be up to him to tell you, if he has a mind to." He put the knife back on the counter. "Just take it. It's not worth anything with all those crazy symbols on it. Gives me the willies anyhow."

Nick set the guitar case down and picked up the knife. The handle felt warm in his hand. Purposeful. He couldn't explain it but, like the guitar, it too felt, well, right.

He unclasped the case and slid it in next to the guitar and closed it. Just as he was about to leave he stopped and turned around, remembering why he came in in the first place.

"Mr. Falcon?"

"Yeah?"

"This guitar, do you know anything about it?"

He couldn't quite read the expression this time, but it looked careful.

"That guitar came in here thirty years ago, around the time I first starting working here. Big heavy guy brought it in here, but I can't remember his name. Didn't get much for it as I recall. Sorry, chief, that's about all I know."

Nick frowned. He was about to leave again when another approach occurred to him. "It's kind of weird, but this guitar kind of reminded me of one I saw this guy playing last night."

"No kidding?"

"No kidding. I think his name was Paul Brammell. Paul Brammell and the Lonely Dancers."

Falcon let out a low laugh, but he looked a little pale.

"If that's what they were called then someone is either pulling your leg or has a pretty sick sense of humor."

Nick pulled his chin back like he wasn't buying. "How's that?"

"Paul Brammell, *the* Paul Brammell I knew of at least, well, he's been dead for thirty years."

Now it was Nick's turn to be surprised. He felt the fine hairs at the nape of his neck prick up.

"Dead? *Thirty years?*"

"As a doornail. That was big news here in 1981. The whole band was killed when their van wiped out up on 9B near that wicked curve at 251. Long before your time, chief. He was driving and went through the windshield, so I heard. They had to peel what was left of him off the old oak tree they hit, the one on the Sutherland's property they used to call the Hanging Tree. Damn shame, too. They'd just released their first album. Real tragedy. They were coming down from Albany, I think. Stopped to do a show here before getting back to New York."

Nick rubbed his chin. Why would a band stop in Wyvern Falls for a set if they were already that far up on the circuit? The Feast of Saint Anne's Carnival was a popular local event, but nothing that ever drew much more than some local bands as far as he knew. A British rock band with an album? Not likely.

"Not for nothing, but why would they have been playing here? In Wyvern Falls?"

Falcon looked relieved, like he was on surer ground. "No big mystery there. Amelia Evans, the singer's girlfriend, lived here. Pretty little thing, that one."

Nick nodded thoughtfully and chewed his lip. "Yeah, I wish there was a way to find out . . ." The words trailed away with his thoughts. *Thirty years ago? What the hell was this all about? What if . . .*

". . . yourself."

He realized Falcon had been talking and shook his head.

"Sorry . . . what?"

"I said, 'Ask her yourself'."

"*What?*"

"I'm not a broken record, chief. She's still here. In Wyvern Falls. Works up at the Greek restaurant on Main. Hell, I just saw her yesterday. Must be pushing forty-five but still looking mighty fine if I don't say-" He was cut off as Nick threw a "Thanks!" at him and the bell over the door was tinkling.

"God-damn kids, Tommy muttered to the empty shop, his head shaking.

Outside, a slinky-looking guy with stringy hair and a soiled jean jacket was walking up the opposite side of the street when he saw the guitar being removed from the display window of Accardo's, which froze him in his tracks. The man, who went by the name of Larry Miller, or "Boots" as his friends called him, dressed like he was twenty even though he was pushing fifty, had John Deere bill cap and scuffed work boots. He lit up a Marlboro and pretended to have an animated discussion on his cell phone while he kept his eyes glued to the shop.

When Nick finally emerged and practically ran uphill on Main Street, Boots hit a speed dial key on his phone. Somewhere in Manhattan, a phone rang.

After three rings, a sharp, irritated voice came on, "What is it?"

"News flash, boss. You're not going to believe this one."

"Unlikely. Go ahead."

"That old guitar, Paul Brammell's old guitar?" Boots could barely contain the excitement in his voice. He relished the opportunity to finally have some *important* news. It'd been a slow month in the old home town.

The silence on the other end of the line felt impatient

When no response was forthcoming, Boots finally continued, the first pin pricking at his enthusiasm. "Well, some kid just bought it from Accardo's.

Looked awful excited about it too."

More silence. Then: "You called me about a kid buying a guitar?"

Miller felt the pin become a nail. "Not just any guitar, b-b-boss" He stammered "Paul . . ."

"Shut up."

Bucket of ice followed. Miller clapped his jaw closed. One did not mess with the man. Bootsie's first rule of survival. Or was it his second? His memory wasn't as good as it used to be. There was an extended silence this time. The digital clock on the phone measured three digital minutes. There was something else bothering Boots like a vague itch. Something about the kid. He kind of reminded him . . .

The voice cut off his thoughts: "All right. It's probably nothing. Just keep an eye on him. Don't call unless it's important. Got it?"

"Got it, boss." He felt his excitement coming back and added, "Ace as in Aces!": one of his catch phrases even though he had no idea what it meant.

But the line was already dead.

-3-

WHEN IT came to Greek restaurants, there was a limited range of options in Wyvern Falls – well, only one option actually – and that was Xeno's. Or officially: Xeno's Greek Restaurant, as it was proclaimed in pseudo-Greek capitals on the menu and in blue-and-white letters above the awning, along with an amateurish pen-and-ink sketch of the Acropolis, in case there were any lingering doubts. Opened in 1991, it was owned and run by the Zerba brothers and quickly established itself as one of those casual yet step-above-the-typical-step-above-the-typical-dinner type of places that thrived from the get-go. Tony Zerba, the elder of the two, was the brains and social front of the restaurant, as he had a natural charm and the obeisant charisma suited for the role. More often than not, he was the one handing out menus and seating the guests. His brother, Dimitri, aka "Pashamou," seemed to be permanently installed behind the open cook counter at the back and seemed to have decided from an early age that yelling in his deep baritone was the only way to communicate with the world. With his big hulking frame, bushy mustache, and bad comb-over, he resembled an angry giant Zero Mostel in a Pillsbury Dough Boy outfit. He also somehow combined churlishness and good-natured humor into one personality, which often led to some comical misunderstandings with the various employees. It was sometimes difficult to differentiate whether he was really angry or really happy.

Probably both.

Nick had been there on and off over the years but mostly for a Sunday brunch or late snack. He tried to recall if he'd ever seen a waitress approximating Amelia Evans' description and came up blank.

The owners had made a half-hearted stab at an upscale décor – a predictable white-and-blue Mediterranean theme with appropriate photos on the walls, tile floors, and white-washed tables and chairs with white plastic tablecloths. Along the length of the left wall, the top half was mural of, presumably, the Greek countryside, while the bottom half was a meandering stone wall affair with sea shells and narrow ponds and fountains in an almost successful attempt to simulate some sort of Grecian coastal grotto. In one corner, a young man was set up with a Korg keyboard, busy filling the air with kitschy renditions of favorite Top 40 hits of yester-year, ladled out at a soft volume that seemed to float the songs around the room.

Nick greeted the hostess and opted for the counter at the back. After muscling the guitar case in front of his feet, he ordered a gyro salad and a Snapple. Being a Saturday, the restaurant was about three-quarters full with the lunch crowd and the three waitresses and one waiter had their hands full. None of the waitresses fit the bill – they were all in their 20s and the one waiter looked like a vaguely annoyed Harvey Korman from the old Carol Burnett Show.

The woman behind the counter who took his order looked like she might be the Zerba brothers' mother, so it looked like he was, in Val Carr parlance, S.O.L. He wanted to ask the counter lady but he couldn't come up with a legitimate way to phrase it without sounding bizarre:

Hi, is there an Amelia Evans working here?

Perhaps, why do you ask?

Well, I just wanted to ask her a few questions about her dead boyfriend and his guitar . . . did you know he played a gig here at the Carnival last night? How cool is that?

That ought to go over well.

So instead he wound up working his way through his gyro salad. (He loved the crispy strips of spiced lamb and seared onions, but carefully laid the little grape leaf wraps aside.) From the kitchen came the bellowing voice of Dimitri announcing orders: "Souvlaki! Souvlaki! Souvlaki!" or "Hot food! Hot food! Hot food!" Apparently they were taught that it was necessary to repeat everything three times, loudly, in Greek Cooking School. At one point, there was a crash and the sound of breaking plates and the cook roared like a lion. A string of Greek curse words ensued. Nick wasn't sure, but he thought he saw something resembling a meatball flying in the air past the opening of the cook's counter and, a moment later, one of the waitresses came banging through the swinging doors in tears, apron knotted in a bunch.

He dragged out his lunch a little longer but finally decided he'd have to come back another time. When the older woman behind the counter finally drifted up (after racing into the kitchen to cuff Dimitri upside the head after the waitress incident), he asked for the check and added, in a tone he hoped sounded casual, "Oh, by the way, is Amelia working tonight?"

"Amelia? She doesn't work weekends anymore. Who wants to know?"

"Just an old friend."

That earned him a disapproving look up and down. "Excuse me for saying so, son, but you look a little young to be chasing around that woman's skirts." Seeing Nick's cheeks go red and the surprised look on his face, she recanted and added, "That wasn't a nice thing to say, was it? She'll be in again on Monday night. Or she might drop by in to pick up her check. I can give her a message if you like."

Nick tried to think quickly. He noticed her name tag said *Maria*. "Ah, well, she doesn't actually know me. Personally that is. This is about someone she knew a long time ago."

Maria's eyes narrowed. "You're not some missing son she never talked about or anything now, are you? If so, you can turn around and walk straight back out that door. That woman's had enough trouble in her life already."

Cripes, what kind of woman was this Amelia Evans? He thought. *I just came in here to ask a few simple questions . . .*

"No . . . oh no. Nothing like that." He realized he was chewing on his thumbnail. "It's not that important. I'll try and stop back during the week though. Thanks!" Another string of curses came from the kitchen, followed by the clanging of pans. There was a flare from the grill and a cloud of black smoke billowed out into the restaurant area. Maria turned to deal with this new disaster and Nick took the cue and, picking up his guitar, left.

Xeno's had a double set of doors to the front sidewalk on Main Street. Nick wasn't paying much attention – actually he was looking at his feet – as he exited out the second set of doors more quickly than normal.

The next set of events happened in rapid succession.

As he was pushing open the door with his guitar case, someone from the other side pulled it open simultaneously. With the resistance removed, he flew forward, losing his footing. The result was a flailing tumble of arms and legs as someone cried out. Nick found himself entangled with a woman in a sloppy tango that lasted three steps before the two of them landed on the sidewalk in an awkward embrace. The guitar case slammed to the ground and snapped open, half ejecting the Firebird. Shaking his head, Nick found himself staring inches away from a pretty elfin face with big brown eyes, heavy mascara, long straight brown hair pulled into a loose ponytail, and bangs. At first glance, he might have mistaken her for a high-schooler. Then he saw the slight pouches under the eyes, the fine crow's feet, and the first suggestions of lines settling around her mouth.

Nick Carr had just found Amelia Evans.

It was an awkward moment. In the Hollywood version of the scene, he would have thrown caution to the wind, circumstances be damned, and given her a resounding kiss on the lips right then and there. And, if the startled, amused expression on her face was any indication, she might not have minded. But then reality seeped its way into the frame. Nick realized he was lying tangled on a public sidewalk with a woman old enough to be his mother and a few gawkers had already appeared.

He gained his feet and found some semblance of the manners his parents had drilled into him from an early age. Bending over, he was able to extend a hand and help her up. She had on a pair of 501 jeans, leather sandals, and a low cut T-shirt. Although she didn't seem be to sporting too much in the cleavage department, she cut a fine figure and the overall effect was that of a hip, middle-aged woman looking after herself without bowing to the excesses of plastic surgery or living in utter denial of her years.

Plus, she had a winning smile.

She let out a rich, almost musical little laugh and, with an amused sigh, said, "Well! I've had men knock me on my ass before, but never quite like that, I'm afraid!"

Nick blushed again for the second time that day. Suddenly he was a little awkward kid again, one whose shoes were too big, hands too large, and who was too afraid to risk using his voice in case it cracked.

"Oh God, I'm sorry," he blurted out.

She dusted herself off, as if falling down with a stranger was an everyday occurrence. "It's quite alright. It was an accident. Are you okay?" She seemed more concerned about him than about herself and without hesitation brushed off his arms and the front of his shirt, apparently oblivious to the effect she was having.

"My apologies," he managed in a voice that sounded more normal. Then without thinking, he stuck his hand out. "Nick Carr." Just as readily, she clasped it and shook it, her grip firm and cool as she looked directly into his eyes.

Soothing, he thought, *this woman is soothing personified.*

"Amelia. I'm afraid I . . ." Her words trailed off as she looked down at the opened guitar case at their feet and the guitar half out of it. Her complexion went white as a sheet and, cupping a hand over her mouth, in a little voice said, "Oh, my."

Then, before Nick could respond, she fell straight into his arms in a dead faint.

It wasn't clear whether or not a damp towel really worked but Nick had seen it in a movie or on TV somewhere and it was all he could come up with on short notice. He didn't have any chapters in his playbook on "What to do next when a beautiful middle-aged woman passes out into your arms in front of a local restaurant in the middle of the afternoon," so he improvised. Somehow he manhandled her over to the one of the old fashioned benches the Village had installed some years back – no easy task with even a small woman like Amelia. A 105 pounds of dead weight is a 105 pounds of dead weight. Fortunately, it was only a matter of a dozen feet. Once he had her installed with some semblance of respectability, he ran in and was able to get one of the waitresses to rush him a white towel and glass of water.

He dabbed her forehead with the dampened towel until, after a minute, her eyelids fluttered and she came to with a start.

"Oh . . . my God, where am I?" she said, clutching Nick's arm for support.

"It's okay. You'll be fine." He said, not sure if either was really true.

He held up the cup.

"Here, uh, have some water."

That did seem to help. The color crept back into her cheeks and she made a couple of slow blinks. "I'm so sorry. It's just that…that guitar…" She looked around and saw it was back in its case, leaning against the bench. She held the cup in both hands in her lap, like a little girl. Nick had to admit, older woman or not, he hadn't minded that hand holding his arm.

Not one bit.

She's got to be pushing fifty, pal. Cool your jets.

Amelia glanced over at the case, quickly, then back. "Where on earth did you get . . . it?"

Nick debated coming straight out with it – why he was here, why he'd bought the guitar, the unbelievable coincidence of running into her like this – but even as the words organized themselves, they didn't seem right. In fact, the picture they suggested was beginning to look a little, well . . . *creepy*. But lying wasn't one of his natural talents either. So he decided to, as his old high school history teacher Mr. W. used to say, skate right up to the edge of a lie.

"I just bought it today actually. Saw it hanging in the window at this place, Tony Accardo's, way down on lower Main. He almost added: "And not only that. I'm pretty sure I saw your old dead boyfriend playing it onstage last night. How's that strike you for laughs and giggles?"

He had a hunch the last line wouldn't have flown too well. Amelia rolled her eyes. "At Fat Tony's? Pete . . . I mean this old guitar was hanging in the window at Fat Tony's, all this time and I never saw it?" She looked straight into his eyes again, as if he actually might now the answer. Another thought ran through his head: *Well, no, I've only been alive on this planet twenty years and your ex has been dead thirty according to the latest gossip, so I can't say with any certainty it's been there all this time, but maybe.*

The hand reached out and touched his shoulder. Amelia was a real toucher, it seemed. "You want to be careful at place like Fat Tony's. You're better off bartering with the Devil they say." She said it as if she was half joking, half not.

"Well, actually, this guy named Tommy runs it. Tommy Falcon?" The way she said, "Fat Tony's," like an old those-in-the-know reference, only reminded him of their age difference.

She laughed. "Tommy? In that case you're *definitely* better off dealing with the Devil." Then her expression grew sad and she looked off into the distance. For a split second, Nick was aware of the whole moment: the warm sun of a spectacular summer afternoon, the chirp and chitter of finches and sparrows arguing in the flowering pear tree nearby, the languid atmosphere of a river town in late June, sitting on a bench with a very pretty (and much older) woman, all this juxtaposed with the undercurrent of something darker, more bittersweet.

The reality of time, separation – the reality of loss.

She patted his hand and he snapped out of it. "Look, I really should be going. I need to pick up my paycheck and do some grocery shopping. It's been very nice meeting you." She stood up, found a smile for him, and turned towards the front door of the restaurant. Nick followed suit and stood up as well, reaching for the guitar case, sensing something slipping away. Suddenly, he heard his own mouth speaking as if its own accord:

"Amelia?"

She paused and half looked back.

"Look, this may sound completely out of line, but would you have any free time available this evening?"

She responded with an amused look he interpreted as patronizing.

He felt his spirits slide a few degrees.

"Nick, that's really sweet. But . . . you're a little *young* . . ."

He interrupted her with a wave of his hand, "Oh no, nothing like that. I didn't mean a date or anything. I mean . . . okay, this kind of weird . . . it's just that, well, Mister Falcon filled me in a little bit on the history of this particular guitar and . . . look, I know this is all really bizarre but I have a couple of questions I'd like to discuss with you. I understand this might be painful, but I think it's important. It's kind of hard to . . ."

"Okay."

"What?" He wasn't sure he'd heard correctly.

She must have seen or sensed some of the sincerity in his expression.

"I said, *okay*. After all these years . . . it's probably time to talk about it. You live in town?"

"Voelkner Avenue."

She opened her purse and, rummaging around, produced a Uniball pen and a dog-eared taxi company's business card, which she scribbled on.

"Why don't you swing by around seven."

And she was gone.

The front door of Xeno's eased shut after her and Nick was left standing vaguely confused at what had just happened. Assurances to the contrary, *had* he just made a date with a middle-aged woman? He wasn't sure. She'd written an address and apartment number on Locke Place, which he recalled was one of those semi-rundown areas with rows of clapboard buildings down near the river on the south side of town. The kind with balconies and sway-backed roofs. Then he remembered he needed to call Mike and their new drummer, Ramon, to confirm their band rehearsal for Sunday evening.

First, he had to get home a set up his new guitar. The guys were going to be amazed.

A lot more than he guessed, as it turned out.

At 7:05, Nick parked his old Mustang on River Road, half a block from the address on the business card. Partly because it was better lit, mainly because it was the closest parking spot he could find. Not that the Ford would be a prime target for carjackers or would-be thieves. Hell, they'd probably pay him to get it out of the neighborhood. Please – make room for something worth stealing.

He'd left a message on Mike's cell phone and spoken with Ramon briefly. They had a rehearsal set up for 6 P.M. on Sunday over at a place called the Fenmore Factory – really an old foundry that had been refitted as a self-storage facility that also leased some rooms as rehearsal spaces. Then he'd gone down to his dad's workshop in the basement and spent an hour cleaning up the Firebird, first removing the old strings, then using tarnish remover to rub out the hardware and Pledge to clean up the body and headstock. He took apart the volume, tone controls, and toggle switch, cleaned them, and reassembled them with the efficiency of a soldier field-stripping his main weapon. Last, he restrung the guitar, adjusted the tie rod in the neck, and set the action.

He also saw that the botched repair job on the body wasn't as bad as he thought. He decided he might be able to tap out the wood filler and do slightly better job himself, maybe even one good enough to look almost new.

After a sulking dinner with his parents and younger brother (his sister was on a sleepover at her girlfriend's house), he'd put on what he thought of as his "New York Rocker" look: a black T-Shirt, black jeans and black lace-up shoes. And a vest. He'd seen a picture of Tom Waits from the late 70s dressed similarly and tried to cop it occasionally.

Before leaving he'd paused outside his brother's bedroom door. Adam was loading some things into his backpack.

"Hey kid, I heard about Henry. Don't worry, he'll turn up. He probably had to get away from his old man for a bit."

Adam had nodded absently in return.

"Mom told me what happened at the Fortune Teller's tent last night. You might want to stay away from older ladies in the future . . ." Sensing the joke falling flat he'd added, "Going out to the carnival again tonight?"

"Maybe. We're going to hang out at Pete's first."

"Well, keep it clean, okay?"

"Okay."

He'd picked up the guitar and headed out.

The building Amelia lived in was in a row of semi-connected buildings with second floor porches, probably built around the turn of the last century, tired structures with rickety exterior staircases, white-washed clapboard, grey slate roofs, and diamond-paned windows. There were some brick buildings from the 1930s that looked like garages and warehouses, one or two giving the impression they were still being used. Her particular apartment was on the second floor and at least offered an angled view of the Hudson River, which in places downriver like Tarrytown would probably fetch a cool million. There were two weary looking Adirondack chairs and a yellow pine table on the porch, along with some fresh-looking hanging planters filled with pansies and African violets and a Ficas tree in a large clay pot. If nothing else, Amelia had something of a green thumb. He rang the buzzer and suddenly wondered if he should have brought flowers or something, but no, this wasn't really a date now, was it? A moment later, the curtains behind the door brushed back and there was the sound of several locks being opened.

Then he was looking at Amelia's flashing smile and his doubts evaporated.

"Hi. It's me," he said.

"It's you!" she shot back playfully. The door opened wide and she invited him in.

Her apartment wasn't large and the furniture looked like second-hand chic but it looked clean and well-cared-for. The couch was yellow pine with flower-patterned overstuffed cushions and pillows along with a coffee table and chairs. The walls were slatted white-washed paneling and a large framed lithograph of John Lennon hung on one wall. There was a galley kitchen off to the side and a closed door that presumably led to the bedroom. The apartment also had a white brick fireplace with a slab of oak for a mantelpiece with some lit candles on it, some framed pictures, and a large mirror. The wide pine planked floor had a mellow sheen and a thick piled throw rug in the middle. A fresh vase of violets was on the end table. There was a small pine book case with paperbacks and a small desk with a laptop computer and printer. A pair of sliding French doors led out to the porch. Next to the door was a sagging Ikea TV stand with a flat screen television and a DVD/VCR player. A stereo receiver was tucked in on top and, on either side, a pair of Advent speakers like old monoliths from the Golden Age of Analog. Overall, it had the look of a well-used but comfortable river cottage with a woman's touch.

"Come in," she said. The stereo was tuned quietly to a classic rock station. Tom Petty was telling him that even the losers get lucky sometimes.

"Make yourself comfortable," she said as she walked off into the kitchen. "Do you want something to drink? Iced tea? Juice? Beer?"

"Iced tea sounds good."

A few minutes later, she came in with a tray with a couple of tall glasses and a bowl of corn chips.

There was a slightly awkward moment while seating decisions were made. He wound up on the couch while she opted for the chair. The cushions were sprung and for a moment Nick thought the sofa would swallow him up, but, after some adjustments, he got himself situated. Amelia sat on the edge of her chair, knees together, at the same time looking both like a proper lady and girlish.

Nick took his glass and a tentative sip. It had the sharp taste of sun-brewed tea bags with fresh lemon and a hint of honey: home-made. What a concept.

The lack of conversation began to weigh in the air. From the speakers, the Screaming Trees quietly barreled through *Sweet Oblivion*. Mark Lanegan's raspy vocal sounded angry and pleading. Finally, there was an awkward tangling of words as both Nick and Amelia tried to start up some conversation at the same time.

"Look, I know this is—"

"Did you have any trouble find—"

She let out a little laugh. Nick suddenly understood; she was as nervous as he was.

He raised his glass. "Please. You go first."

"Well . . . you're here. So I guess that answers the question about finding the place. And now you want to ask me about a very painful time in my life. The most painful thing I ever experienced actually. They say time heals all wounds, but that's all a big, big lie. What a bunch of crap. Did you know that?"

Nick was wondering if he really should go through with this. If she should go through this. What the hell was he thinking? He set his glass down and was starting to rise, "Look, maybe this isn't such a great idea . . ." but the hand on his knee stopped him.

"Sit down," she said in a more assertive tone. "You literally walked into my life out of the blue, with Paul's guitar, and then asked me about what happened. Nobody's done that in thirty years. *Nobody*. You asked, and I'm going to answer. I *have* to answer. And you have to listen . . ."

Amelia took a deep breath, set her glass down on the coffee table, and began to talk.

"God, I was so young. Sixteen going on thirty. You think know everything at that age and adults don't know a damn thing at all. Everything you're experiencing–love, music, fashion, alienation, insecurity, disillusionment–that you're the only one who's really experiencing these things for the first time. *Nobody understands me*. Nobody *gets* me. Or my friends . . ."

"I really didn't have a lot of friends in high school, believe it or not. What a time. Garish eye shadow, hairspray and Spandex, stiletto-heeled boots and Duran Duran."

"Then came Paul."

"I didn't even really know about the Lonely Dancers until a party that year. My best friend, Robin – she was such a punker – she was always into the latest screwball bands out of New York or London. The Sex Pistols, The Clash, New York Dolls, James White and the Blacks, Pearl Harbor and the Explosions, The Dead Kennedys, some real wild stuff. Robin was a year older than me but she sometimes seemed *ten* years older. She was so street-wise and experienced. And *tough*. If some guy she didn't like got fresh with her, she'd crack him in the jaw. And she could do all sorts of things from fixing cars (her dad was a mechanic) to fixing guitars. Anyhow, we were having a party at one of the other girl's houses – I think her name was Sherrie…mousy girl, red hair and freckles – and suddenly Robin pulls out a bunch of albums she'd picked up in the city earlier and the one on top was a band called Lonely Dancers. New group out of the U.K. That was Robin – fearless. First to smoke, first to make out with a boy. First to go into the city and scour record stores in the East Village. It was a lot different back then. Back then, New York was wild and crazy and dangerous. Times Square was all massage parlors and peep shows. People got mugged and shot and killed. But in Robin went and out Robin came. Her hair dyed pink and moussed up, black eyeliner. But back to Sherrie's party. Someone put the album on the turntable, cued it up, and suddenly we're shaking and dancing and snapping our fingers to this really cool song. *You're Dreaming*. God, what a song."

Amelia absently hummed a few bars as Nick sat frozen, goosebumps up and down his arms. He could even hear the riff echoing in his head. "At some point I must have said 'who are these guys?' and Robin shoved the album sleeve in my face. It looked like some sort of Propaganda Art. Russian or something. And I said 'wow, these guys are *cool!*' and Robin said 'Glad you like; we're going to see them next Friday.' And she pulls out an envelope with tickets. 'What!?'

"Next Friday. SUNY Purchase, as in White Plains. They're opening for The English Beat. And you and I are so THERE!' and she probably hooted her Robin hoot and snapped her gum."

"We went. I don't remember much about the show, and I was hardly a music expert. But there was something about Paul. He wasn't overly handsome; he just looked different. Cool. And there was something sad about his eyes. Like a man who had gone to far places and seen hard and painful things but who was still searching for the good things he knew were still there. That doesn't make much sense, I know, but that's the best I can do. And he looked so different. Did I say that? English. With his cuffed jeans, leather bowling shoes, and spiky blond hair and his cheekbones . . . he really had great cheekbones!"

"I don't remember exactly how it happened, but I do know this, somehow Robin managed to get us backstage after the show – she was something, could talk the pants off a hustler that one – and suddenly there we were, a group of sixteen- and seventeen-year-old girls, backstage with the band! They were so charming. Those English accents and English quips. He was such a gentleman, Paul. Some, well okay, a *lot* of the musicians we met up with in those days were just nasty or full of themselves. But Paul wasn't like that. When we were introduced, he took my hand gracefully and bowed his head, like one of those knights in a movie, and looked at me with his sad eyes and said, "Paul" and then something like, "Pleased, I'm sure." Like I was the Queen of England or something. And he had a little smile that just lit up his face. Like it was all some private joke between you and him. My silly teenage heart flew out the window and just like that, I was in love."

With that, Amelia stifled a sob and hid her face in her hands.

"I'm sorry. I need to take a break. I think I need a drink. Can I get you anything? More iced tea?"

"Actually, that beer is sounding good right about now." She disappeared into the kitchen and reappeared a few minutes later. This time, the tray had a bottle of Corona with a wedge of lime plugged into the neck, what looked like a glass of cranberry juice and, to Nick's surprise, a pack of cigarettes (Newport's) and a lighter, along with a chipped ceramic ashtray.

"I hope you don't mind. I haven't had a cigarette in ages but I keep a pack around for emergency stress events. I think this qualifies."

Nick shook his head. "No worry. It's your . . . place." He almost said "your funeral" but caught himself in time.

She slit open the cellophane with a fingernail and a moment later was in the "two straight fingers holding lit cigarette" pose. She blew a few puffs up and sideways like a silver screen Hollywood actress. Nick wondered if there was a special finishing school women went to learn proper smoking techniques.

"Do you want one?"

"No, thanks, I don't smoke."

"Good for you." She held up her glass. "Cheers."

Nick clicked her glass with his beer and took a sip. The smell of tobacco quickly filled the room. Amelia got up to open the porch windows and turn on the ceiling fan. Then she sat down again, this time with her legs tucked up sideways, and took a long pull off her drink. "Vodka and cranberry." She said in response to Nick's raised eyebrow. "Another old standby."

She took another long pull on the cigarette, then ground it out in the ashtray, making a face. "Awful things." She ran a hand through her hair absent-mindedly and Nick was struck at the absurdity of the situation. Here he was in a middle-aged woman's apartment, a woman he had just met hours earlier, no less, whose dead boyfriend's guitar was in the trunk of his car, on a Saturday night. After seeing said dead boyfriend perform the previous night. After his ex-girlfriend's boyfriend . . . too complicated. "Just roll with it, Nick," he told himself. "Just fucking roll with it."

There was something else pressing on his mind as well. No getting around it, he found her very attractive. Sexually. Was he crazy? What would Mike say? Or any of his other friends? This was crazy.

And it was about to get a whole lot crazier.

-4-

DESPITE BEING twenty years old, Paul Brammell took a shine to young Amelia. "It was a different time," she explained. "Things weren't all whacked out and uptight the way they are in 21st century. Today, there'd be police investigations, community outrage, and national news over what in 1981 no one would bat an eye at."

Nothing apparently happened that night other than some late night drinking (and a little pot), a run to a local bar called Whities in downtown White Plains, and some madcap drunken antics up at the Valhalla reservoir. Paul got her phone number and, except for Robin making out with a roadie, everything stayed respectable.

Amelia skimmed over the details of how the relationship developed, except to say the Lonely Dancers were touring up and down the Eastern seaboard to promote the new album, focusing on New York and Boston and Philly and any surrounding college towns, and within a month she and Paul had become 'an item.'

It was all very exciting and glamorous, particularly for a girl who had spent her whole life in a small town on the Hudson. They quickly developed a routine for meeting up. Amelia was living at home but it was an unhappy situation. Her father had been killed in a motorcycle accident two years earlier and her older brother, Gary, had become reclusive and withdrawn. His career seemed to be focused on working at the local video store and skateboarding and getting stoned. And not necessarily in that order. Their small house on Vanderbilt Street still had an aura of tragedy about it and her mom had gone all religious in the course of the year before. Mr. Evans' portrait had joined a pantheon of Madonna's, Christ images, and statues of a dozen saints Amelia had never heard of on a table set up in the bay window. For Amelia, it was all a little weird and spooky and she missed her dad terribly. He'd been a foreman at the GM Plant in Tarrytown and the 1200cc Harley that'd he'd married to a telephone pole a month afterward had been his pride and joy – it'd taken him three years to restore it.

Curfew wasn't strictly enforced, but even so she had to be discreet. So Paul would call and, if her mom answered, he would say he was from the phone or gas or electric company. He'd say he'd like to schedule an appointment for nine. Or ten. And that would be Amelia's cue to run down the street to the pay phone on the corner at whatever time he indicated and he would call and set up the plan. If he was in the area, he would pick her up in town in the van the band rented. If not, she would hop the Metro North – usually to the city – and meet him. Somehow in her religiously-addled state, her mom never picked up on the fact it was the same English voice calling from the utility company, or that there were so many appointments made that were never kept.

It was a wild adventure. Especially the nights in the city. The Lonely Dancers were riding the wave of up-and-coming bands on the verge of breaking through on the New Wave scene. New York City was still in its fast and hedonistic days and there was no telling whom you might find yourself rubbing elbows with. One night she was standing at the bar at Max's Kansas City when Paul said, "I'd like you to meet my friend Davie…" and she found herself looking straight into the face of David Bowie, who had just come out of the bathroom with coke smeared all over his upper lip. One time, she found herself wedged between Lou Reed and Deborah Harry listening to a rant by Jane (aka Wayne) County. Later that night, she wound up in the men's room stall (it was beyond disgusting) at CBGB's doing coke with Iggy Pop. Another night, they were hanging out with David Johannson and Joey Ramone at the Mud Club.

It became a whirlwind: partying, late nights, the famous and the not-so-famous. One night, they rode the D train all the way up to the Bronx and on another, they lay on the beach at Coney Island drinking schnapps out of paper bags and smoking cigarettes on the boardwalk.

The world became a big party.

Naturally there was a down side. Paul had his groupies and there were more than few cat fights and bitchy screaming matches. Despite bringing Robin along when she could, their friendship cooled – a typical scenario when you get swept up in a relationship and things are moving at a lightning pace. Resentment begins to build, the 'Hey, you didn't invite me to that party' or 'you got to see the Clash and didn't call me!!!?' and so on. Within two months, they stopped talking altogether. Her grades at school suffered because she was missing so many classes. Her mom was withdrawing into her born-again world and it was all Amelia could do not to pack her bags and move out for good.

Then there was Paul's manager.

Amelia didn't like him at all but wouldn't go into details. Only that he was a creep and she didn't like the way she'd catch his eyes walking all over her breasts and ass when Paul's back was turned and she'd feel as dirty and violated as if he'd physically touched her. She tried to bring it up but Paul would shrug it off with "Aw, he's a right bloke, just ignore 'im" or something similar. After the third time he sounded irritated and after that she clammed up.

The Lonely Dancers were getting some air play and *You're Dreaming* actually made it to the Billboard Top 100. Granted, it was down around 86 but it got them on the map and their label, Polydor, wanted them in the studio in July to record their next album. They had already been cutting some demos of new material at Gramavision in SoHo during off hours and in and around their touring schedule, which was being pushed harder and harder.

They talked about Amelia moving out and joining them on the road but decided it would have to wait until after the recording started. There was no room in the VW van they were renting and, once they were in the studio, Paul would at least be staying in a motel for more than one night.

"But you were *sixteen*." Nick interjected.

Amelia laughed. "Nick, back then you could walk in pretty much any bar in New York City and get served without an I.D. Heck, there were girls younger than me hanging in the scene. As long as you acted older. That was the trick. God, we thought the world was ours. We'd just keep going up and up and up, rich and famous and in love. We even talked about where we'd retire – some remote island in Greece, where Paul said he would become a goat herder and I'd pick olives and bake him bread by the Mediterranean . . ."

Her eyes momentarily got a faraway look, then she shook her head sadly.

"And then it all ended."

A silence followed that hung in the room uncomfortably, unsure where it should go. Amelia didn't make a sound but Nick could see streams of tears running down her cheeks. That made it even sadder somehow.

"Would you rather not talk about this?" he ventured.

She shook her head in response and, still not saying anything, got up and went to the kitchen to make another drink. When she came back she had a fresh beer for Nick as well, along with a box of Kleenex. This time she sat next to him on the couch.

Her eyes were glassy with tears. "No . . . I really have to get this out . . ." After a moment, she regained some composure and picked up where she'd left off.

"It was the first night of the carnival – Feast of Saint Anne's. The night Paul was killed. The whole band was killed. That was the night my world ended."

"It's funny when you think about it, they weren't even supposed to be playing here that night. They had done a quick tour – Syracuse, then Ithaca – and were supposed to be playing Max's the following night. Paul said they were going straight to Manhattan – they had the graveyard slot available at Gramavision and wanted to get some tracks down – and that we should meet up in the city before the gig. Then he called from the road and said the recording slot had to be cancelled and Richard, their manager, had heard there was a cancellation at the Carnival Night's band tent. He'd suggested the boys swing by Wyvern Falls for an impromptu set and see their 'number one girl'." She smiled vaguely at the reference to herself.

"Paul said, 'It'll work out fine. Bit-o-fun for local birds (his term for my girlfriends) and I get to see my little dove a night early. Sound like a plan?'"

"Sounds like a plan, Stan," was my scripted response. One of the many routines we'd developed in the past three months.

"See you in a bit then. Oh, Amelia?"

"Yeah?"

"Love you, dove."

"And me you, Stu."

"He sounded so confident a sure of himself in the world. I was so excited to see him . . . and those were the last words I ever heard from his mouth."

"I was at the beer tent with a bunch of friends, giggling and smoking cigarettes, when we heard the sirens and saw the ambulance and police cars go racing through town. I was on Cloud 9. My whole town was going to see *my* Paul, and me with him, and I'd be *somebody* for a change. It wasn't really all as selfish and self-serving as that sounds. You have to understand, I was sixteen, had been miserable for the years leading up to this, and, for the past three months, I felt like Cinderella (a New-York-City punkified Cinderella, mind you). I felt like, like it was finally *my* time. I thought God was saying; 'I took your dad away, I turned your brother into a basket case and I turned your mom in a Christmas fruitcake who worships Velvet Jesus paintings, so here you are. A little bit of happiness. Take it. You deserve it."

"God can be so cruel . . ."

"We didn't understand what was happening at first. *Of course.* How could we? I remember looking at my watch thinking 'I wonder if he'll be here soon . . . if there's an accident I hope they don't get stuck behind it!'

They'd missed the sound check already but they didn't really need one by that point. That's how good they'd gotten. Then I remember Ellie's mom coming running up to us – her husband Gene was the town sheriff back then – and grabbing me by the shoulders, shaking me and saying,

"God, I'm so sorry, I'm so sorry! You need to come with me right now! I'll take you!" I was thinking, "What on earth does she mean? Is she on drugs?" while at the same time I got this terrible feeling, that feeling that your whole existence is unraveling and will keep unraveling until there's nothing but blackness."

"She took me to the police station. Someone got me a cup of coffee. One of the deputies came in. Actually it was Roy Hendricks – yes, our police chief, but he was a wet-behind-the-ears rookie back then – who came over, put his hand on my shoulder, and, looking at me with those sad grey eyes of his, said 'Amelia, I'm afraid I have some bad news I'm going to have to tell you. Really bad news. It's about your friend Paul. There's been an accident.' And I started screaming."

"I'll spare you the gory details. The van had been coming down Route 9B and went off the road on that wicked curve near 251. It's called 'Dead Man's Curve' for a reason. The van tumbled into the woods until it hit a tree. They said the brakes failed. The mechanic who looked it over later said the whole vehicle was pretty much in violation of every New York State inspection requirement he was aware of and it was a blue wonder something like that hadn't happened earlier. There was talk about investigating the rental company and the garage that issued the previous passing inspection but I don't think anything came of it. Probably because they also found trace amounts of alcohol and amphetamines in Paul's blood and he'd been driving. They wouldn't let me see the body – the police were adamant about it. Too much of a mess and I heard later that Paul had been nearly decapitated. Roy and another deputy, Terry Denunzio (he died of a heart attack a few years ago), were first on the scene and both lost their dinners, it was that bad."

"That was more or less it. I really didn't have any say-so. I was just a girlfriend and under-age at that. Back then, if you were under 18 you pretty much didn't exist. The record company paid for someone to claim the bodies, there was a small service at a church in the East Village, and his body was sent back to his family in England. A place called Kent. I didn't go to the service in the city and I don't think anyone really wanted to see me, or if they did no one reached out. Even Robin was withdrawn and avoided me. A few of my other friends put together a private ceremony with a candle-light vigil over at the Village cemetery by the old Presbyterian Church. Some of their mothers chipped in and put a small stone there in memoriam."

"Over. Poof. My whole future – or that wonderful fantasy I was living for three months – gone up in smoke. I went numb for a long time. But life went on . . . ." She blew her nose into a wad of Kleenex and her chest hitched up and down with sobs. "I'm sorry . . . it's really not much of a good story, is it?"

For a moment, Nick didn't say anything. He felt helpless, yet at the same time wished there was some way he *could* help. So he did the only thing he could think of, which was to put his arm around her shoulder. He felt her stiffen, then it was if the tension just leaked out of her body as she leaned into his clumsy embrace.

He wasn't exactly sure how much time passed but at least a couple songs came and went on the stereo. At some point, he realized he was stroking her hair and her head was on his shoulder. His t-shirt was damp with her tears. Aside from the music drifting out of the Advents (Benjamin Orr was singing *Drive* at this point), the apartment was quiet, like a still life: evening study of young man with older woman in river-side apartment. Then, he realized she was looking up at him, searching his eyes for some sort of confirmation or answer and he was aware of how close her face was to his, how long her eyelashes were – bedroom eyes someone might have called them – and that her lips were slightly parted. Without even thinking, he cupped the line of her jaw and kissed her.

Amelia kissed him back.

Tentatively at first.

It was the wildest sex Nick had ever had.

There had been an interlude on the couch of making out for what seemed like hours, the kind of interlude only experienced by two lovers trying to feel each other out for the first time. Nick had a little buzz going on and the voice in the corner of his head was yelling "This is crazy! What in the hell are you doing!? You're twenty years old! She's, Christ, what, forty-six? Have you gone insane!!!??" And the answer was "yes-maybe-dunno" but either way that voice was easy enough to ignore. It felt right at least. After a while, his curious hands inevitably found the more private parts of her anatomy, cupping a breast here, rubbing down her crotch there, all the while she had this incredibly sensuous way of kissing, light and forceful one moment, sometimes playful, sometimes aggressive so that at one point he thought, "I had no clue what kissing was until tonight. No clue at all."

On the fifth trip to the beltline, he slid his hand in and was rewarded with a gasp in his ear followed by a flick of her tongue and a nibble which drove him wild. She responded by a gentle squeeze to his groin. Not long after, by silent agreement, pants went flying across the room (followed shortly by a bra that landed across the TV set). He was amazed and surprised at how firm her body was.

The voice was getting smaller – "It's crazy, I'm telling you, she's forty-six. Call the guys with the butterfly nets, Nick Carr has gone completely insane" – but he flicked it aside for good as she stood up from the couch, flashed him a girlish smile, and clasped his hand firmly. The bedroom he was led into was small, almost filled by the queen-sized mattress on top of a box spring beneath a thick down comforter. Next to it a pine nightstand and a mismatched dresser ran along one wall. In the gloom, he could make out some pictures on the walls but there was little time to take in details. He found himself on his back with Amelia straddling him in leopard-print panties. Above him, her breasts stood at attention with puffy nipples that drove him even crazier. She grasped his hands, brought them up to them, head tilted back in ecstasy. In the moody moonlight coming through the window, she could have passed for a woman, well, 30 years younger. Easy. Then, without any warning, she sat up, pulled his erection out of his underwear and eased him in. She was quite tight. This time, he was the one gasping.

The first time, he lasted fifteen minutes. The second, half an hour.

The night passed in a semi-delirium. There were patches of sleep followed by intermittent sex. It was beyond anything he had ever experienced. He wasn't sure where she went to school, but the one he learned from (granted mostly from online video streaming on his home computer late at night, perhaps not the best source) didn't actually teach him most of what he was experiencing this night. This was sex on a whole other level, one he had never imagined.

Not that he had a long resume to refer to. His first actual sexual experience at fifteen had been a disaster. He had been drunk *and* sick and wound up faking an orgasm to save face, thank god for condoms. His last, the finely-feathered Francine, had been more of the magnitude of sex with a sack of potatoes compared to this. And as for Sabina, that relationship had never really progressed beyond making out and copping a little titty as they say. So Nick was getting a crash course in sex ed and as luck would have it, he was a quick study.

In the dim half-light of dawn, he found himself snuggled next to her, stroking her breast. "Good genes?" he inquired.

"No, Yoga. Lots of it," Amelia replied. Then she rolled out of bed, wrapping the bed sheet around her, and shuffled off into the living room. When she came back, she had the pack of Newport's and the ashtray with her. She opened the bedroom window, which overlooked a wall of trees. This time, when she offered him one, on a whim he took it.

"God, I'm really corrupting you tonight, aren't I?"

Nick laughed. "Well, I know it's a cliché, but, what the hell, you only live once." It wasn't as bad as he thought, probably because of the menthol. The two of them sat propped up in bed, smoking, the ashtray on the covers between them. A slight breeze played with the curtains. Amelia took a drag, blew it towards the ceiling and toyed with the edge of the comforter.

"Nick?"

"Yes?"

"It's been a long time for me. Too long. But you don't have to stay, you know."

He thought about that a moment. "Do you want me to leave?"

She sat looking off into the dark.

"No."

Both cigarettes were put out together.

Nick woke to bright sunlight pouring through the open window and what sounded like a convention of birds chattering in the trees outside. His mouth tasted like dead ashes, his bladder felt like it was about to burst, he had a pounding headache, and his groin was sore.

But he also felt like a million bucks.

He made a fist, shook it at the ceiling, and, grinning, said, "Rock and roll!"

Next to him, the bed was empty but a minute later Amelia came through the door in a terrycloth bathrobe with a small tray and two steaming cups of coffee.

"Rise and shine, sailor."

She couldn't hide her age in the morning light, to paraphrase another classic song, but that she didn't try made it a non-issue to Nick. Sure, there were dark smudges under her eyes but her cheeks had a flush and there was no mistake about her smile. Plus, he had a hunch he wasn't exactly looking in top form himself after the previous night.

"I need to use your bathroom first," he said.

"Of course. There's a spare toothbrush in the medicine cabinet."

When he came back, she was propped up on one elbow, gazing out the window, the sunlight bathing her face. Her eyes were half-closed. The bathrobe was slightly open, revealing a tantalizing peek at one breast. If he had been an artist, it would have made for an excellent portrait. In that moment, Nick was struck by an epiphany; the bittersweet grasp of how fleeting beauty, love, and life were at same time as they were so utterly, stupefyingly amazing. He felt a pang somewhere in the deep waters of his soul.

And a less metaphorical pang in his groin. Amelia half turned to him and smiled, breaking the spell. Or shifting it.

"You're not going to give this old girl a break, are you?"

"Nope."

He must have dozed off but snapped awake as she jumped on top of him. He shook his head groggily. Then he remembered.

"Shit! What time is it?"

"10 a.m. Give or take."

He tried to half-roll out of the bed. "Crap! I'm supposed to be at work."

"Work? It's *Sunday*."

"The hardware store – I have to work today. I should have…shit – I'm already late." He ran into the front room, trying to collect his clothes. A nearly impossible task – it looked as if they'd undressed in the middle of a tornado the previous night. One sock was swinging lazily from the ceiling fan. Another was on the curtain rod. The contents of his jeans had scattered when he'd tossed them across the room. As he was zipping them up, he realized Amelia was standing in the door to the bedroom, bathrobe half open.

"Nick?"

"Yes?"

"Do you remember what you said to me last night?"

He tried to re-run the snippets of conversation (pillow talk) that had gone on in between bouts of sex. *What . . . which conversation? Her favorite color? Her bra size? The deteriorating situation in Pakistan?*

He was coming up blank.

Watching the distress on his face, she smiled and shook her head. "About being a Rock Star."

The penny dropped. Ah. At one point, he told her about his band, his dreams. His song writing and what it meant. Without mentioning the Lonely Dancers.

"Yeah . . . what about it?"

"Did you mean it?" It came out as a straight challenge. "*Really* mean it, that is."

He wasn't sure where this was going. Pop quiz: life aspirations? She was looking at him with a very serious expression. His hands dropped to his sides and he looked back at her just as seriously.

"Yes. I did."

Crossing her arms, she appeared to turn this over. "Then if you're ready, let's get rolling. For starters, you're not going to work today."

"I'm not?"

She pushed away from the door jamb and disappeared into the bathroom. Her voice echoed around the tiles "No. You're not." When she reappeared, she had a pair of scissors, a towel, and a bottle of hydrogen peroxide.

"First, we're going to start with a haircut. Then a shower. Then you and I are going to take a little trip into the city."

"We are? For what?" Nick realized he was sounding like he'd eaten a couple of dumb pills for breakfast.

"Shopping. If you really want to be a Rock Star, then you have to dress like one. Starting today."

Nick just nodded, not entirely sure what in the hell he'd just gotten himself into.

-5-

ACROSS THE street in the brick archway of an old garage that had been closed for over ten years, Boots was having another cigarette. Boots was a Camel man. On the ground of the garbage-strewn entrance were two Camel butts from the night before. He noted the old Mustang was still parked down the street.

So the kid likes older nookie, he thought to himself, a greasy smile playing across his lips. *Who would have guessed?* That made him think of a few selections in his video porn collection, ones with clever titles like *Naughty Teen Students* and *My Best Friend's Mother* or the slyly imaginative *Young Dicks/Old Tits*. One calloused hand rubbed at his crotch. *I might just have a date tonight and take advantage of myself*, he thought.

First, he decided it was time for another call to Manhattan.

"Make it good."

Larry/Boots felt momentarily annoyed. Once, just once, he'd like tell that voice off, the way he did in his morning conversations with the mirror when he was shaving. To be the man he knew he was . . .

"I'm hanging up."

"Wait!" he said, his voice cracking with nervousness. "News update, Boss. The kid who bought Brammell's axe yesterday? I think he just spent last night banging Brammell's ex! *All* of last night."

There was a pause on the other end. Then: "Really? You're sure of that?" Boots could almost hear the purr in the voice, like a dangerous cat whose attention has been pricked.

"Sure as Sam," he replied. "He's been there all night."

"What a strange development. Perhaps it *is* time for a visit to the Falls. You're absolutely sure of this?"

Boots stepped back into the shadows as the door on the second-floor

213

landing opened. As he glanced up, his jaw dropped and the phone fell right out of his fingers and clattered on the asphalt, its screen shattering. "No way . . . Holy Fucking Shit!" he hissed. A tinny voice called from the ground "What!? What!?" then went dead as Larry's sprung work boot stepped on it. He was running halfway down the block before it occurred to him what had happened and even then he didn't stop. No fucking way he was going to stop. His eyes were wide and his nicotine-stained teeth were stretched in a grimace of fear.

He'd just seen a ghost.

An honest-to-god living ghost.

They took the 11:15 Metro North down to Grand Central. Amelia had whipped up some scrambled eggs and toasted up some frozen cinnamon-raisin bagels with honey and after a hot shower, Nick felt halfway human again. He had a giddy feeling in his stomach he hadn't felt in years.

The feeling of doing something completely crazy and spontaneous. Something that would unquestionably piss off his father.

"So what was CBGB's like?" They'd picked a pair of window seats and Nick was idly watching the Hudson go by as the train raced southward. On the opposite shore, the thickly-forested slopes were turning the deeper green of summer, broken up by the signature cliffs of reddish-brown rock that looked like lumbering old giants half-dozing in the sunlight.

"It was a complete dump. It smelled of beer and old vomit, every square inch of the place was covered in graffiti, band flyers, and posters and back then it was packed solid pretty much every night. The bathrooms in the basement were beyond disgusting and the layout was terrible – you had to squeeze past the stage to get to them. And then you had to be half drunk to actually *use* them. But according to Paul, the sound system was one of the best of any club in the city and it was a scene that made a lot of bands."

From down the car came the rich baritone of the conductor accompanied by the double click of his ticket puncher. The voice had a sing-song, almost Cajun drawl to it: "Tickets, tickets. Good to go, good to go. In this corner . . . good to go . . . tickets, tickets, please . . ."

When he came up to Nick and Amelia, the conductor, a ginger-haired middle-aged man with a thick nose and glasses – like so many Metro North conductors, he appeared gruff yet neatly buffed and polished – paused and raised an appraising eyebrow at Amelia. Then he saw her hand on Nick's thigh and gave Nick a quick wink before picking up his sing-song dialogue: "Well done, good to go . . . good to go . . ."

They made the rounds of the various vintage clothing stores, starting with What Goes Around Comes Around on Broadway, looping over to Andy's Chee Pees before threading their way down into the East Village.

Amelia was depressed to see that all the second-hand boutique stores along Broadway had all but vanished, especially Canal Jeans, and had been replaced by designer clothing stores like Armani, Banana Republic and Guess! Jeans. (My God, they turned New York into a New Jersey shopping mall!). They found a vintage red-and-black Motocross jacket with a Triumph patch on one shoulder for a couple of hundred at Ancy's. When Nick balked at the cost, Amelia whipped out a credit card and paid for it before he could protest.

He wasn't sure what to think or even what it might imply. Did this mean they were an item? Was this her way of getting her hooks into him?

What was she really thinking?

"This doesn't mean we're going steady." She said as she fussed with the collar, as if reading his mind. She'd insisted he wear the jacket out of the store. "You can pay me back when you get signed."

"Look, Amelia, I can't afford . . ."

She shushed him with a finger to his lips. "No cant's today. Cant's won't make your dreams come true. Can's will. Understood?" Then she brushed his lips with hers. He felt himself respond but the next moment she was pulling him out into the sunlight and down the street. He had to admit he felt different. The clothes make the man as they say.

Amelia was distraught when they got to the corner of Seventh and Second Avenue to discover Loves Saves the Day had been closed. "It was even featured in *Desperately Seeking Susan*!" which drew another blank look from Nick. At another thrift shop further down on St. Mark's, however, they managed to find a pair of skin-tight jeans, hi-top leather sneakers that looked like bowling shoes, a white T-shirt with a Union Jack on the front and a black one with The Jam logo on it and a British RAF roundel. Another stop on St Mark's got Nick's ear pierced and scored knee-high boots, a tight leather skirt, and a leopard-print blouse for Amelia. She came out looking like she dropped ten years in a minute. Nick bought himself a pair of Ray Ban knock-offs and a garish-looking boa scarf for Amelia.

They found a café called Versagé on the opposite corner from Love Saves The Day (although apparently Love hadn't) run by some pony-tailed Israeli dude who insisted on comping them drinks just for looking like the most colorful couple in the place.

They wound up at an outside table long Second Avenue having a late brunch of Eggs Benedict and Samosa's. Nick was feeling that, since the day before, his life was on a horse that had shot out of the barn and was showing no signs of slowing down. When he'd ducked in the bathroom at the back of the restaurant to take a leak, he didn't even recognize the guy in the mirror. It was as if this morning the old Nick Carr had been left in a box someplace and this New Guy – he wasn't really sure who he was yet – was running around with his wallet and car keys. This guy in the mirror had blond hair that was moussed up in a spiky ducktail haircut, the new clothes gave him the vague aura of a young punk rocker with a British slant, and the gaunt look from lack of sleep made him look edgy. Even a little haunted. All he lacked was a cigarette tucked behind one ear.

He thought he looked kind of cool.

Amelia was laughing. "Twenty, thirty years ago no one would have looked twice at us. Now we're a colorful couple!?"

Nick turned the word "couple" over in his mind a few times, back and forth. He wasn't sure if he liked it. But he wasn't sure he didn't, either. "Is that what we are now, a couple?" It came out sounding harsher than he intended.

The smile dropped off Amelia's face. She looked she'd been slapped.

"No. I didn't mean that at all."

"What did you mean then?" Nick couldn't believe what was coming out of his mouth. It had a cutting tone and a slightly British accent. He also couldn't believe how quickly the atmosphere between two people could turn to ice, as if someone had tossed a bucket of liquid nitrogen on it. Even more to the point; why was he being such an asshole?

There was a minute of silence, then a stricken look crossed her face and she dropped her napkin and stood up. "I'm sorry. This was all a stupid idea. I don't know what I was thinking. I think I should go." She moved to brush past him and head for the gate but, as she did, Nick surprised himself by reaching up and pulling her down into his lap in one snapping motion. Her shoulder jarred the table, spilling their drinks and her one booted foot kicked up, upsetting the table next to them. There was a startled cry as an elderly couple's lunch catapulted into the air and landed upside down (one crepe landed half on the man's head), but Nick wasn't paying attention. He had Amelia straddled across his knees, his other arm wrapped around her waist as if he'd pulled off a tango dip, and he looked into her surprised, upturned face. There was a tear at the corner of one eye.

"Jesus, Amelia, I didn't mean that!" he whispered. "It's just . . ."

"What did you mean then?" she replied, echoing his earlier question.

Then he very gently bent down and kissed her.

When he broke away, she blinked twice, then, grabbing his cheeks with both hands, kissed him hard on the lips. There was a commotion going on at the tables around them but it seemed to be coming from the end of a very long tunnel. For the space of a few moments, there was just his face, her face, and the few inches separating them in the entire universe.

And then they kissed again.

What in the hell!?

Then another sound broke into his awareness. It took a minute to categorize it: it was the sound of hands clapping. They broke apart to see the restaurant owner stepping over, clapping as hard as most of the patrons sitting at the sidewalk tables, along with a few people walking by (except for the elderly couple, who wore identically put-out expressions on their faces), and Nick and Amelia became acutely aware they were the center of attention. No small accomplishment in New York City even in the jaded 21st Century.

Nick looked up at the owner, then at the horrified couple across from them. The older man had finally gotten around to removing the crepe from his head. His wife was fussing over him with a bunch of napkins.

"Oh God, I'm so sorry!" He pulled Amelia into a somewhat respectable sitting position on his lap. She wrapped her arms around his shoulders.

The owner was shrugging like this was an everyday occurrence. "What? Don't be! That was beee . . . autiful!" He bowed to the elderly couple while waving the waiter over and promised to buy them dessert and a couple of drinks. "So charming! You two make a great couple! Be good to each other! Be very good to each other!"

-6-

MIKE AND Ramon both did double takes when Nick showed up at the rehearsal room at six o'clock that night. Mike actually said, "Dude, I think you have the wrong..." before catching himself.

"Christ." He looked Nick up and down. Then a standard Gallagherism: "*Nnyarrr*!"

"Not too shabby, eh?" Nick did a palms-up gesture, followed by a quick turn-around. "But wait until you see this." While Ramon was fidgeting and fiddling with his drum kit, he opened the guitar case and pulled out the Firebird and held it out to his bass player like it was a holy relic. "Check it out."

Mike strummed a few chords in that sloppy way only bass players not familiar with guitars can, then picked out a few simple leads.

"Sweet."

He flipped it back and forth a few times, looking it up and down, testing the weight and balance. Suddenly, the guitar was snatched out of his hands.

Nick flipped it upside down. Then back again. Then back over again.

The crack was gone.

He ran his hands over the back, not trusting what his eyes were telling him. The guitar was flawless. No sign of any cracks, damage, or repairs of any sort. The Firebird body was unmarked. He sat there frozen for a moment, icicles dancing up and down his spine.

"Dude, what's wrong?"

"Wrong . . . wrong?" Nick fixed a smile on his face. The effect was ghastly. There was a whole truckload of wrong going on here. But then a line from an old 70s movie he had seen weeks ago on TNT popped into his head and he amended it, faking the tick of a broken robot: "Wyvern Falls, where nothing can go wrong . . . go wrong . . . go wrong . . ."

Mike cracked up and Ramon, who had been sitting behind his kit like an expectant retriever waiting for the word "go!" did a test roll around the drums and finished off on his crash cymbals. Most drummers are like hyperactive kids, Nick decided. They can't sit still for more than a minute without using their hands or feet. Ramon Arturo had been an amazing find: he combined precision, love of alternative rock and energy with his Latino sense of rhythm.

He was also a very good-looking kid. Girls went crazy over him.

He flashed Nick a big grin; "Let us play, *amigos*."

Nick warily plugged the Thunderbird into the MKII Marshall Head (via his effects pedals which included a Morley distortion box and a digital delay) and let a few notes rip. The sound coming out of the 412 cabinet was a snarling roar.

Did the guitar repair itself somehow?

It didn't make any sense . . . but it was . . .

He shrugged and kept playing.

They went through the first half of the set list before Nick decided something wasn't working and called for a break. The songs were sounding flat, lifeless. Everyone was playing their parts, everything sounded fine, but it was like a vodka tonic made with Grey Goose and flat tonic water.

No fizz.

Nick took up a seat on the metal stool next to his amp, legs crossed, arms crossed, tapping his fingers on the guitar. Mike was standing by his own amp – A Fender Bassman – fiddling with his Rickenbacker 4001, while Ramon made fiddling adjustments to his kit – tuning the snare, tweaking the high hat, testing the foot pedal.

After a minute, Nick stood, stepped up to the microphone, and play a few notes which quickly became a riff. He worked it back and forth a few times before Ramon jumped in with a tight little back beat on the high hat and snare. Mike shrugged and laid in a simple driving bass line. Without thinking, Nick started ad-libbing a vocal line: "We've got a one-way ticket tonight . . . Rock and Roll, Lock and Load . . ."

They ran it through a few times, the second time Nick adding in a chorus. Mike caught the buzz and suggested a half-time sequence as a bridge that built up into a lead. Nick felt like the guitar was alive in his hand. The lead played itself. In another twenty minutes, they had written another five similar songs. Rough, but more or less there.

They stopped playing for a few minutes, looking at each other in mutual amazement. It had been that simple. Mike looked around the rehearsal room, nodding. "Wow. *Trés* cool. Okay, Nick, what gives?" Nick struggled for words. He wasn't convinced there was any way to say this without sounding utterly loony tunes. Instead he looked up, his face paling.

"Mike, Friday night, what was your take on the band we saw, you know, the British one – Paul Brammell and The Lonely Dancers?"

Mike looked at him strange. "Who?"

"The British band. The Lonely Dancers. The one I said was totally amazing. Right before 75RPM went on."

Mike said nothing for a moment as he tried to decide if Nick was pulling his leg or not. Finally, he said. "Dude, the band before 75RPM was Bone Cancer, Chaz's punk band out of Nyack. And they sucked. I thought you must be high or something . . . Nick, man, you okay?"

Nick wasn't actually feeling okay. Actually, he was feeling quite a few neighborhoods away from okay. He'd be willing to swear on a warehouse of Bibles that the band he had seen on stage was the Lonely Dancers. Hell, he had never even heard of them before Friday night.

Had he?

No. He had not.

And there was no way, drunk, high, or otherwise, that he would have mistaken Bone Cancer for them. Mike was right – Chaz's band sucked. They were a bad imitation of a bad imitation of Queens of the Stone Age.

What in the hell was going on?

Should he tell Amelia? Somehow that didn't feel right either. *Who then? Tommy? Tommy…no.* There was one other person he could ask. He just had to find him.

Frank Percy.

Just then, there was a knock at the door of the rehearsal studio. Mike set down his bass and opened it. Amelia was standing there in her high boots, tight jeans, a wide-collared black blouse and sunglasses high up on her hair, which had been teased out in a classic Chryssie Hynd cut. She had cool mauve lipstick which matched her nails and just a trace of eye shadow. For a moment, no one said anything. Then Ramon let out a low whistle. Amelia snapped her gum and stepped into the room, pulling a letter-sized flyer out of her purse.

"You boys interested in actually getting out there and playing a gig?" Nick looked around. Mike gave him a "what the hell, why not?" look, Ramon was nodding, his eyes glued to Amelia. Nick turned to her as nonchalantly as he could manage and said, "Sure."

Amelia flashed him a smile and handed him the flyer. "That's good to hear, because you're playing tomorrow night."

Nick looked it over. It was a simple job breaking out Monday night's Highlights for the Carnival: raffles, an added ride for kids only, a special Portuguese cook-out at one of the tents, and the schedule of the four bands playing that night. Second on the list was their band, The Unexpected.

"How the hell did you . . .?"

She smiled. "I still know people. Actually, Tommy Falcon set it up.

Apparently, he thinks well of you." She turned to leave, then gave him the classic over-the-shoulder look back. "Call me later if you want to stop by."

She gave a quick wink and was gone.

Nick looked over at Mike, who was mouthing the word "hot" as if it was too hot to say aloud. There was a rare moment where Ramon was at a loss for words, then he got back on track. "Smokin'!" Twirling one drumstick absentmindedly, he turned to Mike. "Did you see that shit? That was four alarm, baby! Four alarm!" Then it dawned on him and he looked at Nick, eyes going wide. "You? Her? No shit! You're the man! You devil! That was one smoking senorita!"

Nick let out a sheepish grin. "Yeah." he sighed, "she is that."

He looked at the flyer. Their first gig. No joke. Then it hit him.

"Okay, boys, we have some serious rehearsing to do."

Two hours later, he sat on the hood his Mustang in the parking lot, smoking a Newport out of the pack he'd picked up earlier at the local 7-11. Amelia was filling his thoughts and heart (and, yes, groin) with a dull ache. He felt like a junkie who'd just gotten his first taste of smack after years of staying clean. Ramon hadn't been exaggerating: she'd looked like she'd stepped right out of a magazine. The kind printed on glossy stock with slick photography, slick typography, and the kind of models that make you want to drop everything and move to London or Florence or Sweden or wherever the hell it is that the models they find are created.

He also had that uncanny feeling that his life had jumped the tracks and this new one was a runaway toboggan on an icy slope, one where any little bump might shoot it off on another trajectory, or tumbling end over end, like...

a body...
through the windshield...
hitting a tree.

Nick shook his head and tossed the cigarette away on the gravel. Then he jumped back into the car and took off back towards town.

It took all of forty-five minutes to find Frank Percy.

That included a stop at Wyvern Falls liquor (now open on Sundays!) to pick up a pint of bourbon using a fake I.D.

Frank was over at one of his usual haunts, this one being on the bench near the fountain at Hamilton Park, one leg bent, pork-pie hat pushed down his nose. He was waving an unlit Pall Mall in one hand, half mumbling/half singing a Barry Manilow song, of all things, a can of Colt 45 nestled in his lap. He looked like he was wearing the same clothes he was when Nick last saw him two days previously. As Nick came up and sat on the other end of the bench, Frank switched into a nonsensical rant:

"You know the horseman rides, come September . . . stay off the moors, Johnny . . . and stay off the whores. What the hell, no one gives a damn anyway . . . I won't get any bolder now that Hell's Angels wanna wear my lead shoes . . ."

"Frank?"

"God-damn Jesus Christ Copa banana…"

"Frank," Nick said a little louder.

"I used to be a one-legged lion tamer . . . did I tell you that?"

"Frank!" Nick said, nudging his foot.

The slouch hat got pushed up. Frank squinted at him with one eye closed, like a Japanese gangster. "Who's calling?"

Nick held out the bag of bourbon. "Jim Beam."

"Then I'm listening."

A hand groped out for the bag but Nick pulled it back just out of reach.

"Got a question for you, Mister Percy."

"Mercy, mercy! Go ahead, I'm on the line."

"Friday night. The Carnival. You introduced the bands. The third band was 75RPM. Who was the band before them? It's very important Frank, what. . . . was . . . the . . . band?"

"Christ almighty on a stick. Which band you mean?" He gave a half-hearted swing at the brown bag, "Mistah Beam can tell me . . ."

"Frank, what was the band!?"

"It's hard to hear the music of life when you're just a lonely dancer . . . Band? I don't remember any band…but a Band of Brothers, brother."

Nick was getting frustrated. Finally, he just dropped the bag in Frank's lap. He was about to stand up when suddenly Frank grabbed him by the collar of his jacket and pulled him in close. He smelled like discount booze.

"It's payback time, Dicky Dicky. Peter Paul Pumpkin Eater sez so . . ...off the moors, sonny . . .'cos Brammell the Camel's got a two-way ticket tonight . . . Hell sells and love bites!" Then his eyes seemed to go wide.

"Damn! She's sweet on you, ain't she? But he's coming back for more!" Then he let go of Nick and, unscrewing the cap, took a healthy swing of Kentucky bourbon and launched into a garbled version of Sinatra's *Fly Me To The Moon*.

Nick backed away, shaking out his jacket. He didn't know what to think but one thing was certain, this whole thing was getting weird. Really weird.

Ten minutes later, he was down on Locke Place knocking at her door. After a minute, the curtain was pulled back and, after a quick glance, the sound of locks being pulled and he was face to face with Amelia. She looked at him intensely and pulled him inside by the collar of his jacket, locking the door behind him. Then all he knew of was her lips all over his, questing, probing biting.

He couldn't get her blouse unbuttoned fast enough, while her hands had his pants down in twenty seconds.

Her bra shot across the room and landed in a flower pot. A moment later, she took him in her mouth.

This time they didn't make it past the front room.

Typically, Valery Carr was out of the house by 7:40 in the morning, which gave him enough time to swing by the Portuguese bakery in town to pick up coffee and a roll and get to the office by 8:00. When Nick swung by the house at 9:30 on Monday morning, however, his dad was sitting at the kitchen table, waiting for him.

At any other time, it would have appeared as just another typical weekday morning in the Carr household, right down to Val Carr sitting at the head of the restored farmer's table with the morning paper, mug of coffee at the ready, except for two things:

1) The paper was neatly folded on the table and not in his father's hands.

2) His father was just sitting there, arms crossed, his face expressionless except for the deep crease in his brow.

Neither sign was good. Together, they were very bad news.

He didn't even do a double take at Nick's makeover as his son came in, hurried through pouring out the last cup in the Braun coffee maker, and tried to make a hasty exit. He froze in the doorway to the front hall as his dad spoke up, not turning around, just sitting there, arms crossed, looking straight ahead.

"Frank Garrety said you didn't show up to work yesterday," he said evenly.

Nick felt as though ice was seeping through his veins.

"I, uh, something came up, I, uh . . ."

"Sit down." It wasn't a request.

Nick felt panic rising in his throat. Then, oddly, something else on the tail of it. The smell of leather? Metal? Blood? With it, a calm settled over him like a cloak and he stepped quietly over and took a seat at the table opposite his father.

The line between Val Carr's eyebrows grew deeper as he took a better look but gave no other acknowledgement to the blond-haired punk standing in for his son. Nick took a deliberate gulp of his coffee, set the mug down, and folding his hands together leaned forward and looked his dad back directly in the eye.

The wall clock ticked off a full minute and neither spoke nor flinched.

Finally, his dad rubbed his jaw with one hand, a standard Val Carr pre-talk maneuver. His head shook slowly.

"Son, what in the hell are you doing!?"

"What do you mean, 'what in the hell am I doing?'" He was surprised at the challenge in his own voice.

Nick expected his father's fist to hit the table – another standard Val Carr maneuver – but instead his dad looked up at the ceiling with a "see what I have to deal with?" to the heavens. His head was still shaking. He looked down again at Nick, the muscles in his jaw clenched.

"Don't crack wise with me, son."

"Or what?" Nick shot back. "You'll beat the crap out of me? The all-purpose solution Valerie Carr uses for all life's problems? Beat it to a pulp?"

Nick couldn't believe his own ears.

Who was this? Testosterone Nick?

"That's a great fucking . . ."

"Enough!" His dad roared. He held his hands out like he was about to crush the air between them, but instead set them carefully on the table. "I bent a limb to get you that job with Frank. Right now you're going to call him up and apologize and pray like hell he's in a forgiving mood, because by God..."

"*Bollocks!*" Nick interjected.

"*What!?*" His father was incredulous.

"Goddammit to hell, son, what has gotten into you? You drop out of school, you live in this fantasy land of thinking you're a rock star, now I hear you're slumming with a waitress who's old enough to . . ."

This time he wasn't cut off by words, he was cut off by a Yankees mug of coffee sailing through the air, just narrowly missing his head.

It ricocheted off the cupboard behind him and shattered on the floor.

To his credit, Val stayed where he was, partly because Nick hadn't moved either but mainly because of the look he saw in his son's eye. It was a flat, murderous look. The kind that says the next wrong word is going see blood spilt. He'd seen that look plenty of times in the army before a serious fight broke out. It was a look he'd worn himself on more than one occasion.

On plenty of occasions actually.

But never on his own son before.

Nick stood up, easing his chair back, still wearing that eerily expressionless face. For a moment, Val wondered if he was going to leap across the table at him. He also noticed something else – the ten-inch knife in its sheath at Nick's hip. It seemed that this Monday morning was an occasion for all sorts of firsts.

For the first time in his life, Val felt fear towards his own son.

Nick did call Frank Garrety, however. Not because his dad insisted on it, but because Garrety deserved better and Nick knew it. The truth was, he liked Garrety. He liked his easy-going banter, he liked the way he treated employees and customers fairly, and he liked the way he always managed to find Nick the more interesting jobs to do, like designing the window displays or assembling the floor models. Not because of Nick's dad, but because he knew Nick was a quick study, stuck in a job that was well beneath him.

That didn't stop him from assigning Nick toilet-cleaning duty on occasion just to keep him humble.

The afternoon rehearsal was a disaster.

The sound was off, the band was out of synch, the songs were a mess. The PA kept feeding back and at one point Nick was sorely tempted to pull a Pete Townshend and just ram his guitar through his speaker cabinet. However, recognizing that was an inadvisable strategy *before* the gig, he restrained himself and called an end to the rehearsal.

The sound check at 6:00 PM went marginally better and Nick's confidence went back up a few degrees. Even so, he was edgy as a caged cat and after pacing backstage for ten minutes told Mike and Ramon he'd be back in a bit and went for a long walk out past the carnival grounds to the low cliffs at the south end of Raadsel Point.

There was a good spot near the point that Nick liked to think of as his "thinking rock" – a rough boulder near the top of the cliff that offered a panoramic view of the Hudson River partially hidden by a copse of cedar trees. A few yards away, chunks of old masonry lay jumbled in the undergrowth, remains of a Revolutionary War fort that was once sited there.

He lit up a cigarette and sat there a while, blowing smoke up at the darkening sky, arms crossing his knees. It was another brilliant sunset, the kind only the peculiar atmospherics of the Hudson Valley can offer; the deepening cliffs of the west shore, the rich salmon and amber hues and deep Cerulean blues, as if this was a spot where Nature could loosen her skirts and show off a bit.

It was also a spot Nick had found by accident ten years ago after running out of the house. That had been back in the day, when Val Carr had been a drinking man and had decided his son needed a little lesson in discipline.

His mom had packed up Nick and his sister and little brother and they'd left for a month following that episode. They went to live with his grandparents over in Port Chester. They only came back after the bottles went down the sink drain.

For good.

It felt like his thoughts were in a whirlwind. When his Mother had told him earlier what had happened to his brother's friend Henry and the horrible stuff that had been going on up the road at Castle Krell he had simply shrugged. It might have been a vague news announcement from a remote country.

"What the hell's wrong with you!?" his mother had asked in that tone that was both concerned and angry at the same time.

He didn't know. All he had room for was Amelia . . . and music . . . and those strange memories that kept tugging at his thoughts as if he was really someone else . . .

-7-

THE FIRST BAND wasn't a hard act to follow – a barely competent Green Day cover band whose singer was off key more than he was on. Twenty minutes before 9:00, Nick found himself over at the beer tent.

"Hey, rocker dude."

He turned to see Sabrina wedged in next to him, giving him the once over. A few times. With a blazing look he hadn't seen since…since she first hooked her claws into him back in high school. It took him a moment to remember he was the same Nick Carr he had been then, or even three nights ago. The whole debacle of Friday night already seemed years in the past.

Emotionally, he also felt equally detached. Even a few nights ago, he would have gone moon-eyed just talking with Sabrina again but at the moment he felt as cool as a box of iced cucumbers.

Still, she did look mighty fine. *Mighty Fine*, as Mike would say.

"Hi, Sabrina. You seemed to have misplaced your Neanderthal."

She rolled her eyes. "Vince? He's over at the poker tent blowing his paycheck. It's not that serious. He's good for a little excitement but a little short for conversation."

"Really? I'm pretty sure he thinks your personal property."

She touched his elbow lightly, ignoring the jibe.

"What gives with the new look?"

"Guess I was due for a change. The old look was looking old."

She was giving him one of her better sideways flirt looks. Not her best, but a pretty good one.

But Nick was feeling coated in Teflon.

"See your band made it on the bill tonight – looking forward to seeing what you got. Any songs in your set about me?"

Nick felt a hint of a cold knot in his gut. Christ, as of last week pretty

227

much every song in the set was about her. But that wasn't really the case anymore, was it? Two nights ago, he would have folded for this moment. Now he felt as if he was seeing her for what she was: a bitchy, oversexed high-school girl accustomed to getting her way.

He shook his head and lied. Half lied, really. "Nope. Sorry."

She looked at him a moment. Then jabbed him in the ribs. "Liar."

Nick was about to jab her back when suddenly he felt a light tug on his arm and Amelia was standing there, looking amused.

And hotter than ever, if that was actually possible. Nick wondered if he should check his sleeve for scorch marks. Amelia raised one eyebrow and, leaning forward, whispered in his ear (but loud enough for Sabina to catch), "I thought I warned you about flirting with little girls." Then loudly:

"Come on, Bad Boy, you've got a show to do."

Nick looked back at Sabrina, expecting to see daggers in her eyes.

Instead, she surprised him with a confused look. As if she couldn't comprehend not just being one-upped in the female pecking order, but as if realizing that against Amelia it was Game-Set-Match before it even began. She managed to get out a "Who's the mom, Nick?" Amelia was already pulling Nick away but she looked back over her shoulder at his ex, shook her head and stifled a laugh with her fingers.

"Not yours, apparently."

Nick almost felt bad for Sabrina. She actually looked surprised. Then he remembered his last little get-together with Vince Voelker.

Almost, but not quite.

Backstage, if one could call the temporary plywood platform set up for the bands a stage, Nick had butterflies in his stomach. Then Amelia was there, holding his face in both her hands. Her cool hands he corrected himself. Cool and calm.

"You're going to do great. Get up and knock them dead." Then she planted a kiss square on the lips. Ramon tapped him on the shoulder.

"C'mon, lover boy. Our fans and fame await."

Then he found himself strutting across the stage like he owned it, slinging the Firebird over his shoulder, and plugging in the jack while flicking on the Marshall as he passed it in one fluid motion.

Just like an old pro would.

Then a casual glance over at Mike, who gave him a curt nod, back to Ramon, who was grinning wildly, and then one . . . two . . . three

They were off. Like a rocket.

There's a certain feeling, a moment pretty much impossible to adequately convey in words, that every musician who plays in a band exists for. It's sort of a transcendent, otherworldly experience when everything falls into sync, an awareness of being connected with each other, of different people (in this case three) sharing something almost mystical, a harmonious dialogue told through the language of music. It's a high that's higher than any artificially-induced experience, like a flood of pheromones flushing through the system, goosebumps up and down the arms, an out-of-body experience, where time ceases to exist and each note slows down into an eternity. Because, unlike any drug, this is it, this is the real thing, this is what it's all about. This is why one endures the incessant humiliation, the bad gigs, the horrible deals, the nightmare auditions, the getting screwed out of pay, because, in the end, this is the truth behind all of it, what no moronic A&R rep or self-important record company exec could ever fathom or even have a remote clue about: The Experience.

Typically, it only occurs for a momentary interlude, perhaps for an entire song if the connections are just right.

For Nick and his band mates, it was the entire set.

Nick glanced over at Mike, Mike glanced over at Ramon, Ramon back at Nick, and they all *knew*.

This was it.

Like three interlocking pieces of a synchronized musical puzzle, the three of them ran with the new songs Nick had blocked out with them the other night. The audience sensed it. More people filtered into the music tent.

Hands were tapping hips. Feet were tapping the ground. Heads were nodding to the beat.

Nick would never have thought such a thing was achievable. It was a vaguely reckless, dangerous feeling. Part of him was in control, part of him was hanging on for dear life.

Riding the lightning.

The Firebird felt alive in his arms, the Humbuckers lending the chords a throaty growl. Most of the lyrics – *all* the lyrics actually – he was ad-libbing. Coming from somewhere, nowhere, pulling them out of the ether:

"Don't even say you're sorry,
It's all one elab-or-ate scam,
When the frosty hours are dead and gone,
I promise that you'll be damned…"

At the back of the tent area, where the light was less and the shadows were more, Boots stood smoking a cigarette, a plastic cup of Schlitz beer in one hand. Next to him stood a dark haired man with a crew cut and a beer gut, arms crossed and an intense expression on his already-intense face, lips compressed into a thin line. He was trying to decide if this was all some elaborate, warped practical joke and, if so, who was behind it and how much money it was going to cost him.

This man's name was Richard Sloan. "Dicky" to his friends and enemies.

He wore black jeans, black snakeskin cowboy boots, and a black-and-gold silk windbreaker, the collarless kind with elastic sleeves and a name embroidered on the left breast. This one said "Brooklyn Britches," a somewhat ghastly attempt at fashion made ghastlier given that he was pushing sixty, but then Dicky Sloan was never a wellspring of good taste when it came to clothes.

Or dialogue, as even Boots could testify.

"Fuck a duck. Fuck a goddamned duck," was all he had said in the last five minutes. He'd spotted Amelia as soon as they arrived, standing near the front of the stage, and had positioned himself next to one of the spotlights so that, even if she did look in their direction, all she would see would be a vague shadow behind the glare.

Still looking good after all these years.

Real good.

A little smile crept across his lips and, without realizing it, he pursed his lips, then made a small double kiss that sounded wet and obscene. Then his eyes narrowed as he looked over at the stage at Nick.

At the guitar.

And the jacket.

And the hair.

Then Nick and the band kicked into the next number. Out of the PA came the opening riff of *You're Dreaming*.

Dicky felt his blood turn to ice.

Thirty minutes later Nick walked off the stage shaken, yet feeling gold plated.

There had been some truly weird moments when he wasn't sure what was going on. After jumping into *You're Dreaming*, he'd looked over and swore Mike wasn't there playing bass. The guy standing there was wearing a V-neck sweater and black leather pants and playing the Rickenbacker left handed. And when Nick had glanced back, Ramon had been replaced by the Lonely Dancers' drummer in his biker jacket with the Triumph patch on it.

He felt this giddy, woozy feeling of
[slippage]
The music was flowing like a current.
Timeless.
Carrying.
Looking down he saw with a detached sense of alarm that somebody else's hands were playing the guitar – longer and flatter than his own. The

audience seemed different.

Strange.

Spiked hair. Mullets. Tight jeans. Girls with big starburst haircuts. Blue eye shadow. Glitter?

Some looked like corpses.

Grinning. Desiccated faces.

Screaming.

Screaming skulls.

A man in a leather jacket screaming.

Tires screeching. Glass shards.

Look ma, I'm flying!

And the taste in his mouth. Blood. Dirt. Bark.

Correction: *Grave dirt.*

He thought he was going to pass out. Then he glanced down stage right and saw Amelia there.

Young. So beautiful.

Like sunlight at the end of a very long dark tunnel.

She loves me.

Not you.

She loves me.

Not . . . What's happening?

Shrieking

Amelia's face crumpling into grief. Tears streaming down her cheeks.

Goddammit! That motherfucker . . .

Then blackness.

The pulse of the backbeat, the hum of the amps. A throbbing bass-line

Awareness.

What song? What . . .?

Nick realized he was singing:

"I'm wide awake,

It's 3 AM and the world's a mess

I'm in overdrive.

I think we're screwed up: fighting like dogs over scraps of love . . ."

A guitar riff he'd never heard before – a second guitar he could hear clear as day even though they were a *three*-piece band – counterpointed his rhythm with a scaling riff that stepped up and then reversed itself, repeating in a loop.

[Slippage.]

He felt a fourth presence on the stage with him. Off to his left, he glimpsed a shadow . . .

"I'm going insane. It's my first official gig with a full audience and this is how God works it: enjoy! Oh, eh, sorry about the losing your mind bit!" Then without missing a cue, he jumped into the opening chords of their final song in the set, a ripping version of The Who's *Substitute*. Mike managed to get a suitable "dive bomb" bass sound out of the Rickenbacker and the audience was going crazy.

Then, just as abruptly, it was over.

Nick took a bow, then, brandishing the Firebird over his head with one hand, said simply "Thank-you! We are 'The Unexpected'. Goodnight!" The entire tent erupted in applause.

Nick Carr wasn't the only one enjoying some otherworldly moments during the show.

When the band launched into *You're Dreaming*, Dicky Sloan, for one of the very few times in his life, felt paralyzed. Not just the song. Suddenly he would have sworn on his mother's grave (if he could remember where the hell she was buried) that up there on stage the young buck from town had been replaced, actually fucking *replaced*, by Paul Brammell himself.

Even worse, he could feel Paul's eye's searching the crowd until they settled on him, trying to hide his bulk in the shadows, and, for a second, Dicky Sloan was a bad boy, a very bad boy all over again and needed to be punished. For all his tough-boy posturing, abusive bullying, and cutting sarcasms, there was a moment when Sloan felt cold, unbridled fear.

It was at the end of the song when from across the stage Paul ("it was Paul") pointed his finger like a gun at Dicky and made like he was popping him off: one-two-three shots.

He'd seen enough.

He grabbed Boots by the upper arm and, pulling him in close, whispered instructions in his ear. Then he let go, shook his hand as though Boots' jacket was riddled with germs (it probably was), and, wiping it on his own pants leg, high-tailed out of there.

Over by the PA board, Tommy Falcon stood, stubby hands clasped behind his back. He was wearing a black cowboy shirt and a pair of lizard-skin boots that would have put Sloan's footwear to shame. The PA system was his after all – one of the many routine little favors he did for the carnival (and more importantly the mayor – it was always good strategy to pile on the favors with the local government and Falcon's currency wasn't restricted to the kind issued by the U.S. Mint) was to loan the equipment for the bands.

It was no big deal for him to arrange for Nick's band to be on the bill tonight. That was strictly a freebee. Tommy had known Amelia since she was a gawky doe-eyed girl and, though they hadn't talked in years, still thought of her as a little sister who could do no wrong in his book. He knew all too well what it was like to come from a broken family. But at least he had his three brothers to fall back on.

He was also a man who kept a sharp eye out for his surroundings and he quickly spotted Dicky Sloan hovering over in the shadows like a leprous toad. He immediately knew whatever the reasons for his sudden appearance in Wyvern Falls after so many years, none of them could be good ones. Which put up a few red flags in a row: this kid coming out of left field and buying Paul's old guitar, Amelia showing up asking for the same kid's band to have a slot on the bill, Dicky Sloan showing up in the audience. And hell, while we're at it, what had inspired him in the first place to pull that damned guitar out of storage after thirty years and hang it in the window the previous week.

Just what in the hell was going on here?

He looked over at Amelia and saw her running up on stage and planting a big kiss on the kid's lips.

"Oh boy," he thought. "I sure as hell hope you have some idea what kind of trouble you're stepping into, lady." He was afraid he already knew the answer.

At the back of the stage, Mike and Ramon were clapping Nick on the back at the same time. Ramon was pushing a mug of beer into his hands and showing pretty much every one of his pearly white teeth.

"Shit man, we rocked. *You* rocked. We are rock stars tonight, amigos! All of us in the gutter but some of us are looking at the stars!" he said and let out a big "Woop!" People were coming around from both sides of the stage and suddenly one detached from the crowd and ran up, surprising Nick by grabbing his arm. He was about to make a comeback on Chrissie Hynde's line from *Message of Love* but instead did a half-spin and found himself looking into Sabrina's face for the second time that night.

"You were amazing!" Then she shrieked: "Holy Shit!" like she'd seen the Pope himself just take one. Nick thought it might be the sincerest look he'd ever seen on her face. Then her face softened. "That was great Nick, really, *really* great!" and, grabbing his face with both hands, planted a smacker on his lips, then another, then ran off before he could even react.

"What the . . .?" He was looking around but there was no sign of Amelia.

Mike was grinning ear to ear as well and from somewhere Ramon had gotten hold of a cup of ice and dumped it down the front of Nick's T-shirt.

"Gotta cool off little lover boy, save some ladies for the rest of us!" Nick jumped back and, pulling his shirt out from his belt, grabbed the ice and got most of it down the back of Ramon's sweat-soaked T-shirt. Then he realized there were a group of young teenage girls – maybe two dozen – pressing in and asking for his autograph.

"What the . . ." he repeated. He didn't know what to say. A couple of young Latino girls squeezed in on either side of him, while a third snapped a couple of photos with her cell phone, leaving Nick momentarily blinded by the flash. Band posters were thrust in his face along with pens.

"Sign!"

"Can you sign this, *por favor*?"

"Ooh, can I get your autograph?"

He almost panicked. It all looked great on TV, or, better yet, in his daydream fantasies but this unexpected onrush of girls invading his personal space, demanding of him, touching his hair, his jacket, his face, in reality kind of freaked him out.

Creeped him out as well.

One girl whispered his ear. "Sonia wants to be your friend. Do you like her?" A shy, dark-skinned girl no older than thirteen was forced in front of him, giggling.

Nick held both his hands up in mock surrender. "Ladies. I'm flattered. But I, uh . . ." *think! Think!* "I really have to load my equipment and get out of here."

A sea of frowns met his gaze.

"But you'll be seeing us again. I promise. The Unexpected. Expect us!"

Picking up the Firebird in its case, he high-tailed it out the back of the tent towards the parking lot. Passing the bathroom cabin, he had a flashback to Friday night, then almost jumped back as again a shadow detached itself from under the eave and came forward.

His stomach did a somersault before he realized it was a man of much smaller stature than his good friend, Vince Voelker. This guy looked maybe a 120 pounds dripping wet and had scraggly hair, a John Deere cap pulled down on his head, and greasy hair shooting out from the sides.

He had a cigarette dangling from one hand and something else being pushed forward in the other. It took a second for Nick to realize it was a business card.

"Eh, you're Nick Carr, no?" The guy had a reedy voice. Nasally. With a twang.

Nick relaxed slightly. "That's me."

The card was thrust at him. "The Boss wants to see you. Sez you'll be needing management if you wanna get anywhere. He handled some big name acts and thinks you guys got potential. Call this number. He wants to talk. Soon. Real soon."

Nick hesitated, then took the card and looked at it. It said:

Mirage Management, Ltd.
Richard Sloan, *Executive Director*
Entertainment * Music * Select Artist Representation

It gave an East Village address, phone, and fax number, along with a cell number. No website, Facebook or Twitter information. Odd. Nick glanced at it and filed it in his wallet. "Sure. Um, whatever."

The guy just kept staring at him, like a disconnected robot waiting for input. Then he blinked and grinned. "Ace as in Aces, bud! You work with the Boss, you going places. Scout's honor."

Nick had a hunch this guy wasn't much of a scout and might be more than just a few cards shy of a full deck, but nodded. "Sure thing."

He was also a little dubious about what places he might go with a manager like this.

He was still feeling at a loss about Amelia. What the heck had happened to her? Where had she gone? He was trying to cycle back to what had happened during the gig. Did he do something wrong? Did he upset her? All he knew was this sudden sense of longing and emptiness in his heart. He loaded his guitar and amp, then circled around back towards the beer tent. Ramon and Mike texted him about a party over on DeGraw that they were heading to but of Amelia there was no sign. A couple of people stopped him and complimented him on his set but he hastily disengaged himself. He ran into Tommy Falcon near the poker tent.

"Mister Falcon!"

"Hey there, big guy."

"You haven't seen, ah, Amelia around, have you?"

Always a consummate actor, Tommy played the "aw-shucks-don't-know-nothin'" routine. "Well, uh, no. She was at the show, I think. But I haven't seen her since."

Nick tried to check the rising desperation in his gut. "Did you see her leave? C'mon, Mister Falcon. It's important!"

Tommy decided to give in a little. "Yeah, well, I saw her headin' towards the parking lot right after your show ended – you boys really were something, you know. Anyways, she didn't look too happy. Son, maybe you should let things rest a spell."

The words floated right past Nick's ears without even registering. "Uh, thanks, Mister Falcon! See you soon!" And he was off.

Tommy stood there a moment just shaking his head. "Kids."

-8-

NICK RAN back to his car at a near sprint, his breath coming in whoops. His new attachment to Newport's wasn't doing wonders for his stamina. He even looked inside the Mustang, half-believing she might be waiting for him there.

Not for any rational reason.

He stood there for a moment, hands on the top of the door frame, when he heard a crunch in the dirt behind him. He turned around in time to be slammed up against the car.

Apparently his good friend Vince Voelker was in the mood for a return visit.

Vince held him up against the door, gripping Nick's upper arms with the iron clamps he had for hands. There were a few major differences involving this encounter however.

For starters, no sooner had Vince thrown him up against the Mustang than Nick, or at least the Nick Carr typically in charge of this body, fell down the rabbit hole. The eyes looking out of his features went blue and steely.

Vince got in his face again:

"Apparently I didn't make myself clear the other night, chump," he said through clenched teeth.

"What in the bloody hell are you talking about, *wanker?*" Nick heard himself respond in an unmistakable English accent.

Vince made a face that said: *what the . . .?* Then, "Sabrina, asshole. She dumped me tonight. She was all Nick this, Nick that. Well, guess what, dipshit, tonight I'm going to rip the Wonder Nick's fucking balls off."

So much for the school of simple Vince threats.

But this Nick wasn't eating any of it.

"I wouldn't advise it . . . fucker. Let go of me right now or *your* balls will be the first thing coming off this evening. Your limp little excuse for a dick goes second," he hissed.

Vince compressed Nick's arms even more, then froze. He felt an icy prick in his groin and, glancing down, was shocked to see a six-inch knife blade poised directly under his manhood, the blade having already cut through his shorts.

That got his undivided attention.

Then he glanced back up and saw something even scarier: nothing but pure cold murder in the eyes looking back at his.

No anger, no hatred.

What he saw looking back at him was his own death. For a split second, he saw himself writhing on the ground, his surgically-removed testicles rolling around in the remains of his underwear like a pair of soft-boiled eggs, an odd looking appendage lying on the grass in front of him which he understood, with growing horror, was his own severed penis. The pain unbelievable – and then he imagined the blood spurting as it forced its way around his clenched fingers, from the femoral artery severed after the knife had continued on its trajectory through his groin. He saw that clear as a perfect ultra high-definition television picture.

His eyes were big as marbles. Nick moved his face closer and whispered, "Suggest you piss off quickly and permanently."

Vince Voelker didn't need to hear that suggestion twice.

He let go and backed away very carefully, hands open in a placatory gesture. When he had backed out of arm's length, he turned and ran like hell.

He left Wyvern Falls the next day.

Permanently.

When Nick came to, he found himself lying face up in soft grass at the side of a hill. Grey-white clouds chased one another across a starlit sky where a crescent moon slid in and out of view. The grass smelled good – the heady aroma of newly-mown clippings that seems so integral to the definition of summer. The temperature had cooled off a bit and as Nick lay there, he had a fleeting wish he could just stay like this forever, suspended in a peaceful cocoon of timelessness gazing at the heavens above, the breeze sweet and soothing, the stiff leather of the motocross jacket like a protective armor.

A few bats flitted overhead, describing overlapping arcs.

Nick tried to ponder a few critical questions, such as "where the hell am I?" and "how the hell did I get here?" But in his relaxed state, the need for answers seemed unimportant and removed.

Finally, he rolled over on his side and gazed at a small gravestone.

That got him sitting up with a start.

He was in a cemetery.

The Wyvern Falls Cemetery, apparently, being that he could now see the long tapered steeple of the Presbyterian Church over the next rise. What the fuck was he doing sleeping in the cemetery? Happened to be in the neighborhood, swung by for a little nap just for laughs and chuckles? Then as the weak moonlight emerged from behind a cloud he saw the engraving on the tombstone:

In Loving Memory,
Paul A. Brammell
June 29th, 1961 – June 29th, 1981
A gallant flare you made against the dark!

It was his birthday, then. Today.

This was getting really weird.

Brushing himself off, he stood and lit a cigarette, trying to gather his thoughts, which was hard when they all kept getting their ends tangled: Sabrina, Vince, a dead band that shows up for their gig 30 years after getting wiped out in a road accident, the lead singer's guitar surfacing in the window of a pawn shop, running into the same man's ex and falling into pretty much an instant relationship with her, changing his whole look and getting laid and his first gig, smoking, and, and, and . . .

". . . too much monkey business for me to be involved in," Mister Berry once complained.

"Too much monkey business to even remotely fucking figure out," Nick amended. What happened to his sleepy small river-town loser existence? It was like some whimsical trickster had shown up, crumpled his ho-hum life into a ball, and chucked out the window of the train car, just as it jumped the tracks and went crashing into the canyon.

He blew smoke up at the stars.

He was quickly understanding how easy it was to get addicted to the damn things. They gave you the sense of doing something when you had nothing to do.

They also gave you cancer, emphysema, and made you reek something horrible.

He held it before him between his thumb and forefinger. Mister Cigarette: The Real Gift Giver. With that, he took one more drag, then flicked the butt toward a nearby tree.

Amelia? Where the hell was Amelia? He needed to see her.

More than that; he simply *needed* her.

As he turned to leave (hoping his car was somewhere obvious – hadn't thought of that!), something snagged his ankle.

"What?"

Looking down, he saw blackened hand clutching his foot.

Even as he watched, a second hand was working its way out of the ground, scrabbling for his other foot.

"Jesus Christ!" he screamed, twisting his leg around. Digging in with his other heel, he wrenched backwards and wound up landing on his ass. Even worse, whatever had grabbed him came up half out of the ground with him.

It was a rotting corpse, with tufts of rotten blond hair and the putrefied remains of a motorcycle jacket with a few shreds of a T-shirt underneath. *Impossible!* Nick thought, *Amelia said they sent the . . .*

The thought was interrupted as the thing yanked itself up further and landed right on top of Nick. The skeletal fingers clutched and clawed at Nick's jacket until the face drew even with his. The smell was dreadful – the ancient smell of old rotted meat mixed with dirt and god knew what else – and Nick gagged.

A garbled voice came out from between the working jaws:

"Hi . . . mate . . . so you wanted . . . to . . . be . . . a . . .rock-and-roll star?" it said, as a bunch of meaty earthworms writhed out of the eye sockets, plopping down on the front of Nick's t-shirt, "Got . . . me . . . an . . . early . . . grave . . . it . . . did? Shagging . . . me . . . old . . . bird . . . are ya?"

Nick was paralyzed with terror but produced a suggestion of a nod. The corpse clawed its way closer until the rotting mouth was close to his ear:

"Tricky Dicky . . . has been naughty . . . got . . . to-pay 'is dues . . ." Unable to control himself, Nick snapped his body in the opposite direction and vomited.

Or thought he did.

There was a sense of

[slippage]

And he found himself doubled over, a dry retch coming out of his mouth. He was staring at the grave maker. Still in the cemetery then. But no corpse. No vomit. Just smooth, freshly-cut grass.

Sitting up, he saw there were smudges of dirt across his t-shirt, but, after lying around in the grass, that could have been from anything. He stood up and brush off his jeans. *Amelia*, he thought, *I need to find Amelia. Tell her everything. I need to find out what the hell is going on here.* Reaching into his front jeans pocket to fish out his keys, he felt something else in there, clunky and metallic. Pulling it out, he saw that it was (of all the damndest things) a pair of small rusted cutters with old yellow grips with faded letters on it that said "Hotchkiss Auto-Body."

"What the fuck?" Nick stared at them in disbelief. It didn't make any sense. Blackouts. Tools appearing in his pockets. Cameos by dead and decayed rock singers. What was next? Career counseling from Elvis? Guitar lessons from Jimi Hendrix? Alien abduction?

He was about to chuck them away when changed his mind and shoved them in his jacket pocket.

What the hell.

Ten minutes later Nick was at Amelia's.

He knocked again, harder this time. He had a hollow feeling in his gut that she wasn't home. Even worse, that something had happened. It took him a moment to register that the door had swung inward after his last knock.

He stepped cautiously into Amelia's apartment.

"Hello?"

Nothing.

"Amelia? It's me. It's—"

"—the little lover boy," a vaguely familiar voice finished for him. At the same instant, a flashlight flicked on, blinding him, followed by the dead click of a gun being cocked.

Nick shielded his eyes with his arm, feeling his heart flood with dread. His dad kept a few pistols and sidearms around the house. He understood exactly what that sound meant. What he didn't have a clue about was what was going on here.

His voice came out about a hundred percent bolder than he felt.

"Who's there? Where the hell is Amelia?"

"Oh, she's having a little chat with the boss, catching up on old times. Now I would stay very still little lover, unless you want to eat some bullets . . . turn around, hands behind." The flashlight clicked off and a somewhat short man stood up and walked over to Nick. The cold weight of a gun barrel pressed against his temple, then he felt a pair of hand cuffs click over his wrists, painfully tight. The man smelled of tobacco and clothes that hadn't been washed in a week. His mouth smelled like it was more like a year.

In the half light of the doorway, Nick could see it was the same scrawny man he'd run into earlier in the parking lot, the one trying to hook him up with a manager.

"C'mon, little boy, yer going for a walk with Boots," he sneered, pulling Nick by the arm with him. "Change in plans: You don't need to call the Boss anymore – you get to meet him direct and in person. *Tosh*, and to think I thought you was a ghost. Shee-it. Yer just a little punk. Boss gonna have fun with you. Then *I* might have some fun with you! Make you squeal like a pig. You betcha! Ace as in Aces!"

The warehouse was in walking distance. Further down the road on the next street over on Bellevue was a district of old warehouses, some still in use, some abandoned. One was eking out an existence as the Wyvern Falls Home Builders Supply, Inc. and another the power station for Metro North, dating from the turn of the last century. Nick also learned that at least half the streetlights were broken and that the neighborhood was more or less abandoned this late on a weeknight. They only saw one person on the way over and he looked like a passed-out tramp, dead drunk, a worn-out jacket draped over his head and a loud snore puffing it up intermittently. The man's pointed shoes were lying flat in opposite directions. Boots pulled Nick in tight and slipped the barrel of the pistol up against his spine.

They crossed the street to a low building with rows of slanted skylights. Boots pulled out a keychain from his belt and, after a few tries, unlocked the heavy padlock, drew the bolt and, sliding back a massive iron door, pushed Nick through, closing it and sliding back in place a massive bar. An elephant would have a rough time getting through it.

Outside, the bum slid down the coat with one dirty hand and took a pull off a half-empty bottle of Jim Beam. Then he managed to get unsteadily to his feet and, after one fall, stumbled away into the darkness.

Nick wasn't sure what to expect when he stumbled into the main area of the warehouse, but it certainly wasn't the bizarre sight that met his eyes. It looked like a movie set of someone's bizarre idea of a 1970s bachelor's pad. In the middle of the expanse of stained concrete floor was an orange-and-brown shag carpet with an overstuffed faux leather (a.k.a. vinyl) couch. With it was a coffee table and pair of end tables in the ubiquitous style one sees described in Craig's List postings as "mid-century modern" or, in layman's terms, cheap 1950s junk. One table even sported a lava lamp. There was also a scattering of recliner chairs, a modern Samsung 52-inch flat-panel TV on a black-and-chrome stand, a water bed off to one side with a heavy dark stained pine headboard and a tangle of sheets, and a kitchenette area and dining space with another "mid-century modern" table and chairs.

The tall multi-paned windows had all been painted over black or boarded up and the skylights had black-out shades.

Beyond the furnishings, the warehouse was filled with an assortment of oddities. One area was a stockpile of music equipment – mostly old PA systems, speaker cabinets, guitar and bass amps, monitors, etc. – which, based on the accumulation of dust and cobwebs, hadn't seen action in some time. Two cars occupied another corner, one a 1959 Buick Special, the other a 1975 Chevy van which, based on the gold fleck and pseudo-Boris Vallejo fantasy art airbrushed on the sides, appeared to be a refugee from an old van-in. Also, there was an old Triumph 500cc motorcycle in bad need of restoration. The other side of the warehouse was filled with an assortment of crates, old furniture, and six long rows of industrial metal shelving twelve feet high and filled with a variety of boxes waiting to make their way to Chinatown, boxes containing merchandise that the ATF, also known as the Bureau of Alcohol, Tobacco, Firearms and Explosives, would find extremely interesting.

However, what Nick Carr focused on were the three people in the central area of the floor. The first was a tall man with a black crew cut, matching cowboy shirt and boots, and a beer gut to go with it. He had a bullwhip in one hand and a sawed-off shotgun in the other. The second was tough-looking middle-aged woman whom he had never seen before lounging on the couch. She looked slightly overweight, had garish make up, what looked like a Tina Turner wig, and had made a hideous attempt to dress like a woman half her age. That included a tube top and tight jeans that only drew more attention to the belly forced to roll out over her belt.

The third person, hand cuffed and tied with duct tape to an old metal chair set in front of the coffee table, her shirt in bloody ribbons, was Amelia.

Nick felt the gun barrel pressed into the base of his spine as Boots' grimy hand pushed him forward.

"I got him, Boss. I got your little boy for you . . .. hee-hee."

"Bring him here, Bootsie . . . go help yourself to a beer if you like. Plenty in the fridge."

Boots brought Nick up and suddenly did a little jig like some sort of weird trailer-trash leprechaun. "I did pretty fucking good, didn't I? Ace as Aces! I'm the dude, right, huh? Huh?" He paused in with one foot in mid-air as he found himself with sawed-off double shotgun barrels an inch from his forehead.

"Can it, shit-for-brains."

Nick had a wild moment where he thought maybe he should do something dramatic like do a diving roll and go for his knife (which was still sheathed at his belt – Boots hadn't even noticed it). But this wasn't some B action movie and he had an over-riding hunch that doing anything foolhardy would get him killed. Or seriously maimed.

As if to assure him of this, "Boss" swiveled the gun until it was resting under Nick's chin. Up close, Nick could see the he had the doughy face of a man-child, with the pasty complexion of someone who didn't get out in the sun much. He also had pouty lips with large but sparse eyebrows over a pair of deep, dark, and utterly soul-less eyes.

The kind of eyes that would think nothing of pulling the double triggers and blasting his head apart like a ripe melon. Nick felt his guts turn to jelly.

The pouty lips compressed into a grim little line. "Tonight's star attraction has arrived. What's your name, son, and don't tell me Paul or I will be inclined to pull both of these triggers." He had a slightly southern accent.

"Nick, Nick Carr." He swallowed with some difficulty. To say he wasn't scared with two twelve-gauge barrels shoved up under his chin was an understatement. Yet at the same time, he felt strangely calm. "And who exactly are you?"

The man-child face turned into something approaching amusement. "Who . . . am I?" Then he chuckled. "Of course, of course." He stepped back, turned, and, stepping over to Amelia, caressed her cheek with the end of the bullwhip. Amelia whimpered in response. The eyes looking through her tangled bangs looked terrified. "Well, little darlin', you want to tell your little man here who I am?"

"Dicky Sloan," she mumbled.

The backhand slap happened so fast that it was only after Amelia's head snapped back that Nick registered the "crack!" Then the whip was cast aside and Sloan stepped up to Amelia and positioned his crotch on her face, putting the shotgun barrels to her head.

"Don't ever call me that," he hissed. Then he smiled. "It's Richard' for you, got it, bitch?" Then he sidled in closer, one pudgy hand rubbing his crotch suggestively. "Would you like to say hello to little Richard?"

Nick felt himself stepping forward, his temper rising. He froze as Sloan pointed the shotgun at him again, this time cocking both the hammers. "Sit down, little one. I think its story time."

Boots came up, popping the top on a can of Coors. "Story time! Cool."

Sloan looked at him flatly until Boots mumbled an apology under his breath and slunk over to the recliner chair. Then Sloan wheeled around. "Oh gosh, where are my manners? I haven't made introductions!" He stepped over and placed one hand on Nick's shoulder, the gun leveled at his gut, and guided him over to the couch where he forced him to sit down.

"Nick Carr, meet Toby. Toby, Nick. Boots you already met, and Amelia . . . Amelia I think you know?" He gave a lecherous wink. "And quite well I understand. Quite well indeed! But maybe . . ..maybe not as well as you think." He uncocked the shotgun and paced around the perimeter of the furniture, the gun resting on his shoulder.

And he began to talk.

"Well, Mister Nick Carr, you might be interested in the whole story about Miss Amelia here and the English twit you were so eager to imitate. You had me going, you know! Good Lordy, you had me going tonight! Imitation is flattery! But flattery will get you nowhere, man. (W-e-e-l-l-l, maybe *vivisected* in my book . . . but let's wait and see.)

Sloan paused, ran a hand through his crew cut, and shook his head like a bear waking up. "Sheeez, now where was I?"

Over on the couch, the woman named Toby lit a cigarette and, without looking up, said in a hoarse voice, "Amelia. You were going to tell him about Amelia."

Sloan fixed her with his blank stare: "You mean when she fucked me?"

He turned to Nick. "Didn't she tell you that? The night after her old man bit the dust. She didn't tell you that?" He looked up at the ceiling and laughed. "Oh Lord in Heaven! Always looking for her daddy."

Sloan walked over to Amelia, who was hanging her head and refusing to meet Nick's eye. "Who's your daddy now, honey?" He purred. ". . . please."

"Don't."

Sloan made as if to slap her again, but then changed his mind. Instead he pulled up one of the chairs, swung it round so he could cross his arms and rest his shotgun on the back rest, and said, "Okay, story time, bucko."

This time there was no psychotic charm or bravado. He stared at Nick until Nick reluctantly returned his gaze. Nick also noticed for the first time that Sloan had unnaturally long lashes, giving him a feminine look

"Once upon a time, there was a band of three young men who called themselves The Lonely Dancers. They weren't a bad little band, these lonely boys, and they had some potential. It was the early 80s, bands were popping up every which way, New York was a-hopping and wild. Punk was over but New Wave was in full gear. CBGB's was packing them in every night, Max's Kansas City was still a hot spot, and so were the Mudd Club, the Palladium, and the Ritz. I was managing three bands then; Phyllis Killer, Love in Black and The Wyos. But Paul Brammell and the Lonely Dancers were a cut above anything I had on my roster. I could smell it on them. So I signed them and started shopping their demo which we recorded at Gram-o-vision over in Tribeca.

"Good times. Good times. The Saints were marching in, hurrah! I got them signed within a month on Polydor. (Here Sloan examined at his fingertips as if they were gold-plated). The album was recorded in three weeks. It had a lot going for it: tight songs, tight harmonies, and they had the right energy and the right look. Sometimes I wonder if they even knew."

Nick looked up. "Knew what?"

Sloan looked like he was pondering a deep philosophical problem. "That this was it. This was as good as it would ever get. Oh, they had the one good album in them with a semi-hit or two. But they had already shot their wad and didn't even know it. Paul thought they were just getting started. I knew they were already finished. He'd played me the demos for the next album. They sucked. Complete crap. Your first album you've been writing your entire life. It's the second album that shows what you really got. And Messrs Brammell & Co had nothing.

Nick was confused. He said quietly, "I don't understand. Why would you have their demos?"

Sloan grinned. "Why? Why? I was their manager, that's why. And that's why I had them killed."

There was a wrenching sob from Amelia and her head tilted even further down. Nick didn't need to consider what he knew of these situations – at least how they played out on TV or in the movies. To know this one wasn't good. Not good by a couple of big neighborhoods.

When a psycho-crazy guy with a bull whip and a shotgun tells you straight out he's responsible for multiple homicides, it can only mean one thing: he's going to be adding you to the list shortly. And with that knowledge, a strange sort of calm settled over Nick like a blanket. His odds of survival were quickly diminishing but he had at least two wild cards in his favor: a six-inch knife and a pair of cutters.

It was something, at least.

Nick made like he was having trouble ingesting a particularly ludicrous claim: "You had them killed. Uh-huh. And exactly why would you have done that?"

Sloan smiled. "The money of course. Things were fast and loose in those days. I was being audited by the IRS, my other two bands couldn't get signed to save their lives, and there was a little issue with my um, backers."

"I took out a substantial insurance policy on them – standard procedure for all my acts that I invest in – so I guess you could say they were worth something after all! Fucking English twits! But I collected a cool 2 mil. Nice? Nothing to tie me to anything. Hell, I was at CBGB's watching one of my other bands self-destruct onstage that night. Lead singer of Phyllis Killer was zonked on heroin. That'll do it."

Amelia let out a muffled sob.

"But hey, it was enough to get my little business here started and keep my feet wet in show business. But I'm afraid, dearly beloved, that is not why we are gathered here tonight. We are gathered here because some little groupie slut couldn't keep her skirt and panties on and some gullible little dipshit thought he could rattle my cage for a few greenbacks. Just couldn't let the dead stay buried, could we? So my question to you, my bucky lad, is what is the real reason you're playing dress up as a lead singer I had eighty-sixed thirty years ago? What's with resurrecting his equally dead songs onstage? Bringing public attention to matters best left forgotten?"

With that, he walked over and picked up the bullwhip and gave it a couple cursory snaps. "Answer carefully, or this will be a long and painful night for both of you. I promise . . . I do, I do!"

But Nick wasn't looking at Sloan. He was looking at the middle-aged train wreck with the Tina Turner wig. Wheels were turning in his head. She had been deliberately not looking at him since he'd shown up.

"And just what is your role in this little class reunion? Toby isn't really your name is it?" She took a quick pull on her cigarette and blew it sideways out of her mouth, still avoiding his gaze. Sloan looked perplexed. Boots took another pull off his can of beer and belched. Nick felt light bulbs clicking on somewhere in his head.

If it could have been possible, Nick would have drilled her with his eyes. "No, I don't think Toby is your name at all. I think its Robin. As in Robin Hotchkiss. No surprise Amelia didn't recognize you. You look like the type that's been putting some hard miles on over the years. And I think you're the one who did the dirty work, didn't you? You killed three young men, didn't you, you fucking bitch?"

With that her eyes turned to him with a fear-stricken look, like a deer frozen in the headlights.

Nick heard himself shouting, "Because you cut the fucking brake lines!!!"

That was when Amelia screamed.

Boots' eyes were as big as saucers and the can of beer slid unnoticed out of his hand, toppling to the concrete floor. Sloan was looking wildly back and forth between Nick and Robin with a look that ran through surprise, confusion, then amusement.

Amelia was staring at Robin in disbelief and said in a trembling voice, "It's you? Robin . . .Oh . . . my . . . God. Paul? Why? Why would you do such a thing? You were my . . . best friend!"

Robin regained her composure and, like some eerie Hollywood special effect, her expression went from slack-jawed shock to bitter rage in seconds. She took a final drag off her cigarette (the ash was a good inch long by this point) and stubbed it out in the ashtray.

More like stamped it out.

"You always were so fucking naïve, Amelia. Wide-eyed little Miss Innocent, bats her eyelashes, crosses her knees, goes all girlie-girlie and gets a free ride to fame, getting her hooks into the coolest singer on the scene back then. Paul should have been *mine*." She was spitting the words out. "But it's always the fucking pretty things that get it all, isn't it? That's the way it always works. I was the one who dragged you to that show, who got you introduced to the band, and you stole the fucking lead singer!!"

Amelia was shaking her head, sobbing, "What are you talking about, it wasn't like that at . . ."

"*You fucking slut!*" Robin cut her off. "You had it all, the parties, the boyfriend, hobnobbing with the coolest celebs, you had your ticket out of this hell hole and me? I had nothing. Some fucking friend! God, if you only had a clue how much I hate you!" Robin made a bad imitation of a crybaby: "oh poor me, poor little pretty me!" Then her eyes narrowed. "Well, screw you and the horse you rode off on. When Dicky here came to me one night with a plan to get back at you *and* make a shit load of cash, I was all fucking ears, honey." She sat back with a smirk. "It was so fucking easy, too. We set it up so Paul had to call from the Sunoco up on Route 9 where I was waiting. The phone booth was off to the side where it's dark. While Paul was making the call to Richard, it was a cinch to sneak under the van and work the brake line loose. With that piece of shit-on-wheels no one would ever bother looking. Do you know how much money we made? Ha! It was . . ."

"I think that's enough tales out of school, kiddies," interrupted Sloan as he stood up. "And I think it's time for Amelia and Nick to go for a ride. In – hold on to your hats buckaroos – an old van!" He pulled Nick up by his arms and motioned Boots to untie Amelia. "Get her out of that chair and let's get moving. Time for a trip down Memory Lane . . . ooh, what is this?" he added, spotting the knife at Nick's hip.

Nick winced. "Fuck!"

Sloan unclasped the knife and pulled it free, holding it up to the light. "Wow! Now that's quite a pig sticker!" Nick would have almost found this funny it wasn't for the shotgun, the homicidal eyes, and the fact that the woman he had recently taken a fancy to was strapped to a chair with her shirt in bloody ribbons.

Sloan was turning the blade this way and that when suddenly it appeared to twist of its own accord and struck at his face like a snake.

"Christ on a stick!" he screamed, whipping it away from him across the room. Nick heard it clattering across the floor as a ribbon of blood blossomed across Sloan's cheek. Right then there was a tentative knock on the sliding iron door.

Sloan motioned with his head for Boots to see to it while he positioned himself behind Nick, the twin barrels of the shotgun pressed into the base of his spine. Robin sprang to her feet and stood behind Amelia, pulling a pistol out of her waistband and putting it to Amelia's neck.

There was another polite knock at the metal door and, after some effort, Boots got the bolt shot back and slid it open halfway.

Frank Percy stood there, right hand poised in mid-knock. His eyelids were at half-mast.

"Avon cawling . . . shpare a drink?"

Boots looked back over his shoulder at Sloan and raised his hands in a "your call" gesture when a shadow stepped in from the side.

Nick blinked twice.

The shadow revealed itself as Tommy Falcon and, unless Nick was mistaken, the large-caliber pistol he put up to Boots' temple was the very same one he had been re-assembling the day Nick had come by his shop.

It looked a lot bigger and a whole lot scarier in one piece.

Boots got shoved backwards into the warehouse at the same time Nick heard the unmistakable deadly click of the revolver's hammer being cocked. All of Tommy's 'jovial Elvis' shtick had vanished.

The steel blue eyes were cold as diamonds.

"Well, well, well," Sloan said, "Old friends are just falling out of the woodwork tonight. Hold it right there, Tommy, or the kid gets his spine blown in half."

Then Boots stumbled and fell and Amelia screamed again.

After that, things happened pretty fast.

-9-

NICK HADN'T been idle throughout the history update either. While Robin had been going through her little tirade, he'd made good use of the clippers in his jacket pocket. Rusty as they were, after working the grips open and closed a few times, he was able to get it working. By the time Sloan had plucked the knife out of its sheath, he had already clipped the chain and was holding his hands behind his back strictly to maintain appearances.

Time can be a funny thing, though. Like the last few minutes on the classroom clock on the last day of school, it seemed to slow to an agonizing crawl, when in fact it was all over in barely a minute.

Just as Boots stumbled backward, Nick whipped his body around and knocked the shotgun aside with his forearm. It was one of those things that, had he thought about it, he would never in a million years have attempted it. But events seemed to have taken on a life and purpose of their own.

The roar of the shotgun, even in the big open warehouse, was deafening. The left side of the couch next to Robin exploded, along with the Lava lamp. A stray piece of double-aught buckshot went through Robin's left cheek, pulverizing one of her molars as it exited. As she stumbled backward, Amelia dropped to the floor.

Nick, his hearing obliterated for the moment by a loud ringing, kept twisting as the shotgun continued to arc toward Amelia. He pushed it upwards out of harm's way, plunging the clippers with all his might into Sloan's thigh. The second barrel went off, shattering some of the glass skylights, as well as a couple of rows of the florescent lighting system, which triggered a sequential blackout of most the overhead lights in a dramatic cascade of sparks and shards of glass tubing.

Sloan was making a high-pitched scream like a little girl and Robin was taking aim at Amelia. Before she could fire there was a loud *pkow* from the Ruger Blackhawk .44 Magnum in Tommy Falcon's hands, which destroyed most of her knee cap and shattered her leg.

That was all she wrote for Amelia's ex-friend for this event.

Sloan grabbed Nick with his free hand, throwing him with surprising force into the coffee table, which sent him into a tumbling sprawl.

With sparks cascading down from the overhead lights and the lighting intermittent, Sloan hobbled over to the Chevy van and got in through the passenger door. Tommy got off one shot that took out the passenger side window and one more that put a large hole next to the head of the sword-bearing barbarian painted on the side (who naturally had a semi-clad woman clinging to his leg). Before he could squeeze off another, Boots was up and grappling with him. Amelia swore she saw Nick yank open the back door of the van and leap in as the engine roared to life, the headlights coming on, as, with a squeal of tires, the vehicle plowed through everything, slamming through the swinging garage doors at the back of the warehouse and off into the night.

After a brief struggle, Boots found his skull on the receiving end of the wooden grip of the .44, which broke his cheekbone. Then Tommy's left fist connected with his jaw and knocked him out cold.

The van was gone, Sloan was gone, Nick was gone. (So was the Triumph motorcycle, but that wasn't noticed until later.) Robin was screaming in agony and the acrid aroma of spent gunpowder and the ozone of blown electronics filled the air.

Tommy ran over to Amelia and knelt beside her. "Good Lord, are you all right?"

The jury was still out on that one, but it appeared the damage looked worse than it really was. Sloan had only been toying with her before Nick had been hauled in. After a quick once over, Tommy cradled her in close and ran his fingers through the messy tangles of her hair. "You're gonna be fine, darlin,' you're gonna be just fine."

Amelia was clutching Tommy's shirt and sobbing, but she pulled away and looked up. "Tommy, you have to catch them. Dicky . . . Nick is in the van!"

Nearby, Robin was wailing. "I'm dying, oh god, I'm dying. Somebody please help! *Aaggghh!*"

Tommy patted Amelia on the head and, standing up, walked over to Robin, the .44 still in one hand. Seeing that hand cannon in close proximity convinced her lips to restrict themselves to a quivering grimace and, through clenched teeth, she said in a much tinier voice, "I'm . . . going to die . . . you killed me!"

Tommy shook his head. "Woman, if I wanted you dead, you and I wouldn't be talkin'. Best shut up before I change my mind though."

With that, he pulled out his cell phone with his free hand and punched in 9-1-1.

Sloan fishtailed the van as he spun out of the warehouse parking lot. The driver's side fender was crumpled in and the headlight knocked askew but the American-made circa 1975 six-cylinder engine was cranking out the RPMs and the van leapt up River Road like some nightmare apparition from the age of disco and bad haircuts. No sooner had the van jumped onto Main Street than the radio sprang to life, tuned to a classic rock station and, apropos enough, to ELO's hit *Strange Magic* with Jeff Lynde lamenting through the van's souped up speaker system:

"Oh I'm never gonna be the same again
now that I've seen the way it's got to end...
What a strange magic . . ."

Zooming up to the four corners of Main Street, Sloan veered left onto 9B and headed north out of town. He'd ripped the clippers out of his thigh and tossed them into the passenger seat, squealing like a pig as blood spurted out through his fingers. The wound was more painful than life-threatening but it would have to wait. First on Dicky Sloan's To Do list was to get the hell out of Dodge quickly and efficiently. Second depended on whether he wanted to:

A) Head across the Hudson at the Bear Mountain Bridge and back down the Palisades to New York to tie up some loose ends or . . .

B) Take the 'Fuck-it' option in which he tools all the way up to Canada and catches a flight out to some remote corner of the earth where he can lay low (possibly Argentina) and work out his next move while the storm blows over.

Trouble was it was too early to know just what level of shit-storm he was currently in. Keeping the pressure on his thigh with his right hand while hunching over the steering wheel, his left hand worked the wheel in a white-knuckle grip as the speedometer inched up past sixty, then sixty-five. The van zoomed past a 30mph speed limit sign and one of those helpful electronic speed-check readout jobs that warned: "Your actual speed is: 67mph!"

Fortunately, most of the Wyvern Falls law enforcement community was out at the carnival with the rest of the shift on standby at the main station.

For Dicky Sloan, all his old chickens were coming home to roost. Well, three of them at least.

The van with its garish fantasy art careened up Route 9B, which, luckily (or unluckily) for Sloan, was devoid of southbound traffic. Jeff Lynde's continuing pronouncements from the world of 1975 about *Strange Magic* was only underscoring, even augmenting, the surrealness of the situation. The song seemed to go on forever and a half – a common ailment of 70s hits – but part of this in fairness could be attributed to Sloan's perception shift.

[Slippage]

As events played out to their inevitable conclusion.

Sloan looked ghastly in the uplit glow from the dashboard. It didn't help that somewhere in the last minute he'd tried to wipe the sweat out of his eyes and left a broad smear of blood across his face.

"Oh, Dicky, Dicky, Dicky, this can't be happening! No, no, no! We had plans, you and I . . ."

Sloan was unaware he was singing along with ELO in an off-key shriek as the van pulled into the straightaway past the entrance to the old Van Eyckmann estate. The needle on the speedometer was edging past 80 and the Chevy engine was showing its age. It rattled and shook, the pistons developing an alarming knock as black smoke blew out of the exhaust pipe.

Also showing age was the merciless music promoter who had sat unblinking through countless contract signings (although those had been farther between in the past ten years), the almost psychotically-detached wheeler and dealer who had negotiated many shrewd and very profitable concert tours, merchandising deals, and last, last but not least, the seemingly fearless counterfeit goods supplier who had bullied his way into the Canal Street market in more recent years – those versions of Richard Sloan had unraveled and fallen away like a cheap knock-off dress made in a back-alley sweatshop.

In their place was a terrified, injured, and unbalanced man-child tipping over into the realm of lunacy.

Boots, had that noble soul and sidekick been conscious and present, might have done a repeat performance of his panicked flight the previous day, seeing the man he revered so in this present state.

(Sob) "Dicky, Dicky, what are we going to do? Why, why, why is this happening? Get away, got to get away, old boy! I can rebuild . . . I can start a new agency in Buenos Aires. There was that guy, Juan Carlos, I helped get signed back in '99 . . .I have friends! People who like me! Fucking Tommy Falcon. Dead! He's so fucking dead . . . hee-hee and Amelia, that pretty little cunt . . . I'll send for her; I'll send . . ."

"You'll what, mate?"

It took Sloan a good heartbeat or two to realize another voice had spoken. Another voice distinctly not in his head.

Not at all.

Richard Sloan had an extra passenger with him.

Three, as a matter of fact.

Sloan looked back as a blond-haired face leaned forward in the flickering light coming through the windshield. Two dark-haired faces were on either side.

"This isn't happening. Not to the Sloan-meister! No way baby!" The tires of the van squealed as the road began its left twist into Dead Man's Curve.

The 'JCT 251' sign shot by in a white blur.

"Funny us all being together again, eh, Dicky?"

"Don't call me that! Nobody calls me that! You're dead! All of you! Get out of my van! I command you!"

"Sorry, no-can-do, mate. Command all you want; you have an appointment to keep with the guy downstairs . . ."

The faces of Lonely Dancers, at first a photo image of three young British musicians in their prime, mutated into something old, ghastly, and very dead.

Dicky screamed.

The van's tires did too.

". . . *Strange Magic . . . it's just a . . .*"

Pulling into the curve, Dicky realized he was suddenly alone and dropped his hand in relief. Because it was just a—

Three stone-faced figures straddling the curve of the road. Hands clasped behind. A British New-Wave fashion snapshot circa 1981.

Paul Brammell's eyes boring into Sloan's screaming visage.

Sloan's hands – it all came down to instinctive reflexes and the basic desire not to hit something – wrenched the wheel at the last moment. Gravity and the basic laws of physics kicked in. The van's old tires made a last effort at maintaining purchase before the treads flailed off. The over-taxed pistons of the Chevy Six could take no more and one rod fired through the engine block into the cab and took most of Sloan's bloody right hand with it through the roof. Then the van did a rolling tumble with all the grace of a somersaulting rhino, barreling through the air, windows shattering, metal crumpling, hub cabs flying, branches snapping.

It was all like a horrifying choreography.

The van sailed out of its third roll and the front end angled down into a tree stump, slamming the bulk of the engine up into the driver's seat, crushing Sloan's lower body as his upper torso separated and ejected through the shattering windshield. It did a weird back flip and was impaled upside down on the stump of a broken limb on the old oak tree. On the Sutherland's property.

Hanging.

The van smashed back down on its mangled tires with a muffled crump, one skewed headlight beam bouncing up, then down, then coming to rest on Sloan's corpse, as if it was some macabre art piece:

Severed Torso #15: Music Biz Payback.

Dicky Sloan had finished his one-way ticket. In the opposite direction from another crash so many years before.

A moment later, there was another screech of tires as a motorcycle fishtailed to a stop. Then the sound of someone vomiting.

-10-

AMELIA WAS sitting on the toilet, hunched over and crying, when there came a knock at the front door. It had already been an award-winning evening, what with getting kidnapped and tortured by the industrious Dicky Sloan, discovering her best friend of thirty years ago had not only betrayed her but was the instrument of Paul's death and directly responsible for destroying her life. Then seeing her lover take off after Sloan and, if what Tommy heard over his police band was true, had just been killed in another accident, up on Route 9B. And if her instincts were on the money, at the same spot where Paul had died all those years ago.

For the last half hour after Tommy had dropped her off back at her apartment (she had all but physically manhandled him out the door, insisting she would be fine, she just needed to be alone, rest, and no, absolutely not go to the hospital), she had sat on the toilet, a straight-edge safety razor in her right hand, trying to get up the courage to draw it across her left wrist.

It was hell of a lot harder than she had imagined.

Perhaps she lacked the single-minded decisiveness of a true suicide. Perhaps after all, she was a coward and a failure, even when it came to ending her own life.

Or perhaps she had already survived so much that it seemed like a monumentally stupid idea.

There was the knocking again. This time, it was a fist banging on the door.

For a moment, she considered ignoring it and carrying through with her "plan," but then whatever was left of her self-pitying attempt fluttered away. Whoever was at the door apparently had no intention of going away anytime soon and, as her dad once said, "If you can't finish the business, don't start it."

She had a hunch it was Tommy back with more news – unless it was the police – so back went the razor blade into the medicine cabinet. She tightened the belt on her terry-cloth robe, did what she could with a few quick strokes with the hairbrush, and, frowning at the smudged mascara and dark circles under her eyes, walked out to the front room.

Just as the glass in the door window shattered.

Ordinarily Amelia would have screamed, but it appeared she was all screamed out for the evening. Instead she simply stood there, arms at her side, tears running down her cheeks while she waited passively for whatever latest dark joke the Gods of Irony had visited upon her.

Apparently, all they had left in their joke box was Lawrence 'Boots' Miller. After fumbling with the inside locks with his hand, Boots invited himself in. Boots wasn't exactly looking top of his game either. His cheek had swollen to the point that one eye was nearly shut and the offset state of his jaw suggested he wouldn't be doing any heavy eating for some time yet, particularly if the broken teeth just visible to one side and the stream of blood bubbling past his lips were any indication.

Amelia was trying to remember how things had been left back in the warehouse but her mental eight ball was coming back: Reply hazy, try again later. She could only recall that Boots had been left sprawled on the concrete floor, out cold. Tommy hadn't thought him much of an additional threat at the time.

An assessment that would have to be seriously re-evaluated, based on the bone-handled six-inch knife gleaming in his right hand.

"Oh, goody, look who's home!" he attempted to say, though it came out sounding more like "*Ohthuddy, okkooshome!*"

Amelia continued to just stand there. The knife was looking like a practical and immediate solution to most of her life's problems. Boots waved it slowly back and forth across her face as if he could mesmerize her with it. Instead it was only making her dizzy.

"Into the bathroom, Missy. It'll be easier to clean up. After I have some fun with you." Or: "*Intooshbafroom Mishy, shittle ebeshierto clean up afta Ihaffshumfunwidyu.*"

Amelia was in full agreement. At least with the first two statements. She walked backward, still watching the knife blade, using her hand to guide herself into the small bathroom she had just recently exited. Life was turning into such a series of revolving doors these past few days. The bathroom was looking like an abysmal stage set for her last act in life. The 1930s black-and-white tiles were stained and in one corner patched with concrete. The sink was a third-rate Ikea job whose white chipboard frame was sagging with age and humidity. The medicine cabinet and mirror over it were about the same quality and vintage, and the bathtub was one of these deep old art deco things with a good eighty years of rust and lime stains to prove it.

The toilet was probably the one item in good condition – a high pressure SAC that practically sucked the air out of the room when you flushed it.

At least she would go out in a room with a top quality crapper.

Boots pressed her backwards until she sat down heavily on the rim of the tub. The wicked-looking blade caressed back and forth across her throat. His sour breath with its coppery tinge of blood filled the air, quickly overwhelming the dish of Target potpourri by the sink. The blade then played across her breasts while Boots grinned a lopsided grin, eyes gleaming with dimwitted sadistic lust. His free hand worked at the zipper of his soiled jeans.

The blade prodded, then neatly sliced open her blood-stained blouse. Her small breasts, still bleeding from the long marks made by Sloan's bullwhip, fell loose. Boots breathed heavily. He placed the blade horizontally across her throat while he worked his penis out of underwear that hadn't seen the inside of a washing machine in weeks.

Amelia closed her eyes.

She'd already decided to force the issue to a speedy conclusion rather than face what was certainly coming next.

What did come next was over in seconds.

There was a slurred "Wuh?" from Boots' mouth and the blade was lifted abruptly away. Amelia's eyes flew open in time to see Boots spin around and swore she glimpsed over his shoulder a thatch of moussed blond hair and a biker jacket. What she was spared was seeing the six-inch knife, seemingly of its own accord, arc up and then swiftly down, burying itself in his crotch to the hilt. He let out a muffled grunt, then by his own hand the knife was torn out, described a second arc and this time plunged into his sternum with enough force to topple him backward into the bathtub.

The last thing Amelia saw as she pitched forward and fainted was Boots collapsing into the tub in a spray of bright arterial blood.

This time it was like a frame dropped out of badly-edited movie. One moment she was falling forward into oblivion, the next, she was on her back in the middle of her bed, in her bedroom, looking up past two very concerned faces looking down on her.

One was Tommy Falcon.

The other was Nick Carr.

The world went fuzzy and grey around the edges, like old insulation, then snapped back as Tommy cracked a vial of smelling salts under her nose.

"Stay with us honey," Tommy said in his deep rolling voice.

She struggled to sit up, finally managing it with Nick's help.

"Easy," he said, putting a glass of water to her lips.

She took a couple of sips, then touched his jaw with her finger tips, trying to process that he was real.

"You?"

"Me."

"Really?"

"Really."

Then the image of Boots and the knife and the tub rolled over in her mind and she tried to bolt out of the bed. Tommy and Nick held her in place with a bit of effort.

She cried out, "Oh, God, he's in the bathroom!"

Tommy kept his grip tight. "No, he's not. He's gone. Forever and for better, Amen."

That was all he would say on the subject. Nick had gotten there first and, after a good two minutes of flipping out, settled into an eerie calm and got down to taking care of business, once he figured out Amelia was only passed out. Fortunately, she was one of those old-fashioned types who kept her address book right next to the telephone and, better yet, Tommy's cell number was penciled in next to his home one. Tommy listened to Nick's summary on the situation, not saying a word until Nick had finished, and then "Don't touch a thing, chief. I'll be there in five minutes."

He was there in three.

After a quick once over, he pulled Nick aside and put a firm hand on his shoulder. "Son, I'm gonna need some help on this. It's a nasty bit of business but I have an idea how we might set things to rights. Only two things you need to know: Amelia is like family to me and I will do anything I have to, to protect her and to see her done good. The other is that, should anything ever get out of the bag on this, I and I alone will take the drop on this. You were never here tonight." He squeezed Nick's shoulder and looked him hard in the eye. "Got it?"

Nick swallowed but looked him right back. "Got it."

"Good man. Now let's get to work."

It had taken the better part of two hours to get Boots' body wrapped up in a heavy tarp Tommy had brought with him and to get the body muscled into the back of a beat-up pick-up truck Nick had never seen before and never would again. Boots might have been a 130 dripping wet, but dead weight is dead weight and both men were breathing hard by the time they got back up to the apartment. Half an hour with rubber gloves, Clorox, tile cleanser and brushes and there was little even a determined forensics team would have found. Not that anyone in the law enforcement community would be particularly eager to find out where good old Boots Miller had gotten off to. Tommy had taken off in the truck, leaving Nick to stay with Amelia.

Within a week, the truck would be at a junkyard in New Jersey getting compressed into a cube of scrap metal.

A couple of days later, a certain Canal Street businessman with a Tong tattoo on his left wrist would get a surprise when the shipment of grey-market refrigerators contained a little bonus in one of them, a decomposing corpse with a note pinned to the soiled Levi jacket breast pocket:

"Recommend finding new supplier, negotiations didn't go well. Signed, WF Glee Club"

In Boots' wallet was also a carefully prepared business card that read:

Mirage Management, Ltd.
Robin Hotchkiss, *Executive Director*
Entertainment * Music * Select Artist Representation

In his other pocket was a beat-up disposable cell phone with a text message from three days ago on it:

"Boots, fucking Chinks! Moving into some action in Spanish Harlem. C-Town is next. Time to kick some slant-eye butt! – RH

A few days later after that there was a police report of several Asian-looking men seen in the vicinity of Robin Hotchkiss's house over on Croton Lane in the Barrows and, although there was no clear sign of forced entry or foul play, there was also no sign of Miss Hotchkiss.

Except a pair of crutches lying on the floor next to her bed, along with one of those hard-plastic leg casts that strap on.

Tommy Falcon was a big believer in harsh justice. Especially when someone messed with his friends.

Before he left in the pick-up truck that night (or morning – it was more like 3:30 a.m. by that point), Tommy pulled Nick aside again. He wasn't sure what Nick had or hadn't figured out. The kid was bright but the whole business with the knife and Boots didn't add up to any rational answers but definitely a few uncomfortable ones, so he told him to stick around with Amelia a bit and he would check back later in the day. He also asked Nick to give him the sheath for the knife off his belt. When Nick hesitated, he said, "Son, I don't know the whole deal with this thing, but what I do know is that it can be mighty dangerous. I think our good friend Boots would agree. It may have worked for the Good Guys this round, but I wouldn't want to bet the bank on it next time, yeah?"

Nick thought about the gruesome scene he had walked in on hours before. He had a feeling he would be revisiting it more than a few times in his nightmares in the weeks to come.

Nick was also quite sure he didn't want something with such terrible potential – or history – within ready reach of his hands. He'd read somewhere that some blades get a taste for blood and begin to yearn for it.

A ridiculous concept. Of course.

But maybe one he didn't want to test.

Nick found himself back in Amelia's apartment feeling awkward and unsure of what to say or do next. There was the inescapable and bittersweet sense that things had changed, in himself, in his view of the world, between them, everything.

For the past few days, he had been flying unbelievably high then somehow everything had become, well, incredibly fucked up. He found her sitting on the couch in the front room and, for lack of a better strategy, he walked over and sat down next to her, putting his arm around her shoulder as she put a hand on his knee.

They both spoke at the same time:

"Nick, I'm so sorry . . ."

"Amelia, I don't know what to . . ."

Then they simply held each other for a while.

Then a kiss. And then another.

In his ear, she said in a sultry voice, "Hmm . . . let me go and, baby, I'll drop . . ."

He didn't until they got into the bedroom.

-11-

NICK CAME into the kitchen around 11:30, surprised to see his dad sitting there at the kitchen table.

"Deja-vu all over again," as Yogi Berra once said.

Val Carr didn't look at all surprised. This time there was no newspaper, no coffee. He was just sitting there, hands in his lap. Outside was about as picture perfect a summer day as one could order, if one were ordering a moderate one in the 70s with a light breeze and a few cumulus clouds chasing each other across the sky. From somewhere out the window came the drone of a neighbor's lawnmower and the faint scent of newly-cut grass. When Nick came in, he motioned to an empty chair at the table. Something was different in his dad's demeanor. Nothing he could put a finger on, but something definitely different.

Non-confrontational.

Nick pulled up seat.

The silence stretched out for a good two minutes. Finally, his dad spoke up:

"You missed the funeral this morning."

Shit, Nick thought, mentally kicking himself, *I completely forgot* . . .

As if sensing this, his Dad made a dismissive gesture with his hand. "That's not what this is about. I got a call from Tommy Falcon. Just a little while ago."

Nick had thought the day was finished with surprises. Apparently he was wrong. That Tommy Falcon might be on close enough terms to simply call his dad raised all sorts of questions. For starters, it suggested that there might be more than a few things about his dad he didn't know anything about. He folded his fingers together and said nothing.

After another span of minutes, Val Carr looked up at the ceiling, as if seeking some divine inspiration. Then he leveled his gaze at his son.

"I heard you had a pretty rough time of it last night."

Silence.

His dad glanced around, as if to reassure himself they had the place to themselves, then, much to Nick's surprise, he pushed his chair back, stood up, walked over, and put one leg up on the chair at Nick's end of the table, clasping one arm with the other.

"Son, look . . . I know I'm hard on you a lot. Hell, hard on you pretty much *all* the time . . . but you're still my son. You might not believe it, but truth is I just want what's best for you."

Another lengthy pause while the crickets zinged in the grass outside. "Tommy and I go back a ways." A brief chuckle while he studied Nick's expression. Then, "*Why* isn't any concern of yours. And I'd hardly recommend him as a role model . . . but then again you could do a hell of a lot worse. Bottom line is, his word still holds water and he said you handled yourself well last night. Whatever happens with you and this Evans woman . . . as long as you do right . . . hell, it ain't for me to judge. We clear?"

Nick was stunned. He didn't trust himself to speak, as tears were welling up in his eyes, and there was a faint quiver in his lower lip he didn't care much for. But, tightening his jaw, he nodded.

And if there weren't enough surprises being dished out today, he felt his dad's hand on his shoulder. Maybe the first time in . . . ten . . . fifteen years?

As if sensing this, his dad spared him any further embarrassment and simply added, "Go on, get the hell out of here and get yourself some rest. And check on your brother when you get a chance. He's been having a pretty rough time of it himself . . ."

That was about as close to tacit approval as one could hope to get from Valery Carr. Nick gave a little fist bump on his dad's knee as he stood up then went upstairs to crash.

It was around 6:00 p.m. when he pulled up to Amelia's apartment. On his car stereo, Karl Wallinger of World Party had been singing *Way Down Now*. Nick wasn't quite sure why he was back or what he intended to say, but he had a hunch he might. Neither prepared him for who was sitting at the top of the stairs, waiting for him.

Sabina Torres.

She was wearing a tank top and white cutoff shorts – a somewhat conservative choice in the Torres fashion book – but with the same sandals he'd seen her in the previous . . . Friday? It seemed like years ago. Her pile of hair was pinned back high on her head and he noticed she had an envelope dangling between her fingers. She was looking at him with a curious expression.

He looked at her back.

Finally: "She told me everything. Well, maybe not *everything*. But enough. Nick . . . I'm so sorry. I really am." Looking carefully in her eyes he was convinced it was true. *Almost*.

But maybe he was getting past cynical for his years.

Sabina held out the envelope. "She asked me to give this to you." A wry smile. "And *no*, I didn't read it."

He took it and glanced at the sealed lip, then tore it open and flicked out a short note written in Amelia's loopy, girlish script (with hearts above the 'i's):

Dear Nick,

How do I even begin to say what these past few days have been like for me? You swept me off my feet (literally!☺!) and into a whirlwind weekend I will never, never forget. You have no idea what that meant, or how wonderful it's been after so many years of fear, sadness, hating myself. You're so sweet, and tender, and such an amazing lover!

I know you must think me weird, but what we shared was so very special and I will never, never forget it. But you must also know that this could never work. Maybe in another life time, another age, but there are too many obstacles here: Paul, what happened with Dicky and Boots, the past – it could never simply be just you and me and that just wouldn't be fair. You deserve better. Much better than I could ever give. Nick, you're so young and your whole life is ahead of you! Follow your heart and I know the girl of your dreams will someday walk right out of one of your songs and into your arms.

All my love,
Amelia

PS: And thank you. This is not a proper way to end things but I'm not much good at goodbyes. But you have given me such a wonderful gift – finally I will leave Wyvern Falls and see what life has in store…but please don't look for me, I want to leave things as they were last night.
PPS: Sabina is not as evil as she looks!

Snorting, Nick shook his head and, stepping past Sabina, pushed open the door and glanced around. There was no question, Amelia was gone. There was a distinct absence of her *thereness*. He took a quiet walk around the apartment, trying to process the reality that so much had unfolded here in the past four days – an entire lifetime – and it was already over like a stage set abandoned by its actors. All her personal items were gone. All that remained were pieces of old furniture. Each with an episode, a story. Now mute and lifeless.

He felt a flooding sense of longing, bittersweet and tinged with sadness. Then it was gone. Or at least put away carefully into that box he would need in the future. The one labeled "Song Ideas."

He folded the letter, put it neatly into his jacket pocket, and stepped outside into the cool evening. Sabina was still standing at the top of the stairs, giving him a searching look, one he'd never seen before.

"Care to take a girl to the carnival?"

"Sure. Why the hell not?"

III. LORENZO KING
AND THE DUNDERBERG IMP

"...he that runs races with goblin troopers, is likely to have rough riding of it."

-Washington Irving, "The Legend of Sleepy Hollow"

-1-

IT WAS ALMOST a scene worthy of an old Norman Rockwell Saturday Evening Post cover: the study at the back of the 1930s Cape Cod on Van Cort Lane with its knotty yellow pine paneling and crown moldings with their motif of alternating playing card cutouts: clubs, diamonds, spades, hearts in black/red/black/red pattern. There was an efficient-looking mahogany desk with a brass lamp and a side table with an antique Atwater radio rubbing shoulders with a dispatcher's shortwave unit and several shooting match trophies. Angled near the corner of the desk was a framed photo of the Wife and a photo of the Two Daughters in a "We Love You Daddy!" frame (two pretty high-school girls standing by an overlook in the Mohonk Mountains sporting identical "boy-what-a-great-day!" grins). There was a blotter with a perfectly-arranged pen holder and a "Greetings from Niagara Falls!" ashtray that hadn't seen a cigarette butt in ten years. The overstuffed couch with its floral pattern said "yes, a woman put me here" and a few ships models arranged around the room, including a 40" one of the racing schooner Bluenose in a glass case. On the walls was a collection of framed photos of pistol matches, awards, various group photos of police doing various group police things, including one taken of a hunting trip in Montana back in 1988. One stood out from the pack: a photograph of an eagle-eyed young man in a state trooper's uniform with his Sam Brown belt and a hefty pistol, leaning against a patrol car phased out in the early 1980s, a man who looked like he still had the world by its horns and could handcuff and take it down in a regulation choke hold if necessary; a man who looked ready, willing, and very capable of enforcing the laws he had sworn to uphold and protect.

There was a noticeably older version of that very same man sitting in the old-style captain's chair before the desk, hooded grey eyes still sharp as an eagle's but now with a perpetual squint from many long years of watching New York State's highways and byways for trouble. The hair was now gray but still in a regulation cut, courtesy of a twice-a-month visit to Mikhail's Barber Shop across from the old Alhambra Theater on Main Street, and he was in his faded workshop Levi's but still looked every inch the police officer.

This was Roy Hendricks, current police chief of Wyvern Falls and the whole family-man-in-his-study scene looked pretty good if you glossed over the fact that the wife in the photo was dead some three years and that he had been sitting there for the past five minutes with barrel of his .357 Magnum in his mouth.

A cough of static came through the dispatcher's unit, followed by Lieutenant Raymond Sanchez' deep voice: "Chief, you there?"

The abrupt noise in the cozy-sized room almost startled Hendricks into ending his career right then and there.

Hendricks carefully released the hammer on the Smith & Wesson and, opening a side drawer, placed it in there and locked it. There were only two safety mechanisms keeping him from blasting his brains all over the ceiling of his quaint American study and they were called Andrea and Pamela, the two girls in the framed photo. His wife, Helen, had been subtracted from life's equation by a felon his badge, gun and even the laws of New York State were powerless against: cancer. The black gulf of depression that had subsequently opened in his heart had been, and still was (to him at least), unimaginable.

Sanchez was a good officer. A bit of a ladies' man with a boxer's physique and a deep voice that resulted in an unusually high amount of phoned in "problems" from women popping up during his shifts, he had the hallmarks of an outstanding policeman: calm, confident, and methodical. He was also wasting his time in a small river town like Wyvern Falls and Hendricks was looking to convince him to move on to the bigger leagues in White Plains or even New York City. It would mean losing an indispensable member of his force but Hendricks wasn't one for holding people back.

Sanchez' voice came through again. "Hello Chief, are you there? Copy."

No "yo's" or "'sups" for Raymond, who seemed to be on a mission to prove himself the well-spoken and cultured Officer Sanchez. Can't bust on him for that, Hendricks thought. In fact, I wouldn't mind if a couple of other officers took their cues from him. The ones who acted like they were dressing up as cops and that high-fiving the local homeboys was part of winning a popularity contest. He took another long look at his dead wife's picture then, with a sigh, reached over and picked up the mic.

"Copy. What's up?"

Another cough of static. For all the technology, Sanchez sounded like he was talking from a tin can. "Roger that. The guy from LiveEye NY? Lorenzo King? He just arrived." Hendricks felt his spirits sink further. He'd gotten the courtesy call from King's network the day before but that didn't help much. He was already getting a hinky feeling that this year's carnival would be problematic, even though he couldn't have articulated why exactly. Hendricks wasn't much for omens, horoscopes, or any other sort of "flighty" rubbish, but he did trust his instincts and they were starting to see little yellow and orange flags popping up here and there. No red ones just yet, but it was early in the game. Either way, the last thing he wanted was a pestering, self-important reporter who, by all accounts, was a legend in his own mind stirring up trouble.

But he wasn't going to fix much sitting on his ass at home.

He shook his head and pressed the mic.

"Thanks, Lieutenant. I'll be there in ten."

-2-

LORENZO KING still saw himself as the next big thing in the New York media, an investigative reporter who thrived on exploitative journalism. Selling himself as a tough and aggressive type who'd worked his way up from the streets of Spanish Harlem (he was from an affluent neighborhood in Suffolk County), King combined unwavering ambition, tireless energy, and an ego of epic proportions into a compact, meticulously groomed and dressed five-foot seven-inch frame. Long before he had stood before that microphone on his very first job as a reporter for NY1 – landed with a dramatic audition tape he'd made with the help of his cousin Ricky – his concept of himself as *Latino Media Legend Numero Uno* had already coalesced. It was simply a matter of the rest of the world catching up to this amazing fact.

And in fairness – for a while at least – it appeared that might be in the cards for Mister King.

Aside from his weekly blog "Lorenzo Sez" and regular appearances at any public event, he was a firm believer that any opportunity that put his face in front of a camera (and subsequently up on YouTube, Twitter, Facebook, and every other available media outlet) was worth pursuing.

Whether it was a "big-ticket news item" like uncovering a local election scandal or something as mundane as the opening of a pre-school day care center in Queens, your man El Lorenzo was there.

However, as anyone who has worked in media and entertainment will tell you, fame is a fickle mistress and can elude even the most earnest efforts. While LiveEYE NY had its dedicated core following, in the last six months its ratings had slid into the horse latitudes with more viewers gaining interest in the show in the follow-up slot, Ghost Seekers International. And, despite King's best attempts to inject some new life into the show (he had a habit of referring to himself in the third person as

"The Lorenzo" or "El Lorenzo"), June had turned out to be a slow news month and ultimately news made the show. The only big-ticket items had been the gay marriage issue (definitely a no-fly zone topic for the homophobic King) and the endless skewering of Anthony Weiner in the Post and Daily News, which had become the proverbial flogging of a dead horse, though admittedly the Representative's combination of sneering mug and last name seemed tailor-made for such skewering. Then someone at the show got a tip about this carnival up the river that still ran of all things – can you believe it? – some sort of old-fashioned Carnival Freak Show. Possible angle of exploiting society's unfortunates. Minorities involved. A long shot, a desperate news scrap that would on any normal day be ignored, but it was slim pickings this week. King had been mortified but his producer hadn't been.

LiveEYE's ratings hadn't just been slow this week; they had been swirling around in the toilet all spring. A lesser man would have been in a panic.

"Get your ass up there King and make some hay for us, bud," His producer had said, "LiveEye NY is becoming TiredEyeNY and that doesn't bode well for your so-called job security. People are getting tired of your same old shit. And lately your ratings have been wallowing in the dumpster, in case you hadn't noticed."

King was one of those types who was Teflon-coated when it came to negative news regarding themselves. He responded as if he hadn't heard, "*Mierda*, Sammy. The Kardashians are in town – we're doing a scoop tomorrow night at Kiss and Tell – and you want to send me chasing fucking midgets at a freaking carnival at some piss-ass river town up on the Hudson?"

Actually, that was a stretch – the Kardashians *were* in town but not necessarily scheduled to be at one of New York's trendier night clubs this coming weekend. And he thought they were about as clever and entertaining as a bunch of discount doormats at Target. But they were a guaranteed news item and any celebrity he could tack his name to was good news in his mind. That wasn't even the point. The point was he was The Lorenzo. And the King called the shots. Not the other way around. Or at least he would in two weeks, when the new contracts were signed and his new reality show started shooting: City Streets, about the trials and tribulations of a street-wise (and extremely good-looking) Latino news reporter on the hard-bitten beats of New York. Then Sammy and that shit-ass New York "news" show could kiss his ass.

At the moment though, Sammy wasn't listening, which was also typical: ". . . forget the goddamn *Hardcashians*, buddy, they wouldn't even talk to you last time, or any time, remember? Besides, you owe so much on your tab at Kiss and Tell they wouldn't serve you a glass of fucking water.

AJ'll be your camera man. He'll meet you at Grand Central tomorrow. Call him to confirm. And I'm sending along an intern – nice Japanese kid from NYU. You can show him the ropes and he can fetch your coffee and shine your shoes and talk chop-suey, right? But next time I hear from you, your waxed Latino ass better be on a Metro North train tooting up the Hudson. Come Monday, I want to see some very angry and very exploited-looking midgets streaming from my website. Yeah? Otherwise, we're looking at switching your slot with that new Ghost Seeker's International show. They're getting some traction, bud."

Lorenzo was working on getting his teeth unclenched. He hated being called 'Bud' even if Sammy called everyone under fifty at the show that, and the snipe about Ghost Seekers International was a straight-out jab and twist. Sammy knew he was pissy about that bunch of twenty-something lug heads fresh out of a bad college dorm party and quickly cashed in on the whole Ghost Hunters and Haunted reality show bandwagon, with their infrared cameras, bogus equipment, and even more bogus staff titles. On top of that, he hated having AJ as a camera man. Alan Jefferson Parker was a vet from the first Iraq War, a towering bald black man with the shoulders of a linebacker who wasn't much for indulging King and his "mystique." And the last thing he needed was some geeky intern tripping over his heels and pestering him with idiotic questions.

"God, how long must a professional wait for a decent personal assistant and a stylist? Where the fuck was the stylist?"

-3-

BY THE TIME King arrived at the American Hotel in Wyvern Falls, his mood had gone from foul to seething.

The intern had been worse than he'd expected: a chattering over-eager kid named Hideki Hasegawa who insisted he was big fan of "the King" and was keen to move to America, start his own game show, and become a "Repubrican" because he understood they had all the money and lived in gigantic houses called "Macks Mansions."

On the train ride up, King had become convinced he was about to make the switch from "Celebrated Investigative Reporter" (in his own mind at least) to "Foreign Intern Killer" and could already see the seventy-two-point headline on the front page of the Daily News: "King Krazy: Celeb Reporter Strangles Assistant!"

The cameraman, AJ Parker, wasn't any help either. He took up a separate seat on the Metro North Train with his gear, put his feet up, crossed his massive arms, and went to sleep for the whole trip. King suspected he was shamming for most of it but he knew better than to call him on it. AJ was a good cameraman but at six-four not a guy you wanted to mess with. At least he kept his mouth shut, did his job professionally, and pretty much ignored everything else, like it or not.

Then, when they got out of the cab at the old three-story wood building that looked straight out of an 1880s postcard, King felt his spirits sink even further. The American Hotel was a by-gone relic with full-length porches on the first and second floors, gabled dormers on the top floor, and just generally exuded a vague air of antiquity. A horse-drawn carriage would have looked more appropriate on the short half-circle drive than the ailing Ford Crown Vic 'Ecu-Taxi' that had just dropped them off.

The three of them stood there on the sidewalk with their luggage, looking up, one smiling, one indifferent, one with a look that ran between stricken disbelief and white fury.

"You . . . you booked me in . . . in *this*?" King was trying to convince himself that this was some sort of ludicrous joke.

Hideki nodded enthusiastically. "*Hai!* Taste of America! Website said it very historic!"

"But this is a fucking dump!"

"As long as it has a bed and a bar it works for me," Parker said, shouldering his RED ONE Video camera and equipment bag like they were child's toys.

King pulled a comb out of his pocket and ran it through his already perfectly groomed hair, a habit he did so frequently he wasn't even aware of it. With his shark-skin suit, Italian leather shoes (knock-off Gucci's) and clear lacquered nails, he looked perfectly groomed from head to toe, the proverbial city slicker almost ridiculously out of his element.

He shook his head resignedly, wondering how much worse this snowballing fiasco of a news scoop could possibly get.

A whole lot worse as it turned out.

The check-in desk was right out of a movie set. King had no frame of reference on how low tech it was, so he could barely understand it. Aside from a discreet smoke detector and sprinkler system, it appeared that the main lobby, with its dark wainscoting, plaster walls, yellowed lithographs, photographs, and one oil painting of the Wyvern Falls of yesteryear, hadn't been updated since. Even the threadbare carpet might have been original. The heavy-looking furniture had been reupholstered in the 80s, and ashtrays had been removed since the smoking ban caught up ten years ago, but that was about it.

As to the pictures (which only Hasegawa took time to look at), the oversized painting was a reasonably well-executed oil of The Mill and the Lowgate Bridge in the village, along with the picturesque falls that were the star feature of the village at the tail end of the eighteenth century. There was also a photo of the old Alhambra Theater on Main during its heyday, assorted other landmark buildings in town (most which now only existed in such historic images) and one photo of a Fireman's Parade from July Fourth, 1936. There was also a lithograph of Philipse Manor, another of the old Dutch Church in Sleepy Hollow, along with another unusual photo of Franklin Roosevelt chatting it up with Margaret "Daisy" Suckley on the vast porch of Wilderstein Manor near Rhinecliff.

The hotel had a traditional check-in desk. The kind made of solid oak gone black with age and with a key rack and letter cubby behind it. It also featured an old-fashioned ledger that you signed with your name and address and in return you received an actual metal key with a room number tag attached to it, the kind you turned a door lock with.

The man working the counter was thin, serious and a just little disconcerting in an Anthony Perkins sort of way, although physically he looked more like the Australian actor Guy Pierce. His thinning sandy-colored hair was combed back perfectly straight and the eyes peering over the rimless spectacles studied King and his companions as if weighing up whether they might run off with just the towels and bed sheets or perhaps might take the television and mattresses as well.

"Will you be staying with us longer than two days, Mister King?"

"I don't believe so, Mister . . .?"

"Oh, the name is Templeton. Gerald Templeton. Now the reservation was for three single guest suites, yes?"

King almost burst out laughing. *Suites? In this place?* He stifled his snicker with a cough but Templeton caught it anyhow.

"Did I say something funny, Mister King?" The face was smiling, one eyebrow raised, but something in his tone sounded serious. Maybe even a little dangerous. But King couldn't contain himself. The place reminded him of the Bates house in Psycho, even if it was smack in the middle of town. The next thing out of his mouth was, "I just hope your mother isn't downstairs in wheelchair, rotting away."

Templeton looked puzzled, and slightly affronted. "Why would my mother be in a wheel chair downstairs? She's in the kitchen cooking."

King shook his head, "Never mind." He knew the sound of a joke falling flat on its face when he heard it. Mercifully, the American Hotel had made one concession to the 21st century: a credit card processer. He handed over his Capitol One ('What's in your wallet? The only credit card left I can keep piling debt on!'), frowning.

Not for much longer.

LiveEYE NY had pulled all corporate cards a year ago when some bean counter in finance decided the recession was catching up a little too close to the UPX network's coffers. Now everything had to be expensed and lately it was taking up to two months to get reimbursed. And things were getting tight. King owed money to a few persons (like his supplier and his bookie for starters, his landlord and his ex-girlfriend for seconds) who weren't concerned with observing the niceties of the judicial system. Jacinta's brother "knew people"; *hombres* who would think nothing of breaking a few (or several) parts relating to his anatomy if a little persuasion was deemed necessary.

But this new deal with the Groove network would change all of that. The Lorenzo was going to finally get his day in the sun, his ship was finally coming to port, Hail, Mary and all the saints and amen!

Templeton handed back the credit card Asian fashion – with both hands – while ticking off the standard hotel-rules bullet list ("Check out is before 11:00 a.m., our Continental breakfast is served from 7 to 9 a.m., this brochure will provide you with a map and the location of several restaurants and other points of interest in the village") followed by the requisite "I do hope you enjoy our stay with us," delivered with just a hint of sincere efficiency.

King handed AJ and Hideki their respective keys. They had enough time to chill out before grabbing some dinner at whatever passed for a restaurant this far from the civilized streets of New York, then it was off to the carnival to sort out the lay of the land. AJ could get some establishing shots, King could get a sense of what the actual angles on the story might be. Get down with the little people. Chat up the half-pints and find out what their grievances were. They had an appointment with the carnival manager – George Ramos – the following afternoon and no doubt King would have to take his usual approach: a fast attack with a variety of insinuating questions, get him on the defensive, peck at him this way and that until he slipped (they almost always do) and they got a clip or two they could juice up with some clever editing.

Unscrupulous, sleazy carney overseer exploiting society's outcasts!

And these freaks . . . *what kind of terrible existence did they endure?* Mental torment, physical deformities, psychological issues, deviant sex lives etc. etc. He'd have to get Hideki to just shut up and stay the fuck out of everyone's way and maybe, just maybe, they could squeeze enough bitter drops of juice out of this lemon of a story to fool the public into thinking it was lemonade.

Then King saw the group of people coming down the stairs.

"Yo, boys – if it ain't Marc Anthony!"

King felt his entire body seize up. Looking like he'd just stepped off a college campus was Joel Hewitt, so called lead investigator and producer of the Ghost Seekers International, and, in king's mind, Public (and Private) Enemy Number One. In addition to the five-member investigative team (Garth Winslow, Karen Liu, Freddie Stern, Ann Constantine, and Bob Weiss), Joel had a production team consisting of:

Camera A Operator – Jim Farrell
Camera B Operator – Rick Petricello
Director of Photography (DP) – Mark Rubenstein
Camera Assistant (AC) – Claudia Rainey
Sound Engineer – Tom Grant
Personal Assistant – Sheila Walters

All of which underscored with a blinking bold line the current meagerness his own production team – or what he liked to refer to on air as his "run-and-gun squad," hinting at some sort of medium/large scale renegade staff operating under him:

Camera A Operator – AJ Parker
Personal Assistant/Intern – Hideki Hasegawa

"Very funny," King said, putting on a forced smile that taxed the muscles in his jaw. One thing his father's side had given him was an award-winning set of chompers and Lorenzo flashed them at every opportunity. From the get-go, Hewitt had struck King as the sort of hyper-active, over confident gung-ho fun guy who masked a cruel streak most people didn't seem to want to see. It also annoyed him endlessly that this white suburban brat from West Hampton Beach not only mis-appropriated every ghetto-culture buzz-word he could lay his hands on, but that his "docu-soap" paranormal show had eclipsed King's ambitious (and lamely derivative itself) effort in the ratings.

One bogus knock-off show was being one-upped by an even more bogus knock-off show.

All of which crossed King's mind in a split second. He had the uncanny ability to rewrite on the fly the fiction of his life so that the chapters all painted him as the winning model of success, no matter what the reality of the paper they were written on was saying otherwise.

All this took a shuddering hit as he found himself shaking Joel's hand with Joel's other hand thumping him on the shoulder like some long-lost school chum.

"*Booya*, my friend! What shakin'?"

"What brings you to this fine establishment?"

"Here? We're filming an episode here in the American Hotel this weekend. This place is crawling with ghosts! Talk about haunted! EMF readings are off the charts here, bro – this place is *Schiznit*! And we heard the carnival here rocks. How about yourself? Long ways from the mean streets of New York, man! What gives?"

Hewitt's tendency to mangle together all sorts of slang and lingo tended to tie King's brain up in knots. Distantly he heard a series of troubling key-words stumbling through his head – weekend . . . shooting . . . hotel . . . here – but he rallied his thoughts and say, 'Oh, just here following a lead on a possible story . . . heh, nothing too exciting."

Another clap on his shoulder, hard enough to make him wince.

"I doubt that, bro, you're always onto something dope. The Latin Lightning, that's you, man!"

King couldn't decide if he was being insulted or praised. Knowing Hewitt, probably both.

Hewitt was already moving on, pausing and looking up at Parker as if he were a statue that had mysteriously materialized in his path.

"Ah, AJ! Call me if you need a real job, homey!"

Seeing Parker's eyebrows go up slightly and giving a non-committal look that suggested he wasn't anybody's homey, Hewitt, never one to be off his game for long, turned back to King and said "See you around soon, bro!" Then to his team: "C'mon, Seekers, let's do a little sight-seeing and score some chow!"

Before he stepped out through the hotel's double oak doors, he said to Templeton, who was standing at the front desk and doing whatever perpetual busy work hotel clerks do at front desks, "Yo, Gerry, my man!" and, without waiting for a reply, left.

Templeton looked up with a distracted, vaguely annoyed look, as if he'd heard some nitwit shout an inappropriate comment from another room.

King stood a moment, smile still frozen on his face as he muttered, "Not if I see you first" through clenched teeth. Then Hasegawa was in front of him and holding up the slim point-and-shoot camera (a very sleek and hi-tech Canon model not available in the U.S.) with which he had been snapping away.

"See, I take a very nice picture of you with Mister Hewitt. He is very popular in Japan!"

"That's wonderful," King replied in a tone that suggested it was anything but. But he countered with a quick adjustment to his lapels and, snapping his cuffs, said, "Keep your eyes open though, my friend, because soon *El Lorenzo* will be a household word in Japan . . . and everywhere else!"

-4-

KING STOOD on the midway at the Feast of Saint Anne's Carnival, arms crossed, his right forefinger tapping on his left bicep. The flat cast of his eyes and compressed lips did not suggest a man in the best of moods.

This entire trip was turning into a debacle that was looking like it would wind up making him the laughingstock of the year. His first order of business when he got back to the City would be to track down the little *cabrón* who'd put Sammy up to this imbecilic excuse of a story and have him hung by his *cojones*.

In keeping with the continuing downward trajectory of this whole trip, the rooms had been pretty much a disaster. Calling the rooms at the American Hotel suites had been akin to calling a dilapidated old Volkswagen Beetle a luxury ride.

The rooms were spacious but that was about all that could be said in their favor. It had been more like a walk through a time portal into, say, the 1930s. The ceiling and wall fixtures hadn't been updated since then, the bed was some iron-framed thing with a sprung mattress and the 19-inch Zenith television was an ancient relic from the Lost World of Analog. Oh . . . and the bathroom? It was a shared cubby down the hall with cracked black and white tiles and a naked bulb hanging down from the ceiling. At least the suite sported a shower – it was a freestanding cut-rate job clumsily installed in one corner of the room, next to a wall-mounted porcelain sink with rust stains and an art deco mirror above it. The plaster on the walls was cracked in many places and the baseboards worn and scuffed. On a wash stand by the tall windows was a vase filled with fresh summer flowers, an almost bizarrely incongruous touch.

Only the short line of coke King had done with the quick, efficient movements of a well-oiled ritual had saved him from completely losing it, though the cramped bouncing ride out to the carnival in one of the ubiquitous local Ecu-Taxis that were found all over town did little to improve his mood.

There was a brief upswing as they stopped by the police station in the village and got some good establishing footage, the drama enhanced by what was a chaotic night already at the precinct, with King peppering Chief Hendricks (just as he arrived at the entrance no less) live on camera with all sorts of questions about the exploitation of society's undesirables and such at the local carnival. King kept the energy up reasonably well with insistent questions like, "Chief, were you aware of what's been going on here under the very noses of your very own police department every year here in this so-called All-American Carnival? Do you have any comment on what we understand to be some sort of Freak Show at your carnival?" Followed by allegations of abuse of civil liberties…etc. etc. with Hendricks giving back a look like "Who the hell is this guy?" which only played out even better on camera.

All utter BS of course but enough to edit into a semi-decent opening for the story. Since when had a sensationalizing show like LiveEYE NY been about the truth anyhow?

People didn't want truth these days. They wanted entertainment.

Things were looking up.

Then they got to the carnival.

As far as carnivals went, it was pretty good sized and hit most the usual bullet points of what a typical carnival should be, but Lorenzo King was not exactly the type who found a mobile version of the Coney Island he once visited as a kid in the 1980s high entertainment. In that department, his style was more in sync with the West Indian Day Parade in Brooklyn or even the San Gennaro Festival in Little Italy (although he'd decided it had pretty much lost its cojones since that fascist Giuliani went on a blitz to squash anything New Yorkers considered fun back in the good old 90s). No, the issue here was that growing certainty - auto re-editing of the El Lorenzo success story aside - that there would not be any lemonade made here tonight other than the sugar water they were passing off as such at the concession stand nearby.

This whole adventure was turning into a disaster of epic proportions, compounded by the bitter fact that his rivals were here in this very same town making giant vats of lemonade that their viewers would be chugging by the gallon next week.

It was almost, almost enough to bring a tear to King's eye.

That tipping point was only moments away.

After Parker had shot some opening footage at the carnival entrance with King (who looked every inch the savvy N.Y. City reporter in his Armani suit), Hasegawa had gone ahead to scout out the main attraction of their story, dashing up and down the midway with his iPad like the proverbial kid cut loose in a candy store.

King had just done another additional take – he still preferred to use a hand-held microphone as he thought it gave him a certain air of authority – making sure Parker only shot from what he considered his most photogenic side (the left) when Hasegawa came dashing up.

"This is Lorenzo King," King was saying for the fifth time, as always lifting his chin up slightly when announcing himself, "Reporting to you live in the Village of Wyvern Falls, a quiet Hudson River community where, if our sources are correct, a yearly carnival hides a deep and terrible secret . . ."A big fan of the Keith Morrison every-word-and-gesture-is-dripping-with-insinuation school of investigative reporting, King trailed off with a dramatic turn of his head and calculated lift of the right eyebrow, suggesting the deep and terrible secret might only be one of dozens lurking in this seemingly typical American carnival.

Then the dramatic snap back of his head with his signature statement: "You'll see here it first – on LiveEYE New York."

Suddenly Hasegawa was at his elbow, chatting excitedly that he'd located the source attraction for their story.

"Where? Where!?"

For a moment, King lost himself in a combination of desperation and excitement. Hasegawa had demonstrated an unbounded enthusiasm for all things American which, loath as he might be to admit it, King was finding infectious.

They had arrived at the end of the midway where a bunch of trailer rides were parked among several concession stands. Sandwiched between a garish ride titled "Hell House" and another called "Buccaneers on the Spanish Main" was what looked like the scrubby country cousin to the two, a beat-up-looking thing with a sun-bleached sign that read:

"Hudson Oddities"

And below that in smaller print:

"Strange and Fabulous Creatures!"

Barely legible, printed in flowing Victorian-like ribbons that made up the framework of the sign were further details: *Snake Lady of Kaaterskill Falls! The Headless Horseman! The Ghost of Chief Croton! The Spitting Devil! Spider Boy! Rip Van Winkle! The Dunderberg Imp . . . and more!*

Apparently such things were of little interest to this year's carnival goers as there was not a single person in line for this ride. Even more embarrassing, in his haste to get around the jammed-up line of people waiting for Hell House, King had stumbled into the pint-sized proprietor of "Hudson Oddities," knocking the man's hat – a grey plaid 1960s looking

280

Fedora – into the dirt and stepped on it with one 'Gucci'-clad foot. (Had he being paying attention, he might have noticed a peculiar thing: for a moment the hat looked like something else entirely, a red conical type once called a 'sugarloaf hat').

King was looking left and right impatiently, hands on hips, saying, "Where the hell is it?" as Hasegawa finally caught up with him shouting "Heer! Heer!"

It took King a moment to process that the Japanese intern was pointing to a midget-sized man standing at the flimsy metal gate next to him. The midget, who looked like the oldest and ugliest carnival worker King had ever seen, said something like "Flikker" (which sounded vulgar) under his breath and, with cat-green eyes glaring, yanked his hat out from under King's foot. After dusting it off and batting it back into shape, he placed it back on his head.

King had a painfully incredulous expression on his face, like a man who wakes up to find the Porsche that was in his driveway the night before has been replaced by a go-cart.

"Here? Here?" he echoed back, looking from Hasegawa to the man, then at the trailer ride with growing comprehension.

Then the diminutive man next to him spat out, "*Na!* Heer! As in Jacob Heer! That's I – I who own this attraction!"

King looked down, as if seeing him for the first time. The fellow was oddly dressed. Squat and blocky in build, he looked like a caricature of a 1930s or 40s carnival barker, with his creased leather shoes, old man pants, and vest with a stiff-looking white shirt that was yellowed with age. "*Qué chingados!* This is your show?" King fell into his smooth voice, the "wow-this-is-really-amazing" tone that was always a red flag to those who knew him. Parker, standing nearby with his camera at the half-ready rolled his eyes. Hasegawa was nodding enthusiastically.

Heer was apparently attempting to smile, but it came out more as a grimace. "*Ja*, it is my show. A dollar each and a dollar a piece!" He glanced over at Parker. "But not the *Swarte* Piet with da kamera – no kameras allowed!"

King was smiling in an equally unfriendly way. "The...who? Ah. Well, my little friend . . ." he said, pulling out three bills from his wallet and stuffing them into Heer's vest pocket, "Policy can't stand in the way of investigation, and it's your show we are here to investigate!"

Without waiting for a response, he motioned for Parker to follow him. With his cordless mike thrust forward like an avenging sword, he grabbed Hasegawa's arm with his other hand and pushed through the door and into the trailer.

-5-

INSIDE, the poor lighting made judging distances and dimensions a hit-or-miss affair. King paused for a moment, trying to get his bearings. The attractions were set up in cubicles following a zig-zag route that snaked through the trailer from front to back, so that only one booth could be seen at any given time. All the interior surfaces were black, lit with cheap fluorescent lighting fixtures, and a series of Day-Glo foot prints had been painted on the floor to eliminate any guesswork on which way one should proceed.

The first booth contained the so-called Snake Lady of Kaaterskill Falls. It was even worse than King expected. A bored-looking young woman was in a bathing suit (with badly painted scales on it) in the midst of what was clearly a stuffed sheet made up to simulate a giant coiled snake's body. The illusion might have fooled a four-year-old, but barely. King, however, with an almost diabolical grin stitched on his face, played along as if this was par for the course while making it painfully clear he would take this nose-diving fiasco of a story and ram it straight into the ground.

The microphone was thrust towards Snake Lady, who raised one skeptical eyebrow in response. Parker shouldered his RED ONE and started filming.

"So, Miss . . .?"

"No names please." . . .

". . . So, Miss Nonamesplease, it has come to the attention of our LiveEYE audience…"

"Who?"

". . . you've never heard of LiveEYE New York? Were you raised in a —never mind. We're here tonight to look into the exploitation of society's unfortunates like yourself!" He glanced back at his cameraman.

"We on?"

Parker gave him back a look that said, "Sure, why not?"

"So, Miss, how did you find yourself trapped in these . . . shall we say 'horrendous' circumstances?"

'Snake Lady' snapped the gum in her mouth. "Well. . . not much to tell. I'm in college. It's summer. I just needed a job . . ."

King gestured with his open hand. "Of course . . . you just . . . 'needed' a job! Isn't this how it always begins? Come LiveEYE viewers ..let's see what else this abusive den of society's unfortunates can reveal for us!"

From there, it became even more surreal.

The Headless Horseman turned out to be a guy wandering around a cage with a cheap black cape costume that clearly built up his shoulders to hide his head, plastic cones held together with black duct-tape to make his black engineer boots look like someone's vague idea of riding boots. Spider Boy looked like a local ninth-grader in some home-made spider get-up sitting half-way up the wall in a nylon rope 'web', with judicious use of the synthetic spider webbing found by the bag in every dollar store around Halloween. Black lights had been positioned to give a dramatic up lit effect but the result was more comic than scary.

The Spitting Devil was another young kid wearing a latex Halloween mask. By the time they reached the back of the trailer where a wrinkled old man smoking a corn-cob pipe purported to be Rip Van Winkle himself (if one ignored the cheap dress-shoes with cardboard buckles taped to them and the white beard with its elastic band showing), King's delivery had taken on that of a diabolical farce.

The exit door of the trailer slammed open and the three of them piled out, King half dragging Hasegawa by the arm. He was looking wildly about, convinced by this point this was all some elaborate practical joke – most likely put on by Hewitt & Company – and that any moment they'd all step out of their hiding places and declare him officially punk'd.

When that didn't come to pass (Hewitt & Company were, in fact, at that moment finishing up a round of Bud-in-a-cup while watching a second rate Queens of the Stone Age cover band called Bone Cancer over at the nearby music tent), King's mood tipped over into seething rage, with the Japanese intern the immediate focus of it.

"Do you think this is funny? I get strong-armed into dragging my *culo* up here for this shit-ass excuse of a story – a fucking fourth rate freak-show run by a Keebler fucking elf? Have you ever heard of fact checking? Verifying your fucking sources?" (The point that King himself had neglected to do this either was clearly not up for discussion.) With the microphone still in his right hand, he had Hasegawa by the arms and was shaking him. "Are you on a fucking mission to turn my career into a laughing stock?" he snarled.

King might have escalated even further at that point had it not been for the massive hand that landed firmly on his shoulder.

"Give it a rest," Parker said in his deep baritone.

King shrugged Parker's hand off with an angry twist of his shoulder but he let go of the intern and stepped away, lips in a tight line. The look on Hasegawa's face was rigid fear, but King had been mistaken in thinking he had been the cause of it.

Hideki Hasegawa had been born and raised in Kyoto, the oldest son of a senior manager at Daimaru, one of the older department store chains in Japan. From an early age, however, Hideki had suffered from what his father termed an "overactive" imagination and an obsession with monsters and horror movies. His father, who personified the classic Japanese businessman, was at a loss on how to deal with his son and did his best to ignore it, convincing himself that this was all youthful nonsense that would fall by the wayside once Hideki stepped up to the plate to become a responsible adult, as any first son was expected to do, despite increasing signs to the contrary. Mrs. Hasegawa, however, harbored no such illusions. She had recognized from the get-go that Hideki shared her psychically sensitive abilities, which ran deep in the history of her family, and that his psychic ability was in fact much stronger than her own. A discreet but also very stubborn woman, she quietly guided her son (without his even being aware of it) to develop his natural ability.

Everything might have continued on a more or less normal course until the events on the family vacation to Yoshino, a mountain village in the Nara Prefecture, which was known for its particularly famous Sakura cherry trees. It was also known for a few other things, including its dolls. It wasn't the incident with the dolls at the museum (which was creepy in its own right) but what happened at the mausoleum of Emperor Go-Daigo where things went off the rails.

The popular story was that, in the 14th century, Sasaki no Kiyotaka, a court advisor to the then Emperor-in-exile, gave him some appallingly bad military advice and, as result, was ordered to commit seppuku or ritual suicide. After his death, Kiyotaka returned to haunt the court as a ghost or yurei in the form of a troublesome *tengu* demon.

It was during the tour of the Emperor's tomb that Hideki became aware of a certain man hovering around the fringe of their group who had joined them along the way.

Something about the man wasn't quite right, and Hideki found his eyes being drawn to him again and again. Nobody else appeared to take notice, although Mrs. Hasegawa felt increasingly nauseous as the tour wore on.

Hideki's two younger sisters seemed oblivious.

It was as they were standing by the tomb itself that something horrible began to happen before the young Hideki's eyes. The strange man transformed, his features becoming hideously distorted as he elevated into the air, feet turning into massive claws, and arms evolving into wings. Horns and fangs sprouted from the thing's face, along with a grotesquely long nose, its homicidal eyes locked onto Hideki's as it rose and floated up over the tour group.

And Hideki, his hands balled into fists, screamed at the top of his lungs.

The demon lunged at him.

Hideki discovered he was a fast runner.

His father had been furious and ashamed at his son's behavior. Following the return home, there had been many late nights with Hideki's parents arguing. At one point, his father was determined to send him to the National Defense Academy of Japan to knock some sense into him; at another, there was talk of packing him off to his strict bachelor uncle who had a farm up in Hokkaido. Then, in his sixteenth year, Hideki went through a phase where he became fascinated with magic – going as far as studying after school under an eccentric local woman named Miko Teruhi (whose specialties included locking and unlocking a collection of odd Edo-era mechanical devices) – which had Mister Hasegawa livid. Hideki's mother had firmly brushed aside all these schemes and it was Hideki who finally devised a face-saving solution, after many years of discord in the Hasegawa household, by announcing his desire to attend college in the United States to study media communications of all things. The heart of this plan was nothing more than a scheme Hideki had developed as an excuse to get out of household (and society) he felt increasingly at odds with, while giving his father an out that would appear prestigious, at least on the surface.

The choice of New York University had come out of an internet search and the rest, as they always say, was history.

The real point of interest, though, was how Hideki's version of the Freak Show trailer was radically different from Anthony King's and even AJ Parker's, though the latter found himself increasingly uneasy through their tour, even as he was coming to the conclusion he would ditch this whole job – to hell with the pay – and head back to New York the next morning.

The Hideki Hasegawa version of the trailer was a nightmare.

Even the trailer itself looked considerably different, older and more antique, like something from another era, an era when the freaks weren't just physically deformed or medical outcasts of the human race but perhaps something else altogether.

A darker and more horrifying window into those things lurking in the more shadowy realms of existence, perhaps.

The Snake Woman of Kaaterskill Falls wasn't a gum-snapping college girl trying to earn a few extra dollars (or cents if the evening turnout was any indication), but something much older and more terrifying. What he saw was something resembling a hybrid of human and snake, with an elongated, vaguely feminine face. There were no arms per se, but stubby appendages that ended in flipper-like claws. A pair of bulging mounds might have suggested breasts. The rest of the body was more like an oversized, legless lizard than any serpent, and the entire body was covered in gleaming scales that gave off a fetid, fishy smell.

The eyes were purely reptilian though, and when the thing made a guttural attempt at communicating – which, amazingly, Lorenzo King seemed to not only be unfazed by but actually understand – its narrow black tongue flicked out and lanced at the air, noting the three men's respective scents. As it did, the mouth made a grotesque popping sound (not unlike snapping gum) that revealed two sets of opalescent fangs.

Hasegawa had been through this drill before (however closely it always seemed to push him to the brink of his sanity), and he was well aware that those around him didn't always see things, shall we say, the same way. So, instead of running screaming from the trailer, he clenched his teeth, balled his hands into fists, and toughed it out, though his body shook and shuddered with the effort.

The Headless Horseman wasn't the traditional rogue spirit of a cursed Hessian but something similar – a Gaelic nightmare sometimes referred to as a *Dullahan*, a smallish creature that held its disconnected head in one arm, a head the color and aroma of moldy cheese with a maniacal grin not unlike a Jack-o-Lantern's. It was a creature referred to in the rare sixth volume of *Volksmärchen der Deutschen*, written in 1785 by a German folklorist named Johann Karl August Musäus, whose tale did, in fairness, inspire Washington Irving's classic creation.

Hasegawa wasn't much concerned with the finer points of literary lineages, however, only that the thing standing next to the rotted skeleton of a horse followed him with its dreadful eyes, a ropey string of drool glistening from one side of its mouth.

The Spitting Devil he witnessed was a frog-like creature the size of bear, with a broad catfish head rimmed with teeth and surrounded by a grisly collection of barbels that trailed off like stiff tentacles. It was squatting in the far corner of a cage that held a large iron tub filled with mossy-looking water. Rip Van Winkle was an ancient looking thing which bore more relation to the moldering mummies of ancient Egypt (except for the wispy and yellowed remains of its beard and hair) than to any living creature, dressed in the ragged remnants of its original eighteenth-century clothes. It stared at the three visitors with rheumy eyes that didn't look quite sane.

The last booth, the one labeled Dunderberg Imp, was empty, though by this time King – who was three steps ahead of Hasegawa – was all but charging out the exit and he didn't appear to even notice.

The Japanese intern wasn't sure why he'd given the lead about the Carnival Freak Show to King's producer over at the station. Partly he had been trying to prove himself useful; partly he genuinely wished to help the host of New York's LiveEYE show. But now part of him was wondering if perhaps some other, more sinister influences were at work here.

King stood by the exit area of the trailer shaking his head. He felt himself hovering on the edge of a meltdown moment that not even his auto-editing success fantasy could pull him back from.

"Fuck-fuck-fuck-fuck . . ." He was muttering, barely suppressing a hysterical giggle. "Oh, this is good…this is rich! The LiveEYE viewers are going to love this fucking story! I can't wait until I…"

"How about a little wager then?" interjected a thickly-accented voice, pronouncing the word wager "vay-jerr."

"I . . . a what!?" King wheeled around to see Jacob Heer standing in the shadows by the edge of the trailer, a long-stemmed clay pipe held in one gnarled hand. The deep-set eyes glittered green in the semi-darkness.

"A wager . . . a challenge as it were. *Gatver!* All your soort always want things easy – all handed on big silver platters! A wager, I propose . . . and should you win, not just a story, but you earn something better . . . perhaps?"

King made a palms-up gesture in the air – "Why not? The whole world's gone mad anyhow" – along with a smile didn't look altogether friendly.

"Okay, I'll bite. What kind of a wager are talking about?"

Heer's stubby fingers tapped his chin. "Oooh, nudding difficult. Let me see . . . how about boats . . . what do you know about sailing boats?"

King, who knew as much about sailing boats as he did about nuclear physics (although he did have an uncanny nose for when something unusual might be in the wind), shot him a wary look. "I *might* know a thing or two. What is it you have in mind?"

Heer cocked his had as if enlightened. "Boats, *ja!* A sailing boat race up the Hudson, I think. I let you sail my boat, as Captain of curse! Surely even a *pisvlek* like you can manage someding simple as that? If you win, you take prize, *ja?*"

The midget detached what appeared to be a leather purse from his belt and a moment later, a large coin sailed through the air. King caught it with a deft motion. It was a very old and heavy Dutch guilder cast in silver. He held it up to the light and saw it had a crude-looking stamp of a lion and a date of 1647.

"A sample. The prize would be a chest full of such coin, and odder silver treasure wort very much, *ja*?"

King suppressed a laugh. "A treasure chest. Are you for real, *amigo*?"

"Oh *ja*, for real."

"And what kind of boat are we talking about?"

"A boat with sails, of course."

King shook his head. "Well . . . I probably would be a little rusty on my sailing skills. It's been awhile," he said, failing to mention that "been awhile" actually meant "never." He didn't add that he was terrified of any water outside of a waist-deep swimming pool.

Heer took a pull on his pipe, grinning with yellowed teeth. "Ohh *ja*, I supply you with sailing crew. You just give orders; they make the boat go where you tell them. Simple. You skipper my boat from, let's say, Raadsel Point, past der Anthony's Nose to Shattemuc Island. First to pass the island wins the treasure. We work out details lader. We'll make race Monday night with the tide."

King had skeptical written all over his face and stood with one arm resting on the other as he rubbed his chin with his fingers. The whole thing didn't fit quite right. It had the whiff of a hustle. Still . . .

He glanced back at Parker, who was just getting off his cell phone and shaking his head. Hasegawa was standing rigid as a fencepost, staring at Heer with eyes as big as saucers.

"What do you mean, 'first past this Shattemuc Island'?" King asked.

The yellowed grin broadened. "Well, it wouldn't be a race widout anoder to race against, *ja*?" Heer made a quick gesture with his hand. Around the corner came Joel Hewitt followed by his entire Ghost Seekers entourage.

"Yo yo yo, if it ain't Marc Anthony! Hey bro! What's this I hear about you and me having a little boat race?"

-6-

KING stood by the river bank, alone. It seemed close to twilight, but it was hard to tell. There was a mist that obscured everything, although he sensed the Palisades looming just beyond his range of sight. He was on a dark sandy beach near the Raadsel Bay Condominiums, a gated community on the shore just north of the Hudson Yacht Club. The water lapped patiently with a sing-song murmur and although there was no wind, the fog was moving in swirls and eddies. The air smelled of brine.

The little beach was littered with driftwood which, as he looked closer, turned out to be bones bleached by the salt and sun: thighbones, a partial ribcage, a half-buried skull, and the fan of a pelvis. Some were human; others appeared to be animals of sorts.

He also realized with a start he was dressed only in his underwear – the white Fruit-of-the-Looms of his childhood. He also realized that he had a raging hard-on, the kind you got only as a kid, rock-hard and painful. The sand felt cool and gritty between his toes. He was aware of a shape out there in the water, standing in the murk.

He was also keenly aware that he didn't want to know who it was. The gurgling water was a slurred voice, calling his name:

"Lorenzo . . . oh, Lorenzo . . . the water's fine . . ." It sounded like someone struggling to speak through running water. "Why don't you join us, Lorenzo? We can play our secret game . . ." followed by a husky grunting sound, followed what might be an air bubble popping.

King felt sick to his stomach and fear rippled through his limbs. He knew the voice, of course. It was his Uncle Jorge.

The figure was closer. It was definitely his uncle – a considerably decayed, water-logged version of him, at least – and time and the elements hadn't been kind to him, either. Remnants of fish-white skin hung from his skeleton, which also sported stringy clumps of seaweed, which appeared to have coagulated into rudimentary eyes in the sockets. In life, Jorge had been a fiercely attractive man who always exuded an overcharged aura of sexuality which always had the ladies (and men of a certain stripe, too) swooning over him.

In death, the sexual aura thing wasn't working well for him anymore, though King wasn't surprised to see an extended tent in the crotch of his uncle's designer pants.

Good old Jorge had been always been hung like a racehorse.

Closer now, and another figure materialized next to his uncle: King's sister Rosalita. Of course. Her head hung down as it often had been for the balance of her abbreviated life and she stood slightly back from their uncle like a timid actress in a small supporting role. Her hair, which she always worn down to her waist, had been ravaged by the ocean. A tiny crab was tangled near her forehead, one pincer moving feebly in the misty air.

They were now only a few feet away and King could see that the clumps of seaweed gathered in their eye sockets were alive and moving. His scream came out as a little whimper and sweat broke out on his brow as he tried to move, but he was frozen in place.

Jorge's decayed hand made a sort of caressing motion in the air before him and King felt it around the knob of his own prick, along with that curious wave of disgust and excitement he had always felt, beginning with the first time his uncle had touched him there in real life.

"Rosalita wants to play with you too," the gurgling voice was saying. ". . . We all want to play with you down here . . ."

Rosalita apparently didn't agree with this assessment, since she was shaking her head left to right and back and a watery sob issued from the strings of hair. Seaweed mercifully hid most of her face. Then his uncle was intimately close to him, the odor of rot and dead-fish decay making King's guts roil. He squeezed his eyes shut, trying not to visualize the lipless teeth streaming sea water and black worm of a tongue almost touching his ear.

"But me first Lorenzo . . ."

King snapped awake in his bed with a whooping gasp of air.

The cloying stench was still in his nostrils, even as he continued to gasp.

Then he bolted to the waste basket just in time to throw up the remnants of his dinner.

Minutes later, he was sitting on the edge of his bed in the dingy room, a pocket flask of Grey Goose vodka in one shaking hand. The hands of the old plastic alarm clock on the night stand read 3:05 AM. Of course. The suicide hour.

And the exact time uncle Jorge had finally done his sister and him and a bunch of other kids a favor by jumping into the surging currents off the northern tip of Manhattan one night in 1987, at that dangerous area of whirlpools and eddies where the Hudson meets the East River known as Spuyten Duyvil.

He'd used the low railroad bridge there that connected Manhattan with the Bronx.

Spuyten Duyvil Bridge.

"Spouting Devil" as the Dutch phrase went.

They'd found his corpse two weeks later off Staten Island. The games had begun when King was eleven and his sister twelve, and had continued on and off for several years. They'd told no one. Uncle Jorge had been very clear and terrifying on that point, threatening each of them with harm to the other.

Nor had King ever talked about it with his sister, despite several attempts. She would always bow her head and clam up. As kids, they had been close. As teens, she'd withdrawn into herself until, just shy of her eighteenth birthday, she waded off into the waters off Rockaway Beach one April morning while partying with a bunch of friends. The coroner ruled it an accidental death.

Lorenzo knew better.

All of this was old history though, and he hadn't had the nightmares since his early twenties.

He'd read several books on how to recover from such things, books which were subsequently disposed of discreetly and far from his apartment in Queens. Over time, the memories of his childhood molestation had distilled into a small hot ball of shame and guilt he'd buried deep in his mind.

Or perhaps he only thought he'd had.

Perhaps those events had been shaping him all along, even suggesting things about his desires he'd rather not examine too closely. King took another swig of vodka, grimacing as it bit into his raw throat. The warm glow in his gut that followed dispersed the terrible thoughts swirling around his brain somewhat. He also realized his cheeks were wet with tears.

How long had it been since he'd last cried?

Five years? Ten?

Certainly not at his mother's funeral. Jorge had been her younger brother. She'd never understood why King had focused so much of his rage towards her.

Three a.m.

What a terrible hour. That wondrous hour of despair when all the darkest voices, the blackest tendrils of depression nibble and murmur at your psyche. When that little Eeyore in everyone's thoughts grows fangs, sunken cheeks, and take on that haunted, hungry look.

Why bother? What's the use?
Come join us.
We all like to play down here.

And now he had gotten himself tangled up in this stupid business with a boat race on the Hudson. What the hell had he been thinking? A chance to make a quick buck? More than that. Part of him, that part of Lorenzo King that lived way deep inside, buried beneath years and years of layers lacquered up into a brittle façade, was beginning to self-destruct. Though he didn't fully recognize it, King was growing bored with his own image. Perhaps in a perverse way, this was a chance to prove himself. And stick it to that asshole, Hewitt.

He didn't get any more sleep that night.

-7-

"WHERE'S Gerald?"

The woman standing behind the front desk at the American Hotel was a dead ringer for the man who had greeted them night before, except for the light make-up, oversized librarian glasses, and thick taffy-colored hair styled in a seductive wave. She was also wearing a tight skirt and suit jacket that seemed somewhat formal for such a run-down place.

She looked up over her glasses and gave King a quick smile.

"Gerald . . .? Oh yes, my twin brother! Gerald always works the second shift. I'm Geraldine Templeton. I generally work mornings around here."

Despite feeling haggard with lack of sleep, King felt his flirtatious side automatically kick in and he leaned over on the counter towards her. Why not? She was exceedingly attractive and a sharp dresser. He caught a faint whiff of perfume that suggested roses and a hint of cedar.

King put on one of his better dreamy smiles and breathed deeply.

"Dolce & Gabbana?"

Was that a light blush on her cheeks? She gave him a slight *you're teasing* look in return. "Oh no, Jeanne Lanvin."

"Of course," King said with the authority of a connoisseur, "Elegant and fresh. I like it. It suits you."

Definitely a blush on the cheeks now. King felt himself warming up. "Mister . . .?"

"King. Lorenzo King. You may have heard of me . . . I'm on television." King puffed his chest out a little more and adjusted his shirt cuffs. He was glad he'd chosen the tan suit, it felt appropriate for a little summer morning flirt even though it was already past eleven. "We checked in last night . . . Geraldine? Such a . . . pretty name."

It was anything but. In fact, it sounded as pretty as a bunch of clanking gears in his head, but he was on a roll. And when *El Lorenzo* was on a roll, he usually got what he wanted (he thought).

Geraldine ran her finger down the ledger, leaning slightly closer as she did so. The starched shirt of her suit was buttoned too high to reveal any direct cleavage but the shape of her bust suggested the pickings would be fine.

"Oh, yes, I see it here. Lorenzo King. Oh. As in the star of LiveEYE New York?" She was too modest to do more than raise an eyebrow but King returned with a tilt of his head, his smile widening. He was all but preening himself. "And now the Ghost Seekers International team are with us as well. We don't get a lot of celebrities here in the Falls let alone our hotel, although last year Philip Seym-"

"Well, I don't have the opportunity to get up in this area very often," King cut in. "In fact, I was hoping you might be able to recommend – or even show me – a decent local place for dinner?"

Geraldine drew herself up. "Oh, I don't think that would be proper, Mister King, you see I'm not that type of girl . . ." She tried to look affronted, though her eyes clearly suggested she *might* definitely be that kind of girl if a certain notable TV celebrity was persistent enough. But before King could deliver his follow up line, there was a heavy "ahem" as someone behind them cleared his throat.

AJ Parker stood in the archway that connected to the front hallway, massive arms crossed and looking at each of them in turn with flat expression, then shaking his head. Next to him, Hasegawa stood gawking at Geraldine as if he'd never seen a woman before.

"Ah . . . didn't realize I had an audience," King said.

"I didn't either," Parker said dryly, "Mister Hasegawa and I were looking to score some lunch and we thought we'd see if you'd like to join us. Now that you're finally up."

"I, uh…why not! Let's see what this fine town has to offer . . . speak to you soon, Geraldine. Or do you prefer Gerrie?"

Geraldine seemed to have recovered herself. Parker was all but glaring. "*Miss Templeton* is fine, thank you."

"Yes, yes, of course!" King said with a wink, as if this was all part of the flirting game. I like when they play hard-to-get, he thought. "Well, I'm sure I'll see you later."

As he brushed past the two men in the archway towards the front door, he heard Hasegawa mutter something that sounded like, "Wow, amazing foo-ta-nah-rey!" Which he misinterpreted as something else.

"Yes, a little out of your league, *amigo*. Not to worry, I can give you some pointers," he added.

Hasegawa smiled, made a quick bow and replied quietly "*Kekkou desu.*"

No thanks.

They wound up grabbing brunch over at Mooney's Bar & Grill on Main Street, where King insisted they eat right at the bar A tall bald guy with a beard named Jeff was on duty, and, while he wasn't much impressed with King's credentials, he was at least friendly enough and didn't mind a little conversation on what was clearly a slow day.

King had finished up a decent Eggs Benedict and was toying with his third cup of coffee. Parker was taking his time with a massive spinach and mushroom omelet with a side of French toast, while Hasegawa went at his scrambled eggs and Canadian bacon with obvious relish. The jukebox by the end of the bar was playing *Ashes to Ashes* by David Bowie. Robert Fripp's discordant guitar riffs wandered out through the air along with the song's funky popping bass notes.

King swirled his coffee cup with the air of a connoisseur. "So, Senor Jeff, what can you tell me about a little man who runs a show called Human Oddities up at the Saint Anne's Carnival?"

The bartender was using a white cloth to wipe off water spots from a clean rack of glasses that had been delivered a few minutes before. He was wearing a green and white striped shirt with a black bow tie but the rolled-up sleeves and heavy apron gave him a casual air, enhanced by hairy forearms with a large sailor's anchor tattoo on one of them.

"Well, I'd say someone was pulling your leg."

"Pulling my leg how?"

"Any way but straight. There hasn't been a Human Oddities show at our carnival since, heck, the 1970s maybe? Before my time anyhow. My family moved here when I was in the first grade. Was run by a guy who used to call himself the Dunderberg Imp. A stage name, of course."

"Really?"

"Really."

"Well, that's quite funny. Because this man you say calls himself the Dunderberg Imp challenged me to a race last night, up the Hudson." Jeff the bartender didn't answer right away, but kept on polishing a glass, checked it against the light, then started on another. He had a street-wise air about him. King wondered if he might find a rap sheet in his background in addition to a Navy service record.

"Well, Mister . . . what did you say your name was?"

"King. Lorenzo King."

"Well, Mister King, if a short little guy calling himself the Dunderberg Imp challenged you to a race up the Hudson, then I can definitely give you one solid piece of advice."

"What's that?"

"Grab your suitcase, turn around, and go back to wherever city it is you came from as fast as you can."

"Ah, I see." King sipped his coffee.

Jeff studied him a moment. "No. You don't. But you will."

"So who is this 'Dunderberg Imp', if you don't mind my asking?"

That got a chuckle. "Originally? Something of a local legend, if you believe in such things. Brought over by the Dutch. A sort of malicious goblin who they said would vex sailors up and down the river in the old days, conjuring up freak storms and currents, running ships aground and drowning their crews if they didn't pay their respects to him. Supposedly, he lurks with his little team of imps over on Dunderberg Mountain, always looking for an opportunity to trip up some unsuspecting human for the sheer hell of it. Most people just laugh at such things but I don't. This isn't some quaint little prankster out of a Washington Irving tale. This is a guy who will rip your guts out and laugh his ass off while doing it. But if you do find yourself in such a circumstance, just try to remember two things: when you pass Dunderberg Mountain, which marks the entrance to the lower Hudson just opposite Anthony's Nose, tip your hat. The second is that his jurisdiction, or sphere of influence if you like, doesn't extend past Shattemuc Island to the North or much south of Raadsel Point. Anywhere between there and you're fair game."

King blinked his eyes indulgently. Someone was pulling his leg and it wasn't just some midget up at the carnival.

"Well, well, Senor Jeff, no offence, but you're sounding like the innkeeper in a second-rate horror movie. Next you'll be telling me "stay off the moors," or "beware the Jabberwock." No, my mixologist friend, I don't believe in spooks and local legends and such. I do believe in this, however," With that, he pulled the old Dutch guilder from his jacket pocket and flipped it around his fingers.

Jeff wasn't impressed. "All the silver in the world isn't worth your life. But hey, it's your funeral." He looked like he was ready to add something else, but just then King's cell phone jangled out a digital ringer version of Ride of the Valkyries

It was a local number and not one that he recognized.

He made a dismissive "excuse me" gesture and moved down to the other end of the bar.

"Lorenzo King?" It was a woman's voice. Latino, from the sound of it.

"Yes, you've found him. Who's this?"

"My name is Olivia Hernandez. Word has gotten around you're in town. Some guy named Sammy gave me your number at the station." She sounded upset and a little hoarse. Still, King wasn't in the mood for theatrics after a sleepless night on a rock-hard mattress. And he made a mental note to have a little talk with Sammy Bag-o-Doughnuts about being free and loose with his cell number.

"Well, I'm sure you didn't call up to chit-chat over Lotto numbers or my recommendations on my favorite nail salon. What can I do for you, Miss Hernandez?"

There was a pause as she measured the rudeness of his response. She pressed on. "It's my son, Mister King. He's gone missing. And I don't think he's the only one in town either. And I'm not convinced the police are taking my case seriously enough. There've been rumors."

King rolled this around his head a moment, mentally underscoring the key points:

-Missing Son.

-Not The Only One.

-Police Not Serious.

-Possible story. Also possible bullshit.

He took a deep breath.

"What is it you would like me to do, Miss Hernandez?"

"Meet me out at the carnival ground. I'll show you where he was last seen."

King weighed it up. Hopefully, she wouldn't turn out to be a complete dog like most of the overweight, starry-eyed crazies he usually got calls from. The ones whose idea of lifetime achievement would be living in a hair salon on top of a shopping mall next to a twenty-four hour McDonald's. *El Lorenzo* had to maintain standards, no?

That's what he kept telling himself anyhow.

-8-

THE CARNIVAL grounds lost much of its allure in the harsh light of the afternoon June sun. The ground looked trampled and littered, the locked-up rides and trailers couldn't hide their rust, dents, and dings. The paint looked old and flat, the myriad of light bulbs fly-specked and dead. Not that Olivia Hernandez needed any kind of negative backdrop to make her look good.

Lorenzo King was all but pawing the dirt when he found her by the entrance to the midway area just after 2:00 p.m.

"Miss Hernandez?" he asked, flashing his most dazzling smile. He was thinking he might have to revisit his earlier assessment of this backwater river town. It appeared to have one or two possibilities after all.

She was dressed in a simple cut-off shorts, sandals, and t-shirt get up.

She still looked like a class act.

He put out his hand. "Mister King, humbly at your service! *¡Tienes los ojos más bonitos del mundo!*"

You have the prettiest eyes in the world!

She returned the kind of tight smile that said she not only doubted that but was already anticipating any of the other ten dozen lines he would follow up with.

"Thanks for coming out here."

It was one of those lazy summer afternoons where the bees hummed drowsily about their business, a seagull or two made on occasional swoop overhead just for the heck of it, and a light breeze ruffled the treetops. The patchwork of cumulus clouds spanning the valley turned the river and hills into random studies of light and dark. After so much time in the steel and concrete canyons of New York City, Parker and Hasegawa were soaking up the open vistas of Raadsel Point, both unaware that they each wore identical unassuming smiles of contentment.

King, on the other hand, had both eyeballs glued on Miss Hernandez. In his mind, he was already well past the first drinks and onto the second round of sex. It wasn't until she cleared her throat a couple times that he realized he hadn't introduced his cameraman or intern.

"Oh, ah, yes, my colleagues, Mister Parker and Mister Hasegawa . . ." After greetings were exchanged, he added, after noting the lack of a wedding band on her left hand, "So tell me about this son of yours . . ."

There wasn't a lot to the story. They had been at the carnival last night, the last event they had gone to was the Red Baron's Daughter fortune telling tent, which had made her uncomfortable – especially the part where the fortune teller had made her son hold what looked like a bullet and concentrate, and the dreamy look he'd had afterwards, like someone in a trance.

"There was something strange about her, I swear . . . like *una bruja* – a witch." She put a tissue to the corner of her eye where tears were threatening to spill out – she was holding it together for now, but barely. After a few fitful hours of sleep, she knew she must look like a wreck. They were walking down the midway, which was closed up and empty at this hour. King made a soft laugh. "Well, Miss Hernandez – can I call you Olivia? No? Miss Hernandez, then. It is hardly a crime to tell fortunes. And it's the 21st Century. Publicly calling out people as witches probably won't fly with my LiveEYE viewers."

She shook her head, annoyed. "You don't get it. She did something. I know she did. My son has never behaved like that . . ."

She took a moment to realize King was no longer listening. He had stopped dead in his tracks well before they had gotten to the Red Baron's Daughter tent. The Hell House trailer was there. The Buccaneers of the Spanish Main trailer was there. But between the two, where the 'Human Oddities trailer had been the night before, was nothing.

Not only was there nothing, there was no indication that Jacob Heer and his ride had ever been there at all.

There wasn't even enough space to hold a trailer.

"AJ, did you ever check the footage you shot last night?" King was standing with his hands on his hips, trying to come to terms with what his eyes were telling him. Hasegawa had run over to the spot where there should have been a trailer, a decent-sized trailer, not one so much smaller than the one they thought they walked through the previous night, and was pacing back and forth, running his hands through his spiky black hair in frustration.

"Of course. Just a few spot checks, but it was all there." Parker cupped his hand over the small monitor mounted on the top of the RED ONE video cam and worked the touch-screen controls. A crease deepened between his eyebrows.

"No shit," he said after a minute of fiddling.

"No shit what?" King said stepping over and trying to get a look.

"No shit as in 'no-footage-of-the-trailer-no-shit'."

"I don't understand."

"See for yourself, chief."

Parker angled the camera so King could see the monitor. It showed the footage shot at the entrance earlier the previous night and then a clip walking up the midway. Then, in the midst of a pan shot from the Hell House ride, the image scrambled, then abruptly went black. The time code in the corner continued to run but no audio, no visual, just a big nothing. Seven and a half minutes of non-footage. Then a bunch of blotchy pixels appearing, resolving into a shot looking to the opposite side of the midway with Lorenzo glaring at Joel Hewitt, then marching off.

King stepped away, making an open hand waving gesture. "What the fuck is this? Did you check the back up?"

"This is the back-up," Parker replied, then holding up a slim black SSD card. "This is the original. Same problem. Now-you-see-it. Now-you-don't."

King shook his head. "That's impossible. Did the footage get corrupted!? Do you even know how to fucking operate this camera?" His voice rose in pitch, the first notes of hysteria creeping into it.

Parker straightened his shoulders. "Easy, boss."

"How can it be blank? There's a time code . . . did you put the fucking lens cap back on?"

Parker shot him a flat look in response.

"Then how, then . . .?"

Olivia, who was clearly running out of patience with all this, finally interjected, "About my son, Mister Ki . . ."

King wheeled on her, eyes flaring. "I don't care about your fucking son right now!" he snapped, "We have a fucking problem here!" He paced back and forth, muttering, "Could it be Hewitt? Is he behind this?

Could it be . . . could it be . . .

He was oblivious to Olivia standing there, taken aback, glaring at him in shock and anger.

Hasegawa looked back over his shoulder, dumbfounded, and Parker's face was alarmingly bland, as if he was contemplating knocking King's lights out for making such a nasty comment to a lady or simply turning around and walking out of the whole thing. Both which were true.

For a moment, an uncomfortable silence hung in the air, then Olivia walked up to King and slapped him hard across the face.

"*Pendejo!*" she spat at him. Then, with the air of fierce dismissal only certain Latino women can pull off, she spun around and walked away.

"Screw you too!" King said, spitting in the dirt after her. He turned to Parker. "Come on, I think it's time to talk to the manager of this carnival – Mister Ramos – and find out what the fuck is going on here." He took a few steps towards the trailer area before realizing no one was following him.

He looked back at Parker. "What, you got a problem, too?"

Parker waited a moment before answering. "Not anymore. I'm quits on this job. Oh, yeah… and you're a real asshole." With that, he shouldered his gear and started walking back towards the parking lot where Olivia had gone.

King yelled after him. "Yeah? Well fuck you, too! You think you can just walk out on *El Lorenzo*? I'll make sure you never work in New York again! Your career is fucking *finito*, asshole!"

Without looking back, Parker flipped him the bird over his shoulder and just kept walking.

King wheeled on Hasegawa who was still gaping at him in shock.

"What?" He stood for a moment snapping his fingers absentmindedly. Then he said, "We don't need him. We'll shoot on your handheld. Come on, we have fucking work to do!"

Minutes later, he was pounding on the door of the manager's trailer, which had been parked in front of the rest of the carnival like a first line of defense. It was a thirty-year-old Catalina that was clearly a battered veteran of America's back roads. The variety of bumper stickers on the back end were a snapshot of various observations and destinations (and even radio stations like "WXLK 96: Kickin' Country!") through time. Near the side door, unobserved by Mister King, was one with a smiley face next to: "Take It Easy, Life Is Short."

King's last knock met only empty air and very nearly rapped the snarling face that emerged from the shadows of the door, which had been yanked open with enough force to rattle the frame.

George Ramos wasn't a particularly tall man but what he lacked in the vertical department, he more than compensated for with sheer ugliness. Barrel-chested with short, bow legs, he wore a stained t-shirt charmingly referred to as a "wife-beater," plaid slacks that might have been washed in a sink a few weeks before, and a pair of old-style suspenders with the "U" and double buttons at the end. Above the hunched shoulders was an oversized head so scarred and seamed that it gave the immediate impression of a man violently at war with everything in life. The long, almost ape-like arms with their complex tattoos and gnarled fingers enhanced that impression. He had thick greasy hair pulled back in a pony-tail and in his hands he was working an old dish rag that smelled suspiciously like hand lotion.

There was a nearly comic moment as Ramos crossed his eyes at the fist hanging inches from his thick nose, then King registered the hostility blazing off the man in waves (along with his old-man smell of sour sweat and tobacco) and quickly withdrew his hand. For a moment, he wondered if the face before him might simply open its massive jaw and bite his fist off at the wrist.

"George Ramos?" he got out.

"Who the fuck are you?"

"Lorenzo King, LiveEYE New York. We had an appointment? Now if you don't mind I'd like to ask you a few questions . . .?"

"Who?"

King repeated himself without success.

"Never heard of you. What's that gook doing with the camera?"

King looked back at Hasegawa. "Him? Oh, he's shooting video. Of you."

"Really? No shit. You can do that with a regular camera?"

"Well, that's hardly a regular camera, but yes, you can."

"And he's filming me?"

"Yes, he is."

Ramos surprised him by flashing the intern a big smile with even bigger teeth. Then he turned back to King. "You from some sort of TV show?"

"Well, yes, as I said before. I . . ."

"Yeah, I heard you the first time, buddy. Don't you guys use, I don't know, real cameras or something?"

King drew himself up. "Of course. I had to send our camera man back due to a . . . uh, technical issue."

"You don't say."

King was getting frustrated. Ramos was clearly toying with him. And enjoying himself.

"I do say. Look, I have several questions that—"

"—Well goody for you. You want that I should give you a medal or something?"

"No, Mister Ramos, I want you to tell me about the Human Oddities ride and Jacob Heer! I want to . . ." He trailed off as Ramos doubled over. It took him a moment to realize the carnival manager was laughing. "May I ask what is so funny?"

Ramos had a hoarse, choking laugh that suggested late nights with cheap whiskey and too many cigarettes.

"Oh, that's a good one, *amigo,* you interrupt my afternoon beauty nap to ask me about that old fucking wives' tale? Boy, you city shits aren't as smart as you try to look, you know that?"

King was trying to remember if he had shaken Ramos's hand or not, while trying to grasp the other implications of just what a beauty nap might actually be.

"I can assure you, Mister Ramos, it was no wives' tale we witnessed last night. In fact, this Jacob Heer even challenged us to a race."

"Oh, I just bet he fucking did, Mister Smarty-pants Reporter, I just bet he did. And I bet he offered you this week's winning Lotto numbers, a whiff of Lady Gaga's panties, and a guaranteed cure for baldness to go with it. Now, if you don't mind, I'm late for an appointment with myself. Now fuck-off, faggot."

With that, King found the trailer door slammed in his face.

He snapped a sarcastic smile at Hasegawa, who was still filming with his point-and-shoot.

"You heard it here first, folks. This is Lorenzo King, speaking to you live from Raadsel Point in Wyvern Falls, New York," he said, as if this had been just another routine interview.

One thing he did know was that Ramos had been lying. His mouth may have been cracking wise but the eyes had told a different story.

George Ramos had looked nervous.

-9-

BY 6:00 SUNDAY night, Lorenzo King was well and thoroughly drunk.

They'd wound up walking a mile and a half back to the village, by which time King's feet were in agony from his Gucci knock-offs. Fortunately, many of the businesses were still open on Main Street and in short order he was able to procure a) the least garish-looking pair of Reebok sneakers from a run-down-looking shoe store called Geronimo's; b) a pack of sports Band-Aids from Emblidge Pharmacy and finally; c) a liter of Grey Goose vodka from Hudson Liquors. The last establishment turned out to be run by a tall, jocular Brit named Alan Woodger who had apparently retired early from a successful career at the BBC in London.

King waited until he got outside, plopped himself on a bench next to one of the flowering pear trees that lined the street, unscrewed the cap, and took a hearty swig with the bottle still in its brown paper bag, oblivious to the irony of mimicking a classic street drunk with a fifty-dollar bottle of booze, not to mention one wearing an Armani suit with a pair of bright new sneakers that looked like they'd been borrowed from some sort of disco astronaut.

On any other day, particularly a fine summer afternoon like this one was, this act might have solicited the attention of the local law enforcement community, but, as luck would have it, they were seriously occupied elsewhere at the moment.

So, after three stiff belts, King felt the knot of emotions twisted up inside loosen up a bit. Hasegawa was busy texting someone (one of his friends back at NYU, who would soon be receiving some interesting updates from the Hudson Valley region) and King simply sat there, legs splayed and smiling to himself in a not-so-jovial way.

Another person might have appreciated the way Main Street angled up obliquely to where it crossed Hudson Avenue/Route 9B. (Technically, heading north into the village, Route 9 became South Hudson Avenue, then North Hudson where it continued past Main). It was lined with classic brick-and-stone row buildings dating back to the late 19th Century – most of the original wooden buildings had been destroyed in a fire in 1874 – and the village was well sighted on the sloping terrain between the river and the eastern highlands. Many of the original brick structures had survived due to a severe economic slump in the late 60s and early 70s, coupled with an acrimonious town board then that couldn't agree on anything. As fate would have it, this resulted in most of them escaping the wrecking ball of that wonderful urban renewal era when some architectural wizards decided that shiny brick-steel-and-glass boxes were just the ticket to replace all those dumpy old buildings around the country. The upshot was that, by the 1980s and beyond, at least a few people came to their senses and decided those "dumpy" old buildings might be worth saving after all, and many found a second lease on life as trendier stores, cafés, and restaurants. There were a few oddball failures (like the second-rate shoe store King had scored his Reeboks in) and one or two had fallen into disrepair, but most of the stalwarts still stood: the old Alhambra Theater, which looked like an exotic Hollywood movie set; the stodgy looking municipal building; and the neo-classical Hudson Savings and Loan building, built in the days when banks actually used to pay customers for the privilege of using their money instead of the other way around.

Overall, the main business and shopping district of the town had an open and inviting flavor. Somewhere in its development, an able-minded town planner had ensured that the building and street layouts took maximum advantage of the steep grades and scenic vistas. Like many river towns, it featured a sometimes confusing network of steep streets and alleys once you were off the main drag, but the overall effect was a picturesque, somewhat upscale village that invited one to pause, take a deep breath, and soak up the view.

All of this was lost on King, however, as he stared blearily off into nothing, trying desperately not to see the stark reality lurking through the half-delusion that was his career. The final straw had come earlier with a call while walking back to town; the City Streets deal had fallen through.

The network suits were skittish and early focus group test screenings hadn't gone well . . . sure Mister Lorenzo . . . call us if you have something else . . .

He felt himself tilting dangerously into the territory of self-pity, where the doors were opened by an overwhelming urge to tear up and mumble, "Why me? Why me!?" Instead, what had come out of King's mouth was,

"Shut the fuck up!"

"Nani?" Hasegawa had looked up, surprised.

"Eh?" Unlike King, he had appreciated the layout of the village and in fact had already taken over fifty digital pictures of it.

King hadn't been paying attention. He was looking up into the well-trimmed branches of the pear tree, where a bunch of sparrows and finches were chatting (or arguing) animatedly and it wasn't clear if he was addressing them or the unwelcome thoughts in his head. Then he'd patted the intern on the shoulder like an old friend.

"It's a tough game, amigo . . . a tough game. You go up, up and up . . ." (here he made a flying gesture with the flat palm of his hand) "Then down and down . . . and when you're down they just start kicking you...." he'd said, implying that his career had fallen from Herculean heights.

"You want a hit?" he'd said, tilting the bottle towards Hideki. The intern had shaken his head quickly.

"No thank-you, Mister King! I stay with *mizu*!" He'd said, taking a mini-sized plastic bottle out of his back pack.

"Yeah . . . I'll miss you too, amigo..."

The intern looked concerned, "Don't worry, King-san, I will find way to make this up to you, restore honor, and make you lots of money!"

"I'm sure you will..." King said, deflatedly.

Hasegawa's face grew serious. "In Japan, there is a saying, '*na na korobi ya oki*' – 'seven times fall down, eight get up.' So . . . fall down a hundred times, get up one hundred and one. Keep getting up! I help you!"

By the time they'd made it back up to the hotel, King was developing a decided weave in his step. At the lobby desk, Gerald was back on duty, looking up quizzically as King entered, leaning on Hasegawa for support. King waved the bottle in its bag in a mock salute: "Ah, to the man with the best-looking sister in town! I say: *salud*!"

From there, Hasegawa had got him up the stairs and into his room where, after another couple of swigs, he'd passed out for a bit.

It was around 8:00 when he was roused out of a half slumber by someone pounding at his door.

"Eh? What the fush do you want? Go away!" he yelled.

When the pounding didn't stop, he forced himself out of bed, feeling the first hammering throbs of a major headache coming on behind his eyeballs. Hasegawa was back, this time with a tray containing a steaming mug of hot coffee, a bowl of chicken soup, and, mercifully, a bottle of aspirin.

He was chattering away excitedly, but it took a few moments for King's alcohol-addled brain to process what he was saying.

". . . big story, Mister King . . . all police at castle out of town! Get you cleaned up and we go right away! Big news! Kidnapped children found, taxi waiting outside. We clean you up and get you there! Big story make you famous again, *hai*!"

King took the bowl of soup with both hands and gulped it down, followed by the coffee and three aspirin, then ran over to the sink and splashed cold water on his face. He looked a mess and his eyes were bloodshot but he cleaned up as best he could and put on a pair of wrap-around Ray-Bans.

Somehow, Hasegawa had procured an efficient-looking Prius Eco-Taxi driven by a young college kid (Corey Hunt, according to the license in the sleeve by the dash) who was more than happy to put the Toyota through its decidedly non-eco paces. When Hasegawa had tapped him on the shoulder with a twenty-dollar bill and urged him to take them up Route 9B as fast as possible to a place called Krell Castle, his face lit up. The twenty had disappeared into his shirt pocket and, looking up into the rearview mirror, he said, "Shit, yeah! Fuck all this green-driving crap. Let's see what this puppy really has under the hood!"

Before they'd even buckled themselves up in the back seat, he'd put the pedal to the floor and they tore off out of the drive, fishtailing onto South Hudson and right through a red light, narrowly missing a Domino's Pizza delivery car.

They actually got airborne for a second or two as they shot over the Low Gate Bridge – a scenic stone-arch affair built by same masons who had constructed the beautifully detailed Kensico Dam down in Valhalla – then were off like a rocket up North Hudson and out of town. King managed to wait until they'd screeched to a halt in front of the tall iron gate of the castle before throwing open the back door and vomiting. When he looked up, he saw they were right next to a large van with the Ghost Seekers International logo on it.

The second time he threw up, he made sure it was on their front windshield.

-10-

CASTLE KRELL was a derelict mansion located a few miles north of Wyvern Falls, a fairytale looking structure (from a distance at least) sited on the high ridge overlooking the Hudson.

When they arrived, the castle grounds were bordering on chaos with police cars everywhere, strobing lights, and cops running back and forth. There hadn't been enough time to properly secure the crime scene before the Ghost Seekers team had shown up, adding further chaos by tromping everywhere with their own cameras, lights and special paranormal detection gear – EMF meters, ion detectors, EVP listeners, and such.

Someone shouting: "This place is assed-out, boss, I'm getting readings all over in the 20k Hertz range! Holy . . ."

"Crackalackan, crew!" Joel yelled back from the front steps of the mansion, "Get it down, bro, this is sure shot!" He had his gimme cap on backwards and, with his GSI sweatshirt, outrageous high-tops, and cargo shorts looked like he might have just escaped out of an MTV spring break hosting gig.

King was trying to narrow down what exactly was happening, an effort complicated both by the clear lack of organization and his level of intoxication. Even so, he might have gotten something of a story had he targeted one of the lower-ranking officers standing on the fringe of the grounds, such as the pair of disgruntled-looking cops smoking cigarettes by the entrance gate, the ones who hadn't batted an eyelash when King had stumbled by. Instead, he'd zeroed in on the blond-haired guy he'd seen the night before at the police station whom he'd pegged as a plain-clothes detective.

He intercepted the man just as he was stepping away from a

veterinarian's van, of all the damndest things, and thrust his microphone in his face.

"Sir, can you comment on reports of a sex-trafficking ring operating here at . . . what do they call this place? Castle Skull? LiveEYE New York viewers are demanding answers! Hasegawa, you getting this all on tape? Sir? Sir . . .?"

The man, who he would later discover was, in fact, a detective by the name of John Easton, pulled up short and gave him a confused look, trying to follow the microphone that was wandering unsteadily in front of his face. The detective glanced around quickly with an alarmed look, but, before King could repeat himself, the air was split by three gunshots fired in quick succession.

All eyes went to Police Chief Hendricks, who was on the front steps of the mansion, his Glock pointed up in the air, his expression seriously PO'd.

"That's it, you're all under arrest," he snapped.

Someone – it sounded like Ricky Petricello – said "Hey you can't . . ." but was silenced by a fourth gunshot.

The next thing King was aware of was his arms being yanked behind him and the cool metal kiss of handcuffs being clapped on his wrists.

Then he passed out.

-11-

"LORENZO . . . the water is fine, Lorenzo…"

Mist over the river, the gurgle of water. The muddy sand squelched between his toes.

The aroma of decay, of dead fish. The briny tang of saltwater mingled with something deeply unpleasant, of viscous things that should have stayed in the darker regions of the ocean where they died.

A watery belch.

His sister was standing before him, naked, head down. More tiny crabs had taken up residence in her tangled hair. Some of the flesh had been nibbled away and what remained was fishy blue-white. The fingernails of her right hand had gone black. The left one was mostly bare bones. The right one reached forward and touched his crotch, tentatively. Asking. Lorenzo was paralyzed with terror.

He didn't see his uncle, but he sensed his presence everywhere. Around him. Watching. Encouraging.

Another watery belch escaped his sister's mouth, the hideous rancor of escaping gasses. And yet, perversely, his crotch was responding . . .

King was shaken awake.

"Huh?"

"Bad dream, King-san! You having very bad dream!"

Hasegawa was bending over him on the hard wooden bench, a damp washcloth in one hand. King looked around blearily, his head throbbing. They were in a small holding cell, a modern-looking place with a polished concrete floor, stainless steel toilet and sink in one corner, and a glass door with an electronic lock.

The Wyvern Falls police precinct might be in an antiquated building, but they'd at least overhauled their holding cells in the basement back in

2007, just before the recession turned the entire country's economy upside down.

A digital clock high up on the wall said 3:05 AM.

The entire Ghost Seekers International team was crashed out along the opposite wall, minus all their equipment, of course.

King was trying to recall how they'd all gotten there but it was a blur of disjointed images. He vaguely recalled being hauled into a processing room where he had been photographed and then had his fingerprints scanned.

After that, things went mercifully blank.

"What...happened?" he croaked out.

Despite the late hour and circumstances, Hasegawa looked clean and alert.

"Big stuff – everyone got arrested! We are all being kept overnight to 'cool our heels,' the police chief said!" A concerned look came over his face. "This very bad news for Hideki-san though – I get arrested, get sent back to Japan. Big disgrace!"

King didn't have an answer for that. His mouth tasted like a garage dump, his whole body ached, and it felt as though someone had driven a spike through his left eye. The muscles in his lower back were clamoring from lying too long on the bench.

And why was he suddenly having nightmares about Uncle Jorge and his sister? That was buried way in the past. Done and dead, long moldering in their graves.

Why weren't they staying dead?

3:05 a.m.

That had some resonance.

He put his hand to his forehead and closed his eyes.

Monday was going to be a long, long day.

The longest day in his life, as it turned out.

12.

IT WASN'T until four o'clock that afternoon that they were all released. Ultimately, the list of original charges – obstructing a police investigation, tampering with evidence, disorderly conduct amongst others – were dropped by Hendricks, under the condition that they all packed up their suitcases and hightailed it out of the Falls that evening, though the network was going to facing a stiff little fine for the whole mess.

They would have been released in the morning if it hadn't been for the fight that broke out between Hewitt and King.

It had occurred just after the meager breakfast had been served (toast and orange juice). King's foul mood had been getting pricked at by Hewitt's increasing "buddy up" behavior with a couple of curious cops outside the door, then, to up the aggravation quotient a notch, Hewitt had walked over, sat down next to King, and clapped him on the back with a wink, saying "Hey, hey, chill, bro, I got some juice around here so we'll be out soon . . . beside you and me got a little race up the river tonight, yeah? I mean we're talkin' about one phat box of silver, may the best bro take all!" King had been sitting with his elbows on his knees, staring off into space and trying not to scream.

"I think we just better drop it, Joel. The whole things sounds like a . . ."

"No way yer assing out on me now, bro!" Hewitt had interrupted,

"Otherwise, I'm just gonna have to score with yer sister's ass tonight, hehe!"

It was a joke meant in bad taste (as if the Hewitts of the world knew any other kind) but the result was instantaneous.

No sooner had the last words cleared the Ghost Seeker host's lips than King's left fist connected with his right eye. An instant later, King was on him, screaming and punching and the two men rolled across the cell floor. Hewitt had a good fifty pounds on his opponent easy and nearly as hot a temper – it only took a moment before King was getting the worst of it, which later would be tallied up as a split lip, a swollen jaw, and some bruised ribs.

The fight might have gone on longer than it did – the Ghost Seekers team didn't appear to be in any rush to intervene – if Hideki hadn't stepped in. No one could completely agree on what exactly happened next, only that the young Japanese intern stepped nimbly over, waited until he saw an opportunity, then somehow grabbed Hewitt's right hand with both of his in a symmetrical grasp, thumbs pressing into a pressure point. This was executed with a deft twist of Hewitt's wrist that instantly had him on his back and howling uncle.

King gained his feet and get in one last kick (a lucky shot that caught Hewitt in the testicles) before being hauled back by the two Ghost Seeker's cameramen. Moments later, the guards were in and King was being manhandled off to a separate holding cell.

At around 4:30 a ragged and disheveled Lorenzo King stumbled into the lobby of the American Hotel, half supported by Hasegawa with one hand holding a plastic bag of ice to his chin. A horrified Geraldine Templeton looked up from behind the desk with a gasp, then raced over to assist the two of them up the stairs.

"Oh, Mister King, this is dreadful! Let's get you up to your room immediately and I'll have a hot bath drawn down the hall!" she said disapprovingly, the excited look in her eye suggesting that a little drama was anything but. Word had already gone through the town, first about a bunch of children rescued up at the Castle and then about the debacle with the Ghost Seekers team and Lorenzo King.

This would fuel the gossip fires for months to come, with the Templeton's finding themselves unwitting centers of circumstance but for the moment, the first priority was putting things back to rights and that involved getting King cleaned up and out of sight. An agreement had already been imposed by the police chief that the Ghost Seekers team (sans Hewitt) would come by an hour later and quietly check out, adding, "Do not pass Go, do not collect two hundred dollars, do not blink so much as a goddamn eye at each other or all of you will be in for an extended vacation in our basement spa again. Am I speaking plain English or does Lieutenant Sanchez here have to write it out in capital letters?"

That got quick nods from all involved.

It might have all ended right there, our two rival parties going their separate ways and exiting out stage left and right, but for the notes.

One of them appeared under King's door at just past 6:00 p.m. The note was a folded piece of yellowed paper with bunch of ragged words written in pencil on it, suggesting its author was a little out of practice with such things. It read:

See you at the main dock, 9 of the o'clock sharp unless – as Ghost-man say – you are chickenshit lady-boy who wish to go home and cry to mommy . . .
—JH

This was followed by a crude sketch of what looked like a little sugarloaf hat.

King picked up his cell phone and dialed a number. A moment later, he was talking to his second cousin Ritchie in Queens who picked up the phone as if he had been just sitting there waiting.

"Hey, Ricky, Lorenzo. I need a favor, man. You guys used to have a boat right? Yeah? Look, I got a bit of an opportunity here but I need a crash course in racing boats . . ."

Ricky, a good natured guy but not overburdened in the brains department, was immediately excited. Two years younger, he all but worshipped the ground Lorenzo stood on.

"Wow, cool, man! What kind of boat we talking about?"

King thought a moment. "A sailing boat."

A pause.

"Oh, well you know we had a power boat, man. But a boat's a boat, right? The front is the bow. The back is the stern; you'll need to know stuff like that. My buddy, Jimmy Scarpa, though – his dad has a sailboat over in Sheepshead . . . I can call him if you like. I bet he'd love to help."

King thought about it. The Jimmy Scarpa his cousin was referring to did time at Rikers for dealing. It would also be one more hand in the till. "Look, Ricky, find out what you can from Jimmy, then I need you to get your ass on the next Metro North train up here. Just you and only you. Got it?"

"No problem! Got you covered, bro! We're on it!"

King somehow doubted that. But beggars couldn't be choosers.

"Okay, here's how you get here . . ."

Five minutes later, King was about to doze off when his cell rang. The call was from Sammy back in New York, who, after working King's ear over for a few minutes with most of the choice expletives in his extensive catalogue, proceeded to inform King that he was fired and his show cancelled. This was wrapped up with ". . . and don't bother coming back to the office to pick up your stuff – it'll be in the trash bin out back!" King had responded by walking over to the window in his room, throwing up the sash, and hurling the cell phone well out into South Hudson Avenue, where moments later it was run over by a black Cadillac Escalade with tinted windows.

The driver was a hawk-faced man with grey hair pulled back into a pony-tail and wearing Bausch & Lomb sunglasses.

Over at Mad Anthony's Inn where Hewitt and his staff had moved, a similar note appeared under his door on the second floor:

See you at the main dock, 9 of the o'clock sharp unless – as Big-King man say – you are lady-boy chickenshit who wish to stay home and play wid himself . . .
—JH

Downstairs in the low-ceilinged dining room and the 18th century tap room, guests were startled at a resounding thud that might have been someone's fist hitting the wall, followed by a door slamming hard enough to rattle the crystal on the tables.

King arrived by taxi at five minutes before the appointed hour. The village's public docks were situated just south of Raadsel Bay Yacht Club and Marina, where a building once called The Wyvern Falls Canoe & Boat Club had been converted into a waterside bar and clam shack. The harbor was guarded by a small breakwater and lighthouse before opening out into the river proper. To the north past the yacht club were the Raadsel Bay Condominiums, a gated community of neat-as-a-pin buildings with a New England sea-side flair and immaculate lawns. From there, the bay curved from a low beach and woods into the bluffs of the point itself, which from a bird's-eye view was shaped like the wing of a dragon (or Wyvern and one version of the town's history claimed this was the origin of its name) that had flopped down at the river. The winking colored lights of the carnival could still be seen across the bay and a stiff breeze was kicking up white caps on the water. From the marina came the jangle of metal halyards and lines and, on the converted mast on the narrow front lawn of the yacht club, the RBYC ensign snapped in the wind. Any sailor would have agreed it was looking like a fine night for a brisk sailing race.

King felt his guts twist in fear.

And shock.

The first thing he said when he saw the two 'boats' moored at the dock was "Holy shit!"

He wasn't sure exactly what he had anticipated finding at the docks – something more of the magnitude of a twenty- or thirty-footer perhaps – yet for some reason, the scene he and Hasegawa were presented with as they pulled up was both absurd and completely appropriate at the same time.

There were two ships moored at the roughshod heavy wooden public quay (in contrast to the neat and efficient docks of the yacht club next door). One was a sleek-looking yacht, the seventy-seven-foot ketch "Solomon's Seal." By boating standards, it was an antique-looking thing – dating to the early 1930s, in fact – with its teak upper decks, shining brass hardware, and old-style round portholes. One half-expected to see a dashing Errol Flynn-looking skipper in the back with a pencil-thin moustache and sailor's cap, dressed in crisp whites, possibly with a Hollywood starlet in Capri pants and loose cotton blouse. In fact, the half-dozen crew members visible on its decks looked like something out of an old 30s movie (a couple even wore striped shirts, Greek caps, and bandanas tied around their necks) and the elderly man in the stern who was in charge of the vessel evoked the ghost of Errol Flynn after a fashion.

By comparison to the other ship, however, it was positively modern.

The second ship, the "Vander Dekken" according to the letters across the stern transom, had apparently escaped out of a different and much darker version of Hollywood. It was a hundred-foot, three-masted galleon that looked like an apparition from a pirate movie. Just over ninety feet bow to stern, she had a prominently raked deck, sweeping hull, and ornate, if ancient–looking, detailing around the aft gallery and foredeck. Old-style Dutch pennants flew from her topmasts and the tarred rope rigging snapped and thrummed in the breeze as if the ship were eager to be off. Her crew also appeared to have been plucked out of the chapters of history. Most were clad in tar-stained breeches, loose shirts, and an assortment of caps and scarves, except for a handful dressed in more formal-looking attire on typically saw in 17th Century Dutch paintings. Even stranger was the group of what appeared to be armored Japanese mercenaries clustered on the main deck.

Between the two ships, seated on a stool at a makeshift table of a few boards thrown across some wooden crates, was Jacob Heer. Next to him was an old-fashioned wooden seaman's chest with iron clasps and knotted rope handles. The Ghost Seekers team were already there as well. Hewitt – sporting a real shiner of a black eye, King was pleased to see – and three of his investigators were admiring the ketch, which was a fine-looking yacht that looked sturdy and fast. Bob Weiss and Freddie Stern were with the director of photography, goggling over the galleon, while one of the cameramen, Jim Farrell (who had the surfer/slacker dude look down pat), was setting up some establishing shots with the help of a tripod. Weiss was going back and forth with one of his meters muttering, "Did you see that? Did you hear that?" while making sure the second camera man was capturing his scripted "panic" looks.

Cousin Ritchie was nowhere in sight.

Hewitt's personal assistant, Sheila Walters – looking like a poster girl for sandy-haired cute-and-bubbly communications majors tailor made for morning news show careers – was, however. She came rushing up to King and eagerly inquired if he needed time for his own cameraman to set up shots. She was very excited that the ships were to be provided with period-dressed crews.

King clenched his fists, "Um, no, my intern here will get some photos for the record, but…"

"His camera man quit, Sheila," Hewitt interrupted as he walked up, "Hey, do you need to borrow one of mine, bro? Oh, and hope you don't mind, Heer says you get the hot-rod racing galleon!"

King pulled himself up, straightening his suit self-consciously. "Fuck you," he spat, eyes taking on a narrow, dangerous look. Sheila gave a mortified "oh my" and stepped backward with a "this wasn't on the test" expression, but, before anything could go any further, Heer's voice cut the air between them, decisive as any referee's.

"*Na, na geents*, save yer spit and *patoons* for der race! Now sit yerselves down and bend yer ears, as der are a few rules both must abide by!"

King looked at him, incredulous. "He isn't serious? You're not actually expecting me to race on that freaking thing?" He pointed to the galleon. "You said 'boat'. Not ancient pirate ship." He felt a whine creeping into his voice and hated it, but added, "Why do I have to get that clunker? This isn't a race; this is a joke!"

Heer glared at him. "Ship, boat. No madder for a real man. For sure you can manage to skipper, no? You give orders like a big *ezkel* on television, how about der real world, eh? Or do you wish to stand und cry like a little baby? Maybe I should just hand der prize to der Ghost-master here right now . . .?"

King all but puffed up like a partridge. He made a dismissive shake with his head. "Pffft, no. Of course I can handle it. El Lorenzo can handle *anything*."

And for a second he actually believed he could.

Hewitt blustered in. "Yeah, it's just a big sailboat."

Heer snorted in response. He pointed a stubby finger at the two crude-looking stools placed in front of the table, which had an ancient-looking chart on it, held down by belaying pins. He looked mean and eager. Aside from glaring looks, King and Hewitt seated themselves without any further exchange and Heer got right down to business.

"Now, here is der way this will work. Each of you will skipper one of my boats, Hewitt on 'Solomon's Seal' der (he pointed to the yacht); King on 'Vander Dekken.', *ja*?" When King protested, Heer silenced him with a sharp chopping motion of his hand. "Not yet. Now, both boats are provided with a full crew to sail them, led by a first mate – no worry, you'll know immediately who he is. However, you give the orders. They do whatever you tell them. The race starts with both boats crossing the two channel buoys at the center of river here," he tapped the chart with his finger, "off Raadsel Point. The course will take you past Dunderberg Mountain and Anthony's Nose here, then to the finish line off Shattemuc Island here, where I will await at der dock with the prize." He rubbed his chin. "Let's see . . . the finish will be marked by two large buoys, each well-lit by a large lantern."

"Now, mind me on this. Rule one: when passing Dunderberg Mountain, it is required that you tip yer hat as a matter of courtesy to the imp who is said to live across der river from there, or risk his wrath and ire – which may or may not cost you der race. Rule two: only der skipper can give commands. Anyone else interfering will only cause confusion with der crew. Give your orders to the first mate, he will relay them. Rule three: one must complete the course, start to finish, in order to win. No exceptions.

Is this clear?"

Hewitt jumped in first. "Whoa, shorty! First, what the hell is this whole biz with hat tipping and the 'imp' thing? Some sort of joke?"

Heer looked back at him evenly. "No joke, the Dunderberg Imp is not a joke. You show respect, you tip yer hat, or it will cost you."

"Cost me what?"

"Cost you your life, smart guy. What else?"

Hewitt squinted at the carnival man, trying to decide if he was joking or not. It didn't look like it.

"And what exactly is the prize?"

Heer smiled, then pulled the sea chest out so both men could see it clearly. Though not overly large, by the grating sound it made, it was heavily laden. Yet Heer had dragged it out with one hand effortlessly. He flipped the lid open, revealing its glittering contents in the yellowish glow cast by the old-fashioned dock lights: silver coin, plate, candlesticks, and steins, a heaping assortment of antique treasure.

"All one hundred percent silver," Heer said with an unpleasant grin. "Just over five-hundred thousand dollars by today's market," he added, reading their thoughts. From the Ghost Seekers crew that had gathered around, someone let out a low whistle.

"And one final rule: The prize, this treasure, can only be taken after the race is won."

King glanced over again at the ungainly-looking galleon, then at the sleek-looking yacht. "But this isn't even fair – there's no way I can win. That ship looks like it can barely sail! That yacht has to be twice as fast!" He glanced around quickly, mentally adding; *and if my cousin doesn't get here quick I will be completely and truly fucked . . .*

Heer made a clucking sound that might have been a laugh. "Oh, looks are not everything, Mister King. I assure you, she can go quite fast and her crew knows her well. It is most certainly a fair match or what kind of race would this be? No, it is your wits and guts that will decide who wins the silver this night! One must be resourceful."

Mark Rubenstein, the director of photography, chimed in with what was definitely a Brooklyn accent: "Hold tight, Mister Here – where's the catch? You trying to tell us you're willing to fork over five Hundred-K in loot for a simple race up the Hudson? That does not sound right. In fact, that sounds like a whole different continent from all right." That got him looks and nods from the Seekers crew. Hewitt was giving Heer a shrewd look that said he'd seen a hustle or two in his lifetime as well.

Heer sat back, steepling his gnarled fingers together. "Oh, I did not say the race was 'simple.' I said that not at all."

Rubenstein decided he was on a roll. For a guy who was clearly Jewish, he sounded remarkably Italian, "But the winner gets the silver. That chest of silver," he clarified with his finger.

"That is correct."

Rubenstein didn't look like he was buying whatever Heer was selling. He let out a cynical laugh. "Well, pardon me for saying, but the stuff in that chest looks pretty old. I mean, just how many races have there been, and how many people have won it? What, you have a whole warehouse of this stuff just lying around?"

Heer looked at the DP with something approaching a sneer.

"I said no such thing. This is what I have."

Rubenstein, a gangly young man with curly black hair and a classic wise-ass face, was looking around with a "do you believe this guy?" expression.

It was King who spoke next, however.

"So what is the catch?" he said levelly.

"The catch? Both of you are der catch. Someone always makes mistake and tries to break der rules. It seems to be human nature."

"And how do we know you'll make good on handing over the prize when the race is over?"

Heer scratched his chin as he considered this. "Someone from each team can stay with the chest. The girl there," he pointed at Sheila Walters, "And . . . well, the little yellow-skin is all you have. They can wait at the dock at Shattemuc."

Rubenstein cut in again, "So how many people have actually ever won this race?"

Heer kept grinning. "None."

"None?"

"*Na.*"

"Care to share with us what happed to the previous contestants?"

"Yes. They are all dead."

"Joel, allow me to tell you this; *do not* – I repeat – *do not* do this."

Rubenstein was in Hewitt's face with one pointed finger. "Forget this whole thing. Let's go back to the hotel and do the show like we always do and get the fuck out of this loony town. There's plenty of electro-fucking-whatever readings to be taken, plenty of spooky infra-red video to shoot, hell, we got enough already to concoct two episodes. But do not do this." Rubenstein had been trying to convince Hewitt for the past few minutes to call the whole thing off. The vaguely crazy look on the lead investigator's face said he wasn't even considering it.

"Oh, we're going to do it, stop being such a chicken-shit wangsta, bro. We're gonna give our fans something they never seen before."

Hewitt was standing with his arms crossed, eyes going back and forth at the two ships. "This fucking rocks!" he said. Then he looked over at King, who was standing by the gangway leading onto the galleon's deck with the grim expression of a man facing certain doom.

"Yo, Marc Antony, you think you can take us in that pile of junk?"

The smile on King's face was ghastly. "You can bet your jockstrap on it, *Xerox*." Behind him, Hasegawa was continuing to snap pictures of the galleon from every conceivable angle. He was very excited by the Japanese mercenaries on the galleon. "Classic Ronin – from old Japan!" he'd explained. "Very authentic!"

But where the hell was Ritchie?

Sheila Walters had just rushed up to Hewitt with her ever-present iPad. "Um, Mister H? Our shooting schedule shows that tonight we were supposed to . . ."

"Can it, short-cakes." Hewitt cut her off, "We going to be making television history tonight."

"Ay, a night of history to be sure, mine little *Klootzaks!*" Heer had just stepped up to the area of the dock between the two boats, hands on hips. A dented brass trumpet was slung from his neck. On both vessels, the crews were preparing the ships to get underway. There was the patter of bare feet on wood, the thrum and whine of pulleys and lines as canvas was hauled up or unfurled. The only thing odd was the complete absence of any sort of shouts, yells, or conversation; both crews worked in a spooky silence.

"Now here's how this will play. I will take the missy here," he pointed to Hewitt's assistant, "Und the little Japan-man up to Shattemuc Island once the race has started, where we will greet the winner at the dock there, *ja?* When I see both ships cross the starting line, you will hear one blast of my horn, and the race is on." He grinned. "It's time to begin, the tide is near peak. And remember the rules!" Touching the assistant by the elbow, he led her over to Hasegawa, then ushered both of them back to his table, speaking in low tones.

King stood looking at the galleon for a moment, his guts churning. The little devils of doubt were piping up a little louder now: *you can't swim . . . what if the ship capsizes? . . . you're going to lose, what the heck do you know about sailing? Look how dark and swift the water is . . . an old rotten bucket like that — probably sink a few hundred yards from shore . . . look how the wind is picking up . . . you'll die doing this!*

Clenching his fists, he shook his head and stepped over to have a quick word with Hasegawa. The intern was clearly amazed that he was going to be in charge of a galleon.

"Wow, you sail ships too? Most impressive! Don't worry, I take good pictures when you win race!" He rolled his eyes towards Hewitt, who was having a team huddle nearby. "He's a real jerk, you can beat him . . . easy!"

King straightened up, looked nervously around over the Japanese intern's head. "Yes, yes, that's the plan . . ." he said distractedly. Was that a taxi pulling into the parking lot?

On the ketch, the Ghost Seekers team filed onboard excitedly, like a bunch of school kids going on a field trip, minus their director of photography. Even when Hewitt threatened to can him on the spot, Rubenstein had been adamant.

"Then fire me, Joel. I'm still not going to be any part of this. Not for all the silver on the planet. Goodbye."

King stalled by the gangway leading onto the Vander Dekken. Sailors were clambering out on the yards, unfurling the sails.

There was a commotion in the parking lot, then not one but four guys came running up onto the dock. King's felt his heart sinking.

Ritchie, an overweight Hispanic man in his late 20s with a goatee, close-shaved head and tattoos all over his arms (mostly of the snarling lion/tiger variety that mimicked the posters of the mixed martial arts school he trained at) came huffing up with a thin, shifty-eyed guy with a pale complexion and a bad toupee: the infamous Jimmy Scarpa. The two others King didn't recognize. One looked like a nerdy Shakespearean actor in some sort of black outfit and cape, the other was a tall, obese dude who looked like a theatrical redneck. His cape was hooded. Both were carrying futuristic-looking rods that seemed oddly familiar.

King was shaking his head. "Come on, Ritchie, this isn't a fucking party. I told you—"

Ritchie held up his hand, an excited look on his face. "Don't worry, cuz, its cool! It's cool! My man Jimmy can really help us – he knows everything about sailing boats! And these other two guys here, Kenny and Andrew, are my bros. They train with me at the school! Kenny here runs the Queens chapter of Jedi Knights with Andrew. They know their shit, man, it's cool! We got your back covered!"

"*Queens? Jedi Knights?*" King stammered, "What the fuck are you talking about?"

The one named Kenny, who up close appeared more like a computer nerd trying to pass himself off as some sort of urban rocker dude/martial arts master, muttered, "It's Kenneth, actually." Then in unison, the two strangely-dressed men both dropped to one knee at the foot of the gangway, bowed their heads, and leaned on the poles, which King now realized, with growing horror, were full-sized light saber props from the Star Wars movies. They even lit up, glowed, and gave off the signature "vvvvrrrew" sound.

"We are at your service, my lord," Kenny said solemnly.

For one of the few times in his life, Lorenzo King was at a complete loss for words. Finally, he got out: "This isn't happening . . ."

While Ritchie tried to calm down his cousin, Jimmy was glancing around nervously, like he was sizing everything and everyone up. Meanwhile, a second car had pulled up and three more Queens Jedi Knights came running up on the gangway: a mousy blond-haired girl, another guy with spectacles who looked every inch the computer programmer, and a tall black kid with a neatly-trimmed moustache. They immediately huddled as Kenny gave them some sort of instructions, pointing to the galleon and to the river. The guy named Andrew stood with folded arms and with his blond crew cut and piercings tried to act like he owned the place. He looked about as dangerous as a beached whale.

King was trying to control his rising anger. "Ricky, what the hell have you done? I asked you to . . ." But it was too late.

"Hey, we got to get on board, the tour boat is leaving!" his cousin said enthusiastically. Then next thing King knew, he was being dragged onto the ship.

Nearby, Rubenstein stood, gawking.

Minutes later, the two vessels eased away from the docks and tacked out past the small lighthouse and into the river proper, a waning crescent moon and evening star adding suitable accents to the night sky. When Rubenstein turned back around, the diminutive Dutchman and interns were gone, along with the chest of silver. What looked like an old 1950s Buick was gliding up the ramp by the Metro North station (which, like many up and down the Hudson Line, had been meticulously restored to its early 1900s charm) but he didn't recall seeing them actually get in it. He turned back towards the bay and looked at the two ships heading out under a press of sail and shook his head.

Behind him in the parking lot, a police cruiser slid quietly into one of the spaces. Lieutenant Sanchez killed his lights and got out of the car, taking in the empty dock with its table, the tall man with his hands in his pockets at the end of the wharf, and the two ships heading out past the point.

He leaned against the open door and rubbed his chin.

This wasn't good.

-13-

IT WAS nearly 9:30 when the shortwave unit coughed again.

"Chief, you there?"

Hendricks was seated at his desk in his usual position, though this time with the barrel of the revolver under his chin. From the old Atwater on the sideboard, *On The Beautiful Blue Danube* was wafting quietly out in mono, courtesy of 105.7 on the FM dial.

This time, Hendricks simply released the hammer, flicked the safety, and placed the pistol on his desk. He leaned over and snagged the mic.

"Copy. I'm here."

There was a pause while Sanchez chose his words on the other end.

"You're not going believe this, but looks like we have another situation developing. Over."

"Copy that. What kind of situation is that?" Hendricks felt the first rumblings of his stomach acting up. He was already wrung out from the past forty-eight hours and the near disaster up at Castle Krell yesterday Now what?

"Uh, that Lorenzo King from LiveEYE New York? Apparently, he's gotten himself involved in some sort of race up the river. In a goddam old-fashioned sailing ship that looks like a galleon. Over."

Hendricks felt his blood-pressure start its creep towards the red line. "Roger. Race against who?" He was afraid he already knew the answer. Another pause. "The Ghost Seekers International guys. Guess they didn't hear you too well earlier. Over."

Then he added, "Oh, and you'll never believe this either. King was joined by a bunch of people dressed up as . . . well I'm pretty sure they were Star Wars characters. Over."

Hendricks mouth compressed into a thin line. Goddamnit all to hell, he thought. He looked at the pistol. A momentary fantasy of using it in a variety of ways on both parties crossed his mind.

"Chief, you there?"

"Copy."

"I've got their photography director with me . . . what's that? Sorry, director of photography . . . a Mark Rubenstein, here with me at the main village dock."

"Copy that. I'll be there in five."

Sanchez acknowledged and the line went dead. From the Atwater, the Cleveland Philharmonic continued to ply away at Strauss's waltz, oblivious to this latest turn of events. Hendricks made a fist and did a controlled tap on his desktop.

"Son of a goddamned bitch."

<h1 style="text-align:center">-14-</h1>

THE CARNIVAL rolled on into its fourth night.

The lights continued to twirl and flash. Screams, yells, and the cacophony of rides, buzzers, and ringers wafted through the evening sky, along with mixed aromas of fried foods, beer, and cotton candy. The merry-go-round's calliope gasped its lunatic melody and the roller coaster sang out its metallic clatter. By the card tents, the poker rounds continued to get grimmer and quieter and, at the huge blue and yellow music tent, a band known as The Unexpected wrapped up their first (and to some, supernaturally-tinged) gig to unanticipated and very enthusiastic applause. For the few people looking out at the river – and that included the high-school couple at the top of the Ferris wheel – the sight of the two sailing ships racing up the Hudson wasn't overly unusual. Though much larger, to the casual observer the Dutch galleon wasn't much different from the replica of Henry Hudson's Half Moon frequently seen up and down the river and large sailing yachts were not out of place. In fact, with the recession still dragging out the economy, it was the large gas-guzzling motor boats that had become the rarity.

So, for example, to the couple in their swinging seat on the Ferris wheel, in this case a certain David Van Coort and a Francine D'arby, the latter currently on the A-list for both the hottest legs and the hottest black chick at Wyvern High, the two ships were simply a romantic accent to a scenic panorama. And an opportunity for the young Van Coort to finally make his move – successfully – out of the dreaded "friend zone" and into an area a little more exciting for both of them.

Aboard the *Vander Dekken*, however, it was a slightly different story. King had been led to a position on the quarterdeck and given an archaic-looking overcoat and flat brimmed hat by the head officer, who indicated with gestures that he should put them on. None of the crew spoke – they seemed to communicate almost telepathically with quick glances, which to King was nonsense. His guess was that they were all professionals hired by Heer, probably like the ones they had at the Pirates on the Hudson event he'd covered the previous year – the kind that had hidden wireless mikes and receivers. Still, the coat seemed ridiculous and musty smelling until he felt the first bite of cool air out on the river. He was certainly glad for the ridiculous sneakers – the worn planks of the deck were smooth to the point of being treacherous.

Sailing on the Dutch galleon was both a terrifying and an exhilarating experience for King, whose entire boating experience had previously been limited to a Circle Line cruise around New York Harbor (he had stayed in the center of the boat the entire time, petrified) and a single ride as a kid on the Staten Island Ferry.

The sloped quarterdeck – the raised deck aft of the main deck where the captain and his officers would typically be found – offered an excellent view of the *Vander Dekken* in action. It was accessed by a short ladder along the gunwale on either side and had a heavy wood balustrade at which King stood, gripping the rail with both hands until his knuckles were white.

Behind him was a raised housing where one of the crew operated the whipstaff, the hinged wooden lever that operated the rudder. Contrary to most Hollywood movies, the classic ship's wheel was a relatively modern sailing invention that didn't appear until the early 1700s.

Behind the quarterdeck was a short and sharply-sloped poop deck that ended in an ornate rail with an oversized lantern mounted atop it. Forward of the main deck was the raised forecastle (or "fo'c'sle" in sailing lingo) and beyond that the jutting bowsprit. The ship had two masts rigged with two large square sails, each with a shorter mast on the quarterdeck rigged with a triangular lateen sail.

For the first ten minutes, as the crew tacked the ship out into the river south of the point, King was petrified, clutching the quarterdeck rail for dear life, convinced that every tug and pull of wind through the sails was going to capsize the vessel and send all of them to their . . .

Come join us.
We all like to play down here.

. . . watery deaths. The constantly shifting motion of the ship was unnerving at the very least and for the first ten minutes he was frozen in place, all his energies focused on keeping the contents of his stomach where they belonged.

Quite the captain you are, *El Lorenzo*, he finally thought. At least the fear and adrenaline were proving to be an effective antidote to his hangover.

He had no idea if the ship was in any way safe or seaworthy, though the crew seemed confident enough going about their tasks. The timbers groaned and creaked, the rigging rattled and sighed, and every so often the entire ship would lurch as the canvas sails caught the breeze. The river gurgled as it sluiced around the hull and occasionally the breeze would bring with it snatches of carnival sounds from the point.

Meanwhile, his cousin Rickie was clearly having the time of his life, along with the so-called Jedi Knights. He ran back and forth on the quarterdeck like an excited kid, clambering up and down the small poop deck three times. Jimmy Scarpa, on the other hand, hadn't said two words since they left the docks, instead standing off by the port gunwale smoking a cigarette. He'd spent the last five minutes below decks before reappearing. The Jedi Knights (Queens Chapter) had assembled on the main deck. where they rehearsed a series of pseudo-Japanese sword routines with their Light Sabers trying to impress the cluster of armored Japanese soldiers who stood impassively, arms folded, nearby. Kenny however, joined King on the quarterdeck, where he stood apart at a respectful distance. He had attempted to engage the first mate and officers without result.

Nearby Solomon's Seal put up her full spread of canvas and heeled over as she maneuvered towards the starting line. For the most part, the Ghost Seekers team stayed huddled in the aft cockpit, except for one daring soul – it was the cameraman, Farrell – who had positioned himself in the bow with his video camera.

King had no real idea what he was supposed to do, other than standing on the quarterdeck and trying to look important.

Ricky ran up and stood next to King, hands on rail and taking deep exaggerated breaths. "Do you believe this thing? This ship is like totally cool, man! How did you land this gig?"

King was clenching his teeth, calling on every ounce of self-control he had available.

"Just lucky, I guess. Ricky, does Jimmy have any fucking idea how to sail this thing? I think he was downstairs shooting up."

Ricky gave a shrug and smile that said, "hey, who cares, this is fun right? Then he said, "Hey, Jimmy, you cool with helping sail this thing?"

"Yeah, yeah, sure," he responded, looking anything but.

Ritchie smiled. "See? No problemo!"

King glanced over at him. "Jimmy, exactly what kind of boats did you sail on out of Sheepshead?"

"Well . . . nothing like this, of course."

"Did it even have sails?"

Scarpa mulled this over. "Yeah, *some*."

"It had 'some' sails?"

"Yeah, it was like, a Sunfish."

"A fucking Sunfish?" King smacked his forehead with his palm.

"Ritchie, you brought a guy who knows how to sail a ten-foot trainer to help me sail a galleon! *Hijo de puta.*"

Scarpa flicked his cigarette over the rail. "Yo, I don't need this shit." he said, before disappearing down below for a second time. Ritchie was unfazed, giving a "So-what-the-hell-can-a-guy-do" shrug.

King turned to his right. "And who the hell are you again? Kenny?"

"Kenneth. And I'm a Sith Lord and Jedi Master."

"No kidding? You never know who you'll run into around here. So, you have any more knowledge about racing boats than my good buddy, Joey Brooklyn?"

Kenny let out a soft chuckle, which came off slightly staged. "I'm afraid not. I am, however, well versed in various martial arts and sword fighting and, with my fellow knights, will shield you from harm."

"Martial arts? You have a Black Belt or something?"

Kenny looked off into the distance. "Well . . . not exactly. I've taken classes in many styles, though, and train regularly."

"Oh, that's wonderful. I feel so much safer now!"

King was feeling the first icy fingers of panic.

Why does every damn thing in my life go so horribly wrong? Why? Why?

Suddenly, from somewhere nearby came the long deep blast of a horn.

King swore it came from the cliffs over Raadsel Point. Ritchie was convinced it was from the sky above. Over on Solomon's Seal they thought it sounded from the west bank of the Hudson.

The Ghost Seekers team put up a ragged cheer.

Kenny clasped his hands behind his back and cocked his head to one side.

"Either way, it appears the race has begun."

Ritchie let out a whoop, "Ándele! Ándele!"

King crossed himself. The wind was coming down from the north-northeast.

Solomon's Seal heeled over and picked up speed. Meanwhile the *Vander Dekken's* sails began to lose air and flap about uselessly.

"What the hell is happening!?" King shrieked.

The Dutch sailing master stood by the steering house with arms folded, the four other officers gathered around him, not saying a word. They were short men with stocky builds and looked weathered, ugly, and unfriendly. King had to admit that their make-up and costumes were good. Their collars, doublets, and pantaloons might have been plucked out of a museum.

"Why aren't we moving?" King yelled at him.

Nothing.

King paced back and forth. Ritchie looked nervous. On the main deck, the Jedi Knights stopped their routines and looked around, puzzled.

"What the fuck! Make this ship go!"

"Tell him put the ship on a port tack, heading north-by-northwest. As close-hauled as she'll go," Kenny chimed in from the port rail. King couldn't have been more surprised if a monkey had stood up and expressed a quadratic equation.

"What!?"

"Just tell him."

King did.

The master nodded, eyes glancing about. The crew sprang into action, hauling on various sheets to pull the yards around as the ship adjusted its course. The air filled with the sound of lines racing through blocks and pulleys, the crew dancing about in eerie silence. The sails filled with wind again and the galleon surged forward, masts creaking, shrouds and stays thrumming.

King was gripping the rail again as the ship picked up speed.

"I thought you didn't know anything about racing boats." Kenny shrugged. "I don't. But sailing ships I do, at least sort of. I used to be addicted to that PC Game, Sid Meier's Pirates. And I have an excellent memory."

King didn't know whether to be impressed or to burst out laughing. Then, remembering the stakes, he decided – in a rare moment of self-control – to hold his tongue. Instead he clapped one hand on Kenny's shoulder conspiratorially.

Feeling bold, Kenny added, "I think part of the game here is you need to figure out the correct thing to tell them, then they'll do it."

"Tell me everything you know, and I'll buy you a dozen of those light sabers."

It turned out Kenny had a lot to talk about.

On board Solomon's Seal, things were even livelier.

It turned out that Tom Grant, the sound engineer, grew up crewing on J24s and knew a thing or two about boats. Hewitt insisted on manning the ship's wheel – a classic wooden one with spokes in the aft cockpit – which led to a few screw ups at the start. Their first mate was also unhelpful. He looked like an elderly Errol Flynn in whites with a traditional captain's cap and a pipe that appeared to let out smoke but only a trace of tobacco smell. He sat in the very stern, arms crossed and not saying a word. Karen Liu, one of the less hysterical of Hewitt's investigators, kept smacking her EMF meter, cursing, "I think this damn thing is busted! The readings keep showing as stuck on maximum. But that's just plain impossible."

Freddie Stern was experiencing similar impossibility issues with his air ion counter, which was registering off the chart readings for both negative and positive ions. Meanwhile, Joan Constantine was below in the main cabin, having problems with her i9 compact thermal camera. At first, she wasn't getting any readings on the crew at all, although the Ghost Seekers team registered perfectly. Then she wasn't registering any thermal image of herself, which had her confused and uneasy. That only added to her mounting anxiety about her missed period, which she was praying wasn't connected to a clandestine fling she'd had with Hewitt the month before after a wrap party.

It took some minutes of conferring for the investigators to sort out that the key to getting the ship sailing correctly was to figure out the correct way to phrase orders to the first mate. They, too, were thrown at first by the eerie way the mate would simply glance forward and the crew would instantly respond, though their conclusions took more fanciful routes than King's did over on the Vander Dekken.

"We may be witnessing genuine psychic phenomena," Garth Winslow said excitedly. "I think these guys are truly telepathic!"

Hewitt fixed him with a skeptical look before remembering he was live on camera.

Rick Petricello was using the infra-red cam – a signature gimmick topped only by the even more ludicrous "You Are There" head cam. – As Hewitt's face wobbled into view, the investigator switched on his best "concerned and serious" expression and whispered, "Folks, we may be witnessing actual telepathic phenomena with the sailing crew here, possibly enhanced by the ghostly presences here on this purportedly haunted yacht…"

Almost on cue came a loud thump, to which two investigators cried, "Did you hear that?" followed by a very human "Goddamnit!" as Joan emerged out of the main cabin hatchway, rubbing the top of her head.

Solomon's Seal was sailing close-hauled on a port tack, well ahead of the galleon wallowing just past Raadsel Point. Tom Grant had quickly coached everyone on keeping to the high side of the boat (which the ship's crew did automatically) to counter the ship's heeling as the wind caught the sails. She certainly made an impressive sight, cutting along the dark waters of the river under a full spread of canvas, spray coming off her bow as it bit into the foaming waves like a thoroughbred. Aside from the two lights in the stern and the soft glow of lights out from the portholes, she only carried two ship's lanterns mounted just above the deck on the main shrouds; red on the port side and green on starboard.

The wind picked up and the point and the sounds and blinking lights of the carnival slipped away into the darkness.

Aboard the *Vander Dekken*, King and his crew were finally getting their act together.

With the proper orders given and the ship finally trimmed correctly, she made way, gaining speed though on a more oblique approach up the Hudson than the yacht racing ahead of her. With her blocky forecastle and square sails, the galleon had to sail at least 20 degrees off the direction of the wind, so she would have to take a much more acute zig-zag course up the river.

On the plus side, as Kenny explained to King, she would probably make up for the deficit with her superior speed – her larger amount of canvas would work better in the strong wind. One thing he'd learned from his years of playing Pirates was that, in a stiff breeze, a galleon could get up to 12-14 knots while (at a guess at least) the yacht might make 10 or 11 tops.

Kenny also had the foresight to request from the first mate a chart of the river so they could work out some sort strategy, as well as their route. As long as the wind kept up, it was all a matter of time and angles. More or less.

Scarpa hadn't been seen since he'd disappeared below. Ritchie had gone down to check on him and said he was in the main cabin 'taking a nap'. King, always amazed at his cousin's good-natured naiveté, knew better. He had never been into heroin himself – Bolivian marching powder was his game – but, as the saying goes, it takes a junkie to know a junkie. Sure enough, when Kenny dragged him in to the main cabin to look over the charts of the river, the illustrious Mister Scarpa was sprawled in the signature glassy-eyed half-doze in the small captain's bed built into an alcove with a privacy curtain.

The cabin had a cramped, vertigo-inducing aspect with its sloped deck, low beams, and oppressive atmosphere. The small diamond-paned windows were latched tight and wouldn't have offered much air circulation regardless. There was also a small door that led out into the stern galley.

A heavy desk was in the center of the space, along with a variety of chairs, chests, and a few lanterns slung from the beams. There was bric-a-brac such as a rack of rusty swords, some small oil paintings, and some exotic nautical decorations (including a sextant, a set of Javanese masks, and an antique telescope) but King barely registered any of this. He was still overtired, stressed, and, within the confines of the cabin, on the verge of becoming sea-sick. He stayed only as long as it took for Kenny to show him a rough guess as to their best route to the finish line.

Part of the guesswork was related to the fact that the charts were clearly hundreds of years old, part was due to the possible variables in wind and current. But Kenny estimated that they should be able to make the finish line at Shattemuc Island (also marked as Polei-polei) within forty minutes, give or take.

King was inwardly grateful to finally have someone who he felt was of some use – Kenny suddenly found himself elevated to top of the "Buddy A-list" – though not grateful enough to explain what the ultimate prize was at the end of the race. And he certainly had no intention of sharing any of the loot with the whacky Jedi Knights or the strung-out Jimmy Scarpa. Ritchie would have to be thrown a token share, but only afterwards, probably parceled out so he wouldn't blow it all at once or give it all away. Ritchie might be one of the few people King actually cared about, but he was also shrewd enough to know that his cousin needed to be kept on a "need-to-know" basis and that right now it was best to keep him well in the dark.

-15-

CAPTAIN FOWLER arrived at the marina almost at the same time as Chief Hendricks.

Just before the recession had hit, Hendricks had wrangled a state-of-the-art police launch out of the village budget and, as of this night, was counting every single one of his lucky stars for his foresight. It had only been used on a handful of occasions, usually to assist a local fisherman with engine trouble and once to apprehend a drug-runner who had stolen a power boat out of the yacht club (that had garnered the front page of the WF Gazette along with the predictably badly-shot photo), but never in his wildest dreams did Hendricks think they would need it to head off a night race between a galleon and a yacht.

And it wasn't as if what King and Hewitt were up to was exactly illegal, though Hendricks could certainly muster up some sort of reckless endangerment charge or such. It was more personal. He had ordered them out of his town for nearly jeopardizing the Castle Krell crime scene and now here they were, still screwing around on his turf like a couple of hot-headed teenager's drag-racing.

Except on sailing ships instead of hot-rods.

The police launch had been something of a coup. A custom-built 44-foot fast patrol boat originally commissioned by the Greek Coast Guard, Hendricks had gotten it for a song when that country was going through a fire sale to liquidate some of its assets the previous year. The cost of shipping had nearly topped the cost of the boat itself. With its sleek bullet-shaped hull, raked cabin, and sporty WFPD livery, the launch was the envy of rival police departments up and down the river and a personal source of pride for Wyvern Falls. She was powered by twin Volvo-Penta D12-650 diesels that combined cranked out an impressive 1300 horsepower. With her throttles opened up, she could rocket up and down the river at 40-plus knots.

Hendricks had appropriately named her 'Themis'.

The goddess of divine law and order.

Fowler had brought along three of the best divers in the WFPD at Hendricks request. Fowler himself was a skilled boatman from a long line of them, as was Lieutenant Sanchez, who had proved a quick study as well when it came to handling high-performance watercraft. One family legend had it that the first of his family to arrive in the area was originally a member of Captain Kidd's disbanded crew, which fed neatly into the local folklore of that notorious pirate's gold being buried somewhere on Raadsel Point. Fowler only let out the whole story on rare occasions, which only polished it with more legitimacy over the years. If pressed by a friend, his usual stock explanation was, "Well, never let the facts get in the way of a good story."

Hendricks was having a quick word with Fowler and Sanchez in the cockpit while the other three policemen untethered lines and got the ship underway. The twin Volvos were letting out a throaty burble as the launch eased out of its special berth next to the yacht club.

"How do you want to play this?" Fowler asked the police chief. All the policemen were wearing black Summit Outerwear lifesaver jackets with bright yellow life-vests. Fowler was at the helm with one hand on the throttle, the special WFPD bill cap tilted on his head at jaunty angle. Hendricks let out a chuckle. "Good question. I don't remember that the Coast Guard training course covered galleon interception."

Fowler smiled. "Nope, don't think it did."

Not for the first time, Hendricks noted that Fowler had a particular way of speaking that reminded him of old broadcasts of Franklin Roosevelt – a Hudson River dialect one didn't hear much of anymore. He looked out through the sloped Plexiglas of the cockpit windows. "So, I guess we'll just try to head them off and talk them into pulling over. This'll be one for the books."

"Sure will. Better get yourself a seat, Chief. Things are going to get wet."

No sooner had they cleared the small harbor with its old style lighthouse, then Fowler pushed the throttles forward and the boat shot out into the river, engines roaring, a rooster tail of water shooting out in its wake.

The patrol boat swung out wide into the river, cutting through the roughening waves with a repeating slam that was enough to rattle the fillings in everyone's teeth. The wind had picked up, shifting around until it was coming off the compass from the northwest. From the rime splattered cabin, Hendricks, who was blessed with exceptionally good eyesight, was surprised to see the two ships much farther up the river than he would have thought possible, even factoring for the strong tide. They were just disappearing around the next bend in the river, which would line them up for the next leg taking them past Anthony's Nose, the sharp promontory situated just north of Dunderberg Mountain where the river made a westerly jig.

How the hell did they get up there so fast? He wondered. He also saw something else he didn't quit care for – a low heavy fog rolling in from the highlands around the mountain, accompanied by occasional flashes of lightning.

Fowler raced the launch up the river, the hull all but skimming on the surface as they ate up the distance. But as they came around the next bend, they came upon a completely unexpected scene. The captain eased back on the throttles and the engines settled into a rumbling cruising speed. Hendricks clambered up onto the foredeck with a pair of binoculars, a megaphone slung over one shoulder, not believing what his eyes were telling him. From the opposite shore, a strange layer of clouds was crawling down to the waterline and creeping across the river, like some sort of bad dry-ice movie effect.

He looked over at Fowler and shouted, "You ever see anything like this before?"

Fowler shrugged. "Heard of it, but I've never *seen* anything like it before."

Even as they watched, the sails of the two ships disappeared into the mist.

-16-

IT WAS SHORTLY after the fog descended, and what began as a little prank by Hewitt, that things began to go terribly wrong.

It started with a half-joking suggestion from Tom Grant.

He'd been leaning back on the cushioned bench at the back of the yacht's cockpit, keeping an eye on the trim of the sails, when almost absently he said to Hewitt, "You know, it'd be pretty easy to knock them out of the race by jamming their rudder."

Hewitt, who had been hamming it up at the ship's wheel like he was a seasoned pro at skippering yachts (a routine slightly marred by the way he was wearing the skipper's cap backwards), glanced at his sound engineer.

"What?"

Grant had been enjoying his unexpected rise in status with the team since they'd gotten underway. In the past year, Hewitt had barely said two words to him. Now, he was being treated like his best buddy. The other investigators had bunched towards the front of the cockpit and, if he wasn't mistaken, Bob Weiss and Karen Liu had been giving him increasingly annoyed looks. And the way Garth Winslow was pointedly not looking (or talking) to anyone else was becoming painfully obvious.

Only Freddie Stern was making any effort at checking the EMF meters and ion detectors. Joan Constantine had taken up standing on the steps leading down to the main cabin, gripping the hatch coaming and looking like she was in a serious struggle to keep her dinner down.

Grant continued to study the shape of the main sail. "Jam the rudder on King's ship. Then she can't steer. Bam! Race over. We get the prize."

Hewitt looked nonplussed. "We can do that? I mean, *how can we do that?*"

Grant considered a moment. "Well, we should have some sort of gaff or fending pole on board. If we can get close enough, I can jam it in their rudder. By the time they get it sorted out, we'll be coasting across the finish line."

Hewitt made a nasty little grin. "I like it! Make it so, my man!" He motioned to the silent first mate, then at the galleon off to their starboard side, "We're going to pay a close visit to our competition, keep us sailing smooth, yeah?"

The Errol Flynn face was expressionless. But there was a slow nod. Grant got up and, easing past Joan, disappeared into the main cabin. A few minutes later, he reappeared with a long wooden pole with a metal hook and point at the end. He also had something slung over his back.

It was an old-fashioned bolt action rifle.

"What the hell is that?" Hewitt said. The rest of the Ghost Seekers crew looked alarmed.

Grant laid down the pole and unslung the rifle. "Check this shit out – I found this in the locker as well! It's an old Springfield 30-06."

Hewitt's face lit up. "Is it loaded?"

"Oh, yeah."

"Cool. Give it up."

Then he looked over at the first mate. "I'm ordering you to get us in as close to that galleon's rear-end as possible."

"Stern," Grant corrected him, "He has to get us as close to the galleon's *stern* as possible."

Aboard the *Vander Dekken*, King was becoming a little surer of himself, though his heart still threatened to vapor-lock at any unexpected lurch or noise. In fact, a steely sort of determination began to set in as, in his mind, the race had become less about any prize and more about sticking it to Hewitt and Company. The money would be his of course – King would not be denied his rightful due – but, more importantly, King was already seeing how this could play out as a brilliant kick-off to his new show. Gutsy New York Reporter (Hispanic star from Spanish Harlem, no less) slam dunks Obnoxious White Frat-boy rival in historic race up the Hudson River by quick thinking and seat-of-the-pants ingenuity! Bold and daring! A man born to lead . . . and win! Kenny had now assumed a position at King's right hand. While the tall and obese Jedi – it turned out his name was Tim Fallon – had also taken up residence on the quarterdeck, standing alongside his master with folded arms and the self-important air of a loyal sidekick. His double bladed light saber (which cost him a small fortune on eBay) was slung over his back. To his credit, he was the only one of the group to hold a legitimate job as an IT contractor for a shipping container company. The rest of the Jedi had gathered on the forecastle, while Ritchie had taken up a position on the poop deck. He'd pilfered some clothes out of a locker in the main cabin and now looked like some strange amalgam that could only be described as "Joe Queens meets Blackbeard the Pirate."

The four Dutch officers continued to stand apart by themselves, ignoring any attempts to engage them in conversation. The rest of the crew stood by on the main deck, clambering up like nimble monkeys when required, while the group of odd-looking Japanese mercenaries kept to their tight phalanx in the middle of the deck before the main mast, impassive as statues.

Jimmy Scarpa remained lolling on the horizontal plane down in the captain's bunk.

As they'd rounded the last bend, they'd been spooked by the rolling fog coming down off the opposite shore and, by the time Kenny had suggested to King to direct their first mate to change tacks and begin the next leg up towards the Bear Mountain Bridge, the mists had all but enveloped the two ships.

The *Vander Dekken* was on a port tack, charging up the river at a good clip, with the wind off her port quarter and her sails braced around as far as possible. Solomon's Seal was just off their starboard beam, a ghost conjured from the golden days of yachting with her full press of canvas and short bowsprit.

A mile up ahead, the high promontory of Anthony's Nose loomed to the north with Dunderberg Mountain to the southwest, the elegant span of the Bear Mountain Bridge just coming into sight.

Kenny made sure (through King) that the sailing master was to keep them out of the shallows on either side of the river, though how they could manage without any modern navigation devices was anyone's guess — which posed some serious questions as to the legality of this vessel, when considered with the complete lack of any basic safety equipment, such as life vests.

The wind continued to "box the compass," as the saying goes, until it began blowing up out of the southwest. The galleon's sails swelled out even further, the yards and rigging groaning with the strain. They were fast approaching the Bear Mountain Bridge, the galleon surging through the billowing mist like some sort of Flying Dutchman apparition, when someone gave a yell and pointed to the port side of the ship.

King ran over, along with Kenny and Fallon.

Out of the fog, Solomon's Seal emerged, seemingly on a collision course with the galleon's stern quarter. Up on the poop deck, Ritchie jumped up and down, waving his hands, "Hey, yo, back off, amigos! You freakin' crazy?"

Still the yacht came on.

King was by the port rail, one hand gripping the ratlines of the main mast, a scowl on his face.

"What the hell are they doing?" he half-yelled at no one in particular, the words snatched away by the wind.

Kenny leaned over the rail, frowning, one foot on the small cannon lashed to the deck. From the high stern, they were nearly ten feet above the water line. Fallon jumped up into the rigging like an oafish buccaneer. He unslung his light saber and raised it above his head threateningly.

"Back off, knaves!" he bellowed.

King winced.

Kenny looked alarmed. He spotted Tom Grant at the broadest part of the approaching ketch's deck, one arm twisted through a halyard, so that he could angle his body out from the boat as far as possible. More disturbingly, he saw the long gaff balanced in Grant's left hand.

He quickly calculated distances and angles.

"Not good, not good," he muttered to himself. Then he yelled at King at the top of his lungs, "He's going to spike our rudder! Hard to port!! Tell him hard to port NOW!"

The crew responded instantly, the groaning and creaking from the masts and rigging suggesting that they were being stressed to the breaking point. The deck canted suddenly, all but tumbling everyone off the starboard side (for one precarious moment Jedi Fallon swung out over the water and was nearly thrown off into the river) before the ship righted herself, sending everyone sprawling, except for the ship's crew (including the Ronin) who, aside from leaning slightly, were able to defy physics and remain standing in place.

There was a heavy thud and the sound of wood splintering.

Then they heard the screaming.

It might have worked out as Grant intended but for the rogue wave that surged the ships together just as Solomon's Seal cut across the *Vander Dekken's* stern, batting aside the small wooden dinghy tethered off the galleon's stern quarter. The plan had been simple enough: get in close, jam the gaff into the galleon's rudder to kill her steering ability, sail on, win race.

But, like so many things, overconfidence and a lack of adequate experience resulted in a completely different outcome.

Tom Grant was familiar with the nimble characteristics of a modern twenty-four-foot racing boat – the J24 – but inexperienced with the risks of putting large sailing vessels within tight proximity in a heavy sea. As he thrust the gaff at the narrow space between the galleon's rudder and its hull, his aim was thrown off as the other ship did a sluggish swerve. The gaff was knocked askew and clattered away into the water, nearly wrenching Grant off his perch and into the roiling waters of the Hudson.

Which might have worked out for the better.

Instead, as the yacht passed by, a surge forced the two ships together.

Grant was thrust headfirst into five hundred tons of solid wood hull, instantly crushing his skull like an eggshell. Then as he collapsed, the two ships ground together, mangling his body to a pulp. The spray of blood and snapping bones was all but lost in the chaos of cracking wood and tangling rigging.

People were screaming from the cockpit of the yacht as Grant's body dropped mercifully from sight.

The force of the impact and the course change of the galleon swung the ketch around until the ships were nearly parallel alongside each other.

Aboard the *Vander Dekken*, the demise of Mister Grant went unobserved – from the high stern superstructure it been a matter of "now you see him, now you don't" – but the fun was just beginning. King and Kenny regained their feet and clambered to the starboard rail, trying to sort out what was actually happening. The ever-gallant Tim Fallon leapt to rigging near them again, furious at whatever business the Ghost Seekers crew had been trying to pull. In his excitement, he had turned on his light saber – a hi-tech Ultra-Saber with a Destiny-Blue blade – and was holding it above his head like some sort of geeky, obese Zeus.

Like many insecure, emotionally under-developed misfits, Fallon had an irrational temper, honed by years of revenge fantasies and school-yard beatings. Even so, in his heart he never truly meant to hurt anyone.

So it was with a flash of utter horror that he felt an unseen hand pull his arm backwards and hurl his glowing UltraForce™ light saber ($349.95 on eBay) into the cockpit of the Solomon's Seal.

Although the tip of the saber was rounded, it flew as straight and true as a perfectly-balanced spear and with uncanny force (certainly much more speed than would have physically seemed possible) into the open, screaming mouth of Garth Winslow.

The results were extraordinary.

And definitely not pleasant.

The polycarbonate blade (which featured an actual laser and proprietary magnetic ball system) skewered the back of Winslow's throat and shattered as it burst through the upper part of the spine. His head snapped back, his eyes bulging in shock and agony, a choking gurgle leaking out of his mouth, followed by a gush of blood and a fried meat smell, as the laser cooking the inside of his mouth in brilliant electrical arcs of Destiny Blue.

The screaming intensified.

Joan Constantine fell backwards into the main cabin in a dead faint.

The rest of the Ghost Seekers team simply sat frozen in place, unable to process this sudden and traumatic course of events.

Joel Hewitt, however, looked furious. Still standing by the ship's wheel, he shouldered the Springfield and worked the bolt to chamber a round. Next to him, the first mate continued to sit unperturbed, as if this was all just part of routine night sail. Except for his eyes, which flared with malicious glee.

"You are so assed-out, mother-fucker," Hewitt snarled.

He took aim at Fallon looming above and fired.

Given the short range and the size of the target, it wasn't at all surprising that the bullet found its mark, even considering the pitch and roll of the two ships and Hewitt's lack of shooting expertise. The rifle was loaded with soft-point 180-grain bullets and the resulting effect on Fallon's abdominal section was catastrophic.

He let out a deflated "Oh," and slid down until his knees were resting on the bulwark rail, one hand still gripping the mainmast stay, the other grasping his belly. King and Kenny stood next to him, gaping in shock, as did Ritchie up on the poop deck. From the forecastle of the galleon, the rest of the Jedi Knights (Queens Chapter) looked on in horror.

With a creak and snap of rigging and spars, the two ships separated, the wind snapping through the upper part of Solomon's Seal's main sail, now torn in several places.

Tim Fallon pitched forward silently and tumbled down into black waters of the Hudson.

The two ships drifted apart and there were a few drawn-out moments in which it seemed time went on hold while this inexplicable turn of violent events sank in.

If more sober minds had prevailed, it might have stopped then and there, but it didn't.

And naturally, in all the excitement, neither King nor Hewitt remembered to tip their hats to Dunderberg Mountain as their respective ships finally eased past and into the final leg of the race.

From the peak of that squat-looking mountain – at just over a thousand feet it was really more of a rounded hill – the clouds appeared to gather and swirl, punctuated by angry flashes of lightning.

A peal of thunder rolled and boomed across the river.

-17-

HEWITT WORKED the bolt on the Springfield and chambered another round, oblivious to anything but the bloodlust thrumming through his veins. This was an altogether new experience for him, a quantum leap from mere bullying and cruel pranks. He had actually just shot and killed another human being.

With a high-powered rifle.

And it felt good.

He felt invincible. Powerful.

He swung the rifle toward his next target and grinned. "Yo, Marc Anthony . . . *smile!*"

Over on the *Vander Dekken's* forecastle, the three Queens Jedi's were shouting – the girl was screaming ('ohmygod, what-what did you do to Timmy!!!') – while the tall kid with the mustache had figured out that the swivel cannon mounted on the rail next to him might actually be loaded. With hands that didn't seem to be controlled by his own thoughts, he grasped the long handle at the back of the cannon, aimed down towards the cockpit of the drifting yacht, and pulled the lanyard.

There was a deafening "bang!" as the swivel gun fired, sending a scything load of chain-shot, musket balls, and nails at Solomon's Seal.

Karen Liu and Freddie Stern were killed instantly. Rick Petricello would live on for a few more minutes as the torn femoral artery in his thigh bled out.

Amazingly, Hewitt was only hit by a flying link of chain that clipped his left ear and a nail that tore a small ragged wound in his right side, but it was enough to throw off his aim.

The bullet only winged King – cutting a divot out of his shoulder – and sent him flying backwards onto his ass on the quarterdeck. Kenny had already fallen backwards, hands around his face, sobbing. Nothing in his years of so-called martial training had ever prepared him for this. Ritchie, seeing his cousin wounded, leaped down to the quarterdeck, narrowly missing a third bullet from Hewitt, who was having an unbelievably good sharpshooting run, oblivious to increasing pain from the rifle stock kicking into his shoulder and the blood streaming from his head where half his ear was now gone.

Never the brightest bulb in the box, Ritchie stood up after seeing that his Lorenzo was still alive and shook his fist at the yacht.

"You son-of-a—" he screamed. Then Hewitt shot him, right in the forehead. The back of his skull blew out and Ritchie King, only son of Carlos and Juanita of Flushing, Queens, was no more.

On the forecastle, the Jedi Moustache Knight was onto the next swivel gun, this one mounted near the corner where in battle it could be trained on enemy boarders, preparing to give the cockpit of Solomon's Seal a second dose of carnage. He didn't see Jim Farrell re-emerge from the forward hatch of the ketch with a flare-gun, a 26.5 mm vintage WWII German model he'd found below, and aim it directly at him. There was a crack and a flaming contrail shot across the two ships.German model he'd found below, and aim it directly at him. There was a crack and a flaming contrail shot across the two ships.

Before he could fire the second swivel gun the Knight (real name: Ed Dewitt) found himself hosting a 12-gauge Army surplus Geco flare charge in his chest. Even as it ignited, he fell back, his hand jerking back on the lanyard and yanking the swivel barrel up, with the ensuing blast cutting the ketch's foresails to ribbons.

Lorenzo King dropped to the main deck, the injury to his shoulder searing, splattered with blood and gore from his cousin. He crawled up to the deck cannon there, which some unseen hand had had the courtesy to run out of its gun port. A deranged look was in his eyes, his normally coifed hair matted and standing up in tufts. He looked up at the quarterdeck rail, where the four ship's officers now stood, looking down at him like a portrait of a somber 16th Century Dutch tribunal, their arms folded. Like their counterparts on the Solomon's Seal, they seemed unperturbed by the violence and carnage around them.

The ship's master nodded.

King grinned.

He grasped the leather lanyard in one hand, glancing through the open gun-port down the cast iron barrel of the six-pounder cannon. Barely ten yards away, Hewitt still stood in the back of the yacht, gun swinging around wildly as he sought out another target.

King held his breath, instinctively waiting for the roll of the ship to aim the gun downward.

Hewitt rose up in his sights.

King's eyes flared. "I'm cancelling your show, *amigo*," he hissed.

He yanked the lanyard.

-18-

OVER THE PEAL of thunder, Hendricks clearly heard the signature crack of rifle fire followed by the heavier boom of cannon fire. Nothing like the howitzers one might hear on any given day from the West Point artillery range, but there was no mistaking it nonetheless. The distant screams, warbled and distorted by the wind, didn't bode well either.

He glanced over at Fowler, who stood at the wheel, head slightly cocked, his eyes saying he didn't like what he was hearing either.

Not one bit.

Up ahead, the bend in the river that swung past the Bear Mountain Bridge was still blanketed in rolling fog.

"I'll get on the radio for back-up," Hendricks said. "You get us over there quickly and carefully, Wes."

Fowler nodded, "Got it."

Without being asked, the three other officers reappeared on the deck of the boat armed with Heckler & Koch G36 assault rifles.

Fowler eased the engines to quarter power and they headed into the mist and lightning.

Over on Shattemuc Island, Hideki and Sheila waited uncomfortably on a bench out on the long pier that formed part of a marina built out from the south part of the island. A light pole powered by one of the marina's generators gave off a fickle glow and beside them was the heavy sailor's chest Heer had left. They'd driven across the short causeway connecting the island to the western shore where Heer had dropped them off, along with the prize chest, giving them explicit instructions they were to wait at the end of the pier until the winner arrived.

"What about you? Where will you be?" Sheila had inquired. "I mean; don't you have to give them the prize or something?"

Heer looked at her a moment, eyes gleaming. "I have business to attend to…but I will return, I assure you of that. Meantime, sit back and enjoy the show! I promise that you will find this event most entertaining . . . most entertaining. *Ja*!"

Now part of a trust, Shattemuc was home to the now-dilapidated ruins of a once exotic Hudson manor (more of a small castle actually) but was still maintained for summer boat tours. It even sported a clam shack and bait store, though both were still boarded up for the season, the latest in many local victims of the recession.

Sheila had made several nervous attempts at small talk but Hideki seemed preoccupied and, after a handful of monosyllabic responses, she gave up. The way he simply sat, fists resting on his thighs, looking out at the empty expanse of river with intense focus (empty but for the rolling mists, and flashes of lightning to the south) was utterly strange and unnerving to her.

Not creepy, but strange. Alien. The world of Sheila Walters was made of chatty busybodies constantly talking over each other, clamoring to be heard or at least announcing their presence.

This young Japanese man was completely out of her scope of experience.

The roar of the cannon was deafening.

It all but leapt out of its mount, the carriage shooting back on its wooden wheels and nearly crushing King's foot.

His head was so close to the muzzle that the concussion all but blew out his hearing, except for a high ringing sound.

The cannon ball didn't come anywhere close to Hewitt, but it did smash through the base of the main mast which, after a suspenseful moment, toppled over in a cacophony of snapping rigging and splintering wood. It fell into the water with a resounding splash and, acting like a sea anchor, began to drag the yacht away in the current.

Hewitt was all but out of his mind, firing the rifle into the air and laughing like a lunatic.

"Fuck you, you Fakin' Jack! You can't kill me! Hahaha!!"

To King, it sounded like Hewitt was yelling from a box filled with cotton and all he could think to do was to sit back on his haunches, a dazed look on his face, as his rival jumped up and down in the cockpit of the yacht, hooting and firing the rifle gain and again.

Then a movement in the sky over head caught his eye.

Something was spinning, tumbling through the air.

King's mind was having trouble processing the data his eyes were feeding him. Then they went wide with utter surprise.

A much smaller (and if possible, more grotesque) nightmare version of Jacob Heer was barreling though the air like the world's ugliest and most strangely-dressed acrobat. He glimpsed gargoyle-like features that were now distorted impossibly wide, the nose hooked out and flaring, ears tapering off into twisted points. A conical blood-red sugar-loaf hat was on his head and the misshapen, bulbous body was now sporting some sort of jerkin along with leather pantaloons and curly-toed shoes.

The whole effect was repulsive and yet compelling to watch, like a horribly deformed person suddenly observed on a normally familiar street.

All this was registered in a glance, as was the rusty hand scythe, the type often used by Dutch farmers to thresh wheat back in the old days, which, interestingly, still appeared to have a gleaming razor-sharp edge.

King watched this from the deck of the *Vander Dekken* as if in a dream. Nothing in his media career – his entire life for that matter – prepared him for the scene that quickly unfolded.

There was a whickering sound, then a thud as Heer, tumbling end over end, bounced off the foredeck of the yacht and ricocheted off into the sky again like the world's most bizarre rubber super-ball, followed by a deranged laugh that trailed off in a weird Doppler effect. Jim Farrell was looking with almost detached awe at the stump where his arm used to be. (The lighter thud he'd heard was his previously-attached appendage dropping on the teak deck, still gripping the German army-surplus flare gun.) This was followed by a splattering rain of blood as he stumbled backwards a few steps and fell, half tangling himself with the ship's rail as he passed out and slowly bled to death.

Hewitt continued on with his maniacal laughter, working the bolt again, the spent cartridge tumbling down into the cabin and leaving a slight burn on Joan Constantine's cheek. He focused down the barrel, trying to shoot at the improbable target Heer was making as the Imp – for clearly that is what he was – tumbled through the air back at the boat again. *Crack!* went the Springfield, followed by a grunt as the scythe whistled through the air and eviscerated Hewitt's midsection.

The Ghost Seeker dropped to his knees as his guts poured out like tangled sausages, the rifle clattering to the deck alongside him as Heer bounded off again. The imp's hideous giggle trailed away into the wind. A second later, he was back, reappearing next to Hewitt and pulling back the investigator's forehead to expose his throat.

Heer's eyes glared with malevolence as he raised the scythe.

"You dare to take on the Great Dunderberg Imp, *apenkind?*"

Hewitt's eyelids fluttered. But he said, "Fuck you, you ugly toad."

The blade came down and Hewitt was silenced for good.

King came to his senses long enough to panic.

He stumbled over to the four Dutch officers who continued to stand impassively on the quarterdeck, even when he knelt before them.

"*Mierda!*" he said hoarsely, "How can you just stand there?? . . . Help me!"

Four sets of eyes looked impassively at him, cold as marbles. None of them blinked.

"*Pudrete en el infierno!*" he spat.

Rot in Hell.

There might have been a glimmer of understanding. The one that was the sailing master made a sound like a suppressed laugh.

From somewhere forward in the ship came another whistling thud and a scream.

King got moving.

He had just run through the entranceway on the main deck when he turned to see Heer tumbling down from the forecastle in that bizarre end-over-end somersault, hitting the deck once and catapulting towards the door.

King slammed the door shut just in time. There was a thud and the tip of the scythe appeared through the seam, inches from King's head. Then it wriggled as Heer tried to work it loose from the other side. King backed up, horrified, then ran back into the main cabin. Behind him, the door splintered as the imp went at it with maniacal fury. Jimmy Scarpa was standing by the open stern window, hands on the sill, looking out dreamily. He looked over at King, his reflexes clearly operating at half speed, and said, "Hey, man . . . there's a pretty little boat out there . . ."

"What?" King's ears were still ringing from the cannon blast and he wasn't sure he was hearing correctly.

Scarpa gave him a lopsided smile, his eyes bloodshot. "Yo, man . . . can I go home yet? I can row-row-row a boat gently down the stream . . ." he slurred.

King ran over to the window and looked out. At first, he saw nothing but the rolling mists falling away behind and the ship's wake. Then he looked down and saw the wooden dinghy, tethered to the stern of the galleon.

He was frozen in fear at the prospect of jumping – what if he missed? – when from behind came the sound of splintering wood followed by a curse in low Dutch.

King patted Scarpa on the shoulder, a ghastly smile on his face. The dried blood and gore didn't improve matters either.

"That's the most useful advice you've given all night. *El Lorenzo* says . . . *gracias!*"

King clambered out onto the narrow stern gallery. From inside came the patter of running feet.

"*Sayonara!*" King said, then jumped.

He almost missed the boat.

The galleon was drifting off course – as no one was giving directions any more – but still making headway and it was no easy matter to jump from one moving object down into another. King's feet missed the back end of the dinghy but he struck it with his thighs, his crotch just missing the stern post, then landed on his head. Then the back of his head struck the bench and he saw stars.

He heard a yell, followed by a splash and something striking the front of the boat.

King righted himself, head smarting and all, then spotted a pair of hands gripping the gunwale at the bow of the boat.

A moment later, Jimmy Scarpa's water-soaked head appeared, spitting water. He looked like he'd taken a whopping injection of sober in the past few moments.

The grotesque face of Heer popped up over the rail of the stern gallery. The wicked looking – and now very bloody – scythe wavered in the air next to it. He shouted something that sounded like '*Kutaap!*' Then he shot out and up in to the sky like a human cannonball.

King scrambled forward, snatching up a spare oar lying at the bottom of the boat. First he freed the towline that was tied off on a cleat on the bow. No sooner did he do so than the weight of Scarpa hanging on the front of the bow slewed it around.

"Get off! She's mine!" King snarled without even thinking, and whacked Scarpa a good one on the head with the blade of the oar. When he still didn't let go, King smashed his fingers next, first one hand, then the next.

There was a gurgling splash as Scarpa dropped off and fell away in the current.

King glanced around wildly, crouched in the dinghy with the oar clenched in both hands, a feral look on his face. His lips were curled back in a snarl. The Imp's snicker sounded from first one side then another, the combination of the Doppler effect and the wind making it difficult to pinpoint. Meanwhile, the galleon disappeared into the darkness and mist while the current continued to pull King and the little boat north.

He closed his eyes briefly, part of him wishing it was all over, at the same time knowing everything had irrevocably gone far past the point where it could ever be put back to rights, that no matter how this turned out he would be eternally fucked, in big capital letters.

He heard another whistle and snicker.

His eyes flew open and the imp was tumbling straight at him out of the sky, blade glinting in the pale starlight.

Instinctively King shifted his weight back in a classic batter's crouch, the heavy oar gripped like a bat.

Heer popped out of his tumble, his malicious grin changing briefly to an 'O' of surprise just before the side of his misshapen head was met by the full impact of the ship's oar.

King had really gotten all his weight into it, maximizing the swiveling action of his narrow hips.

There was a resounding crack of wood and breaking bone. At least a couple of rotten looking teeth went flying, then Heer smashed down onto the gunwale, hard enough to shatter the wood, then bounced off in a spinning arc that ended with a loud splash in the river.

King crouched there for a minute, features locked in a deranged rictus, and, when nothing happened, he dropped the broken oar and sat down on the center bench.

Nothing but the wind and sluice of water, the dinghy bobbing up and down in the waves.

King swiveled both of the main oars in their oarlocks, dropped the blades into the water, and began to row.

How much farther until he was safe? King wondered.

He had lost all sense of time and direction.

His shoulders and upper back were screaming, and blood continued to ooze out of his wound. It felt as though he had been rowing for years. Then suddenly he could see the channel buoy, and, perhaps fifty yards beyond that, the dock.

There was a figure standing on the dock.

Someone was calling his name.

King didn't even realize he was crying.

-19-

SHEILA HAD finally given up around 2:00 in the morning.

"I don't think they're coming," she'd said, more to herself, since Hasegawa had continued to stare silently out into the river.

"Did you hear me? Hello? Mister Japanese guy? I think they forgot about us here . . ." She looked at the chest. Was there really half a million dollars of silver in there? It really didn't matter much to her either way. Her father was a superintendent of a nearby school district and made easily double what the governor of New York State did (go figure that one), and her mother was an investment banker with JP Morgan, so money wasn't exactly an issue in the Walters' domicile.

"Plus," she thought, "silver was so . . . heavy."

Meanwhile Hideki was in the Zone.

He had been catching random images of the events unfolding out on the river and continued to sit silently, mortified, outwardly appearing tranquil but internally screaming.

He knew something else, too.

And waited.

Sheila had stood up many times in the past couple hours, pacing up and down the dock, doing a few half-hearted yoga stretches, bored. She was cold, hungry, and fed up.

When she repeated her observation twice more with no response, she finally blurted out, "Fine, I'm leaving." And walked away towards the causeway, dialing the number of the local Eco-Taxi she'd logged into her iPhone earlier.

Just in case.

Ten minutes later, she made it to Route 9B, where she stood next to the dilapidated looking wooden sign that read "Historic Shattemuc Island: Tours daily!" After a few minutes, she looked around guiltily, then rummaged around her purse and pulled out a crumpled pack of Virginia Slims she kept for special emergencies and lit one up.

Hasegawa simply sat and stared ahead.

Half an hour later, he heard the creak of oars.

He stood up, trying to ignore the pins and needles in his legs and feet from remaining motionless so long, then walked stiffly out to the end of the pier.

The dinghy took shape out of the dark mists.

Hasegawa cupped his hands around his mouth and yelled.

"King-san, you've almost made it! Keep coming! You've won!"

He jumped up and down.

Twenty yards away, emerging out of the fog, King looked up blearily.

He felt cold and dead as a cemetery urn inside.

And no longer wholly sane.

For the past half hour, he had been he had been listening to his dead uncle.

"Where are you going, *tu eres mi príncipe, si* – my little prince, yes?" Jorge's voice a watery gurgle in the river, murmuring sweet nothings mixed with witty observations about King's life and career.

"The great Lorenzo . . . will they broadcast this final episode…your magnum opus? You were always my favorite, Lorenzo . . . did I tell you your mother knew about us? She couldn't face the truth . . . weak like your sister…you never would have been that good anyhow . . . join us! The water's fine!"

Or was it all in his head? He wasn't sure. The only thing he was sure of was that he felt horrible. His whole life had been one big sham, a whopping lie he had invented.

El Lorenzo.

He was a joke.

And had done bad, *very* bad things tonight.

Then he saw the figure on the dock.

Rosalita.

Stark naked, skin and bones.

His sister was calling to him.

Telling him . . . unpleasant things.

He didn't notice that the current had shifted – the lower Hudson was after all a tidal basin, more of a fjord than an actual river – and now he was being pulled back down the river.

Into the realm of Jacob Heer.

All he was focused on, though, was his sister standing on the dock. He didn't want to see her, her nakedness, or think about the things his uncle had made them do together when she was alive while he videotaped. The oar handles dropped out of his hands and began to trail backwards in the water.

"Join us, Lorenzo . . ." the chorus of voices whispered, "Join us down here . . ." Something bumped against the hull of the rowboat. Shapes appeared to be drifting just below the surface.

"But I can't swim," he whimpered. "I can't."

His lips were trembling.

"You don't need to . . . all we do is play down here, Lorenzo . . ."

He let out a sob, then fell backwards in the boat.

It bobbed as someone – or something – climbed into it.

He felt drops of salty water dripping on his face, and, looking up from his upside-down perspective, wasn't surprised to see the imp standing there, dripping wet, a venomous look on his face.

He wasn't surprised at all.

The Imp of Dunderberg looked seriously PO'd.

The scythe came down.

Hasegawa saw King slump in the rowboat as it slid back into the darkness. He kept calling, not really understanding what was happening, yet sensing the presence of the dead and watery things nearby.

He thought he heard a whistling *thunk* just before a jagged fork of lightning laced across the sky to the south followed by a hollow boom. King was gone.

The race was over.

-20-

THE BIRDS started in around 4:30 a.m.

First a few tentative chirps, then a few bursts of chatter.

Across the river, the Palisades took on a dim, rosy glow.

A new day was breaking over the Hudson.

Hasegawa was sitting on the bench at the dock when the black Buick pulled up. The door opened and a haggard looking Jacob Heer stepped out.

He was in his suit again, though his jaw was tied up in a crude-looking sling and his left eye was black.

Still, he seemed in good spirits as he strolled up to the bench and the sailor's chest next to it.

"They never learn, they never learn, stupid *Klootzak*," he said to no one in particular. Hasegawa continued to sit, on his hands this time, his face expressionless.

Heer gave him a crafty look, then opened the chest and peered inside. Silver coins and plate met his eye. He let out a satisfied grunt, closed the lid and dragged it back to his car.

"Drop by if you're ever interested in a little race," he called over to Hasegawa, grinning. When he didn't get a response, he muttered, "Stupid yellow-man," and slammed the door closed. A minute later, the Buick was silently gliding over the causeway.

Only then did Hasegawa pull his hands out.

His normally immaculate fingernails were chipped and rimed with dirt. The front pocket of his windbreaker bulged slightly with the toolkit he'd carried with him everywhere since he'd been sixteen, a gift from an old teacher.

Hideki smiled.

-21-

HENDRICKS WAS sitting at his desk in his study.

One hand lay in his lap, the other propping up his chin.

He looked lost in thought.

The gun was lying on his desk, disassembled next to a cleaning rag, the bullets replaced in their plastic cartridge box with its orderly slots.

That night a week ago had been one of the spookiest crime events in his career, and he'd logged a few of those over the years.

I don't know why I took this job, he thought, not for the first time. *Next time I get a hint of anything like this past week approaching, I'll book a fishing charter off Montauk — no, make that Key West — and get the hell out of here for a week. I'm getting way too old for this shit.*

Of course, he would do no such thing. The Roy Hendricks of the world liked to gripe and grumble as much as anyone, but they could no more turn their backs on what they saw as their duty than they could reprogram their own DNA. Taking care of things was hard-wired into them.

It was their purpose.

Fowler had eased them up the river, the launch's Volvo engines rumbling like a pair of testy thoroughbreds chomping at their bits. The launch was equipped with a Marinesonic sonar system but Fowler didn't seem confident about it.

For starters, he had been having trouble getting a clear signature of the two ships they were trying to track. And, though river traffic tended to be light in the evening, if the sonar was malfunctioning he didn't want to risk a close encounter with a barge or worse, a small tanker. Like many river men, he preferred to rely on his senses and instincts rather than technology.

The wind and currents of the river could be treacherous and the rolling mist – one of many Hudson River weather phenomena – made both sight and sound difficult to gauge. Overhead, the night sky could be seen through patches of cloud, although visibility was an intermittent hit or miss affair.

They were just passing under the Bear Mountain Bridge when Solomon's Seal drifted into sight, its mainmast and rigging trailing in the water.

"Jesus Christ," one of the officers on the foredeck had said. "Looks like a slaughterhouse."

Hendricks had clambered up onto the side deck next to the cockpit. "Call Peekskill PD and have them join us. Looks like this is now a search and rescue mission," he had said to Fowler.

Joan Constantine was the only remaining survivor of the Ghost Seekers team onboard. They found her sitting on the stair leading into the main cabin, wrapped in a blanket and shaking uncontrollably, clearly in shock.

A quick search of the yacht had Hendricks and his men stumped – how in the world had a bunch of reality TV show people managed to sail a seventy-four-foot ketch?

There was no sign of any sailing crew.

A nip of brandy from Fowler's hip flask put a little color back into Joan Constantine's cheeks. She continued to babble on about a flying dwarf slicing up people and a strange crew that stood by and watched people dying without raising a finger and how could anyone do such a thing? Hendricks had a hard time figuring out just what on the hell had really happened. The Ghost Seekers host – Hewitt – had died from having his throat slit ear to ear, but why was a man sitting in the cockpit with his head impaled by a Star Wars prop and another tangled in the bow with his arm neatly removed, and what was the story with all the shrapnel and carnage at the back-end of the yacht?

Hendricks had seen the ugly results of violence gone awry plenty of times in his career, but nothing even approaching this. And the more they discovered, the weirder it all became.

There was clear evidence somebody – or *somebody's* – with professional experience had managed to sail the ship out this far. The rigging knots and the way the sails were set were clearly the work of seasoned sailors, but there was no sign of them at all. The ship itself had turned out to be registered to a David Hilderman out of the New York Yacht Club, but Hilderman was deceased (killed, in another weird circumstance, at Taron Hall just up the road nearly seven months before) and the yacht had been reported missing.

The whole situation then went into a whole new level of weird when they discovered the dinghy with a headless corpse in its stern – the deceased identified by the wallet in the front pocket as none other than Lorenzo King – and, to really clinch the title in Hendricks' All Time Most Fucked Up Cases, a call had come in ten minutes later that the head of the late LiveEYE New York's host had been discovered – impossible as it was – impaled on the lightning rod atop the steeple of Wyvern Falls' Dutch Reformed Church on South Hudson, more than five miles away. The rod was an antique cast as a folksy interpretation of the Dunderberg Imp with its conical hat tapering to a point, in homage to Washington Irving.

Of the galleon, there was no sign either, despite a coordinated search by multiple police departments up and down the river.

"How does a whole galleon simply disappear?" Hendricks had asked Fowler later at the police station, as they worked on tackling the monumental amount of reports that had to filed. "You saw it yourself. Where is it?"

Fowler had a careful look that suggested he already had a few theories on that topic, but wasn't keen on airing them.

"I have no idea, Chief, I have no idea. It may show up yet . . . who knows?" Perhaps some other time, when things had settled down and he and the Chief were, say, enjoying a day off out fishing for striped bass or maybe shad on the river, he might share a thing or two about ghost stories he'd heard as a kid (and maybe one or two things he'd seen himself over the years) but tonight had clearly not been the time, especially with all the other strange things going on during this year's carnival.

Fowler had a hunch they could look for that missing galleon a very long time and not find it.

Unless it wanted to be found.

The girl had been treated at Philipseburg and then transferred to a psychiatric hospital. There had been fallout from the TV network, the families from the cast, insurance claims and whatnot, but little that could be pointed towards anything but the recklessness of the crews themselves. Mark Rubenstein had made a statement for the local news from the American Hotel the following night, claiming he had tried to talk all of them out of this foolishness and they had gone on anyway, out on the river in unfamiliar boats with no safety equipment.

George Ramos, the carnival manager, was cleared as well. There were no records of a Jacob Heer in his carnival, let alone any rides resembling a freak show, and all his paperwork looked to be in order. As best as anyone could tell, the call into the network that had tipped them off about this had been some sort of hoax.

Hideki Hasegawa had given his statement, which hadn't been very helpful. He claimed he didn't understand English particularly well and couldn't verify much, other than that he had met a short man called Heer, had been told to sit on a bench on the dock at Shattemuc Island to wait for the race to finish, and that had been it.

No mention of any treasure.

But the young Japanese had found the area intriguing and interesting, and was planning to stay local for the time being. Although not at the American Hotel.

So many of the statements about what had happened were so inconsistent and borderline ridiculous that Hendricks had begun to wonder just what really had happened, and whether a lot of alcohol (and perhaps drugs as well) might explain a good chunk of it....

Hendricks sat back and took a sip of the B&B in the small snifter next to the gun.

Hell of a week. Time for a vacation, I think.

He looked over at the picture of his two girls. The photo of his wife was in the top drawer of the desk. He had decided he needed to let her ghost rest for a while. Besides, he was getting tired of their one-sided conversations. Pamela would be going off to college the following year. It was summer. His job wasn't going anywhere – it was a lifetime appointment – and he'd decided a little family vacation was in order. He'd been delighted when both girls agreed. They were at that age when the last thing most young girls wanted was to hang out with their old man. But there'd been an opening at a friend's a beach house out at Montauk for two weeks that he'd gotten at a "professional discount," and he'd promised there'd be plenty young men for them to chase around the beaches out there.

Hendricks let out a sigh.

Something had changed in him in the past two weeks, partially related to the horrible things that had occurred in the village (and maybe a little to do with the look of that traumatized woman, Constantine, who somehow reminded him of his youngest daughter) that resulted in some sort of spark, a glimmer of light as it were, that suggested there might be a way out of his tunnel of grief after all.

He wasn't sure how he would make it, but he knew it started with one small step forward.

IV: HEY DUMMY!

"Fasten your seatbelts, everybody. It's going to be a bumpy night."

-Fats, *"Magic"* (1978)

"But everybody knows dummies can't talk…."

-Rod Serling

-1-

DARCY VAN WORT sighed and counted the bills again.

It hadn't been a good night. But then again it hadn't been a bad night either.

Who was she kidding? It had been an embarrassingly *terrible* night, especially for a Saturday.

Dunderberg Ring Toss just wasn't the money-making cash cow it used to be.

That at least brought a faint chuckle to her pursed lips. The booth she had been working at the Feast of Saint Anne's Carnival since 1978, with its cute variable sized elves with their pointed sugar loaf hats, belted jerkins, and hose would never make the Fortune 500 list but at least it used to be a steady money maker.

Not for her, of course. Darcy's presence here was strictly volunteer.

All the proceeds from the booth went towards the Children's Reading Program at the Wyvern Falls Public Library where she had worked part time as an assistant since . . . oh gosh, was it 1981? Where had those thirty years flown to? Which sent her mind rifling through all sorts of uncomfortable information out of the index cards of her life:

-Fifty-seven and never married.

-No boyfriend on file (and all those disastrous attempts in the Personals column of the Wyvern Falls Gazette had been assiduously erased from the cards).

-Parents deceased. No info on any other family aside from two cousins over in Croton who never called except on Christmas.

-Residence: a tiny cottage-sized house on Larson Street brimming with tchotchkes, a dazzling collection of doily things and plenty of lace curtains.

-Two (overweight) cats, Mister Pippins and Mister Poppins. And also in the master file Mister Akins (now deceased), her old piano teacher, who, starting when she was ten would place his hand, high up on...

"Slam!" went the drawer in her head.

If nothing else, Darcy Van Wort was a veteran of the mental redirect, ranked *experten* when it came to matters of avoidance and denial. It was hard to deny the truth of the small pile of bills in her hand, however, which sent an ice pick of dreadful possibilities through her thoughts. *They may not want you back next year. This may be it – (lace) curtains for you, ol' Darcy- kins!" This was followed by a flurry of self-pitying questions: "Why? What's wrong with kids these days? The little ones used to love my little Dunderbergies...*

True, the little polyurethane figures were looking a little tired and a little dated. (A little? The biggest elf/imp in the middle seemed to speak up: *Open your eyes, lady! We look like refugees from a 1940s Christmas display. After an extended layover in the town dump!).* Darcy shook her head side to side quickly. "I just need a chance to . . ."

The thought trailed off as she remembered she needed to stop by Mister Ramos' trailer to hand over the evening's till. As if of their own accord, her hands reached into her purse and transferred twenty dollars into the booth's earnings. "It won't help much, but it might help a little, and after all, it's for the children. Why can't everyone see that?"

This was followed by another thought:

Bob Johnson.

She snatched at it like a lifeline.

"I have to see Bob Johnson first! I brought him a little dessert. Of course! Certainly I can put off my unpleasant little trip to Mister Ramos for a few minutes. I have to check on Bob Johnson and make sure that he's okay."

Mickey & Johnson' was a new addition to the carnival's entertainment tent this year. Or, as Darcy thought of it, a "new Old Fashioned" addition, because Mickey & Johnson was a classic ventriloquist act, the kind that went out with Charlie McCarthy and Edgar Bergen and black-and-white television sets. The kind of good old-fashioned (white) entertainment that these poor children, particularly those children raised on nasty songs ("Hip" and "Hop"? It even *sounded* dirty) and wearing black nylon caps like a bunch of pint-sized gangsters, could use a little more of! And, oh dear, those young girls dressing like loose women and...and...

Darcy shook her head again in that rapid, palsied nod. *Mister Johnson . . . stay focused Darcykins! . . . there's something about him.* His complexion wasn't healthy for starters, and he smoked that god-awful pipe . . . and, yet, he seemed like he might be a gentleman. No question he was a throwback to another era – a good era – with his neatly Brylcremed hair and Errol Flynn mustache. He looked a tad underfed (*gaunt, even - Miss Darcy, the man looks like he hasn't had a decent meal in years!*), so she'd taken it upon herself to bring him a small dish of her grandmother's Famous Bread Pudding. The entertainment tent was next to the Red Baron's Daughter tent. Darcy hadn't actually seen the so called "daughter" but she had heard that there was quite a commotion there just last night, but she had a hunch Mister Johnson was probably back in his trailer by now, doing whatever it was entertainment professionals did after their shows were over for the evening. She already had constructed a scenario in her mind where Bob Johnson was kicking back with his favorite magazine – she saw him as a Field & Stream type or even Home Woodworker (though why a travelling vaudeville act would read a home woodworking magazine she hadn't quite worked out yet), probably smoking his pipe and with a bottle of beer at his elbow. No, she corrected, a glass of Cutty Sark on ice. A gentleman like Bob Johnson would probably be a quality Scotch drinker.

The trailers for the "working folk" were strung out in a loose line at right angles to the parking lot past the entrance to the Raadsel Point campgrounds, just behind a loose wooden fence and a copse of old spruce trees. She knew which Johnson's was as it was nearly impossible to miss – a large silver Airstream that might have dropped right out of the 1950s. Nearby was his 1962 Ford F100 pickup. The Airstream was parked a little farther away from the others. Cary O'Donnell, Mister Ramos' liaison between the village clerk's office and the carnival (and Darcy's primary resource for critical intel like the locations of certain feature attraction's trailers), had mentioned that Mister Johnson was apparently a man who valued quiet and privacy. And after seeing that little gleam in her friend's eye, she added: "We-l-l-l, just be careful, Darcy, you can't always be sure of these travelling performer types." What she didn't add was that she had met Mister Johnson once and thought there was something downright weird about him. Especially the way he slow blinked. Like a robot or something.

The lights were on in the trailer.

There was a radio quietly playing what sounded like an old-time talk show – actually, it sounded like Jack Benny – and she could also hear a man's voice that had a barky, high-pitched quality. It was Bob talking in that preoccupied way she knew men talk to themselves when working on a hobby like wood carving or fixing a fishing pole. Gathering up her courage the way some older, single women in small towns clutch at their skirts when nervous, Darcy knocked softly on the trailer door.

Bob kept chattering away to himself, however, and the Jack Benny routine continued on the radio.

"*. . . so the thief said again, 'So, what's it gonna be, your money or your life?' . . .*

I said, 'Hold on, I'm thinking, I'm thinking . . .'"

Darcy knocked again, slightly harder.

The sound of an audience laughing, canned chuckles and chortles from yesteryear.

The door was apparently unlocked. It swung inward.

Bob's voice was louder now, though she still couldn't quite make out what he was saying. She realized that it sounded curiously muffled, as if he was talking into a blanket or something.

The voice paused for moment and she thought she heard Bob say something like "Come on in" before resuming his sing-song chatter. Darcy hesitated, looking at the foil-covered dessert tray in her hand. On the radio, Benny had launched into another routine. She heard someone say, "Whattya raised in a barn!? Come in and close the door!" Followed by more canned laughter.

Taking that as her cue, she stepped up into the trailer.

The first thing she saw as she stepped into the entryway was a terrifying nightmare face that brought her up short and nearly had Grandma's Famous Bread Pudding decorating the linoleum floor. A sharp gasp escaped her lips. Then she realized it was a mask, one of those angry scowling things carved out of ebony wood with little white shell eyes, pointed teeth, and daubs of red paint. On top was a thatch of fuzzy straw. Gaudy hoop earrings were fastened onto the crudely carved ears. The phrase "Fuzzy Wuzzy" – a term she'd read in some old National Geographic story once – popped into her head and almost set her giggling. It had been something about New Guinea cannibals and one of the Rockefellers who wound up on their menu during a good-will trip. For a thrilling moment, she wondered if this mask was from the same place...perhaps the same tribe that had done such a horrible thing...then dismissed the idea as ridiculous.

There were few other decorations, mostly vaudeville posters from Mickey & Johnson performances years past, some of which looked to be as far back as the '40s and '50s (which could also be filed under the "Ridiculous" column, since Bob Johnson didn't look a day over forty!). There was a small kitchenette and seating area with Formica countertops, chrome edging, and vinyl cushions that all but screamed 1950s. The kitchenette was spotless. In fact, it looked as though it had never been used, though Darcy quickly put that scenario down to her image of Bob Johnson being a neat freak.

Like herself. Nothing worse than a man who doesn't maintain order in his home.

There was a small passageway that led into the front area where Bob continued to chat away with himself.

Perhaps he's on the phone, Darcy thought. She debated whether she should call out or knock on the wall or something, but hadn't he said "Come in?" Or had that been the radio? Darcy wasn't quite sure anymore. She'd never been one to think fast on her feet. "Always to-ing without dh-inking," her mother used to say to her, half reproachfully. "And dumb as a box of chickens," her father would chime in, not so affectionately.

So, without further "dh-inking," she stepped into the next room.

It took a full minute for her mind to process what her eyes were registering.

The main living/sleeping compartment had been converted into a sort of workshop. Sort of. There was a Philco radio on a shelf through which Mister Benny was delivering his routine from yesteryear. On either side was a cushioned bench that could be pulled down into beds. The small Airstream windows had sliding curtains of polyester fabric in a color sometimes known as Pepto Pink.

From there, the Airstream interior designer's template for the all-American trailer and the Bob Johnson version of it parted company. For starters, there was the string of shrunken heads, real human heads, white human heads to be specific, hanging from the ceiling. All around the walls hung various masks and hideously-carved wooden flutes that should have (and once had) been lining the walls of a New Guinea which doctor's hut. And there was a macabre bookshelf/cabinet filled with all sorts of strange paraphernalia: jars of various liquids, assorted dolls and sculptures, assorted organic parts of undetermined origin. Then there was the make-shift table, or perhaps altar was a better term, on which were the remains of a small disemboweled goat.

But the shock and awe didn't end there.

Positioned on a bench - a long, oversized cooler actually - to the right, stiff and lifeless, was Bob Johnson. Staring unblinkingly into space, propped up like the world's most realistic life-sized doll.

Sitting at the desk on a high stool, back to Darcy, was Mickey, Johnson's black-haired, mustached Mini-Me caricature of himself. From Darcy's vantage point, she could see Bob's pipe stuck at a jaunty angle into its mouth, even issuing little puffs and whorls of smoke.

She could also see the large primitive knife gripped in one of Mickey's little wooden hands, poking curiously through the steaming entrails of the animal.

Mickey was doing all the talking.

In Bob's voice.

The clatter of the dessert tin bouncing off the floor sounded like it was a mile away. Darcy's eyes went back and forth between thousand-yard-stare Bob and the pint-sized version of him made of wood, springs and rods, levers, and paint (and human hair, though she didn't know that), like the victim a particularly gruesome practical joke. She was also vaguely aware of a thin, keening sound which was the scream trapped in her throat trying to escape.

She wanted to leave ("run like the Dickens," as her mother used to say, run, rabbit, run!) but it felt as though someone had super-glued her feet to the floor. Part of her registered the sound of the trailer door closing all by itself, but that data was shuffled aside as her brain processed the fact that Mickey/Bob was still talking, and addressing her in his sing-song voice.

Without turning around.

"Hey lady! Holy macaroni! Pull up a seat...have some eats!" There was a pause as the little wooden head swiveled slightly in coy over-the-shoulder acknowledgement:

". . . and Bob's your uncle!"

The knife glittered in the candlelight.

Another little puff of smoke came out of the pipe.

-2-

"YOU ARE *not* taking me to a Nudie Show, James!" Karen Evershaw said in a laughing voice that suggested the "not" might be up for negotiation. Jim Franks raised his eyebrows in mock surprise, an impish grin on his face. A slight, good-looking man in his early thirties, his finely-drawn features, intense green eyes, and unruly thatch of straight black hair put him dangerously close to the "pretty boy" camp. This was offset, however, by an extremely bright mind and a keen sense of humor.

"No-no-no-no, I said *Skin Show*, not *Nudie Show*. It's a classic American carnival thing, and is attended purely in the interest of paying homage to tradition."

"Is that a fact?"

"It is in fact a fact, Jack. Of sorts."

They were walking along the midway where the concession stands began. The Feast of Saint Anne's Carnival was roughly laid out in a horseshoe shape. First were the kiddy rides like the Bumble Bee and the Red Baron and the carousal, followed by trailer rides and game booths along the outside. The larger rides like the Ferris wheel, Yo-Yo and the Crazy Coaster were clustered around the center. At the top of the horseshoe was the midway, which continued through the main concession stands and, beyond that, the beer and music tents. They had just picked up a pair of Dutch funnel cakes after getting their photos taken at the Fantasy Foto Booth and were walking leisurely towards the opposite leg of the horseshoe, where the more adult oriented entertainment was, such as the 'Red Baron's Daughter' fortune teller, the vaudeville stage, and, of course, the aforementioned *Skin Show*. The photo booth was one of those kitschy things that took your photo and superimposed the faces on a stock pair of bodies – Karen had insisted on the 80s Brit Rock Band, which turned the two of them into leather-clad punks with spiked-up mullets (the other choices had included Saturday Night Fever, WWI Ace and Damsel, Hawaiian Hula Dancers, and, somewhat creepily, the Pair of Dolls). Five dollars later you received an eight-by-ten print in a garish plastic frame, which Karen insisted would have place of honor on her teacher's desk.

Out on Raadsel Point, it was about as perfect a summer night for a carnival as anyone could order, a cool breeze coming off the river and sighing through the treetops. It was Tuesday and the third night they'd gone to the carnival. A quintessential June evening: lights flashed and spun, laughter, screams, and the entire familiar soundtrack that was part of every fair and carnival across the country filled the evening air.

Karen dabbed a smudge of powdered sugar from Franks' nose and gave him a flirtatious kiss on the lips. An English teacher at Wyvern Falls High, everything about her announced "woman" in bold letters: the striking combination of thick and luxurious chestnut hair, strong brown eyes, sensuous smile, and swimsuit figure that was the ardent subject of many student (and a few faculty) fantasies. Two years older than Franks, she generally played the mature woman role but that could go out the window on a dime when her impish side surfaced, which it had a habit of doing frequently in his presence.

It was one of the things he secretly loved about her. That and the way she insisted on calling him "James" - it was something of an in-joke between them - sometimes as in Fleming's infamous secret agent, other times as if he was a butler as in "James, could you fetch me a cocktail….?" During college, Karen had spent a year at a school in England and could mimic a British schoolgirl accent almost perfectly, particularly the lispy "Ssshropshire."

To his friends, Franks was clearly someone who didn't take himself too seriously, though, like many things about Franks, it had taken Karen a little time (and a lot of guesswork) to figure this out. A careful man and sometimes too clever for his own good, he could deliver an utterly absurd statement with such measured seriousness that often people just went straight ahead with him on it, with the result that many jokes went beyond the point of no return.

He was still amazed and unsure of what she saw in him. Their first few dates had gone disastrously as she had really run him through his paces. He'd never really received a full explanation, though she'd once mentioned in passing "Oh, it was kind of like a product testing phase. You have to smack it on the table, throw it against the wall, and stomp on it a few times to see how it holds up."

They didn't get as far as the Skin Show tent though, before something else caught his attention.

"You've got to be kidding," he said in a deadpan voice.

They had just strolled up to the mid-sized entertainment tent where assorted acts went on each night. The easel and placard they faced looked like a leftover from carnival attractions of yesteryear.

At a first glance, it looked like an antique, until one saw that it was a reasonably good recent print dry-mounted on FoamCore. So . . . a new poster made up to look like an old classic, then.

It had a 1940s color palette and showed the typical guy-in-a-suit-with-a-dummy-in-his-lap drawing with the headline "An Evening with Mickey *and* Johnson – Fun and Laughs for the Entire Family!" The man, dark haired and with a pencil-thin moustache, had an exaggerated smile and raised eyebrow in mock amusement as he looked at the ventriloquist doll who looked equally amused, eyes glancing sideways and mouth open. A small voice balloon was displayed next to his head with the caption "Hey Dummy!" At the bottom of the poster in italic print it read: "Sponsored by Electrico Productions" with a logo that suggested a man in a fedora with sparks emanating from his hat.

Next to the entrance was a talker in top hat and tuxedo (one that had clearly seen better days), an elderly looking man who kept up his routine with a loud and almost passable W.C. Fields banter. "Come one, come all, a classic ventriloquist act from yesteryear, folks! The one and only Mickey and Johnson! Come on in, good for a laugh, good for your health, completely one-hundred percent certified organic!"

"We are so not doing this!" Karen said with a throaty laugh.

"Oh, we *so* are!" Franks shot back, eyes twinkling. "Come on, it has a built in auto-creep factor to it! Like having Christopher Walken show up... *anywhere*. The show starts in ten minutes. Come on, I've never actually seen one of these acts outside a movie."

She nuzzled his ear with her lips. "I don't know; I was kind of getting a little curious about that Skin Show."

Franks stopped, drew himself up stiffly and stared off vacantly at nothing. In a staccato Anthony Hopkins voice, he said, "Abracadabra, I sit on his knee. Presto, change-o, and now he's me! Hocus pocus, we take her to bed . . ."

He was cut off by a light cuff to the head.

"Stop! You keep that up and the only thing you'll be taking to bed is an old Playboy magazine..."

Franks snapped back with a perplexed look. "I still have those?" Then he caught her up in a hug and kissed her. "Come my little bunny, suffer me on this and I'll buy you a whole bag of carrots." In a quieter voice, he added,

"Then we can run home and bouncy-bouncy..."

Karen kissed him back, then touched his lips with her forefinger.

"Maybe. If you play your cards right, sailor."

They walked up to the talker and Franks pulled out his wallet. As he paid for their tickets, Karen glanced over at the poster again.

Something about it seemed off. Was it the sly, sideways glance of the dummy or the clearly artificial expression depicted on Johnson, as if the artist had been trying to suggest some sort of deeper, more sinister secret? The smile faded from her face. Part of her suddenly felt uneasy, and, for a brief moment, she considered trying to talk Jim out of the whole thing, redirect him to something better. Safer.

Even as a little girl, she had been very careful about which dolls she played with, especially after that incident when she was nine years old . . . but she also knew Jim was just as stubborn as she was and would only dig his heels in harder.

They walked through the entrance into the dark gloom of the tent.

-3-

THE TENT was surprisingly full.

It took Franks a moment to process this. He wouldn't have guessed a ventriloquist dummy act would have been much of a draw in the 21st Century, even as a novelty act, but as he looked around he began to understand that this wasn't your typical broad demographic either.

For one thing, a good third of the audience looked like they'd been shipped in from a retirement home like Pine Meadows (just east of the village) and a good majority of the rest were a mix of Portuguese and South American. Only a handful would have checked off 'White Caucasian /Other' on their Census forms.

Not for the first time, Franks mused about how odd it felt to be a minority in his own country.

Like many Hudson River towns, the racial demographic in Wyvern Falls had changed drastically over the past twenty years. Many of the old Dutch and English families had given way to Portuguese and Spanish/Hispanic surnames, to the extent that leaders in the diminished black community - many of whom could trace their bloodlines back to the 1600s - felt somewhat resentful at their minority status being usurped. As someone who had grown up in a small white-bread town in Maryland, where the one black family in his High school years was considered a fascinating novelty ("We've seen photos of your kind before!" the Mayor had supposedly said) and then lived in the mish-mash melting pot of New York City for much of his professional career, the current ethnic mix of the village that had become his home in the past two years still struck him as a surprise somehow. It was an anomaly that didn't fit any preconceived context, like walking into Saint Petersburg, Florida and discovering a thriving Eskimo community.

The tent was filled with folding chairs and the stage was a large trailer that had been adapted to include such items as rack lights and sliding velvet curtains. A small set of stairs had been added to allow access to the front of the stage and at the back of the tent was a low wooden platform with a soundboard and a spotlight. The air had the peculiar musty and old-hay smell that only carnival or circus tents seem to have.

No one paid much attention to the elderly man – a man with thick wooly grey hair and the thick, wide features of a native South Pacific islander – who sat in the corner in an old but neatly ironed suit with his hands folded in his lap. A man with an old and badly-healed scar that ran from his right ear down across his throat.

Franks and his girlfriend found a pair of empty seats near the front, sandwiched between an Ecuadorian couple with three kids and a row of elderly people, at least three of whom looked like they already nodded off. As a veteran of countless meetings and presentations in his career, Franks could sympathize. Something about being in a dark room filled with people triggered the snooze response. He'd lost track of the number of times he'd half dozed through most of them.

The murmur of the audience died down as a tall elderly gentleman in a top hat and tails strutted out onto the stage with the confidence of a seasoned emcee. With his narrow frame and sharp features, he might have been descended from the Carradine's or even the Barrymore's, though the white goatee and mustache suggested he'd also make a viable candidate for Uncle Sam.

He drew up at the center of the stage, hands folded, acknowledging the crowd with a nod, first right, then left. His eyes glittered in the spotlight. "Ladies and gentlemen," he said in a stately voice, "It is with great pleasure that I introduce our next act, a classic performer…er, performers…from the traditional days of old, the likes which have not been seen in many years! Please, join me in welcoming . . . Bob Johnson and Mickey Muldoon!"

With one hand held aloft, the emcee glided backwards as the curtain drew back, revealing a narrow stage with an empty chair on it. There were a few moments of prolonged silence. Someone coughed and a chair squeaked.

Then, from the back of the audience a voice barked, "Hey, wake up, dummy! That's our cue!"

Heads craned, bodies turned. The spotlight poked around the audience, looking for the source.

After a few failed attempts at confused searching, the light settled on a man standing in the back corner of the tent – Bob Johnson in a grey flannel suit, a fedora cocked jauntily on his head, and on his face the perplexed look of a man who had awoken in a completely unexpected location, not unlike a B actor in a classic Twilight Zone episode. Cradled in his arms was Mickey, looking up at his partner with a big "cat-that-got-the-canary" grin, a pipe sticking out from his clenched teeth.

"Hey…that's my pipe!" Johnson said with an exaggerated double-take, plucking the pipe out of Mickey's mouth and popping it into his own, "and aren't you just a little young to smoke?"

"I'm old enough to put up with your jokes, and believe me you, theyrrree gettin' old!"

A few tentative laughs followed this.

"You're sayin' my jokes are old?" Johnson shot back.

"I'm sayin' if they get any older, they'll be wearing dentures!"

More applause.

Johnson chuckled, his eyes doing that eerie slow-blink. "Well, then I guess I better walk out a few new ones, because it looks like we have a full house to entertain…" Johnson strolled towards the stage in a stiff, slightly awkward gait. But he drew up short when he came next to Karen. Mickey's curiously realistic eyebrows shot up in mock surprise as the spotlight zeroed in on them.

"Now here's a dame after my own wooden heart . . . say, Lotus Blossom, where have I been all your life?"

Karen looked over at Franks nervously, but pulled out a smile. "Someplace I haven't," she replied evasively.

"Oooh, a live one, Bobby! Definitely not your type then . . . *hehe.*" Micky gave Johnson a sideways look, then his head swiveled back to Karen. "But you interest me - you interest me very much! What musical music we could make together! Did anybody ever tell you you've got curves like the Pennsylvania Turnpike?"

Karen's smile grew forced. But before she could respond, Bob Johnson cut in with a disapproving cluck, "Now, Mickey, that's hardly an appropriate way to talk to a lady . . ."

"Well . . . hey, buddy boy . . . I don't need to talk to her, you see . . . I can read her thoughts!"

"Read her thoughts? Why that's clairvoyance!"

Mickey's head did a swivel double take, "Claire? Her name isn't Claire!" The audience broke out in sporadic laughs as the head swiveled once more and the over-sized doll eyes locked onto Karen. They glittered, looking eerily human. In that split second, she felt icy finger tips walk up the back of her neck and she had a premonition – more of an intuition actually – that she knew exactly what the doll was going to say next, as one eyelid fell half-closed in a leering wink. ". . .Your name is . . . Karen . . . and you've been keeping secrets, little lady . . . does Jimmy boy here know? Hehe."

Karen looked like a deer that had just been caught in the headlights.

Franks, who had been sitting with his arm on the back of her chair, felt her stiffen. The atmosphere in the tent suddenly felt thick and oppressive. And he picked up on something else – an underlying hint of decay, mold, and...rot. Franks realized his right hand was clenched into a tight fist and, for a split second, he had an overwhelming urge to punch the dummy square in the face and go on punching until it was smashed to bits. What the hell was happening? And, on the heels of that, an ugly thread of suspicion in his thoughts: what secrets?

Johnson must have picked up on this, as he abruptly took a step back, Mickey's face taking on an open-mouthed "yikes!" look. "Easy there, buster, steady as she goes, bats outta Hell oh-oh-oh . . ." Then the head swiveled toward Bob and, strangely, the dummy said in a quiet, trembling voice, "I can't go to Rabaul again, Mickey, those Japs'll get me next time for sure!" Then Johnson's eyes did that weird slow blink like a drugged patient just coming to and he was walking away, Franks and his girlfriend apparently forgotten.

He paused in front of a young-looking kid of ten or eleven whose rimless glasses, neat-as-a-pin shirt and slacks, and chin-up demeanor all but shouted 'I'm smart!" Even his hair looked ironed and pressed into place.

The audience shifted nervously in their seats. The act was foundering. Even a dummy could sense it.

"Ah, and who are you, my fine looking laddie?" Mickey said, abruptly jumping back into his excited self again.

The kid stood up unexpectedly, hands on hips. "I'm Danny Riedel," he announced, "and I'm the smartest person in my class!"

"Whoa, short-fella trousers. I'll make the jokes around here!" Mickey shot back.

Danny blinked, his face a study in seriousness. The cleft between his eyebrows deepened, "I'm not joking!" he insisted, "I won the Regents' spelling bee this year, my grades are top of my class, I'm doing a work study at a senior citizen's home and volunteering at the ASPCA, in fact I . . ."

"Okay that's enough . . . that's enough . . . goodbye, little kid, goodbye!"

"But Danny sounds like a boy after my own heart," Johnson countered.

"Yeah, and after my job!" Mickey cut in. "Goodbye . . . goodbye, you pint-sized Bieber!" Johnson stepped forward again towards the stage in his awkward gate.

It might have ended there, but Danny was not a boy to be denied. Still with his hands on his hips, he stomped his foot on the ground.

"Hey, you stupid puppet, don't you walk away from Danny Riedel when he's talking to you!"

The tent grew quiet.

Without turning around, Mickey said, "He's the stupid looking one, if you ask me."

"Now, Mickey, he's no more stupid looking than me."

"Yeah, that'd be asking for the impossible wouldn't it, Bobby-boy?"

Danny stomped his foot again. "Hey dummy, I'm talking to you!" he shouted.

Mickey's head popped up over Johnson's shoulder, looking back at him, "But I ain't listening to you, four-eyes!"

"Well you better, because I'm a star!"

Johnson continued walking toward the stage as Mickey kept his eyes locked on the kid with a look that was all but malicious. "Sorry, kid, there's only room for one star in this show . . . and you ain't glittering. In fact, pee-yew, you stink! Don't quit your day job - oh wait, you can't even work, half-pint! Ha!"

As Johnson mounted the stage, Danny's eyes grew narrow and mean. "I'll get you for that," he said under his breath. Next to him, a middle-aged man with graying hair and the pinched expression of a concerned accountant put a hand on his shoulder, "Now, honey, that's no way to talk to an entertainer..."

Danny turned on his dad. "I don't care, Franklin, I don't like this stupid show anymore!" and shrugging the hand off, spun around, and marched out of the tent in a huff.

The father stood up with his palms out and, with an "aw shucks" smile, said to no one in particular, "Boys. What can you do?" and followed him out.

Aside from a few uncomfortable glances, no one was really paying attention.

Except on stage, now launching into a Biblical skit about the creation and Adam and Eve ("And then God created Earth," Johnson explained,

"Crash, bang, boom!" came the response), Mickey paused after his line and his eyes swiveled towards the still-flapping tent entrance with what might have been a crafty smile.

The kind that might be saying "We'll see who gets who."

-4-

"I REALLY, really don't want to talk about it," Karen said the next morning.

It was only 7:30 but already the day seemed like it was threatening to topple over into disaster. They were sitting on the back patio of Franks' house, a flagstone terrace under a canopy of old sugar maples and a massive oak that, along with the landscaped garden and BBQ area, gave it a shaded, grotto-like flavor. The house, at 65 Crichton Avenue, had been a steal for Franks when he'd bought it in a short sale a couple of years previously. A meticulously restored 1884 Victorian with a slate mansard roof that Franks jokingly referred to as the Munster's House, it combined a tasteful if sometimes eclectic mix of classic architecture and modern renovation

Franks was sitting with his feet up on the teak patio table, a steaming cup of coffee in his lap, listening to the chatter emanating from the boxwood tree at the back of the yard that they called the Bird Community Center. Karen had been sitting opposite him, idly leafing through a gardening magazine. Much as he hated himself for it, the ventriloquist's insinuating comment from the night before had been sitting there in a back corner of his mind ever since, like a little a malevolent imp twiddling its thumbs.

He'd broached the subject with his usual sense of twisted humor, this time with a fair imitation of the Mickey's sing-song bark: "Hey, little lady. what kind of secrets have you been keeping, eh?" Karen had given him a narrow-eyed look in response, not sure if he was joking or not.

Franks wasn't sure himself.

Karen had gone back to her magazine with redoubled intensity, as if the article on proper mulching was a drawn-out and complex physics equation.

Franks fixed her with his intense gaze, brows half-raised.

Typically, this would result in a drawn out Mexican standoff until Karen, exasperated, would give in with a roll of her eyes followed by one of her stock sighs.

But not this morning.

To Frank's surprise, she abruptly threw down the magazine, stood up and walked back into the house through the kitchen. She didn't slam the door but closed it quietly, which felt more ominous, somehow sad.

Even the sparrows and finches lurking in the boxwood quieted down. Franks sat there for a moment, marveling at how quickly this morning had gone wrong. Not for the first time, it struck him how tenuous personal relationships could be – one moment cruising along calm waters and the next going to hell right over an unseen waterfall.

He rolled his eyes towards the sky, but if anyone was up there listening they didn't answer.

"Hey."

Franks was standing in the doorway of the master bedroom. At the back of the house on the second floor, it featured tall windows with an oblique view of the Hudson and a marble fireplace. With its warm hues, wood floors and high ceilings, it felt both spacious and cozy at the same time. The queen-sized mahogany sleigh bed was piled with pillows and a down comforter that looked inviting enough to sleep a year in. Franks called it the Rip Van Winkle Sled.

Karen was standing in front of the oversized vanity they'd scored at an antique shop in Cold Spring, fidgeting with an earring and wearing nothing but white lace underwear. Her thick chestnut hair was tied up in that careless way only truly sexual women can manage, and the way she stood with her weight on her back leg and both hands at her right ear only emphasized the sensuous curves of her figure. If any of the male student population had been standing in Franks' shoes at that moment, they probably would have simply exploded.

Franks could barely contain himself.

Karen glanced at his reflection in the tall vanity mirror but didn't say anything.

Franks rubbed his arms. "A little cold in here!"

A trace of a smile?

He glanced at his watch. Plenty of time before he had to get over to his studio in Irvington. Besides, he was the boss (or at least half-owner) of Kinetic Media, an interactive media company he'd founded two years ago with his business partner, Brom Mulder, a friend of his since childhood, who was the business brains of the operation. Brom could sell ice to

Eskimos and have them as excited as school kids about it. He was at the office punctually every morning at 8:30, but Franks, like most creative types, rarely rolled in before 10:00.

Still rubbing his arms like he'd stepped into a blizzard, Franks stepped up to Karen, placed his hands on her shoulders, and nuzzled her neck. One bra strap seemed to slip off under his itinerant fingers. Karen turned her head slightly, made a rueful smile, and quietly said the five cruelest words a woman can ever say to an aroused heterosexual man.

"I just got my period."

-5-

"TALK ABOUT a bucket of cold water in your face," Franks said. He was sitting at a small window table across from his friend John Easton at a café called Julep, on Tarrytown's Main Street. The café, an eclectic place that was half restaurant, half gourmet store, featured a dizzying assortment of exotic and rare foods; anything from olive oil imported from the Aria Private Reserve in Greece to honey-baked Mexican pecans. Easton looked a little peaked – kind of like hell actually – and Franks had offered to buy him lunch before dropping him off over at Philipseburg for a check-up. Easton wasn't giving up any details, but apparently it had something to do with the incident over at Castle Krell that was buzzing around the Wyvern Falls rumor mill. Franks was really curious to hear what that was all about, particularly the part involving the reason behind the bandages on his friend's neck ("What, you doing the tango with vampire?" he'd asked when he'd picked Easton up at his house that morning. "Yeah, something like that," had been the reply) but he was also treading carefully. There was the issue of Vivienne hanging uncomfortably in the air between them like bad laundry, though Easton was being evasive about it. She'd run out on both of them a few days earlier – as Easton's girlfriend and as Franks top web designer – but Franks felt personally responsible, as he'd had a hand in setting them up together the previous fall. So, for the moment, they were playing the *hang out and talk about anything else but* game.

Franks sat back, taking a long sip of a cool glass of iced mint tea. The remains of a saffron-marinated chicken pita sat in front of him. Easton had barely touched his jerk pork Panini and salad.

"It's like the ultimate ace up their sleeve," Franks continued on his rant. "The all-purpose opt-out card in the early phase of any relationship. 'I just got my period.' It's not like you can call them on it. 'Really? Can I check?' That's simply not allowed in the rules. Now if the relationship has gone into long-term territory, your significant other will generally give you a heads up as in 'I think I'm getting my period,' or laying out the 'I Just Got My Period' card beforehand, as a general courtesy announcement over morning coffee. Or at least simply in the spirit of fair play: 'in case you had sex on today's agenda . . .' But damn! When they play that card on you just as you're about tackle them and chew their clothes off? That's just plain inhumane. It should be against the Geneva Convention."

Easton shrugged and made a half smile.

"Well," he finally said, "I wouldn't make too much of it. I think she's pretty keen on you and this may just be one of those rocks in the road you stub your toe on." He didn't add that he was certain that this was the case. Chalk it up to one of his intuitions.

Franks mulled this over a moment, a thoughtful look on his face. Outside, Main Street was fairly quiet, being mid-week, though Julep was fairly busy. The owner, a heavy-set Egyptian named Omar, was sitting by the register charming a pair of Scarborough housewives with some Tunisian cheeses. Although he'd grown up in Brooklyn, Omar could lay on the exotic Middle-Eastern merchant *schtick* in spades when it suited him.

He returned his gaze to Easton. "Look, John, I'm really sorry about what a mess this whole thing is turning out to be with Vivienne."

Easton, who had been sitting with his fingertips resting against his mouth, looked back at his friend directly. He let Franks squirm for a moment, then smiled. "I'll be fine, Jim. It's not like this is the first time in the history of mankind something like this has occurred. The world hasn't ended last I checked." Of course, for the past few days, that was exactly what it felt like, in his heart of hearts at least. But, if nothing else, Easton was a survivor. The best strategy was to simply plow ahead and not think too much.

And he'd had plenty to keep his thoughts elsewhere this week. Nearly getting strangled to death (or worse) by an undead WWI pilot had seen to that.

"It's kind of funny, though," he continued. "In today's romance culture, they always put such a premium on lost loves and soul mates and all that rubbish, but they tend to gloss over the fine print. The disclaimer that reads, '*Meeting your long lost soul mate is not necessarily a guarantee of a successful or ongoing relationship. Actual results may vary.'"

That got a laugh out of Franks.

"But reality is a little different, isn't it? So many variables come into play – timing, circumstance, context – mostly things that are completely out of your control. I guess those are the things that make relationships and romance so elusive and maddening and so desirable at the same time. Kind of sad to think we live in an age when people think they can just go online and order it up like a new pair of shoes. Kind of takes a bit of the fun out of it, yeah?"

Franks laughed again. "Amen to that, chief" One of the things he liked about Easton was the Brit's cynical optimism. Suddenly, the day was looking just a little bit brighter.

More importantly, the air felt heck of a lot clearer.

Franks pulled out his wallet. "Lunch is on me. Come on bud, let's blow this pop-stand and get you over to Doktor von Helsing and make sure you're not in immediate danger of turning into a vampire or investment broker. That'll really make a mess of your love life. Well, the former at least. I hear investors get all the girls these days"

Easton chuckled, "Damn straight – and they're just vampires who can work in the daylight."

6.

THE AIR IN the hut was stifling.

Combined with a temperature of nearly a hundred degrees (and a relative humidity approaching those same three digits) were the sweet and sour aromas of human sweat, urine, strange herbs and ointments, oily smoke and, underneath all of that, the more troubling smell of rot, decay, and death.

The man sat on the crude stool, his khaki U.S. Army Air Force uniform drenched dark brown with sweat. On either upper sleeve were the stripes of a technical sergeant. Above that on the right shoulder was the circular Fifth Air Force patch with its blazing comet and Southern Cross star pattern, on the left, the wing patch of a combat airman. There were only two other occupants of the hut (three if one counted the wooden ventriloquist's dummy propped up next to the airman); the fierce-looking New Guinea witch doctor, naked but for a soiled loincloth, and the young New Guinea boy squatting by the hut entrance, eyes wide with fear. The witch doctor was lean and sinewy and short, his mahogany colored skin glistening with sweat. His hair and teeth gleamed red with betel nut oil, an assortment of animal teeth and tusks pierced his nose and ear lobes, and his face was an intricate map of tattoos and raised patterns that suggested – even to the uninitiated – the darkest and most arcane secrets, not just in the nightmare realms of mankind but of other things waiting beyond. To gaze on them too long was to invite nightmares and perhaps the risk of drawing the attention of things and entities best left alone.

The necklace of human teeth is terrifying enough, but it is his eyes that are the scariest – abnormally large with the whites always visible completely around them, they were hypnotic black holes of power and madness. It was rumored by the surrounding tribes that he could break bones and even burst a man's heart at a glance and, when one was in close proximity, it was easy to understand why.

The boy, Yauwii, – whose nickname was Shell (as in the oil company), sat on his haunches, trembling with fear. He hadn't wanted to be part of this, to bring the white soldier man here, but the man had been clever, persuasive, and persistent. And he had offered lots of money – not the less valuable Australian bills but American money. Shell, like many boys from his village north of the Allied airfields at Port Moresby, had drifted down to pick up work as a tent-boy for the American servicemen whose ranks were regularly growing on the island: running miscellaneous errands, mending clothes, cleaning shoes, and so on. At first, there had been occasional raids by the Japanese but these had grown more infrequent and all but stopped after their airfields at Lae and Nadzab on the opposite coast had been captured in September. Life had gone reasonably well for Shell in the sergeant's tent which was shared with three other enlisted men. Free chocolate, cans of sweet pears, condensed milk. The cans of Australian Bully-Beef they freely gave him, claiming it was something called horse meat. He got to watch the sergeant practice his routines with the puppet, which he said he used to do back home as an entertainer, though Shell wasn't exactly sure what that was.

Then had come the massive attack on Rabaul.

The 1943 calendar stuck to the tent pole had a box circled that said Tuesday, October 12th.

It seemed that every plane the Americans had went up in the air that day. The fighter planes, the bombers, especially the big ones with four engines, taking off from airfields. Airfields with names like Durand and Jackson but usually referred to by the airmen simply by their distance from Port Moresby: Twelve-Mile Drome, Seven-Mile Drome and so on. The roar of planes filling the skies, milling about in chaos before finally sorting themselves out by squadron and heading northeast towards the Owen Stanley Mountains and beyond, to the Bismark Sea, to an island called New Ireland and to the fortress that had become the Japanese Gibraltar of the Pacific; Rabaul.

The sergeant was a waist-gunner for a B-24 named "Devil's Child" which sported a re-worked Vargas pin-up girl in a red outfit, featuring pointed ears, a barbed tail, and, of course, bare breasts. It was in this plane that the sergeant, perhaps not the most stable of personalities to begin with, cracked somewhere over the deadly skies of the Japanese stronghold. Shell never understood the specifics, he wasn't there when the Nakajima Ki-43 Oscars and the Mitsubishi A6M3 Zero fighters swarmed in among the bombers like angry hornets, their 12.7mm and 7.7mm machine gun shells riddling the B-24's metal fuselage and turning it into a sieve, or when a 20mm canon shell blew out the chest of the other waist-gunner opposite the sergeant's position, turning him into a mangled caricature of a human being. And how the sergeant screamed and screamed and screamed in terror and madness as the fighters lined up with blinking lights on their wings and fuselages, the glowing yellow tracer bullets looking like every single one is arcing directly at him. Nor how he half crouched behind his swivel-mounted .50 caliber machine gun half covered in gore, the frigid air of twenty thousand feet blasting through the half-shattered Plexiglas and riddled aluminum, the hammer-clatter of the Browning machine-gun as he sprayed erratic fire at the incoming enemy aircraft. Nor one surreal moment when a Japanese pilot pulled up alongside the crippled bomber and stared in surprise at the American gunner in the waist position who was laughing uncontrollably and firing in every direction wildly, the moment dispelled when defensive fire from the other American bombers stitched holes in the Japanese plane, sending it spiraling down into the smoke and chaos of Rabaul harbor.

Shell had no concept of what it was like to sit in the big droning B-24 being knocked about by the concussion of the heavy Japanese anti-aircraft shells probing for the correct altitude, the clatter of shrapnel against the aluminum hull sounding like fistfuls of pebbles being thrown at the plane, wondering if the next shell will be the one that sends the ungainly Liberator cartwheeling down through the heavens, perhaps with its wings shattered and its terrified crew plummeting to their deaths.

Fate has not marked "Devil's Child" for destruction that day, however, and the grim-faced pilot and co-pilot finally feathered the runaway prop on engine #3 and, with a lot of ingenuity and luck, are able to nurse the bomber out of the reach of the enemy fighters and head toward their home base. It was the wounded tail gunner who finally crawled back and gave the pilot the lowdown on what has transpired in the waist section (after vomiting what was left of his powdered eggs and toast from the morning chow tent) and tries his best to comfort the sergeant after seeing to his own moderate injuries. Numb with shock and pain he sat with the sergeant, who had settled into a vacant stared crouch, and they share a Lucky Strike.

What Shell does understand is that when the sergeant's plane finally straggled back to Jackson Drome where it made a semi-crash landing, nothing was the same. The sergeant has gone quietly "longlong" – crazy – and his routines with the wooden puppet grew increasingly strange. In his puppet voice, Shell sometimes heard the sergeant say things like "I can't go back to Rabaul, Bobby, the Japs are going to get us next time for sure!" and "We got to get out of this mess . . . cut me legs? Shoot me foot? hee-hee" and Shell felt sad. The sergeant had been so kind and generous to him (even if he was a little odd) but the defining moment came almost by accident two weeks after the first major attack on Rabaul. Rumors had been circulating around the tents and it was on yet another sweltering New Guinea morning that, while quietly polishing the sergeant's boots, he found himself in a fierce grip, the sergeant's face only inches from his own, an unlit pipe stick out at a jaunty angle.

"I don't want to die! I don't want to die, boy!" the sergeant hissed through clenched teeth. Shell was confused and scared, his natively sharpened senses picking up the coppery aroma of fear seeping out of the man's pores. The sergeant was shaking him back and forth so hard he wondered if his head will simply snap off, bounce on the rough floor boards, and roll down the path towards the aerodrome.

Scared and now crying, Shell heard words coming out of his mouth that he instantly regretted, "I know man. He can help! I know man. He can help!"

He was not aware of how many times he repeated this until the words finally got through the sergeant's panic and the shaking finally stopped. The man was staring at him like he was seeing him for the first time.

"What? What do you mean? Who?"

"Pouri-pouri man! He help masta!"

"Who?"

Shell doesn't want to speak the name Saguma, the terrible and powerful witch doctor who lived by himself miles away from the boy's village. Speaking his name aloud was very dangerous – it could even summon him he had been told – but the name escaped his lips nonetheless. It is as if the sergeant had shaken it out of him.

"Saguma? Who is Saguma?" the sergeant asked. His voice sounded of desperation, and craziness.

"Saguma is pouri-pouri – ogowili, a sorcerer man, he can do anything . . . but mebbe nogut, dangerous for masta." Shell was having second thoughts, already regretting he said anything, as much as he wanted to help. He had only glimpsed the witch doctor once, at a distance, and even then he felt his blood turn to ice. For weeks afterward, he slept badly, plagued with nightmares of Saguma creeping up the ladder of his family hut, or crawling over the thatch roof like a giant malignant spider to snatch him in the middle of the night and devour him painfully, a morsel at a time, as told in the whispered stories the children of his village share.

As if on cue, Shell heard the doll-boy speaking from his perch on a nearby cot.

"Come on, laddie-boy, help us out here! Give it up! That's what friends are for! Where do we find Mister Linguini, er, Laguna, I mean, Saguma?"

It took a lot more cajoling but the sergeant and his doll-boy were persistent and that afternoon, as if in a dream, he found himself leading the sergeant and his doll-boy friend into the jungle north of Port Moresby. Although he had never actually been to the witch doctor's hut (and never had been told exactly where it was), it was if his feet were drawn there by magic.

It was as if the witch doctor was summoning him.

The ritual took place over the course of three consecutive nights.

The witch doctor was able to help, it turned out, for a price. Two-hundred thirty-seven dollars and seventeen cents, to be exact – the precise amount that the sergeant had stuffed in a can in his foot locker. There is a ritual that will allow the sergeant to transfer his soul to the doll-boy for long periods of time, putting his living body into a sort of stasis, making it more or less impervious to death, though doing so requires continual maintenance of the doll – hair, fingernail parings, urine, etc. (and, of course, blood and semen) to keep the receptacle or housing properly functioning (like a refrigerator) and linked to its host.

There are cleansing rituals to be performed, then a series of spells and cocktails of such ingredients as Sudi-Sudi (a preserving oil), tree chugger tongues, soma and the phallic-looking Kadimbi mushroom, smoked mountain lotus paste and the crushed feathers of a New Guinea harpy eagle. White sage and frankincense resin are mixed in. A new puppet head and hands were fashioned out of the reddish brown wood of the *Totara tree from pieces carefully chosen by the witch doctor and refitted over the existing doll mechanics. Saguma explained very slowly to the sergeant the process for the soul transference and the upkeep of the respective bodies.*

On the third night, the transference is performed.

It is one of the most terrifying experiences of Shell's life.

The witch doctor murmured a series of guttural incantations. Shell didn't understand the words but they sound ancient and alien, sometimes crawling around his ears like deadly snakes, other times buzzing like angry insects.

The sergeant simply sat there, glassy eyed, drenched in sweat, the puppet boy poised nearby on a special stand not unlike the baby-in-a-manger pictures Shell had seen in the book the missionary people show in the village now and then. At some point, the witch doctor babbling a phrase over and over and over again and Shell swore he saw the dried, shrunken heads (human, boar, frog, bird and such) strung all around the hut start shaking and making chittering sounds, like laughing monkeys. Smoke and incense fill the hut along with a rhythmic thumping that sounds like a dozen tiny drums. Shell crouched in the doorway, terrified and yet curious.

Saguma gestured for the sergeant to approach the stand and its wooden resident.

Shell's eyes darted around the interior of the hut as he realized that the heads aren't just chittering, they're chanting:

"Kissalife! Kissadet!" hiss the human heads.

"Kissalife! Kissadet!" The boar grunts.

"Kissalife! Kissadet!" The frogs croak.

Saguma produced a small bird of paradise feather with its end sharpened to a needle-like point and, as the sergeant stepped up, stroked the back of the white man's neck in an almost sexual caress. His eyes were wide with malice and, even though Shell was just a child, he sensed that the witch doctor was enjoying all this in the same way some men of the village enjoy making war on other villages; because wreaking hell can simply be fun.

"Kisalife! Kissadet!" the chorus of voices filled the hut.

The drums reached a crescendo then stopped abruptly.

The sergeant's mouth yawned wide and his tongue slid out.

The witch doctor pricked it lightly with the sharpened bird feather and bent the man's face over the doll, whose mouth has also opened.

The sergeant, who was as high as a kite on the intoxicating potions he had been taking for three nights straight, vaguely felt a moment of fear and a tearing sensation throughout his mind and body. In his ears was a sound like a roaring wind, and the thudding of his heart seemed to bounce off the wattled walls of the hut.

"Kiss of death and kiss of life." Saguma said tonelessly and a single drop of blood dropped into the doll's mouth.

The sergeant's heart stopped.

For a moment, nothing happened.

Then the doll's eyes flew open.

The sergeant slumped down to his knees, then toppled over on his side.

Shell felt like his breath was trapped in his throat. He almost jumped straight up into the air as the doll abruptly sat up and said,

"Hey, buckaroos, this stuff really works! Packs a heck of a hangover though — my head feels like it got turned into a block of wood!" The head swivels side to side and the eyes blink. "Pee-yew, smells like someone left a dead goat in here!" It looked up at the witch doctor and did a comic double take, "Oh, I guess that's just your aftershave! Waddya call it, buddy — Spoiled Vice?" Then it looked at its tiny wooden hands, which it opened and closed experimentally before looking around the room, pausing as it saw Shell sitting in the doorway. The mouth (with its carefully inlaid set of real human teeth) grinned. With a wink it said, "I guess its show-time, Shelly-boy!"

Then the doll-boy jumped up and locked its jaws on the witch doctor's throat.

-7-

DANNY RIEDEL had become a man – or a boy actually – on a mission. Since the previous night, he had leant his considerable intelligence to the objective of getting back at the "Carney Guy and his Stupid Doll" as he's come to term them in his head.

"Nobody makes me look stupid . . . *nobody!*" he said sitting at his desk in his immaculately laid-out bedroom. Little about the room said "boy." In fact, it looked more like the room of a third-year physics student at Yale.

The Riedels lived at in equally immaculate Tudor-style on Shadybrook Lane in the upscale tract neighborhood just northeast of Wyvern Falls High School sometimes referred locally (and somewhat illogically) as "The Mews," a name that supposedly originated with a wealthy-but-misguided Anglophile who lived there in the 1950s and fancied himself a writer of sorts. Nearly all the houses were spacious Cape-Cods or Tudors built postwar with sprawling lawns, appropriate landscape features, and a scattering of tall trees, all with two-car garages, large back patios, and, occasionally, a swimming pool as well. It was an idyllic suburban neighborhood that looked like it might be better suited to somewhere in Connecticut than tucked in a Hudson River town.

Danny's bedroom was large and decorated in a clean Restoration Hardware manner – before that company's featured color palettes took a depressing turn into the realm of industrially bleak greys and browns – and, instead of the usual posters kids his age typically favor of bands, movies, or even babes, there were framed photos of Einstein, Stephen Hawking (autographed), Oxford University, and Johann Sebastian Bach. The last was added after Danny discovered that Bach's analytic recall was such that he was able to dictate his final composition – a chorale prelude for organ – to his son-in-law while on his deathbed and that when the notes of three staves of the final cadence are mapped in the Roman alphabet his name can be found. Analytic recall was something Danny knew a thing or two about. Even while he was doodling on the graph pad in front of him, his mind had turned over dozens of detailed scenarios for orchestrating the ventriloquist's humiliation, which he had already determined will not pose much of a difficult problem. The only question was which one he will enjoy the most.

Another thing Danny was familiar with, yet nearly powerless to control, was his temper. Even as an infant, he possessed a level of anger way out of proportion to any event causing it: the sin of not clipping the crusts off his sandwiches or an extra cookie denied might be rewarded with a viciously-thrown bowl or milk bottle, accompanied by an hour (sometimes two or three) of full throttle, pedal-to-the-metal screaming. Now at the ripe old age of eleven, he had learned to combine his outbursts with cunning, employing a variation of the old saying - get mad *and* get even.

When Danny Riedel got mad, it possessed him like a living entity, absorbing all his thought processes and focus whether awake or dreaming. Frequently he wouldn't sleep at all, or only for a fitful hour or two.

These fits might go on for days, even weeks, sometimes resurfacing months later.

In fairness, his aberrant behavior wasn't entirely his own fault. Danny's rages and hysterics were only eclipsed by those of his mother, whose behavior could instantly flip into the realm of lunacy at any given moment. Mister Riedel's stock coping response to any of these episodes – mother or son – was an almost breathtaking level of denial, usually accompanied by one of his various "hands up in the air" gestures or sometimes "hands over the ears" while chanting "I'm going to my happy space . . .I'm going to my happy space" over and over again like a mantra. Still, in the pecking order of the Riedel household, Danny was reigning champ, a ruling *L'enfant terrible* as it were, and it was no surprise when he announced to his parents that night around 7:30 that he was going for a bike ride around the neighborhood.

His mother had been sitting on the couch in the living room watching Storage Wars on A&E while his dad was reading a Rose Kennedy biography on his Kindle Fire HD.

Dressed in a conservative light-yellow golf shirt and pressed Bermuda shorts with a T-Tech backpack, Danny paused near the family's 54" HD TV with one disapproving eyebrow raised. On the wide screen an elderly couple were jumping up and down like monkeys in their excitement over a bunch of porcelain figurines they'd just scored. Danny shook his head. "Alice, I can't believe you watch this rubbish." He addressed his mom without looking at her. She ignored him. From his leather easy chair, his father looked up over his Kindle.

"Be careful out there, honey, and make sure you're back before sunset."

"Shut up, Franklin," Danny replied, without his usual conviction. He was focused on his mission for the night, which would decidedly take place after sunset. But then he added, "I'll be back before 10:30 – I'm going to stop by Gerald's and watch a special on quantum physics theories on the Science Channel at 9:00."

Later, when he was talking with the police about what happened, Franklin Riedel would recall that as odd – his son was never in the habit of explaining himself or saying where he was going.

-8-

DANNY KNEW *exactly* where he was going.

Hacking into the Wyvern Falls' antiquated municipal database system had been child's play for him. He was able to get directly into Cary O'Donnell's computer at the Village Clerk's office and find the exact lot number assigned to Bob Johnson's trailer. The RV lot next to the campgrounds was frequently used from April to December by everyone from retired seniors, vacationing families, migrant workers, modern gypsies, and of course carney folk. And ever since the incident two years ago in which an elderly couple had been attacked by a drunk migrant worker (who also was on the FBI Most Wanted list), the police chief had insisted that every single trailer parked there have a permit filed with the clerk's office along with a lot assignment so the Parks Department could also monitor usage of the water and electrical hook-ups. Although not a foolproof system by any means – as revealed by the false papers filed by the woman who had claimed to be the Red Baron's Daughter – it at least discouraged less than savory characters by making it clear they were under scrutiny.

Nor was a young kid riding his bike out to the carnival grounds likely to attract any undue attention. Even in the 21st Century, Wyvern Falls was still enough of an insular community that people generally left their car doors unlocked and let their children play unattended, unlike towns such as Newburgh whose poverty and drug trafficking had made them as dangerous as the Bronx.

Danny steered his mountain bike around the main parking lot towards the section where the vacationer trailers were – another of the police chief's unofficial mandates was keeping them sectioned off from the carney workers – next to the large log cabin meeting/community house which featured a large set of bike racks out front. Pulling up, he found a spare slot and locked up the bike with two Kryptonite U locks using a special key. Although many of the bikes were Nirves and Diamondbacks and such, there were enough high-end mountain bikes to make a bicycle thief's jaw drop. And yet to date there had never been a single bicycle stolen out on Raadsel Point.

It was closing in on 8:00 PM when Danny approached the silver Airstream trailer sitting apart from the others. According to the night's program he had checked earlier, his good friends Mickey and Bob would perform until 9:00, giving him plenty of time to slip in and out unnoticed. The nearest lot to the Airstream was empty, cordoned off by yellow police tape after an incident the previous weekend involving a fortune-teller woman. ("Exactly why you can't trust those, those weirdo gypsies!" his mother had said. "Now, dear, it's not nice to judge people just because they are different from us!" his dad had responded.) Danny wasn't completely clear about what had happened, his network of friends was limited (only one actually, and qualifying Gerald Van Cortlandt as "friend" was a stretch), but he had heard that the Van Dorn kid had been killed, though the murderer had been caught and killed in a gunfight with police up the road.

The town would buzz about it for weeks, along with rumors of a bizarre race up the river supposedly involving ghost ships – which Danny dismissed as nothing more than the typical over-imaginative hysteria of under-developed minds.

Still, things had changed this year, despite the veneer of business-as-usual at the Feast of Saint Anne's Carnival. There was no question however that the heart had dropped out of it.

Communities are like living organisms unto themselves and now, after not one but three simultaneous (and from the word in the pipeline, extremely unpleasant) experiences, many of the local people at least had instinctively pulled back. More parents were staying home this week watching movies with their kids or going shopping at the mall. Some families had sped up their vacation plans without really considering why.

Nothing as overt as an outright boycott of the carnival, more of a "neighbor had a tragedy, maybe we shouldn't be out partying" subtle pulling back on the usual fun and games. There was still the outside traffic from other towns – Cold Spring, Tarrytown, Peekskill, and Ossining, to name a few – but ride attendance was down, ticket sales had sagged, and food vendors who, by the fifth and sixth nights, would weigh whether or not they could stretch their supplies to the end of Night Seven without restocking, now frowned at the surpluses on their shelves.

The carnival had taken on the vaguely dilapidated air of a party that had lost its steam.

If Danny Riedel had been a little less under-developed in his social skills, he might have been more aware of this and, things might have turned out a lot different for him. And if the police had been a little more on top of their game and if either of Danny's parents had been a little more of a Pack Leader, to quote Cesar Millan, it might have just turned out to be just another night at the tail end of the village's annual carnival.

But the village police were exhausted and hadn't attached any major significance to Case #6:2011vwf040, a missing person's report on local library assistant Darcy Van Wort filed by her friend Karen Evershaw, due to a note that had turned up the next day in Miss Van Wort's neighbor's mailbox in a plain envelope – no postmark – that read:

Dear Whelma,
Ran out last minute for a few days, finally met a new and exciting man in my life!
Details to come! ☺
Darcy

The neighbor, Whelma Fitzpatrick, couldn't recall the last time she'd seen Darcy's handwriting and the officers who'd retrieved it hadn't gotten around to sending it off for analysis.

If they had, they might have determined that it wasn't written by Miss Van Wort at all.

And Danny, who, for all his intelligence could suffer his own surprising lapses of common sense, was completely unaware that, due to poor ticket sales, the evening's last – actually all – performances by Mickey and Johnson had been cancelled.

The trailer was unlocked.

Danny walked up with the confidence of someone keeping an expected appointment and knocked, tilted his head as if listening to a response and said, "Yes, it's me," for the benefit of any unseen observers, surprised as anyone that the door was open. He'd anticipated a slightly more difficult entry and had come equipped with a special ultra-flat hook/latch made of hardened polymer, similar to the ones used by firemen to gain access to homes without breaking windows.

It was really quite amazing what one could order online these days.

The inside of the trailer was dark, although there was still an hour of sunlight left so he could see well enough. Danny was impressed with the Zugai masks (which he photographed with his Droid), ignored the old posters and spotless kitchen, and went straight to the back room when he didn't find anything resembling a laptop in the front area.

Unlike the shock-and-awed previous visitor, Danny wasn't blown away at what he found in Bob Johnson's work room.

"Well, well, what do we have here?" he said with an appraising smile. "Bobby-boy is certainly into some interesting hobbies!" The work table had been cleaned and put away, the poor goat of the previous Saturday long disposed of at the town dump, but the shrunken heads and shelves containing assorted jars and accoutrements were all still in place, along with a bunch of framed photos. Danny, who had pulled on a pair of surgical gloves immediately after entering (he also had a lint-free cloth that he would use to wipe off the main door handle when leaving), got quickly to work, sorting quickly through all the available storage spaces with the methodical efficiency of an expert thief. He'd spent years practicing his techniques at home and, later on, anywhere he could.

He carefully took photographs of anything of interest, including the heads, the jars and their labels, a box of what looked like women's jewelry, a large wooden toolkit filled with an assortment of carving tools, saws, and paints, and, even more macabre, what appeared to be a box of human hair, teeth, and nails. There was also a narrow closet filled with all sorts of uniforms and costumes that presumably were used to play different characters as part of the act. Nothing overtly incriminating (although there were two lockers under the bench seats that he decided were beyond his limited lock-picking abilities) and, even slightly more frustrating, no computer.

The crux of Danny's plan was hinged on his target owning a computer. Even an old one. "What kind of person didn't own a computer these days?" he wondered. Cripes, even his grandmother owned one and she was an ancient sixty-one years old.

Well no matter, he decided. It wasn't critical. He took out a couple of DVDs he'd prepared earlier and, after a few minutes consideration, hid one at the bottom of the tool box and the other under the liner of a drawer. The DVDs contained a large assortment of hardcore sex – torture and snuff films, along with some truly bizarre necrophilia footage that he'd downloaded using a Wyvern Falls Middle School teacher's PC that he'd hacked into a year before. The school's firewall had been set up by complete rubes – he'd routed his access through Eastern Europe using stolen credit card information lifted through some dupe in Nigeria and, as an added bonus, included a few extra documents loaded with stolen credit card data. In a few hours, after a carefully-placed phone call to the Wyvern Falls Police Department, Danny was confident the law enforcement community would be showing up with some very interesting and pointedly direct questions at the top of their list.

If all went as planned, this would also involve an extended stay on Cell Block C at the Sing-Sing Bed & Breakfast for Mister Johnson.

Danny's interest in such matters was pretty much clinical; what emerging sexual inclinations he had so far developed were wholly focused on older women. Ever since he had caught The Graduate one night on TNT, he had been fixated by the idea (except that in his fantasy the woman in question was a Harvard professor or a Supreme Court judge) and his efforts with such highly illegal matter were simply as a means to an end.

The issue that Mister Johnson didn't appear to own any sort of technological device beyond an old radio was problematic but something that could be easily remedied, perhaps by simply taking an old laptop from the dump, smashing it up and planting it in the woods nearby, as if the owner had gotten angry with himself over a clearly disgusting habit. Cross-checking with the photos he had taken with the Droid, Danny made sure everything was back in its place exactly where he'd found it, then carefully exited the trailer, wiping down thethe door handle as he left.

It never crossed his mind to check out the 1962 Ford F100 parked nearby.

If he had, he would have noticed in the waning light someone wearing a fedora sitting in the driver's seat, apparently reading a newspaper and with an unlit pipe sticking jauntily out of the side of his mouth.

And he may or may not have noticed the other head that had been peering over the top of the truck seat, watching the trailer the whole time through the cab window with the deceptively half-lidded look of a cat studying its prey.

Just as Danny disappeared through the trees as he walked towards the area with the bike racks, there was a whine and rumble as the Ford's eight-cylinder engine was turned over.

-9-

A GURGLING scream came out as a half snarl.

The witch doctor staggered around the hut clawing at the puppet whose teeth are chewing away at his throat. He got two fingers in the thing's mouth to pry it off and merely succeeded in getting them bitten in half.

The doll was much more powerful than he had anticipated. The fear he had clearly seen in the sergeant. What he hadn't seen was the boiling rage underneath it. A rage honed and burnished like a gleaming hand grenade from years of taunting and abuse as an odd over-imaginative child growing up in a Depression-Era country, from years of humiliation by hard-eyed audiences at carnival side-shows in the years leading up to the war.

Something has gone wrong with the act of transference. He had seen similar things before – the change causing the mind of the person involved to dissolve into instant madness – but nothing like this. The madness was already there, lurking, waiting to spring out like a 'Manuvatemplal', or demon of the night.

But there was no time to contemplate his slip in judgment. There was a fierce, tearing pain at his throat, followed by a whistling sound which he realized was issuing from his shredded neck. As his knees dropped to the dirt floor of the hut, he pried the doll off with one final burst of strength, his eyes wide with fury, and hurl it against the wattle wall, sending shrunken heads flying in all directions.

In the doorway, Shell simply stared, so horrified he couldn't even manage to get a scream out, his eyeballs seeming to make a concerted effort to jump out of his skull. The doll-boy bounced and rolled and when it popped up, Shell saw something gleaming in its hand: the human-bone-handled dagger belonging to the witch doctor. The one with the wickedly sharp blade inscribed with odd symbols. Outside, what sounded like monkeys were screeching, perhaps sensing or smelling the violence going on within their proximity. The coppery aroma of fresh blood mingled with the cloying smells of sweat and smoke.

Saguma was still kneeling, clutching his torn throat that was now minus its larynx, looking like the world's angriest (and certainly most oddly-decked-out) worshipper, when the doll launched itself through the air and buried the knife in the witch doctor's right eye.

Shell suddenly found that his legs could still work after-all.

He turned and tore off through the jungle.

A moment later came the patter of small feet.

-10-

WHEN DANNY came home, his father had already gone up to bed even though it was only 9:30.

His mom had progressed to the even more mentally challenging 'Gene Simmon's Family Jewels' and barely acknowledged her son's return, except that, as he was heading up the stairs, she half-turned her head distractedly and said, "Oh, a package came while you were out. Your father put it up it your bedroom."

Danny froze and looked over at his Mom. At thirty-one, Alice Riedel's once-perky features were already beginning to settle into slack-jowled and over-medicated middle age. For a moment, Danny glimpsed the old woman she would become, a revelation met with a small "*hmmph!*" of critical dismissal.

I would never marry a woman who would let herself go like that, he thought. Then his mouth switched to Track B.

"What kind of package?" he heard himself ask.

"Oh, a pretty big one. UPS dropped it off."

Danny's eyes narrowed. "UPS? This late at night?"

His mom was still watching the television screen, though she now had a vaguely annoyed expression. "Well, he had a brown shirt, brown pants, and a brown cap that said UPS, so I guess that means yes, honey . . ."

Danny felt an odd tingling sensation at the back of his head that he didn't like. Not at all. There was no reason for any package to be delivered to him, by UPS or anyone, at all. Today, tomorrow, or in the foreseeable future.

He had the distinct and unpleasant feeling he was being out-maneuvered.

The door of his bedroom swung slowly open.

Danny looked around the room warily, like a safari hunter suspecting that the lion he was after has come down with a major case of the smarts and set its own trap.

A large oblong cardboard box was propped up in the leather Oxford tub chair in the far corner of the room next to the expansive bookcase. It looked to be just about the right dimensions to contain a ventriloquist's dummy.

Danny stepped into the room, his socks moving soundlessly across the thick wall-to-wall carpeting. His lips were set in a determined line as he crossed over to the chair, but the way his eyes darted around the room betrayed his uncertainty. Even so, he stepped right up to the box, looked it over, and, noting the clear packing tape, lack of any official labels or postmarks (although the letters U.P.S. had been hastily written in black marker in large crude capitals all over it), and marveled, not for the first time, what unbelievable dolts his parents were. He'd heard of a case recently of some kid supposedly filing for a divorce from his parents and wondered (also not for the first time) if he should seriously look into it. In the meantime, there was the issue of this little mystery gift to be dealt with. After a moment's thought, Danny went over to his desk – a broad Restoration one in dark cocoa with wood file cabinets and burnished steel hardware – and, opening the center drawer, pulled out a wicked-looking letter opener that looked like something out of The Lord of the Rings. Walking back over to the chair, he pondered the box a moment, then suddenly plunged the ten-inch blade into the side of the box. He did this half a dozen times at various different spots until he was satisfied that whatever might be inside wasn't alive (or at least would be leaking blood) before he took the opener and, holding it blade down in his fist, sliced along the box's top seam.

Then, tearing open the two flaps, he stepped back and stared at the contents.

Inside the standard packing box was an old beat-up storage box that looked like something out of the vaudeville era, with its frayed edges, striped covering, and old stickers. In this box was an indentation lined with water-stained silk in the approximate size and shape of a dummy. The smell of mildew and mothballs wafted out.

The box was empty, however. Or rather, in the cavity where the head would rest was a small pile of smashed-up, iridescent slivers, that looked like a couple of broken up DVDs. A closer look revealed that they had clearly been chewed to pieces. Above that was a small Post-it note pinned to the liner.

In crudely-written block letters it read:

Thanks for the snack, bucky! See you soon!

Danny snatched the note, looking at it and at the slivers of chomped DVD discs in disbelief. Then he crumpled the note and threw it angrily across the room, plunging the letter opener into the box where the head would be.

"I'll get you, you little prick! Just you wait . . ." he hissed.

On the nightstand next to the bed, the screen of the silver gadgety-looking projection clock gave off a pale blue glow. The large digital numbers read 2:17 AM. Smaller readouts indicated that it was also 70.3°F, the date was 01.07 FRI and the moon was in its NEW phase.

From somewhere beyond the window came the forlorn cry of a whippoorwill. Within the room came a quiet rustle of linen as Danny turned over in his sheets. His sleep had been fitful, really more of a series of short dozes, but he was prepared at least.

Underneath the covers he was fully clothed, including his hiking shoes. He didn't know exactly what Bob Johnson might try but there was no doubt he would try something – and a hunch said it would likely be something on the order of a surprise during the night.

The clock went through two additional numerals before Danny slowly pulled his blanket down and, reaching over instinctively, found his glasses and put them on. There was no moon now but a pale light filtered in through the dormer windows of his room from a nearby streetlight. The box had been removed hours ago to the oversized trash bin by the garage, but now, in the shadowy light, he could see something else had taken up residence in his favorite reading chair.

It was silent in the bedroom – the pregnant silence of anticipation – and, in the darkness, light glinted off the lenses of Danny's spectacles and glistened off the eyes of his mysterious nocturnal visitor across the room. Danny didn't gasp or scream, though his hand began to slowly and very carefully ease its way towards the Droid in its leather holster at his hip. He was curious, however, about how anybody or anything could have gained entry without triggering the ADT Home Security system and even more puzzled by what his little visitor was holding up in its little hands.

It looked like a two-foot long bamboo tube.

Even as he grasped the significance of this and jerked the covers up, there came a soft and hollow "pfffft" and he felt a tiny sting near his throat. His hand dropped away from the Droid as the paralytic poison from the feathers of the rare blue-capped Ifrita in which the dart had been dipped made quick work of his nervous system.

For the first time in his eleven years, Danny felt fear, terror, and helpless panic.

He heard a rushing sound in his ears and the hammering of his heart in his chest which diminished to a quiet flutter as the batrachotoxins kick in.

Then he heard a light thud as his visitor dropped down to the carpeted floor.

A moment later, a pair of eyes appeared at the edge of his bed.

-11-

AS ANY HIKER who has explored the woods and trails up and down the banks of the Hudson River can tell you, the ruins of old buildings and houses can be found practically everywhere. The combination of large swatches of undeveloped (or no longer developed) land, combined with a history of industry and wealth dating back to the first half of the 17th century, meant that a lot of stuff got built, thrived for a time, then became forgotten or abandoned. Whether it was the sprawling foundations of an old factory, the collapsing shell of a once glorious mansion, or the moldering remains of a neglected cemetery, the region has some of the richest archeology of modern western civilization to be found in the entire country.

One of the biggest industries to dominate the Hudson River Valley throughout most of the 1800s, an industry which generated enormous wealth, corruption, and (predictably) vast amounts of bad behavior by politicians and business owners, is one that, today, would sound absurdly ludicrous to the ears of even the poorest citizen in the area: ice.

Like the oil industry, wherever there is a high-demand product that can be controlled by a limited number of enterprising individuals, complete fuckery will result, usually in such a manner that those who can afford it the least will be squeezed the most. That is practically a law of human nature.

The ice industry in the Hudson Valley proved to be no exception. While today an entire bag can be bought at a local corner store for a couple of dollars, in the 19th century the growing need for and understanding of refrigeration, combined with a period when cold winters froze up much of the river, ice was king. Strung up along the mid and upper river region, the vast icehouses were built to store the blocks harvested throughout the winter months to be meted out downriver to the swelling population of New York City – an increasingly lucrative market, as immigrants poured into its tenements and needed more food and, to preserve it, more ice. By the early 20th century, however, the advent of modern refrigeration and ice-making technology, along with a crackdown on political corruption in New York's Tammany Hall, spelled the end of the ice business. The vast warehouses needed to store it were torn down or left to fall into disrepair and, by the middle of the century, were relegated to old picture books or the fading memories of a passing generation.

Some of the smaller icehouses persisted, however, particularly if they found a second life by being repurposed for other uses. One such building, built of double-walled brick with peeling white paint and faded lettering that read Knickerbocker & Sons, still stood in the strip of woods on the shore of Raadsel Bay just past where Wyvern Falls Creek emptied into the Hudson and the campgrounds began. It had found some use as a refrigerated storage building until the early 1960s and later was used by contractors to cache equipment and supplies when the Raadsel Bay condo complex was developed in 2001, but it had remained vacant ever since.

Now it stood mostly hidden among the trees, its surrounding parking lot overgrown with weeds and heaving up in places, a half-forgotten relic of another age, except as the occasional topic at town meetings when some busybody (usually one of the elderly condo residents) petitioned – always unsuccessfully – to have the building torn down. And yet, like so many similar structures up and down the river, it seemed to have a strangely-charmed life of its own, somehow escaping the wrecker's ball and yet not enticing enough to interest artists or developers in fully bringing it back. Few people knew that the building still had electricity (which, given the state of the wiring, made it a fire trap) and fewer still – only one to be exact – knew that the back storage room was still in use as an ice house.

Because he was the one who had recently set it up.

The ice blocks were no longer harvested from the river or local ponds of course. They were produced from an antiquated ice-making machine that had been jury-rigged and cajoled back into working order by this industrious user, but the room still worked quite well for its original purpose, and the heavy chain and industrial padlock on the massive cooler door had been carefully selected for their rusted and neglected appearance. Only a very close examination would reveal the fresh scratches and traces of oil around the keyhole.

Danny arrived around midnight, rolled up in an old carpet over Bob Johnson's shoulder in a fireman's carry. To any onlookers, the ventriloquist might have simply been another local trying to get rid of some old household stuff, illegal dumping hardly being headline news in a place like Wyvern Falls. Only a vigilant observer would suspect that his purpose was, in fact, more sinister, starting with the New Hampshire plates on the Ford truck he'd left at the small scenic parking area near the water.

There had been an awkward moment when, shortly after the pick-up eased into the parking space, the paralytic had worn off and Danny had started to whimper and struggle within the rolled-up carpet. In the act of swinging the carpet out of the truck bed, something had tumbled out and landed in the tufts of tall grass that grew around the rough log posts that defined the edge of the parking area. Bob had only glimpsed the object out of one slow blinking eye but, when he took a step over to look, a puzzled expression on his face, the kid struggled more and he was forced to put the roll down.

Not that he would have understood what the object was. The slim black Samsung Droid was completely outside his knowledge of electronics and technology. As was pretty much any gadget made after the 1940s.

He'd unrolled the carpet next to the truck (with its ticking V8 engine) and, while pinning Danny's chest with one hand, reached into the plastic holder in his shirt's breast pocket with the other and extracted another slim needle-like dart. Bob's eyes were cold and dead as he pricked the boy's neck and waited for the batrachotoxins to kick in again. It wasn't an exact science by any stretch. In the past. there had been several "accidents" when he'd used too strong a dose and induced heart failure in his victims. On others, he had used too light a dose and had been forced to resort to cruder solutions, including a ball peen hammer. That had been messy.

Inside the cooler, Danny was transferred to an old-fashioned mortician's table and strapped into place. Though paralyzed, his eyes were able to move around just enough to take in that he wasn't the only occupant in the cooler, though he was the only one that appeared intact. Since he was unable to scream, the best he could manage was a tear at the corner of one eye. It pooled, then ran down along the rim of his glasses.

Overhead, naked bulbs in rusted hanging industrial fixtures gave off an uneven light. The roughly twenty- by thirty-foot space was half-filled with large blocks of ice and crude metal shelves. The concrete floor was a patchwork of cracks and mysterious stains and, in addition to water, other substances oozed their way towards the rectangular drainage grates.

Danny's head rolled to the left and saw a familiar figure lying horizontally on a large slab of ice next to the table he was on. Even in profile he recognized the face – it was Miss Van Wort, the assistant from the Wyvern Falls Library.

Despite his interest in older women, he could have done without seeing her naked body. From his earliest years, when he'd read voraciously anything from Stephen Hawking to Skeptics Magazine, Danny had dismissed any concepts of God or religion until that perspective had finally tipped over into blatant contempt toward anyone who expressed belief or faith in such topics. And yet, without even a second thought, he found himself praying, pleading to God or any higher being who might be available, to help him somehow, anyhow, get him out of this predicament.

He'd heard the phrase "There are no atheists in foxholes." Now he was actually experiencing what that sentence really meant.

Meanwhile, Bob hummed to himself as he went over to his improvised workbench and sorted through his tools.

The song was *High Deedle Dee-Dee* from Walt Disney's 'Pinocchio'.

-12-

SHELL WAS running full tilt through the New Guinea jungle with an agility he'd never known he possessed. Blind terror lent speed to his feet as he leapt over fallen logs, dashed through stretches of Kunai grass that cut his skin like razors. He pelted past totara and acacia trees, some hanging with vines, the occasional python, and fist-sized spiders in their webs. Giant woolly rats, boars, and fanged frogs scattered as the boy crashed through the foliage, followed by the persistent patter of tiny feet.

It was while thrashing across the stream near his village that he finally stumbled on a submerged mangrove root. He half-turned in the muddy water to see the doll leaping through the air, the witchdoctor's wicked-looking knife flashing in the dim starlight. There was a splash, then a searing pain along the side of his face. His bladder let go in the tepid water as a tiny fist grabbed his woolly hair and pulled his head half out of the water to deliver the final death cut.

He knew he was about to die, that he was about to pay the ultimate price for what really amounted to nothing more than good nature and basic good intentions.

But the descent of the knife was interrupted by a series of whistling thuds and splashes.

And shouts.

A rain of spears and stones were flying through the air. One particularly well-aimed rock bounced off the doll's head, taking a chunk of wood, paint, and human hair with it. With that Shell found his head released, barely noticing a series of splashes as the thing ran away, disappearing back into the night and darkness.

Just before he passed out, he felt hands scrambling at him, drawing him out of the water.

The side of his jaw felt like it was on fire.

Then he surrendered to the bliss of unconsciousness.

The doll made it back to the hut and paced about, frustrated.

Had the boy survived? Probably. What will happen next? Will the secret get out? What to do?

First there was a more pressing matter to attend to.

In the course of the three-night ritual, the sergeant had come to understand that there was a 'transference' – that a magical bridge had been formed between man and doll allowing his essence, his anima, to go back and forth. The incantations and mix of ingredients that included his own hair and nails (and a few other things like urine, bits of skin, and a trace of semen) had formed this bridge between him and the doll. The witch doctor had told him that not only can he make himself more or less invulnerable by "occupying" the doll, his human body was less susceptible to such trauma as shock and wounds while in combat. But there were limitations. While transferred to the doll, he cannot control his human body. And while this state will prolong his life considerably – the elixirs and magic will slow the aging process of the human vessel extensively – he was not immortal and still had certain vulnerabilities. For instance, if the doll was destroyed while his soul was trapped in it, he would die. And the human body must be maintained, as it also acted as source of harvesting for the hair, nails, and such that must be renewed in the doll, since over time they would lose their potency and the bridge would weaken.

The sergeant was enlightened to many of the secrets of the transference ritual but not to all – like any good magician the witch doctor kept a few trump cards up his metaphorical sleeve – and, more critically, before finding out the actual method of transferring back into his human vessel, the sergeant had, in his haste and excitement, eliminated his immediate source of information.

There was an almost comic moment as the doll stood over the lifeless body of the sergeant, jumping up and down and then grabbing the human's head and shaking it in its tiny hands. Time was running out. The growing rumble of drums in the distance announced that a war party was preparing to come after him and he was reasonably certain the reception wouldn't involve hugs and smiles. For the most part, the New Guinea natives had proven themselves indispensable in helping Allied airmen, often at the risk of severe Japanese retribution, but the sergeant knew they could be deadly and fearless as well. There had been least some documented instances of U.S. bomber crews surviving crashes or bailouts in the mountains to the north but wound up on the dinner table of their native rescuers. While he considered this dilemma, he at least had the foresight to gather many of the items scattered around the hut that he would need and stuff them into the large army duffel bag he brought earlier.

He was just in the process of placing a sacred spirit flute in the bag when he heard a whistling "thunk!" as a spear sailed through the hut, narrowly missing his head and embedding itself in the wattled wall. A moment later, a fierce-looking face appeared in the entrance, topped by cloud of woolly hair and a halo-like headpiece fringed with bird feathers.

The man leapt into the hut brandishing an Australian Army-issue machete. Oddly, he was dressed in a combination of traditional and modern clothes: a long yellow skirt bound with a hide belt and a white tank-top T-shirt. His name was Lowai, he was

Shell's father, and he had arrived well ahead of the rest, determined to have first shot at destroying this thing there had been talk about in the village these past nights. The doll wasn't concerned with introductions however, as the blade whistled though the air where its head had been just moments before. It tumbled forward between Lowai's legs and swung the witch doctor's dagger at the man's Achilles tendon. But Lowai hadn't earned his name Hasu-Hasu — lightning — for nothing. He leapt straight up like a cat on a hot plate and landed swinging.

The fight that followed was short and brutal.

Shrunken heads flew, statuettes were knocked askew, an angry-looking coconut head (with white shell eyes and tiny jagged shell teeth) went rolling out the entrance. The inside of the hut was hacked to pieces and Lowai was cut many times, though none of the wounds were fatal. At one point, a scattered candle set the walls alight and in short order the walls smoldered and burned , hampered only by a heavy rain earlier in the day. The doll had proven a nimble target as well, time and again avoiding the deadly machete blade making glittering arcs through the air.

But then the doll stumbled — over the leg of the witch doctor's corpse, ironically — and had one of its diminutive feet severed. A second later, it found itself pinned under a heavy calloused foot, its knife-wielding hand immobilized by Lowai's left hand.

The doll made a half bark/ half snarling sound and snapped its bloodstained teeth in frustration. Lowai bared his own teeth in a ferocious grin as he angled the machete across the doll's neck, preparing to sever it.

To his puzzlement, the doll's eyes flick left, then right, then the eyelids drop half-closed as it ceased to struggle. Too late he heard a rustle behind him and had only managed to half turn his head before he felt a searing pain in his chest. He looked down to see the tip of his very own spear emerge to the left of his sternum in a shower of blood. His eyes went wide with shock and anger as he collapsed and the last thing they registered before he died was the American airman standing there with a blank expression, outlined against the smoke and flames.

-13-

THE SILVER SAAB 9-5 rolled into the parking area at just past 1:00 PM. on Friday afternoon.

Although Jim Franks was driving, the car was actually Karen's. His old '96 Range Rover had been towed to the shop with a dead alternator that morning, and with Karen off for the summer, it had simply made sense for him to borrow the car for the day. It was increasingly obvious the 4x4 – which was really beginning to look and act its age – was way overdue for retirement, but Franks was having trouble letting go. Not only was it a veteran of his bachelor days in the city, it was the last year the British vehicle retained its rugged lines before being redesigned as a more upscale SUV, or 'Soccer Mom Mover', as Franks dryly referred to them.

Plus, he loved the old Rover and joking about getting a rifle and rack for it and an Aussie hat for him so he could run off to wrestle crocodiles and chase rhinos for Marlin Perkins. Secretly, he just harbored a nostalgia for driving something that harkened back to the days before speed dialing and instant texting, when people didn't feel the need to express themselves with emoticons.

Still he couldn't deny the Saab was a pleasure to drive with its efficient interior and tight gear shift. It made him feel like he was driving a stylish airplane, which made sense, given its pedigree.

Since it was a brilliant day in the low 80s and a slow one at the studio over in Irvington, he'd rung up his girlfriend and talked her into a lunch date. They'd picked up food to go from the Portuguese deli on Main Street and taken a ride out to one of Frank's spots out on Raadsel Point. ("I bet you bring all your girls out here to seduce them," Karen always joked. "No, only the most seducible ones," Franks would typically respond.)

Further out on the point came the distant sounds of the carnival getting packed up. Most of it had been broken down the night before and two thirds of the rides were already gone, though some of the workers would loiter at the camp grounds over the weekend.

Once again, the Feast of Saint Anne's Carnival was over. And, for more than a few people this year, that was a good thing.

Usually there was a tidy finality to the way the carnival packed up and left town, its members dispersing to destinations as mysterious as the ones they came from, but this year it felt like there were a lot of loose ends and unresolved questions lying about like uneasy ghosts.

And unfinished business.

To Franks and Karen Evershaw, aside from the rumors of what had happened up at Castle Krell and the strange deaths of LiveEYE NY reporter and the Ghost Seekers International crew, the mystery of what happened to Darcy Van Wort was around the top of the list.

Along with the undeniable sense that something had gone slightly askew with their relationship, courtesy of an insinuating remark made by a ventriloquist's dummy.

The two of them sat in the car looking at the bay, Franks in a black open-necked golf shirt and fatigued pair of jeans, Karen in a snappy floral print summer dress that accented her curves. A lone sailboat was motoring out of the Yacht Club, heading towards the open river, and a few cumulus clouds were taking their time wandering across the sky. Not for the first time, Franks idly wondered what it would be like to own a sailboat he could use to putter around on the river. If this month was any indication, it wouldn't happen anytime soon.

"I slept with Mark," Karen said abruptly.

Franks felt the sliver of suspicion make a twist in his gut. Mark, as in Mark Everston who was cousin to the Raadsel Bay Yacht Club Everston's, was Karen's ex-husband. They had been going through a messy divorce when she'd first met Franks. He had a split-second twist on his idle yachting fantasy: perhaps he could instead invest in a derelict torpedo boat and blow the yacht club to smithereens during one of the Everston clan's frequent soirees. Or at least make a strafing pass or two with a deck-mounted .50 caliber.

"You've been wondering since Tuesday night."

Karen had been staring straight ahead as she spoke. Now she turned and looked at him directly.

"It was two months after we started dating. You were in Vancouver that week with your designers at some big media convention. I'd gone back to the house to get some things. Mark had just lost his mother . . . we had a few drinks. It just happened. It was a huge mistake and I feel awful about it. I would give anything to take it back, but I can't. But I also didn't think any good would come of it if I told you."

Franks felt like his jaw was locked. "So why tell me now?"

Karen let out a bitter laugh. "You don't hide yourself half as well as you think, Jim. Ever since that, that little shit of a dummy opened his mouth, it's been eating at you. I could tell. Because it breaks my heart."

Franks let this simmer for a minute as he sat back, arms folded. He felt his emotions working into a maelstrom and he didn't want them to get the best of him. Even so, he couldn't help the next question out of his mouth.

"Anything else you've been keeping from me?"

"Yes."

Not the answer he'd hoped for.

"Jesus," he muttered, thinking, *Now what? An affair with one of her students? Cheated on her taxes? A chronic gambling addiction she's been hiding?*

Karen dropped her hands in her lap and gazed out the windshield again. A pair of geese were bobbing past in the water, looking for handouts.

"I know why Vivienne left John so abruptly."

Franks blinked. *Christ*, he thought, *this is beginning to turn into a bona fide soap opera.*

"And . . .?"

"And I can't tell you."

"Can't or *won't?*"

"Both. I made a promise to her and I won't break it. It's something she'll have to break to him when she's ready."

Franks put his palms to his forehead. "Great. Just wonderful. Any other headlines you want to run out while you're rolling?"

A pause. Then, "Yes. One."

Franks threw his hands out in an "and . . .?" gesture.

A longer pause, then,

Just that . . . *I love you.*"

That was the left hook.

Franks was stunned. There it was: the 'L' word. It hadn't been brought up yet in the seven months they had been dating, but had been avoided and dodged to the point that *not* bringing it up felt like a weird game. Franks knew what he felt, knew without a doubt that he loved her back to the deepest levels of his heart, but the divorce with Mark (along with her ex's verbal abuse and out of control drinking) had been like a specter between them.

He felt his eyes begin to water and suddenly the air in the car felt like it was choking him.

"I . . . I need a second." He threw open the car door and walked a few steps over to the thin beach that ran along the shore. It was mostly made up of dark sand, rocks, and bleached oyster shells.

Franks took a couple of deep breaths. The breeze ruffled his hair.

Behind him, he heard the car door click shut. He was preparing to turn and announce that he loved her too when his thoughts were interrupted. An unexpected robotic voice came out of the grass near the wood post in front of the car.

"Droid."

His brow creased in puzzlement. "What the . . .?" Then he looked up as the Saab's engine started, startled to see Karen had moved over to the driver's seat. Behind the glare of the windshield, he could see she was crying.

"Karen! Stop!"

He was too late. She threw the car into reverse and spun out of the parking lot, leaving him with a stricken and confused look on his fa And an empty stomach. They hadn't even eaten lunch.

From the weeds, the Samsung phone announced itself again. "Droid."

He didn't fully register that an old Ford pick-up drove past a moment later, following the Saab back into town. He'd been distracted by another odd sound, what sounded like the click and whirr of a fan over in the woods.

But that didn't make any sense.

-14-

FRANKS BENT over and fished the phone out of the grass.

Someone had just left a message, according to the blinking voicemail icon, but when Franks double tapped the desktop he got a surprise instead – the owner's photo gallery. The content of the images couldn't have been more bizarre if he'd stumbled across a collection showing the Pope in his underwear.

He also noted that the battery icon was showing the phone was about to go dead. First he tried to call the unit's voicemail but hung up when he realized he didn't have the pass-code. Whoever owned it had a lot of messages in their mailbox though – it announced that it was full. Without hesitating, he pulled out his iPhone and pulled up a program he'd recently installed, a Bump App called ImageSwap that worked between wireless devices. Initially, he'd gotten it so he could share photos between his and Karen's phones. Like all great apps, it worked via a very simple interface: one held the two devices more or less next to each other (or 'bumped' them) and you could simply use your finger to drag one phone's image gallery over to the other.

A few precious minutes were spent loading up the app on the Droid and, by the time he was transferring the photo gallery onto his iPhone, the Droid's battery icon was blinking red. A moment later it gave up the ghost with a final announcement in its flat monotone "Droid" and went dead.

If it hadn't, a few things might have turned out differently.

Then again, perhaps not.

Karen wasn't answering his calls. Neither was John Easton. Only later would he learn his friend was at that moment flying in a biplane over the river with a bunch of kids. Franks debated about running home but decided he needed to make stop first. He could think of only one name at the top of his list who might shed some light on his questions: Tucker Brooks.

The Wyvern Falls Public library was on Verplanck Avenue off the upper side of Main. Another imposing Federalist style building (apparently there was a municipal code mandating that style for public libraries in small towns across the country in the past), it sported a few surprisingly modern improvements, including a computerized index system, a DVD rental section, and Wi-Fi access. Nothing too drastic, but enough at least to keep its chin up on the rim of 21st century technology. It was also the base of operations of the man who was both the head librarian and (in quite a few minds at least) arguably the smartest person in Wyvern Falls, perhaps even the county: Tucker Brooks.

Even Danny Riedel would have, albeit grudgingly, agreed.

Little about Brooks suggested this, however. A massive hulk of a black man with a lazy eye and hands the size of catcher's mitts whose demeanor suggested more of a benign, half-drowsing bear than the town's resident genius, Brooks possessed an encyclopedic knowledge of everything he'd ever read – which was extensive – along with a near photographic memory.

He was one of those anomalies that confound analysts and educators alike, a SUNY Purchase drop-out who had decided setting up shop in a small town library suited him just fine, though he maintained correspondences with an odd mix of people ranging from Smithsonian curators, a renegade physicist or two, a well-known Russian chess champion, and a network of jazz musicians, along with some local deli owners and the manager of a White Plains pet shop.

Something about the structure of the library, with its quiet atmosphere, subdued lighting, and ordered knowledge residing within its walls, suited him perfectly. A safe and solid fortress of calm for a man with a troubled and pain-filled childhood – of which little or nothing was ever revealed, even to his closest friends. There were rumors that his off-the-charts intelligence had been triggered by a serious beating from his father as a child once (another version had him similarly waking up a genius after a gang put him in the hospital with severe head trauma), but any probing into his past were met with Zen-like deflection and the one person who seemed to have any inside knowledge on his past, the previous head librarian George Steenberger, was in his grave for six years now.

Tucker – everyone referred to him by his first name – was well-liked in the community and especially by the parents for the soft-spoken yet inspiring manner with which he ran several children's reading groups, including one for the mentally handicapped. Kids loved him. And since he taken over the library, he'd revitalized its role in the community by introducing several programs including ongoing art exhibits, a digital Hudson Valley literature program, and several historical displays, including some life-sized Revolutionary War soldiers on loan from the West Point Museum.

He was also a fanatic about chocolate – with milk in the summer months and as hot cocoa in the fall and winter – and seemed to have an inexhaustible supply of Jacques Torres bars stashed in secret locations throughout the library and in his apartment over on Elm Street.

When Franks showed up on Friday afternoon, he made sure to bring a large container of custom-made iced chocolate milk (with a ropy swirl of hot fudge) from the Columbian pastry shop down the street as an offering.

All he had to do was to tell the owner was, "One Tucker Shake to go."

Tucker looked up from the central carousel desk as Franks came in. Predictably, with it being a fine Friday afternoon with the carnival just ended, the library was fairly deserted. The head librarian was watching *The Young and The Restless* on his laptop – following daytime soap operas was one of his peculiar hobbies – with his chin propped up on one hand and a half-dreamy look on his face. He pulled out his ear buds as Franks came up to the desk and shook his head sadly, though one eye noted the shake.

"This is terrible," he said quietly.

"What's that?" Franks responded, half whispering out of habit even though the library was all but empty.

"Well, Victor just came home and told Diane to pack her bags because they're going to get married tonight."

"And…?"

"B-but now Nikki's hit the bottle again. She ran into Victor at the stables to give him a birthday present and they wound up having sex – but they still can't be together – and now Nikki found out Deacon and Meggie were behind the plot to break them up. She'll have to go back to rehab now. Did you know 17.6 million adults in the U.S. have a drinking problem as of this year?"

"At least I know I have plenty of company. You know, Tucker, I'm starting to get concerned about you. Your hanging out with these books all the time and all. Remember that Twilight Zone episode with Burgess Meredith? About the books?"

Tucker grinned, "Yeah . . .'Time Enough at Last', first season, episode nine, based on a short story written by Lynn Venable."

"Now you're *really* scaring me. You need to get out of this dump a little more often. Anyhow, I brought you a present," Franks said as he placed the shake between them.

Tucker shrugged. It was a well-played routine between them.

"White man bearing gifts. I-I-I'm the one who should be scared."

He always spoke slowly and with an occasional stutter. Then he saw the iPhone appear on the desk. "What do you have for me today?"

"A bunch of pictures. Really weird ones, in fact. I'm hoping you can tell me something about them."

Tucker made a quick "gimme" gesture with his paw of a hand. "L-let's see what you got."

Franks came around to the other side of the desk and showed him the gallery in question, after which the librarian produced a USB cable from one of the drawers and hooked up the phone to his laptop. A minute later, he was fanning through the images while making repeated "hmmpf" sounds. With his other hand, he called up websites on the library's main workstation, typing almost simultaneously on each keyboard with surprising agility.

The clatter of tapping keys sounded harsh in the subdued environment of the library, despite the spaciousness of the place. The main room was essentially a large box with a small rotunda at the top, with the second floor stacks along open galleries on all four sides, accessed from staircases at each corner. The rotunda with its heavy glazing seemed especially designed to diffuse light coming in. Hanging globe lights dating from the 1910s cast a soft glow through the room, while more modern energy-efficient LED pendant lights had been added around the central desk area to give the buffed brass and mellowed oak woodwork the aura of an old-fashioned command center. The combination of classic décor and hi-tech accents made for an odd mix.

Franks looked over a nearby 'Profiles of Pirates' display that featured assorted books in the library's holdings, along with individual bio-cards on glossy stock that Tucker had put together and printed himself as part of a monthly education theme. He was looking over the one on Captain Kidd, featuring the classic image by Howard Pyle, and reading about the legend of Kidd's treasure being buried out on Raadsel Point when Tucker interrupted his thoughts.

"Okay . . . okay . . . I think we got something, Jim"

Franks put the card back on the display rack. "Talk to me."

"Well, what you got is w-weird all right." The image filling up the entire screen of the laptop showed the inside of Bob Johnson's trailer with the shrunken heads and paraphernalia. "The trailer is an Airstream, a model introduced in 1951, but the sculptures, shrunken heads and such pre-date that and are definitely from New Guinea – I would guess WWII, based on what I've found in these other photos." He fanned to one that showed the closet with its door open and various jackets hanging inside. He pointed to one that was clearly a vintage Airman's uniform. "See that '5' patch on the shoulder? That's Fifth Air Force. Organized under General Kenney in 1942 and based out of New Guinea until moving up to the Philippines and eventually to Japan after the war ended. Also, you can see an old A-2 leather flight jacket in there and you can just make out the hand painted Skull and Crossbones on the back (you see that?). That's an outfit called the Jolly Rogers. 90th Bomber Group. Definitely Fifth Air Force. And there are a lot of little things in these pictures that reinforce that." He pulled up another image that showed the shelves with their jars and vials. "See, there's a wooden cup – some sort of souvenir – that says "Rabaul – 1943" in tiny lettering at the base and that rubber thing is a Lyster bag that our guys used to store purified water in the jungle."

Franks was puzzled. "Okay. But what about all this other stuff. Are those heads real?"

"Oh, I'm pretty sure they're real. They look like genuine shrunken human heads. And look, at least five of them are Caucasian. If it was just that, I would simply say that whoever this trailer belongs to has a bit of a weird taste when it comes to interior decoration. But it's all this other stuff together that's t-t-troubling me."

Franks raised his eyebrows. "Tell me," he said.

"W-well, this is all heavy duty stuff. Extremely *rare* heavy duty stuff. And we're not talking someone's weird New Guinea cannibal collection. This is for performing black magic rituals. These are ingredients, tools, and parts. Very bad mojo here, my friend. V-v-very bad."

"Shit," Franks said, then looked around to see if anyone had heard. He pulled out the dead Samsung phone. "But my question is, how did they wind up on this Droid?"

Now it was Tucker's turn to raise his brows. "You got these from that?"

"Yeah. Found it in the parking area at the top of the bay."

"Well, that's easy. These pictures were taken right here."

"Right here?"

"S-s-sure, as in right here in Wyvern Falls. At the Point, at least."

Franks, who had been leaning with his hand on Tucker's shoulder, looked at his friend in shock. "How the heck do you know that?"

Tucker flipped to one of the shots that included the front window of the trailer. Using the magnifying lens tool, he zoomed in. Through the slightly opened curtain, the spruce trees were just visible – though pixilated – along with the back-end view of an old pick-up truck. Next to the truck was a leaning pole with a rusted metal chit nailed to it that read '17'.

"That's a lot marker for a camping slot at the point. Your mystery photographer took these shots f-from inside a trailer there at-at . . ." He right-clicked on the image and an info menu popped up. ". . . in and around 8:00 PM last night." As if on its own accord, Tucker's left hand brought up a menu on the library workstation. He typed in a few key words into the catalogue search engine menu and a second later was met with a short list of entries.

"We don't have a lot on this stuff. You got a minute?"

Franks was half-thinking about Karen and had an aching need to get home and set things to rights between them. But there was something about this whole situation – here, the library, talking with Tucker – that seemed imperative. *Urgent.* He'd known Tucker for years now. From the first time he'd set foot in the library, walked up to the front desk and introduced himself, there'd been an unmistakable sense of déjà vu as he'd instinctively shaken the big man's hand and a sureness they would be friends, but he'd never seen the librarian this excited and agitated before.

"Sure, I guess I got a minute."

Tucker's mitt-like hand patted him on the shoulder. His touch was surprisingly light. "Sit tight and hold the fort. I'll be right back."

Franks was absently studying the glass case nearby that housed a life-sized mannequin of a 17th century Lenape Indian warrior and considering various plans for making things up to Karen, when Tucker returned with some oversized books.

"Sorry, t-took longer than I expected. I'm short-staffed with Darcy out. She was like having three of my regular assistants . . . and this new girl Helen I have here today seems more interested in talking to her boyfriends than restacking things."

The two books were *The Fifth Air Force* by Steve Birdsall and the second was a large blue volume titled *The Jolly Rogers: History of the 90th Bombardment Group.* He laid the blue book in the space between the two computers so both of them could look it over properly. The book had the musty odor of one that hadn't been opened in a very long time.

"Not really a popular item," Tucker said, as if picking up on Franks' thoughts, "And n-not my usual area of interest." He pulled out a pair of reading spectacles and put them on with practiced care. Then he went through pages, running his finger down the paragraphs and over the photos at a pace way too fast for Franks to follow. Like many book worms, he murmured to himself while doing so.

From what Franks could see, the book was a dry collection of "just the facts" writing, grainy and badly shot photos, punctuated by occasional crudely-drawn doodles and cartoons that were probably only funny to the faces in the faded pictures.

"What are you looking for?" he asked.

"I . . . uh, oh, s-s-sorry," Tucker said, a sheepish grin on his face. "I forget sometimes. A lot of people don't read like I do . . . just looking for clues . . . clues and mo—"

"Stop," Franks cut in, putting his hand down on the page Tucker was about to turn. Suddenly, the hairs at the back of his neck were standing straight up at attention. A cold knot formed in his gu.

At the top right hand of the page was a close-up photo of a man with sergeant's stripes on his sleeve kneeling in an outdoor tent next to a native kid. The man had a pencil-thin mustache, a pipe sticking out of one corner of his mouth, and he was making an exaggerated *this-is-great-fun!* face. The native boy was clearly hamming up a "hey-what-the—?" sideways glance of the classic wary customer. But what turned Franks' blood cold was the ventriloquist's dummy propped up on the man's knee, its mouth slightly open, and its big eyes looking straight at the camera.

Staring out of the pages of a book printed sixty-six years ago. Then he realized he'd seen the sergeant before too.

"Holy shit!" was the only thing Franks could think of to say. It seemed to work, so he said it again. Then he jabbed the photo with his finger. Under the image the caption read "Sergeant Bob Johnson and his good 'ole pal Mickey try out a few lines – talk about a tough customer!"

"I've seen those two . . . there's no way you're going to believe me on this, but I swear to God Karen and I saw them at the carnival this week."

Tucker didn't respond right away. He sat, hunched over the computers and books like a big and very scholarly bear, and rubbed his chin.

Then he surprised Franks by saying softly, "Oh, I believe you."

His fingers reached over to the laptop and tapped the space bar. After a pause while the computer came out of sleep mode he went back and forth between the gallery images until he came to another shot that showed the trailer window again. The picture taker had been trying to get a close up of the row of shrunken heads above the window and had inadvertently gotten a shot of the pick-up truck in the background. Zoomed in, the pixels looked smudged, but one could just make out the top part of the head and eyes peering out the back window of the truck.

"I would say that's your man," Tucker said. Then one large finger pointed at the flat-eyed face on the screen, "Hey, Dummy, what tricks have you been up to?"

-15-

THE WARRIORS *arrived at the witch doctor's hut only to find it engulfed in flames. It was not clear if it was put there deliberately or somehow made it there of its own volition, but the corpse of Saguma was propped in the entranceway, a macabre sight that was charred and cooking, its eyeballs burst and jaws open in a silent scream. The group of New Guinea men – there were twelve of them – stood there mute, like bizarrely-attired apostles with their horns and feathers and animal bones. Then they fanned out and shortly picked up the trail leading south towards the American airfields.*

It was a strange incident in Army Air Corps history when the 90th Bombardment Group's commanding officer was dragged out of bed just after midnight to deal with a group of angry natives claiming that one of their tribe had been murdered and his son seriously injured by an American serviceman whose tracks led directly to the group camp in the hills overlooking Jackson Drome.

The night was hot and sultry and the banner some wit had erected over the nearby trail leading down to the airfield – the one that read "Thru these portals pass the best damn mosquito bait in the world" – isn't kidding. Standing outside the operations hut with a bunch of guards, MPs, and a handful of his officers, the C.O. Colonel Art Roger, was not a happy man as he swatted at the bugs plying for his neck and face. Someone fired up the generator and the surrounding lights strung from poles had been turned on again, their pulsing glow lending an even more surreal aspect to the event.

The contrast between 20th century soldiers and their stone-age counterparts was otherworldly, a scene that might have been cooked up by an overly-imaginative Hollywood writer. As one historian would point out after the war, "it would have been closer in time and understanding and relative civilizations if suddenly we had found ourselves fighting over medieval Europe or in the French and Indian Wars or with Cortez and the Aztecs" and never had this been better underscored than at the confrontational meeting this very night.

Colonel Rogers was trying to process that one of his men had not only been accused of murder – that he at least understood – but also of taking part in a forbidden witchcraft ceremony to boot. The latter was most certainly not in his Army Air Force Regulations Manual.

Sergeant Bob Johnson, who had a semi-celebrity status in the group for his ongoing shows and participation in USO events, had been located and now sat out of sight in the CO's office. Rogers knew better than to incense the natives any further by letting them see the source of their anger and he was doing his best to handle the situation firmly but with kid gloves. The non-commissioned area of the camp had been put into an uproar earlier, when the natives tried to drag Johnson out of his cot and haul him off, and a brawl had ensued when his fellow tent-mates intervened. Matters came to abrupt halt when one soldier drew his .45 sidearm and fired several shots into the air. Order had been restored but a larger contingent of villagers had been spotted approaching from outside the camp to lend their solidarity.

"I assure you this matter is being treated most seriously," Rogers was saying to the local named Pok, who opted to take charge of the posse. A charismatic man with dashing good looks accented by a mustache and an intense gaze, Rogers – who inspired the bomber group's roguish nickname – was also debating as he said this how seriously he should take the clearly loony-acting sergeant sitting inside. When Pok and his fellow warriors started to protest, Colonel Rogers raised his hand calmly and said in a loud, clear voice, "Sergeant Johnson has been detained and is being questioned as I speak. Major Atkins here will take you to the ANGAU office over by ADVON Headquarters and, after taking your statements, will assist us in a thorough investigation of these charges. In the meantime, anyone not directly involved in giving statements should return to their homes immediately or they will be removed forcefully." Angry glares were met with his firm gaze and unmistakable aura of authority. Not one to repeat himself, Colonel Rogers turned on his heels and headed back to the sweltering confines of his office where he was already certain he would have to deal with this all-too-surreal situation in a manner the Army was best suited to: by burying it. Johnson's service record, which had been reasonably solid to this point was sitting in a folder on his desk. Accompanied by his aide, he entered and picked it up, while nearby a disheveled Sergeant Johnson sat in a chair, flanked by two guards.

"Hey, Colonel, what's the rumpus? Seems like the natives are restless tonight!" said the dummy in Sergeant Johnson's lap.

Rogers didn't respond. Instead, he tapped the folder in the palm of his hand and studied the sergeant. It hadn't escaped his attention that the dummy was splattered with blood (most of it, including a fair amount of gore, centered around the mouth area) and that Sergeant Robert 'Woody' Johnson had a serious case of spaced-out eyes. Never a big fan of ventriloquist's acts himself, the Colonel had indulged the sergeant's eccentricities around the base in the past in the interest of keeping morale up. Many of the men seemed to genuinely appreciate the distraction and there'd been no harm it.

Until now.

Lacking any response to feed off, Mickey swiveled his head and whispered to his partner, while the two guards glanced about nervously and kept a tight grip on their M-1 rifles.

"How do you want to handle this, sir?" the aid quietly asked his commander.

Rogers handed him the file. "Get him cleaned up, have his belongings packed up, and get him shipped out of out of here at dawn. Sergeant Johnson here is going for extended — make that 'very extended' — leave to Townsville and then back to the States."

"But what about the investiga—"

"There'll be no investigation, Corporal," Rogers said curtly, cutting him off. "In case you forgot, we're in the middle of a war here and we haven't exactly won it just yet. The last thing we need is an American serviceman who's clearly nuttier than a Christmas fruitcake embroiled in a trial involving witchcraft and murder. Do you have any idea what the press would do with this? Christ, we're having a hell of a time getting men and supplies around here as it is. Now get him and any trace of him the hell out of here. He's giving me the creeps."

"Yes, sir!" the corporal said, snapping off a stiff salute.

From there, the efficient damage-control machine of the Armed Forces kicked in and Sergeant Bob Johnson, Serviceman #36 419 851, and Private Mickey McPherson, no known number, began their curious journey of falling through the cracks of the system.

After a brief evaluation by Army psychologists back in San Francisco, Johnson was shuffled through a series of hospitals at increasingly obscure bases until at one point he was listed as officially AWOL after wandering off a base in the middle of New Mexico. No effort to track him down was made nor was there any notification to his next of kin (an aunt in Schenectady). His paperwork was quietly swallowed up in the unfathomable sea of bureaucracy that only governments seem capable of.

In New Guinea, the tides of war surged forward and, within three months of the incident, the Fifth AF Bomber Command (and Colonel Rogers) moved up to Nadzab and the futile attempts to pursue the case met with polite assurances and deaf ears. A World War was on and there were much bigger things to be concerned with. Port Moresby had become a back seat in the war arena. And with life and death part of the daily routine, the memory of Sergeant Johnson and Mickey quickly faded from the minds of his fellow servicemen — literally, as many were killed and relatively, as the rest were rotated out — except for the occasional conversation around the crude base bars or mechanics' shops that go along the lines of "Hey, remember Sgt. Johnson and that dummy of his? They were pretty good!" or "You should have been at that USO show with Gary Cooper when one of our own guys did a pretty decent routine . . ." until it seemed that Bob Johnson and his chatty little dummy were never there.

But, for them, their story was just getting started.

-16-

"KAREN? Karen?"

Franks had gone through the house three times but still couldn't find any trace of his girlfriend, which was odd because the Saab was in the driveway, her purse and keys were on the kitchen counter, and, even more troubling, the front door was unlocked. He went around the yard twice and the garage once, growing increasingly concerned.

Karen never left the front door unlocked.

Although Wyvern Falls wasn't exactly a hotbed of crime and burglary, it was one of those things she was fanatical about, to the extreme of even accidentally locking Franks out on occasion when he was simply out mowing the lawn.

It was when he had walked back into the kitchen that it occurred to him that something there wasn't quite right. Stepping back to the archway that connected it to the dining room, it took him a moment to pick up what wasn't right.

Then it struck him: it looked *staged*.

The keys, the purse.

Then he saw something on the floor by the stove. It was a tiny dart. Next to it were several drops of fresh blood.

Franks was startled by someone pounding on the front door. From the way the leaded glass was rattling in its panes, it sounded like they were doing it with a giant mallet. Placing the dart carefully on the counter, he jogged down the hallway to the front of the house and threw the door open.

Standing there on his front porch in black jeans and a black *Go Army* t-shirt was Tucker, one giant fist about to come down on the door again. For a moment, Franks was afraid he was going to get conked square on the head.

"Uh, s-sorry Jim," Tucker said sheepishly, dropping his hand to his side, "but we got to go."

Franks was befuddled. "What!? Tucker, I can't go anywhere, Karen's disappeared . . . I think something's happened. I think I need to call the police!"

Tucker put one massive paw on Franks' shoulder, "I know," he said, "That's why you have to come with me. I think it h-h-as to do with why Darcy d-disappeared." He pointed to his car, a bright blue 1971 Dodge Charger R/T with a spoiler and black racing stripes sporting 15-inch chrome mag wheels that had been left idling half onto Franks' lawn.

"Now. We gotta hurry."

"*You saw her!?*" Franks said as he buckled his seat belt. No sooner had he done so then Tucker floored the gas pedal. The Charger's 440 cubic inch V8 roared to life and the big Goodyear tires bit, sending a fair volume of Franks' lawn sailing through the air. Across the street, old Mister Evans, in the process of sweeping his front walkway, nearly dropped of a coronary in front of his tidy Sears Roebuck house.

The massive car took off like a rocket.

Despite the spacious interior, Tuckers' bulky six-foot-three frame made it look cramped. This particular model featured bucket seats in black vinyl, a pistol grip shifter, and one of those heavy-duty steering wheels that all but disappeared in the librarian's hands. As an absurd touch, two small Pinky and the Brain stuffed animals were wedged on top of the dashboard. Franks instinctively had his legs braced wide in the passenger seat, feeling oddly vulnerable with the old-style waist-only seatbelt.

The Charger was living up to its name as they flew down the streets towards the river, getting the attention of more than one gawking passerby.

"I came out the front d-doors of the library to try and catch you but it was too late. That's when I saw the old Ford F100 pick-up going down Main Street. S-same as in the photo. It looked like th-that guy was driving . . . and Karen was in the front seat like sh-she was sleeping."

"You're sure it was her?"

"Oh *yeah*," he said definitively, giving Franks one of his sheepish grins. "Every guy in town is *sure* when it comes to s-seeing your girlfriend. No offense." Tucker gunned the car through a yellow light as they crossed Hudson and the car went momentarily airborne with the steep incline of the road, dropping back down to terra firma with a sickening jar that bottomed out the shocks and rattled Frank's teeth.

"Why were you trying to catch me?" Franks asked, once he got his senses back.

Turner expertly swerved around a clueless mom who was opening her

SUV's door on the traffic side of the street while talking on a cell-phone and glanced briefly at his passenger. "I saw it in one of the photos. On the shelf. Darcy's Kitty-Cat earrings. And when I called Cary O'Donnell at the village clerk's office to find out about the plot arrangements at the Raadsel campground she said she'd been worried about Darcy and her interest in one of the carnival guys."

"Bob Johnson?"

"The one and only."

Franks considered this. On one level, he was seething that anybody, let alone a carnival quack, should have done anything to the love of his life. On the surface was a dangerous calm. "Shouldn't we call the cops or something?" he said evenly. There was only one cop he could think of he would seriously consider calling – John Easton – and he hadn't returned his message yet.

"I already did. I got the distinct sense the dispatcher wasn't taking me too seriously. She said they would send someone to, to look into it. You know what that means."

"We're the ones looking into it."

"You're th-the man."

Franks had to admit that truck him just fine. He was looking forward to an interesting and fruitful discussion with Mister Johnson and his sidekick. Then something else strange sank into Franks' thoughts.

"Hey, Tucker?"

"Hmm?"

He pointed at the dashboard. The Charger was zooming down Main past a row of old shops including Accardo's pawn store. "Is that an eight-track player?"

"Damn straight."

"And . . . .it *actually works?*" Incredulous, he realized he had been listening to The Beach Boys for the last few minutes. Michael Love was singing *I Get Around* and had just been explaining that "my buddies and me are getting real well known - the bad guys know us and they leave us alone."

Tucker glanced at the console. "I had to re-magnetize the heads and replace some parts, but she works like a charm. Every so often I'll find some tapes at a tag sale or on Craig's List."

Franks held on as the car swerved onto the overpass ramp at the Metro North Station. "I would have thought Sly and the Family Stone or the theme from Shaft would have been a little more appropriate for the whole black guy/70s muscle car shtick."

Tucker let out a laugh. "That's only for the ladies."

The trailer was empty and the pick-up truck was gone.

Except for a couple of run-down-looking trailers and one sad RV that looked like it was held together by a lot of wishful thinking, the parking grounds were deserted.

Tucker had fishtailed the Charger to stop in a spray of dirt and pine needles next to a stand of old spruce trees, and a moment later they were jogging towards the Airstream. Tucker was armed with a tire iron he had retrieved from the trunk. Franks had a flat-eyed look on his face as they reached the trailer door and, finding it unlocked, started to yank it open. The next thing he knew he was sitting on his ass in the dirt to the side. In one fluid motion, Tucker had reached with one massive hand, grabbed Franks' shoulder and thrown him down to the ground backwards. Franks got as far as 'What the hell are you—?" when he saw the deadly bundle of rusted knife blades swinging back and forth on a chain hung from the entrance roof. He felt a sick feeling in his stomach as he realized how close he had come to having either his face or neck cut to ribbons.

"Had a hunch he might have left us a greeting card or two," Tucker said softly. "Better let me go first."

For all his bulk, the librarian was nimble and as light-footed as a cat. Two more nasty surprises had to be disarmed before he gave the All Clear. One was a classic hand-grenade tripwire in the hallway, the other turned out to be a bowl of acid set to tip from the top shelf of the closet when the door was opened. When he stepped inside, Franks found his temper had cooled considerably.

"Where the hell did you learn how to deal with this stuff?" Franks finally asked.

"I did a stint in Special Ops," Tucker said off-handedly.

"Really?" Franks was impressed.

Tucker grinned. "Nah, just kidding. I just read a lot."

Franks gave him a sidelong glance, not sure which way his leg was being pulled.

"Sure. Right."

Aside from the booby traps, however, the trailer had been thoroughly emptied out from top to bottom.

Except for the note taped to the window.

Written in pencil on a piece of standard ruled paper, it read:

I'M LATE, I'M LATE! FOR A VERY IMPORTANT DATE!

"Shit," Franks said, a growing sense of helpless fear pervading his thoughts. That sent his heart racing while a series of random thoughts shot through him: *What if she's gone? [She's dead.] She loved you. You fucked up. You lost her. [She's being tortured.] Why did you have to pick up that goddamn phone?*

The two men were sitting outside on top of one of the roughshod picnic benches provided by the Parks Department.

"Any bright ideas?" he asked.

Tucker was hunched over, hands crossed, frowning. His right forefinger was tapping restlessly.

"Well, at least we have enough to get the cops off their asses. Hand grenades are highly illegal, even if we were technically breaking and entering. But this isn't good, my friend. I think we're running out of time."

Franks was sitting with his right hand cupping his left fist, subconsciously making a meditation grip. He couldn't believe it was all coming down to this. Two guys sitting around going "Oh fuck. Well at least we gave it the ole' college try."

He nearly jumped as a whirr and clang came from the trailer. Tucker kept staring forward at nothing. "Compressor," he said, "For the refrigerator. The power's still on."

That triggered a memory, a scrap of conversation he'd had or overheard recently. A joke? No, something John Easton had said the other day when he was driving him to the hospital. About a ridiculous case where some guy had been tapping off the IBM utility line to power his house undetected for twenty years and only got caught after he sold the house and forgot to disconnect it.

"Bit of a Dummy!" Easton had added.

It took Franks a moment to realize he was looking up at the sky, stunned.

The refrigerator.
The power's still on.
You picked up the goddamned phone.

"Holy shit!" he said and this time he jumped off the bench, whacking Tucker on the back as he did. "We got to move, bucko. I think I know where they are!"

17.

IT *WAS A* slow process, but Bob Johnson was a patient and methodical student. At first, it took a bit of trial and error to work out the process of exchange between man and puppet. The witch doctor had tried to explain it, but of course Johnson didn't really understand it – it was like trying to explain to someone how to ride a bike before they'd gotten on – but once he figured it out it was relatively easy and he eventually was able to do it on the fly.

The other stuff was more difficult.

Maintaining the Johnson body when he wasn't in it. He'd grabbed many of Saguma's supplies before escaping the hut, but learning what to do with them was a whole other conundrum.

That had taken time and effort.

In that sense, the carnival circuit was a perfect match for his research, particularly in the early days just after the war, a circuit that often led down the stranger back roads and byways of America. In New Orleans, he had found several good resources (after working through a lot of fakers) versed in the black arts, and there had been the half insane sorcerer he'd hooked up with in the Bayou for a week, the gibbering man with the cataracts. Most of his so-called spells had been bogus, but his divination skills with live animals had been useful, as had been his supply of knives.

There had been the pansy in Seattle he'd met who he'd played along with to learn the man's doll-making skills – he'd had his own shop near downtown – and the poor guy thought he'd made a friend and lover, revolting as it was to Bob, and found his death instead. At least he'd had a decent stash of money in the apartment upstairs from the shop.

And so it went. A scrap of information here, a useful technique there.

Staying in the doll most of the time, increasing his longevity. And developing new skills.

But it hadn't dawned on him until years later that there was a price to pay for all *these endeavors, one that the New Guinea witch doctor had neglected to mention.*

Or perhaps it had been in the fine print.

He was slowly going insane.

Arguably Bob Johnson had never been one to score high points in the healthy and balanced department but his quirks had essentially been harmless before the war and the subsequent events in New Guinea.

But combining sociopathic behaviors with black arts and a fragile psyche was not proving to be a good lifetime strategy, especially over decades. On one or more levels Bob realized that this couldn't go on as indefinitely as he'd hoped. For starters, the flesh and blood body, despite his best ministrations and techniques, was beginning to decay, and, in this case at least, was a critical component of the arrangement. When Bob's physical body went, his soul, anima, whatever one wished to call it, would expire not long after.

But there was one thing he would like to accomplish before that happened.

At some point recently Bob had decided he wanted a family.

One that involved a wife, a mother, and a son.

And of course . . . they'd need their little puppets too.

-18-

THEY FOUND the Ford pick-up behind the old ice factory, half covered with an old tarp.

It only took minutes to get here and this time the cops had been called and were on their way. But neither Franks nor Tucker were ones to sit idly by and wait for the cavalry, however prudent that might be. The point became moot when they both heard the scream.

From Karen.

It was Franks who found the way into the old Knickerbocker & Sons ice house. Forcing open a rotted set of hurricane doors (the lock and chain simply pulled out), he found a short flight of steps leading down to an entrance walled off with plywood that, from the amount of mildew and spider webs, had been installed quite some time ago. Franks put his shoulder to it and the flimsy barrier buckled and fell inward with a shower of dirt and debris. Brushing off the worst of it (including a couple of large, but confused spiders), he stepped gingerly into the gloom of the basement, Tucker close behind.

Low-ceilinged with extra-heavy beams and drainage piping, the basement had apparently become a repository for all sorts of junk over the years. Everything from old file cabinets, metal signs, car fenders and hoods that looked like they dated back to the 1930s were strewn about, covered with dust, cobwebs, and mold. There was even an upright piano in one corner, burst open, with bundles of broken wire hanging over the remaining keys like an exotic plant. Feeble light came in from a few heavily barred, slot windows.

The place looked like a junk picker's paradise - if one could simply avoid dealing with the new tenant who'd taken over the main floor.

A thud and muffled cry from upstairs had them hopping over the debris as quickly as possible toward a large wide stairwell near the far left wall. This led up to an entrance loading area on the first floor, barred by massive wooden doors. Behind them, a second set of doors, apparently leading into the main area, were closed. To the north side appeared to be the shipping clerk's area with its counter and window. To the south side was what looked like administrative offices.

They chose the former office and found themselves in a half empty room with plaster and wainscoting that had another window and door opening onto the main warehouse floor. Most of the glass had been shattered years ago and, as they stepped carefully across the debris-strewn floor, they saw a truly bizarre tableau before them.

The main floor was opened up to a sloped roof two stories up. Along the length of the building, which was perhaps sixty feet, was an array of beams, gantries, and pulley and hook systems. Rays of light gleamed through sooty glass panes, most which appeared intact. Dust motes whirled lazily through the warm summer air and, from one high corner, came the hum of a wasps' nest. It was an almost idyllic scene that as a print might have been labeled: "Antique Warehouse Study in Yellows and Browns." Provided, of course, that one didn't allow one's eyes to drop to the bottom part of the scene. Then, everything slewed towards the horrifying.

Although he had been setting up shop since the week before, Johnson hadn't had sufficient time to organize things properly and consequently his work area had an improvised, ad hoc look to it.

Not that his visitors were deeply concerned about this.

To one side was a work bench with various ventriloquist's dolls and doll replacement parts scattered on it. There were some open crates, an old Air Pilot kerosene lantern, a lathe, several haphazard piles of lumber, and a spray booth. Near one corner were several issues of Home Woodworker, some with pages carefully flagged with Post-it notes. On the opposite side was a battered industrial sink, some shelving on which many jars and accessories had been hastily stored, and an old Dutch folding table on which the Philco radio was softly playing Benny Goodman.

On the far side, the warehouse was sectioned off by a one-story refrigerated room sealed by a medieval looking wooden door with massive latches and iron hinges.

In front of that though, were the strings of shrunken heads, desiccated body parts, one complete hanging human skeleton, at least a dozen scalps of recent vintage, and an assortment of rare New Guinea tribal masks, voodoo statues (including a terrifying one of Baron Samedi on his cross – Lord of The Dead – made out of a real human skull and hair), a bunch of surgical equipment, and an old artificial respirator.

On one small surgeon's table was strapped Danny, minus his lower legs, with a leather gag tied around his mouth, his eyes bulging in terror and pain, despite the morphine drip being fed into his arm. The legs, still in their shoes, had been set carefully aside next to his head. Before an oversized oak workbench, facing away from them, was Bob Johnson, with shirtsleeves rolled up.

Strapped atop the bench like the proverbial human sacrifice, stark naked, was Karen. Her entire body glistening with a purifying oil from Johnson's own recipe book. For one horrifying moment, Franks thought the ventriloquist was doing something to her, from the motions his arms were making, but a moment later Johnson half turned, revealing that he had been brushing something carefully along the edge of a ceremonial *kris*, or dagger, while humming to himself.

Karen was shaking her head back and forth and then stopped, eyes widening as she saw Franks peering over the broken interior window sill, with Tucker right behind him. He could see tears streaming from her eyes and, clenching his teeth to stop from yelling her name out, instead put a finger to his lips and then motioned for her to not keep looking at them. She simply closed her eyes and turned her head back up towards the ceiling.

Sitting off to one side on the table was Mickey in a slightly slumped *Off Duty* pose.

Even as Franks and Tucker were trying to figure out their next move, the humming stopped.

"You boys like what you see?"

The voice came from behind them.

A *woman's* voice.

Or rather, a woman's voice trying to sound like a little girl.

In unison, Tucker and Franks slowly turned their heads.

The back of the shipping clerk's office was a floor-to-ceiling wall of wooden shelves and cubby slots – some with moldering ledgers and boxes and various debris – but in the central area, where a cabinet had been, a shape was just barely visible in the gloom.

Sitting there on the shelf was a ventriloquist's dummy. Even in the shadows, a glint of light reflected off the open eyes. The straight, page-boy cut gray hair was nearly identical to Darcy Van Wort's, Tucker realized.

As was the high-pitched voice.

The two things that were decidedly un-Wort-like were the lacy American-Girl-style dress and the hefty ball peen hammer lying across the little lap.

Tucker motioned "go!" to Franks, pointing towards the open warehouse and the table where Karen was strapped, the tire iron gripped firmly in his other hand.

The Darcy doll dropped to the floor with a light thud, the hammer clasped in her diminutive hands.

"Hi, Mister Brooks!" she said a chirpy yet slightly knowing voice.

"Would you like to play with me?"

The hammer swayed back and forth.

Tucker's only response was to shake the tire iron. He may have been a man of various odd habits, but talking to dolls wasn't one of them.

The Darcy doll ran in a looping circle around the librarian just as Franks threw open the door and ran into the warehouse.

At the table, which Franks noted had all the classic trappings of the quintessential sacrificial altar (thought he would have been willing to testify without hesitation that the offered victim was in no way a virgin), Bob Johnson had finished up his knife-sharpening exercise and picked up a large glass of some viscous-looking liquid and was gulping it down, apparently to prepare for the next phase of whatever ritual he was up to. His demeanor and casual 50s attire suggested nothing more than just another guy enjoying an afternoon cocktail or two, provided one ignored the deadly *kris* held blade-down in the other hand.

Franks paused long enough to snatch up the first thing he could find to use as a weapon – a fractured piece of two-by-four on the floor – just as Johnson spotted him.

To his surprise, Johnson raised the glass in a half salute and said cheerfully, "Well, hey, there, fella, care to lend an old man a helping hand?"

"You son of a—" Franks said as he charged head first, swinging the two-by-four.

The blade came around more quickly than he would have guessed.

In the shipping office, Tucker was hunched in a semi-squat position, keeping himself facing the doll as she looped around him. In her girly Darcy-voice she giggled and said, "This is so much fun!"

She ran three complete circuits, putting Tucker's nerves on edge, before suddenly cutting in. Tucker swung with the tire iron and missed as she dodged between his legs and, a moment later, he howled in pain as the hammer connected with the side of his shin, dropping him to one knee.

The doll kept running, sprinting partly up the opposite wall like the world's weirdest skateboarder executing a half-pipe, before coming back straight at Tucker, hammer swinging.

He rolled to the side as she shot past – just missing his head with the ball peen – feinted right, then ran left to circle back at him. This time, he dodged sideways and swung again, and again met empty air. The doll was just too damned quick.

"Ha! Ha! Missed me!" she giggled, nimbly jumping back.

The cat-and-mouse routine went on a few minutes more, Tucker aware of his panting breath and pounding heart (and a bunch crashes from the other room), cursing himself for his sedentary lifestyle. There was little time for regrets, however, as the doll went on the attack again, pulling a reverse and this time a zig-zagging approach.

In the gloom, it was hard to get an accurate read on distances and Tucker swung wildly again, this time connecting with one of the doll's legs, cleanly snapping it, but even as he did he saw the hammer coming down too fast in an overhand strike. Reflexively he threw his left arm up.

He heard the *crack* of his ulna and radius fracturing a moment before the fierce bolt of pain registered, but then he was rolling on his back, knees pistoning up, and ejecting the doll over him. He rocked forward as she landed in a tumble and, trying to gain his knees, failed and did a half spin as a wave of nausea enveloped him.

The Darcy doll tried to stand up, couldn't, then began to drag herself forward awkwardly using one leg and the busted stump of the other. The mouth opened as if in excited anticipation and Tucker could see, to his horror, that it was lined with human teeth.

Then, using his good hand, the tire iron swung down, square onto the wooden skull, smashing it.

Again and again.

Torn hair, shattered rods and levers, one eyeball rolled away, trailing gossamer wires.

Tucker, angry, terrified, and howling like a wounded bear, kept swinging until the doll was nothing more than a pulverized mess.

Then he dropped the tire iron, bent over, and threw up.

Franks felt the blade slice through his shirt and into the meat of his upper shoulder, even as the wood in his hands connected with the side of Johnson's chest. Then his momentum sent the two of them sprawling into the shelves, knocking bottles and shrunken heads and statuettes every which way. Franks gained his feet first, stepping back with the two-by-four held like a bat in his hands, hair hanging in his face and a wild look in his eyes.

Johnson stood up and slow blinked, a big smile on his face. Franks swung at his head and was surprised when the ventriloquist caught it with lightning speed in one hand, an inch from his face. "That's not being very nice!" he said cheerfully.

Franks' response was an equally swift left roundhouse kick that caught Johnson square on the jaw. Johnson's smile became a sloppy grin and then, swinging his head drunkenly, he rolled his eyes up and collapsed.

Franks looked down at the unconscious form.

"That's because I'm not in a particularly nice mood today, asshole."

A moment later, Franks was over at the table, using his pocket knife to cut through the leather thongs binding Karen's wrists to the oak top. He was just about through the second thong when he caught a movement out of the corner of his eye.

It was Mickey's head swiveling towards him.

The eyes flicked open.

"Hiya buddy!" Mickey said. He slowly got onto his feet while Franks took a step back, distantly aware that his shoulder felt like it was on fire, and that the burn was spreading.

Mickey pounced.

It was something of a ludicrous wrestling match: a fashionably dressed art director tumbling around on the warehouse floor in a death grip with the ventriloquist's dummy, but there was nothing funny about it to Franks. He'd taken several vicious blows to his face from the tiny wooden fists and had narrowly missed getting his nose (and, once, his ear) bitten off several times. Franks had taken a couple of nips to his arms in the confusion and lost a clump or two of hair, but with dawning horror he realized something else was going terribly wrong – his entire shoulder had gone numb, as had the side of his face – and it felt as if all the strength was draining out of his body.

He finally wound up on his back and understood that this was about to end badly – very badly – for him. His right arm went all funny and just fell away, only his left hand, gripping the dummy's neck, was keeping his enemy at bay.

As if sensing this shift in the fight, Mickey relaxed slightly. The smell of spoiled meat wafted out of his mouth as he leaned forward and said, "I think I'll have your larynx for lunch, laddy." Franks could clearly see the badly stained human teeth lining the mouth and the painted rubber throat hole as the jaws yawned wide.

Then: *thwunk*!

Mickey's head vanished.

It took Franks' now-fuddled mind to register the breeze, the swinging two-by-four that had connected squarely with the doll's head, and the same head being sent arcing and tumbling though the air, trailing wires and springs – like a very large and hideous softball – to ricochet off one of the beams and land with a shattering crash on one of the iron drainage grates on the floor, sending pieces every which way. The remains of the head rolled to a stop on its side, one eye shattered, a large chunk of its wooden head broken off, revealing a hollow brain cavity inside.

The broken jaw opened just slightly and the other eye went half closed in a sly wink.

The body was tossed aside (along with the two-by-four) and Franks stared up into Karen's face. She crouched over him, stark naked, tears in her eyes, and placed a cool hand on his cheek.

He could barely feel it.

Paralysis was spreading through his body. He felt his consciousness receding.

"Darling, what's wrong? What's happening?" she whispered, alarmed.

"Everything's fine," he slurred, "I-I . . .lo—" but he couldn't finish. His tongue wouldn't move.

"Shhhhh," she sobbed and bent to kiss him.

Then, as the darkness seeped in, he saw the figure appear over her shoulder. He also saw the knife was coming down, but he was helpless . . .

-19-

THE CRACK of the .30 caliber rifle, even in the open ice house, was deafening.

The hand with the blade stopped in mid-air, the owner thrown off by the impact of the steel-jacketed round entering and exiting his chest cavity. The blade made another attempt at its target – Karen's naked back – but was stymied again by another bullet in the chest.

And another.

And another.

Seven rounds in all, sending Bob Johnson staggering back against the big table, the *kris* clattering harmlessly to the floor.

Over by the open side entrance to the ice-house stood an old man with fierce aborigine features, his close-cropped woolly hair now white, the scar on the side of his face still livid against his black and leathery skin. In his arms was an old Army Surplus M-1 Garand, standard issue to so many G.I.s back in World War Two.

Bob Johnson stood for a moment longer, gaping in surprise.

Then the man with the rifle shot him through the mouth.

There was a metallic *katching* as the empty M-1 clip ejected out the top of the breech and clanged off the floor.

This time Johnson dropped straight on his face.

A moment later, the man was at Karen's side, covering her with his short-sleeved shirt. He tried to pull her away but she wouldn't budge.

"What's wrong with him!?" she cried. "I think he's dying!"

"Give me some room," the man said in a surprisingly young-sounding voice, "I will try to help, but it may be too late."

She looked at him with mascara-streaked eyes. "Who are you?"

"My name is Shell. Like the oil company. I've come many years and many miles to end this."

-20-

JIM FRANKS snapped his eyes open.

He'd been having a dream, an awful dream, where he was paralyzed on the oak table in the warehouse, his head half-turned while he watched Mickey tearing into Karen's torso next to him. He could hear the grisly grunting and tearing sounds, then the dummy reared its gore-splattered head, holding the torn-out heart muscle in his tiny hands.

Mickey grinned: "You know the heart is always the sweetest part, bucko!"

Then it was over.

Outside the bedroom window, the sky was just lightening with a hint of the new day arriving. The first few birds tentatively spoken up, alerting the neighborhood that, once again, darkness has passed and the coming light is on schedule.

The sheets felt cool in the queen-sized master bed. In the twilight coming though the tall Victorian windows, he could make out Karen's form lying next to him, sleeping on her side as she usually did. He took a deep breath and let it out, then another, just because he could. Breathing.

Such a simple thing that we take for granted every day.

Breathing. The basic function of being alive.

The elderly Japanese owner of the Karate dojo he'd trained at had given an entire meditation lecture on it just the week before.

Must appreciate. Something so simple.

Franks understood.

Karen had filled him in later on what had happened, with some help from Tucker.

It turned out that the paralytic on the knife wasn't a fatal toxin, it was intended to numb the victim while certain . . . *work* . . . was performed. Like a powerful anesthesia.

Fortunately, neither of them had to find out just what work Johnson had in mind.

The police did show up ten minutes later, along with a couple of much-needed ambulances. Before they did, however, the man named Shell had gathered all of Johnson's accessories into a pile outside, located some dried kindling, and burned it.

Karen, who refused to leave Franks' side, had said, "Isn't that destroying evidence of a crime?"

Shell had given her a fierce look. "Let them put me in jail. These things must be destroyed. They are evil, and no man should possess them, as they will possess him. Like they did him," he added, pointing to Johnson's prostrate form.

Karen shuddered.

After that, the subject was closed.

In the refrigerated cooler, they found the body of Darcy Van Wort, along with several other earlier projects Bob Johnson had apparently attempted and failed. Police Chief Hendricks, who looked exhausted, stood by with arms folded and a steely look in his eye, wondering if finally, just possibly finally, this nightmare of a week was over.

He also wondered if this whole fiasco of Carnival Week might cost him his job, appointment or not. He decided he didn't much care. In the meantime, Lieutenant Sanchez did a remarkable job of handling the crime scene.

Shell had been whisked off in handcuffs to the police station for questioning and to be booked for murder and for destroying evidence, though he was released twenty-four hours later at the police chief's discretion when, according to the coroner, Bob Johnson had already been dead. For years, according to the report, which, of course, utterly stumped the investigation.

"How the fuck can I arrest my only suspect for murdering a dead man?" the chief ranted at the White Plains coroner later in his office, "Can you explain that?"

"It's certainly one for the books," Lon Cheever, the coroner, had replied, thinking about another corpse currently cooling on a slab at his office that was *also* most certainly one for the books.

Sanchez had also been there for that conversation, twirling a pencil in his hand. ". . . and yet, Mister Johnson was able to perform live, in a deceased state, for an audience? Is there any possible medical precedent for this?"

"I'm looking into it. Believe me, I'm looking into it," the coroner had answered.

Danny was still alive – barely – and would require many operations and months of therapy. They were able to reattach only one of his legs. But as subsequent events would show, it would prove a positive life-changing experience in a terrible way. Danny's atheist days were behind him for good.

Tucker would have his arm in a cast for a couple of months and Franks, amazingly, would walk away with only superficial cuts and bruises. Still, they kept him at the hospital for three days on I.V. antibiotics for the bites alone.

But he was lucky.

Shell had come by the hospital to say goodbye and wish him luck. He reluctantly explained bits of the history of what had happened, and what little he knew about what Bob Johnson had accomplished in his own horrible way.

"We cannot cheat death, and the price to do so is terrible."

"That's what my plastic surgeon says," Franks had replied. "But seriously, what do you think was in that glass he was drinking just before I hit him?"

Shell considered this. "No way to know for sure – something new he was working on perhaps. In a way, Mister Bob was a pioneer, finding knowledge far beyond and far more evil than what the witch doctor I introduced him to ever knew."

"Well, either way, Shell, we owe you a big-time. I don't want to think about what might have happened if you hadn't dropped by when you had."

"Then don't," Shell had replied.

"Anytime you need anything, anything, just ask. It's yours."

A sad look had come over the New Guinea native's face. "You owe me nothing. I was responsible for all that happened." After a few moments of silence, he had added, "But I was a child . . . I wanted to help . . . and caused so much death instead. You see? This is the terrible truth of life sometimes."

Franks got it.

"You awake?"

Karen let out a sleepy chuckle, "Maybe."

He turned over and put a hand on her shoulder, then let it slide around to her breast, where he lightly touched her nipple. He was thrilled to find she had slipped into bed naked after he had crashed the previous night.

"Definitely," she amended a moment later.

Then she turned her head towards him so he could kiss her full on the lips.

He felt his groin stiffen and that irresistible urge begin to take him, but, instead of his hand moving lower towards that wonderful spot, he instead cupped her cheek and looked intensely into her eyes.

"Karen?"

"Yes?"

"What you told me . . . out at the Point? When everything went to hell in a hand-basket?"

He felt her body tense slightly. Their eyes remained locked.

"*Yes?*"

"I didn't get the chance to tell you . . . I just wanted to tell you that I love you, too. Big time."

Her whole face lit up.

"I love you. *Big time*," she whispered.

The rest that followed didn't require words.

That evening, they were sitting out on the back patio finishing up dinner. Karen had thrown together a dinner of pan-seared chicken, angel hair pasta with pesto sauce, and fresh garden tomatoes in balsamic vinegar with chopped onions, olive oil and fresh garden basil.

Not for the first time, Franks wondered how on earth he had hooked up with such an amazing cook for a girlfriend.

Franks had his legs crossed, a glass of Portuguese white *Dao* in one hand. After three days of awful hospital food and pumped full of antibiotics, the food and wine left him giddy. The wine was light and fruity – a perfect summer wine, he decided.

Overhead, crows started their own conversation. Franks wondered if they were complaining about the neighborhood going to hell with so many finches moving in.

Karen had just taken the plates in and was coming out to refill her own glass.

"Honey?"

"What?" Karen said, as she took the bottle out of the ice bucket and filled her glass. She stood looking at him, one brow raised, a little smile playing on her lips.

"Well, I just wanted to apologize. For screwing up our rescue operation and everything. You ended up saving my ass back there. I thought it was supposed to be the other way around . . . like in the movies."

She laughed. It was rich and musical.

"James, the fact you even came for me was enough." Her eyes took on a dreamy look. "No one ever did that you know . . . not even my ex."

"Seriously? Not even—"

"-eriously," she said, cutting him off. She put down her glass and stepped around behind him, resting her hands on his shoulders. She was the only woman he'd ever known to do that. "Besides, I think we can agree it was Mister Shell who earned the honors."

"Well, perhaps," he said finally, "In case you were wondering though, I still love you."

That got another smile. "I know, you just said it a few minutes ago."

"Ah . . . I'm just trying it out you know . . . getting used to saying the 'L' word and all. Practice makes perfect and all that." He looked like he was enjoying himself. But in a way he also felt energized, like some magic line had been crossed and thought, "Funny how a single word can do that."

Karen bent down, snuck one hand down his shirt, and said lazily in his ear, "You can practice all you want, but I think this teacher wants a lesson . . ."

Later that night at the morgue, the fluorescent lights suddenly flickered on. The click of the door being opened sounded abnormally loud in the sterile underground space, as was the subsequent patter of small feet.

They walked past the storage doors and straight to the row of gurneys with their sheet-covered residents awaiting the following morning's autopsy procedures. It had been a busy weekend with the unusual backlog coming in from Wyvern Falls. The body count alone was one for the books this week.

The footsteps paused.

There was the whisper of a sheet being pulled off and softly dropping to the floor.

Then another.

On the cold metal gurney, Bob Johnson's eyes flew open.

As did Darcy Van Wort's on the one next to him.

He looked over and smiled.

"Hello there, pumpkin!" His voice sounded oddly garbled, with a slight whistle due to the damage at the back of his throat.

It might be time for someone else to take up the reins on the routine.

But at least the new formula he had been tinkering with seemed to be working. And the second set of dummies he'd hidden in the truck . . . the cops had even found them and left them.

Things were sure looking up!

"Hi, Sugarpop!" Darcy said.

They looked at each other.

"It feels so naughty to be naked," she added coyly. Then she reached down and hoisted up her dummy. "It was so smart of you to have made their siblings as well . . . we'll have such a happy family!"

"You betcha, Darcy-kins!" Bob agreed, picking up a newer, if slightly cruder version of Mickey. "Or Bob's your uncle!"

The next day, Lieutenant Sanchez and Captain Fowler were sitting in the police chief's office.

"You have got to be kidding me. This is not . . . fucking . . . *possible*," Sanchez was saying. He was having great difficulty grasping what the handful of photos on the chief's desk were telling him.

Hendricks was sitting behind his desk, fingers steepled, surprisingly calm. It was the first time he could ever recall hearing his top lieutenant use a four-letter word, let alone in his presence.

Fowler was sitting with his leg crossed ankle-to-knee, British fashion, rubbing his chin. "These were taken at White Plains Airport at 7:34 AM. this morning?"

"From airport security cameras. Tickets were paid for in cash. Destination was Washington D.C. – Dulles actually – with a transfer to San Francisco that was never boarded. Dulles is looking through their footage to see what they got right now. I just heard from the morgue. Their bodies are unaccounted for as of now."

Sanchez picked up the photos again. "Sir, this is just way too . . . too weird and creepy. I mean, it definitely looks like Bob Johnson and Darcy Van Wort but that's utterly impossible . . . and those dolls . . . what on earth do you make of them?"

Hendricks looked uneasily at his lieutenant. "There are some things you don't want to think too much about, Lieutenant."

Fowler gestured with his fingers. "Maybe it's time you rang up that Easton fellow?"

Hendricks shot him a sideways look, "I was afraid you were going to say that."

EPILOGUE

July 11th, Mooney's Bar & Grill, Main Street, Wyvern Falls

THE THREE MEN sitting at the bar that Monday night pretty much had the place to themselves. The regulars were off duty at the other end and, aside from a few college kids and their dates playing pool by the far seating area, the place was empty except for the men, Pat Mooney, and a bored-looking waitress who was counting the minutes until her shift ended.

On the old Wurlitzer jukebox, a band called Johnny Society came on, rocking it out with a catchy little number called *Don't Talk Me Down.*

Jim Franks had a beer in front of him – a Bavarian white ale – and a bowl of mixed nuts. To his left sat John Easton, nursing a single malt as usual, and, to his right, Tucker Brooks had a steaming cup of hot cocoa which Pat Mooney had reluctantly produced with a shaking head.

Mooney sauntered up and spread his hands on the bar, eyeing Franks and Tucker up and down with a sad face but mischievous eyes. "So, what's this I hear about you two boys getting beaten up by a couple of dolls? Say it ain't so."

"It ain't so," Franks replied soberly, "They were Keebler elves, two dozen if memory serves, and they were heavily armed."

Tucker nodded his head in agreement. "Yeah, ghetto elves with brass knuckles. They fought dirty. But we got the better of them in the end."

Mooney chuckled and ran a hand through his silver hair. "Your mothers would be proud. Next round is on me, then."

Franks turned to Easton. "How you healing up? And what really happened up at Castle Krell?"

Easton took a pull of his scotch. This time, it was a ten-year-old Dalmore with a deep amber cast. He was particular to the smooth and slightly peaty taste. He waited until Mooney had drifted out of earshot and then gave them an abridged version of the story.

"Holy shit," Franks said, "And I thought I was having a weird week."

He'd given Easton a recap of his own adventures earlier over the phone, which was when the detective suggested they meet up for a drink. "Maybe we should get Tucker here to put this all into a book, like the ones he keeps threatening to write. Not that anyone would believe any of it."

"I wouldn't," Tucker agreed. Then he looked at his cast and shoulder sling. "I'll never look at ventriloquist's dummies quite the same way again, though. I promise you that."

"Amen," Franks said raising his beer. "Here's to not trusting dummies. And fortune tellers."

Glass clinked as the salute was met.

The mood grew somber as the moody voice of Nicole Atkins now filled the bar singing *Neptune City*. She sounded like a female Roy Orbison singing for a David Lynch soundtrack.

"So now you've joined the ranks of dog owners?"

Easton nodded. "After a fashion, I suppose. I'm calling him Rovsky. But it's more like he's adopted me. And I'm not sure 'dog' is an accurate term. 'Giant hairy beast' is more accurate. Like a werewolf crossed with some sort of bear, yeah?"

"I bet your house is a lot safer."

"That would be a pretty safe bet," Easton agreed.

"So what happened to the Japanese kid?" Tucker asked, leaning over. "That whole business with Antonio King and the Ghost Seekers International crew was unbelievable. Not a healthy week for television shows here in Wyvern Falls. Not that the cultural landscape of American media will be any the worse with them gone."

"That's a terrible thing to say," he added hastily. "Nobody deserves to die like that. I heard they found that guy's head on a church steeple."

Easton thought about this. "Yeah, that was a pretty rough one, right? But not the first time I've seen someone pay a hefty price for a bad decision. And a lot of these media types think their celebrity status makes them armor-plated. Perhaps there's a grain of truth to this Dunderberg Imp business. I know I'll be sure to tip my hat if I ever sail past his mountain, superstition or not." He looked over at Tucker. "But to answer your first question, the Japanese kid – Hideki is his name – contacted me last week about helping him deal with a bit of antique silver plate he's come into and navigating the international laws of donating some of the proceeds to a charity he wants to set up in Antonio King's name. Something about helping abused children."

"Why the heck would he want to do that?" Franks asked.

"Why don't you ask him yourself?" Easton responded, half turning, "I asked him to join us and if I'm not mistaken, that's him coming through the door right now . . ."

It was 3:00 AM and the lights were still on in the White Plains morgue. The assistant to the county forensics team, Osterman, had been carefully re-photographing the remains of Case #4450-86299, Klaus von

Richtenstein, with particular focus being paid to the glyphs and runes which could just barely made out on the corpse's face.

The office had located relatives of the deceased, who had insisted on immediate cremation and an unmarked burial in Potters Field. And of course Osterman couldn't allow that to happen. Not after what he'd uncovered in the books "borrowed" from the evidence locker – books the police had seized in the investigation.

There was unbelievable knowledge to be uncovered and delved into, at least for one with a methodical and curious mind . . .

Two days later, John Easton drove south along the Taconic Parkway in the Mustang. The amped-up stereo system was playing The Pretenders' *Pack It Up* and Chrissie Hynde was letting it rip about a weenie ex-boyfriend. She sounded seriously PO'd.

Rovsky was sitting in the shotgun seat, massive head out the half-rolled-down window. Easton looked at the dog and grinned, still not sure what to make of him.

He'd decided it was time to take a week's vacation and head out to Montauk Point on Long Island where Roy Hendricks had invited him to hang out. The police chief had invested in a condo there and offered to put up the detective and his dog so they could get in a little striped bass fishing and let things cool down in the Falls.

Easton had never been there but the prospect of a long drive, a beach house, and some fishing was looking like an excellent plan.

Nothing to worry about but getting plenty of sun, sand, and sea.

-THE END-

NOTES FOR THE CURIOUS

SO, HERE we are again, dear reader, at the end of another adventure (or four) in our strange little town up here on the Hudson. I hope you found the stories entertaining, thought-provoking, and maybe even a little informative. I know I did as they were being written.

That's kind of the scary part – I'm not entirely sure where these stories are coming from, let alone how they're coming about. There's more transcribing than actual writing going on, I can tell you, like I've been assigned some mysterious narrator by the guy upstairs.

But that's kind of half the fun, isn't it? That and poking around all the local history and legends that are rife here in the Hudson Valley to see what ghosts get scared up. And believe me, there are a lot of them running around here. Even before Henry Hudson and his crew showed up to get the colony party going the native Indians had had plenty of time to build up a hefty backload of spooks and hauntings.

And the history continues to be made. Like everywhere across the United States, demographics are changing, customs are changing, life is changing.

And yet in so many ways, they're not.

I think people always enjoy a good story, one that takes them away and out of their lives for a little bit. And I like to think that what goes on here in Wyvern Falls is in many ways a microcosm of the country at large.

So I hope you stick around and join me for another tale or two and see what these local characters get up to. They'll be here. I promise.

In the meantime, since a fair amount of these stories are drawn from actual events and history – that thing we call the "real world" – here are some additional notes to satisfy your own curiosity and hopefully encourage you to explore your own horizons a little further.

The Red Baron's Daughter

I've always been drawn to WWI aviation as a kid (along with those terrific Enemy Ace comic books), but it has only been in recent years that I uncovered much grimmer and even disturbing accounts of what these so-called Knights of the Air endured and the terrible price they paid, including the Red Baron himself. Firsthand accounts quickly strip the romance right out of this history, where the average life expectancy of a new pilot was less than two weeks.

Aside from the fictionalized von Richtenstein, many of the scenes depicted in the back-story are intended to be accurate. Richtofen did in fact receive at least one macabre photograph from an admiring fan showing the mangled remains of one of his victims, which was found amongst his personal belongings after his own death in 1918. On the back of the grisly photo was written:

"Sir: I witnessed on March 17, 1917, your air fight and took the photograph which I send to you with hearty congratulations, because you seldom have the occasion to see your prey."
With fraternal greetings,
Baron von Riezenstein, Colonel and Commander of the 87th Reserve Infantry Regiment

Certainly Richtofen developed an increasingly morbid interest in collecting trophies from his victims whenever possible, many which were sent back to his family estate. And, like many aces, over time he developed a death wish, when killing eclipsed their psyches and they continued to fight until they were killed, despite the opportunity to retire from front-line duty. It can be clearly seen in the contrast of the fresh-faced portraits of these men when they first went off to war with the haunted and gaunt, thousand-yard-stare looks of their last photos taken.

Still, credit should be given to them. Having flown in antique biplanes, I cannot image what guts (and perhaps insanity) it took to actually take these flimsy things into combat and shoot at each other, often while doing outrageous and many times fatal aerobatics. For further reading I'd recommend W.W Windstaff's (a pen name) merciless and blackly humorous memoirs as a WWI pilot, Lower Than Angels (Enigma Books, 1993), Aces High by Alan Clark (Barnes & Nobel Books, 1999), They Fought For the Sky by Quentin Reynolds (Rinehart & Company, 1957) and, for the definitive account of the Red Baron, The Red Knight of Germany by Floyd Gibbons stands above the rest for details. Major Thaw was in fact the commander of the 103rd Aero and his biography, like many of his fellow pilots who started out fighting in the Lafayette Escadrille (the American volunteer squadron that would later become legitimized as the 103rd Aero once America got officially involved) reads like some sort of made-up action book hero beyond anything Hollywood could ever dream up. As does Frank Luke, the American 'Balloon Buster' who served as my template for Luke Evans. For experiencing WWI aviation first hand, there is no better resource in the United States than the old Rhinebeck Aerodrome near Rhinebeck, New York, which maintains a museum and flying show of these astonishing aircraft. Special thanks to Hugh Schoelzel (President) and Dan Fleming (Head of Marketing) at Old Rhinebeck (www.oldrhinebeck.org) and apologies for taking liberties with the office there – I really have no idea what's on the second floor of the house aside from the bathroom. Hugh is an ex-TWA pilot and can often be found piloting the museum's whackier contraptions, including that refurbished 1910 Bleriot XI. I heartily recommend visiting the museum and supporting this rich chapter in American history and, for the more intrepid, taking a flight in their 1929 New Standard biplane over the Hudson. It is worth every penny I assure you.

Sometimes in the process of researching these stories, all sorts of stuff get pulled into the mix deliberately but sometimes – subconsciously or perhaps by some other design – other stuff just seeps in. I freely confess to co-opting the idea of the German legend of Lorelei, the siren of the Rhine River who supposedly lures sailors to their deaths, but I had no idea until after I wrote the story that the myth has been ascribed to a certain section of the Hudson River as well and, even stranger, the original location in Germany is near a castle called Reichstein – uncannily close to the protagonist in this story whose name I thought I just pulled out of thin air. But that's what makes this all sort of fun. And spooky....

The Lonely Dancers

At least some of this story is drawn from my own personal experience as a musician and especially the eight years I spent playing the New York City music scene. That included more than a few gigs at the legendary CBGB's among others like Kenny's Castaways, the Bitter End, and even Max's Kansas City during its brief revival in 1997-8. But much of this goes further back to the ancient days of vinyl records and the shops that sold them and that time during college when you are first convinced you are getting into stuff that is really, really cool. For me, one of the most iconic albums for me (it still is 30 plus years later) was an album Strange Man, Changed Man by a band called Bram Tchaikovsky. It had everything: great songs, tight harmonies, well-crafted lyrics, and that uber-cool album art by The Rocking Russian. I confess to shamelessly co-opting his Russian Propaganda Art style for my own band, The Jag, during our early days on the NYC alternative circuit. During the course of writing this story, I was able to track down and purchase a copy of this great album and played it constantly as an inspiration. The Lonely Dancers is a bittersweet tale of love and loss and one of the little-talked-about truisms of the music industry – some bands really only do have one really successful album in them. Whether that was true of Bram Tchaikovsky is not for me to say let alone suggest – this is fiction folks – but running through this story is my not-so-thinly-disguised homage to a band I strongly feel deserved a lot more success and recognition than they got.

There is, however, a bizarre postscript to this story. Six months after it was completed, videos of a Bram Tchaikovsky gig 30 years ago began to surface on the internet, in an eerie parallel to the time frame in the story. Even stranger, six months after that, a Facebook page for Bram Tchaikovsky showed up. Intrigued, I contacted them and came clean about my homage to them and ultimately wound up talking directly with Micky Broadbent, who was equally baffled at this whole turn of events. He has no idea who posted the videos either, nor that they even existed. So, special thanks to Mister Broadbent and Peter Bramall for granting permission to use their likenesses and related references, etc. Micky Broadbent was able to fill me in one the real story of what happened (nothing so tragic or melodramatic as my tale I'm happy to report) and I'm excited to say they are looking to re-master the very same Strange Man, Changed Man album that was such a huge influence on me. I strongly encourage you to visit their Facebook page at:

https://www.facebook.com/pages/Bram-Tchaikovsky-Official/201890943246493

As of this writing they are negotiating with Warner Bros to get 'Strange Man Changed Man' remastered, so please give them your support – they deserve it!

Also special thanks to Bram's original drummer, Keith Boyce, who personally answered my first inquiry about the band and what it was like making that album. There was a loopy surrealness to receiving his email just as I was walking down the meat section of Stop & Shop thirty years after first hearing that album that so influenced my life, my wife looking around with vague embarrassment at people as I jumped up and down yelling, "This is so cool!"

There are plenty of bands, some well-known, some obscure, that shaped the music-scape of the late 70s and early 80s and I heartily recommend tracking down their albums and buying them: Bram Tchaikovsky, The Motors, New Math, U2 (Boy and October, at least), Tom Waits, The Jam, just to name a few. A full listing can be found on the Wyvern Falls website (www.wyernfalls.com) under Mooney's Jukebox. The bathroom in CBGB's is accurately described as the hell-hole it was, and Andy's Chee Peez really is (or was) a great second-hand clothing store. I still have a mod jacket I bought there. Arguably, my band mates and I were Johnny-come-latelies to the NY music scene by the time The Jag got underway in 1990, but I still remember the city the way it was in the 80s from my occasional visits there, back in the day when what made New York cool was its essential lawlessness. You could walk into a bar and buy a drink when you were sixteen and not get carded. I know I did. Of course, special thanks to my band-mates: Mark Wyszynski, Carlos Cabrales, Chris Conway and Chris Valentine, as well as a bunch of drummers who were either forgotten or spontaneously blew up, with special mention to Tedd Dolhon, whose tales as a musician back in the NY scene of the 70s and 80s are fabulous and endlessly entertaining.

Lorenzo King and the Dunderberg Imp

Washington Irving's short story, The Storm Ship, is somewhat short on particulars when it comes to the sub-story of the Dunderberg Imp, outside of his description and his propensity to vex sailors in the region of the mountain bearing his name. The fact that this update on that tale didn't roll out on tamer lines as well can be squarely blamed on my neighbor Wendy, who, during a conversation where I mentioned the early concept, said offhandedly, "Oh, except I'm sure this Imp is the kind of guy who will rip open your guts and leave them trailing along the ground..." and I then thought, "I hadn't pictured him that way, but now that you mention it...".

From there, it all went off the rails.

Special thanks here to Police Chief Joe Burton and Captain Scott Craven of the Ossining Police Department for taking the time to sit down and brief me on how the department actually functions day to day, as well as the latest procedures in booking suspects, how the department supports the community, jurisdictions, etc. The reality was quite a bit different from my original ill-conceived notions garnered from one-too-many movies and cop shows and although the police station in Wyvern Falls is nothing like the one they are in charge of, I think it's good policy to create fictional elements of a story out of creative license rather than ignorance whenever possible. Thanks as well to Patty Sacchi for setting up that meeting.

Hey Dummy!

An homage to every creepy ventriloquist's dummy story ever told and, in particular, my two favorites, Magic (1978) and Dead of Night (1945), the latter which I admittedly borrowed a few lines from, this tale draws on my extensive research on the 5th Air Force in New Guinea in WWII for my non-fiction book, Combat Recon, and has its back story in much historical fact, minus the witch doctor business, of course. The campaign in New Guinea is – and will continue to be – a source of amazement and frustration to me, not just due to my own great uncle's involvement but because it is such a quintessentially American story – a rag tag bunch of guys (5th AF) pull it together and defeat a superior and better-equipped force (the Japanese) against all odds, using good old American ingenuity and "by-the-bootstraps" unconventional tactics. It's very odd that the corner of WWII history that produced the Air Force's highest scoring aces (Dick Bong and Tommy McGuire) and some of the wildest and most innovative air war tactics is shuffled aside and all but forgotten now, in the 21st century. These guys really deserve a lot more attention.

Researching the economy of ice houses along the Hudson underscores the fact that in every century it always seems to come down to the same old crap, doesn't it? A few people zero in on a necessary commodity and then proceed to get rich by screwing everybody else. Sound familiar? Of course it does! I can only imagine what today's oil industry will look like in the next century...

For a comprehensive history of the Hudson River Valley for this story I drew heavily on Tom Lewis' The Hudson (Yale University Press, 2005) and highly recommend it.

Again, special thanks to my Number One Fan and supporter, my wife, Tomiko, who always gives it back to me straight and doesn't flinch (visibly at least) at some of the weirder by-ways these stories occasionally wander into. I'm eternally grateful to Tam Hernandez, whose oh-so-critical editing has taken this manuscript to a level I could never have achieved by myself. Big thanks is also in order to Anna Cabreras for her legal assistance and proof-reading, Carlos Cabrales for always answering my "nickel & dime" legal questions, Mark Wyszynski for his candid feedback (and being such a best friend and comrade-in-arms, particularly during our unforgettable/forgettable years performing together), Tom Laemlein for supplying random historic tidbits and being a terrific friend, Jennifer Kelly Laemlein for her additional proof-reading and edits, my parents and step-parents, of course, and anybody else I may have not mentioned by name.

Last, super big thanks to Washington Irving himself, the pioneer who paved the road for all fiction writers in the U.S. and who still ignites our imaginations to this day. His presence is still very much alive here in the Hudson River Valley, especially around Halloween. Trust me on this. I regularly stop by his grave site in Sleepy Hollow Cemetery (yes, it's behind the Old Dutch Church) to pay respects and, whether or not he likes it, his influence permeates all these pages. By my desk in my office, I keep an inspired warning by him about those who come to this area of the Hudson River that might be applied to my own little village of Wyvern Falls. It reads:

"...However wide awake they might have been before they reached that sleepy region, they are sure, in a little time, to inhale the witching influence of the air, and begin to grow imaginative, to dream dreams, and see apparitions."

-Robert Stava, Ossining NY, 2013

ABOUT THE AUTHOR

Robert Stava is a writer who now lives in the lower Hudson Valley
just north of NYC, apparently not far from that half-imaginary village he sets
so many of his stories in, Wyvern Falls. Originally from Cleveland, Ohio, he
grew up in the Finger Lakes region of New York State and after going to college
for Fine Arts wound up making his career in advertising at Y&R and J. Walter
Thompson in NYC. He went on to become a multimedia Art Director and later as
Creative Director ran the 3d Media Group at Arup, an international U.K.-based
design and engineering company before catapulting into the
wild world of writing horror fiction and design.

His first novel "At Van Eyckmann's Request" was published in 2012.

He is also author and designer of "Combat Recon: 5th Air Force Images from
the SW Pacific 1943-45" (Schiffer Publishing, 2007), a historical account based
around his great uncle's service as a combat photographer during WWII.

Visit his author site:
www.robertstava.com

and the official Wyvern Falls feature site at
www.wyvernfalls.com

or follow him on Twitter:
@robertstava

www.ingramcontent.com/pod-product-compliance
Lightning Source LLC
Chambersburg PA
CBHW051535250626
47157CB00001B/50